VANISHED!

As soon as the children had gone, Katherine rushed to the telephone to call the Toronto police again. It rang as she reached it.

'Yes?' she cried, 'Craig?'

'No, Mrs Fraser,' the Toronto officer said. 'I'm sorry. And I'm sorry we took so long getting back to you; we wanted to be sure –'

'What? Of what?'

'That there's no trace of your husband. He's not in any hospital in the area; he's not in jail; he's not in the morgue. He didn't register at any hotel other than the Boynton. He didn't charge any meals or rent a car. Mrs Fraser –' The officer cleared his throat. 'He probably wasn't even there. We checked with the airlines. Mr Fraser didn't fly to Toronto last Tuesday.'

JUDITH MICHAEL

Possessions

WARNER BOOKS

A *Warner* Book

First published in Great Britain by Sphere Books Ltd 1984
Reprinted 1984, 1985 (twice), 1986 (twice), 1987, 1988,
1990 (three times), 1991, 1992
Reprinted by Warner Books 1993
Reprinted 1994, 1995 (twice), 1997, 1998, 2000

Set by M Rules
Printed in England by Clays Ltd, St Ives plc

ISBN 0 7515 0582 X

Warner Books
A Division of
Little, Brown and Company (UK)
Brettenham House
Lancaster Place
London WC2E 7EN

We dedicate this book to Harry Barnard, whose boundless love and encouragement we deeply miss.

PART I

Chapter 1

'**K**atherine!' The voices echoed in the brightly lit rooms.
'Wonderful party . . . terrific food! . . . so good to be here . . .'
And to each other, still at the tops of their voices, they shouted,
'Didn't know they threw these parties . . . did you?'

The voices rose above the music from the record player and
swept through the house and out to the terrace where couples
danced in the warm June night or stood on the low stone wall
to view the spectacle of Vancouver's skyline across the Bay.
And Katherine, with Jennifer and Todd's help, opened new
bottles at the small bar and moved back and forth between the
kitchen and dining-room, keeping the steaming casseroles and
platters on the buffet heaped with food.

'The guest of honour salutes a terrific hostess,' said Leslie
McAlister, lifting her glass. 'And,' she added with a small
bow, 'Jennifer and Todd. Your mother should hire you out to
friends when they entertain.' She put her arm around

Katherine. 'Very impressive, being the reason for such a party. Why didn't you tell me you threw such terrific affairs? If I'd known, I wouldn't have let three years go by since my last visit. On the other hand, why haven't you come to San Francisco so I could give a party in your honour?'

'You should have come sooner,' Katherine agreed. She was trying to twist the cork out of a champagne bottle. 'Craig does this so easily, but I can't seem to –'

'Let me.' Leslie took the bottle from her. 'It's one of the first skills single women learn.' With a flourish, she pushed up the cork with her thumbs, at the same time covertly studying Katherine, comparing her to the plain, shy Katherine Fraser she'd seen only sporadically for the past ten years. She was still shy: slightly alarmed at the boisterousness of her party and looking surprised when her guests praised her, but she was a little prettier, especially now, with the excitement of her party brightening her wonderful hazel eyes and giving her pale skin some colour. And though she and Leslie were the same height, she was slimmer; she doesn't worry about her hips, Leslie thought ruefully.

Still her educated eye saw that Katherine wasn't nearly as attractive as she could be. Her heavy dark hair was pulled back and held tightly by an elastic band, stretching the skin at her temples, her lipstick was the wrong shade for her skin, and her dress was too plain for a figure that demanded drama. Leslie, who worked at being stunning and sophisticated, making a virtue of kinky red hair and a sharp jaw, felt her fingers itching to redo Katherine. Silently she laughed at herself. Never content; not only did she spend her days as an executive of an exclusive department store that catered to the whims of wealthy customers, she couldn't wait to go to work on a friend who seemed perfectly satisfied with herself.

The cork popped neatly from the bottle, trailing misty tendrils of champagne vapour. 'Oh, well done!' cried Sarah

Murphy, small, round, with black alert eyes. 'Men always spray it everywhere, but you have such finesse! You must entertain a great deal. Katherine, on the other hand' – she tapped Katherine playfully – 'never entertains, yet here she is giving such a lovely party. And without a husband in sight. Where is Craig, my dear? Usually I see him leave like clockwork every morning, but I haven't seen him since Tuesday.'

'He had to go to Toronto –'

'With a party coming up? It must have been terribly important to make him disappear and expect you to –'

'Cope,' Leslie finished smoothly. 'And isn't she admirable? One might be envious – if one were the type.' She smiled sweetly. 'Katherine and I were catching up on our news; do you mind if I monopolise her before I leave for the airport?'

'Oh, my, no,' said Sarah. 'Of course not; Katherine's been so anxious to see you –' She followed them, still talking, until they hid behind a cluster of guests at the piano. Beneath the noise of the party, they burst out laughing.

'Thank you,' Katherine said. 'She's a wonderful neighbour and she'd do anything to help us if we needed her, but she's a little hard to get rid of.'

'Hinting,' Leslie scorned. 'I can't stand people who haven't the guts to be honestly nosy.'

'Or honestly anything,' Katherine added as they went through the glass doors to the terrace. 'You never liked anyone who lied.'

'That's why we latched on to each other: the two of us, so damned stubborn about the truth. So how come we don't see each other more often?'

A shout from the living-room broke in, rising furiously above the sounds of the party. 'You son of a bitch, you have to accommodate the Quebecois –'

'Accommodate the French!' came an outraged response.

'We're already taxed up to our necks to pay for them. Our money should stay in the west –'

'So that's what you want, eh? You'd do anything to get out of paying taxes!'

Katherine's face was frozen with panic. 'They can't fight; it would ruin everything.'

The outraged voice rose higher. 'Pretty free with accusations, Doerner! You're known for that aren't you? Especially false ones!'

'What the hell –! Listen you bastard, that was two years ago. And when I found I was wrong, I paid the costs and it was over. Who do you think you are –'

'Oh, shit!' someone else cried. 'Do you two have to come to blows at every party?'

Leslie looked at Katherine's face. 'Shall I try to break it up? Sometimes a stranger is a good distraction.'

Katherine shook her head. 'I should do it. Damn, why isn't Craig here? He'd know what to do; one of those men is his partner. Well –' She straightened her shoulders. 'I'll be right back.'

In the living-room she made her way through a crowd surrounding two men, their faces contorted with anger as other guests held them apart. Katherine drew a shaky breath and, forcing a smile, raised her voice. 'It's like an American western, isn't it? But shouldn't we have a saloon and a dusty street where you can pace off?' She heard a ripple of laughter and the two men reluctantly smiled. She put her hands on their arms. 'We do have a bar; can I offer you drinks instead of bruises?'

'Far more civilised,' one of them said. 'Mrs Fraser, I apologise. If some people weren't so free with accusations –'

'The bar! The bar! Drinks, not bruises!' came cries from the guests. A short, grey-haired woman mouthed an apology to Katherine and took the other man's arm, turning him towards the bar. In a moment, Katherine slipped out and returned to the terrace.

Leslie was watching from the doorway. 'The perfect hostess,' she said admiringly. 'I thought you said you don't give many parties.'

'We don't give any parties. We used to, years ago, but we haven't lately; Craig doesn't like them.' Katherine was trembling but a feeling of pride swept over her. 'I did stop them, didn't I?'

'You did. Without making anyone angry. Who are those guys, anyway?'

'Carl Doerner, Craig's partner in Vancouver Construction; I have no idea who the other man is. My house is full of people I don't know.'

'Katherine! You're not serious.'

'Yes I am. We don't have many friends, and I wanted to impress you. So we invited Craig's business acquaintances and people I'd met at Jennifer's and Todd's school.'

'But they came to your party.'

'They wanted to meet my friend, the Vice President of Heath's of San Francisco. You're a celebrity.'

'If I am, it's the first time. And I didn't make this terrific party; you did.'

'If I did, it's the first time.' They grinned at each other and Katherine felt the warmth of Leslie's closeness. It had been almost the only warmth in high school and two years of college, and afterward, until she met Craig. Leslie, brash and curious, had breached her shyness and given her a chance to know how good a friend she could be. But then, on a vacation in British Columbia, Katherine met Craig Fraser and, within a month, married him. And Leslie, returning to San Francisco after the wedding, decided to make herself the first woman vice president in the fifty-year history of Heath's of San Francisco.

'The years disappeared,' Katherine said, thinking back, trying to answer Leslie's question of why they saw each other so seldom. 'And you haven't visited us very often.'

'Look who's talking!' Leslie retorted. 'You've never come back to San Francisco. Ten years, and never one visit.'

'Craig wouldn't go. I asked him so many times; he just refused and wouldn't talk about it.' Katherine gazed unseeing at the lights of Lions Gate Bridge, strung across the Bay, fastening West Vancouver to the glittering Vancouver skyline. 'Do you remember the time I called you, when I was so lonely? We'd been married about three years and had only a couple of friends, and Craig was starting with Carl Doerner's company, and I was always alone with the babies – it was when you were breaking up with what's-his-name – and we nearly drowned our telephones in problems and tears. What *was* his name?'

'I have no idea. Seven years ago? How could I possibly remember?'

'You were so miserable, I thought it was an undying love.'

'It probably was, at the moment. I haven't found one that lasts. I don't see many, either. You and Craig; a few others. Though don't you think you could find someone else if he suddenly – Sorry, ghoulish question.'

'Well it is, but everyone thinks about it. And I suppose I could love someone else if something happened to Craig.' She smiled at Jennifer, who came onto the terrace carefully balancing two plates of steamed shrimp. 'Thank you, sweetheart. Would you and Todd like to go upstairs now? I can take over; you've worked so hard and it's getting late.'

'Todd's already goofing off,' Jennifer said resignedly. 'He's talking about Atari games with some computer guy. I like being the hostess. See you later.'

Amused, Leslie said, 'Seems you've been displaced as hostess. Speaking of computers, my wild oats brother has become a computer whiz. In fact, I hired him a while back, figuring a good job might make him an upright citizen. Fingers crossed and daily prayers; so far he seems to be making it.' She paused. 'So do you. You look happy, Katherine.'

8

'I am.' Through the open doors, Katherine heard fragments of conversation and a chorus reviving old folk songs to a piano accompaniment. She felt she was floating on the bright lights and colours of her beautiful house, and wished Craig were there, to share it. We've got to stop being so solitary, she thought; we should make more friends, entertain more.

'I'm sorry I won't see Craig,' Leslie said, as if picking up Katherine's thoughts.

'I am, too. I can't imagine why he isn't back; he promised he'd be here to help with the party. Can't you stay over? He'll probably get here just when you leave.'

'I really can't. A couple of odd things have come up at the store and I ought to earn my salary by looking into them. I wouldn't even have come up for the conference, if you weren't here. You'll just have to bring the whole family to San Francisco.'

'I will. I don't know what Craig has against it, but we'll –'

'Katherine.' Carl Doerner was in the doorway. 'Could I see you for a minute?'

'I'll get some more wine,' Leslie said, and left them alone.

'I apologise,' he said. 'No excuse for such childish behaviour. I'm on edge, lots on my mind, but still . . . Katherine, have you heard from Craig?'

'No, have you? I thought he'd be back by now.'

'I just called him at the Boynton. He's not there.'

'Of course not. He's on his way home.'

'They don't have a registration for him.'

'They must have; that's where he stayed. But it isn't important, is it? He's on his way home.'

'Katherine, have you heard from him? All week?'

'No, he's probably been busy. So was I, with the party –'

'Does Craig use other hotels in Toronto?'

'No. Carl, what is this? Craig is on his way home; there's no mystery about it.'

9

'Probably not. But when he gets here, will you have him call me? Right away.'

Something in his voice finally reached her. 'Are you worried about Craig?'

'Of course not. Just – have him call me. All right?'

She nodded, frowning slightly as he walked away. Behind her, someone said, 'Wonderful house, Katherine. So much room to move around.'

'We built it,' she answered. 'Three years ago. It is beautiful, isn't it? Craig and the architect worked out every inch.'

What does that mean – no registration at the Boynton?

'Talented fellow: he and Doerner built our office building.'

'And that new motel in Burnaby? Didn't they do that?'

Of course he was registered. Carl was impatient and didn't ask them to check.

'Mom!' Katherine looked down at Todd's mischievous grin. 'There's a whole bunch of chocolate cake in the kitchen. It's for us, isn't it?'

She smiled. 'How much have you eaten?'

'Just a taste. Jennifer said I better ask you.'

'How much is "just a taste"?'

'Uh . . . two and a half pieces: Jennifer only had two.'

'Quite a taste.' She kissed the top of his head. 'One more small piece. And don't forget to brush all that chocolate off your teeth before you go to bed.'

'Sure. When's Dad coming home?'

'I guess tomorrow. He'll probably call and let us know.'

He would have told me if he'd changed hotels.

'He promised me a balsa aeroplane model.'

'Then he'll bring you one. Goodnight, Todd. Sleep well.'

Unless he changed his plans at the last minute.

'Nice boy, Katherine. The picture of his father.'

But whenever he changes his plans, he calls me.

'Katherine.' Leslie was carrying her overnight bag. 'I've

10

got to go or I'll miss my plane.' They walked to the front door and she looked at Katherine appraisingly. 'A sudden problem?'

'Why?'

'Furrowed brow, faraway look. Can I help?'

'No, it's not serious, just something that I can't explain. I wish you could stay longer.'

'Next time. Or you'll stay longer in San Francisco. You will come? Promise?'

'Promise. As soon as Craig can get away.'

'Don't wait too long; I really have missed our talks.'

'So have I. I didn't realise how much until now.'

'You could come alone, you know.'

'Oh. Yes I could. I'd rather not, though; and wouldn't you like a visit from the whole family?'

'Of course. Come soon, then. I'll give you the key to the city.' They put their arms around each other. 'So damn good to see you. Letters and phone calls aren't enough. Why the hell we let ourselves get so wrapped up in our own lives –' And she was gone, waving from the front gate as she got into the taxi.

Just as Craig did when he went to the airport on Tuesday.

Three days earlier. Tuesday morning. He held her to him as the taxi pulled up, but he was looking off in the distance, already thinking of Toronto. He kissed her, told her he loved her, and was gone, waving as the car pulled away. An ordinary trip, no different from the dozens he took every year to meet with suppliers, architects, other contractors with whom he and Carl did business. Back on Friday, he had promised at breakfast, to help with the party. An ordinary trip. *But why wouldn't he be registered at the Boynton?*

Her exhilaration had vanished; her party had changed. Her guests still gesticulated and smiled, talking rapidly, but the sound and brightness had dimmed, as if muffled by a curtain. I'll find out for myself, she thought, and ran upstairs to call the hotel. 'No, Mrs Fraser, he didn't register,' the clerk said. 'We certainly wouldn't make a mistake about one of our regulars. That's what I told Mr Doerner when he called, and if he hadn't got angry and hung up on me, I would have told him that Mr Fraser did have a reservation but he didn't arrive. We assumed he'd changed his plans. I wish I could help you, but I can't. He isn't here, Mrs Fraser, and he hasn't been, all week.'

He isn't here, Mrs Fraser. He hasn't been all week. Katherine sat on the bed and looked blankly at the wall. He hasn't been all week. Laughter drifted up the stairs, glasses clinked, and the chorus at the piano belted out 'The Big Rock Candy Mountain', but the sounds were far off, the air dark. He isn't here, Mrs Fraser. He hasn't been all week.

Chapter 2

On Saturday morning, the debris of the party lay strewn about the house. Katherine sat at the kitchen telephone, watching her children clean up the dining-room. 'We need a *maid*,' Todd grumbled, stacking plates precariously on the floor.

'*We're* the maid,' Jennifer responded.

'If Dad was home,' Todd said, 'Mom would do it with us, like she always does.'

'She's waiting to hear from Daddy,' said Jennifer. 'She's worried.'

Todd looked up from his stack of plates. 'She didn't say she was worried. She just said Dad would be late because he got busy in Toronto.'

'He always calls, doesn't he?' Jennifer demanded. 'He calls in the middle of the week and he calls if he's going to be late and this week he didn't call at all.'

'Mom!' Todd yelled. 'Has something happened to Dad?'

13

Katherine came to the door. Her legs felt heavy, her eyes scratchy from being up all night, waiting, watching the blazing porch light grow feeble as the sun rose. She was too tired to lie convincingly, and her children were expert at catching her in contradictions – and anyway, she thought, they deserve to know what's happening. 'I don't know where he is, Todd. He's probably tied up with some business people and he'll call us as soon as he can.'

'But where *is* he?' Todd insisted.

'I said I don't know,' Katherine snapped. More gently, she said, 'I'm waiting for him to call.'

The telephone rang and she flung herself across the kitchen to answer it. 'You haven't heard from him?' Carl Doerner asked without preamble.

'No.' In her disappointment, her legs gave way and she sat on the stool at the counter. 'But if he's really busy . . . Couldn't something important have come up at the last minute? Something in another city?'

'He's heard of telephones, hasn't he? Katherine, tell me the truth: you have no idea where he is?'

'Why would I lie to you? Carl, I'm *worried*; Craig always calls on business trips, and he promised to be back on Friday. I'm going to call the Toronto police.'

'Well, hold on a minute now, slow down. Craig's a big boy; we don't have to panic just because we're not sure where he is. Something unexpected probably did come up. Chances are he'll walk in any minute and we'd feel pretty silly, wouldn't we, if we had half of Canada out looking for him?'

'Half of Canada? I only said –'

'I know, I know, but I think you should wait. You watch, he'll waltz in safe and sound, wondering what the fuss is all about. I think we ought to give him time to finish his business and get home. But have him call me as soon as he gets in, will you?'

Jennifer was beside her. 'What did he say?'

'That we shouldn't worry.' Katherine turned on the burner beneath the tea kettle. 'And he's right; Daddy can take care of himself. I think we should get to work. What would he say if he came home to a house that looked like it was hit by a cyclone?'

But all day, and into the evening, as the three of them cleaned the house, all Katherine could think of was Craig lying in the street, victim of a mugging or a hit-and-run driver or a heart attack. But wouldn't someone have found him and called her? Not if a robber had taken his wallet; that happened all the time. So she had to call the police. And if Carl didn't think she should, that was just too bad.

Still, she waited a little longer, until Jennifer and Todd went to bed. 'Wake us up when Daddy comes home,' Jennifer pleaded.

'We both will,' Katherine said. 'Don't you think he's anxious to see you too?' But when she dialled the Toronto police, her voice failed. She felt ashamed, as if she were calling Craig a criminal – someone to be searched for, hunted down, his name bandied about by strangers. An anonymous officer at the other end was saying, 'Yes? Hello? Yes?' and at last, knowing she had to do it, she forced out the words. 'My husband is missing.'

'Yes, ma'am,' he said, so matter-of-fact Katherine wondered how many missing husbands he dealt with each week. 'When did you last see him?'

'Tuesday morning when –'

'He was coming here? Toronto?'

'Yes, he went there often, on business, and he –'

'What airline did he fly?'

'Airline? I don't know; he didn't tell me. Probably Air Canada.'

'And his hotel in Toronto?'

'He always stays at the Boynton. But I called them and –'

15

'Did he have a reservation?'

'Yes, but he never . . . he never got there.'

'Never got there. When did you expect him home?'

'Friday. Yesterday afternoon. We were having a party for a friend of mine from San Francisco –'

'He didn't call or write?'

'No! If he had, I wouldn't be calling you!'

'All right, ma'am, I know this is a strain, but if you'll just be calm. We have to ask these questions; it's our job. Give me a description now.'

Katherine pictured Craig, sitting at his desk, organising neat piles of paper and binding them with rubber bands or string. 'Six feet tall,' she said. 'Light brown hair and beard, brown eyes –'

'Weight?'

She paused. How odd, she thought. 'I don't know.'

'About –?'

'I guess . . . about one seventy? He takes a size forty sweater.'

'Scars or distinguishing features?'

'A scar next to his right eyebrow, not a big one but you can see it. That's all. He's really – he's not unusual – just nice-looking.'

'Shoe size?'

'I don't know.' He must think I'm a terrible wife not to know these things. 'I don't buy his shoes.'

'Right.' He went on and on, asking about the people Craig went to see, companies, banks – 'I don't know, I don't know,' Katherine repeated – and then for their charge card numbers, and she read them to him. 'All right, Mrs Fraser. We'll get back to you as soon as we can.'

'Tonight?'

'Or tomorrow morning. Sit tight, ma'am; give us time to check everything out.'

That night again, as the hours dragged by, Katherine huddled in a corner of the couch, drinking tea, listening for the sound of Craig's key in the front door. The house creaked and shifted in the dark and she held herself rigid, afraid to investigate the sounds. At dawn she put her head back to rest her aching neck, and fell asleep – to be awakened two hours later by the furious sibilance of Todd and Jennifer's whispers.

'He must have called,' Todd said. 'And Mom's waiting for him here instead of upstairs in bed.'

Jennifer bit her knuckle. 'She said she'd wake us up if he called. She's down here because she doesn't like to sleep alone. Parents don't like to be in bed by themselves.'

'I'll bet he called and he's on his way home with my balsa model.'

'Who cares about your balsa model? I just want Daddy!'

We all want him, Katherine thought, her eyes still closed. And he hasn't called. Sunday morning and Craig hasn't called. She opened her eyes and stood up, aching as if she had not slept at all. 'We all want him,' she repeated aloud. 'And it's hard for us, not knowing where he is. I think when he gets home we should ask him to be more considerate next time he goes away.'

Todd scowled. 'Maybe a truck hit him. Or a train. Or a meteor.'

'Meteors don't hit Toronto,' Jennifer scoffed.

'They do too. They hit everywhere. Even Vancouver. One of them could smash into our house and wipe us all out.'

'Cheerful thought.' Katherine smiled. For a brief moment everything seemed normal: Todd and Jennifer, the morning sun slanting into their bright living-room, a beautiful ordinary June day. Soon Craig would walk in, just as Carl had predicted, apologising because he got so busy he forgot to call, explaining his change in hotels, telling her she should know

17

better than to worry; he could take care of himself just as he took care of his family. 'I think we would have heard if a meteor had smashed into Toronto,' she said. 'Now, look: I'm going to take a shower and I think you'd better do the same. Isn't this the day for that picnic on Grouse Mountain? What time are you being picked up?'

'We're not going,' Jennifer declared. 'We're going to stay home and wait for Daddy.'

'You are going,' said Katherine firmly. 'If he gets home before you, we'll come up and find you. Come on, now, let's get moving. Todd? Jennifer? *Please*.'

But after all it was not an ordinary day and as soon as they were gone, Katherine rushed to the telephone to call Toronto police again. It rang as she reached it.

'Yes?' she cried. 'Craig?'

'No, Mrs Fraser,' the Toronto officer said. 'I'm sorry. And I'm sorry we took so long getting back to you; we wanted to be sure –'

'What? Of what?'

'That there's no trace of your husband. He's not in any hospital in the area; he's not in jail; he's not in the morgue. He didn't register at any hotel other than the Boynton. He didn't charge any meals or rent a car. Mrs Fraser –' The officer cleared his throat. 'He probably wasn't even there. We checked with the airlines. Mr Fraser didn't fly to Toronto last Tuesday.'

'That's impossible.' Katherine's throat was tight.

'No, they have no record of –'

'Of course he flew to Toronto.' Her voice rose. 'I saw him leave for the airport on Tuesday.'

'Mrs Fraser, don't you understand? *He never used his ticket*. Either something happened to him in Vancouver, before he got to the airport, or he never intended to take that flight.'

18

'How dare you! How dare you accuse my husband of lying to me! Who do you think you are —' She put down the telephone trying to draw a breath. She heard the officer repeatedly calling her name, but his voice in the receiver was so tiny and distant she knew it had nothing to do with her. She hung up on it.

But in a minute, with frantic urgency, she dialled the Vancouver police. Craig never lied to her. Something terrible had happened to him, and if the Toronto people were telling the truth, it happened in Vancouver. Right here, and all week she had had no idea of it. She'd been happy and busy, planning the party, and the only time she'd thought of Craig was when she felt annoyed with him for not being there to help her. And all that time he was ill, or injured, or dead. I should have known, she thought. When he didn't call.

'My husband is missing,' she said when a policeman answered, squeezing the words once more through her locked throat, and then she nervously paced her living-room, waiting for someone to arrive.

Two young officers came, carrying clip boards and printed forms, and they checked off categories and carefully wrote Craig's description as Katherine recited it for the second time that day. They asked for a recent picture and Katherine gave them one and then, synchronised and efficient, they took turns asking questions and writing answers. As she told them what the Toronto police had said about the airlines, Katherine caught a look between them. 'What is it?' she asked. 'If there is something you haven't told me —'

'No, ma'am,' one of them said. 'We were wondering what you haven't told us.'

Katherine shook her head. 'Nothing.' A wave of exhaustion from two sleepless nights engulfed her and she closed her eyes. If she could just sink into bed and turn away, shut out everything . . . But the officers were rustling impatiently and

19

she forced her eyes open. 'Nothing. What else could there be?'

'Ah . . . your husband's lady friends?' the officer suggested. 'Any you know of, that is. Lots of wives don't, so you shouldn't feel ashamed if . . .' His voice trailed away at Katherine's look.

'What we mean,' the other one put in helpfully, 'is that people don't just vanish without a reason. Husbands have *reasons* for disappearing. It wouldn't necessarily be a lady friend. You understand' – he was so earnest, Katherine thought, and so clumsy; why were boys sent to do this job? – 'we're not suggesting anything in particular. Maybe the two of you were having problems? Or your husband piled up gambling IOUs? Maybe he's been despondent lately? Have you looked for a suicide note? They have *reasons*, Mrs Fraser, that's all; we're certainly not here to criticise you or your husband – that's the way things *happen*.'

'Not to us.' Katherine's lips were stiff and she was too tired even to be indignant, as she had been with the Toronto officer. 'My husband and I have been married for ten years and I know he wouldn't stay away if he could help it. You don't know anything about him; you don't know what happened to him.'

'No ma'am; that's true. But *did* he like the ladies?'

The telephone rang and Katherine raced to the kitchen, her heart pounding. 'My dear,' said Sarah Murphy, her voice rippling with curiosity. 'Is everything all right? I just glanced out my window and saw the police car.'

Katherine's shoulders slumped. 'Sarah, I can't talk now.'

'It's not a heart attack, is it? Craig, I mean? Katherine? Is Craig all right?'

'Craig isn't home. Sarah, I have to go –'

'But he did get back. Didn't he?'

'Sarah, I'll talk to you later.'

20

'Yes, you don't want to keep the police waiting. But Katherine, I'm here, you know, if you need me.'

'Yes –'

'I'm always here, always available.'

'I know. I'll call you later, Sarah.'

The police officers were at the front door. 'We'll send out a bulletin on your husband, Mrs Fraser, and we'll let you know if we hear anything. But you really ought to look around for clues; that's probably the only way we'll find him.'

Don't they understand that my husband may be dead? Katherine watched them walk past her flower gardens and disappear beyond the hedge. Then, without planning it, she found herself sitting at Craig's desk. Not looking for clues, she thought; that was ridiculous. But perhaps he'd left a schedule of appointments; places she could call. That was all she was looking for. She felt like a trespasser. It was Craig's desk; she never used it. Superstitiously, she thought she might be making it more likely that he was dead. 'Oh, don't be stupid,' she said aloud, and quickly pulled open all the drawers.

Gradually, she stopped feeling guilty as her puzzlement grew. Going through drawers and pigeonholes, lifting and putting back neat folders and packets of papers, she found Craig's notes on buildings Vancouver Construction had built, sketches for the wood carvings he made in his spare time, copies of expense forms he had submitted for business trips, including frequent trips to Calgary (he'd never told her he had a long-term job in Calgary), past-due membership notices from his private club, a batch of unpaid department store bills, and lined pads of paper covered with scribbled numbers – added, subtracted, multiplied, crossed out with angry Xs, then repeated in different combinations.

Katherine pondered the numbers. Craig always paid the bills; he'd never even hinted about debts. We'll have to talk

21

about it, she thought, as soon as he gets home. Then, behind a box of business cards in the bottom drawer, she found a small picture, torn raggedly from a larger one. Disquieted, she gazed at the lovely girl laughing into the camera; someone she had never met. *I didn't know Craig kept a picture of an early love. Something else he never told me.*

'Mom!' Todd cried, throwing open the front door. 'Mrs Murphy says the police were here. What happened to Daddy? He isn't dead, is he?'

Jennifer jabbed him with her elbow. 'Don't *say* it.' She looked at Katherine. 'What did they want?'

'I asked them to find out if Daddy's been in an accident.' Katherine steadied her voice. 'They can check hospitals faster than we can. That's all they're doing. How was your picnic? Tell me about it while we make dinner.'

They were subdued, but they talked and helped her as they did every evening and once again, for a few peaceful moments, Katherine thought that everything would be fine; how could anything bad happen when her house seemed so normal? And then they heard the front door open and with a yell Todd and Jennifer tore through the dining and living rooms with Katherine just behind them. But it was not Craig; it was Carl Doerner.

'The door was open,' he apologised, striding in. 'I didn't hear from Craig; did you forget to tell him to call me?' He stopped in the middle of the living-room, his back to Katherine. When she was silent, he let out a long sigh and turned to face her. 'Nothing? Not a word?'

She shook her head.

'Damn, damn, damn.' His large head, with its mane of grey hair, moved slowly back and forth. 'I'm sorry, Katherine. I hoped it wasn't true.'

Uneasy, Katherine turned to Todd and Jennifer. 'Would you set the table? I'll be there in a few minutes.' Jennifer made a

22

disgusted sound but the two of them left the room. 'What does that mean?' Katherine asked Carl.

'He's skipped. I wish I could spare you this, but –'

'What are you talking about? Skipped? You mean run away? He had nothing to run away from. And he wouldn't anyway. You know him, Carl; he's not the kind of man to run away from anything.'

'Katherine, I'm sorry.' Restlessly, Doerner moved about the room, shoving furniture out of his way. Katherine thought how out of place he looked in the bright room with its flowered furniture and drapes – like a shaggy bear in a summer garden. 'I'm sorry,' he repeated, his voice heavy and slow. 'But Craig's been stealing company funds for over two years.'

'Stealing! Carl, are you mad?'

'Nearly seventy-five thousand dollars. The accountant caught it, and Craig and I had it out and he admitted it: he made up fake companies, sold them fake materials, authorised payments to himself – it's complicated, but I can show you how it worked if you want. He asked me to give him a week and –'

'It's not true!'

'He asked for a week to raise some money, and I believed he meant it, so I promised not to go to the police.'

'I don't believe it; there's been a –'

Doerner pulled a thick envelope from his pocket and held it out to her. 'Statements. From the accountants, the solicitors –' When she did not move, his hand dropped. 'Goddamn it, Katherine, why would I make this up? Craig was more a son to me than a partner; I was going to retire and sell him the company in a couple of years. Now what the hell am I going to do?'

'Craig stole?' Katherine asked numbly. 'He stole from the company?'

'That's what I said.'

23

'Well, you're wrong. Why are you so sure it was Craig? Why are you blaming him –?'

'I'm not blaming him; *he admitted it*. Said your house set him back more than he expected, and there were other things – he wouldn't say what – but he said he'd pay it back, every damn cent. And I trusted him! I let him go!'

'When?'

'What?'

'When did you and Craig talk about . . . about the money?'

'Monday. Last Monday. He said he'd have some of it by Friday and a plan to pay off the rest. He was crying. Damn it, so was I. Now what the hell can I do? I don't want to charge him with embezzling!'

'Wait, please, just wait a minute.' Katherine was dizzy. Doerner had pushed the furniture out of place and the room seemed to be shifting, like the deck of a ship in a storm. Monday. And on Tuesday, even though she asked him to stay home that week, he rushed off to Toronto.

He kissed me goodbye and said – I'm sorry; I love you.

She clasped her hands. 'What are you going to do?'

Doerner grunted. 'Up to now I've kept my word. But damn it, he betrayed me! Don't you see that I've got to report this? Too many people are involved – the insurance company, our solicitor, the accountant – I have no choice; I have to go to the police!'

Like a missile, Todd flung himself across the room at Doerner. 'You can't go to the police about my Dad, you bastard; you're a *liar*!'

'Todd!' Katherine pulled Todd's battering hands away from Doerner and knelt to hold him against her. As he buried his face in her shoulder, crying noisily, she saw Jennifer watching stonily from the doorway.

'Just a minute,' she said to Doerner. Taking Jennifer and Todd by the hand, she led them upstairs. 'I promise we'll talk about this in a few minutes.' Her voice was shaky and she cleared her throat. 'But I want you up here. I do not want you downstairs. Is that clear?' When they nodded, their eyes wide and blank, she went slowly downstairs. Doerner was still in the middle of the room.

'Betrayed his kids, too.' His face was dark. 'Son of a bitch. Bad enough he let me down, but to do that to you and the kids . . . by God he deserves whatever he gets! I treated him like a son but now he's going to pay –!'

'Carl, don't go to the police. Please. Can't you wait? One more day, just until tomorrow. Craig must have been on his way home when something happened . . . he's ill or hurt . . . you don't know! If he really did take that money he wouldn't run away; he'd make it up to you. We'd both make it up to you. Please, Carl. You've waited this long. Please.'

Doerner flung out his hands. 'What the hell. One more day. Tomorrow's Monday; I'll call you at noon. I can't wait any longer than that.' Katherine nodded. 'Well, then.' He sighed. 'He really left you in the lurch. I wish there was something –' He waited but Katherine was silent. 'Well, then –' Another moment and he was gone, passing beneath the porch light that was blazing for the third night in a row.

A few more hours for Craig, Katherine thought. I don't even know if he needs them. Or what else he might need. *Not knowing* was a leaden weight inside her, so heavy it made her feel sick. She thought of the dinner they had made and could not imagine eating it.

But they all picked at it while Katherine told Jennifer and Todd sketchily, what Doerner had said. 'We only have his word for it,' she finished, refusing to think about the envelope he'd offered her; it could have been anything. 'We won't know the real story until Daddy gets back. All we can do is wait. We'll hear from the police, or Daddy will walk in the front door and explain everything.'

'Daddy wouldn't run away,' Jennifer said.

'Of course not.' Katherine remembered the jokes she'd heard about wives who preferred to think that an overdue husband was injured rather than unfaithful. Which do I want, she wondered grimly. Craig in an accident or Craig running from a crime?

It kept her awake for another night in their cold bed. *Craig, I want you home.* She was crying. *Please come home. I want you safe, and everything the way it used to be.* But the next day, when Doerner called exactly at noon, she had nothing to tell him. And so he called the police.

An hour later, a different pair of officers appeared at her door, older than the first two, with different questions and a keener scrutiny of Katherine and her house.

'Nice,' said one, pacing off the living-room and admiring the view through the curved wall of windows. 'My wife,' said the other, 'always wanted to live in West Vancouver. Too expensive for us; too expensive for most people.' When Katherine did not respond, they sat down and asked questions, hammering at her husband's purchasing habits, travel, debts, gambling, women, gifts, drinking, drugs . . . But Katherine had become cautious. She did not mention Craig's desk with its unpaid bills, scribbled numbers and overdrawn notices from the bank. Instead she told them, truthfully, that her husband had not changed in the ten years they'd been married; that he was generous to his family but careful with money; that he did not gamble, drank very little, dressed simply and did not use drugs.

After an hour, the policemen exchanged glances. 'We have to know about his private life, Mrs Fraser,' said one. 'We've issued a warrant for his arrest, and of course we'll find him if he's alive, but it would be easier, especially for you and your children, if we had the names of his friends.'

'You mean women.'

'That's what it usually comes down to.'

'There are no women,' she said without emotion. She seemed to have none left. Like an automaton, she repeated her denials, looking at her hands, feeling the room slide away as waves of sleep lapped at her.

'Well, we'll be off,' they said at last. 'Unless there's something more you want to say.' Katherine did not move. 'You know where to reach us if you think of something.' She nodded. 'Well, then, we'll be talking to you. And Mrs Fraser.' At the altered voice, she looked up. 'We'd appreciate it if you didn't leave town.'

In less than an hour the first reporter rang her doorbell. Katherine, now as wary as a trapped animal, stood in the doorway, keeping him on the porch. 'I have nothing to tell you,' she said.

He waved his pencil as if conducting with a baton. 'Mrs Fraser, did you and your husband quarrel? Did you have – um – intimate problems? Did your husband buy jewellery? Give gifts to friends? Did he travel often? Where did he stay when he travelled? Hotels, or – um – with a friend?'

Katherine clung to the doorjamb, shaking her head. 'It's none of your business,' she said and slammed the door in his face.

But on Tuesday morning, her husband's picture with his faint, sad smile looked up at her from the front page of the *Vancouver News*. 'Craig Fraser,' she read, 'a partner in Vancouver Construction, a firm which has built some of Vancouver's major office buildings and residences, is wanted by the police for questioning in connection with a seventy-five-thousand dollar embezzlement from his company. He has been missing since last Tuesday, when, according to his wife in a statement to the police, he said he was going to Toronto. Mrs Fraser refuses to speak to reporters. Police in Canadian

27

provinces and the border cities of the United States are searching for him; an arrest, they say, is expected shortly.'

The stark words and Craig's picture – a public figure, a wanted man – were like a strong wind slamming shut a door Katherine had tried to keep open. For the first time she let the thought form and settle within her. *He is not coming home*.

Chapter 3

Ross Hayward put down his newspaper and looked out the window as the plane descended over Vancouver. Bordered on two sides by water, the city's skyscrapers seemed to float in the early morning sun with a haze of mountains on the horizon. It reminded Ross of the city he had just left; someone from San Francisco could feel at home here. The thought made him glance again at the newspaper in his lap. He had read and re-read the story of embezzlement and flight, but it was the photograph that he had been studying for two days: the bearded man with his faint, sad smile. 'Possibly,' he murmured. 'But probably not; too incredible to believe . . .'

In the terminal, he found a telephone directory and looked up Craig Fraser's address. He did not call ahead; he had to surprise the wife and watch her face; otherwise, he'd have had no reason to make the trip.

*

'You must go there,' Victoria had said the day before. 'Telephoning won't do.' She had burst into his conference room just ahead of his protesting secretary, stopping the Staff Assistant to the Mayor of San Francisco in the middle of a sentence. 'Ross, I must talk to you. Now.' Her hair was windblown and the silk scarf at her neck askew – the first time in his thirty-five years that Ross had seen his grandmother even faintly dishevelled or permitting herself to show emotion in public.

He pushed back his chair at the head of the conference table. 'I think you all know my grandmother,' he said, aware that Victoria was on first-name terms with many of these men and women, dining and sitting on Boards of Directors with them, and entertaining them in her home. She greeted them brusquely and Ross took her arm. 'If you'll excuse me a moment – you can criticise my plans without the static of my biased opinion.'

The City Director of Planning waved a hand. 'We haven't discussed rents.'

'The figures are on page forty. If you'll go over them, I won't be long.' Ross ushered Victoria through a door into his office, leaving behind San Francisco's top government officials who'd been studying and debating his architectural plans for months. And it would be months more before they approved every detail so that work on the three hundred million dollar project, called BayBridge Plaza, could begin. He wanted to be with them, defending his ideas, speeding the process along, but his grandmother demanded his attention. He sat beside her on the couch. 'Tell me what's happened.'

'Look at this.' Her trembling hand held out a copy of the *Vancouver News*. 'Tobias saw it at one of those international news stands. Craig's picture –'

Her voice broke on Craig's name. Ross looked at the front page picture, read the story and looked again, remembering

Craig. Slowly he shook his head. This was a stranger, with a high forehead, full face and deep lines on either side of his nose, disappearing into a heavy beard. Not Craig, who had been thin and boyish, hair falling over his forehead, shadowed hollows in his cheeks. Still, there was something about the smile, and the clinging sadness of the eyes . . .

'Of course there's the beard,' said Victoria. 'And he's much older. But the eyes! And that smile! Ross? Isn't it Craig?'

Ross shook his head, anxious to get back to his meeting. 'I doubt it. There is a resemblance, but only a suggestion of one; it's interesting, but –'

'*Interesting!* What is the matter with you?' She sat straight, her eyes blazing at him. 'Do you think I don't know my own grandson? And even if, perhaps, I had some doubt, I thought I could count on your curiosity and stubbornness – but all you do is wave aside this *interesting* resemblance. What in heaven's name is wrong with you?' She saw him glance at the door to the conference room. 'Well – you want to get back. Why don't you simply agree to do what I ask? Then I'll leave you alone.'

Ross laughed and gently adjusted the scarf at his grand-mother's throat. 'All right; what is it you're asking me to do?'

'Go up there. Find out the truth for me.'

'To Vancouver? My dear, you can't ask me to drop every-thing to search out a stranger just because he seems to resemble someone you haven't seen for fifteen years.'

'Will you stop being so cautious! I don't think this is a stranger and I'm asking you to find out for me. For heaven's sake, who else can I ask?'

'Tobias,' Ross suggested. 'Claude –'

'For some favours. Not this one. Ross, *I must know.*'

Ross was re-reading the story. 'He's disappeared, it says. I wouldn't be able to see him.'

'His wife. His children. Photographs. Good heavens, boy, are you going to make me beg?'

'No.' Ross smiled and took her hand. Of all the family, he felt closest to Victoria. He would not make her beg. 'But I can't get away this week –' His private telephone rang and he made a gesture of apology as he answered it.

His brother's voice charged at him. 'Someone just called to tell me Craig's picture is in yesterday's *Vancouver News*.'

Ross tensed. 'It's hardly that certain.'

'You've seen it?'

'Yes. There's a curious resemblance. Nothing more.'

'I am going up there to find out. Read me the story so I'll have all the information.'

'Derek, wait a minute. I've already made arrangements to go and there's no need for both of us to be there. I'll call you when I get back.'

'*You're* going to Vancouver? To check out a long shot on Craig?'

'I'm going to Vancouver –'

'What the hell for? It's nothing to you if he –'

'– And I'll call you when I get back.'

Victoria smiled serenely as he hung up the telephone. She straightened her scarf and ran a small brush through her white curls. 'Thank you. How clever of you to keep Derek out of it. What a dreadful mess he might have made.'

Ross bent down to kiss her cheek. 'I would have gone anyway. For you.'

'I never doubted it, my dear. When will you go?'

'Tomorrow.'

From his taxi, driving through the city streets and across Lions Gate Bridge to the suburb of West Vancouver, Ross noted the buildings that had gone up since his last visit, six years earlier. He had just opened his own firm in San Francisco and had

32

been meeting with Vancouver city planners about the restoration of decaying neighbourhoods. At the end of the day, he'd gone back alone to the European boutiques of Robsonstrasse to shop for Melanie and the children. Might Craig have been here then – even, perhaps, passing him on the street? For God's sake, he thought; of course he hadn't. Craig had been dead for fifteen years, and this trip was a waste of time.

The houses of West Vancouver were built into wooded hills. Set back from the road, they offered passersby glimpses of natural wood and stone, wide windows, and terraced yards. As Ross opened his window to let in the scents of June, the taxi came to a stop beside a boxwood hedge. Beyond it, at the crest of a gentle slope, was a house smaller than its neighbours but skilfully designed to look larger by taking advantage of the contour of the land. Two children, a boy and a girl, ran down the walk and stopped a short distance away, watching gravely while Ross paid the driver. Turning, he got a good look at the boy and drew a sharp breath. Everything else faded; only the boy was clear; his compact body, his thin face tilted in curious examination, and the impatient gesture with which he pushed blond hair away from bright brown eyes.

'I guess you're not a detective,' the boy said. 'They all have cars. And you're not a policeman. So what are you?'

He was about eight, Ross thought, and it might be nothing more than coincidence.

'What *are* you?' the boy repeated.

'Not a detective,' Ross said to the boy. 'Have detectives been here?'

'Not yet – I don't think – but my Dad was supposed to be home last Friday and lots of people are looking for –'

'We don't answer questions from strangers,' the girl broke in.

'But you ask them,' Ross said, smiling at her. She was about nine, his son's age, and she promised to be a beauty, with heavy dark hair and high cheekbones in a delicate face. Her mouth was more determined than her brother's and her enormous hazel eyes were bold. For the first time, Ross wondered about their mother.

'It's our house,' the girl said firmly. 'We're supposed to ask questions. I'll bet you ask plenty when strangers come to your house.'

He smiled again, liking her spirit, wanting her to like him. 'You're right, I do. Especially when they don't introduce themselves. My name is Ross Hayward. I'm an architect, I live in San Francisco and I've come to see your mother, to talk to her about your father. I'd like to help,' he added, though he had not intended to say any such thing. 'If there's anything I can do.'

They studied him, shading their eyes against the noon sunlight. The girl made the decision. 'I'm Jennifer Fraser. This is my brother Todd. Mother is in the house and I think it's all right if you come in. You can follow us.'

'Thank you.' Ross followed them up the curving walk, thinking, *Jennifer. Her name is Jennifer.* As they reached the front door he slowed. The children had left it open and for a fleeting moment it seemed to be an entrance to a mysterious cave.

'Don't worry,' Jennifer said impatiently. 'I said it was all right for you to come in. I'll get mother.' She ran off as Todd led Ross through an arch into the living-room.

After the shadowed entrance hall, the brightness was striking. A curved wall of windows looked south and west, across the deep blue of the bay to the city of Vancouver and, beyond it, to Vancouver Island. Though the house was only about two hundred feet above the water, the expansive view gave an illusion of greater height and also made the living-room seem twice as large as it really was. Ross, the architect, the builder, scanned the room, running his hand along the window frames.

'Well done,' he murmured, admiring the vision of another architect and builder.

'I beg your pardon?' a voice said behind him, and he turned as Jennifer came in with her mother.

'I was admiring the windows,' he said. 'They're very fine.'

'My husband designed them.' She stopped, keeping the length of the room between. 'I trust Jennifer's instincts, but I'd rather not have visitors right now, so if you'll just tell me why you've come –'

He walked to her and held out his hand. 'Ross Hayward,' he said, watching for her reaction as she briefly put her hand in his, but there was nothing; either she did not recognise the name or she was so exhausted she could not respond. He could see her exhaustion: an aching weariness etched in her face, her body swaying slightly as she took her hand from his and rested it against the doorjamb, her neck muscles tense with the effort of holding up her head. But the architect and artist in him saw beneath her pale exhaustion, the delicate structure of her face – high cheekbones, a broad, clear forehead, long-lashed eyes with a faint upward turn at the corners, a generous mouth. Her dark hair was pulled carelessly back, but a few tendrils escaped the rubber band that held it and they clung to her cheek. In better times, Ross thought, she could be a lovely woman, and he found himself wanting to help her, to ease the strain in her face, to see her smile.

Instead, she frowned, meeting his searching look with her own puzzled one. Twice she began to say something, then caught herself. Finally, she said, 'I asked why you've come. If you won't tell me, you'll have to leave.'

'Mrs Fraser,' he said. 'Does my name mean anything to you?'

'Your name?'

'Hayward.'

She shook her head. 'Why should it?'

35

'Your husband never mentioned it?' Again she shook her head and Ross, watching her closely, said, 'He never . . . used it?'

'Of course not; why would he? He has his own name.'

Ross nodded. He looked at Jennifer and Todd, standing silently behind their mother. 'I think –' he began gently.

'That's not fair!' Jennifer cried, knowing what was coming 'We let you in! You can't tell us to leave!'

Katherine felt a chill of warning. 'Maybe we should go along with this,' she said slowly to Jennifer. 'I don't know what it's about, but – why don't you and Todd wait in the front yard? I'll call you as soon as Mr Hayward finishes all his secrets.'

'Mother, it's not fair!'

'I know. I want you to do it, anyway.'

Jennifer shrugged glumly. She took Todd's hand. 'Come on. Nobody wants us.'

Ross and Katherine watched them leave. 'I like them,' he said. 'I have two of my own, about their age –'

'Do you?' she responded distantly, and Ross fell silent, feeling the awkwardness of his intrusion. Why should she be interested in anything about him, except why he had come?

'Could we sit down?' he asked and led the way to the couch where they sat at opposite ends, facing each other. Katherine could not take her eyes off him. Tall, broad-shouldered, with an easy stride, he had a narrow, tanned face that was stern in repose, then suddenly lightened by the warmth of his smile. His dark eyes were deepset beneath heavy brows and unruly dark blond hair, and he wore his clothes with the confident air of a man accustomed to wealth. He was everything that Craig was not – and yet, somehow, the longer Katherine looked at him, the more he reminded her of Craig.

'I'm sorry,' she said, turning away, picking up a thread from the carpet. 'I know I'm staring, but you remind me of . . .

36

something about you reminds me of my husband. I don't know what it is, you're really quite different from Craig, but something about you . . .' She faltered. 'It's absurd, I know; I suppose I'll see Craig everywhere, now that –' She stopped again and took a breath. 'What is it you want?'

Ross opened his briefcase and took out the newspaper folded at the picture he had been looking at on the plane. 'I saw this yesterday in San Francisco.' He held it out, but Katherine recognising it, made no move to take it. A little awkwardly, he put it on the couch between them. 'I have a cousin,' he began. 'Or I had one. Craig Hayward.' From an inner pocket he pulled out a small photograph and laid it beside the newspaper. 'This was taken in 1965, when he was twenty-two. He was home from college for the summer, in San Francisco. A month later he was killed in an accident. At least, we thought he was killed. But when we saw this newspaper, it seemed a good idea to talk to you.'

There was a silence. 'Yes?' Katherine said politely. Relief was sweeping through her and she barely glanced at the picture. He had nothing important to tell her. 'I still don't know what you want from me.'

'Some of my family,' Ross said carefully, 'think the two pictures are the same man.'

Katherine frowned. 'I thought you said your cousin is dead.'

'We thought he was dead.'

'Well, it doesn't matter whether he is or not. My husband has nothing to do with him. He has a different name; he comes from Vancouver, not San Francisco; and he doesn't look anything like your picture. Even if he did, what would it mean? The world is full of people who look like other people and no one thinks anything of it. I'm sorry you've had a trip for nothing, but you're wasting your time, and mine, too, so if you'll please go –'

'You're probably right,' Ross agreed, but he stayed where

he was, looking from the photograph to the newspaper picture and then around the room. 'But as long as I'm here, I'd appreciate it if you'd answer a few questions. If you don't mind.'

'I do mind.' There was something about his voice, too, that reminded her of Craig, and she was becoming uncomfortable.

'Mrs Fraser,' said Ross quietly. 'Do you really believe your husband told you everything about himself? Isn't it possible that he had some secrets from you, that he kept a part of himself separate?'

'No!' Abruptly, Katherine stood up, hating him for making her lie. 'It is not possible and it is none of your business; nothing here is any of your business!'

He sat still, looking up at her. 'I want a few answers. Then I'll leave. The more you help me, the sooner that will be.'

'I can't help you! Can't you understand that? Can't you understand that I have no interest in you or your cousin? You said yourself there was probably nothing in it; what more do you want? You walk in here and accuse my husband of being someone else, which is ridiculous; you show me a picture that doesn't look at all like him; and you expect me to let you talk all day about it? I have other things to think about and *I want you to go*. I don't even know why you came here, trying to upset us –'

'I'm not here to upset you. I'm here because my grandmother sent me.'

The unexpectedness of it caught Katherine in mid-flight. She tried to picture Ross's grandmother – how old she must be! – sending him to Vancouver on a wild goose chase. Ross leaned forward. 'You see, Victoria is absolutely certain this is her Craig, her grandson, and she asked me – instructed me,' he added with a private smile of such tenderness that for a moment Katherine liked him. 'Instructed me to drop everything and come to Vancouver to confirm it.'

'And if you found it wasn't true?'

38

'I would tell her that and she would accept it. After all, she'd already lost him once.'

'Lost him.' For the first time, Katherine picked up the picture and really looked at it. A thin young man, clean-shaven, wearing a sports shirt open at the neck, tilting his head and smiling, but with an air of sadness, as if a thought or a memory haunted him. Shakily, she sat down. The eyes were like Craig's. The face was Todd's.

Ross was watching her. 'You see why I wanted answers.'

Stalling while she tried to think, Katherine asked, 'What does that mean – lost him?'

'He disappeared. There was a sailing accident in San Francisco Bay and we never saw him again. We assumed he drowned and was swept away. The current is especially strong near the Golden Gate Bridge, where it happened. But he was very strong – a champion long-distance runner in high school and college. It's possible that he was able to swim to shore. And then walk away.'

'But why would anyone do that?'

'I don't know. Shock, perhaps. He'd jumped in the water to save his sister when she fell overboard.'

'And – did he?'

Ross shook his head. 'She died.'

'That's . . . terrible. But still –'

'Her name was Jennifer.'

'Oh.' It was like a long sigh.

'And Craig never could face his own failures. He always ran away from them.'

The way your husband did. The unspoken words hovered in the quiet room. But we don't know that, Katherine argued silently; we don't even know if he's alive. She thrust the picture at Ross. 'Your grandmother is wrong. It's nothing more than a resemblance. My husband didn't even have a grandmother, at least none that he knew. He had no family at all, he

39

was an orphan, just as I was. It was one of the things we talked about: how much we wanted a family.'

'No family. Who brought him up?'

'Oh, foster parents, but we meant we wanted a loving family. The Driscolls fed and clothed him but they didn't –'

'The Driscolls? That was the name he gave you?'

The note in his voice stopped her. 'Do you know them?'

'My cousin and I used to play a game – that we were kidnapped and gave our kidnappers such a hard time they paid us to escape from them. We made it up from an O'Henry story we liked, called "The Ransom of the Red Chief." One of the kidnappers in the story, and in our game, was named Driscoll.'

In the silence Katherine heard the pounding of her heart. It's because he's so serious, she thought; he makes these coincidences sound more important than they are. 'I'm not interested in your childhood games,' she said, making a move to stand up. 'And if that's all you have to say, you'll really have to leave. We have so many things to do –'

'You have nothing to do but wait,' Ross said coldly. 'Look, damn it, I don't like this any better than you do. I didn't even want to come up here – I thought it was a waste of time – but now I have the damnedest feeling that it's not. In any event, there are too many things I can't explain, and I don't like loose ends. I'd think you wouldn't either; don't you want to know the truth? I want your help; whatever you can give me –'

'I can't give you anything!'

'Photographs. Letters. A diary. Didn't your husband have a desk? Craig always had one at home, with everything sorted out alphabetised, organised into neat packs held with rubber bands or pieces of string that he'd collect and wind around his finger.'

'So what?' Katherine cried. 'Millions of people organise their desks that way!'

'Or,' he went on, watching her. 'You can tell me what you thought when you looked at this picture. Todd. Is that right? I

40

think it is; when I first saw him, I thought I was looking at Craig at that age. Craig and I grew up together; he was only two years older – that would make him thirty-seven now; is that your husband's age? – and we were as close as brothers, especially since neither of us liked Derek, who really is my brother. Derek is one year older than I. We all came in a rush, as Victoria liked to say. Jennifer, too: if she'd lived, she'd be thirty-three now. And Todd is the image of Craig at seven or eight. Which is he?'

'What?'

'Todd. Is he seven or eight?'

'Eight.' Katherine walked to the arch that led to the entrance hall. Through the open front door she saw Todd and Jennifer sitting crosslegged on the grass, not talking, not moving. Waiting. For their father, for news of their father, for something to happen. She shivered. Something was happening. She turned back to Ross, thinking that she liked his face, its strong lines, the steady, absorbed way he looked at her, his smile when he talked about his grandmother. Briefly, she wished they could like each other, because she had no one to talk to. No one had called, no one had come by, not even Sarah Murphy, since the newspaper story about the embezzlement had appeared two days ago. But there was no way Ross could be their friend.

'I want you to leave,' she said again. He was silhouetted against the wall of windows and she could not see his face; when he did not answer she went on. 'You've told me your story, this crazy story that you're determined to believe, no matter what I think. Well, I'll tell you what I think. I'm sure there was a Craig Hayward who resembles my son, but it's just a coincidence and that's your problem, not mine. I married Craig Fraser, I've lived with him for ten years and *I know him*. You can't walk in here and tell me I don't know my own husband, that he's kept a lifetime of secrets from me about San

41

Francisco and a grandmother and an entire family I never heard of. Do you think I'm a child? I'm sorry you're disappointed, but not one word you've said is the truth . . . well, I suppose you do have a cousin named Craig, or you did, but nothing else is true, nothing else, *nothing else . . .*'

Her words fell away in the silent room. Ross walked towards her and she saw his dark eyes, oddly gentle in his stern face. His voice, when he spoke, was so quiet it took her a minute to feel the impact of his words. 'My cousin, Craig Hayward, his sister Jennifer, my brother Derek and I grew up in San Francisco, in a neighbourhood called Sea Cliff, and spent our weekends swimming or sailing or hiking in the mountains. Craig always said that someday he would build a house high up, with a curved wall of windows overlooking mountains – or water.'

Instinctively, Katherine looked past him, through the curved windows, at the sunlit bay at the base of their hill.

'He read a lot,' Ross went on. 'Mostly spy stories and histories. He was good with his hands and liked to make wood carvings, especially figures of people. But his favourite carvings were the soapstone ones made by Eskimos. Like this one.' He picked up an eight-inch black whale that Craig had bought a year ago from Hank Aylmer, a friend who bought carvings in Eskimo villages to sell in the United States.

Katherine closed her eyes, wishing Ross Hayward gone. He waited, and in the dense silence, she felt the force of Craig's absence. She had been too bewildered, too busy making telephone calls and talking to the police and trying to deal with Jennifer and Todd to feel the reality of it, but in that moment the full impact struck her. She stood in her house and Craig was nowhere in it. She felt him everywhere but he was nowhere. It was not the same as saying: Craig isn't in the living-room or the dining-room or even in Vancouver. It was as if she had to say, *Craig is not.*

Didn't this man understand that was what she had to think about? Why did he force this relentless outpouring of information on her when she had to think about a house without Craig? She opened her eyes to tell him, but as soon as she did, he began talking again.

'And my cousin liked the construction business. We were in it together: our grandfather, Hugh, who died in 1964; his sons Jason and Curt; and the three of us – Craig was Jason's son; Derek and I are Curt's sons. Every summer we worked in our family's company; we'd done it since we were kids, sweeping out offices, doing errands, tagging along on site inspections, later helping with blueprints. Craig loved it; he couldn't wait to finish college and work full time. He was on a job with my father the summer Jennifer was killed and he disappeared. Are there any photographs in the desk in that room?'

Trembling, Katherine folded her arms rigidly to keep her body still. She didn't have to tell him anything. Without her help, he would have to leave; she would never see him again; she could forget he'd ever been here.

But she knew it was too late for that. Because he was right: she did want to know the truth. Walking around him, she went into the study and took from the top drawer of Craig's desk the picture she had found. Wordlessly, she handed it to him and together they looked at the lovely girl laughing in the sunlight.

Ross let out a long breath. 'Dear God.' Once again he opened his briefcase and handed Katherine another picture, this one of four people on a sailboat: Ross on deck, hoisting the sail; the young Craig of the first picture at the wheel; a stranger, handsome and aloof, in the cockpit, and beside him the lovely girl, shading her eyes as she watched the sail rise up the mast.

'Jennifer,' Ross said simply. 'Craig's sister.'

Chapter 4

Derek Hayward refilled his glass with the special Scotch his grandmother kept on hand for his visits and looked thoughtfully across the room at the woman his brother had foisted on the family: a Canadian housewife as out of place in Victoria's elegant home as a field mouse among orchids. Katherine Fraser. Wife of Craig Fraser. Who, if Ross had it straight, was in fact their cousin Craig Hayward. Long gone, long forgotten. They'd thought.

Why the hell had Ross been in such a hurry to bring her here? Without giving them a chance to talk about her, even to get used to the idea of her, he decided *on his own* to invite her and her offspring to meet them. And without a whimper Victoria went along. So here they were – a family dinner. Even Jason and Ann, coming out of hiding in Maine to meet Katherine Fraser and hear about their son, their golden boy. Who, after all, didn't drown fifteen years ago. Who

44

had only run away. And now, it seemed, had done it again.

Derek smiled thinly. Trust Craig, he thought, to act like Craig. Absently swirling his Scotch, he watched Katherine as she talked to the rest of the family, and wondered what she was like beneath that drab façade. There had to be more, he thought; Craig had always liked good-looking women. But this one had no poise or sophistication, no glamour, no beauty . . . well, maybe. Good bone structure in her face, unusual eyes – might be interesting if she fixed herself up and stood straight instead of dragging down every line of her face and body. He shrugged. What difference did it make? If she really was cousin Craig's wife – and the photograph she'd shown Ross seemed to prove it – the only thing that mattered was that she was here, a stand-in for her husband, and they'd have to find out what she wanted from them, and what she really knew about Craig.

The others were clustered about her at one end of the vast drawing-room of Victoria's penthouse. Almost fifteen years since they were all together, but still they were more interested in Craig's wife than in each other. Even absent, the son of a bitch managed to make himself the centre of attention. Something else he'd always done.

Derek looked away, giving the room a cursory inspection as he did on every visit, to make sure Victoria was keeping the place up. It was worth a fortune; far more than the fortune that had been spent on it since his grandfather bought the top two floors of the building and remodelled them twenty-five years ago. The old man had been a genius, Derek reflected. Long before restoration became chic, he made the Hayward name famous for the kind of expensive custom work that rebuilt without destroying the best of the old. And everything he knew went into his own home, from the smallest carved mouldings to the huge marble fireplaces and the ceiling-high Tiffany window. Superb workmanship. It had been at the heart of every lesson Hugh Hayward's grandsons learned under his direction and still remembered and used, even if it was in the modern glass and steel towers that Derek preferred. At least, Derek amended, I remember, and I suppose Ross does. Who knows what Craig remembers?

Craig again. Always there. Intruding. Across the room, that Canadian housewife stood between Ross and Victoria, reminding everyone that he was alive and could turn up any day. Possibly in Vancouver but, now that Ross had brought her here, just as likely in San Francisco, back to their big happy family and the construction company that Derek had been running for years without interference.

'A fearsome, ferocious frown,' Melanie commented lightly, coming up beside him. 'Who's the latest target?' She followed his gaze. 'Oh. Ross's new toy.'

He took a moment to approve her sleek good looks and the curve of her silk dress, then asked casually, 'And what do you make of her?'

She pursed her lips. 'A good wife never comments on her husband's toys.'

'My dear Melanie, you know better than to suggest that my brother collects other women. Or plays with them.' Shifting his glass, his hand brushed her bare arm. 'If you're looking for reasons to divorce him, you'll have to look elsewhere.'

'And if I find some?'

'It would amaze us all.' He watched Ross bring Katherine a glass of wine.

'Amaze you! Haven't I told you, over and over –?'

'Over and over.' He smiled at her. 'Proving how easy it is to complain about a husband without giving up his bank account.'

'Derek, Melanie,' said Tobias, behind them. 'Deep in a sinister plot?'

'Exchanging recipes,' Derek said smoothly. 'How are you,

Tobias? Still well? Still writing your book on – what was it? Cannibalism?'

'Love,' Tobias corrected cheerfully. 'I think you have them confused, Derek.' His blue eyes were wide and innocent above the neat white beard that quivered as he spoke. 'And then of course, the family history, as you also know. Perhaps I should interview you for both books. With your unique viewpoint –'

'I think Victoria wants you,' Derek cut in, seeing his grandmother look around the room. 'Aren't you being her good brother and helping host this festive affair?'

Tobias shot him a quick glance, his eyes briefly penetrating, then wandering and amiable again. 'Claude is helping, which he enjoys, so I can tiptoe about, listening, which I enjoy. How did you and Melanie resist discussing our newest family member?'

'Excuse me,' said Melanie abruptly, and walked across the room, casually inserting herself between Katherine and Ross. 'We've hardly met,' she said to Katherine. 'Everybody's monopolising you, but after all it was my husband who found you, so I should get a chance, don't you think?'

Katherine felt as if a light had flared beside her, exposing everything about her that was wrong. Next to Melanie's blue silk dress her linen suit was wrinkled and plain; her hair was dull compared to Melanie's gleaming ebony; her pale skin washed-out beside Melanie's golden tan. And she knew, as she pulled her shoulders back, trying to stand straight, that Melanie's gliding walk across the room came from a confidence and wealth she did not even know how to imitate. In the luxury of Victoria's apartment, amid these wealthy people, Katherine felt as strange and uncomfortable as a foreigner.

Still, she was the centre of attention. Ross had told her she would be, when he invited her to meet them. 'It's your family, too; you should know them and let them get to know you, let them get used to the idea of you and the children. After all –'

He had looked bemused for a moment, realising anew the enormity of what had happened. 'After fifteen years, to discover someone you loved is not dead but alive, and married, with children –'

'He may . . . not be alive,' Katherine had said.

'I'm assuming he is. But even if he isn't, you have a family in San Francisco and everyone has a lot of catching up to do.'

He had made it seem so simple. And in the two days before they flew there, as they tried to imagine that unknown family, Katherine became excited about the Haywards and Jennifer and Todd overcame their confusion enough to be intrigued by the idea of suddenly having grandparents, as well as the prospect of their first aeroplane trip.

'But I still don't see,' Jennifer said on Sunday, when they were high above the earth and she could tear herself from the window, 'why Daddy never told us he had a family.'

'That's the nine millionth time you've said that,' Todd grumbled, frustrated because he had lost the coin toss and would not get the window seat until the trip home.

'Well, *I* want to know why he didn't tell us, even if you don't,' Jennifer retorted.

'He probably didn't like them,' Todd said. 'You don't *have* to like people just because they're your family. We probably won't like them either. I bet they aren't even Daddy's family; I bet it's all a stupid mistake. I wish we weren't going.'

'Me too,' Jennifer confessed. 'It's scary. Daddy would have told us if we had grandparents. Why did they invite us? We should have stayed home.'

'Maybe they're going to kidnap us,' said Todd. 'And hold us for ransom.'

'Who'd pay?' Jennifer demanded.

'Daddy, of course,' said Todd. 'Only he's not here,' he remembered. 'So nobody will and they'll never let us go and we'll be prisoners for ever and ever.'

'Oh, enough,' Katherine said between weariness and amusement. 'It seems pretty clear that the Haywards are Daddy's family, which means they're our family, and I'm sure they're not scary. Ross said they want to meet us, and maybe all of us together can figure out why Daddy never told us about them. Or we won't know until he comes back and tells us himself. But no more guessing, all right? Just think instead how nice it will be to have an instant family to help us.'

An instant family. Waiting for them. In a way, Jennifer was right: it was scary. But, sitting on the aisle of the huge aeroplane, watching her children inspect their wrapped silverware and small dishes of food, Katherine recaptured her eagerness. The Haywards would be a place to belong, an anchor to cling to when everything else seemed to be collapsing. And someone to talk to about Craig. There was no one else; Katherine had tried to call Leslie, but she was out of town. With the Haywards, she wouldn't be alone anymore.

Her eagerness was in her face when Ross met them at the airport. By the time they reached Victoria's building, it was in Jennifer's and Todd's, too, though they clung to Katherine's hands in the elevator, and hung back as Ross led them into an apartment where a cluster of people awaited. 'Craig's family,' Ross said quietly.

A circle of piercing, measuring eyes surrounded Katherine. *Craig's family.* Impossible. But no one contradicted Ross when he said it. *My husband's family. And I never knew they existed.*

'Victoria Hayward,' Ross said into the brief silence. 'Craig's grandmother. Katherine Fraser.' The two women faced each other. Eighty years old, Victoria was as tall as Katherine and as slender. With skin like finely-webbed parchment, and short, pure white curls about her head, she had a regal beauty that made Katherine nervous. Beneath that calm gaze, she felt young, and inexperienced.

Their hands met, Victoria's cool and dry, unexpectedly firm. 'Welcome, my dear,' she said with a faint smile. 'You come as a surprise.'

'And Todd and Jennifer Fraser,' Ross said, bringing the children forward. Victoria glanced at them and her body went very still. Behind her, a woman gasped. Touching Todd's blond hair, Victoria said, 'Your son. And you named your daughter Jennifer.'

'Daddy chose it,' said Jennifer. 'It was his favourite name, he said.'

'Yes,' Victoria murmured.

Todd looked at her challengingly. 'Are you our grandmother?'

'Incredible,' Victoria said. 'Even the voice –'

'I am.' A small woman, her shoulders hunched, came forward, holding out her hands to Todd and Jennifer. 'Your grandmother.' She smiled tremulously at Katherine. 'I'm Ann Hayward. Craig's mother. And Jason –' She gestured towards a tall man with a dark, weathered face. 'His father.' It was Ann who had gasped when she saw Todd and now she put her arm around him, her face radiant. 'It is incredible, isn't it? Jason? The resemblance –?'

Todd squirmed in embarrassment but Katherine was watching Jason, who had not moved. His face was blank. 'Yes,' he said. 'Craig looked like that once.'

Ross continued his calm introductions. 'Tobias Wheatley, Victoria's brother; my wife, Melanie; our children, Jon and Carrie; Claude Fleming, a friend of the family. And my brother. Derek Hayward.'

Derek nodded to Katherine. She recognised him from the photograph: the handsome, aloof stranger in the cockpit of the sailboat. He was still aloof, taking no part in the talk that was starting and stopping, like a reluctant motor, in the small group of people.

'There's a bunch of Atari games in the library,' Jon Hayward said to Todd. He was a year older, with blond hair and his father's deepset, dark eyes. 'Do you want to play? You too,' he added magnanimously to Jennifer and Carrie.

'We can beat them,' Carrie whispered loudly to Jennifer. Small, blonde, lively, just ten years old, she bounced on her toes. 'Jon always gets impatient and plays like a gorilla.'

'Mom?' Todd asked. 'Can we?'

Katherine hesitated, not wanting to be left alone, and Jennifer, watching her, said, 'I'd rather stay here.'

Katherine shook her head. This seemed planned, as if Ross had instructed his children to clear the youngsters from the room. 'Of course you should go,' she said. 'Have a good time.'

She watched the four of them run off and followed the family into the drawing-room. A few steps in, she stopped, overwhelmed by brilliant colours and textures: silk-covered apricot walls, pale yellow velvet furniture and muted Persian rugs. With the red-gold sunset flooding in through high windows, the room seemed lit from within and Katherine drew a breath of pure pleasure. 'It's the most beautiful room I've ever seen,' she said softly.

'Yes,' said Victoria, pleased. She sat in a wing chair beside open French doors that led to a balcony, while the others stood nearby, pouring drinks, filling small plates with hors d'oeuvres from a table beside the piano, and asking questions of Katherine. Only Derek stood apart. Katherine kept glancing at him, puzzled by his aloofness, vaguely aware of the power of his separateness: he was the kind of man others would want to impress, to make a dent in his still, smooth surface.

'– Craig look like?' Ann was asking eagerly. 'I couldn't tell from the newspaper pictures; they're so fuzzy . . .'

'I brought photographs,' Katherine said, taking a packet from her purse and handing it to Ann. Immediately, Ann gave

51

it to Victoria. Katherine flushed. Everything begins with Victoria, she thought. Ross told me, I should have remembered.

Victoria went through the pack slowly, handing each picture to Ann as she finished with it. She was very pale, and her lips quivered, but she finished the pile in silence and then stared fixedly through the French doors.

'Did Craig still hike in the mountains?' Ann asked, looking at the photograph of all of them in the Grouse Mountain cable car. 'Did he have staff working for him?' she asked when she came to the picture of Craig and Carl Doerner at their desks. 'I have his trophies for long-distance running,' she said, holding a picture of Craig on a bicycle. 'I can send them to you, if you'd like.'

Tobias, too, was looking at the photographs, commenting and passing them on to others who made their own remarks. From the tangled voices, Tobias said, clearly and sadly, '. . . And wondering all the while, what stranger would come back to me.'

A silence fell. 'Not to me,' Katherine faltered. 'He's not a stranger to me.'

'Oh dear, oh dear,' Tobias lamented. 'I'm so sorry; I didn't mean to upset you. I was quoting a poet. Wilfrid Gibson. I have a habit of doing that; popping up with quotations, which, alas, my family usually ignores. When I taught at University, my students had no choice but to listen. I do miss that. You mustn't take it personally. Though Craig is a stranger to us, you know.'

Jason walked past Tobias to Katherine. Tall and thin, he had the tough gnarled hands of a man who worked outdoors, and his gaze was restless, searching the room. 'Ross said your husband is in the construction business. His own company?'

'He has a partner.'

'How much does he own?'

'One-fourth.'

'One-fourth?'

'He was going to buy more,' Katherine said defensively. 'In fact, Carl planned to have Craig take over when he retired.'

'How much did he make?'

'I don't know.' She was defensive again. 'It depended on how many jobs they had each year and Craig didn't like to talk about money. We always had enough.'

'Well,' Jason said. Katherine held her breath, waiting for someone to say, *Enough of stolen money. He embezzled from his company.* But no one did. They won't talk about it, Katherine thought. In fact, she suddenly realised, they were asking questions, but no one was really talking about Craig at all.

And she and Jason had talked in the past tense. As if he were dead.

She looked about the room. Derek was watching her, his narrow face and deep eyes so absorbed it was if he had erased everything else, holding only Katherine in the path of his vision. Flustered, she looked away, at Claude Fleming who had not yet spoken, at Ross, who was more distant than he had been in Vancouver, and beyond them, through the French doors.

The kaleidoscope of San Francisco stretched from Victoria's balcony at the crest of Pacific Heights far down to the misty water of the bay. The view blended with the mirrors and tapestries on the apricot silk walls so there seemed to be no barrier between the rooms and the sky and the city below. They were suspended above the earth on the golden light of early evening. A magic place, Katherine thought, and wondered if Craig had felt the same way when he was here.

When he was here. He had spent his growing up years in these rooms, with these people. It was impossible to understand. *Where are you?* Katherine cried silently. *This is your family; I shouldn't be here without you, we should be here together . . .*

'Katherine.' Victoria motioned to her to sit beside her. 'Tell me about your family.' Briefly, Katherine described her father and mother, their small grocery store, and the apartment above it, where they lived together until she was three, when her parents died within a few months of each other and her aunt came to live with her.

'In Vancouver?'

'No. In San Francisco.'

'San Francisco! Ross! Did you know that?'

'No.' He looked at Katherine. 'You never mentioned it.'

'You only wanted to know about Craig.'

'You should have told him,' Victoria declared. 'And where did you go to college?'

It's a test, Katherine decided. And I've probably failed because I grew up over a grocery store. 'I went to San Francisco State College for two years; then I had to go to work.'

Beneath Victoria's scrutiny, Katherine thought – she's comparing me to the women the Hayward men usually choose. Richer, smarter, more beautiful.

Ross brought her a glass of wine and Claude Fleming asked, 'Where did you work?'

'I was a clerk in a jewellery store. I wanted to learn to design and make jewellery.'

'And did you learn?'

'I've made a few pieces.'

'That you sold?'

'No; I gave them as gifts.' *I know what it is. I'm like the bride-to-be, under inspection by the groom's family. But there isn't any groom.* Dimly, Craig hovered nearby and suddenly her longing for him burst within her. It engulfed her and tears stung her eyes. *Where are you?* she cried again. *And who are you*? She wanted Craig, the Craig she knew; she wanted to be home; she wanted the four of them to be together, where they belonged.

'Mrs Fraser.' Claude Fleming stood beside Victoria's chair. 'Does your husband have any distinguishing features? A scar, for example? Or a limp?'

Hope flared in Katherine. They weren't really sure it was the same man. Maybe Todd had been right: it was all a mistake. And she'd been right, too: she *knew* Craig – he would not have kept such an enormous secret from her.

Ross had been gazing across the room at Melanie and Derek, their heads close together as Tobias came up behind them. He turned. 'Claude, you can't dismiss the photograph Katherine found.'

'Or the son,' said Victoria shortly. 'I know you're trying to be helpful, Claude, but the boy is the image of Craig. And the girl is named Jennifer. We've all accepted it.'

'A lawyer looks for proof,' Claude said. 'Not emotion.'

'Lawyer?' Katherine asked.

'Family lawyer as well as friend. Did your husband have any distinguishing features?'

'A scar,' she answered, thinking how curious that the Haywards should ask their lawyer to help them meet her. 'Next to his right eyebrow.'

'And so did Craig,' sighed Victoria. 'From one of Derek's acrobatic horseshoe pitches.'

'It's not conclusive,' said Claude. 'But let it go for now. Mrs Fraser, what did your husband tell you about the Haywards?'

'Tell me –? Nothing. I told you I never heard of the Haywards until Ross came to Vancouver.'

'For fifteen years,' Claude said sarcastically, 'a man does not tell his wife about his family. Parents. Grandparents. A sister. Two cousins. A little hard to believe, wouldn't you say?'

Katherine flushed. 'I don't know what *you* would say –'

Ross put a steadying hand on hers. 'I think he kept us a secret, Claude,' he said quietly.

'Then what the hell *did* he tell you?' Claude demanded.

'That he was an orphan. It was one of the things we – I thought *we* shared. He was brought up by foster parents in Vancouver – he said – and always wanted a family . . .' Her voice trailed away.

'Insane,' Claude muttered. 'Ridiculous.'

And it was then that Melanie crossed the room, pushing between Ross and Katherine, saying, 'We've hardly met,' and making Katherine feel drab and out of place next to the flare of her high colour and blue silk dress.

'Ah,' said Victoria, relief in her voice, as she saw the butler in the dining-room arch. 'Dinner. Ross, will you help me? Derek, you've been avoiding us; please take Katherine in. Claude, you and Melanie. Jason and Ann, I suppose. Tobias dear, we have no one for you.'

'Only the butler,' said Tobias cheerfully and, leading the way, took the chair at the foot of the table, opposite Victoria at the head.

Derek sat at Victoria's right, Katherine at her left, but it was not the intimate family dinner she had imagined. Nine people, at formal place settings on hand-embroidered linen place mats, were spaced about a gleaming mahogany table where eighteen would have been comfortable.

No places for the children, Katherine realised, just as Victoria said, 'The children are being served in the library. In my experience, they're happier with each other than with adults. But if you prefer having your children with you, the arrangement can be changed.'

'No.' Once again, Katherine felt tears sting her eyes. 'I'm sure they'll be happier there.' Feeling alone and troubled, she watched the butler fill wine glasses as the maid served pale green soup in fragile bowls. Except for Derek, everyone was

56

friendly, and no one had said a word against Craig. But something was wrong, and she tried to identify it as she ate her soup and listened to the others talk about an office tower the Hayward Corporation was building in the financial district and a highway overpass they were bidding on near San Jose.

Across the table, Ross lifted his wine. 'We should drink a toast to the newest member of our family.'

'Yes,' said Victoria. 'Welcome, Katherine. We hope –'

She paused and there was a silence. What? Katherine wondered a little wildly. We hope Craig isn't dead or injured and lying somewhere undiscovered? That if he's alive he isn't guilty of embezzlement? That he'll come back to his wife and children and settle his financial problems? That he'll choose to come back to his first family after fifteen years of living a lie? That he'll tell his wife the truth for the first time in their marriage? That Katherine figures out what she's going to do?

'We hope Craig finds his way back to all of us,' Ross finished gracefully. 'Katherine, would you tell everyone about your house? It's very fine, especially the windows.'

She began, but almost immediately Ross took over, explaining how the house and its walls of windows followed the contour of the tree-covered hill, facing south above the panorama of English Bay, Vancouver and Vancouver Island.

'But the view,' Tobias said to Katherine. 'How do you have a view with all those trees?'

'They're so tall,' she said absently, preoccupied with her thoughts. 'We look between them; they're like pillars, holding up the sky.'

Derek looked up sharply. Tobias, too, looked surprised that she had said something interesting. 'A pleasant fancy,' he murmured.

'Don't you love the trees?' Ann asked. 'In Maine we live at the edge of a forest.'

'Craig helped clear them when we built the house,'

Katherine said, remembering his triumphant smile when he and the crew finally pulled out a large tree that was dying but still stubbornly clinging to the earth. 'He liked – likes – heavy work.'

'But aren't you tired of the forest?' Tobias asked Ann. 'Fifteen years of peace and quiet: so excessive. Why don't you move back here?' There was a glint in his eye. 'Jason could rejoin the company and we'd all be together again.'

Slowly Derek turned in his chair. 'Have you taken up family planning, Tobias?' he asked evenly.

Melanie laughed. Tobias looked amiably vague and Claude changed the subject, and at that moment Katherine knew what was wrong with the evening. *No one was excited about Craig.* Jason seemed almost angry, and the others – even Victoria and Ann, who did seem to care that he was alive – were so restrained it was as if they had no feelings about him at all. They'd asked questions, all except Derek, but at the table everyone was behaving as if this were an ordinary family dinner, with nothing unusual to discuss.

She cleared her throat. Her heart was pounding because she was afraid of making them angry. But after all, she was here to find out about Craig. 'Why did Craig disappear fifteen years ago?' she blurted into the murmuring conversations.

The conversation stopped. Everyone looked at Victoria. But Melanie spoke first. 'Why,' she drawled, 'most likely for the same reason he ran out on you.'

'Melanie, be silent,' Victoria snapped. 'You don't know what you're talking about.'

'They weren't married then, you know,' Tobias explained to Katherine. 'Melanie and Ross, that is. So she never met Craig.'

'Superb roast beef,' Derek said pleasantly to Victoria. 'Perfectly rare. Have you hired a new chef?'

'I hired him,' said Tobias. 'But Claude found him.'

'I also found the orchid,' said Claude, touching the plant in the centre of the table, its arching stems of white flowers mirrored in the mahogany. 'Like the roast, it is quite rare.'

'Do you grow flowers?' Victoria asked Katherine. 'Or vegetables? I confess I know nothing about the climate of Vancouver.'

Katherine put down her fork. She was Victoria's guest, and hopelessly inferior to all of these wealthy, self-confident people, but she was desperate to learn about Craig. With her eyes on the orchid, she said, 'I was trying to find out why Craig ran away fifteen years ago. I thought you would help me. With –'

'Money,' said Melanie brightly. 'And didn't we all know that was coming. You said I was wrong,' she told Ross. 'Well, who's wrong now? The minute she found out her husband had a wealthy family –'

'No,' he said flatly. 'I invited Katherine, and she came –'

'For her share of the wealth.' Melanie looked steadily at Katherine's lowered eyes. 'Right? Veteran's pay. Or maybe – if Craig wanted to come back for a piece of the company, wouldn't it be smart to send a sweet wife to test the waters?'

Victoria was watching Katherine. Letting Melanie do the dirty work, Katherine thought. ' "Blow, blow, thou winter wind!" ' Tobias intoned. 'Melanie, you are cold and unpleasant.'

'Or,' Melanie persisted, 'hush money. Not to broadcast Craig's latest mess and whatever else he did in the last –'

'God damn it!' Ross pushed back his chair.

'We don't *know* why he disappeared,' Tobias said hastily. 'Fifteen years ago. We have trouble talking about it,' he added. 'Partly because we don't know. Claude worked with the police –'

'We thought he was dead.' Claude spoke directly to Katherine. 'It never occurred to anyone that he might deliberately have disappeared.'

'We've thought and thought –' Ann exclaimed.

'Lack of information –' began Tobias.

'Trust!' stormed Jason. 'Lack of trust! If that young fool had come home and told us what happened –'

'What did happen?' asked Katherine.

'He wasn't a fool!' Ann protested. 'He was clever and dear and gentle . . .'

So was Craig, Katherine thought.

'The golden boy,' murmured Derek.

'Who wasn't a hero,' said Jason. 'So he ran away, to keep from facing us.'

'More likely,' said Ross quietly, 'he ran away because he couldn't face himself.'

'*Why*?' Katherine's voice was frustrated.

'Cowardice!' Jason boomed.

But Ann cried out, 'He died trying to –' as Claude's court-room voice rode over them:

'It seems he didn't die.'

'That is quite enough!' Victoria stood at the head of the table, her eyes blazing. 'I apologise,' she said to Katherine. 'My family is behaving like a raucous mob.' She swept them with her gaze. 'It is unforgivable.' At her gesture, the butler, wheeling in the dessert cart, stopped in the doorway. The room was still. Slowly, Victoria sat down and nodded permission to the butler to circle the table, offering a selection of desserts. The maid poured coffee. When everyone was served, Victoria said to Katherine, 'Ross told you nothing about the sailing accident?'

Uncertainly, Katherine said, 'Only that there was one.'

Victoria nodded. 'We do find it difficult to talk about. Even after so many years. And especially now . . . with the ending changed. But you shall hear the story.' She took a sip of coffee and looked around the table. 'Claude will tell it.'

'Of course,' Claude said easily. Why? Katherine wondered. He wasn't there. Ross said it was the four of them.

60

'The four of them,' Claude began. 'Craig, Jennifer, Derek and Ross, were sailing home across the bay. It was dusk. The bay is often unpredictable, particularly at that time and especially near the Golden Gate; I am told great concentration is needed to sail it safely. But they had been at a party in Sausalito, with a great deal of drinking, and none of them was capable of such concentration. There was a sudden change in wind direction and the boom swung across the boat. It struck Jennifer, knocking her unconscious, and she fell overboard. Craig immediately jumped in to save her. Ross and Derek – though neither was an experienced sailor at that time – managed to turn the boat around and return to Jennifer. They found her dead. Craig, of course, was gone.'

Again the room was still. Katherine glanced at the closed faces of Ann and Jason, trying to imagine what it would be like to lose both her children on the same day. But it was unimaginable: her thoughts skidded from the idea and she wondered if that was why they had moved to Maine.

'Odd,' Tobias ruminated. 'I thought there was something more to it. Of course I was living in Boston, but I seem to remember hearing that besides the wind, there was also a disagreement, one might say a quarrel, that distracted –'

'You *heard*, Tobias?' Derek asked coldly. 'You never told us you heard voices. Do you also see visions?'

'Katherine should hear the whole story,' Tobias said quietly.

'Craig was quarrelling?' Katherine asked. 'What about?'

'They'd been drinking,' said Claude. 'There were conflicting and, I gather, belligerent opinions on the best way to sail the boat. For some reason, rumours about a quarrel, even a fight, cropped up afterward; no one knew why. I think it would be unwise to resurrect any of them at this late date.'

There was a pause. Melanie's fingernail rang nervously against her wine glass. 'If you please,' said Victoria, and Melanie's finger was still.

'So,' Claude went on. 'Apparently Craig made his way to Vancouver. Most likely hitchhiking. Did he ever tell you, Mrs Fraser?'

Startled, Katherine said, 'How could he? I told you he never talked about –'

'Yes, I keep forgetting. Where did the name Fraser come from?'

She looked at him blankly. 'I don't know.'

'A suburb of Vancouver, perhaps? On the southern edge of the city?'

'Named Fraser?' Ross asked. 'Is there one, Claude?'

'Not far from the U.S. border. I found it on a map. I suppose he passed through it when he was running.'

'Did Craig keep up his carving?' Tobias asked Katherine. 'I always loved those little people he made – so realistic.'

'He went through a stage,' Ann recalled, 'of wanting to make carving his career. Can you imagine?'

'I can't at all,' said Tobias. 'I thought he was anxious to go into the company with Jason and Curt. My, my; so Ross wasn't the only one who wanted to break away.'

They had done it again, Katherine thought: moved on to small talk. She turned to Tobias. 'You mean you think he left to break away? You see, I'm trying to find out what kind of person he was – is.'

'You married him,' Melanie said sweetly. 'You must have known what kind of person he was.'

'Is he dead?' asked Tobias. 'I didn't know we'd decided that.'

'No –!' Katherine burst out.

'It's hard to know,' mused Derek, 'with Craig.'

'It is hardly a decision we can make,' Victoria said. All through dinner she had been intent on the conversation, her eyes following the rest of them. The only time she spoke out, Katherine realised, was to stop an outburst that might have revealed something about Craig. 'Port and cognac in the living-room,' Victoria added, and stood up.

Not everyone had finished coffee and dessert. Katherine understood that she was hurrying them through dinner. *Because she wants me gone.*

It was simple; it was obvious. Why had it taken her so long to see it? Ross had asked Victoria to give a dinner and she had done it, but not because she wanted to. None of them wanted this dinner; none of them wanted Katherine to be there. None of them wanted to talk about Craig.

Or maybe they did, but they could not confront the evidence that he had been alive all these years. And since they could hardly evade it with Katherine there, she was an interloper. *And so is Craig*, she thought. *Even though he's not here.*

What did he do, that his family can't rejoice that he's alive?

As clearly as if he sat beside her, she heard Craig say, Most families are rotten. He had said it often, when they were first married, adding that theirs would be different. Now he seemed so close she thought she could touch him. Rotten, his voice repeated.

'Please,' Katherine said loudly as the others pushed back their chairs. 'Please wait.' They looked at her.

'In the living-room,' Victoria ordered.

'No, please,' Katherine insisted; as long as they were together at the table, she might get them to listen to her. 'I don't understand you. I have so many questions about Craig's life before I knew him, and I thought you would want to know about his life over the past fifteen years. I thought we could share what we know because he never put his two lives together; he kept them separate –'

'That's *all* you want?' Claude asked. 'Knowing what you do about the Hayward family and the company –'

'I don't know anything about them! Don't you understand? I don't know the man I married; I barely know his family; I don't know what to believe – I don't even know if I understand myself. Don't you see?' No one answered. 'Well, then, there is something else. I thought you'd be so happy to know Craig is alive you'd do all you could to find him. You have so much wealth and power' – she ignored the triumphant look Melanie gave Ross – 'I thought you might hire investigators, put advertisements in newspapers, call people you know in other cities where he might have gone . . . I thought you'd help me look for him. And I thought the reason he vanished before might be connected with why he's gone now, and if we knew that we might find him together much faster than I could alone.'

No one spoke. They looked out the window or at Katherine or at the white orchid reflected in the dark mahogany table. Laughter from the library reached them faintly, but the dining-room was silent.

Katherine stood up. She felt lightheaded and dizzy, but, strangely, almost excited. She had to handle it alone, without Craig's help. And if they became angry and turned their backs on her – she would handle that alone, too.

'And I did think you might help us with a loan, just until Craig gets back, because we don't have much money and I don't know what we're going to do. But I wanted a loan, not a gift, and one of the things I wanted to do with it was hire detectives to look for him. Because we have to find him and help him.' She stopped briefly. 'If we can; if he's still alive. I don't know what's happened to him, he may be in trouble, or hurt, but you act as if you're the ones who are hurt, that he's insulted you because he –' She stopped again. No one had mentioned embezzlement and she would not be the one to bring it up. 'He's been – he *is* a wonderful husband and a wonderful father and I love him and I won't turn my back on him, even if you do, and I don't understand how you can talk about flower gardens and wood carvings and orchids when Craig –'

Victoria raised an imperious hand. 'We do not need you to tell us how to behave. You know very little about us –'

'I'd know more if you'd tell me!'

'Do not interrupt me! We opened our home to you and your children; you have little cause to criticise us.'

'I didn't want to.' Katherine's eyes filled with tears. 'But I think you'd be happier if you'd never heard of Craig Fraser at all.'

'Katherine,' Tobias chided, looking at Victoria's tight lips. 'Too much, too much. Don't say more than we can forget.'

'You don't want us here,' she went on doggedly. 'You don't want me and you don't want Craig. But of course it was very kind of you to invite us.' She hesitated, then turned to leave.

'Young woman!' Victoria's icy voice stopped her. She heard Tobias lament, 'Oh, Katherine,' and Melanie murmur, 'How charming; no one walks out on –' as Victoria said, 'How dare you turn your back on me! And where do you think you are going? You have no one else to help you.'

Katherine half-turned to see her – so beautiful in her regal anger it seemed nothing could touch her. 'You don't want to help and I don't need you. Craig and I have gotten along by ourselves for ten years, you haven't existed for us so why should I come to you now? I'll find him . . . and we'll be all right.' Quickly she left the room, trembling so violently she thought she would fall.

But suddenly Ross was there, his arm lightly around her shoulders as they walked through the drawing-room. 'I think you should stay,' he told her. 'What you said about us was partly true, but Victoria was right: there are many things you don't know about us. And there's no question that we'll help you financially. I apologise for my wife's insinuations –'

'You have nothing to apologise for. But I don't want any help from your family. All I want to do is go home, where I belong, and find my husband.'

He started to say something, then changed his mind as they came to the library. Jennifer and Carrie were locked in a computerised race with Todd and Jon on the television screen and it was a few minutes before Katherine was able to prise them loose. 'They have a million games, Mom!' Todd said as they all walked down a long gallery.

'They aren't ours,' said Jon. 'They're great-grandma's. But she lets us play anytime we want, and when you come back –'

'*Are* we coming back?' Jennifer asked, squinting as she tried to read her mother's face.

'No –' Katherine began and that single word, louder than she had intended, met Victoria and Tobias, who were waiting in the entry hall.

Tobias took Katherine's hands in his. 'We've all behaved badly; I'm quite ashamed of everyone. But you will come back, of course you will, now that we've met, now that we consider you part of the family –'

But it was clear he wasn't asking them to stay. Katherine stepped back. 'Goodbye,' she said to Victoria. 'I'm sorry.'

'So am I,' Victoria responded unexpectedly. But then she said to Ross, 'Are you driving them to the airport?'

The last of Katherine's fears of angering them dropped away. 'That isn't necessary,' she said bitingly. 'We can manage on our own. We wouldn't want to disrupt your life – I mean your *dinner* – any more than we already have. Todd, do you have your jacket? Jennifer?' She opened the carved oak door and urged them ahead of her into the small vestibule. 'We'll get a cab downstairs, for the airport. We're going home.'

As she pushed the elevator button, she saw Ross gesture to Victoria and Tobias to stay behind. He followed her into the vestibule. 'Your luggage is at the Fairmont,' he said.

'We'll pick it up on the way to the airport.'

'There may not be a flight for Vancouver tonight.'

'We'll find out.' The elevator arrived and the uniformed doorman slid open the door. Katherine held out her hand to Ross. 'Thank you again. When Craig comes home, would you like us to let you know?'

There was a barely perceptible pause. 'Of course,' he said. 'But I'll call in a day or two to see how you are.'

'Your family wouldn't approve.' Her courage exhausted, Katherine shepherded her children into the elevator and nodded to the doorman. The last thing she saw as he pulled shut the iron grille and started down, was Ross, shaking his head, contradicting her, and Carrie and Jon, who had run out to the vestibule, peering through the grille to shout a farewell to Jennifer and Todd.

Chapter 5

After the golden splendour of Victoria's apartment, the house in Vancouver seemed a cool and earthbound haven. But as soon as they opened the door, Katherine knew it was not. Driving home from the airport, listening to Todd and Jennifer imagining their father waiting for them, she had almost let herself be convinced, until they walked in and Todd called, 'Dad! We're home!' and they came up against the cold emptiness of the dark rooms. The house was exactly as they had left it, nothing out of place, nothing changed. 'God damn it!' Todd yelled, stomping down the stairs after searching the bedroom. Katherine let him. It was better than keeping it locked up inside.

But the next morning she was less patient. 'Just go,' she ordered, wanting to be alone, when they dragged their feet after breakfast. 'Daddy will come back, or not, whether you're here or at day camp. We have to keep going; we can't sit around like run-down toys, waiting for Daddy to come along and wind us up.'

That made them giggle and she was able to send them off to catch their bus, leaving her alone in the quiet rooms. Craig seemed to be everywhere – papers with his handwriting, pictures he had hung on the walls, the banister he had sanded and varnished to silken smoothness, the dent he'd made in the dishwasher when he threw a coffee mug at it in a fit of anger. What had he been angry about? Katherine couldn't remember. Maybe she had done something that reminded him of the Haywards.

If that was it, she could understand his anger. A closed private club, the Haywards. If Craig felt as uncomfortable with them as she had, no wonder he left.

But she still didn't know why he left. Sitting at Craig's desk, she knew she had bungled the evening. She hadn't been clever enough to get past their barriers, and so she had lost the chance to learn more about her husband.

She shuddered, remembering how inferior they had made her feel. Forget about them, she ordered herself. Think about now. Especially about money. The top of the desk was covered with bills for roof repairs, gasoline charges, summer clothes for the whole family, overdue bills, 'last notice' bills, a card from the collection agency, mortgage, utilities, and at least a dozen others coming due the first of July. Tomorrow.

Craig always insisted on paying the bills. Sometimes Katherine had teased him, asking what dark secrets made him so protective. Now she knew. She wondered how long he had been juggling accounts to keep them from being cancelled. Your house set him back more than he expected, Carl Doerner had said. Why didn't you tell me? Katherine silently asked Craig. Didn't you trust me?

Don't think about Craig; think about the bills. Two thousand dollars for the mortgage, due the first of the month. Fifteen hundred dollars in other bills due at the same time. Cash in hand: four hundred dollars in the checking account; one thousand in savings. Think about that. Thirty-five hundred dollars in bills. Fourteen hundred dollars in hand.

But she wasn't even sure of that. How much did he take with him? She picked up the telephone and called the bank. And was told that the checking account contained five thousand dollars.

'How much?' She repeated the account number.

'Five thousand four hundred thirteen dollars, Mrs Fraser,' the voice chirped. 'A deposit of five thousand dollars was made at ten-thirty a.m. on June 16th at the Park Royal branch. Would you like us to send you a duplicate deposit slip?'

'No. Thank you.' June 16th. Two weeks ago. The day Craig stood with her at their front gate at ten-fifteen in the morning and kissed her goodbye before taking a taxi to the airport. Only he hadn't gone straight to the airport. He'd stopped off at the bank in the Park Royal shopping centre and made a deposit. To keep his family going awhile.

He never intended to be home on Friday.

He wasn't dead; he wasn't hurt. He was looking for money to pay back Carl Doerner. That was the whole story: no sexy young girl, no mugging and murder, no heart attack. He'd gone away because things got too much for him and he'd come back when he got them straightened out. And that wouldn't be long. He knew Katherine had only enough money for two months. By leaving five thousand dollars, he was telling her he would be back in two months.

Or he'd decided that in two months she'd be able to manage alone.

Or that was all he could spare.

The telephone rang and she snatched it up. It was a policeman, asking if she had heard from her husband.

'No.'

70

'Or anything about him?'

'Yes.' All of Craig's secrets were becoming public. She told him about the Haywards.

'Well, now, ma'am,' he said doubtfully. 'That's a very strange story. But we'll check with the San Francisco police. And you keep in touch, now; don't forget about us if you hear anything else.'

Don't forget about us. Idiots, she thought, slamming down the telephone. All of them – Carl Doerner, the police, the Haywards – saw Craig's disappearance as a personal insult or challenge. No one seemed interested in her, or what she was discovering: that Craig Fraser didn't trust his wife to share his troubles, or his thoughts. He had just disappeared and left her to clean up the mess.

No one seemed interested. A few friends had made perfunctory calls, duty calls, offering, not sympathy (after all, the newspapers said her husband was a criminal) but – 'Help if you need it, Katherine; if things really get bad . . .' (How bad, she wondered, is 'really bad'?)

For the first time, Katherine recognised how fragile were her friendships of the past ten years. Craig had kept people at arm's length, insisting he and Katherine needed only each other. And Katherine had gone along. Through letters and phone calls, Leslie remained her only confidante; her friendships in Vancouver were casual and pleasant, but never intimate.

Now that had come to haunt her. Most people shy away from those in trouble, as if they might catch it by coming too close, and none of Katherine's and Craig's acquaintances were close or affectionate enough to hold out a supporting hand. Well, she'd do without them; she didn't need them. She didn't need the Haywards, either, or any of her neighbours, whom she had been avoiding because she found herself feeling ashamed of being Mrs Craig Fraser.

She didn't need Carl Doerner, either. He should have known Craig was in trouble at the company, and done something about it. Anyway, he was out of town, his secretary told her, for two weeks.

'I can always talk to myself,' Katherine said aloud, but the sound of her voice in the empty house made her feel even more alone and she turned on the radio, spinning the knob until an announcer's comforting baritone filled the rooms. With his company, she sat at Craig's desk and paid the most urgent bills, putting the others aside. Signing the cheques, she felt a brief surge of accomplishment, until she checked the bank balance. How had it shrunk so quickly? She might not have enough for another month. One emergency could wipe them out.

She paused, her hand halfway to the envelope she was about to stamp. *He had no right to do this to us.*

Quickly she shoved the thought away, with all the others she couldn't face, and when Todd and Jennifer came home, she was ready to think of dinner. 'Not that stuff again!' Todd groaned as she took cold cuts and cheese from the refrigerator. He dropped his knapsack on the floor. 'Why can't we have lamb chops or meat loaf or something *real*, like we used to?'

'You don't like to cook when it's just us, do you?' Jennifer asked. 'When Daddy's on a trip, you never cook a whole dinner.'

'You're right,' Katherine said after a moment. 'I haven't been very creative.' She returned the food to the refrigerator. They'd never seemed like a family when Craig was away and those were the times she used up leftovers or made picnic-like meals. But Craig had been gone for two weeks. We're the family now, she thought. It's about time I began cooking for three. 'Why don't we go out for hamburgers tonight?' she suggested. 'And tomorrow we'll buy groceries for the rest of the week.'

'The kind Daddy likes,' Jennifer said. 'So when he comes home he won't think we changed everything while he was gone.'

Katherine turned away. There had been changes every day since he left: little ones, hardly noticeable at first, and big ones, like paying the bills herself. The longer Craig was gone, the less recognisable home was – as if they lost him a little more each day.

'How are we going to buy hamburgers and groceries?' Todd asked. 'Daddy has all the money.'

'Don't be silly,' Jennifer scoffed. 'Mother goes shopping every week.'

'She gets the money from Daddy,' Todd insisted. 'So if he's not here, she doesn't have any.'

Uncertainly, Jennifer asked, 'We don't have any money?'

And Todd said, 'Who's going to take care of us?'

The wall clock hummed, the refrigerator clicked on, a sprinkler watered the roses on the terrace. The house was alive: solid and familiar. But as if a strong wind had made it sway, the children were afraid. And so am I, Katherine thought, but that idea, too, she had to banish.

'We're going to take care of us,' she said firmly. 'We do have money; we just have to be careful how we spend it.'

'How long will it last?' asked Jennifer.

'Until I start to earn our living.' The words came out on their own. Katherine repeated them silently, wondering when she had made the decision. Writing cheques, she thought; when else? Another change: the biggest so far. 'I'm going to get a job,' she said. 'As a jewellery designer.'

On Dominion Day, July first, Ann Hayward called. 'We want to see you, Katherine, before we go back to Maine. We can be there this afternoon.'

'Here?' Katherine asked. 'Why?'

'To apologise, of course. Such a dreadful evening, and even though you can't really blame anyone –'

Oh yes I can. 'I'm sorry,' she said. 'We're busy all day; I promised to take Jennifer and Todd to the parade and then the fireworks –'

'*Today*?'

She thinks I'm lying because I don't want to see her. 'Dominion Day. It's something like the Fourth of July, but not quite the –'

'Well, we'll go with you. Katherine, we want to get to know you. We certainly didn't have a chance the other night.'

Katherine hesitated. They were Todd and Jennifer's grandparents. But then she remembered Jason's harsh questions. 'Does Jason want to come?'

After a pause, Ann said, 'I may come alone. He's needed at home – we have a shop, you know, for pottery and things.' She fumbled for words. 'And it's taking him a while to get used to the idea that Craig is alive.'

'That would please most fathers,' Katherine said coldly.

'Yes. Of course. But it's hard for him to think that Craig abandoned us, let us mourn . . . It's very difficult. We've started quarrelling again, all the old quarrels about whether Victoria and I spoiled him too much, or Jason expected too much of him . . . But that isn't why I called. I want to see you and I'm sure Jason won't mind if I come alone.'

I don't want to be involved with your family, Katherine thought, and said, 'Maybe some other time.'

'But we're in California,' Ann pressed. 'Much closer than Maine. And I'd be representing the whole family.'

'Some other time. I promised Jennifer and Todd the whole day.'

'Katherine, you have no right to deprive me of my grandchildren!'

For a moment Katherine was tempted to say all right, to

pretend Ann was the mother she'd never had and she was the daughter Ann had lost, to let Ann spoil Todd and Jennifer as her only grandchildren, and perhaps at last to have someone to talk to. But she couldn't do it. Ann was a member of the Haywards' private club; she had been silent, deferring to her husband and the others when Katherine asked for help. 'I'm sorry,' she said reluctantly. 'Maybe some other time.'

'Well,' Ann sighed. 'If you refuse to let us be friends . . .' Katherine said nothing. 'I'm sending you some money. Not a lot, I'm afraid, but after I've talked to Jason I can send more.'

'I don't want it. We're fine; we don't need it.'

'It's already in the mail. Katherine, you should be more gracious; we're not as bad as you think and we can be very helpful to you and the children. It's true that we were confused when we met you; we'd had no time to get used to –'

Katherine listened as Ann repeated everything she had said before, but the evening at Victoria's had convinced her that she had her own life – hers and Craig's and the children's – and she had to hold it together by herself until Craig came back; she wasn't sure why, but she knew it was important. The only promise Katherine would make, because Ann begged her, was that she would not tear up the cheque when it arrived.

Two weeks later, she took it from the drawer where she had tucked it out of sight, and deposited it in the bank.

Her hand shook as she endorsed it and she wrote briefly to Ann, telling her she would repay it as soon as she found a job; as soon as she was earning her own money. The trouble was, she had almost no money, no job, and no prospects for one.

'Sorry, not now,' said most of the jewellery store buyers whom she called for an appointment. 'We're full up with orders. Try us in six or seven months; sometime after Christmas.' Others told her to send in sketches or colour slides

75

of her jewellery. 'However,' they added, 'we buy very little from unknown designers.' Three agreed to see her.

And all three turned her down. 'What is missing,' they all said in one way or another, while inspecting the necklace and earrings she had brought in, 'is the meticulous touch of the professional. This has been your hobby, is that right? It shows, you see. Your technique is very basic, not complex and original; there is no touch of the artist. Truly fine jewellery should make you say, "This would be less beautiful if the design, materials and technique came together in any other way." One cannot say that of your pieces. Look here, at this necklace . . .' And, like the teachers who had criticised her in grade school, each of them found fault with some part of her jewellery.

None of them suggested she come back another time. They dismissed her and turned their attention elsewhere even before Katherine was gone.

There is no touch of the artist. Katherine huddled in the corner of the couch where she sat every night, waiting for Craig amid the shadows cast by the porch light's glare. *Your hobby, is that right? It shows* . . . Craig had said she was good. Everyone said, 'You're so clever, Katherine; so talented.' But it wasn't true; they'd said it to please her.

I'm not talented or clever, she thought. I'm not even good.

A wind came up, slamming the screen door back and forth. In the living-room, shadows swayed, creating new shapes. Everything was changing but Katherine felt bogged down. People spend years becoming jewellery designers, but I expected to walk in and find stores, customers, a salary, all waiting for me. I thought it would be easy because I love doing it. But people don't pay you for doing something just because you love it. You have to be good; you have to be professional. And I'm not.

Leslie might have some suggestions, but Katherine still

76

hadn't been able to reach her. And she wasn't sure she really wanted to talk to Leslie. *All my failures compared to her triumphs.* No, she thought, I'll manage. She walked through the swaying shadows to Craig's desk and put her samples and sketches into a bottom drawer. And the next day she went job-hunting.

'Ah . . . no experience, Mrs Fraser,' said one personnel director after another, looking at her application. 'Clerk in a jewellery store ten years ago. And since then – nothing?'

Only running a house, she answered silently. Bringing up two children. Being a wife.

'Skills, Mrs Fraser?' They all skimmed her application. 'No typing. No shorthand. No data processing. No computer experience at all?' She shook her head. 'No accounting. No bookkeeping. Not even general office experience. You've never worked in an office?' Again she shook her head. 'Or sold real estate?'

'No,' she said.

They shrugged. 'Nothing we can offer you. No skills and you haven't worked for ten years. No track record. The recession, you know; we're cutting back. The only people we might hire would be ones with experience. Sorry. Good luck.'

Good luck. While all around her, doors were closing.

She curled up on the couch, tighter each night. What will I do if I can't find a job? I could borrow on the house. No I couldn't; not without a job. And anyway, how would I pay it back? What will we do if I don't find a job? Fear spun a web inside her. Of course I'll find a job. I just have to be patient. I'll find one tomorrow.

Two days later she swallowed her pride and called the friends who had offered help if she needed it, to ask if they knew of any jobs. Some worked in offices in the city; all of them were married to men who did. But they all said, 'Oh, Katherine, there isn't a thing. The economy, you know;

nobody's hiring. But I'm sure you'll find something; you've always been so good with your hands. And, listen, we should get together for lunch. Not this week or next – things are so busy – but one of these days we certainly will get together.'

None of them said a word about Craig.

The last name on Katherine's list was Frances Doerner, and she sounded as friendly as ever. 'Of course I'll talk to Carl, Katherine, and I'm sure he'll find something for you; every company needs efficient people, don't you think? He's still out of town but as soon as he calls, I'll talk to him and get back to you.'

Not as friendly as ever, Katherine thought as they hung up. Once she would have invited us to dinner. But it doesn't matter. Carl will find me a job.

Still, whatever she earned would be far less than Craig had brought home. If they had been living beyond Craig's salary, how could they live on hers? She sat at the desk, adding and subtracting numbers, thinking of wild schemes that dribbled away to nothing. And the next morning, at breakfast, with no solution in sight, she forced herself to explain their finances to Jennifer and Todd, as honestly as she could. 'So what we have to do,' she concluded, 'is sell the house,' and without warning she began to cry.

They stared at her, sitting stiffly in their chairs. 'We *can't* sell the house,' Jennifer said. 'We *live* here. And we have to be here when Daddy comes back.'

'We can't, we can't,' Todd chimed in. 'Daddy won't know where we are; he'll think we forgot him, he'll think we don't want him anymore.'

'He's smart enough to find us,' Katherine said. She wiped away her tears and swallowed the unshed ones. 'We're going to rent an apartment in Vancouver and he'll call Information to get our new address and telephone number.'

'What apartment?' they asked.

'The one we're going to find tomorrow afternoon. We'll make a list of neighbourhoods we like –'

'Not me,' said Jennifer. 'And I'm not moving, either. I'm staying here until Daddy comes home.'

'Me too,' Todd chimed in. 'I'm staying with Jennifer.'

'You'll do what I tell you!' Katherine's voice rose. 'I'm selling this house because we can't afford it, because your father didn't leave me enough money to pay for it, and since you don't know anything about that, you'll keep quiet and do what you're told!'

Jennifer and Todd burst into tears. 'Why did he go away?' cried Todd. 'Didn't he like us anymore?'

'If he got mad at something we did . . . ' Jennifer said, her words trailing off.

'He would have told us, though,' Todd asserted. 'At least . . . wouldn't he?'

Katherine was slow to understand. 'Told you what?'

'WHAT WE DID TO GET HIM MAD!' Todd bellowed. He scowled at Katherine. 'Like, if he was mad at me and didn't want to be around me anymore.'

'Or me,' Jennifer echoed.

'I could maybe fix it,' Todd went on. 'Or say I'm sorry or something so he'd come back. If he knew. We'd have to find him to tell him, and if we don't know where he is . . .'

'He wouldn't stop loving us, though,' Jennifer said. 'Would he? And leave us? I mean, he never disappeared before, and I did lots of things he didn't like, so I don't see why –'

'Wait. Wait a minute, both of you.' Katherine shook her head. Where did they get such ideas? She leaned forward and held them, feeling guilty for the hurt in their eyes. They needed to believe the world was an orderly place where everything had a reason, but she had no reasons to give them. 'Listen to me. You had nothing to do with Daddy's leaving. It's complicated, but you're not to blame. He loves you.'

Jennifer shook her head disconsolately. 'What else could it be?'

Todd frowned. 'Maybe he's hiding, to test us. And we have to find him. Like the prince in that story who had to climb a hundred mountains and pick a special flower and kill a witch and slay a dragon before he could be king. Or something.'

'That's dumb,' Jennifer said, but softly, because Todd was trying to make her feel better. She said to Katherine, 'If it wasn't us, was it because of what Mr Doerner said that day?'

'No!' Todd shouted.

'It might be,' Katherine said carefully. 'Nobody knows the whole story, though. We can't make any judgements yet.'

'But if he *was* mad at us,' said Jennifer, 'and found a family he liked better, and they didn't do anything to get him mad –'

'That's enough!' Katherine's control began to slip. 'He wasn't mad at you; he didn't find another family. He'll tell you that himself, when he gets back.' She hurried them through breakfast, and out of the house, to catch the bus for camp. And before she could begin to brood about whether she had handled them properly or not, she called the realtor and made an appointment for that afternoon.

He greeted her at her front door with the energy of an inquisitive terrier. 'Mrs Fraser, good afternoon, kind of you to think of us. Let's see what we have here, shall we?'

Clipboard in hand, he moved through the house, talking to himself as he took swift inventory and made notes. 'Good views, good light; oh, very pleasant kitchen. This door goes to –? Ah, garage, yes, a bit messy, but the youngsters can take care of that and also – um, basement, dear, dear, we need a good bit of straightening here, too, otherwise can't see the – ah, water heater. The whole house – you'll forgive my frankness – could use a thorough cleaning. Of course you've had other things on your mind, if one can believe the newspapers,

80

but you do want it to look its spanking cheerful best – purchasers pay more for a happy house than a sad one. Get your youngsters to clean up the garage and basement; it's good for them; help mother sell the place, don't you know.'

Katherine watched the realtor sniff about the rooms indifferent and unsparing, enumerating their faults, ignoring the love and laughter they had held. Once the house had been a refuge; now she was handing it over to be invaded and scrutinised by strangers and bought by someone who would not know or care about the lives that had been lived within its walls.

I don't want to sell it; I don't want to leave. She followed him back to the living-room. Why couldn't it wait? A week; maybe two; maybe a month . . . And lose it all, she thought. Because I can't keep up the payments. Clenching her hands, she thrust them into the pockets of her skirt. 'I was wondering about the price. And how quickly you can sell it.'

'Well now, difficult to say. The market is bad; bad all over; we're all hurting. Now I'm aware that you need to sell – you have my sincere sympathies, by the way; an awkward time for you – what is it? What's wrong? Are you all right?'

Between laughing and crying, Katherine began to cough. Awkward, she thought. It is certainly awkward to be deserted. Catching her breath, she said, 'I thought two hundred and twenty thousand for the house. Is that about right? That's what our neighbours got two years ago.'

'Two years ago, Mrs Fraser, it was a different market. For today that's high. And this is a small house. But we can start there and come down. How low will you go?'

'I don't know. This neighbourhood –'

'One of the best. But in bad times people will take other neighbourhoods if they have to. Tell you what, Mrs Fraser. Leave it to me. You clean up the place; have the kids tackle the basement and garage; they'll look bigger when they're neat.

You do that and I'll get plenty of traffic moving through here. We'll have an offer in no time and I guarantee you'll be satisfied.' He shook her hand, smiled brightly, and was gone.

Melancholy as they felt, it was a relief to have something definite to do. Jennifer and Todd, helping Katherine clean, began to accept the idea that they had to sell the house. 'And someday build another one,' said Todd. 'Just like this. Only with a basketball court.'

Then house-hunters came, tramping through the rooms, opening closet doors, peering into bureaus. One of Craig's favourite Eskimo carvings disappeared. But within two weeks the realtor called to say an offer had been made. 'It's not as much as we'd like, Mrs Fraser; in normal times, we wouldn't even entertain it for a house in West Vancouver. But since you're in a hurry –'

'How much?' she asked, cradling the telephone and reaching for a pencil.

'One seventy.'

'Wait.' Katherine scribbled numbers. One seventy minus his commission was about one sixty. Their mortgage was one fifty-two. Which left her –

'I know it's not what you'd hoped for, Mrs Fraser, but –'

Which left her eight thousand dollars.

'– But it's a bad time to sell a house, especially if you're in a hurry. I'm sure we'd do better if you'd wait a few months or a year, but as things stand, I recommend you accept it.'

Eight thousand dollars. For their wonderful house. 'I'll call you back,' Katherine said. Slowly she walked through the house, running her fingers along walls and doorjambs and curving windows, sitting briefly on the stone hearth where she and Craig had sat in the evenings when the house was being built, imagining the rooms that would take shape from the skeleton of studs and beams silhouetted around them. Our house, Katherine thought. We dreamed of it for years, we watched it grow, we painted and tiled and varnished, finishing it ourselves to save money. We made it. It's our house. How can I sell it on my own, without Craig? It's as if I'm cutting us apart, cutting our marriage apart.

Within her, something seemed to slip, like a cloth sliding off a table, exposing its flawed surface. *That's what Craig has done.*

In the vestibule, the mail was lying beneath the slot in the front door: more bills, an announcement of a sale at Eaton's, a letter, and two large manila envelopes from jewellery stores. Numbly, Katherine opened them. The last ones, she thought. All the photographs and sketches she had assembled so carefully and sent to jewellery buyers had come back, with polite notes.

'Dear Mrs Fraser. Thank you for sending us your designs. We regret that they do not meet our needs at present, but we wish you success in your career.'

'How can I be successful,' she murmured, 'if I can't get a start?' She opened the letter: a paragraph from an insurance company where she had applied for a job as a receptionist. They had hired someone with more experience, but wished her success in the future. How kind of everyone, she thought, to wish me success.

The telephone rang and she ran to it, thinking, as they all did whenever it rang – this time it will be Craig. But it was not. 'Katherine,' Ross said. 'I've been thinking about you.'

Absurdly, her heart leaped. She hadn't realised how isolated she felt until she heard his deep voice and remembered his smile. But then she thought – It's been five weeks since he said he'd call to see how we are. 'I've been busy,' he said. 'Or I would have called sooner. I owe you an apology for that fiasco at Victoria's, especially since I got you into it. We're a lot nicer than we seem, at least some of us; I hope you'll discover that for yourself. Now tell me, how are you? What have you heard?'

'Nothing.' She would have liked to tell him everything, but she couldn't: he was part of that family; he'd probably been thinking about her only because he wondered about Craig. Not much of a person to count on. 'We're just waiting. But I've decided to sell the house and move to a place we can afford.'

'Sell –? Isn't that a rash decision? How much money do you have?'

'Enough,' she said evasively. 'But not if we stay here.'

'But I might . . . you haven't sold it yet, have you?'

'I think so.'

'Look, you obviously think it's none of my business but – how much will you clear?'

'Eight thousand dollars. It's not –'

'Eight thousand! On that house? Katherine, don't be a fool. That's a valuable piece of property!'

'Who do you think you are?' she cried. He was as arrogant and unsympathetic as the rest of his family. 'The market is very bad here and I'm in a hurry; I can't make the payments –'

'I might make the payments. At least until you get a better price.'

'I don't want any money from you.'

'Damn it, it could be a business arrangement. To protect your property.'

I'd like someone to protect me, she thought wryly, but aloud she said, 'I don't want to be indebted to anyone.'

'Especially not the Haywards.'

She was silent.

'But we could help you, if you'd let us.' He waited. 'Katherine, you were the one who said you wanted a loan.' Still she said nothing. He let out his breath in a sigh. 'There's only so much we can do, from this distance. If you were here, we could –' he paused. 'Katherine, what about that? If things are as bad as they sound, what about your moving back to San Francisco?'

It was so unexpected she sat down abruptly on the kitchen stool. 'Moving?'

'You grew up here, you know the city, and if you were close by, we could help you. Forget what happened at Victoria's; it was one night, not a lifetime. If you were here, my kids could help yours, Melanie could introduce you to her friends –'

Melanie. Sleek, polished, disdainful. 'Ross, how many of Melanie's friends have no money? How many of them work?'

'None that I know of,' he conceded. 'But you'd have a family waiting for you –'

Why is he doing this? 'I don't have a family waiting for me. They don't want me; they don't even want Craig. And I don't see how I could leave Vancouver.' The doorbell rang. 'I have to go. Thank you. For calling and for thinking about me.'

A policeman stood at the door. Faintly, Katherine said, 'You found him.'

'No, ma'am. Just stopping by to see if you've heard anything.'

She let out her breath. *Not this time*. 'No, I haven't.'

'No sign of him ma'am? He hasn't called?'

'No.'

Whenever we talk about Craig, she thought, the word we use most often is No.

The telephone rang again. When Katherine answered it Frances Doerner said hurriedly, 'Katherine, how are you? I can't talk: I'm late for my hair appointment; I just wanted to let you know, and I *am* sorry, but I'm afraid I was wrong about a job in Carl's company.'

Carl's company. It was Carl's and Craig's company a few days ago.

'There just aren't any jobs, and of course you wouldn't want them to fire anyone. I'm so sorry I misled you; Carl was very unhappy when he heard what I'd done. So that's the problem, dear Katherine; Carl is determined to keep costs down and I couldn't budge him. I'm so sorry; if there's anything else I can do –'

'No,' Katherine said. 'Thank you for trying. Goodbye, Fran –'

'Uh . . . Katherine, one more thing . . . Carl asked me to tell you he needs the car.'

'The car?'

'The one Craig was using. It belongs to the company, you see, and Carl asked me to tell you he needs it. I am sorry –'

'It's all right. I didn't know it wasn't ours. I'll return it tomorrow.'

'It's so sweet of you to take it so –'

'Goodbye, Frances.'

Her budgets glared up at her – the payments that would be due in two weeks and all the money she had: three thousand dollars. She opened a drawer and took out the cheque from Ann Hayward. She had turned down Ross, but this was different: one cheque, and it was in her hand. One thousand dollars. Plus the three thousand in the bank. And eight thousand from selling the house. Enough to move to an apartment and keep going until she found a job.

Don't think about it; just do it. She called the realtor. A fool Ross had said. Don't be a fool. But he hadn't said definitely that he'd pay the mortgage; only that he might. She wouldn't take it anyway. She'd manage alone, even if it meant selling the house.

But when she had told the realtor to accept the offer, she felt she'd made a terrible mistake. She'd been rash, just as Ross said. But he hadn't advised her; he'd only called her a fool. 'Craig, I need you,' she said aloud. 'I miss you. *Please* call;

86

please come back.' She was crying again. It seemed everything made her cry and she was so tired of it, but there always seemed to be more tears, welling up.

She swivelled in Craig's chair and looked into her living-room and beyond, to her dining-room and kitchen, thinking, with a sick feeling, that they weren't hers any more. Outside, the tall trees stood like sentinels among the bushes and flowers she had planted, but they were no longer hers, either.

You shouldn't have sold it. She heard Craig accuse her. You should have waited. The room was empty, but she heard his voice. You had enough money for two months.

'I couldn't do it,' she argued with his shadowy presence. 'I don't believe you'll be back then. And what if I couldn't find another buyer? Craig, I had to do this on my own.' He did not answer.

Through the window she saw Jennifer and Todd get off the bus and run up the walk. Todd was dishevelled, his face smudged; Jennifer's blouse was torn. What had they been up to? They were almost never rowdy. As they came in, she saw tears on their faces and jumped up to meet them. 'What happened?' she exclaimed as they clung to her.

'It doesn't matter,' Jennifer said vehemently. 'Because we're moving away from here and we won't go back to camp. I never want to go there again; I don't want to see any of those kids ever again.'

'They're liars,' Todd declared. 'I beat up Eddie and I almost broke Mack's head open, but then somebody tripped me. If he hadn't I would've killed them all.'

'But why were you fighting?' Katherine asked, thinking – I know. I know why.

'They said Daddy stole money,' Todd said. 'And ran away, because he was afraid of going to jail. So I beat –'

Jennifer stamped her foot. 'We're never going to see any of them again as long as we live!'

Damn them, Katherine thought, fiercely. Damn the cruelty of children, and damn their parents who talked about us and gave them the ammunition to hurt my children.

'Tell me,' she said, sitting with them on the couch. 'How did they make fun of you?'

'Oh –' Jennifer tried to toss off the words. 'They said we should've put Daddy on a leash 'til he was trained to stay home like other dogs –' The words were lost in a storm of weeping and she burrowed her face into Katherine's shoulder.

'They said their Dads were home,' Todd muttered. 'And we should learn to keep our Dad at home where he couldn't steal. But they're lying, aren't they? Just like Mr Doerner. All those bastards are lying, aren't they? Fucking bastards, shitty bastards!'

'Todd!' Katherine said. 'It doesn't help to talk that way.'

'Yes it does. And they *are* bastards, Mom. They *lied*!'

With her children pressing against her, Katherine sent a silent, futile plea to Craig. What do you want me to tell them? If you're coming back I can make up something, but if you aren't what can I do? I have to face them every day and answer their questions; they're not infants; they deserve the truth.

'We talked about this,' she said at last, feeling Jennifer tense as she held her breath. 'Remember? And I said there was a lot we don't know. I think those kids – stink. They're stupid and cruel and we should ignore them. But what they were saying . . . gets complicated, because it seems maybe Daddy did take money from the company.'

'No,' Jennifer said in a muffled voice.

'It seems he did. But he meant to pay it back. That's why he went away: to get money to pay back what he took. I don't know why he hasn't come home. Maybe he had more trouble getting it than he thought he would. We just don't know. And until he comes back and tells us –'

'If he's alive.' Jennifer sat up and wiped her eyes with the back of her hand. 'We don't know that either, do we?'

'Not for sure.' What would the experts advise, Katherine wondered? Is it good or bad to burden children with the truth? She didn't have time to check; she had to decide for herself. Suddenly there were so many things she had to decide for herself. 'All we can do is hope he's alive and wait to hear from him, or from someone else, if he's been in an accident –'

Once more the telephone rang and Todd dashed to answer it. 'Sure,' Katherine heard him say glumly. 'It's for you, Mom. That lady you gave the party for.'

Leslie. Katherine grasped the telephone as if it were a life line. 'How wonderful that you called,' she laughed shakily. 'Perfect timing.'

'My God,' Leslie said. 'What is it? What's wrong?'

'I've been trying to reach you . . .' Katherine sat down and the words poured out: everything that had happened, from Carl Doerner's first question at the party to the sale of her house and Jennifer's and Todd's fight at camp. She was crying, overwhelmed by reliving it all at once.

'Christ,' Leslie said when she finally stopped. 'Lousy, rotten mess . . . Well, now, hold on a minute; let me think.' There was a comforting briskness in her voice and Katherine felt herself begin to relax. 'We will ignore for the moment the fact that you didn't ask me for help, which makes me feel unwanted –'

'I tried to call; you were out of town. And then so many things kept happening –'

'– We will talk instead about my helping you now. How much money do you need?'

'Leslie, I can't borrow money.' Katherine looked at Jennifer and Todd in the living-room, and lowered her voice. 'Craig has already done that for both of us.'

'Oh. Well, I wouldn't look at it that way, but I can see how you might. So what are you doing for money? A job?'

'I'd love one. Have you got one to offer?'

'Sure. But not in Vancouver. You mean you can't find one?'

'Not yet.' She'd left that out, ashamed to admit it to her successful friend, who had built a career for herself while Katherine invested herself in a man who left her. But now she related her rejections as a jewellery designer, as an office worker – 'As anything; no one will hire me. There aren't many jobs to begin with and why should they take a chance on someone with no experience?'

'Because you're smart and quick and reliable.'

'So I'd make a good girl scout.'

'Well, I'd hire you in a minute. There's a job here you'd be perfect for – assistant to the guy who does our window displays. He's an ass, but you can't have everything. You want it?'

'Leslie, I live in Vancouver.'

'I know.' Leslie's voice was thoughtful. 'But do you have to? I mean, what if you and the kids came here? You really could have that job, you know; I could arrange it. And I could find you an apartment so you'd have a place ready to move into. We could go back to our old days of gossip and chocolates. Damn it, Katherine, this is turning into one of my better ideas! Katherine? Are you there?'

'Yes.' First Ross, now Leslie. But Ross had made only a casual suggestion. Leslie was offering a new life.

Gossip and chocolates. All through high school, into college and work, they would sit up all night in Leslie's bedroom, gorging on candy and bemoaning stodgy teachers, the crudity of young men, and the lack of glamour in their lives.

But what did they have in common now? Leslie was an executive with money and freedom; she was attractive and sophisticated and moved in a fast crowd of professional people. Katherine had been a housewife, but now she'd lost her husband and sold her house, so she didn't know what she was.

'I don't think so,' she said. 'We live here; it's home.'

'Home! Listen, lady, from what you tell me, you're in hostile territory up there. No job, no friends, your kids fighting nasty little campers, and not even your own house anymore. You call that home? What about San Francisco? You lived here longer than you've lived in Vancouver; you probably remember every street sign. Right?'

She was right. Katherine remembered a feeling of home-coming the month before, from the moment Ross met their plane, and memories sprang up at every turn. *Home*. My roots and memories. And now – a job, a place to live, a friend.

'But Craig –' she began.

'Craig,' Leslie echoed. 'Well, what about him? First of all, until you're settled you leave my name and phone number with the Vancouver police and any friendly neighbours you can dig up. He can find you through me. Second, isn't it possible he'd go back to San Francisco instead of Vancouver? To his first family, so to speak? If you're here, too, he'll have everybody in one place, do all his explaining, end all his troubles at once. Dandy for him, don't you think?'

And for me, Katherine thought, aching for Craig and their life together. He must miss it, too – if he's alive. It meant so much to him. He'll come back to it – if he's alive. He'll find us, wherever we are.

Nothing else had worked. The closed doors of the past month surrounded her. What else is there, she thought?

'I'll think about it,' she told Leslie, but the tone of her voice had changed and Leslie heard it.

'Good,' she said cheerfully. 'Let me know when you decide; I'll hire a brass band to greet you at the airport.'

'No,' Katherine said absently, already thinking ahead. 'I won't need a band. Just an apartment near a good school for Jennifer and Todd –'

And it was only when she heard Leslie's laughter that she knew she had made up her mind.

PART II

Chapter 6

The great red cables of the Golden Gate Bridge swooped
low, then swung upward to the top of the four-tiered tower
looming above them as Katherine parked the rented truck at
the side of the road. 'Last chance to be a tourist,' she said
gaily. 'After this, we'll belong here.'

'We'll never belong here,' said Jennifer morosely, lagging
behind as Katherine and Todd jumped from the high cab. 'We
belong in Vancouver.'

'Jennifer,' Katherine urged gently. 'Come and look; it's
quite wonderful.'

'Wow,' Todd whispered loudly, spinning in place. They
were below the north end of the massive bridge, beside a small,
sheltered bay where a few fishermen were casting their lines,
and as they looked up, the bridge seemed to fly across the
water, plunging at the far end into a thickly wooded park, with
San Francisco just beyond it. 'A lot bigger than Lions Gate.'

'It is not,' snapped Jennifer, but then she was silent, caught in the spell of the scene across the water – a city of hills, with white and pastel sun-washed houses and apartments stepping up and down the slopes, a solitary cluster of skyscrapers standing together like secretive friends, and everywhere the sparkle of water, almost surrounding the city, with hills and houses beyond.

'It's a little like Vancouver,' Todd said, to make Jennifer feel better, but Jennifer responded, 'Vancouver is a thousand miles away.'

Katherine barely heard them. She was filled with anticipation. Everything will be all right, she thought; I know where I am. We're not strangers. The city shimmered before them and she said impulsively, 'It's waiting for us.'

'So's Vancouver,' muttered Jennifer, turning away from the shining view before it could soften her determination to be unhappy.

'Look over there,' Todd called, walking along the edge of the small bay towards tall, needle-like rocks, a sandy beach, and, beyond it, a lighthouse. 'Can we go look, Mom?'

'Not today,' Katherine said. 'We're meeting the realtor, remember? We'll come back.' They looked together at the lighthouse on the point of land jutting into the water.

'Lime Point,' said a fisherman standing nearby. 'Great place. Out at the end you feel like you're all alone in the middle of the water. And over there' – he pointed to the left – 'that's Alcatraz.'

'Alcatraz –!' breathed Todd.

'Another day,' said Katherine firmly. 'We do have an appointment.'

In the truck again, they drove back up the road to the highway, then over the bridge, between its huge arcs of red cables, watching the city grow larger. Jennifer stared gloomily out of the window, wishing her mother would stop trying to be

96

cheerful when every minute they were getting farther away from Daddy. It wasn't fair; she hadn't asked them if *they* wanted to move to San Francisco; she just made up her mind and then everything happened at once. She ordered them around, making them help her pack, and she rented the truck – Mother driving a truck! – and had half their furniture put in storage and the rest loaded onto the truck. They watched their house get emptier and emptier and when they walked through it for the last time, she and Todd had burst into tears and Mother was crying, too, kind of quietly. It was so awful – empty rooms with bare floors echoing their footsteps, the windows naked and sad without curtains, the doors like black holes in the blank walls. When Daddy came back, he'd cry, too. Why didn't you call us? Jennifer wailed silently to her father. We waited and waited 'til the last minute but you didn't call and now we're in this awful truck a *thousand miles* away.

Waiting at the stop light just past the thick forest of the Presidio, Katherine glanced at Jennifer: rebellious Jennifer, staring out of her window. She knew she should be comforting her, but she couldn't. From the moment she sat behind the wheel of the truck and backed out of the driveway, her own feelings had overwhelmed her and she was impatient with her children's demands. Sitting high above the ground, she felt the anguish of leaving begin to ease and found herself exulting in what she had done: organised, packed, got away on schedule. By herself she had closed the house. Closed a life, she thought with a chill, but it faded in the light of her adventure: her first one alone since meeting Craig. After the fears and failures and loneliness of the past two months, the rattling truck became a chariot, bearing them away, and no matter how frightening the future, Katherine felt, for the first time that she could remember, that she was the one who would decide its direction.

*

The realtor led them to an apartment near forty-sixth and Irving. Katherine vaguely remembered the neighbourhood, called the Sunset, but she had forgotten how dense it was, street after street of tiny houses squeezed together in unbroken rows that sloped gradually down to the ocean. After the openness of West Vancouver, she felt hemmed in, and when the realtor stopped and she saw the building, her heart sank. In a city where the tiniest, most ordinary house was painted blue, pink or yellow, or a gleaming white, the grey stucco building looked as unfriendly as a prison.

'You've got the ocean,' the realtor recited briskly. 'Just a few blocks away; see it from your doorstep. And of course Golden Gate Park, only a block away. Now let's show you inside.'

'This is it?' Todd asked, looking into the three rooms in disbelief.

'It's ugly,' Jennifer said flatly, and stamped out, to sit on the small patch of grass and scowl at the street.

The realtor spread his hands, 'Miss McAlister said no more than four hundred. Not many places in the Sunset that cheap, you know. Nice place to bring up kids, lots of people want to live here. Good school nearby. And it's a clean building.' Katherine nodded. 'But Miss McAlister sends a good bit of business our way,' he added hastily. 'We wouldn't want you to be unhappy. How about we give you some paint and you and the youngsters can brighten up the place? And we'll start your rent with September. Give you two weeks free.'

Katherine looked around. 'This is four hundred dollars a month?'

'Right.' He peered at her. 'I thought Miss McAlister told you.'

'She told me she would look for something between three and four –'

'Mrs Fraser, you cannot be serious. For three in the Sunset you get nothing. Do you think this is a slum?'

Katherine walked into the dingy bedroom. Four hundred dollars was half a month's salary in the job Leslie had got her at Heath's. She shouldn't rent it. They could go to a hotel for a few days, until she found something cheaper. But she didn't know all the neighbourhoods and this was the one Leslie had recommended. She stood, irresolute, the brief exultation of the trip draining away. Look where her direction had taken them: to three rooms for four hundred dollars a month. 'All right,' she said. They'd stay here while she looked around for herself. She started to write a cheque for September's rent.

'That'll be twelve hundred dollars,' the realtor said, pulling out his receipt book.

'*Twelve hundred* –?'

'First month, last month, and one month security deposit. We have to protect ourselves,' he added seeing the shock on Katherine's face. 'People skip, you wouldn't believe it – or they do damage.'

Numbly, Katherine wrote the cheque. Whenever she thought she knew how much money she had, something came along to make it less. 'Canadian bank,' the realtor said, shaking his head. 'Their dollars are worth about eighty-five cents here.'

The exchange rate. Something else she hadn't planned on. 'Could we settle it later?' she asked, trying to keep her voice calm. 'After I open a bank account here?'

After a moment, he nodded. 'I guess I can trust you for that. How about you make up the difference in next month's rent?'

'Fine.' As soon as he left, she turned back to the apartment. Living-room, bedroom, kitchen, bath. After what they'd had in Vancouver! Stunned by the enormity of it – giving up the space and light of their wonderful house, the terrace overlooking Vancouver, her rose garden, the huge trees and open yard – she shook her head. She had given that up . . . for this. How could she?

'Katherine! Good lord, what have I done to you?'

Leslie stood in the doorway, her eyes meeting Katherine's over the grocery bags she held in her arms. 'God damn it. Katherine, I had no idea. The realtor said it was perfect for a family and the best he could do with a top of four hundred . . .'

'It's all right, Leslie; we'll get used to it. And when we do some painting, it will be a lot brighter.'

'But you ought to have more room.'

'I can't afford more room.'

Their different paychecks loomed between them. 'In that case,' Leslie said, putting the bags on the floor and holding out her arms. 'Welcome to San Francisco.'

Katherine laughed and they held each other tightly. 'Thank you. And thank you for coming; it's good to see a friendly face.'

'Especially in this place.' Leslie backed up and surveyed it, shaking her head. 'Well.' She became businesslike. 'Here's the schedule. A crew of muscular young men will be here as soon as I give them the signal, to unload your truck. They do –'

'Leslie, l can't afford movers. We hired a high school boy in Vancouver and I thought we'd do the same here.'

'They aren't movers; they're maintenance men from one of our branch stores. Consider them a welcome wagon. They do whatever they're told, so have them put every piece of furniture exactly where you want before you let them get away. Then I'm taking all of you to dinner. Don't shake your head at me. It's the same welcome wagon. After this you're on your own, but to start you need something special, so we're going to Henri's at the top of the Hilton. Quite a view, decent food, and wine for the grownups. How does that sound?'

'It sounds like Christmas.'

'Listen, I lured you down here; I have to keep you happy. Speaking of which, I brought you a present.' She pulled something from one of the grocery bags. 'Know what this is?'

'It looks like a bundle of rags.'

'It is a bundle of rags. The most valuable gift a friend can bring someone just moving in. Now, I'm going to the pay phone at the corner to call the muscular men and then I'll help you scrub what I am sure is a grimy kitchen. Jennifer and Todd should help, too, don't you think? Instead of sitting outside looking like the sky has collapsed?'

'Of course. How odd that I never thought of rags.'

With Leslie as organiser, the apartment came to life. Two young men, as muscular as she had promised, unloaded the truck, while Katherine and Leslie, with a mildly grumbling Jennifer and Todd, washed the kitchen and bathroom and all the floors. In the three small rooms, they bumped and tripped over each other, but Leslie joked about it, and as Katherine heard the laughter and saw her own furniture settle into place, the anticipation she had felt that morning began to return.

'You see,' Leslie said later, as they were led to a table in the restaurant. 'All it takes is organisation.'

'Or desperation,' Katherine said lightly. They sat beside a window while Jennifer and Todd toured the room to see the view from all directions, admitting it was pretty spectacular. Katherine gazed at the glowing city below and the curving panorama of lights across the bay – Oakland, Berkeley and their neighbouring towns – and had a moment of pure happiness. Dinner with a friend, her children chattering happily instead of complaining, a home where lamplight and familiar furniture waited and, in two weeks, when Jennifer and Todd started school, a job, a salary, a beginning. We've found a place, she thought as the waiter brought their shrimp and crab appetisers and Jennifer and Todd sat down to eat. Until Craig comes back, we've found a place to stay.

The small details of everyday life are invisible until they must be changed. Katherine changed almost all of them in her first two weeks in San Francisco. She arranged for a telephone and sent their new number and address to the Vancouver police, Carl Doerner, and two neighbours whom Craig might call when he found strangers living in their house. Using Leslie's recommendations, she found doctors and a dentist, and made a list of discount stores she could reach on public transportation. She opened checking and savings accounts in a bank near Heath's, filled out an application for cheque cashing at a neighbourhood grocery store, and, borrowing Leslie's car, was first in line one morning to get a California driver's licence. All her charge cards were in Craig's name, so she applied for new ones in her own name at Macy's and Sear's; she had an employee's account at Heath's. Registering Jennifer and Todd at their new school, she found she'd forgotten to bring their records from Vancouver and sent to their old school for test scores, and to their doctor for their medical histories. And she spent a morning getting acquainted with a neighbourhood pharmacist, the butcher at the supermarket, and the owner of a fish shop down the street.

Best of all, Jennifer and Todd discovered Annie, who lived across the hall, and brought her to meet Katherine. Tall, blonde, lanky, just turned sixteen, she was breezily cheerful, serious about her studies, and mad for new clothes, and therefore always on the lookout for ways to earn extra money – for instance, by keeping an eye on Jennifer and Todd when Katherine began her new job.

'Not that I'm not crazy about them,' she told Katherine

earnestly. 'I'd do it as a favour, except . . . well, you know, things *cost* so much . . .'

Katherine knew. She also knew that since Annie lived across the hall, she could be in her own home, at least part of the time, at her own typewriter, listening to her own records, and still be earning money as long as both apartment doors were open. Once they agreed it was a good deal for the two of them, they worked out a schedule of hours and payment for after school and evenings.

It wasn't that Katherine expected to be going out at night, but just in case something came up, it was good to know Annie was there. Especially for the afternoons. In Vancouver, she'd always been home when Jennifer and Todd arrived from school and the thought of their wandering around on their own while she was trapped at work had frightened her. Now that fright was gone.

One more arrangement made, she thought. It takes a lot of running and planning, to belong. But there was still more running ahead. They went sightseeing.

Katherine splurged and rented a car, and they left early one morning for the Muir Woods. Driving north, they drove through a tunnel with its entrance painted in a huge rainbow. A good omen, Katherine thought, as Jennifer laughed with pleasure when she pointed it out, and a little later, when they stood in awestruck silence beneath the cool grandeur of towering redwoods, all of Todd's and Jennifer's grumbling and disparaging comparisons with Vancouver ended, at least for awhile.

The next few days were packed with exploring: museums, parks, an old sailing ship, a chocolate factory converted to a shopping centre, a zoo with a Gorilla World and a Zebra Zephyr tour train. But most exciting of all, for Jennifer and Todd, was driving on San Francisco's streets: the weird disembodied feeling that made them screech with delight when

Katherine drove up one of the city's steep hills and they saw nothing ahead but sky, nothing of the other side, until the car was at the crest and then precipitously descending, giving them a stomach-clutching view down, down, past a cross street, then down past another, and still down, farther and farther, all the way to the water's edge. Then they would let out a long sigh of relief and pause before demanding, 'Where's the next hill?'

At the end of the week, when school and Katherine's job were both about to begin, they listed the places they'd had to postpone. It takes a lot of running to belong, Katherine thought again, smiling. But what a good start we've made.

Heath's main store turns a cool marble façade towards Union Square. From four tall windows, haughty mannequins gaze at the comings and goings in the Square across the street: couples entwined on the grass, men in tatters sleeping on benches, revival singers and fervent speakers on a stone platform haranguing anyone who pauses to listen, office workers taking a shortcut on the diagonal walks between flower gardens, clipped hedges and tall spiky palms. Katherine stood among the mannequins in one of the windows, holding a silk scarf and a handbag, waiting for Gil Lister to ask for them. Heath's window designer for twenty years, Lister ran his little kingdom with entrenched power and a sharp tongue and only reluctantly had accepted Katherine as his assistant. Short and round, with quivering lips and smooth skin, he established his supremacy the day she arrived.

'Stand there, my dear, no, a little more to the right; now, when I ask for the scarf you will hold it up, so, and wait until I take it from you. No tossing it at me and no scurrying about so that I don't know where you are. Think of yourself as a surgeon's assistant, always alert for what I need, making sure I expend a *minimum* of effort in achieving the *maximum* of my potential. Clear? Not too difficult for you, my dear? Let's try it, then. Stand here – no, a little to the left . . .'

When she was not holding items above her head, her arms aching with the effort of keeping them extended exactly as Lister instructed, she sat at a small desk in a corner of his workroom, copying sketches of window displays, ordering mannequins and sending others out for repair, writing orders for scenery and props, and keeping files on all of Lister's designs and those he copied from designers in other stores. 'It doesn't hurt them in the slightest,' he told Katherine. 'I'm not taking any business from them, and I could put together far more original ideas of my own, but you see how busy I am, my dear, it is appalling the way time rushes past and art suffers first, you'll discover that, art suffers when we have no time to contemplate and create. Still, we don't want competitors to be peeved at seeing their little designs in our windows, so we embellish them to give our customers the prestigious look they expect from Heath's. Hand me that table, my dear, we'll change this from a den to a living-room.'

Alternately amused by his tricks to impress others and furious with his tyranny over her, Katherine could not wait to get away at five-thirty each day, and by the end of her first week at work, she was worn out. Still, getting off the bus on Friday, she realised that for a whole week she hadn't anguished over Craig; she'd been too busy, too tired. Is that good or bad, she wondered? I mustn't let him seem too far away; too much depends on him. And if he were here, she reflected, he'd remember that today is my birthday and I wouldn't feel so low about it.

She turned the corner, leaving behind the noisy congestion of Irving Street with its traffic, stores and restaurants from a dozen countries. Walking home, she began to feel better. It was a quiet, pleasant street of identical tiny houses, each with a garage and a bay window above it, a small patch of lawn in front, with miniature gardens and small trees or bushes, almost like a small village.

Beyond another, identical block was Golden Gate Park, its border of tangled bushes hiding museums and gardens, windmills and lakes, fields, woods, restaurants and numberless paths to explore. Katherine saw Jennifer and Todd on the edge of the park, with Annie, waving at her, waiting to cross Lincoln Way. When they ran up to her she thought they looked conspiratorial.

'The paint finally came,' said Todd as Annie went in to do her homework. 'White and yellow. Pretty dull.'

'Those are the colours I asked for,' Katherine said. 'Do I get a greeting?'

They gave her a perfunctory kiss. 'When do we eat?'

'For heaven's sake!' she exclaimed. 'Can I have a few minutes to be me before I become the cook?'

'Mom!' Todd stepped back and squinted at her. 'You never used to talk like that.'

Damn, Katherine thought, and bent to kiss them. 'I'm sorry. It hasn't been the best week, you know.' She saw them exchange a look. 'All right, let's get dinner. Did you look in those bags to see if we got paint brushes and rollers?'

They talked about school and painting the apartment, and as they were finishing dinner, Katherine said, 'You haven't told me what you did after school.'

They gave each other a quick, secretive glance and shrugged. 'Walked around with Annie.'

'Where?'

'The park. Irving Street. You know.'

'Just walking?'

'Not exactly . . .'

'Then what?' Katherine asked in frustration.

'This!' Todd shouted, and from beneath his chair whipped out a small wrapped package. 'Happy birthday!' he shouted again.

106

Jennifer jumped up to give Katherine a loud kiss. 'Daddy always took us shopping for your birthday so we weren't sure what to get but we hope you like it.' Tears filled Katherine's eyes and Jennifer put her arms tightly around her. 'We love you, Mommy. And next birthday, we'll shop with Daddy again, so everything will be all right.'

Katherine tried to smile. All day she had been remembering the ten festive birthdays that had gone before, celebrated with Craig's flowers, lavish gifts, a decorated cake from one of Vancouver's élite bakeries, and a rousing off-key 'Happy Birthday' sung by Craig, Todd and Jennifer. Now, as Jennifer and Todd put before her a plate of glazed doughnuts bristling with candles, it was all she could do to keep her tears from overflowing. 'Happy birthday,' they sang – and all of them thought what a thin chorus it was without Craig. Then Katherine blew out the candles and, with Todd and Jennifer eagerly watching, opened her present.

'Oh,' she said blankly, then recovered. 'Oh, how lovely; and I've been needing a new one; how did you know?'

They beamed. 'It was Jennifer's idea,' Todd said. 'I never even heard of a blusher.'

Katherine turned the small plastic square in her hand, opened it to reveal the mirror, pressed powder and small brush, then closed it and ran her finger over the tortoiseshell surface. 'I'll use it all the time,' she said, hugging them. 'Thank you – and thank you for remembering.' But she wondered, as they washed the dishes, if Jennifer had thought of a blusher as a way of telling her to pay more attention to herself. She felt embarrassed, and pressured, because she couldn't rouse herself to care about her looks. Each morning, dressing for work, she knew she should try, but a wave of lassitude would sweep over her and she would give up. I'm clean and neat, she told herself; that's enough. Someday I'll do more. If – *when* Craig comes back, I'll want to. Until then – She

107

slipped the small compact into her purse. Just as she and the children were waiting for Craig, it would, too.

Saturday morning Leslie appeared as Katherine was opening the first can of paint. 'I don't believe it,' Katherine said. 'What good timing. Too good, in fact. How come you're here?'

Leslie sighed deeply. 'Do not look a gift horse –'

'Leslie. Why are you here?'

'Long story. I stopped by this morning when you were grocery shopping and your kids were telling Annie you yelled at them last night, and worrying that you must be sick. They also told me you were painting the place today, and I decided to make it a party. Are you sick?'

'Of course not. They told Annie? They must have been more upset than I realised. I guess we all were. I didn't understand that they were in a hurry to eat so they could give me my present –'

'Present?'

'Yesterday was my birthday.'

'Damn it, lady, why didn't you tell me? We could have had a party. Thirty-five?'

'Yes.'

'A depressing age to reach alone. Why didn't you tell me?'

'I guess I didn't want a party.' Katherine began to stir the paint. 'And I had no idea Jennifer and Todd even remembered.'

'Good kids,' Leslie said casually. 'Which reminds me – where are they?'

'At the hardware store. We needed extra brushes. Leslie, you don't have to help paint –'

'I know I don't. That's why I'm doing it. Don't argue. Four painters cut the work in half and double the fun.'

And they did. With Jennifer and Todd, they gathered brushes, rags, rollers and paint, arguing vociferously over the best way to stack furniture and divide the work, and soon the small apartment rang with banter and laughter. They worked steadily, stopping only for a sandwich at noon and by three they were almost finished.

'How are you getting along with Gil Lister?' Leslie asked from the top of a ladder.

'As long as I'm his obedient puppy, we get along fine.'

'I'm sorry about that. I told you he was an ass, but I thought with your artistic eye you'd like doing the windows.'

'I would.'

'But Gil doesn't want your ideas? Pity you aren't a charming young boy with a taste for rotund queers.'

'What's a rotund queer?' Jennifer asked, coming in from the bedroom.

'An overweight eccentric,' Leslie said hastily. 'I don't suppose you've met any.'

'I don't suppose that's really what it means, either,' said Jennifer shrewdly. 'I'll ask my mother later; she doesn't think my education should be censored.'

'My God,' Leslie breathed. 'I've been put in my place.'

'Jennifer!' Todd yelled from the bedroom. 'I think I spilled something!'

'Don't you *know*?,' she called back in exasperation. 'Wait a minute; I'll come and help.'

When she left, Leslie grinned at Katherine. 'I feel humbled. Is she always so damned bright and grown up?'

'Only often enough to confuse me.'

'It would scare the hell out of me. Whenever I think it's about time I had one of my one, I meet one of these kid geniuses and decide I couldn't possibly cope.'

'Jennifer seems pretty normal to me. What do you mean, have one of your own? Are you secretly married?'

'No. And no prospects in sight. But is that a requirement?' Katherine cocked an eyebrow. 'It's at least a convenience.'

'Not always.' Leslie waved her brush. 'Not even necessarily. How many women shed unsatisfactory husbands long before the offspring are even half grown? How many men walk out and leave their wives stuck with bringing up – oh shit, Katherine I'm sorry. I am a full-fledged ass. I got carried away with speechmaking and forgot present company.'

'It's all right,' said Katherine absently. She had stopped painting the wainscot and was looking around, trying to figure out why she suddenly felt uneasy. From her place on the floor, she could see all three rooms at once, looking bigger and brighter in their glistening new colours. Her apartment.

How extraordinary. Her apartment, her home. Filled with her possessions, her children, and companionship. But something was wrong.

The bright rooms had the look of a doll's house: a small bedroom for Jennifer and Todd, two narrow closets, a living-room with a sofa bed for Katherine, a kitchen just big enough for their oak table and captain's chairs. And then Katherine knew what was wrong.

There was no room for Craig. They had made a home for a family without Craig.

Melanie Hayward always asked for Wilma in the Empire Room of Heath's: the only saleswoman, she said, who understood her and always found clothes that were her. It was true that Wilma gossiped about the divorces and affairs and marital tiffs of her customers, but a word from Melanie and she was silent. And Melanie always gave the word, as soon as she learned something new about her circle.

'– taken up with Ivan something,' Wilma chattered as she helped Melanie into a silk sheath with a chiffon scarf. 'Macklin, I think, Ivan Macklin; they've been seen together at Carmel and Las Vegas and her husband told her to drop him or get out. "I'm not running no motel," he says. "Either you –" '

'I hardly think,' Melanie cut in, 'that those were his words.'

'No, maybe not,' Wilma agreed cheerfully. 'Now you can either loop this scarf around your neck or wear it around your shoulders . . .'

By the end of the afternoon, Melanie had spent just under six thousand dollars on five outfits for the winter season, had learned three new items about her friends, and had instructed Wilma to watch for something special for an April gala she was planning at Fairmont. Humming, she browsed casually along the main floor, then stopped abruptly near the Union Square exit. Through an open door in the wall, she had caught sight of two people dressing a mannequin in a velvet evening gown. '*Hand* me the sash, my dear,' the man said testily as Melanie watched, and the woman stretched her arm out for him to take a sash from her hand. What the hell, Melanie thought, remembering the last time she had seen the woman – pale, wearing a wrinkled suit, and ready to flee Victoria's dining-room. What the hell is she doing here? Ross never said a word.

She watched as they put a champagne glass in the mannequin's hand and moved on to dress another in satin and lace. Not as pale, Melanie thought, and the haunted look was gone. But there was something forlorn about her as she stood waiting for the little man's orders, obediently handing him clothing and props and, once, glancing furtively at her watch. Serves her right, Melanie thought, for trying to worm her way in.

But why was she working at Heath's? Driving home across the Golden Gate Bridge, Melanie seethed over it. What was she doing in San Francisco? How long would she wait to call the family and announce that she was ready to become a Hayward and share the Hayward wealth?

Maybe she already had. Maybe they knew and hadn't told her about it. Forced to slow down in the heavy traffic, Melanie clenched the wheel. Of course little Katherine would call Ross the minute she arrived. And he kept it a secret. She swung the wheel at the Tiburon exit and a mile farther, at the base of their hill, put the car in low gear and took the steep road a little too fast all the way to the top. She wondered if he'd told Derek. Or Victoria. Or all of them. Why the hell, she demanded silently, am I the last to know?

'I saw your mousy little friend today,' she told Ross at dinner. 'Working at Heath's.'

He looked up from contemplating a bottle of wine. 'Who?'

'You know perfectly well. Your dowdy Canadian protégè, the one who told us off at Victoria's.'

'Katherine? In San Francisco?'

'Don't put on an act with me. Do you think I don't know you're behind it?'

'At Heath's, you said? By God, that took courage. As a salesclerk?'

'I *said*, don't put on an act. You know damn well she's not a salesclerk. You probably got her the job. And a place to live. Without once mentioning it to me. Who *did* you mention it to? Victoria? Derek?'

'I didn't know about it.' They sat across from each other. Carrie and Jon had eaten earlier, as usual, in the kitchen with the maid and the cook, and, as usual he and Melanie faced each other with no one to break the silences between them or moderate their taut exchanges. 'I haven't spoken to Katherine in weeks.'

'You didn't know she was moving to San Francisco?'

'No. We did talk about it once; in fact, I suggested it, but she didn't –'

'Suggested it!'

'She grew up here; she has a close friend – in fact if anyone is helping her, that's probably who it is. And she has us.'

'She doesn't "have" us. She has nothing to do with us. If you didn't keep dragging her in –'

112

'I didn't drag her this time. She made up her mind by herself and didn't tell me about it. What was she doing at Heath's?'

'Window dressing. Helping a nasty little man who treated her like dirt.' The maid came in to clear their plates. 'What did you do today?' Melanie asked brightly.

He sat back. 'As a matter of fact, this was a red-letter day. I was waiting to tell you about it.'

'About what?'

'We got approval from the mayor's office for BayBridge Plaza.'

'Oh?'

'Melanie,' he said very softly. 'BayBridge Plaza. I've told you about it perhaps a hundred times in the four years I've been working on it. Approval from the mayor's office is almost the last hurdle. A few more approvals – maybe another month of negotiating – and we can begin.'

'I remember. You said it was a big project. Expensive?'

'About three hundred million dollars.'

Her eyes widened. 'Your fee is a percentage of that.'

He shrugged. Reliable Melanie; he always knew what would get her attention. 'My expenses are up, too. I told you I hired seventy new people, and I'll be using outside consultants . . . And I have to buy out a lease on that building I bought a few years ago, on Mission Street. It's been added to BayBridge, but the former owner's still in it. I think he's ready to sell; he was talking the other day about needing money.'

'Anyone we know?' she asked idly as the maid put cups and a silver coffee server beside her.

'I don't know him. His name is Ivan Macklin; he built the building. In fact his name is on it.'

'Macklin? I think I know him. Or maybe only the name. Where did I hear it?' Pouring coffee, she frowned. 'Oh. Wilma.'

'Wilma?'

'My salesgirl at Heath's. She heard he was playing around with someone. Maybe that's why he needs money.' The maid put a bowl of sliced peaches and *créme fraiche* in front of Melanie and left the room. 'Are you going to call her?'

'Who?'

'Ross, don't be tiresome. Katherine Fraser.'

'Of course.'

'I'd rather you didn't.'

'I know.'

Tight-lipped, she spooned the dessert into the bowls and passed him one. 'Are you going to buy out Ivan Macklin?'

'Do you care?'

'Not much. Not at all, I suppose. Not any more than you care that I don't want you to call that woman.'

'I do care; I'm sorry it bothers you. Why does it?'

'I've told you. She doesn't belong; she . . . complicates things.'

'Meaning money.'

'Partly.' She stirred her coffee, then burst out, 'I don't want a helpless woman running around looking for protection.'

'Well at least that's honest.' Pushing back his chair, he stood up. 'But I'm not sure she's helpless. A woman who moves her family a thousand miles and finds a way to support them seems pretty self-sufficient to me. In fact, the only thing she might need is friendship.' He slid open the door to the den. 'I'm sorry if it bothers you, but that much I intend to offer.'

Katherine was filling out shipment forms for returning window scenery to the warehouse, when Ross telephoned. She had thought about calling him for three weeks, ever since they arrived, but his voice was so unexpected that for a moment she was speechless. 'How did you know?' she stammered. 'I didn't think anyone knew we were here.'

114

'I'll tell you at lunch. Can you meet me at one?'

'Today?'

'Unless you're too busy.'

She looked at Gil Lister. 'I only have an hour –'

'We'll try to stretch it. One o'clock then.'

'No, I can't. I mean, I can only go at noon.'

'Noon. Well – all right. The Compass Rose at the St Francis. I'll be waiting.'

He had chosen a place diagonally across Union Square from Heath's and Katherine was there exactly at noon. 'Good heavens,' she said, gaping as they climbed the carpeted stairs from the lobby to the restaurant and were confronted with a riotous conglomeration that included Ionic columns, eighteenth century blackamoors, cobra lamps, Lebanese mirrors, and an art deco bar with huge lucite scrolls at the back and griffons at each corner.

Ross led Katherine past overstuffed chairs and couches grouped around marble and glass tables, across a small dance floor to an alcove where a velvet couch curved beneath a Chinese lacquer screen. 'You've never been here?'

'I don't know how I missed it,' Katherine said. 'It's just the place for people who grow up above grocery stores.'

He chuckled as he gave the waiter their order, then sat back and looked at her. 'I'm glad to see you. How are you?'

'Not bad,' she said, and thought about it. 'Really not bad. I don't have that feeling all the time of being on the edge of a cliff, about to topple over.'

'But you still have it sometimes?'

She looked pensively at a bronze goddess reclining beneath English pewter wall sconces. 'I miss being sure of what will happen tomorrow and the day after. I miss knowing the boundaries of my days – what I can or can't do, what I'm supposed to do, what the people I love can do. I know that none of it was true – nothing was certain – but it was so comforting to think it was. And I miss it. I miss Craig; I miss our times together; I miss our house. I get lonely.' She sat straighter. 'I'm sorry. I didn't mean to whine.'

'You're not whining. Loneliness is a fact, not a complaint.' She looked up at the odd note in his voice, but he changed the subject. 'Why must you eat lunch at noon?'

'Because the man I work for decrees it.'

'Why?'

'He didn't tell me. Don't you make rules for the people who work for you?'

'As few as possible. They work harder and more happily when they have some control over their days.'

'Yes.' Katherine watched the waiter serve scallops and wild rice, and fill their wine glasses. 'Gil hasn't learned that.'

'Gil?'

She told him about her job, making it seem more quaint than difficult and then, as he asked questions, she described their move to San Francisco.

'And all that time you didn't call me.'

'I thought about it. I wanted to do things by myself. And get used to being alone.'

'But you let your friend help you.'

'That was different.'

'Alone means without a man.' It was a statement, not a question, and it startled her.

'I never thought about it. I suppose it does. Right now, anyway.'

He looked at his watch. 'Dessert?' She shook her head, wondering if he was offended. 'You know,' he mused, 'I've never gone in drag, but if that's what it takes to be your friend, I'd consider it.'

It was several seconds before she took it in. He had spoken so seriously, and he looked so normal as he sat beside her – handsome, successful, at ease – that the words made no sense.

116

Then she burst out laughing. 'What an absurd thing to say.'

'As absurd as refusing to call a friend.'

Their eyes met in laughter. 'You're looking much better,' Ross said, thinking how remarkable her eyes were and how laughter transformed her face. 'The city suits you.'

She flushed and looked away. 'And your wife?' she asked. 'And Carrie and Jon?'

'Fine.' He wondered why she resisted compliments. 'You haven't told me where you live or how I can help you.'

'In the Sunset.'

'*Where* in the Sunset?'

She gave him her address. 'But we don't need anything. All we have to do is get used to the fog. I'd forgotten that the closer the ocean, the more fog there is. Todd and Jennifer are inventing a fan to blow it out to sea.'

'How do they like school?' he asked.

'Not as much as they would if they let themselves. But they're afraid school means we really *live* here, we'll never go back to Vancouver, or –' She cleared her throat to stop the waver in her voice, 'see Craig again.'

And there was Craig, Ross thought, as if Katherine's words had brought his shadow to sit beside them. 'You haven't heard from him? Or anything about him?'

Katherine shook her head. 'Everything I do – the apartment, my job, my friends – seems to push him farther away, but at the same time he's always with me. As if he's watching to see how well I can manage alone. I know that sounds silly, but still he's here.'

Ross signalled for their coffee. 'It's not silly. It took us years to get used to the idea that Craig and Jennifer were dead.'

'But Craig wasn't.'

'He might as well have been. He might as well be now. If he's not with you, if he doesn't come back –'

117

'I don't talk about that,' Katherine said abruptly. 'Tell me about your work. You haven't talked about yourself at all.'

'Do you have five minutes more? I'll tell you about a place I designed called BayBridge Plaza.'

'Can you tell me in five minutes?'

'I can start. The other three hours will have to wait until next time.'

She laughed. 'Please start.'

'Do you know what mixed-use development is?'

'No, but I suppose – a combination? Offices and stores?'

'That's it, but BayBridge goes even farther: residences, office buildings, shops, theatres, eating places, and lots of space and light – parks, atria, fountains, gardens, tennis courts – places for people. The whole idea is people – on foot, not in cars, and not dodging cars to get around.' He smiled. 'We're building for pedestrians. It's a dream we've had for a long time.'

Puzzled, Katherine asked, 'Who are "we"?'

'My company. The one I began six years ago.'

'It's your dream then.'

'Well, yes, but my staff is made up of people with the same ideas. What we're trying to do is rebuild cities and towns – or parts of them – without destroying them in the process. Look,' he explained as she frowned slightly. 'In BayBridge, we've designed townhouses – some restored, some new – and apartments in renovated warehouses. Wherever possible, we've kept the past – the city's past – and made it liveable, not only because it's a reminder of our beginnings, but also for variety. And we've designed them in so many shapes, sizes, styles and price ranges they'll attract all kinds of residents, young couples, singles, families, retired people – the whole spectrum. The life of a place is in variety, not sameness.'

He looked at his watch and signalled for the bill. 'The buildings will be low, joined by grass and brick paths. No towers, no high-rises, no concrete, no automobiles. They'll be parked on the periphery, screened by berms and trees and walls. The office buildings will be in a separate group and behind them a shopping mall with a community recreation centre. The whole mall, including the central courtyard, will be on multiple levels to make it seem like a series of separate areas – something like small village squares. It's illusion but it works; even with a hundred shops it's scaled to people: intimate, warm, bright, open, with places to sit outside or in, places for kids to play . . . I can't tell you all at once; there's too much. But that's what we're trying to do in the whole Plaza: keep each building area to a size and scope geared to people instead of the greater glory of engineers and architects and manufacturers of concrete and steel –'

He stopped. 'Katherine, I'm sorry. I go on and on when I have a good audience.'

His vitality and excitement had captured Katherine's imagination. 'BayBridge is a small town,' she said. 'Isn't that it? A community. And if you make enough of them, they'll all be connected, like links in a chain. to make a new kind of city.'

Ross's face lit in a smile. 'Thank you. For understanding so completely and for expressing it more perfectly than I ever did.'

Again, Katherine flushed. 'I have to get back. Thank you for lunch, and telling me about your work; it was wonderful. The best antidote to Gil.'

'Wait; I'll walk with you.' He took her arm as they left. 'How long are you going to work for this tyrant?'

'Until I can make a living some other way.'

He thought back. 'Once you said you were going to design jewellery. '

'It didn't work. I wasn't ready. But I think I'm going to try again. Leslie knows a jewellery designer and she's going to ask him for the name of someone I might study with.'

'Let me know how it goes.' In Heath's doorway, they shook hands. 'I'll call you soon; we'll have lunch again. And one night we'll go back to Victoria's for dinner.'

She met his eyes. 'I don't think so. But I'd enjoy lunch.' Anticipating Gil's wrath, she said a quick goodbye and slipped through the door, almost running to the stairs. But, going down, she smiled at the memory of their laughter in the restaurant.

Another friend.

Leslie McAlister and Marc Landau left the theatre while the actors were still taking curtain calls, to beat the crowd to the street. 'I have a feast waiting in the oven,' he announced in the taxi. 'So tonight we go to my place.'

Leslie grinned. 'Gold dust in the salt shaker?'

'That was last month, to celebrate the success of my custom line. Tonight you will find salt. Do you think I can afford such gestures every time we are together?'

'It would depend on the woman.'

'Ah.' He gestured vaguely, his plump, manicured hand somehow sketching the difficulties of finding anyone who deserved from him more than an occasional lavish gift.

Looking at those pudgy fingers, Leslie marvelled that they could be so delicate, not only at the worktable where he created the opulent jewellery that had made him famous and wealthy, but also in bed. An odd man, she thought dispassionately: soft and balding, but ruthless in business; crude but sophisticated, callously promiscuous but occasionally sympathetic and sensitive. After two years of going out with him, sleeping with him, travelling with him, she still wasn't sure how much she liked him. But the older Leslie got, the fewer the men who were amusing and intelligent, and usually Marc was both. And, she thought as they took the elevator to his apartment, he could be helpful to Katherine.

'If not gold dust,' she said. 'How about a small favour for a friend?'

'Possibly.'

'She's just moved here from Vancouver. She wants to design and make jewellery, but she needs to improve her technique and try out different materials. Can she work with you? She's already pretty good; it wouldn't be for long.'

'You're asking me to reveal to a stranger the techniques I've spent years developing. Champagne?'

'Yes, thank you. Katherine isn't a stranger; she's my friend. And I'm not asking you to give away secrets, just help her learn to work with gold and silver and other materials –'

'Where will she get the money to buy them?'

'She's working at Heath's.'

'My dear Leslie, if she's working when will she have the time? And how much can she be earning? Do you have any idea what gold and silver cost?'

'A lot. But that's not the message I'm getting.' She put down her glass and looked at him narrowly. 'It's just too much trouble, isn't it? The famous designer can't be bothered. She's my friend and I'm asking a favour, but there are a dozen god-damn reasons why you can't lift a finger to help. God, Marc, you are a bore. Never mind; I'll ask someone else. Is there more champagne?'

'There is always more champagne. And I am not a bore or you would not be here. As for your friend, I'll find someone to help her. I have no interest in coaching apprentices, but I know a man who takes small classes; I'll see if he has an opening. As for you, my dear, you seem to be turning into a charitable institution. First your brother – is he still at Heath's, by the way?'

'Still there. But I think he's avoiding me and I'm worried –'

'Spare me the details. And take care, Leslie, that you don't give too much of yourself to others; they suck you dry if you let them.' He picked up the champagne bottle. 'Now may we move on to the kitchen? We should inspect this elegant dinner I have personally prepared for you by standing in line at four exceedingly busy and exclusive delicatessens.'

She laughed. 'But you will help Katherine?'

'My God, I've said I would. Give me a day or two. In the meantime here – and here – and here –' He pulled books from the shelf. 'Tell her to read these. And leave me her telephone number before you go. Now, for the rest of the evening, you are to forget about good deeds. Except, of course, for those that belong in the bedroom. After dinner.'

In a small room above a store on Geary Street, Katherine sat on a wooden stool at a workbench, cutting a leaf from a silver square. As she finished the stem, her saw blade, barely thicker than a hair, snapped apart, and she let out a sharp sigh before reaching for a new one. After a day of holding china and silver while Lister set a banquet scene, her arms ached and it was their trembling as she followed the pattern scored in the soft silver that had caused her to break four blades in one evening.

'It happens to all of us,' her instructor said at her shoulder. 'Keep the blade upright and hold the strokes steady. You'll be fine. You're almost through, you know.'

Fitting a new blade to her saw, she nodded. This time her hand moved in a smoother rhythm, flowing with the softness of the silver, and in a moment the roughly-shaped leaf lay before her. With a small file, she smoothed and notched the edges, making the distinctive outline of a maple leaf. A drawer in her lap caught the silver dust and shavings. When the shape was complete, she clamped the leaf in a revolving vice and turned and tilted it while scoring it with an awl – one line down the centre, shorter lines radiating out. When the leaf's veins were finished she removed it from the vice and placed it in a hollow in a block of wood, where she pounded it to a curved shape with a rawhide-covered hammer. And finally, she polished the leaf on a buffing wheel to a silver gleam.

The finished maple leaf shone in her palm, gracefully curved as if lifted by the wind. She touched it with her finger. It was no different from hundreds of others made by students in classes just like her own – yet it was different. Marc Landau had suggested starting from the beginning with a short course in metals and stones. That was why it was different: it was a beginning. Never again would this be a pleasant hobby to fill her extra time; she would be a designer, an artist, a professional. She carried a sketch pad now, wherever she went, to draw forms in nature or architecture that might be created in jewellery. Every night, after Jennifer and Todd were asleep, she worked at a small table in the corner of her living-room, the only sound the scratching of her pencil as she doodled and drew and threw away and began again.

Craig watched her. She had had a snapshot enlarged and framed and it stood at the back of the table watching her: Craig in khakis and a plaid shirt, leaning against a tree at the top of Grouse Mountain. They had taken a picnic lunch, just the two of them – one of the few times they were ever alone. Craig had told her, as she was taking his picture, that Hank Aylmer had invited them to go with him when he next visited Eskimo villages to buy sculptures. A holiday, Craig said. It would be good to get away.

That was in May. One month before he disappeared.

Leaning against a tree – handsome, bearded, smiling – Craig watched Katherine bend over her sketches. He accused her of leaving Vancouver, of making a home with no place for him, of wanting to be a professional and manage on her own. 'Well, what would you rather I did?' she asked his picture. 'Sit in a corner and cry? Whine to your mother and father or the rest of your family – whom you never even told me about? What should I do?'

She waited, as if giving him a chance to respond. 'Well,' she said after a moment, and turned back to her work. A glint of light from the silver leaf caught her eye and she picked it up. The contentment of finishing it swept over her again, warming her as if she sat in a sunlit clearing. And if a shadow hovered nearby, that might dull the shine of her silver leaf, she did not look up to see if it was there.

Chapter 7

By the middle of October, Christmas materials had been delivered for Heath's windows and Lister and Katherine spent two days in the supply room, checking clothes and props against his master list. Katherine was unpacking linens for a children's bedroom scene when the telephone rang.

Lister took all the calls. This time he barked, 'For you,' and glared at Katherine as she took the receiver. He forbade personal telephone calls at work but, thinking of the children and Craig, Katherine ignored him. 'Hello,' she said, her voice low, her back to Lister.

'Derek Hayward, Katherine. We met at dinner –'

'I remember.' She sat down. *Derek?*

'You're probably busy, so I won't keep you. Will you have dinner with me? Tomorrow night, if you can manage on such short notice.'

'No,' she said without thinking. 'I'm sorry, but –'

'Next week, then. You name the night.'

'No, I'm sorry but I . . . I don't go out to dinner.'

There was a pause. 'Then *I* should apologise; that didn't occur to me. Lunch, instead? Tomorrow? A business lunch.'

'Business?' Katherine turned and saw Lister watching her. 'I can't talk now and I can't imagine what –'

'Family business,' Derek said. 'Making you welcome. That's something more than one of us should do.' His voice was like Ross's, warm and deep, and the words were casual, but they had an edge.

'Who –?' she began, then changed it. 'How did you find me?'

He laughed shortly. 'The family. Twice. Melanie told me she'd seen you at Heath's, and a day or two later Ross told Victoria he'd taken you to lunch, and Victoria told Tobias, who mentioned it to Melanie, who passed that along to me, also. Did you follow all that? It's one of the joys of a large family.'

She would have laughed but he was not joking. 'I've never known what that was like,' she commented. He was silent. 'I have to get back to work,' she said. 'I don't think lunch is a good idea. Usually I just bring something and eat here or across the street in the square.'

'I'll meet you there,' he said promptly. 'And I'll bring lunch. Do you have a favourite bench?'

'I sit on the grass.'

'Then I won't wear my best suit. Until tomorrow.'

But he was wearing a suit when she saw him the next day, waiting at the soldier's memorial statue in the centre of Union Square. 'I might take off my tie,' he said as they sat on the grass in a sunny corner between tall hedges. 'But if I didn't wear a suit on a weekday I might forget who I am. And what are *you* wearing, after all?'

'I confess,' she laughed. 'A suit.' He was handsomer than she remembered, with the same dark blond hair and deepset eyes as Ross, but smoother and more polished. And there was another difference. He made her conscious of the way he looked at her.

'Lunch,' he announced, and opened a woven straw hamper. 'Of course I had very little time to plan it properly, but I think it deserves at least polite applause.'

Katherine watched in astonishment as he took out a wooden box and unfolded it to a small table. Dipping into the hamper again and again like a beguiling magician, he drew out two china plates, heaped them with thin slices of rare roast beef, hearts of palm vinaigrette, and buttered rounds of rye bread, and balanced a silver knife and fork across each one. He poured a ruby red Bordeaux into two crystal wine glasses and handed Katherine a linen napkin.

Katherine had expected sandwiches and potato chips in a paper bag. 'You bought this just for today?'

'You said you wanted to eat on the grass; I bought a lunch for eating on the grass. But of course you're right; we should indeed use it again. In fact, from a strictly economic point of view, which I confess I had not considered, we can amortise the cost to reduce it to a rock-bottom ten dollars each by eating on the grass once a week for about thirty weeks. Can you arrange that? After all, we're right across the street from your office, or wherever it is you spend your time. Which reminds me, what is it you do over there?'

'Decorate windows.' Six hundred dollars for a picnic lunch. She was appalled – and fascinated. 'But that's not what you mean, is it? You're really asking what I'm doing in San Francisco.'

He considered her. Of course that was what he meant, but hadn't expected her to pick it up so quickly. She'd improved, he thought, since the night they'd met: the haggard look was gone and she no longer hunched over as if expecting a blow. But why the hell did she twist her hair in a bun and wear a suit that was too big and the wrong colour for someone with pale skin and no makeup? With surprise he realised how good-looking she was. But she had no idea of what she might make of herself. Which meant Craig hadn't cared. Or hadn't looked. 'I want to know all about you,' he said. 'Start with your job. And where you're living.'

He listened as she talked his face absorbed, and when he smiled at her imitation of Gil Lister, Katherine wondered how she could have thought of him as cold and aloof. Either she had been wrong or he was acting a part. But why would he do that? If he wanted something from her, all he had to do was ask. She liked him and she was having a good time; there was no reason not to be honest.

But their talk circled about, until Katherine looked at her watch. 'I have to go in a few minutes. And I haven't told you why I came to San Francisco. I haven't even talked about Craig. And he's the reason you bought this incredible lunch.'

Derek's eyebrows went up. Underestimated her again. Just because a woman is not glamorous, Victoria used to say when he was dating in high school, it does not mean she is simple. Katherine, without a jot of glamour, was not at all simple. 'I bought the lunch to impress you,' he said. 'But, of course, I want to hear about Craig. I was about to ask if you plan to go back to Canada or stay here. And about his partner. Will he press charges?'

'I don't know. I just want Craig to come back – we can think about Carl then. Oh. That's what was worrying all of you at dinner. You thought I'd ask you to pay back what Craig took.'

'Hardly.' Derek smiled faintly. 'I imagine we could scrape together that amount.'

'Then what was it? Why didn't anyone want me?'

'*Are* you going back to Vancouver?'

'No! At least – not until I hear from Craig. What difference does it make?'

'Some of the family,' he said casually, 'think it might make a difference in the division of Victoria's estate.'

'She's not dead.'

'She's eighty-one. The question comes up – what Craig might get if he were here.'

'You mean money.'

He smiled again. 'That would simplify it. Of course, money. But also, Victoria owns fifty percent of the Hayward Corporation.'

Katherine began to understand what was involved. 'Who inherits her fifty percent now?'

'As far as we know, Ross and I.'

Money and control of the corporation, Katherine thought. Ross and Derek. 'Ross wouldn't try to keep Craig away because of that.'

Derek's face hardened, though his voice remained light. 'Ross would do whatever is necessary to accumulate sufficient power and wealth to use the Hayward Corporation for his own purposes.'

Katherine shivered at the knife-edged words spoken in his pleasant voice. I don't believe that, she thought. She looked across the Square, at crowds waiting for streetlights to change. 'Craig has been gone almost four months. If your family really is worried about what he might do, why isn't anyone trying to find him?'

'Claude hired an investigator.'

She stared at him. 'No one told me.'

'There's been nothing to tell. He's found nothing.'

'But I could give him information –'

'I'm sure he'll call you when he's ready.'

'You still think I might have arranged this with Craig! Isn't that right? Your investigator doesn't trust –' She stopped. At the corner a man moved forward: bearded, with brown hair. He was talking to someone, his face partially turned from her, but the way he held his head, tilted a little –

She clambered to her feet. 'Katherine!' Derek said. The light changed and the bearded man turned towards her to cross the street. Not Craig; not even like Craig. But as if her thoughts had brought him to the square, Katherine felt his presence so powerfully he might have been standing beside her in the warm afternoon sun. Derek's voice faded. She felt Craig's eyes on her, puzzled and reproachful, and she felt ashamed of her laughter and her pleasure in Derek's extravagant lunch. She was as bad as the rest of the Haywards, pushing Craig to the background, forgetting that he was in trouble, thinking only of the present.

Craig, she thought, missing him with the stab of pain that she thought had faded in the crowded weeks. She put out her hand, but no one was there. It's the sun, she thought dizzily. And the wine. And I was up so late last night, making sketches after my class. She closed her eyes against the glare.

Derek's hand, cool and hard, grasped hers. 'Sit down. I'm sorry I upset you.'

In the bright darkness behind her eyes, his voice sounded like Craig's. Everything reminded her of Craig. She opened her eyes. 'You didn't upset me. I thought I saw Craig.'

'You haven't finished your lunch.'

'I can't. I'm sorry . . .' She took a step away from him. 'Thank you – it was so impressive – I hope you can use the hamper again, and amortise the cost –'

'Wait a minute; I want to see you –'

'Goodbye, Derek.' It was as if Craig were pushing her. Almost running, she crossed the street with the crowds, and pushed through the revolving doors that sent her into Heath's, and back to work.

*

130

Two nights later, after Jennifer and Todd were asleep, Tobias appeared like an apparition at Katherine's front door. 'I know it seems rude,' he said, ducking his head apologetically as he walked past her into the living room. 'But one could call it a sign of intimacy. In the general sense' – he sat down and cheerfully began to inspect the room – 'of closeness. To pay a visit without telephoning first.' His inspection reached her face. 'You don't agree?'

'Did Derek send you?' she asked.

Tobias looked bewildered. 'Ordinarily I am not *sent* anywhere, by anyone, but even if I were, what in heaven's name would Derek have to do with it?'

'He didn't tell you we had lunch together?'

'Lunch,' Tobias repeated.

'In Union Square.'

He gazed at her blankly. 'There is no restaurant in Union Square.'

'On the grass. He brought a picnic lunch.'

'*Derek*? On the grass? Not possible.' Tobias sat erect on the edge of the couch, hands on his knees, and cogitated briefly. 'I have learned over the years to believe many unbelievable things about Derek, but not this. What was he wearing?'

'A business suit. If he didn't tell you, why are you here?'

'Well.' They looked at each other. He seemed so carefree, with blue eyes as bright and innocent as a child's, and an open smile above his little white beard. But now and then, unexpectedly, the blue eyes would turn sharp, not so innocent after all, and at others, when his smile dimmed, his face would sag in crêpe-like folds. He's seventy-five, Katherine remembered, but those creases in his face were from sadness as well as age. 'Well,' he repeated, and smiled like a friendly conspirator. Katherine found herself smiling back, liking him, even as she asked herself why another Hayward was suddenly paying

131

attention to her. 'I heard you were in the city. Ross told Victoria he'd taken you to lunch and –'

'Victoria told you,' Katherine interrupted. 'And you mentioned it to Melanie, who passed it along to Derek. But Melanie had already seen me working at Heath's and had told Ross, who then invited me to lunch. And I heard all that from Derek.'

Tobias laughed delightedly. ' "The babbling gossip of the air." Shakespeare,' he added helpfully. 'You'd think he knew our family. I brought you a housewarming gift.' He took a box from his coat pocket and gave it to Katherine, who looked at it nonplussed. 'Open, open!' he cried, as eager as Jennifer and Todd, and Katherine unwrapped it to find a crystal and silver candy dish.

'How lovely,' she said. 'Thank you –'

Tobias was surveying the room again. A come-down, he thought, from the Vancouver home she and Ross had described. Over-crowded; brought too much furniture with her. Good quality, though a trifle shabby; his candy dish looked a bit out of place. But she'd made the room cheerful: light colours, an oil painting that looked like an original, a silk scarf knotted around a lampshade, making it glow like stained glass. Good sense of colour and balance; she'd made the place look larger than it was. One oddity: a small table in a corner cluttered with pencils, buttons, string, sketch pads, construction paper, x-acto knives, and empty, flattened toothpaste tubes. Tobias looked a question at Katherine.

'Homework,' she said, adding almost defiantly, 'I'm studying jewellery design.'

'Ah.' Tobias nodded. 'But – toothpaste tubes?'

'For models. They're so soft I can cut and shape them the way I'd cut and shape silver and gold – if I had any. You haven't told me why you're here.'

'To deliver my gift – which I'm pleased you like – and to talk. My dear, is there anything to drink in your house?'

'Oh.' She was embarrassed. 'I haven't had a chance to stock anything –'

She hasn't the money to stock anything, Tobias thought. 'My favourite is ice-water,' he lied cheerfully. 'Or coffee. If you wouldn't mind –?'

Following Katherine to the kitchen, he sat at the oak table, talking, while she made coffee. 'I thought you should know something about us, since you're here – and you *are* here, aren't you? That is, permanently. Is that correct? You're not going back to Canada?'

Just like Derek. They all want to know when I'm leaving. 'It depends on what Craig wants to do.'

'Craig?'

'When he comes back.' She met his eyes, daring him to challenge her.

'But until then,' he prompted.

'This is where we live. The children are in school and I have a job. If you're trying to get rid of me –'

'No, no, what an odd thing to say; why would we want any such thing?'

'Because of the corporation, and his grandmother's estate.'

'Where did you get that idea?'

'Derek said some of the family were concerned –'

Tobias began to laugh, his pointed beard dancing. 'Katherine, dear Katherine. When Derek tells you someone in the family is worried about something, what do you think that means?'

She filled two mugs with coffee and carried them to the living-room. 'He told me what he meant.'

'Yes, but with Derek, my dear, one looks under the words to prise out the unspoken ones. Now think; who is most worried about Hayward money and power?'

Katherine watched the steam rise from her coffee. She had liked Derek until he talked bitterly about Ross. She had liked

133

Tobias until she heard the sharp glee in his voice as he talked about Derek. 'Does your family always make accusations about each other?' she asked. 'It's not very pleasant.'

'Ah.' Tobias, too, contemplated the steam. 'Do you know how Hugh Hayward made his money?'

'Of course. Construction; the Hayward Corporation.'

'Oh my, no. The company was fairly modest until Curt took over – his son, you know, Derek and Ross's father – though Hugh had made the Hayward reputation for excellence. The real money came earlier, in the twenties, when Hugh smuggled liquor from Europe and Canada. Prohibition, my dear: good Scotch made many a millionaire in those dry days. No one in the family likes to recall it, but I find it amusing that our enterprising Hugh was slipping cases of Scotch past the eagle-eyed law, while he and Victoria danced at charity balls and had their pictures in the newspapers as fine young socialites who donated generously to good causes. "Everyone is a moon and has a dark side which he never shows to anybody." '

' "A dark side," ' Katherine repeated slowly. 'Who wrote that?'

'Mark Twain. Fits the Hayward men like a glove. Hugh was only the first.' He sighed and sipped his coffee. 'I did enjoy Hugh. I still miss him, even after all this time. A huge man, devious, witty, handsome. How he adored Victoria. He would have handled that sailing mess differently, but he'd been dead three years, and Victoria had shut herself off, mourning him, and there was no real authority in the family. Is there more coffee?'

Katherine refilled his cup. Of course, she thought. He came to talk about Craig. 'You mean the sailing accident,' she said.

'Ah, well.' Tobias looked around the room, nodding to himself. 'It was a mess. Not that I ever heard the whole story, but I expect to know it some day. Professors of literature are experts at ferreting out long-buried tales. And as I am writing

134

the family history, of course I must discover everything there is to know. Your husband, my dear, caused me untold problems, since no one would talk about him. These days of course everyone is talking about him because you're here, reminding us.'

He sipped coffee. 'Well. Of course Derek and Craig quarrelled on the boat; actually, they came to blows. Ross says he doesn't know why, and Derek won't talk, and Craig, we now know, fled the scene, so I must wait. Now you, my dear, could learn more; no one has a better right to ask questions and demand answers.' He looked at her with innocent blue eyes. 'You could be my research assistant.'

Katherine longed for Craig. He could tell her whether or not to trust this foolish-looking old man. She did want the truth; she wanted to learn as much as possible about Craig. But only to understand him better – and also herself: how she could live for ten years with a man and never suspect he was hidden in a maze of lies. But if she learned bits of Craig's past, why should she give them to Tobias or anyone else in a family she distrusted?

Tobias sighed and stood up. 'I won't push you, my dear. But you and I could help each other and I'm quite reliable, you know. Well, of course you don't know that, but when you've been part of us for a while –'

'I'm not part of you,' she said. 'I don't want to be part of you. I'm waiting for Craig to come back and since none of you cares about him the way I do, just for himself, I don't need any of you.'

'I think you might,' he said gently. 'Why don't you mull it over and I'll call in a week or so. Perhaps we could have lunch. Not in Union Square, however. My knees, you know . . . sitting on the grass . . .' He shook his head and walked to the door. 'You've improved since that night at Victoria's. You're better-looking and I like your spirit. Craig would be proud of you.'

She looked at him in surprise. He nodded, pleased with

himself. 'Think about that.' He opened the door and was gone, but suddenly his head appeared again, eyes bright blue and smiling. 'We'd make quite a team, you know.' And the door closed behind him.

'Just wait,' Leslie said when Katherine told her about Tobias' visit and showed her the cases of wine, and boxes of cheese, nuts and crackers, that had been delivered the next day. 'Pretty soon there'll be another. Looks like you've been discovered by the Haywards.'

Katherine didn't want another one. She had enough on her mind. She had Gil Lister, day after day, and when she left him she came home to children who were cross and difficult to handle. At night she was restless, hungry for love-making and companionship. She went to her jewellery class twice a week, and Leslie came for dinner, or just to talk, at least once a week, but otherwise life was very quiet, with plenty of time to think. Ross had called twice to see if she needed anything, but he had seemed distracted by problems at work, and something else – something personal – and when he did not mention another lunch, Katherine did not either. No more Haywards, she thought. Maybe later, when I figure out how to deal with them.

But Leslie had been right. A few days after Tobias' visit, Claude Fleming telephoned: not a Hayward but, as he had told her at Victoria's, almost one of the family. 'The top of the Hyatt,' he said when she agreed to meet him the next day after work. 'Just across the square from Heath's.'

He was waiting when she arrived: a tall man in his fifties with carefully-brushed silver hair, observant eyes, and a well-exercised body set off in an expensive suit. When Katherine sat opposite him in the booth, he pointed to the crest of a distant hill where a salmon-coloured, balconied apartment building stood alone against the golden sky of late afternoon.

'Do you recognise it?' Katherine shook her head. 'Pacific Heights. Victoria's. You were there for dinner.'

The waitress brought wine for Katherine, Scotch for Claude, and a dish filled with toasted cereal and nuts. Claude slid it aside. 'Execrable dish. The view, however, is fine. Are you settled in your apartment? And your job? And the children in school?'

Katherine gazed at him a moment. 'Perhaps we should have a meeting of the whole family. I could answer all the questions just once and then find out what everyone wants from me.'

His eyes narrowed. Then he smiled and lifted his glass. 'To your new life. Evidently it will be a lively one.'

Katherine's face was flushed. She wasn't used to talking that way, especially to polished and successful older men who made her feel like a child. She wished she hadn't come. She'd already said she didn't want any more of this strange family that had rejected her in June and now sought her out in October. They made her nervous and when she was with them she acted in ways that surprised everyone, including herself.

'– Hope it is lively,' Claude was saying, beckoning the waitress for another drink. 'Everyone hopes so. As they hope to get to know you better.'

'Why?' Katherine asked. 'To find out why I moved here and if I'm lying about Craig? To keep tabs on me so they'll know, the minute he returns, how big a dent he might try to make in their bank accounts?'

He was taken aback. 'Did Derek put that into your head? All we want is to help you. If Craig has abandoned you –'

'He hasn't!'

'Let us assume he has. It would not, after all, be the first time. After four months with no word or sign from him –'

'It's just as likely he had an accident,' Katherine said stubbornly. 'Or something happened that we haven't even thought

137

of. I won't listen to you criticise him – any of you – you never liked Craig; you don't give him a chance.'

'Some of us did,' Claude said quietly.

'Not the whole family.'

He smiled. 'That's asking quite a lot of any family. But some of them adored him. He was in a peculiar position, you know: the first grandson. There were Victoria and Hugh, with their two sons, Jason and Curt – who were always in competition for one thing or another – and then Jason and Ann produced the first grandson, a year before Curt and his wife had Derek. Not that it was a contest, you understand, but Victoria adored Craig from the day he was born; so did Ann; and as Jennifer grew up, she joined the admiring female chorus. Hugh expected his grandson to be another version of himself – aggressive, dominating, confident; Jason wanted a son who was a legend like Hugh Hayward; and Victoria and Ann called Craig their golden boy: perfect, excelling in all things. I felt sorry for him; there was no way he could live up to any of those demands. Curt, who's retired now and living in Phoenix, never liked Craig; he thought he was coddled and weak. Derek followed his father's lead, but then Derek never could tolerate people on pedestals, especially a cousin only a year older than himself. Ross, far less competitive, was Craig's friend. I suppose it helped that Victoria loved Ross but never could like Derek and he never forgave her. Well –' He gestured with his hand. 'Families. The best of them have their feuds. Ross escaped: went to college in New York, got married, found a job. In fact Curt arranged that; a friend of his in New York took Ross into his firm. Derek stayed here and was running the company long before Curt took early retirement. By now he's doubled its size – took some chances that could have been disasters but proved enormously profitable. A real gambler is Derek. And no one interfered with him, not even Victoria, who's the major stockholder. He became the head of the family by default when Victoria withdrew from everything after Jennifer and Craig were killed – after we thought Craig was killed.'

Katherine saw again the picture of the laughing girl. 'What was Jennifer like?'

'Jennifer.' He waved for another drink and looked inquiringly at Katherine, who shook her head. 'Tobias called her sunlight and shadow. She was lovely, with a freshness that made one regret one's age. She danced through life, taking nothing very seriously, until the last few months of her life, when she became quite preoccupied. Tobias was here at Easter and thought her sombre. I thought she was worried. Certainly Ann and Jason were. She was so changed: distant, stubborn . . . she'd been accepted at Radcliffe but then out of the blue said she wouldn't go. No one knew why.'

After a pause, Katherine asked, 'Why did Ross come back?'

'I think, to be near Victoria. He never explained it, though Derek tried his damnedest to find out. But his return didn't change anything. He opened his own firm of architects, made a remarkable reputation entirely separate from the one Hugh and Curt and Derek had made at the Hayward Corporation, and he and Melanie built a house in Tiburon. There really was no family: Craig and Jennifer were gone, Jason and Ann had withdrawn to Maine, Derek and his father ran the company, Victoria was frantic with grief and then just got more and more crotchety. Nine years ago, when Tobias retired, she gave him an apartment on the second floor of her duplex. He and Ross were the only ones who got along with her. All of them went in separate ways, measuring their lives in different possessions.'

The words caught Katherine's fancy. 'What does that mean? Measuring –?'

'What we own, what we are, what we fight for. Derek, for instance, measures his life in money and power. Wives, perhaps, if you count the three he's had. And things: he accumulates everything from art to gadgets.'

Katherine thought of a picnic hamper. 'And Ross?' she asked.

'Accomplishments, I suppose. How much he can achieve in rebuilding the cities of America. No small dreams for Ross. In the meantime he makes good money – nothing near what Derek makes, but he's hardly worrying – and he cares about money, if for no other reason than his extremely extravagant Melanie, but I've never thought of him as measuring his days in dollars. Or power, though he must know it takes power to make his dreams a reality. Interesting man; isn't it because of him that you moved here?'

'Oh, no.' She was dismayed. 'I didn't even tell him.' And I've only seen him once, she added silently. Six weeks ago. 'How does Victoria measure her life?'

'Once it was the family: how firmly she kept it together. That stopped when Craig and Jennifer died. Well, not Craig – you know what I mean. For the last ten years, she's concentrated on making herself necessary. She's on governing boards of the Opera, the Symphony, the Museum of Art, and a couple of welfare organisations, and she's enormously influential because she really works. It was through her connections that the Art Museum got the Peruvian gold exhibit that opens this week. I recommend it: a brilliant show. Why *did* you move to San Francisco?'

'What?'

'I said –'

'No, I heard you. I grew up here.'

'That's the only reason you moved from Vancouver?'

'I'm not after any Hayward money.'

'I don't think you are.' He looked amused. 'I'll report that to the family. You're a pleasant young woman; you speak intelligently and listen well. In fact you've manoeuvred me into

140

talking about the family when I meant to talk about you. Admirable.'

Katherine regarded him. 'I don't believe anyone manoeuvres Claude Fleming. You wanted me to know about the family.'

He was signing the charge slip and his pen stopped momentarily. He smiled. 'You'll do very well,' he said, and finished writing.

'How do you think I measure my life?' Katherine asked.

Thoughtfully, he studied her. 'By your independence,' he said, and watched the swift changes in her face, from pleasure to confusion.

'And Craig?' she asked.

'Ah. Money, loving a select few, being admired, and successfully running from problems.'

Katherine looked through the window, at the darkening sky. For the first time, she was not sure what to say in her husband's defence.

Leslie brought a bottle of wine and a birthday cake and they all helped set the table. 'How old are you?' Todd asked.

'Ninety-nine,' said Leslie. 'But I'm told I don't look it. Some days I don't even feel it.'

Katherine looked up. 'What's wrong?'

'Nothing serious,' Leslie said. 'It's Friday. Lots of things seem wrong on Friday that are miraculously cured by having two free days. Shit, I forgot; you work tomorrow.'

'Not this week. Gil told me he didn't need me. It's like a holiday.'

'Gil? Being generous? Not in character. He must be up to something.'

'How old *are* you?' Todd insisted.

'Thirty-six.' Leslie tousled his hair. 'Does that seem ancient?'

'Not as ancient as ninety-nine.' He looked at his plate as they sat down. 'Mom, what's this gunk?'

141

'Don't be insulting,' Leslie answered. 'Since it's my birthday, I got to choose the menu and it's ragout of beef.'

Todd made a face. 'It sounds awful. I'm going to McDonald's.'

'You're staying right here,' Katherine said. 'And eating dinner with us. You haven't even tasted it.'

'I don't like it and I won't eat it and I'm going to McDonald's and you can't stop me!'

'Hey,' Leslie said, with a quick look at Katherine's face, 'you want to ruin my party?'

'Todd,' said Katherine. 'I left a box in Annie's apartment. Will you bring it in?'

He shrugged glumly. 'Why not.'

When he was gone, Leslie gave Katherine a questioning look. 'He wasn't like this in Vancouver.'

'I know. He's changed since we came here. He's disruptive at school and doesn't do his work – his teachers say he's acting out all his problems. I can't talk to him about it –'

'You don't talk to us about anything,' Jennifer said. 'You didn't even ask us if we wanted to leave Vancouver.'

'Jennifer, that was a long time ago.'

'Well, we haven't forgotten it. And we don't like anything about San Francisco or this apartment or school or your job or *anything*.'

Katherine and Leslie exchanged a look. 'I have an inspiration,' Leslie said. 'You two need a day at the Exploratorium. Next Saturday. At noon. Be ready.'

'Exploratorium!' Todd cried, coming in with a large box in his arms. 'No kidding? Mom promised to take us twice but she blew it both times.'

'I had to work those days,' Katherine said quietly.

'Todd, you're behaving like a pint-sized bastard,' Leslie said. Taking advantage of his open-mouthed shock, she pointed to his plate. 'Eat your dinner – which is terrific, by the way – and see if you can help me figure out my mystery.'

'Mystery?' Jennifer looked suspicious. 'Are you making something up so we'll forget we're not happy?'

'No I'm not,' Leslie said seriously. 'I think we should talk about that. But this is my party and I don't want grouching to ruin it. If Todd blows out my candles with his huffing and puffing, I won't get my wish.'

Todd and Jennifer smiled. 'So what's the mystery?' Todd asked.

'At Heath's we have a new line of sweaters by a designer named Ralph Lauren; they're very popular, and selling fast. Also selling fast are Calvin Klein blouses, silk, costing two hundred and fifty each.'

Jennifer gasped. '*Each*? Is that the mystery? Why people pay that much?'

Leslie laughed. 'Nope. This is it: more of those blouses and sweaters are gone from the departments than the clerks remember selling. How would you explain that?'

'Somebody stole them,' Jennifer said promptly.

'That's what I thought, too. But the sales records in our computer say they've been sold.'

'The clerks forgot,' said Todd. 'They had amnesia. Did you ask them if they fell down one day and were knocked out?'

'As a matter of fact, I didn't,' Leslie answered. 'I'll give it some thought.'

'Something's wrong with the computer,' Jennifer guessed.

'Computers don't make mistakes,' Todd scoffed.

'Not ever?' Katherine asked. 'What if a person makes a mistake in telling the computer what to do?'

'I've got it!' Todd cried. 'It *is* the computer! A bunch of mice came into the computer when it was cold out and rubbed together to get warm and the rubbing made static electricity that erased part of the computer memory, so you're getting the wrong numbers!'

'Good thinking,' laughed Leslie. 'We'll look for mice on Monday morning.'

'Leslie,' Katherine said. 'What's the real problem? It's more than blouses and sweaters.'

Leslie sighed. 'Nothing like a friend to see inside a person's head. You're right; there's more. There's my fellow vice presidents. Four smug males waiting with tongues hanging out for me to make a mistake so they can kick me off their masculine turf. I don't know what the hell is happening with those blouses and sweaters, but if we're losing merchandise – which means money – they'll look to see who's fouled up store security, and that means me.'

'You?' asked Todd. 'Security?'

'It comes under Personnel. And I'm Vice President for Personnel and Payroll. See what I mean?'

Jennifer was watching Leslie with fascination. 'Is the president a smug male who wants you off his turf, too?'

'He's better than the others,' Leslie answered. 'Though who knows,' she added darkly, 'what really lurks inside a big chief's head? All I want is to be left alone to do my job, and so far he's done that, but one good crisis could change everything . . .' She brooded for a moment, then briskly shook her head. 'Enough of this. You're a terrific audience; you've cheered me up; and I love you all. But we are in danger of forgetting one of the most important parts of this evening. Didn't I see a cake in the kitchen? How can I swallow thirty-six years without chocolate cake to make it go down? And what about that huge box Todd staggered in with? Could that be for me?'

Katherine lit the candles on the cake while Leslie opened the box and lifted out a set of appliquéd throw pillows for her couch that the three of them had made. 'You remembered!' she cried in delight. 'And they're wonderful – just the kind I couldn't find anywhere.' Todd and Jennifer beamed and launched into a lengthy explanation of the difficulties in appliqué.

'But it was fun,' Jennifer said. 'Even Todd liked it.'

'I had this sword,' Todd explained. 'And I kept stabbing these monsters from caves that were about to gobble us up –'

'He means he was sewing,' said Jennifer helpfully.

'Just don't tell the guys at school,' said Todd. 'They'd think I was really weird.'

Katherine stepped back, as if she were watching a play. Her children and her friend sat at a folding table, festive with tablecloth and candles, in the centre of the crowded living-room. On a table in the corner, her models of bracelets, necklaces and pendants glinted in the soft light. The grandfather clock boomed nine o'clock. Nothing in that room, none of the people, would have been there if not for her. Independence, Claude had said, sending a quick rush of pleasure through her. He'd been right, and her pleasure had been real. It would only be for a while, only until Craig returned, but still she savoured it: she had done this alone. I'll always remember how it feels, she thought. Because I've never felt it before.

A few days later, Derek called. 'I have tickets for a private opening tonight of a Peruvian art exhibit. I thought you'd enjoy it, especially the jewellery. It includes dinner – possibly grilled Peruvian goat – but if it's inedible, we can go somewhere else. Can I pick you up at Heath's?'

'Yes,' she said without hesitation. Derek could tell her more about the Haywards and about Craig, she told herself, trying to explain her quick response. She thought of another explanation while filling out shipping forms to return last week's window scenery to the warehouse: she might find ideas for jewellery in the ancient gold work of Peruvian artisans. And besides, she decided as she helped Lister arrange witches and warlocks in a Hallowe'en window, it will be good to get out, and Annie can

145

stay with Jennifer and Todd. But, at the end of the day, meeting the sceptical grin of a jack o'lantern on her desk, she admitted that she had said yes because she wanted to see Derek again.

'I'm glad you're here,' he said as she stepped into his car in front of Heath's and he pulled into the traffic on Geary Street. 'I was afraid you'd turn me down.'

The car was sleek and low-slung, and Katherine felt peculiar, sitting just inches above the street, watching other cars and pedestrians loom over her as Derek whipped through narrow spaces that made her flinch. She looked instead at his smooth profile and wondered how many women turned Derek down, or how often he really was afraid they would. 'Why would I turn you down?' she asked.

'Another Hayward. I thought you might have had enough of us after being inundated for the past few weeks.'

'Oh.' She considered it. Did everyone in that family always know what the others were doing? 'No. It's been very interesting.'

'*Interesting*? Good lord, wait until Tobias hears that.' He turned into the Civic Centre and found a parking place near the Museum of Art. 'After meeting the Hayward clan, Katherine Fraser pronounces them interesting.'

'I'm sorry,' Katherine blushed, feeling slow and dull, and wondering how she was going to get through the evening.

'We'll survive.' Derek walked around the car and opened her door. 'You may even find that some of us are more interesting than others. Let's see what's going on inside.'

He took her arm. Unexpectedly, she was filled with excitement. It had been so long since she went anywhere. It wasn't Derek, she told herself; it was getting away from the house, the children, the job, worrying over money, missing Craig, endlessly speculating about him, worrying about him. Her steps were light as she went into the building on Derek's arm.

But once inside, confronted with the crowd, Katherine's

excitement drained away. Sleek men in black tie or dark business suits, and beautiful women in gala dresses, feathered frilled, beaded and bejewelled, took her measure when they saw her with Derek – and a hundred eyebrows went up, making her feel as dull as she had months earlier, beside the spotlight of Melanie's gleaming presence: as if she had crashed an exclusive party.

Unaware or indifferent, Derek made casual introductions, and Katherine shook hands and murmured greetings, wondering all the while why she hadn't been prepared. It would happen every time she tried to enter the Haywards' world. Derek might have warned her, but perhaps he had no idea how she felt, wearing a blue wool suit and white blouse, and a single strand of pearls Craig had given her for their tenth anniversary, while all around her stood women who outshone even the Peruvian gold in the Museum's exhibit.

I won't go through it again, she thought; I'll leave. Derek won't mind; he belongs here and he'll hardly know I've gone. Yet she made no move to turn and walk out. Something held her and as she answered polite questions from Derek's friends, the thought came: *Craig ran. I won't.*

She pushed the words aside as if they burned her, and changed them. It's research. I'm finding out what jewellery wealthy women are wearing. One of these days I'll be designing for them.

'The jewellery is in the cases along the wall,' Derek said. 'Where would you like to start? The fourteenth century? I'm sorry about the crowd; private parties are never private unless you give them yourself. With luck, dinner will be quieter.'

Dinner was quieter. The guests sat ten to a table and at first the conversation revolved around Derek. For the first time Katherine learned the full scope of the Hayward Corporation's activities in California and the West, from highways, bridges and aqueducts to office complexes and industrial parks. She

147

was stunned by the extent of the company under Derek's control. She had assumed it was like Craig's, constructing houses and office buildings and having a difficult time in the recession. In fact, the Hayward Corporation was only lightly touched by the economy. Offices and industrial parks had slowed, but the contracts for roads, bridges and dams had been signed years before and there was plenty to keep the company busy. Remembering how Craig and Carl had been forced to lay off workers because there was not enough for them to do, and listening to the talk of Derek's huge projects and future plans, Katherine began to think he stood above everyone else, untouched by ordinary problems and fears.

And he seemed untouched by people as well. Men and women came up to him and spoke respectfully, often deferentially, some trying to curry favour, others sharing information. But Derek was the same to all of them. Self-contained, remote, caustic, with power coiled behind his polished social presence, he appeared impressive and inaccessible, unlike anyone Katherine had ever known. 'Now,' he said, dismissing the rest of the table by turning to her. 'It's your turn. I want to know about your jewellery. You're taking classes?'

She answered briefly, reluctant to talk about her work. But he pressed her until she described some of her sketches.

'I'd like to see them,' he said.

She shook her head. 'I haven't found a style of my own yet.'

'What do you think of that one?' He gestured casually at a woman across the room whose neck was encased in diamonds that flashed when she moved her head.

Katherine contemplated her. 'She looks like a lighthouse, warning everyone away.'

Derek's idle gaze swung to her as it had on their picnic. 'You can be quite astonishing,' he said. 'And you aren't even aware of it.'

She flushed and was silent, afraid to say something that was not astonishing. After a moment, he asked a question about Heath's and they talked easily for the rest of the evening. But Katherine was aware of his eyes on her, as intimate and absorbed as if they were alone. He had turned a dinner for three hundred people into a private evening.

She realised, as he drove her home, that he had not mentioned her clothes; he had not even seemed to notice them. Yet he dressed impeccably and fastidiously. So he must have noticed. I'll have to do something about that, she thought, if I see him again.

'I'll call you,' Derek said as she unlocked the door of her building. Holding her hand, he kissed her forehead. 'Thank you for coming. I enjoyed the Incas far more than I thought possible.' .

She smiled, watching him go back to his car, and was still smiling when she let herself into the apartment. Annie was waiting for her, a finger to her lips. Katherine's smile faded. 'What is it? What's wrong?'

'Nothing, maybe,' Annie whispered. 'But I thought maybe you'd want to see this alone.' She held out an envelope. 'A letter from Canada.'

Katherine's heart lurched. There was no return address and the postmark was blurred. No it wasn't; her eyes had filled with tears. She blinked them away and read the name of a town she'd never heard of, in Saskatchewan. What was Craig doing in –

Annie had gone to her own apartment; the living-room was quiet. *Craig, Craig, Craig.* It was like a heartbeat as she tore open the envelope and pulled out a piece of paper. But there was nothing on it. Not a word of writing. Only, as she unfolded it, something that fluttered to the floor. She bent down to pick it up: five hundred dollars in crisp one hundred dollar bills.

Chapter 8

A tremor ran through Victoria's hand as she poured their tea. 'And what will you do now?' she asked.

The money lay on the table between them, beside the silver tea service. Katherine's glance slid past it as she took the cup Victoria handed her. For three days the sheaf of bills had been the centre of attention on her worktable. She had tried to explain to the children what it meant – that Craig was all right and knew where they were; that for some reason he couldn't come back to them yet, but he wanted to help them and so he sent the money. It wasn't very satisfactory but it was the best she could do. Then, Friday morning, while they were at breakfast, Victoria called, surprising her with an invitation to tea that afternoon, and on impulse she put the money in her purse. As soon as they sat down, she pulled it out and told Victoria what it was.

In the silence of the sunroom Victoria sighed deeply, turning the five bills over and over, as if looking for a message.

Katherine watched her. She sat erect, as serene and unapproachable as an empress in a knit suit of the finest burgundy wool, her white hair cut like a cap of small curls. Now and then she raised a thin manicured hand to the antique pendant she wore on a gold chain; except for that, her body was still. Even more than the women at the Peruvian exhibit, she made Katherine feel clumsy and poorly put together.

But Victoria's face was drawn and a vein in her neck was taut as she inspected the money. Katherine looked away, admiring the room where they sat. In the sunlit air, the white wicker furniture shone against dark green ficus trees, wistaria vines, and bushy, flowering plants. There were wondrous mementoes of Victoria's trips around the world everywhere – Mexican papier mâché birds, a bronze horse from Ceylon, Japanese ladies in jade, ebony masks from Africa. It was a lovely room, as beautiful and finely-made as Victoria, but it had the hush of a place waiting for someone to bring it to life.

Victoria sighed again. 'It could be from a friend.'

'No.' Katherine watched her place the money carefully on the table. 'It's from Craig. We don't know anyone in that town, or' – she gave a small smile – 'anyone anywhere who would send five hundred dollars anonymously. You don't seem surprised,' she added. 'Or pleased.'

Victoria picked up the silver teapot and refilled their cups. 'And what will you do now?' she asked, as if Katherine had not spoken.

'Wait,' Katherine answered dispiritedly. No answers here, she thought. No help, either. 'I've called the Vancouver police and they're working with police in Saskatchewan –'

'I'm talking about *you*,' Victoria said. 'Now that you know you're not a widow.'

'I never believed I was a widow,' Katherine shot back.

'Please,' Victoria said coolly. 'You need not shout.'

Instinctively, Katherine replied, 'I'm sorry.' She was edgy.

She had vowed never to come here again, but here she sat, as intimidated as the first time, and making things worse by snapping at Victoria. 'I'm sorry,' she repeated and said quietly, 'I'll wait, for Craig to come back.'

Victoria's hand went to her pendant. 'Now that we know he is alive, you might say *we* are waiting too. After all this time. But Craig clearly has no intention of coming back to us. He has wiped us out of his life.'

Katherine winced. *As he has wiped us out.* She looked at the table for reassurance. *No he hasn't. He sent us money.*

Victoria moved slightly in her chair. 'I asked you here so we could get acquainted. I seem to be the last in my family to do so.'

'You were angry, because of my rudeness. I'm sorry for the way I spoke that night.'

'As you should be. You tend to jump at people, Katherine. And away from them. Quite erratic. You must learn to control yourself. And if you learned to sit straight, you would look like a woman who values herself, rather than a musk-rat cowering in a storm.'

Katherine smiled, but there was no answering smile on Victoria's face. Self-consciously, she straightened her spine, and pulled back her shoulders. Her head came up and her eyes met Victoria's.

'Much better. If you always learn so quickly, you will do very well. Now, then. It seems everyone else has had lunch with you, or afternoon cocktails, or – and we find this most odd – a picnic. What do you think of us?'

'I think you all want something from me,' Katherine replied. 'Different things.'

'And what else?'

'You don't act much like a family.'

Victoria poured more tea. 'Have some cake, my dear; you look quite thin. In what way do we not act like a family?'

'You don't like each other very much.'

Victoria laughed shortly. 'That describes many families, Katherine. But some of us do like each other. Very much.' Looking over her cup, she followed the silver gleam of an aeroplane crossing the city. 'And of course you may be exaggerating. Perhaps you think we dislike each other because you dislike us.'

'No –!' Why do they make every conversation a contest, she wondered? and switched to a neutral subject. 'I saw the Peruvian exhibit at the Museum of Art; it was wonderful.'

At last Victoria smiled. 'Yes, isn't it? I couldn't be at the opening, but I heard about your appearance with Derek.'

There are no neutral subjects with this family. 'Derek told you?'

'Derek tells me nothing about himself. My friends told me about his companion. I could hardly fail to identify you.'

'Did they wonder why he was with me?'

Victoria smiled again. 'There was some curiosity – yes, Polk?'

'Mr Derek Hayward, ma'am,' said the butler. 'On the telephone.'

'He heard us talking about him. We should have said something libellous.' Picking up the telephone, she grinned like a girl, surprising Katherine into laughter. 'Yes,' Victoria said into the receiver, gesturing to Katherine to eat some cake.

Katherine ate a small piece, then another, discovering how hungry she was. Soon Jennifer and Todd would be eating dinner with Annie. Then they would do their homework while Annie did hers across the hall, with her door open. Everything was all right; there was no need to rush home. Except that she was famished. Victoria could have asked her to dinner instead of late afternoon tea. Unless she didn't want Katherine Fraser at her table again until she had a chance to look her over and set some ground rules. *Sit up straight. Don't jump at people. Or away from them.*

'I didn't think so,' Victoria was saying. 'But you may be right.'

Her voice changed when she spoke to Derek: it was cautious, even deferential. It should be the other way around, Katherine thought. But Derek was the head of the family, Claude had said. By default.

'Yes, she has,' Victoria said. 'But perhaps she would rather tell you herself. She's here now . . . certainly you may.' She held the telephone across the table.

Katherine barely greeted him before he said, 'You've heard from Craig?'

'He's sent me some money.'

'And what did he say?'

'Nothing.'

'In the letter.'

'There was no letter. There was nothing. Just the money.'

'No letter. A money order?'

'No. Five one hundred dollar bills.'

'Christ.' Derek was silent. 'Where was it mailed?'

'A small town in Saskatchewan. I've never heard of it.'

'I suppose you've talked to the police there.'

'I talked to the Vancouver police. They don't think they can trace cash, but they're sending Craig's picture to the Saskatchewan police to see if anyone saw him.'

'How did he know where you are?'

'I don't know. I wish I did.'

Again he was silent. 'Not much. But it's a beginning.' As if rousing himself, he added. 'I was going to call you tonight. I'm spending tomorrow afternoon at some vineyards in Napa. Would you enjoy a private tour?'

'Vineyards?'

'I'm a partner in a few small ones. The harvest is over, but you can still see how the wine is made. Or is that something you've already done?'

'No we haven't. I'd like very much to go. Could we bring Jennifer and Todd? They've never seen a field of grape vines.'

There was a pause. 'If you really think they'd enjoy it. I'd thought of dinner afterwards, and it would be a late evening for them.'

'Oh.' Stupid, she thought. He's not the kind for family outings. 'I'll have to let you know. Is that all right?'

'I'll call tonight,' he said carelessly. 'About eleven. Unless that's too late.'

'No, that's fine.' After she said goodbye, she looked up to meet Victoria's quizzical gaze.

'I gather Derek was not enthusiastic about entertaining your children.'

'I should have refused. Weekends are the only time the three of us have together.'

'But Derek is very attractive.'

'Oh, no.' Katherine felt herself tense. 'I mean, of course he's attractive, but – I'm married; I'm not looking . . . I'm only looking for friends.'

'*Craig let you down.*' Victoria's voice was fierce in the softly fading light. 'He let all of us down. I remember' – the words became a reverie – 'a long time ago, I used to count my family to make sure all was well. Especially when a storm came up at night, I would go through the names, and where each one was. Of course I seldom knew where they all were, but when I did, and when I knew they were all right, or at least safely inside somewhere, I was content.'

Surprised, Katherine said, 'That's what I always did when Craig was travelling or the children were spending the night with friends.'

'Indeed. So Craig found another woman to worry about his safety in storms. Perhaps that made it easier for him to forget

155

us. He knew how I counted my family to know if all was well. But he let us think he was dead, he let us mourn, *and he did not care.*'

As if Craig sat in the wicker chair across the room, Katherine saw him, very still, staring into space, an open newspaper on his lap. She had seen him that way so often, especially in the evenings when she finished the dinner dishes and came into the living-room to find him staring out the window at something she could not see. Now she knew he had been staring at the family he left behind. 'He did care,' she said to Victoria. 'He wasn't very happy.'

'Happy enough to stay where he was,' Victoria scorned. 'Happy enough to avoid the telephone, the telegraph, the mail . . . a plane to San Francisco.'

'But not happy enough to talk to me.' The words came slowly, but Katherine felt the pressure in them, tumbling out after years of being denied. 'He never talked about his feelings. There were such silences . . . such *spaces* between us. Once I told him he looked as if he were haunted and after that he closed up more than ever. Now I know why, but all those years I didn't; I only knew that I loved him and he wouldn't talk to me, he turned away, keeping all his secrets –'

Tears filled her eyes. 'I've never admitted that to anyone, not even myself . . . that there were those cold spaces between us and I couldn't reach him – no, I'm not sure that's true. Maybe . . . maybe I didn't try hard enough.' She frowned beneath Victoria's intent gaze. 'Maybe I didn't. I don't know why. I kept waiting for him to change, to come to me and let me share whatever was bothering him . . . Maybe I should have pushed him more, to talk to me – of course I should have; it seems so obvious, now – but we had good things, too, and maybe I was afraid I'd ruin them . . . So the spaces got wider and Craig held onto his secrets . . . oh, if you knew how I hated his secrets –'

She was crying. Swiftly, Victoria came around the table to stand beside her, touching her hair, then stroking it. Softly she kissed Katherine's cheek. 'My dear, we have so much to talk about. So many things I've wanted to talk about for so long –'

'To Craig?' Katherine's tears dried and a soft contentment filled her, feeling Victoria's hand on her hair and Victoria's cheek pressed to hers. 'You've missed talking to Craig –?'

'Oh, no,' Victoria said quietly. 'For fifteen years I've missed talking to Jennifer.'

Ross turned off the projector and switched on the overhead lights. The men seated around the square table blinked in the sudden brightness and fumbled for pencils and pens as he unrolled a large drawing and held it down with a water pitcher and three glasses. When he began talking, his voice was relaxed and conversational. An outsider would not have guessed he was at the last stage of four years of planning, designing and negotiating to get the biggest project of his career underway.

'I'm sorry to go over this again,' he said. 'Some of you have been through it a number of times –'

'Go right ahead,' interrupted one of the developers of BayBridge Plaza seated in a row along the wall. 'When you're spending three hundred million bucks, you can't talk about it too much.'

Ross smiled wryly as the rest of them laughed. That was what had taken two of the last four years; everyone thought it couldn't be talked about too much. Especially the people sitting around the table – representatives from the Mayor's office, the Planning Commission, Zoning Board, Citizens for Environmental Planning, the Community Neighbourhood Association, the Department of Buildings, and half a dozen other groups and agencies – who looked up at him now with satisfied faces, prepared to give final blessing to a project that would transform part of the landscape called South of Market. Picking up a pointer, Ross wondered which of them would bring up the last-minute objections he'd come to expect. He'd been through it before.

'I showed those slides of Quincy Market in Boston, Harborplace in Baltimore, Society Hill in Philadelphia, and New York's South Street Seaport Development, even though I've shown them before, because they're our predecessors. Everytime I think we're drowning in regulations or confrontation, it's comforting to be reminded that others have gone through this, and survived.'

Another ripple of laughter ran around the table. 'I'll go over it very quickly . . .'

He began to talk, leaving out his own feelings: his excitement, four years earlier, when the developers had chosen him over all the architects they had interviewed to design the huge project; his frustration at the delays ('The pettiness of people goes up,' Tobias had reminded him, 'with the amount of money. They can't really imagine something that costs a million dollars, but watch them argue over a four dollar versus a three dollar light switch!'); the nights when he woke in a sweat over the leap he was taking by enlarging his staff from fifteen to eighty-five, to handle the massive volume of work; the days and nights when he lost himself in the pure joy of creating the kind of urban development he had dreamed of since becoming an architect.

But none of that appeared in his factual description as he used his pointer to outline the forty acres where thirty-five buildings would be demolished, twenty-five restored, and twelve newly constructed, in addition to a mall of open shops, theatres and eating places.

'With no building higher than eight storeys,' he said, 'and open spaces connecting residential, office and retail clusters, BayBridge will have the atmosphere of a small town.' He paused, remembering who had first called it that: Katherine, the day they had lunch together. 'A link in the chain of small towns that makes up a city,' he went on, still using her words. 'While still being only a block from the commercial strip of Market Street, two blocks from the Civic Centre, and within walking distance of bus lines and two BART stations. A setting, in other words, for people –'

'Yeh, but the people who're there,' interrupted Ted Taylor, pushing up the glasses that kept slipping down his nose. He was the elected representative of the South of Market Neighbourhood Association and for two years had been having the best time of his life, with the power to hold up a multi-million dollar project just by raising an objection – sometimes just by raising a finger. He was sorry it was almost over; how often could ordinary guys like him force government officials and bankers and international businessmen to sit up and take notice? 'What about the people? Lots of them still living there and running businesses – you're gonna kick 'em out to start construction in the spring?'

'We discussed this last month,' Ross said patiently. 'Twenty-eight commercial tenants and ninety-four residents are still in the area; all their leases had expired by last month but we gave them an extension of six months, to next April, and we're helping them relocate. When we set that up, you agreed. Do you have a problem with it now?'

'No,' said Taylor dolefully.

One down, Ross thought. Now if the rest of them would say they have no problems . . .

'A few figures,' he said, and pulled down a chart like a movie screen against the wall. 'When complete, BayBridge will provide six hundred housing units with an estimated population of fifteen hundred people; it will provide twenty-five hundred jobs in one hundred and forty retail establishments plus another two thousand in office and service jobs. The construction itself will provide one thousand jobs. Revenue from real estate taxes and sales taxes will increase as shown on this chart –'

He pulled down a second one. The City Director of Planning nodded, to show he knew all that already. 'Very satisfactory; one of the reasons we like it so much.'

Two down, Ross thought, and told himself this was not the time to show impatience.

BayBridge had really started when the developers had begun to buy up the land. They had selected Ross Hayward Associates to draw up plans for the forty acres, then hired a consulting firm to evaluate these plans. When the consulting firm gave its approval, the developers bought the rest of the land, parcel by parcel, over a year and a half; arranged financing for the three hundred million dollar project, started the rounds of government agencies for approval of every stage of the Plaza, and began to line up major tenants for the shopping mall and office buildings.

Two years later, they signed a contract with Ross for detailed architectural plans of the whole complex. That was when Ross moved to another office building with space for the sixfold increase in his staff of architects, engineers, draughtsmen, and computer operators.

The last step had been choosing a contractor. One of the developers, Brock Galvez – burly, aggressive, a man who had made vast wealth 'by work and prayer,' he said, 'and the good fortune of buying a Mexican farm that turned out to be floating on a sea of oil' – fought hard to give the job to the Hayward Corporation, but the other developers balked. 'It's Ross's family corporation; no way we're going to give the media a chance to smear us for making sweetheart deals.'

Ross had stayed out of it. None of them had asked him if he wanted to work with his brother and when they chose another firm, and he seemed satisfied, they thought he was accepting the inevitable. It did not occur to them that he had no wish to work with Derek. And, though BayBridge was the major project of the year in San Francisco, Derek had never asked Ross for help in getting the job. It was all above-board.

But the haggling over approvals had dragged on, and at times he'd thought the project would never be built. 'These are the final changes you asked us to make,' Ross said, turning from the charts on the wall. Horsetrading, he added to himself, without bitterness. Everyone has fears; everyone wants a feeling of control. Local residents fear higher rents and taxes when we upgrade the area, so we add a community swimming pool in the lower level of the mall. The Landmarks Preservation Council is worried about proper restoration so we submit a description of all exterior materials and paint colours. Small businesses fret over losing customers to the mall, so the developers offer them space in the mall at reduced rents for the first five years. On and on, until, finally, everybody's had a hand in the trading.

'You asked for additional off-street parking,' he said. Actually, they'd insisted on it as soon as Ross sought permission to close off one block of Eighth street that would otherwise cut through BayBridge's largest park. Why is it, he wondered, that city streets are about as sacred as cathedrals and matrimony? It took seven months of negotiations until they got permission to close off the street, but in exchange they had to enlarge the parking deck. 'This made room for fifty-five more cars,' Ross said, pointing to the extended deck. 'But it meant eliminating the snack bar at this end of the recreation area —'

'You took food out to make room for cars?' demanded an incredulous voice.

Noncommittally, Ross nodded. 'I understand some vendors have applied for licenses for food carts to be placed around the mall and in the parks.' They were making notes now, he saw.

161

'In response to other requests, we've reduced air conditioning and heating energy requirements by adding solar energy reflecting glass on all south-facing windows. And in line with revised building codes relating to earthquakes, we've strengthened building number twenty-eight. As for other buildings –'

He talked on, keeping his feelings to himself, though he knew, with every step he took without arousing criticism, he was getting closer. Almost there, he told himself, elation growing beneath his relaxed voice. Almost there.

'What happened to the day care centre?' asked a young man, looking up from furious note-taking. 'In the recreation area – near the gymnasium – wasn't that where we planned it?'

'Shit shit shit,' moaned a dark man across the table. 'We've been *over* this. The government grant was cut! When we find the money, we'll put the day care centre back.'

'Who's trying to get another grant?' demanded the young man.

'I am,' came a voice from the sidelines where the investors were sitting. 'Someone in my office. We're working on it. You want to see what we're doing, come anytime.'

'I'll do that,' said the young man and made another note on his lined pad.

'Well, I like the whole thing.' The chief assistant to the mayor stood and hitched up his pants. 'Good concept, good feeling for people. Natural neighbourhoods. Our office has approved it; I don't know why the hell we keep going around the mulberry bush; we all know what we're doing. Anybody got a comment on that?'

No one spoke. He asked about schedules and dates; the developers joined the discussion; Brock Galvez said, 'We'll be out there within ninety days of sign-off of all the approvals.' Ross let his elation soar. Done, he thought. Galvez was beaming. 'No more than ninety days; we've waited long enough. We'll outdo Baltimore and Philadelphia and New York . . .

we'll put this place on the map. Best goddam set of plans I've ever seen.'

They stood about, talking, as if reluctant to go their different ways. Ross stood with them, his tall figure relaxed as he joined their casual conversation, but inwardly, he was bursting with exultation. For the first time the kind of vast project he dreamed of would be built, remaking the landscape. And no one had put it better than the mayor's assistant who was just now shaking his hand and leaving the room. *Natural neighbourhoods. A feeling for people.* For the first time, Ross thought. Not a dream on paper. A reality.

He debated going back to work for an hour or two, but he needed to talk. Too much excitement, he thought, steaming inside me; it isn't enough to have something wonderful happen – we have to share it to make it real.

He'd stop off at Mettler's, he decided; buy Melanie a present; take her to dinner. They'd celebrate and make promises and pretend they were at the beginning again, when they'd been able to talk and laugh and love.

On Post Street he parked in a No Parking zone and dashed into Mettler's rareified, vaulted room. It occurred to him that he was only a few blocks from Heath's; he ought to go over and see Katherine. He hadn't called her for a long time; the weeks had slipped by while he pushed BayBridge through its obstacle course. He knew she was all right because everyone else had seen her and reported to Victoria who called Ross twice a week to give him all the news; Derek, of course, reported to no one, but evidently he'd taken Katherine to the Peruvian show. Ross felt a twist of irritation; why would she spend an evening with Derek?

It's her business, he told himself. Browsing along dignified glass and mahogany cases, Ross had other things on his mind. He wanted to get home to Melanie. The enormous success of his afternoon welled up, like a promise that everything would be all right. He saw a salesman watching him, gauging the proper time to approach. A pin, he thought; she likes them. And then dinner. Ernie's. The Blue Fox. L'Etoile. Whatever she wants. We'll talk about us, work out our differences, stop circling each other like suspicious strangers.

'It's Mr Hayward, isn't it?' asked the salesman. 'I helped you last time you were here. And what may I show you this afternoon?'

'The sapphire,' said Ross. 'Do you have it in silver? Or only in the gold?'

'We have a similar one in silver, and these as well –' The salesman drew out two trays but Ross was impatient.

'This one. I'm in a hurry, so if you'll write it up –'

'One moment, sir.' The salesman sped to a spiral staircase leading to the balcony offices. 'I need one of the blue boxes,' he whispered to Herman Mettler's secretary. 'For Mr Hayward.'

She tilted her head to the left. 'In Herman's office.'

Hurrying, he went to a cabinet in Mettler's office, found a box, and turned to go. 'Miss McAlister!' he said, seeing Leslie perched on the desk. 'Have you been here long?'

'Three minutes,' said Leslie. 'Marc is arguing with your boss about the cost of gold, or something equally mercenary. Which Mr Hayward were you whispering about?'

'Ross Hayward.'

'Point him out to me, would you?'

'You can watch me; I'll be writing up his sale.'

From the balcony, Leslie gazed thoughtfully at the salesman's customer, remembering the light in Katherine's eyes when she described their lunch at The Compass Rose. No wonder, Leslie thought, seeing Ross's smile. Married, though. They always are. She watched him stride to the door. He's had good news or bad news and he's off to tell someone. With a peace offering in his hand.

'And what is so absorbing?' Marc Landau said at her shoulder. 'Have you, even from this height, spotted a trifle you cannot do without?' He saw her looking at Ross's back in the doorway. 'Or a man.'

'A friend of a friend,' Leslie said easily. 'Are you finished?'

'Yes. Where would you like to go for a drink?'

'Some place quiet. It's been a terrible day. Too many puzzles all at once.'

Landau was silent as they drove to the top of Nob Hill. Finally, a little cautiously, he said, 'Puzzles.'

'Don't worry, Marc, I'm not going to burden you with my problems. Even if you were interested, they're confidential.'

At that he looked at her. 'Is Heath's in trouble?'

'*I* might be in trouble.'

'But if it's confidential it involves Heath's.' He parked in the curved driveway of the Mark Hopkins Hotel. 'You can tell me all about it over a drink.'

'You know, Marc,' she said, putting her arm through his. 'One of your most endearing qualities is your honesty: confidential news is more interesting than Leslie's problems. Let's talk about something else. Would you do another favour for me? Ask Herman to carry a few of Katherine's pieces next spring. She's taking two classes, but she needs encouragement. Just a few pieces, nothing major. Would you talk to him?'

They sat beside a window and Landau tapped the table with a silver matchbook. 'Is there no end to the favours this young woman requires? Where is her pioneering spirit? Does being a woman entitle her to a smooth path to fame and fortune?'

Leslie gave him a long look. 'You're not serious.'

'No.' He let out his breath and Leslie knew he had meant every word, but was not ready to quarrel with her.

'Katherine doesn't know I'm asking you. And I don't want her to know. I mean that, Marc. When Herman offers her space

165

in his marble palace, he's not to tell her I had anything to do with it.'

'You're assuming – All right. I'll talk to him, and swear him to secrecy. Is this your price for telling me about Heath's?'

'Oh, fuck it, Marc, what a rotten thing to say.'

'It must be.' He looked amused. 'To get such a reaction. I'll help your little friend in any case. So you can tell me just because I ask.'

Below them, the lights of San Francisco were coming on in the gathering dusk. Leslie watched them, drinking her wine and debating briefly with herself. 'Nope. I'd like to but I can't.' Because I can't trust you, she added silently. How pleasant if I could. How pleasant if you even tried to convince me I could. 'Maybe some other time. Tell me about Herman. Did you sign a new contract with him?'

He gave in gracefully – another reason Leslie liked him – and talked about the spring line of jewellery he and Mettler had agreed upon that afternoon. Listening, she admired his neat balance of art and business, and the rest of the evening was as pleasant as Marc could make it when he tried. Then, because she was so tired and wanted to go home and worry quietly about meetings she'd heard the other vice presidents had been having, excluding her, she ended the evening after dinner and once again he gave in gracefully.

Nice, she thought, when she was alone in the blue and white living-room of her house overlooking the Marina. Having someone who makes no demands. Although – she turned off the lights, put on a record of dreamy piano music, and sat in a window seat to watch the ghostly shapes of sailboats swaying in the harbour – it would be nice to have someone who does more than make requests and give in gracefully. It would be nice to have someone who gives a damn.

*

The first time Katherine had dinner with Derek, on the Saturday they spent at his vineyards, she discovered he had ordered their meal when he made the reservation. 'So you don't need a menu,' he said. 'In fact, you can't have one. It's all taken care of.'

She protested. 'I'd like to pay for my own dinner.'

He smiled slightly. 'But when I invite you to dinner I expect to pay. Do you see a way out of this dilemma?'

It had been a wonderful day, hot and dry, with a buzzing stillness in the vineyards that stretched between low hills beneath a canopy of cloudless sky. Leslie had taken Jennifer and Todd to the Exploratorium, and the whole day had been a special time pulled out of her everyday life, free of worry. She didn't want to ruin it by arguing over who would pay for dinner. So she met his smile with her own and she said lightly, 'But if I don't see the menu, how will I know what I'm missing?'

'You can take it for granted that you aren't missing a thing.'

Since then, he had called twice a week, inviting her to dinner or a nightclub. Four times she had said yes, each time telling herself it was the last: she should spend her evenings with Jennifer and Todd, she ought to be working on her jewellery designs, she shouldn't be having a good time while Craig was missing. But she went, because Derek could make her light-hearted even after a day of Gil Lister's insults and dinner with her increasingly sulky children. She went, even if she didn't understand why he sought her out, because she was fascinated by his power and wealth, his charm and attentiveness, and the way he seemed to centre them all on her, making her feel young and very special. And she went because she missed being with a man, and he was the only one who was calling.

The day before the excursion to the Napa vineyards, Leslie told Katherine she had seen Ross at Mettler's, buying one of

Landau's sapphire and silver lapel pins. 'Marvellous looking man; too stern, but when he smiles it's a face to remember.' She paused. 'Why don't you call him?'

'Because he's busy with his own life,' Katherine answered. 'And what would I say? "I'm fine, though you haven't asked in a long time; the children are fine, though you haven't asked; I've heard from Craig, though you haven't asked . . ." He probably knows how we are, from his family, and if he wanted to ask me he would. So there's no reason to call.'

'I find reasons when I want to call someone,' Leslie said.

'I've never called a man. And anyway, I'm married.'

'What does that have to do with it?'

'Probably nothing.' They laughed. 'But I won't call, anyway.'

So there was only Derek, introducing her to the nightlife of San Francisco. 'A favourite of mine,' he said one night when they went to the dimly lit Moroccan restaurant called Marrakech. They sat on a low sofa before a carved brass table and used chunks of bread to eat spiced shredded chicken, lamb with honey and almonds, and couscous with vegetables. After a tea girl washed their hands with rosewater, they sat over fruit and tea, talking in the languorous tones of those who have eaten too much and know they cannot stir for at least an hour.

Derek gave Katherine leisurely descriptions of the people in the restaurant whom he knew. One depended on a rich aunt to make up losses on the commodities exchange; one kept a mistress in Cancun; another wrote books for which her husband was famous as author and television personality. 'And over there,' Derek said, gesturing at the noisy group in the opposite corner, 'are the seven dwarfs. One big happy banking family, mutually protective. They pay off irate husbands who catch cousin Dopey in bed with their wives; they kick cousin Sleepy under the table when he insults a hostess by snoring through the entree; they use cousin Snoopy to spy on rival bankers; cousin Doc tries to cure Droopy who, as you may imagine from his name, has sexual problems –'

'There is no Droopy,' Katherine laughed.

'True. Grumpy is the one with those problems, but Droopy is more descriptive. Now there's another group, at the table just beyond the dwarfs –' And he continued around the room, with caustic, intimate dissections that embarrassed Katherine but also intrigued her, because these were some of the city's top business and professional people, whose pictures she saw in newspaper society pages. 'It's my job to meet them,' he said when she asked how he knew so many. 'And stroke them. They control everything we need – construction permits, zoning, structural requirements, highway funds, bank loans – the lifeblood of our company.' He scanned the tables. 'A dull lot, but we can't survive without them. Some of my favourite characters aren't here, but we'll find them at other places, on other nights –' He broke off, watching a couple cross the far end of the room to sit at a small table. 'Idiotic,' he murmured. 'Here, of all places –'

Katherine followed his look. 'Isn't that Melanie?' she asked.

'None other.' His voice was dry.

'But who is she with?'

'A young – a very young – tennis pro from the Mill Valley Country Club. A tadpole on Melanie's well-baited hook. I think it's time for us to leave. Unless you want more tea –?'

'No. There's no room for another drop. And we've been here for hours.'

'The only way to eat here is to make it an evening.' His voice was preoccupied. 'Ready?'

She stood and slipped into her jacket as he held it. 'Isn't the wrong couple sneaking out before being seen?'

He turned his dark eyes on her with the intent look he always had when she impressed him. Smiling, he took her arm. 'Possibly. I'll explain it sometime.' He led the way between couches and ottomans to the exit. 'On Friday,' he said casually as they waited for the doorman to bring his car, 'a friend of mine is having a party. Do you have something formal to wear?'

'No.' It came out quickly, the dreamy languor of the evening gone in an instant. She could not afford new clothes. 'Craig and I never went out very much. I didn't enjoy it.'

'You love it,' he said flatly. In the car, he drove slowly for once, past Japantown and then into Golden Gate Park – the long way back. 'So Craig must have been the homebody.'

'He worked hard,' Katherine said defensively. 'And he liked being home. Whenever he came back from a trip, he'd close the door behind him and say how wonderful it was to be there, safe and protected . . .' Her voice trailed away. They would kiss, while the children waited their turn, and Craig would tell them about his trip, and pull out little presents, tantalising, one at a time, so that it was like a long, drawn-out Christmas.

'Safe and protected,' Derek repeated. 'Like a womb.' He turned off and stopped at the Chain of Lakes, brooding at the water in the misty light of lamps and a fragile moon. 'Or Victoria's open arms. Or Ann's. After all these years, he was still looking for them.'

'Fifteen years. You don't know anything about him.'

'I know everything about him. Do you really think people change? However, I'm more interested in you. Did you –'

'Why? Why are you interested in me? Everywhere we go we meet beautiful women whom you know – some of them you've had affairs with –'

'Now how would you know that?'

'It's in your voice when you talk about them. You shape your words as if they're soft clay – as if you still feel her, whoever she is, under your hands.'

'Good God.' He shook his head. 'Just when you seem most timid, you come out with something remarkable. How long are you going to hide under your cover? Cautious, careful, wearing dowdy clothes –'

'They're not dowdy!'

'By my standards they are. And you know what I mean; you do a full study of every woman in sight when we go out. Look, I have accounts at every store in town; take a day and fit yourself out properly.'

'On your charge accounts? You can't be serious. You're not keeping me, Derek; no one is. I take care of myself. If you don't like the way I dress, you can go out with someone else.'

'I do.'

'Oh.' Of course. All those other nights in the week.

'But I also expect to go out with you.'

'Why?'

'Partly because I like women who are more complicated than they seem. The rest you'll have to figure out yourself.'

After a moment, Katherine said, 'Derek, I'd like to go home.'

He started the car and drove out of the park, and within a few minutes pulled up before her building. Putting his hand on the back of her head, he kissed her lightly. 'I'd like to help you escape from that prison Craig built. I don't think he kept the key.' Reaching across her, he opened her door. 'Think about some new clothes. You'll be more comfortable on Friday night.'

'I'm not . . . free Friday night.'

'Listen to me.' Holding the door handle, he had his arm across her lap, pinning her in place. 'I expect you to tell me the truth. If you don't want to be with me on Friday, say so. If you don't want to be with me at all, say so. But I will not tolerate your behaving like an adolescent who can't handle a simple relationship.'

171

'This relationship,' she retorted, 'is no more simple than you are. It's easy for you to forget Craig –'

'Never easy,' he murmured.

'– but I can't, and because of that I'm confused about a lot of things and none of them are simple. And I'd like you to remove your arm.'

After a moment he sat back. 'Free to go.'

She pushed open the door and stepped out. 'Marrakech was wonderful. Thank you.'

'And Friday night?'

She looked at his narrow face, the hollows in his cheeks accentuated by the slanting street light, his mouth curved in a challenging smile. 'How formal is it?'

'Black tie for the men; a little more flexible for the women.'

Flexible. She had no money for a flexible formal dress. But as she was about to refuse, she stopped. Why shouldn't she go out with Derek? Everything about him was intriguing – even the cruel wit of his descriptions in the restaurant. And even if she was confused about Craig, missing him, worrying about him, bewildered by the money she was sure he'd sent – he had left her, after all, to fend for herself. Why shouldn't she allow herself the pleasure, and vanity, she got from Derek's attention?

But she needed a dress. I could ask Leslie, Katherine thought. Maybe I can find something on sale. And fix it up. I'll be home on Thanksgiving; I could do it then. Why not? I like being with Derek. And I don't have to live like a prisoner while I'm waiting for Craig.

It was only after she had agreed to Friday night, and was unlocking the door of her apartment, that she realised she had used Derek's description: living in a prison.

Thanksgiving. Rescued, Katherine thought, by Leslie and her brother. Derek had neatly passed over it when he invited her to a Friday night party; Victoria and Tobias had left the week

172

before on a museum expedition to Peru. Leslie had suggested a restaurant, which had horrified Jennifer and Todd. Thanksgiving meant home.

'Then I'll cook,' Leslie said. 'I should, now and then, or I'll forget how. And Bruce makes a wicked pumpkin pie. Wait till you taste it.'

Bruce McAlister, ten years younger than his sister, had flaming hair as crinkly as steel wool, matching eyebrows that shot up and down in astonished arcs, and non-stop speech. If not for Bruce, Katherine thought, and the way he distracted Jennifer and Todd from memories of Canadian thanksgivings, the evening could have been a disaster.

'It's bourbon that does it, I don't even measure, I just pour,' he said when they all gasped at their first taste of his pumpkin pie. All through dinner, as they feasted on Leslie's stuffed turkey and Katherine's cranberry sauce and vegetables he had entertained them with stories of his friends, who lived in an area called the Panhandle. 'A few years ago, when we lived on unemployment and food stamps and love, it was a blast – good guitars, good grass, good women . . .'

'Bruce,' Leslie warned.

'Shit, they know all this.' His eyebrows shot up as he grinned at Jennifer and Todd. 'Anyway things are different, it's depressing the way everybody's so straight all of a sudden, getting married, having kids, buying dishwashers for Christ's sake, working steady . . . Even me,' he added sadly.

Todd was transfixed by Bruce's jumping red eyebrows and gesticulating hands. 'You work too?' he asked.

'I admit it with deep embarrassment, I do indeed work from eight thirty to five *five days a week* and I am grossly underpaid by that posh establishment called Heath's –'

'That's where Mom works!' Todd cried.

'And my sister as well, in fact she got me the job – who else would hire me with my background? – but *she* spends her days on the executive top floor while your mother and I slave away in the basement.'

'I don't remember seeing you,' Katherine said.

'You wouldn't, I never stir from the computer room; do you know that I can make a computer do anything except bake a pumpkin pie?'

And that was when he cut into his dessert and they all got their first taste of what Katherine would have sworn was a bottle of bourbon lightly flavoured with pumpkin. 'Bruce,' Leslie laughed. 'Where's the other one?'

'Alas my sis knows me too well; I do happen to have another one.' Reaching under the table, he brought forth a box. 'Unfortunately you understand, this one has only vanilla, no bourbon, no brandy, just the stuff the poor pilgrims had, and no wonder most of them never survived the winter.'

They laughed and praised the second pie. We laughed most of the evening, Katherine thought later. Laughed and sang to Bruce's guitar playing and went home early, with smiles and left-over turkey, and even when we were alone again we didn't reminisce about Canadian Thanksgivings or our house in Vancouver. Thank God for Bruce McAlister; he got us through the day.

On Friday, Katherine asked Gil Lister if she could leave an hour early. He adjusted the ski jacket on a mannequin and zipped it closed before saying over his shoulder, 'Kiddies sick?'

'No. I have something to do.'

'Something personal?'

'Yes. But, Gil, all the invoices are finished and last week's scenery will be ready to be shipped back by three o'clock –'

'Katherine, we've been receiving a number of personal tele-phone calls at work, haven't we? And we've been having lunches that lasted over an hour –'

'Only twice! And it's been more than a month since –'

'And a number of times in creating a window, you were not where I expected you to be. There is a *laxness*, Katherine, in your behaviour. If this indicates dissatisfaction, if you would prefer to work elsewhere, we should part; I cannot work in an atmosphere of frowns and groans and hostility.'

'I do not groan,' Katherine said tightly. 'And I frown less than you do. I try to be friendly, I don't think I'm hostile, but I would be more satisfied if you let me help design windows instead of treating me like an imbecile or a coat rack.'

Lister's hands paused, then moved on, buckling a ski boot. He stood and bent the mannequin's knee. 'Ski poles.'

Katherine took a breath, then let it out without speaking, and handed him the poles. They finished the scene of a slalom race in silence. 'Ah,' Lister breathed, scanning the slope they had covered with styrofoam flakes marked by ski tracks behind the mannequins who were rounding flag-topped slalom posts. Without warning, he whipped about. 'What would *you* do with it?'

'Bring it to life,' she said bluntly. 'It's dead.' *I'll get another job: I don't have to take his insults.* 'Use only two racers, with a third at the top, bending forward to start, and put spectators along the side, especially children and teenagers. Three-year-olds are skiing now, and Heath's has clothes for them. Put a digital time clock in that corner, and a finish line under it. A mountain background; I've seen one in the storeroom. And I'd have someone holding a trophy for the winner.'

'Would you indeed.'

His voice caught her up. What was the matter with her? How long might it take to get another job? 'I'm sorry, Gil. The window is fine; it's simple and colourful. Do you want to put prices with them?'

'No.' He was tapping his foot and studying the four racers. 'I've never skied, you know; it looks quite exciting. Get downstairs and pack up last week's scenery. Don't seal the boxes; I want to check them. You may leave half an hour early if it is a matter of life and death.'

'Thank you.' She was trembling with fury. He'd let her apology lie there, unaccepted, unacknowledged. But it was my fault, she thought as she packed a box with plastic autumn leaves. I knew he'd be angry when I criticised him. Victoria was right; I jump at people. But then why does Derek say I'm timid?

I wish I knew what I really am.

Exactly half an hour early, she left work and rushed home. Leslie had found a dress for her and was coming at eight, just before Derek arrived, to pass judgement. Dinner with Jennifer and Todd was hurried; they were going back to school for a rehearsal of the Christmas choral concert and for once did not deluge her with complaints about school or fog or how often she was away from home. 'You'll wait for Annie to pick you up after rehearsal,' Katherine said as they were leaving.

'We really are old enough to walk home alone,' said Jennifer. 'But if it makes you happy, we'll wait.'

'It makes me happy,' Katherine smiled. 'Have a good time.'

'You too,' Jennifer said. 'Don't be home too late, though.'

Wondering what that meant, Katherine told Leslie about it when she arrived. But Leslie was not listening. Head cocked critically, she was scrutinising Katherine in her new dress. 'Well, well,' she said at last, softly. 'Very well indeed.'

The dress, found in the stockroom from last winter's Empire Room collection, reduced to one-eighth its original price, was of a timeless style and simplicity: a black cashmere sheath, as fine as silk, moulding Katherine's slender figure, flared at the hem, long-sleeved, with a startlingly deep V-neck edged in tiny scallops. Two black silk cords wound twice around her waist, ending in long fringes reaching almost to the hem.

176

But as elegant as the dress was, Leslie knew the real attraction was Katherine herself: eyes bright, face flushed as she studied her reflection, unconsciously standing straighter because the dress demanded it. Leslie gazed at the delicate lines of her friend's face and figure, disguised until now by worry or sadness, or the slouch of her shoulders, or clothes that had become too big for her when she lost weight after Craig disappeared. 'Wonderful,' she murmured. 'At least as a start. How about jewellery? You must have made a necklace in all those classes you've taken.'

Katherine shook her head. 'I'm not ready to go public.'

'Well, then, the only thing left is makeup and your hair.'

'No!' Katherine stepped back. 'Not now, Leslie. This is enough.' Enough change, she thought, astonished and a little disconcerted at the difference one dress could make. Putting up her hand, she blocked the reflection of her face and looked only at her graceful figure, almost as regal as Victoria's. Lowering her hand, she met her own eyes, pleased and shining, in the mirror. She looked like a young girl, about to step into the outside world, instead of a thirty-five year old working woman with two children. And a husband, she added swiftly. And a husband.

Leslie was watching her. 'Enough change for one day,' Katherine repeated. 'It's only a party, after all; it's not so important.'

Leslie opened her mouth to argue, then nodded casually. 'Fine by me. But I did bring my own contribution –' She opened a white box she had brought with her. 'Just for tonight.'

'Oh Leslie, I can't –!' Katherine began as Leslie took out her silver fox jacket and a black beaded evening bag.

'Yes you can, lady; don't argue. If I want to feel like a fairy godmother, the least you can do is let me feel like one. Someday you'll even let me finish the rest of you.'

Katherine hugged her. 'You make me sound like a piece of furniture – but thank you.' Through the window, she saw Derek's car pull up. 'Thank you, Leslie, you're wonderful,' she said, grabbing the jacket and evening bag, and was out of the building before Derek reached the door. It was one of her rules: he was not to step inside her apartment. She had seen his grandmother's; she had heard about his. She was ashamed of her own.

Norma Burton was celebrating her fourth divorce with a party for her closest friends. 'How many does she have?' Katherine asked Derek. 'Two or three hundred,' he answered, appraising the crowd as he checked Katherine's jacket in the cloak room. 'If she likes you for more than ten minutes, she counts you in. Generous if not discriminating, and very much a child. Let me look at you.' He took Katherine's hand and contemplated her. 'Do you know that you are a beautiful woman?'

She pulled her hand away. 'No. I've never been beautiful. It would take more than a new dress . . .'

'Much more. Colour in your face, the way you stand and hold your head, your eyes . . . Have you looked in a mirror?'

'Yes –'

'At your eyes?'

'Yes. Aren't we going to join the party?'

He took her hand again and pulled her to him, lifting her chin. 'Your eyes are magnificent: enormous and bright –' He paused. 'And now they look alarmed, as if you've come to a precipice. What might you be afraid of? Come.' He tucked her hand beneath his arm and led her to the ballroom. 'I'll introduce you to Norma's grab bag of friends; they are, after all, the evening's entertainment.'

By the time dinner was over and dancing began, the faces and names had blurred, like drifting confetti. Everyone eyed Katherine with open curiosity, the glances moving from

Derek's hand on her arm to her dress and then to her face. Everyone asked where she came from and, when she answered 'Vancouver', how long she would be staying. Women manoeuvred to see if she wore a wedding ring and, when they saw it, asked where her husband was. 'On a business trip,' she answered – so many times she began to believe it. Many of the guests asked familiarly about Derek's new apartment and one couple tried to talk about a shopping complex in Daly City they wanted him to bid on. 'I'll be in my office on Monday,' he said.

'Is your apartment new?' Katherine asked. 'I didn't realise that, when you told me about it.'

'About a year,' he said. 'I just finished putting it together. You'll see it once we get out of here.'

She shivered. She felt small and light, cut off from familiar things, as if she had become one of the bits of confetti in the room. She danced with Derek and talked to his friends, but none of it seemed real. She did not feel drab and insecure as she had at the Peruvian exhibit, but each time she was thoroughly inspected by one of Derek's friends, she wasn't sure it was really Katherine Fraser inside the cashmere dress.

All evening, she felt Derek's closeness: his body guiding hers as they danced, his eyes watching her as she talked to others, his hand holding her arm when they walked across the room. 'On a business trip,' she said again and again in answer to questions, and she thought of Craig as she lied about him, as she moved smoothly with Derek to the music, as she said 'Yes, of course,' when Derek told her it was time to go.

At the cloak room, a huge man, triple chinned and balding, with dimples and curly grey sideburns, greeted Derek. 'I'm told this is Katherine Fraser,' he said, and held out his hand. 'Herman Mettler. I understand you're a jewellery designer.'

Katherine saw in her mind a store she visited every chance

179

she had, dreaming of her own jewellery in its mahogany and glass cases. 'Mettler's,' she breathed.

'The very one.' His voice rumbled like a brass fiddle beneath the high notes of the party. 'You're new in town? Looking for a store?'

'Yes, but how –?'

'One of my designers mentioned it. We're always looking for new work; it's possible we could find you a small space. Depending, of course, on what you have.'

'Of course.'

'Well, bring me your samples. A good selection; I don't make decisions on a handful and a promise. Make an appointment with my secretary; week after next. Derek, good to see you; hope you're well. Give my regards to Angela; lovely young woman. Mrs Fraser, I'll see you soon, I suppose.' And he was gone.

Dazed, Katherine put on the jacket Derek held. She thought of Craig again. What would he say if Mettler took her jewellery? Would he still call it her little hobby?

'Katherine,' Derek said as they rode the elevator to the lobby.

'What? I'm sorry; I was thinking –'

'Don't put too much faith in Mettler. He's not always reliable.'

'He didn't make any promises,' she said. 'So why would I put any faith in him?'

'You were building castles, little one, and you know it. Just remember what I said.'

'I will. Who is Angela?'

'An ex-wife.'

'Whose?'

'Mine. Herman is a little slow; we've been divorced for six months.'

'He thought you were married? And at the party with me?'

Derek was silent. 'Let me tell you about my apartment,' he said at last. 'One of Hayward Corporation's finest.'

He described it as they drove: part of a complex of buildings, some still under construction, at the base of Telegraph Hill on Lombard Street, behind the restored warehouses and new buildings of Levi Plaza. When his company was given the contract, Derek bought the top floor for himself, working with the architect to make one huge apartment instead of the two in the original plans. 'Of course it's big enough for a tribal rain dance,' he said as he led Katherine on a quick tour of the rooms, stopping in the kitchen to take a bottle of champagne from the refrigerator. 'But it has its nooks. For instance –'

He took her to a room enclosed on three sides with glass jalousies, furnished with tufted red velvet couches and armchairs, oriental rugs on a parquet floor, and brass lamps with fringed shades. It was an 1890s parlour – formal and overstuffed – but Derek had made it a joke by putting it in a starkly modern building. 'Angela said it was decorated in early brothel,' he said. 'But she was only hoping.'

'Why did you get a divorce?' Katherine asked. Her head was against the back of the couch, the light from a fringed lamp flickering through the bubbles in her glass. Derek had had three divorces, according to Claude. I've been married almost eleven years, she thought; and divorce never occurred to me.

'We were mistaken about each other,' Derek answered. 'What else ends a marriage? Angela thought she could reform me and I thought she was the only woman who didn't want anything from me. We were both wrong. She's very much like Norma: generous, impulsive and a child. But you, my sweet Katherine, have become very much a woman.'

He barely seemed to move, but his face was above hers, blocking the lighted lamp. He put her glass on the table and brushed her lips lightly with his. Then, sliding his arm beneath

181

her shoulders, he kissed her with a demanding confidence that struck against her like a wave, pushing her back against the velvet couch.

Everything fell away. Her fears about Craig, her helpless rage at Lister, worries about the children, about money, about jewellery design, even the spark of jealousy she felt when Derek talked about women – all fell away. There was only Derek's body on hers, after months without anyone to hold her and make love to her. Katherine felt she was dissolving. His tongue against hers released all the longings she had held back for so long, her arms reached around him and her hips strained upward.

And then, through the roaring in her ears, she heard Craig's voice. The words were muffled, but Katherine knew they were the same ones he had said the first time they made love, when they held each other, laughing and already making plans, because they had been so lonely and now had someone to love.

She pulled away from Derek and sat up, wanting him so much that tears filled her eyes. But as she stood and walked the length of the room, she was not sure whether she was crying for him or for Craig. She kept her back to Derek until she could stop her tears. Then she turned around.

He was watching her, the bones of his face sharply shadowed in the light from the fringed lamp. 'I gather my cousin joined us,' he said ironically.

His cousin. It had been weeks since she thought of Craig and Derek as cousins. No two men could be more different.

Derek refilled their glasses. 'Sit down and drink this. He can't see us, you know, and even if he could, you are allowed champagne every other Friday night, or rather Saturday morning, at precisely one-fifteen a.m.'

She gave a small laugh and came back to the couch. 'I'm sorry.'

182

'Don't apologise. You do too much of that. Has it occurred to you that he's not worth your fidelity?'

'No. That doesn't help, Derek. It's hard enough knowing how to behave without making up excuses. I don't know what happened to Craig, but he's my husband and I'd rather believe he is worth my fidelity.'

He drained his glass and slowly refilled it. 'Would you like to hear what happened the last time we sailed together, fifteen years ago?'

'Didn't Claude tell me? Last June?'

'The official version. He wasn't on the boat. I was.'

'But you let him tell it.'

'I always let Claude tell official stories. Do you want to hear mine?'

'You mean it's different from his. About Craig.'

'All of us.' He looked at her, waiting.

'Of course I want to hear it.' Katherine spoke slowly, still shaking from the heat of her body and the memory of Craig's voice. Derek seemed untouched: cool and remote. 'I've always wanted the truth,' she said.

'The truth.' He smiled faintly, then settled back on the couch. 'We were sailing home across the bay,' he began. His speech was flat, almost a monotone. 'We'd been at a party in Sausalito, very dull, and when we left, Craig decided to sail home the long way, out past the Golden Gate Bridge and then in again, to the harbour. Since he'd appointed himself captain, there was no arguing: we went the long way. But when I told him I was in a hurry, he made a concession and put up the spinnaker; the wind was up and it gave us good speed.

'But then he changed his mind; he got worried about the currents and told us to put on lifejackets – Ross was in the cabin and Jennifer took one down to him – and then said we'd have to take down the spinnaker. I said I wanted it up and we argued about it. "Too much sail," he said. "A strong wind could rip it to shreds." Ross and Jennifer came up from the cabin in the middle of our mutual insults – got drenched by spray, I remember, because by then the boat was heeling and we were going at a good clip and water was breaking over the cockpit. It was the right way to sail – top speed and a roaring wind, spray flying, and waves slapping the boat – and I put my arm around Jennifer and said we liked living dangerously and no one was worried but the captain.

'Of course he couldn't take it: the boat was his turf; the only place he could feel superior to me. Besides, he was crazy about his sister – guarded her like a mother hen. He gripped the wheel and yelled at me to let go of Jennifer; he looked so wild that Ross stepped in, to distract him, and said *he'd* take down the spinnaker.

'Craig hardly heard him; he was so busy yelling – he told me if I didn't like the way he captained the ship, I could swim to shore, if I had the guts to try it in that water. Only an ass would have gone in willingly, but he made it a challenge to manhood, or some such thing, and I told him to shut up and get us home.

'Craig was twenty-two that summer, and I was twenty-one – a couple of kids who happened to be related but didn't like each other. We never needed an excuse to think up insults and that day was no different, except Jennifer was there. She always tried to calm Craig down, especially when he was attacking me, but she didn't have any luck that day, and she was probably frightened, too – the wind was so loud we had to shout; we were soaking wet; and Craig seemed to have trouble controlling the boat and his own temper. Jennifer started to cry and Craig went into a rage, blaming me for her tears, calling me a string of names he'd never used before – looking at Jennifer to make sure she heard – and then he began raving about the way I was managing a building we were constructing that summer, the Macklin Building. Craig spent a lot of time trying to convince the family he knew more than I did, making me out to be incompetent or crooked, or both. But that day he should have known better. He was having enough trouble keeping the boat under control but he had to try to impress his sister. When he sent Ross forward to take down the spinnaker, I went over to try to calm him down but he'd worked himself up to such a pitch he thought I was telling him what to do, and he let out a roar and jumped me.

'Then everything happened at once. He'd left the wheel to get his hands on my throat and just as Jennifer was pulling on his arm, crying for him to stop, the boat changed direction – crossed the wind instead of going with it – because there was no one to hold it on course. The boom swung across and struck Jennifer on the side of the head. I barely saw it – I was trying to get out of Craig's grip – but I heard the thud and a second later I saw her tumble over the side.

'Craig screamed and dropped me. He lunged for the life preserver and marker pole and threw them into the water, yelling to Jennifer to grab hold, to fight. We were moving away from her, very fast, and the next minute Craig dove over the side, screaming her name. Ross was at the bow, taking down the spinnaker, and I grabbed the wheel, but I wasn't an experienced sailor and it took me almost ten minutes to get the boat turned around. Ross didn't know any more about sailing than I did – since then he's become an expert – so he stood at the side, calling Craig and Jennifer, trying to see them. It was getting dark.

'I headed for the light on the marker pole Craig had thrown in, and we finally saw the life preserver. Jennifer was propped in it, like a doll, staring at us. But she wasn't alive; I suppose we knew that long before we got to her. Ross started to retch, and then cry, and I told him to pull himself together and start calling Craig again; he had to be nearby.

'Ross called until he was hoarse, in between whimpering, "My God, my God, both of them –" until I had to slap him to get him to pay attention. I told him to hold the boat and I went over the side and tied a rope around Jennifer and together we got her into the cockpit. I couldn't find a pulse.

'Ross called the Coast Guard. By then it was dark and while we waited for them, we got a searchlight from the cabin and swept the water with it, looking for Craig. But of course there was no sign of him. He was gone.'

In the abrupt silence, Katherine sat shivering, so chilled by Derek's cold telling of the story her bones felt brittle. He had not moved; he had not raised his voice. His face had not changed. He might have been recounting a story about strangers. She clasped her hands, to keep them still. 'Where was Craig while you were looking for him?'

Derek shrugged. 'As Claude said, we assume he swam to shore. There were no other boats in the area and we weren't far from Lime Point. He was very strong and he could have made it. Obviously he did.'

'Lime Point?' Katherine was trying to place the name.

'A small spit of land just below the north end of the Golden Gate Bridge. There's a lighthouse on it.'

Todd walking towards a beach, and a lighthouse. 'Can we go look, Mom?' 'Not today; we're meeting the realtor, remember? We'll come back.' 'Lime Point,' the fisherman said. 'Great place. Out at the end, you feel like you're all alone in the middle of the water.'

Katherine shivered. 'Champagne,' Derek said, filling her glass and handing it to her.

'Thank you.' Her voice sounded distant in her ears. 'Why did Jennifer drown, if she was wearing a life jacket?'

'She wasn't. For some reason she didn't put it on when Craig told her to. But she probably didn't drown. We found later that when the boom struck her one of the cleats pierced her skull. It's likely she was dead before Craig got to her. My grandmother was vehement about not having an autopsy, and she pulled strings to prevent one. It didn't matter to the family; with both of them gone in one day, no one thought of anything but mourning.'

'But . . . I don't understand. How did she get in the life preserver?'

'We assumed Craig put her there – discovered her dead in the water, got her to the life preserver – we never knew why – then was so exhausted he was carried away in the current and drowned. Obviously a faulty theory. But that was why everyone called him a hero. Jumped in without a life jacket to save his sister.'

'And then – swam away?'

'And then swam away.'

'Why?'

'You'd have to ask him.' She shivered again. 'I'd better make you some coffee.'

'No, don't. I'd like to go home. Please.'

He nodded. 'A good idea. It's been a long evening.' His arm was around her waist as they walked to the door. 'I have a place at Tahoe; if you'd like to get away we could go there for the weekend.'

She shook her head. 'Thank you, but you keep forgetting that I have two children. And I'd like some time alone. Could you give me a few days?'

'A few days.' He rang for the elevator and they rode down in silence, and in silence drove to Katherine's apartment. 'I'll call next week,' he said as she opened the door. 'You were an exciting woman tonight.'

She shook her head again, not looking at him. She was worn out and would have liked some comfort; of all the things he might have said, that was the last one she wanted to hear.

All weekend, Katherine was haunted by Derek's story. During the days, she was with Todd and Jennifer, but at night remembering it, even as he had told it in his cold, flat voice, she began to imagine it vividly. Yet the more real it seemed, the less she could understand it. Craig enraged and losing control of himself? Craig physically attacking someone? Impossible. Craig never even raised his voice. When he was angry he withdrew into himself, shutting everyone out. Then, sometime later, he'd begin talking again, smiling and even-tempered, and no one would ever know what his thoughts had been, or how he'd resolved his anger.

And he hated physical violence; he would never lift his hand against anyone.

But what if there were another Craig, who could become enraged, throw insults and wild accusations, lose control of himself . . . and try to strangle his cousin?

And embezzle . . . and desert his family.

Craig, which one are you?

The children slept, the lights of an occasional passing car swept across the sofa bed where Katherine lay, while she relived Derek's story again and again, trying to understand the man she had married.

How many of his silences had been caused by the memory of seeing his sister die?

How many of his secrets had been about Derek, and furies he could barely contain?

Why didn't you talk to me about them?

She went to the front window and looked out at the quiet street.

The first time Craig had talked to her was at the opening of an art exhibit in Vancouver. Katherine was standing before a painting of a man sitting hunched over at the counter of an all-night restaurant, when, beside her, a stranger began talking about the vision of loneliness in that painting and the others in the exhibit. His voice deep and warm, he talked about the way Edward Hopper's people were painted within rectangles –

windows, rooms, doors – to show how they felt trapped, cut off from the world and somehow Katherine had known he was talking about himself. By that time they had exchanged names and were having dinner together.

He had seemed so calm and steady, his dark eyes sombre, his full beard making him look older than his twenty-six years, there had not been a moment when Katherine stopped loving and trusting him. Standing in the window of her apartment in San Francisco, she remembered his eyes, and his warm voice, and the way her skin felt when he held her – the first time she had ever been touched by a man, the first time a man had seen her naked, the first time a man had looked at her with desire.

'*Craig*,' she whispered, aching for him. But then she thought how long ago that had been. She had always believed they had so much love, but all those years, since he first spoke to her, Craig had carried that terrible story inside him, and never let her share it.

If that really *was* the story.

The idea came suddenly. The truth, Derek had said with a faint smile. How did she know? Claude had told the official version; Derek had told his. But Derek himself had said he didn't like Craig. Why should she believe he was telling the truth?

The only one who could tell her was Ross. The last thing Katherine decided before falling asleep late Sunday night was that she would call him the next morning.

But those confused thoughts and questions about Craig had filled only a part of that hectic weekend. Long before it had begun, Katherine had promised Jennifer and Todd – to make up for her evenings out – that those two days would be theirs, to plan any way they wished. And so, just when she wanted to be quiet, the hours were crammed with excursions and chatter, hurtling on buses and cable cars from one part of the city to

189

another, forcing herself, through the clamour of her own thoughts, to listen to her children.

'Look!' Todd demanded. It was Sunday afternoon, almost the end of the exhausting weekend, and they were walking through the Exploratorium, a cavernous museum of scientific exhibits made to be manipulated, examined and played with as painless lessons in science and nature. Jennifer had rushed Katherine to some of her favourites: light bulbs that lit when she clapped her hands, a mirror that made her seem to float above the floor, a strobe light that left her shadow imprinted on a screen after the light had been turned off.

Then it was Todd's turn. 'Look!' he demanded, pulling Katherine with him to a television screen. As he stood before it, his face appeared, transformed electronically into hundreds of different-sized squares that gave him one eye larger than the other, three sections of chin, a two-part nose, a jaw line stepping crazily up and down. 'Terrific, huh?' He tilted his head, turned to look back over his shoulder, stuck out his tongue. 'That's me. Terrific, isn't it?'

'Oh, Todd.' Katherine knelt on the concrete floor and put her arms around him.

'Isn't it *terrific!*' he demanded, standing rigidly within her arms.

'Yes,' she said. And it was. Because after weeks of sullen silence, Todd finally had found a way to tell her how he felt. 'You're broken up into pieces, aren't you?' she said, still kneeling beside him. 'Part of you in Vancouver and part of you here; part of you wanting Daddy home and another part mad at him for being gone. And I guess part of you being mad at me, too, for selling our house and dragging you here and then leaving you with Annie a lot of the time.'

Todd stared at her. 'How do you know all that?'

'You told me, by showing me the pieces on the screen. But, Todd, doesn't part of you love me, too?'

'Sure.' But he did not move. Once he would have put his arms around her and kissed her. My son doesn't trust me any more, Katherine thought.

'Well,' she said. 'We'll have to talk about all those pieces. But for now –' She stood up and looked around. 'What happened to Jennifer?'

They found her at the entrance to a separate room. 'Wait till you see this,' she said with a grin, and plunged in, giving no warning of what was inside.

Katherine felt like Alice in Wonderland: her familiar world disappeared as she seemed to shrink to the size of her children and they grew like giants above her. 'I love it, I love it,' Jennifer chanted, dancing about, and Todd, racing from one wall to the other, stopped briefly to kiss Katherine on her cheek.

'It's the angles!' he shouted gleefully. 'We learned about it in school. There aren't any right angles and the floor is slanted, and the ceiling is, too, and everything's crazy, so *we* look crazy.'

Katherine did not understand, but it was more important that Todd had kissed her, and that once again the two of them had found a way to tell her how they felt. Later, at dinner, she said to them, 'So you want to cut me down to size, is that it?'

Jennifer looked up cautiously from her soda. 'We kind of joked about it. Did Todd tell you?'

'I didn't!' Todd said indignantly.

'You both did,' Katherine said. 'When you took me to that crazy room. Pretty smart, shrinking me down like that. But why can't we just talk, if you're unhappy? Do we have to go to the Exploratorium every time, so I can figure out what's bothering you?'

They exchanged a look. 'It's just that we don't know what's going to happen,' Jennifer said. 'The other kids talk about Christmas and Easter and next summer, but we can't. We can't even talk about next week.'

191

'Yes you can,' Katherine said quietly. 'We'll be here next week; we'll be here for lots of weeks.'

'How do you know?' Todd demanded.

'Because –' She took an envelope from her purse and handed it to them. 'This came in the mail yesterday.'

Jennifer read the postmark, then slowly pulled out the piece of blank paper folded around five one-hundred dollar bills. 'The same as last time. There's no letter.'

'No. But it was mailed in a town in Manitoba. I guess that means Daddy is moving around a lot and still doesn't want us to know where he is.'

'Well, fuck him,' Todd growled.

'Todd! Don't talk about your father that way! Do you hear me? You will not talk about him that way! We don't know why he's doing this. All we've heard is what other people say – we haven't heard his side. And until we do, we'll wait for him, and not forget how he took care of us for years and years, and' – her voice wavered – 'trust him. Because we love him.'

'We can get a bigger apartment with the money,' said Jennifer. 'I can have my own room.'

'No. I'm sorry, Jennifer, but we're only going to use the money when you and Todd need clothes or special things for school, or to pay Annie. The rest we'll put in the bank.'

'But he sent it for all of us.'

Slowly Katherine nodded. 'I know. It's not easy to explain.' *He can't get off this easily. If he wants to support us, he has to let us share his life. When he's ready to do that, I'll be glad to take his money. Until then . . .* 'We should try to make it on our own. We don't know that the money will keep coming. And I think it's important, while we're waiting for him, to try to build our own life.'

Jennifer gave her mother one of the piercing looks that Katherine found so unnerving. 'Is that why you go out with Derek Hayward all the time?'

'I don't go out all the time,' Katherine began defensively, then caught herself. 'I go out with Derek for companionship. He's a friend. Just as you're making friends at school. We all need friends. You should understand –' *Don't overdo it.* 'You can understand that. Now how about telling me what the programme will be for the Christmas concert?'

Deflected, because the chorus was a new experience and they were excited about it, they described again the Friday night rehearsal, and by the time they left the restaurant, no one was complaining about not being able to plan for the future. Because, Katherine thought, we're making one every day.

But later, standing at the window while the children slept, going over and over Derek's story, aching for Craig, trying to imagine him lunging forward to get his hands around his cousin's throat, wondering about the secrets wrapped within his silences, Katherine clenched her fists in frustration.

Craig, which one are you?

The more she heard about him, the less she understood. And even when she decided to call Ross, and ask him about Derek's story, she wasn't sure how much she would know. Because as the weeks and months passed, Craig was becoming a different person. And so was she.

'What would you two think,' she said casually to Jennifer and Todd at breakfast, 'if I decided to do my hair a different way?'

Tilting their heads exactly as Craig did, they eyed her. 'How?' Todd asked.

'I don't know. Leslie had some ideas. I thought I'd ask her.'

'Will you look very different?' Todd asked.

'I don't think so. I'll have the same face.'

'Then why do it?'

'To look my best when I try to sell my jewellery.' She corrected herself, telling the truth. 'Just – to look my best. ' It had nothing to do with business. It had to do with change.

'I think it might be all right,' Jennifer said. 'As long as we recognise you.'

'If we don't,' Todd said ominously, 'we'll go off with some other mother who'll probably be an ogre in disguise, looking for human children to work in her basement, sweeping out the bones of people she's eaten, and the only way we can escape is to tie the bones together into a ladder and climb out –'

'Oh, *Todd*!' Jennifer said. She gathered up her books for school. 'Are you going to change your hair?' she asked Katherine.

'If you and Todd don't mind.'

'I guess we don't.'

'Then I guess I will.'

'About time!' Leslie exclaimed that evening. 'Now – I just happen to have a list. Hairdresser, masseuse, manicurist, facial. What do you call the woman who gives the facial? Face-maker? She who saves face?'

Laughing, Katherine said, 'Leslie, I was only thinking of a new hair style.'

'Hair does not stand alone. Would you paint only one leg of a chair? Listen, lady, I have great plans for you. Here's a salon of experts, waiting to do your bidding – all of them conveniently at Heath's where you get an employee discount. I'll make an appointment for next Saturday at nine. Count on half a day. Yes?'

'Yes,' Katherine said. And on Saturday she floated through the morning in the mirrored peach and silver rooms of Heath's salon – a hothouse fairyland that banished the everyday world. For four hours she luxuriated in scented steam, creams and gels, soft sponges, brushes and puffs, and the caresses of skilled hands shaping her hair, filing her nails, massaging her muscles. Erasing, she thought a little sadly, the last traces of Vancouver.

'The very last,' Leslie agreed that afternoon as they stood before Katherine's full-length mirror. Leslie was ecstatic. 'A new woman. Was I right? I am always right about these things. Katherine, you're stunning. Not, I must say, the conventional beauty of the toothpaste ads. Different. Better. Much better. A new person.'

'I'm not,' Katherine protested, but she was uneasy at how different she looked in familiar surroundings. And when Jennifer and Todd came running in, and stopped dead in the doorway, their mouths open, her uneasiness deepened. 'Hi,' she said. 'How was rehearsal?'

'OK.' Jennifer stared at her mother. 'You told us you'd have the same face.'

'Hey,' Leslie said. 'You're not going to tell me that is not your mother's face.'

'She looks like a princess,' said Todd.

Katherine turned back to the mirror. She stood straight, her head high, as Victoria had instructed, the dark heavy hair she had imprisoned in a bun now closely framing her face, then falling in loose curls to her shoulders. Relaxing her hair had eased the tightness of her skin, and her face seemed fuller, her hazel eyes larger and wider apart, with a more pronounced upturn at the corners. Her high cheekbones and the faint shadows beneath them accentuated the warmth of her mouth. Derek had said she was a beautiful woman. Katherine looked in the mirror and knew he was right.

In a small voice, Jennifer asked, 'Are you going to keep looking like that?'

'I think so,' Katherine said. 'Don't you think we might get used to it?'

'If Daddy could see you now,' said Todd. 'He'd come back right away.' Katherine flushed. She hadn't thought of Craig. 'Can we send a picture, Mom? To the place where the money was mailed? In Manitoba?'

'We don't have an address, silly,' said Jennifer. She was watching Katherine.

He'd come back right away. Katherine glanced at her worktable, where a half-finished pendant lay. She thought of the cheques she had written four days earlier, on the first of the month, signed Katherine Fraser, paid with money she had earned herself. She looked in the mirror at the reflection of a woman she did not yet know, still at the edge of discoveries.

I'm not sure I want him to see me now. The words sprang out. *Because I'm not sure anymore whether I really want him back.*

Chapter 9

The letter was centred on Ross's desk. He skimmed it once more, then moved to the table along the wall where the scale model of BayBridge stood. Smiling to himself, he plucked out one building and replaced it with a modernised version. The last step. Ivan Macklin had written to say he had received Ross's cheque for cancelling the lease and would be moving out. For the first time, the Macklin Building would be empty and Ross could get to work on it.

Part of BayBridge, he thought, sitting at his desk. But more important, vacant. Finally able to be inspected. He reached for a scratch pad and began scribbling notes for the engineers. Preoccupied, he heard his telephone ring twice before he remembered his secretary had taken the afternoon off for Christmas shopping. 'Yes,' he said, still writing. His hand stopped as he heard Katherine's voice.

'I called you last week,' she said. 'When you were out of town.'

He waited. When had they last talked? Weeks ago. And he hadn't seen her since their lunch. Early September; he remembered the kids had just started school. Three months. In the silence, he became aware that she was waiting. He drew an embellished K on his scratch pad. 'How are you?' he asked.

'All right. Fine. Jennifer and Todd are up and down, either happy with friends and school, or dragging around, blaming me for everything; we always seem to be arguing or making up. But otherwise we're . . . fine. Do you know about the money that's come? From Craig?'

'Yes.' He'd kept up with her; he knew she was managing, even putting away most of the money that came in the mail. And he knew how she spent some of her evenings.

'I thought they'd tell you,' Katherine said. 'Did they say anything else?'

'No. How is your job?'

She hesitated, and he knew it because of his distant politeness. 'I guess it's getting better. Now and then Gil even asks for my suggestions. A couple of weeks ago he used my ideas to change a ski window after I'd gone home, and took credit for it when the president of the store liked it. Is that progress?'

'Of a sort,' he said, smiling. 'I understand you've seen Victoria a few times.'

'Twice. For tea. It's wonderful, being with her; I always go home wanting more.'

Ross felt a rush of pity at the wistfulness in her voice. 'What about your jewellery?' he asked. 'Weren't you going to try to sell some?'

'I've been studying . . .' He listened as she told him about her instructor, who was loaning her the tools and equipment she could not afford to buy. But he was thinking about her voice, lovelier than he remembered: low and clear, with a lilt that had not been there before. So, she had changed, probably more than the others had told him. He recalled the frightened, bewildered woman he'd seen in Vancouver and at Victoria's dinner – how much he'd liked her and admired the spirit she'd shown even though her familiar life was crumbling around her.

But damn it, he thought, hearing her animation as she talked about meeting Herman Mettler, how the hell could she be sleeping with Derek? Of all the men she might have found to ward off loneliness while she waited for Craig, how could she choose a bastard who didn't know the meaning of sympathy or friendship?

And why was Derek interested in her? He never did anything without a reason and never paid attention to any but the most beautiful women. Yet gossips reported them all over town, from the Peruvian exhibit to Marrakech, where Melanie said she'd seen them when she was there with a group from her tennis club. So, for some reason, he'd turned his charm on Katherine and she'd been taken in – not the first woman to think Derek Hayward was offering her the world. That was it, of course. Ross didn't know what his brother was up to, but he could understand how a lonely woman who thought she had few options could respond to a wealthy man whose options seemed limitless.

I might have helped her find some of her own, he thought. But too much had intervened: Melanie, his preoccupation with what was happening to their marriage, his work, and Katherine's place in the family as Craig's wife. Derek had no such concerns; Derek reached out and took whatever piqued his interest.

He became aware that Katherine had stopped talking. 'You've made a good start,' he said. 'You can't do better than Mettler's.'

'If he likes what I have. He didn't promise anything and I'm trying to keep my hopes down.' She paused. 'Ross, I want to ask you something. Last Friday, Derek told me the story of the sailing accident. There's so much I don't understand – that doesn't seem right – I wanted to ask you about it . . .'

Ross was silent. He didn't want to talk about the accident. He and Derek still had a score to settle from the events of that day, but they would do it between themselves, not by talking through Katherine. There was nothing he could tell her, anyway, that would make Craig a hero; it was better to remain silent.

In fact, there was nothing much at all he could do for her. She was building her own life; she'd made Derek a part of it; and Ross was in no position to interfere. Or compete, he reflected. 'I think you should let Derek explain,' he said at last. 'I don't think I could add anything helpful.' He felt a stab of regret, liking her, wishing there had been no obstacles between them. 'I'm sorry,' he added. 'Maybe sometime –'

He looked up as one of his staff members appeared in the doorway, pointing to his watch. Ross nodded. 'I'm sorry,' he said again, to Katherine. 'I'm late for a meeting. Good luck with Mettler; I'm sure I'll hear all about it from Victoria.'

'Ross –?'

'I really am late. Goodbye, Katherine.'

But he could not shake the memory of her voice. All through the meeting he heard the lilt of her first words and her bewilderment as she said his name the last time, sliding up in a question he had not allowed her to finish. Because I didn't want to talk about the accident, he thought, knowing that what he really meant was he hadn't wanted to talk about Derek and Katherine.

'We're putting together a schedule for the Macklin Building,' he said to his senior staff, 'I just got Macklin's lease cancellation; he'll be out in sixty days. That takes us to mid-February, which means if we get moving, we can begin work on it by spring or early summer. But we have to co-ordinate it with our schedules for the rest of BayBridge.'

They knew he had owned the building for five years but hadn't been able to do anything with it because Ivan Macklin had insisted on a six-year lease before agreeing to sell. What he had never explained to them was why he bought it: a single, rather ordinary building in a decaying neighbourhood where no one was talking about redevelopment; where the first thoughts of BayBridge were more than twelve months in the future. By now, with BayBridge a reality, his staff might consider him a wizard for knowing where to buy, and when, and how to negotiate with the developers to keep the building, leasing it to BayBridge Plaza. Well, let them believe it, he thought humorously. Who wouldn't like his staff to think he's got superhuman powers?

'We're responsible for the renovation, but the more we can use crews as they arrive for BayBridge, the less expensive it will be. What I need is a firm schedule. When can we have the building inspected? When can we get final schematics for the arcade and the renovation of the upper floors? How soon can we bring in a contractor? There's a problem – yes, Donna?'

'Ross, I can't find an engineer's report on that building.'

'That's what I was about to say. There isn't one.'

'But didn't you get one before you bought it?'

'This building doesn't fit the regular pattern.' He looked at them: co-workers, friends, men and women he trusted. 'I don't know what happened to the engineer's report; it's missing. But I think there's a chance the foundation is weak. It's only a guess, but if I'm right, it will have to be strengthened, and that means we'll need plans for both repairs and renovation.'

'Well, we'll check the original plans,' said Donna practically.

Ross shook his head. 'That's part of the problem. I'm not sure the building and the plans agree. If they don't, and if there are problems in the foundation, I want them corrected as part of the renovation.'

No one asked why Ross suspected a problem in the building. They had a job to do; they trusted him; and they knew he trusted them. Donna gathered up her notes. 'OK; we need a foundation engineer to check the support columns, and the soil they're in. Do you have some favourite engineers, Ross?'

'I'll give you a couple of names. Now, can we work out a schedule for the Macklin Building and what the rest of you are doing on BayBridge?'

They settled down to work. They were the original group Ross had assembled when he opened his firm six years before and they were comfortable together, knowing each other's strengths and weaknesses. Like a family, Ross thought as they left an hour later. But then, as he locked the office door for the night, he contradicted himself. Ross Hayward Associates was not like a family because he had chosen its members to balance and respect each other and work harmoniously as a group. Not like a family, he amended. Not, anyway, like mine.

Melanie was waiting in the living-room when he came in. Her back was to the sliding glass doors that led to the deck and the starry ring of lights encircling the Bay – that magnificent scene that made buyers flock to the Tiburon hills, thinking all their problems would fade away in an atmosphere of such beauty. But Ross knew they didn't. We carry our baggage with us, he thought – the accumulated grievances and tensions of years – and no scenery in the world can even begin to evaporate them.

Melanie was not looking at the view. She was dropping ice cubes into a martini, concentrating on how much liquid each cube splashed on the Bokhara rug. 'You didn't call to say you'd be late. I've been waiting for an hour.'

'I'm sorry. We had a meeting and I lost track of the time. Macklin's moving out, Melanie; I'll finally be able to get into the building.' He watched her examine an ice cube and let it fall into her glass; a splash of gin landed on the toe of her alligator shoe. Stubbornly, calling himself a fool, he went on. 'We talked about this, remember? The night I brought you the pin from Mettler's and we went to dinner –'

'The Wilding's party is tonight. I was going to it.'

They stood a few feet apart in the blue and gold living-room but the space between them was immeasurable. 'Why don't you go, then?' Ross asked.

'Because I'm ashamed to show my face! Everyone there knows about my party; how can I tell them I'm not having it after all?'

'Which party?'

'*Which* party! You know damn well which party! The one you cancelled!'

'I didn't cancel the party. Only the garden and the ball-room.'

'Only! Only! That was where I planned it! Where would you like me to put three hundred and fifty people? In our cosy living-room? In your precious Macklin Building? It was going to be the party of the year – and if you had any sense you'd know that would help your business, too! I've been working on it for weeks – the decorations, the food, the invitations – and you decided, *without telling me*, you bastard – you didn't want it, so you made one telephone call and cancelled everything I'd done. You humiliated me with the Fairmont and with my friends – these things never stay secret! – you had no right to treat me that way!'

Ross walked to the bar and poured a straight Scotch. 'You're right. I apologise.'

'You what?'

'I apologise. It was a cruel thing to do and I'm sorry.'

'Then you'll call them back!'

'No.' He downed his drink and poured another and walked towards Melanie. 'I didn't apologise for cancelling the Fairmont; I apologised for the way I did it. You've already given two parties this year at fifteen thousand dollars apiece. You've spent almost forty thousand dollars in the past six months on clothes and entertaining and trips. We can't afford your Fairmont party. Does it occur to you that I work for a living, that I do not enjoy an infinitely expanding income – *Come back here; I'm talking to you!*'

Ignoring Ross, Melanie went to the bar and filled her glass from the martini pitcher. Watching her, Ross realised suddenly she'd never worn that pin he'd brought from Mettler's. But they hadn't talked that night, either, as he'd hoped they would; Melanie had accepted the gift with a brief kiss and then talked non-stop all through dinner, amusingly, as she could when she tried; mainly about the children.

She was not trying to amuse him now; her face was stony as she dropped ice cubes into her drink, listening to him. 'We're going to change a few things,' he told her. 'From now on you'll have two thousand dollars a month for household expenses. That includes your lipsticks and lace stockings and Godiva caramels. When you want to buy out Wilma's designer clothes or give parties, you'll have to come to me so we can share those decisions. Is that clear? I'm sick of writing cheques for a greedy child who gives me nothing as a woman: no companionship, no sex, not even friendship –'

'You mean you'll write the cheques if I earn them, is that it? You'll buy my services. What do I get for one screw? A pair of shoes? Does a blow job get me a matching purse? What do I have to do to give a party at the –?'

'Be quiet!' he roared. 'You don't have the faintest idea what I'm talking about. Do you know, I thought of going to Victoria this evening, to talk about my day, but I decided instead I'd come home to my wife and share with her the things that are hugely important to me. I thought I'd give it one more –'

'Then you're a fool.'

'Oh, yes; that's quite true. But now that we both know that, I think it's time I stopped being one. Are you clear on how we're going to handle our finances from now on?'

'I will not come to you for permission to spend money.'

'You will come to me for every major expenditure over your monthly budget.'

With a scream, Melanie flung her glass at him. Ross jerked to the side and watched the glass shatter against an oil painting he had bought in New York the year they were married.

'When you calm down,' he said, his voice like steel, 'we will talk about money and anything else that needs settling.'

'I don't want to talk to you!' she screamed. 'You bastard, you're only doing this because Derek was helping me plan that party –'

'*Derek*?'

'You knew that!'

'No. I didn't. But Derek had nothing to do with –'

'You're lying. Why else would you cancel my party? You never did anything like that before!' Her voice rose higher. 'You're always worse when your brother's involved; you're jealous of him because Curt always liked him better – poor little Ross, his Daddy loved his brother best – you even ran away to New York to get away from him. And now you're making my life miserable because he's my friend. Everybody thinks you're so nice. My God, if they only knew!'

Very carefully, Ross put down his glass. 'Melanie, listen to me. This has nothing to do with Derek. This is between us. I don't want to make your life miserable – I don't want to destroy anything – I want to find the way back to what we had a long time ago. There were so many wonderful things, especially in New York –'

'Well there aren't any more! There haven't been for a long time!' She was breathless. 'I've been a perfect wife, I've done everything you wanted – I even moved here from New York

205

when I didn't want to – I left all my friends and my mother and daddy – and you treat me like a child – you're cold and . . . heartless!' Her arms outstretched, she stepped like a tightrope walker around the broken glass. 'I'll tell you what you can do. Draw me one of your fancy blueprints about how you're going to make it up to me for humiliating me in front of everyone. I'll look it over when I get back. See if I like it or not.' In a few steps she was at the front door, yanking it open and slamming it shut behind her.

Ross stood in the silence of the living-room, then slowly walked to the broken glass and bent to pick up the pieces. As he did so, a sound made him glance up. At the top of the stairs, in frozen stillness, sat his children, listening.

Thursday, December 10 was circled on Katherine's calendar. Eight a.m.: Mettler's. As the day approached, Jennifer and Todd grew as tense as their mother. 'He'll think they're wonderful,' Jennifer said, watching Katherine polish a pendant of blued steel, the closest she could come, on her budget, to silver.

Todd jumped on the couch and intoned in a deep voice, 'My dear Mrs Fraser, these are so good they will be whizzed to England and given to the Queen, and when she sees them she'll jump on Concorde and fly to San Francisco and parachute to our doorstep – if she can find it in the lousy fog – and say here's a million dollars, please give me enough jewellery for my family and friends and every single person in the, what's it called, House of Something –'

'Parliament,' said Jennifer.

'No, House of Ordinary, something like that –'

Katherine burst out laughing. 'Commons. Todd, you're wonderful, and I hope it all comes true.'

'Am I wonderful, Mom?'

'Yes.' She was concentrating on a curve in the steel.

'Then how come I never get any attention around here?'

'Oh, Lord.' She put down the pendant. Swivelling on her stool, she held out her arms and Todd jumped down and came to her. 'I'm sorry, sweetheart. There's so much to do before tomorrow morning.'

'Yeh, I know.' He looked at her closely. 'Mom – if this guy likes them, and buys a whole bunch, and you make a bunch of money . . .'

'Yes?'

'You won't need Daddy any more, will you?'

Holding Todd, Katherine's arms tensed. She looked to Jennifer, standing watchfully nearby, and Jennifer came to her rescue.

'That's really stupid, Todd. Do we only want Daddy back because he earns money or because we love him?'

'Because we love him, but –' Todd frowned, trying to recapture his train of thought. But Jennifer had confused him and, a little later, when they went to bed, he still had not puzzled it out.

But Katherine knew he would, and would bring it up again. Because he and Jennifer were beginning to recognise that there were many kinds of need. We'll talk about it, she thought – one of these days. When I know what to say. When I know what I feel about Craig.

He watched her. His picture stared at her over the jewellery samples and sketches she would take to Herman Mettler in the morning. Her chin in her hand, Katherine looked steadily back at him, recalling the small warm details of their life together. But when she tried to recapture her contentment, all the way back to the day Craig took her to their first apartment in Vancouver and made love to her on the floor while they waited for the furniture to be delivered, she could not do it. It was gone. And she had no time to try to retrieve it. In spite of herself, her eyes slid from Craig's picture to her jewellery and sketches, and her thoughts moved ahead, to her appointment and what more she could do that night to make it a success.

'Ah, yes,' rumbled Herman Mettler, arranging Katherine's four pieces like the points of a compass. They seemed small and insignificant beneath his splayed fingers on the polished emptiness of his desk. 'Marc told me you were working in Tony's studio. A strong personality, Tony. Strong influence.'

'Those are my own designs.' Katherine handed him her sketches, bound in a folder. 'So are these.'

'No doubt, no doubt. But influence is like an aroma from a distant restaurant; you find yourself cooking onion soup for dinner without realising that during the day you were inspired by inhaling its scent. However. Let's see what you have. Tony, after all, is better than onion soup.'

Chuckling at his wit, he fanned the sketches like playing cards beside the finished pieces and gave them serious attention. Katherine sat rigidly, hands gripped in her lap. No one had seen her work but Jennifer and Todd. In Vancouver she had been fooled by her friends' uncritical praise into thinking she was better than she was. She would not let that happen again. So she kept her designs hidden, even from Leslie. Now, finding no clues in Mettler's impassive face, she looked around his balcony office. On the panelled walls, framed photographs of film and television stars were autographed, with gratitude, to Herman Mettler. 'Friends,' Mettler said. Startled, Katherine turned to find him watching her. 'Women remember, when we help make them beautiful. Your work has promise; we'll start with a dozen.'

Katherine's eyes widened. 'A dozen pieces?'

'Bracelets, pins, necklaces. No earrings; I have enough to pierce every earlobe west of the Rockies.' Chuckling, he fastened his gaze on Katherine until she realised he was waiting for her to join him in admiring his joke. She smiled. 'Now.' He settled back. 'What I like I buy outright; no consignments. I'll buy the blued steel pendants today; the other two pieces don't interest me. How much are you asking?'

Katherine hesitated. 'I haven't priced them.'

'I assumed you hadn't. There's a skill to it; ask around.' He pondered. 'I'll charge seventy for the seagull; ninety for the snail – nice use of the cornelian, by the way; a centre focus as well as an eye. One of the reasons I said you showed promise. My secretary will send you a cheque for sixty-four dollars –'

'Sixty-four?'

'Forty percent of the price I'll charge. Ordinarily, of course, my price would be a markup of what you charge me. Since you are uncertain what to charge, I've worked backwards. Any objection to that?'

'No. I just wondered.'

'Well, then. I want ten more by the end of February, for our spring showing. We advertise heavily so your name will get around if you deserve it. Use colour; some designers can handle black but nothing here tells me whether you can or not, so don't try. This sketch and this one are good; I'd try to ease the rose, however.'

'Ease –?'

'Enlarge the opening in each petal. In other words, deflower it.' This time he bellowed with laughter, and Katherine, knowing what was expected, smiled with him. Then he returned to business. 'We do well with gold, silver, fine gems, cloisonné. Don't use enamel unless you have other forms than this.'

Stung, Katherine said, 'Tony liked that bird.'

'Tony would. I don't like sculptured enamel. Private preferences, Mrs Fraser. If you want me to make you famous, you'll indulge me. Or you can rely on Tony, who can't do a thing for you. Now pay attention.' He swept together Katherine's sketches and samples and pushed them towards her. 'You have promise. You have a certain amount of talent;

how much I can't say yet and I doubt that you can either, until you've tackled a wider range of materials and styles. Continue to work with Tony if you want, but you would be better off away from his aroma.'

'He lets me use his tools and equipment; I can't afford my own, yet.'

'Use him, then, but don't let his onion soup get into your designs. I'm not buying Tony; I'm buying you. You've shown some facility with blued steel and copper; stay with them if you like. Pity you can't afford gold, but if you do well with this order, we may be able to advance you something in February. When a jeweller does that, it's an act of generosity.'

Shaking with laughter, he stood and held out his hand. Katherine took it and then found herself laughing with him. It was easier this time. She'd just made her first sale.

To celebrate, Leslie brought a bottle of wine to go with Katherine's meatballs. 'A celebration,' she reminded Todd as they finished dessert. 'So what's your problem?'

'Mom,' said Todd glumly. 'She's eight million miles away, thinking about jewellery.'

Leslie regarded Katherine. 'True. Good or bad thoughts?'

'Mostly worrying,' Katherine said ruefully.

'Not surprising.' Leslie watched Todd and Jennifer carry the dishes into the kitchen. 'Mettler's forced you to the wall. Come out of your safe little corner, lady, and your happy dreams of success. Do your thing, deliver your goods and see if the fickle public buys or turns thumbs down. Scary.'

Katherine gave a small laugh. 'You're amazing. How do you know that's how I feel?'

'Because that's how I feel every day. Slightly different, but whenever I make a suggestion or decision it can be knocked down in three seconds by Heath's president or the executive committee. Enough three-second knockdowns and I'm out slinking off to find another job. The big difference is that I'm anonymous, but you have to go public – how else can you make a name for yourself? Good reason to be scared. The dream of making it big . . .' Her attention veered off

'What about you?' Katherine asked. 'What are your worries?'

'Me? I? What makes you think I'm worried?'

'Is it Marc? Or something at the store? I tell you my problems; it's not fair to keep yours a secret.'

'Well.' Leslie spread her hands. 'What a coincidence that you should ask.' She pushed a crumb of cheesecake around her plate. 'Remember the Ralph Lauren sweaters I told you about at my birthday party?'

'And Calvin Klein blouses. You're still trying to figure out what happened?'

'We're pretty sure we know what happened. They were stolen. And maybe other things, too; we don't know yet how much. We did a couple of spot inventories without advance notice, and, in lingerie, we can't account for a box of Simone bras. Twenty-four, at seventy-five bucks apiece.'

Briefly, Katherine tried to imagine having enough money to pay seventy-five dollars for a brassiere. But then she concentrated on Leslie. 'But if they were stolen, wouldn't they –?'

'They didn't show up as stolen. Look. We have a computer system that keeps track of all our merchandise, from the time we get a shipment in the receiving room to the time it's sold and paid for. Today, the computer says every Simone bra that we received has either been sold or is still on the shelves. If we hadn't individually counted every bra and sales slip in lingerie we wouldn't know twenty-four were missing. Don't you understand? *The computer's numbers all balanced.*'

After a moment, Katherine said. 'The computer. You're worried about Bruce.'

211

'One hundred percent.' Leslie sighed. 'And, of course, me. I got him hired to work in that department without divulging his unruly past. And now something is going on – maybe a computer operator making a bunch of simple mistakes, maybe something a lot bigger – and if my brother is involved, I'm involved. All those beetle-eyed vice presidents, you know, watching for me to make a mistake.'

In the silence, they heard Todd weaving a story about dishes that washed themselves or were set to self-destruct if they were not clean in five seconds. Leslie shook her head vigorously, like a pony tossing off a rainstorm. 'I needed to talk and I feel better, for which I thank you, but we're supposed to be celebrating your triumph. So tell me – what are you going to make for His Highness Herman Mettler?'

It took Katherine only a minute to decide. She went to her worktable for her sketch pad. This time she felt confident enough to share her ideas.

'Much, much better!' Victoria exclaimed when she saw Katherine waiting in front of Podesta Baldocchi, framed by the shop's lush jungle of flowers and plants. 'Forgive me for being late, my dear – but let me look at you! Katherine, you are quite lovely. I knew it. I am never wrong about women. Of course I am never wrong about men, either. Ah, and when you laugh you are really quite remarkable.'

Laughing as much from happiness as at Victoria's firm judgements, Katherine turned on the crowded sidewalk and kissed her cheek. 'Oh, my dear,' Victoria murmured. She stopped and looked about, as if unsure of where she was. 'How quickly we forget – and then become greedy again.'

'You're thinking of Jennifer,' Katherine said as they walked to Maiden Lane. She felt a flash of jealousy, but then it passed. Jennifer was dead and it was Katherine, wonderfully alive, whom Victoria had asked to go Christmas shopping, and even the grey drizzle of the afternoon could not dim the way she felt when Victoria admired her – as if she had found both the mother and grandmother she had never known.

'Some time we'll talk about Jennifer,' Victoria said. 'But not now. Now I am going to buy a new dress for Christmas dinner. Do you know it will be the first we've had at home in years?' They turned into Helga Howie. 'Usually I am in Italy, or somewhere, but I thought, what a good idea, this year, for us all to be together. I hope I am not getting sentimental. At my age, it would look like senility. Renee, please,' she said to a saleswoman and in a moment the designer appeared and greeted her as an old friend.

After Victoria introduced her, Katherine browsed among Helga's designs and European imports while Victoria swiftly and decisively bought three knit dresses. 'Done,' she said as they left. 'I do not enjoy shopping. Such a waste of energy. I refuse to do it.'

'You just did,' Katherine pointed out.

'But I did not enjoy it. The only civilised way to shop is to have everything sent home. Why should I disrobe in a store when I have an excellent dressing room of my own? However, I wanted you to meet Renee. Someday you'll buy your clothes from her.'

Katherine laughed. 'Do you know that you spent two months of my salary on those three dresses?'

Victoria paused. 'Did I indeed? And yet you are not using the money that . . . arrives each month on things for yourself?'

'No. Only for the children.' She has trouble, Katherine thought, using Craig's name.

'Well. I want you to help me with my shopping. The last few years I've given money but this year I shall once again give gifts. More sentimentality, perhaps. And difficult. How do I know anymore what most of them want?'

213

'How do *I* know?' Katherine asked. 'I hardly know your family.'

'Nonsense. You've spent time with all of us – a great deal of time with Derek, I gather.' They walked into Gump's and for the first time Katherine discovered the heady joys of shopping with unlimited funds. Victoria had been serious about wanting her help: she asked for advice and most often took it, and Katherine chose what she liked, without looking at price tags. For two glorious hours they delved into the world's finest treasures, buying hand-carved lapis lazuli figures from Chile, Venetian opaline glass, Aynsley cobalt and gold china, suede jackets lined in sable, and Hermes purses for Melanie and Ann. 'Though God knows why,' said Victoria. 'Ann won't use hers in the wilds of Maine and Melanie . . . well, Ross keeps his own counsel but it's my guess their marriage won't last out the year and if so, why am I buying that self-centred woman this magnificent piece of leather? Well, it doesn't matter. She can take it with her when she goes. We'll shop for the children on another day; they aren't ready for Gump's. But I am ready for tea. Come; I have a favourite place.'

It was a short walk, across Union Square. 'Now,' Victoria said, seated on a velvet couch at The Compass Rose. 'Do you like it?'

'It's amazing,' Katherine answered. She did not say she had been there with Ross and that the room reminded her of his warmth three months ago and how different he seemed just this week when he abruptly ended their phone call. She did not even ask Victoria what she had meant about Ross's marriage.

'You need this room,' said Victoria, ordering Brie and fruit and tea for both of them. 'You need a little eccentricity. Your taste at Gump's – impeccable, of course, or I would not have agreed with your choices. But, my dear, to be so proper – at your age –!'

'I don't understand. I thought –'

214

'You thought you were pleasing me.' Victoria fell silent, her eyes on a far wall. 'I want to tell you a story. Fifty-six years ago, in 1925, a young woman discovered that the money she and her husband were living on was made by smuggling liquor into the country.'

'Prohibition . . .'

'Precisely. The young woman's husband was co-owner with his father of a small construction company, but he became obsessed with the thrill of defying the Federal government. We will not discuss whether prohibition was good or bad; he was breaking the law and risking prison, and he continued to do so until Congress repealed prohibition. That was in 1933.'

Katherine nodded. Hugh Hayward, she thought. Tobias had told her. But he said Victoria never talked about it.

'The husband's father had died in 1930, leaving the company in the husband's hands. In his passion for smuggling, he had ignored it. By the time of repeal, when he began to pay attention to it, the company was almost moribund. Then he was struck by a new passion: to rescue the company that bore his father's name. It was not a simple task. The country was in a depression and construction companies were dying no matter how hard anyone tried to save them.' Victoria drank her tea and gazed through the great doorway that looked into the busy hotel lobby. 'By 1934, when it seemed he could not revive the company, he went into his own depression in the midst of the national depression. Day after day, he sat in his room, looking through the window at the world passing by. You should have seen him, Katherine – tall and wonderfully handsome, with a smile that strangers turned to as if it were a beacon. When Ross smiles he looks exactly like him. He had broad shoulders and when he walked into a room he took ownership of it just by being Hugh Hayward. I'll show you pictures of him, but they can't tell you how beautiful he was because you had to be with him to feel his magnetism. Then.

215

to see him hunched in a chair. staring out of the window, his fingers picking at his pants on his thigh – picking, all day long – and his mouth moving as if he were talking, but making no sound . . . It was so terrible I had to get away. I had to get out of that house.'

Katherine let her tea grow cold, afraid to break Victoria's reverie.

'In the fall of 1934, I went to the office of the Hayward Corporation and sat down in Hugh's chair. I had no idea what to do, but I knew that a construction company had to have something to build. So I called on the men who had shared Hugh's smuggling adventures and told them I would build them new houses. They laughed at me and patted me on the head. Never let a man pat you on the head, my dear; it means he is about to put you on a leash or kick you out. However, Hugh's friends were great fools. They had written letters about their business and sexual activities – can you imagine? *They wrote them down*! And Hugh kept them. And I found them. In his dresser, under his boating socks. Naturally, his friends preferred that the letters not become public, so they ceased patting me on the head and the Hayward Corporation, under my direction with the help of two fine men who had started it with Hugh's father, built some very expensive houses in Tiburon and Sausalito and Berkeley – oh, but land was cheap then! – and I tucked the letters into the safe.'

Victoria signalled for more tea. 'And more fruit,' she told the waiter. 'Katherine? More brie?'

Katherine shook her head. 'Please go on.'

Victoria smiled. 'We also had help, indirectly, from money the government was spending. When schools and highways, and even post offices, were built by the WPA, people in the neighbourhood began to think about enlarging or repairing their homes. We could give credit because we had all that smuggling money. Once, we renovated an apartment building

216

in Oakland. We stripped banisters and oak floors, rearranged walls and restored broken mouldings, even replaced stained glass doors and windows. It took a year and a half. We finished on March 21st, 1938.'

The waiter put a plate of grapes and pears before them, and poured fresh tea. 'You are wondering how I remember the date. I remember because on that morning Hugh woke up, dressed himself, and went to work, as if on a normal day. Four years had passed and he knew it, but his depression was gone, so he went to his office and sat down in his chair and began running his company.'

Katherine studied Victoria's expressionless face. 'But it wasn't his company. You'd made it yours.'

'It was Hugh's company. There was only one office and it was his, one desk and it was his. He thanked me for what I had done and sent me home to take care of our sons.'

'But they weren't – how old were they?'

'Curt was twenty and Jason, nineteen.'

Their eyes met and they began to laugh. 'But it isn't funny,' Katherine said. 'It's sad.'

'Certainly. But you see, Hugh was a genius and I knew it. I had kept the company alive, but he made it one of the largest and most influential in the state. And besides the monstrous projects that multiplied after the war – roads, bridges, dams, shopping centres – he carried the idea of restoration much farther than I ever dreamed. And if he took credit for thinking of it in the first place, what difference did it make, since he did it so brilliantly? You see, Katherine, all Hugh took from me was a small company. I never would have succeeded as he did.'

They were silent. Around them, conversations rose and fell, cultivated murmurs and the clink of silver spoons. 'He took more than a company,' Katherine protested. 'He took your *place*. It was important to you.'

'True.'

'And you missed it when it was gone.'

'Oh my, yes.'

Katherine was thinking. 'Would you tell me,' she said hesitantly, 'what Jennifer was going to study in college?'

'Ah.' Victoria's eyes were bright. 'I knew you would understand. Didn't I say I was always right about women? And men, of course. Jennifer wanted to be an engineer.'

'And work in the Hayward Corporation?'

'In fact, we often talked about my financing her own company.'

To finish what you began. You wanted Jennifer to live the life Hugh took away from you. So you could live it through her.

Victoria sighed. 'It's late, and we haven't talked about you. We must make definite plans for you, now that you have an order from Mettler. You'll come to tea so we can talk quietly.' She signed the bill, slipped her arms into her fur jacket, and kissed Katherine on both cheeks. And they walked down the carpeted stairs and through the lobby as clusters of people made way for Victoria's imperious figure and determined stride.

Late that night, Derek called. Katherine had not seen or heard from him in the two weeks since he told her the story of the sailing accident. 'I understand you and my grandmother bought out Gump's this afternoon.'

She smiled to herself. 'Aren't you the one who made a comment about the joys of a large family?'

'I am. But a grapevine is often valuable. Did I wake you?'

'No, why?'

'You sound subdued and it's after midnight.'

'I'm working on a new design.'

'And?'

'I shouldn't be so glad to hear from you.'

'Victoria told me you'd been transformed,' he said. 'But evidently you still say what you think.'

Katherine picked up a pencil and began to shade in the bracelet she was drawing.

'Are you still there?' he asked.

'Yes, of course.'

'I am looking at a stack of invitations for parties between now and New Year's Eve. Most of them will be dull. A few will be interesting if you're with me. Are you free between now and the New Year?'

'Derek, it's only the middle of December.'

'What does that have to do with it?'

'I don't know what I'll be doing. I have to spend time with my children; I have to work at night – oh, you don't know that; I have an order from Herman Mettler – '

'He told me.'

'*He* told you?'

'I was in his store the other day and he mentioned it. Katherine, I have before me invitations to two cocktail parties, three dinners and a New Year's carnival. I will accept them if you will be with me. The dates are –'

Automatically, as he listed them, she jotted them down beside the drawing of the bracelet. 'Derek, that order from Mettler is very important to me.'

'Of course it is.' Smoothly his voice changed, as if he had moved closer. 'And I should be congratulating you. How many pieces?'

'Twelve.'

'A good start. When will they be in the store?'

'Spring, he said. If he likes them.'

'He knows what he's getting, from your samples. I wouldn't worry. Can you be in front of Heath's at five-thirty on Tuesday? Cocktails and dinner in Portola Valley and it's over an hour's drive at that time of day.'

His voice was like a long ocean wave, sweeping everything before it. Katherine drew a box around the dates he had read to her, looked away from Craig's picture, and said she could.

She had only the black dress. She skipped lunch the next day to search through a vintage clothing store she had seen advertised, and took home a high-necked lace blouse, an exquisite velvet and silk patchwork waistcoat, missing some buttons, a white tunic, loosely woven of gossamer wool, a belt of hammered bronze medallions, a cranberry-red fringed shawl, and a filmy silk scarf, long and trailing, in blues and pinks. In Heath's junior department she found a deep green velvet skirt that came just to her ankles. And on Tuesday, after work, she changed in Heath's washroom into the velvet skirt and lace blouse and the patchwork waistcoat, newly fitted with mother-of-pearl buttons.

Combing her hair in front of the mirror, Katherine thought of her children, who depended on her; the jewellery she was making, that would someday earn her living; Victoria, who loved her; Derek, who would spin her through December's festivities – and when she walked from the store, her head was high not only because of her clothes and hair and makeup, but because she was beginning to believe in herself.

Her pleasure was reflected in Derek's face as she stepped into his car. 'Victoria understated it,' he said, taking her hand, but a cacophony of angry horns and shouts from other cars forced him to pay attention to driving. At the first stoplight he looked at her fully. 'Stunning. You've learned to be dramatic. If you'd looked like this ten years ago my poor cousin would have been too intimidated even to come close, much less propose. And if by chance he did make it, you'd have looked past him for something better.'

Katherine's face clouded as Derek turned away, shifting gears to move with the traffic. She smoothed her velvet skirt, the excitement she had felt all day crumbling beneath his casual contempt. 'Derek – take me home,' she said tightly. 'I'm sorry, but I don't want to go, after all.'

He drove on without speaking, then swung the car to the kerb and stopped. 'Because I spoke unkindly of my cousin?'

'Because you spoke with contempt – of my husband.'

Surprise flashed across his face, then was gone. 'I've never disguised the fact that Craig and I were not friends. You like to romanticise the idea of a family, but you can't seriously imagine that sharing a last name automatically brings love. Should I pretend that Craig and I were intimate, loving, filled with respect and admiration and mutuality of interests, when none of that was true? Or should I tell you openly that we never liked each other, and that now, knowing he ran off fifteen years ago, and last summer deserted you and your children, I am less likely than ever to think well of him? Which would you have me say?'

'Neither,' she said almost inaudibly.

'No. Neither would please you. But neither would it please you to go home now. Let me suggest' – putting his hand beneath her chin, he leaned over to kiss her lightly – 'that I promise not to speak of Craig again; that we go to this affair in Portola; and if you feel uncomfortable, with me or with anyone who asks about Craig, we will leave on the instant. Is that acceptable?'

A weight lifted. If he made no demands on her and did not force her to choose between loyalty to Craig and going out with him, she could relax. 'Yes,' she said. 'Thank you.'

He kept his promise that night and a few nights later at a dinner party in a penthouse on Russian Hill when, for the first time, Katherine was completely at ease in a glittering crowd. No longer were eyebrows raised when Derek introduced her; instead there were admiring appraisals. 'Vancouver,' someone said at dinner. 'I was there once. Pleasant. Though not quite *cosmopolitan*, you know. Perhaps it was the lack of our charming hilltop houses.'

'We do have some,' Katherine said seriously. 'Every city has people who need to be looked up to.'

After a tiny pause, there was a shout of laughter from everyone but the critic of Vancouver. Katherine flushed and Derek contemplated her thoughtfully as the other guests began to vie for her attention. By the time dinner had ended and they were dancing, Katherine felt swept up, as if the long slow wave of Derek's voice had become a heavy surf, drowning her everyday problems. Nothing seemed unmanageable. Even Craig's shadow was obscured by the brilliance around her and her increasing confidence. She floated on the swell of voices and laughter, the gleam of candles and diamonds and admiration, Derek's absorbed look, his hand on her arm and his dark blond presence, smooth and remote. She floated timelessly, and nothing seemed impossible.

Two days before Christmas, she was brought back to earth at a buffet supper in Mill Valley.

When they had eaten, a magician entertained the fifty guests with sleight of hand and fortune telling. Moving about the room, he reached Katherine. 'You have seen much sadness,' he boomed portentously. 'You will also see joy. You will hold gold and silver in your hands and a man will come from far away to fall at your feet and beg you to love him and let him live with you.'

The others laughed and applauded but Katherine sat frozen. It doesn't mean anything, she told herself. He could have said that to anyone; no one takes these things seriously. But still it was uncanny. She looked at Derek, who smiled slightly. 'He is less a magician,' he murmured, 'than you are an enchantress.' Instinctively, Katherine drew back. 'God damn it,' he exclaimed. 'Must you feel guilty every time –?' He stopped and took her hand. 'We'll talk later.'

It was as if his lips had brushed her whole body, arousing her with a touch. But the magician had brought Craig back, pulling her in the direction of her memories, and she forced herself to sit unmoving, almost not breathing, until the rush of desire subsided. And when they left, Craig went with them; she could barely say goodnight to Derek, because Craig was in the way, hurrying her inside. She closed the door and huddled on the couch. *What will I do if he falls at my feet and begs me to love him and let him live with me?*

They had always made their own Christmas presents. Craig liked to shop, but Jennifer and Todd made presents in school and Katherine made jewellery or designed and knitted sweaters. This year, when they had to make gifts because they couldn't afford to buy them, Jennifer and Todd grumbled as they set up a tree that was half as big, Todd complained, as the ones they'd had in Vancouver.

'This room is half the size of the one we had in Vancouver,' Katherine said mildly. 'And it would be pleasant if you stopped making a fuss about everything.' She opened the box of ornaments they had brought from Canada. 'You act as if you'd buy me a mink coat if things had been different.'

'Well, maybe I would,' said Todd defiantly. 'Or something like it. Daddy always bought you fancy things.'

Oh, yes, Katherine thought. A shearling coat one year, a cashmere robe another, an antique sterling silver and enamel dresser set another. 'I don't need fancy things,' she told Todd. 'Just us, being together.'

Scowling, Todd hung ornaments on the small tree. 'I wish Dad was here!' he burst out. *'Why isn't he here?'*

Katherine put her arm around him. 'I wish I knew.' She thought of all their other Christmases, when Craig sang lusty carols, put up a huge tree in the living-room, and wreaths on all the doors, and hung six-foot stockings at the fireplace.

Christmas was a time, he said, when everyone could be a child and celebrate having a family – the most precious of all their possessions. It was a time for love.

'I waited for him all day,' said Jennifer. With careful precision she hung the last smiling angel on the top of the tree. 'I kept thinking, *now* he'll walk in the door.'

'Me too.' Todd sat on the couch, glumly picking at a scab on his arm. 'Every time I heard somebody outside I thought it was Dad.' His eyes filled with tears. 'Don't people always come home at Christmas? I mean – isn't that the whole idea?'

Jennifer plopped down beside him. 'We shouldn't even have Christmas. It's a fake, without a Daddy.'

'It's a fake to have Christmas *Eve*,' Todd said, 'when you don't make cookies and things with your mother 'cause she's gone.'

'At work,' Katherine said defensively. 'I had no choice; I explained that to you; I tried to get the day off, but I couldn't.'

'So Todd and I had to do everything,' Jennifer said to the ceiling, asking for sympathy. 'Except, Annie helped us make cookies. And we're going to read the story ourselves.' She pulled a book from beneath a cushion. 'Surprised?' She looked a challenge at Katherine. 'Did you think we'd forget?' Without waiting for an answer, she opened it to the first page and loudly began to read. ' "Marley was dead, to begin with. There was no doubt whatever about that." '

But after two pages, she burst into tears, 'I can't do it!' She threw the book across the room. 'I hate it and I'm never going to read it again!'

Katherine bent to pick up the book and smoothed the creased pages. *A Christmas Carol* by Charles Dickens. Every year Craig had read it aloud on Christmas Eve. Then they would eat dinner and open their presents.

'We had a tradition,' Jennifer sobbed. 'And now we don't any more.'

224

'Not now,' Katherine agreed quietly. 'We don't have it right now.' She sat with them on the couch. 'But we can't stop our life from changing. It started to change the day Daddy didn't come home, and it will keep on until he's with us again. And we're going to change, too, because everybody changes; we can't stop that, either, because we're alive. If we didn't keep busy and happy with new friends and new experiences it would be as if we'd died.'

'What if we change too much?' Jennifer asked.

'We'll still be us. When Daddy comes back, we'll keep some of the new things we've done and we'll drop others, but we'll still be the same people. Does that make sense?' They looked at her dubiously. 'Well, think about it. But in the meantime, we can't sit around crying and complaining all the time. If we do, we'll be as wrinkled as prunes, and then how would Daddy recognise us?'

Todd perked up. 'Prunes!' A smile broke through the gloom. 'Daddy would come to the door and say "Who is this? I thought Katherine Fraser and Jennifer Fraser and Todd Fraser lived here but who is this?" And I'd say, "I'm Todd." And he'd say, "Oh, no, Todd is four feet nine inches tall and he looks like a boy. In fact he looks like me." And I'd say, "I'm Todd the talking prune. Eleven inches tall because I cried all my juices out." And Daddy would say –'

'Oh, shut up!' Jennifer shouted. 'Who cares about your stupid stories! Daddy isn't coming home ever again and I wish you'd turn into a prune and disappear into the garbage can 'cause it's nothing to joke about!'

'Jennifer!' Katherine made her voice firm and unhesitating. 'Your father will come back as soon as he can and in the meantime I expect you to behave yourself and help Todd instead of jumping all over him. Now, I want to open my Christmas presents and watch you open yours and then we're going to Victoria's for dinner. And whatever happens in the future I don't want to hear you yell at your brother or me again because we're doing the best we can. Is that clear?'

Her mouth open, Jennifer stared at her. 'You never talked like that before.'

'I'm trying to keep things together around here,' Katherine said bluntly. 'And I'd like a little help instead of having to fight every step of the way. You're not the only ones who are unhappy, you know.'

'We don't go to parties all the time,' Jennifer said.

'No, but –' *Must you feel guilty every time?* Derek had asked. 'You're right; you don't and I've gone to a few. But we're all going to one tonight, and I'll bet we find a stack of presents waiting for us. Now do we open these presents? Or do we wait until tomorrow?'

'NO!' yelled Todd and lunged towards the small pile beneath the tree.

More slowly, Jennifer followed. But by the time she and Todd unwrapped the zippered sweaters Katherine had knitted them during her lunch hours, she was almost smiling. Katherine exclaimed in delight over the carved wooden candlesticks Jennifer had made in shop, varnished to a shining butternut finish, and the clay paperweight model of the Golden Gate Bridge that Todd had made and painted a bilious orange. By then, they were friends again.

Leslie and Bruce had joined forces to fill a box with Dungeons & Dragons books for Todd and Jennifer. Todd lay on his stomach and plunged into them. 'This is for you,' Jennifer said and watched as Katherine opened a large box and sat in stunned silence. 'For New Year's Eve,' the card said. 'Compliments of Heath's, Leslie and Bruce. Have a ball.'

'Oh,' Jennifer sighed a long breath as Katherine held up the dress – a billowing white taffeta skirt and a black lace top, the collar a high lace ruffle, the sleeves ending in lace ruffles two inches long. 'More parties,' Jennifer said, but she could

226

not resist the dress. 'It's so beautiful! Will you save it, so I can wear it some day?'

'Of course,' Katherine said. 'But you'll have your own wonderful dresses by then.' She held the dress and imagined herself wearing it, dancing in it. Folding it carefully in its box, she thought, New Year's Eve. With Derek.

She caught herself. A new year. Promises and resolutions. Without Craig.

'We'd better go!' she cried, springing to her feet. 'The whole family is going to be there and Victoria does not like people to be late to her parties!'

They hurried. Jennifer and Todd were thinking of a stack of presents, but Katherine, with thoughts of a new year, was reflecting that she had lied to her children. How could anything ever be the same again? If Craig came home tonight, or tomorrow, or the next day, how could they pick up their lives and behave as if they were the same people? They couldn't; of course they couldn't. She'd lied, to herself as well as Jennifer and Todd.

She felt a moment of panic. *We've gone too far.* They couldn't find their way back; they would all have to begin again. Her stomach was churning as it had when everything was coming to a close in Vancouver; all this time she'd thought they could pick up the pieces of that other life and put them together again, but now that had come to a close, too. She could only go forward. It felt, Katherine thought, as if she were lost again, looking for guideposts and a helping hand.

But on the bus she told herself it wasn't the same. She was learning to find her own guideposts. And for a helping hand – if she wanted, she had more than one waiting for her. At a family Christmas dinner at Victoria's.

Victoria answered the door, wearing a full-length gown of silver-blue Italian silk velvet, and greeted Katherine with an embrace so warm that everyone was reminded of her carefully correct one only six months earlier. Coming up behind her, Derek took Katherine's hand with a familiarity both exciting and disconcerting. Todd and Jennifer were gone in an instant, taken by Carrie and Jon to see their new Lionel train, set up in the study, leaving Katherine, as before, to face the rest of the family.

There were greetings and kisses. 'Oh my, oh my,' said Tobias, kissing her on both cheeks. ' "A lovely lady, garmented in light from her own beauty." Shelley, my dear, and you are a poet's dream. May I bring you champagne?'

But Derek was ahead of him. He brought Katherine a brimming glass and a plate of oysters and celeriac. 'Are you occupied with Tobias or can we finish a conversation we began the other night?'

'Derek,' said Tobias gravely. 'I am overcome by your subtlety. But I am leaving; I must search for a book.'

'The tiniest bit rude,' Katherine said lightly. 'Or do I exaggerate?' She saw Ross watching her with a frown. But Derek's hand was on her arm.

'Only a trifle. Shall we finish that conversation?'

Melanie was standing by herself, near the piano. When Katherine looked at her, their eyes met.

'Derek,' Victoria said, coming up to them. 'Will you help Tobias search the library? He seems to have lost Dickens.'

'Dickens?' Katherine repeated. Derek shrugged, briefly tightened his hand on her arm, and left.

'A family custom we are reviving tonight,' said Victoria. 'When Craig and Jennifer, and Ross and Derek were growing up, we would begin Christmas Eve in the afternoon, reading Dickens' *Christmas Carol* – is something wrong, Katherine?'

'No.' *I shouldn't be surprised. His roots are in this family.* 'Craig always read that to Jennifer and Todd at Christmas.'

'So he didn't entirely forget us.' After a moment, Victoria beckoned to Ross. 'Craig kept up our Christmas readings.'

'Did he act out the parts?' Ross asked Katherine.

'All of them. He was very good.'

'So is Tobias,' said Ross.

'Tobias is memorable,' Victoria said. 'He'll read it after dinner, for anyone who wishes to listen. If you would like . . .'

'Perhaps I will.'

Victoria nodded and moved away. Ross was searching Katherine's face. 'You look wonderful,' he said. 'I'm glad you're doing so well.' He put out his open hand, as if asking forgiveness.

Melanie appeared at his side. 'Claude is looking for you,' she told Ross. He hesitated, then apologised to Katherine, and left. Melanie and Katherine faced each other. This time, there was no bright flare; this time Katherine could hold her own. And Melanie did not look well. Beneath heavy makeup her face was drawn and her eyes heavy, and her full-length orange dress, beside Katherine's black one, looked garish. But she smiled so gaily that Katherine found herself smiling back. 'How you look,' Melanie murmured. 'Amazing. I might not have recognised you.' Katherine had to strain to hear her voice. 'Is it the fog? Or sexual variety? I understand either one improves the complexion, though in your case so much is improved you must be having a great deal of variety.'

Katherine's smile disappeared. Her head felt constricted. *What have they been saying about me, among themselves?* Across the room, a movement caught her eye. Victoria had raised her hand to her hair, and as Katherine looked her way, she winked. Katherine was dumbfounded. Serene and regal in her tapestried palace, Victoria winked. Katherine's head cleared; she smiled gratefully and turned back to Melanie. 'I had help from generous friends,' she said pleasantly. 'Instead of ambushes from insecure women.'

'Why you little bitch.' Melanie's smile became rigid. 'If you think you can talk that way just because Derek has been squiring you around, keeping tabs on you so he'll know where your husband is –'

'What?'

'Oh, come. Come now. You can't think he's been seeing you for your charm and wit. Derek? Who can have any woman he wants? I know Derek so well – if you didn't have a wandering husband who needs careful handling if he wanders back, Derek would have trouble remembering your name.'

Katherine drained her glass of champagne. 'Perhaps Derek takes me out because I provide relief from relatives who know him so well. Excuse me,' she added icily and crossed the room to refill her glass.

'What did you do to Melanie?' Derek asked. He took Katherine's arm with a possessiveness that ran along her skin like warm fingers. She saw Melanie watching, and Ross, too, and pulled away. 'And what are you afraid of?' he added.

'Not knowing the truth. Derek, why do you –?' She stopped. This was not the time to ask him. 'Where are the children? Have they been banished?'

'I'm afraid not. Victoria and Tobias plan to turn them loose on that Everest of gifts beneath the tree. Shall we find a quiet corner away from flying Erector sets?'

'I'd rather stay; I enjoy watching them.'

'Criticised and judged,' he murmured. 'We wouldn't have stayed away long in any case. I want to watch you open your presents.'

She looked alarmed. 'Why? Derek, we didn't bring anything elaborate.'

'Then we shall send you home,' he said lightly. 'I like what you've done with your scarf.'

She had draped it around her neck, the fringed ends hanging down her back, altering the look of the black cashmere dress. 'I'm glad,' she said. 'I was afraid black would be too sombre. No one else is wearing it.'

'No one else looks like you. What did you say to Melanie?'

'It isn't important.'

'If I ask about it, it is important.'

'Then I'd better practise my answers. Thank you, Tobias,' she said, as Tobias appeared behind her and kissed her cheek.

'Meaning, you thank me for my kiss?' asked Tobias. 'Or for diverting you so that you need not answer Derek?'

'You, at least,' said Derek, 'are never at a loss. How dull that must be, Tobias. Katherine, we sit together at dinner. I'll see you then.' He went off and Katherine saw him silhouetted against the window with Melanie.

She closed her eyes briefly. In half an hour, the family had entangled her in its web. 'I've been talking to Ross,' said Tobias. ' "We boil at different degrees." '

'Who does?'

'Ralph Waldo Emerson, since he wrote it, but I meant that if I were as angry as I think Ross is, I would boil over. But Ross controls himself. Now what, we ask, is Ross angry about?'

'I don't think it's my business.'

'It is, however, mine, as I am the family biographer. Have you heard rumours of an impending divorce?'

Katherine remembered what Victoria had said. 'No,' she answered.

'How badly you lie, Katherine.' Tobias sighed. 'Did you know that William Congreve wrote, "Tho, marriage makes a man and wife one flesh, it leaves 'em still two fools"?'

She laughed. 'No. But he's probably right. Sometimes.'

'More often than not. I am across the table from you at dinner. Will we be able to talk?'

'Why wouldn't we?'

'Derek might monopolise you. Well, well, look at that; he came after all.'

Katherine followed his gaze. Jason and Ann were coming in from the vestibule and close behind them a tall, handsome man lean and darkly tanned, an older, silver-haired Ross and Derek who ignored everyone to come directly to Katherine. 'Curt Hayward,' he introduced himself. 'My son has told me about you. So have others.' Holding her hands, he stood back to look at her. 'Lovely. You have brought consternation and pleasure to this family. I understand Craig sends you money but keeps his whereabouts a secret.'

He resembled Derek more than Ross: sleek and polished, aloof, smoothly charming.

'He is in Canada,' Katherine said.

'A large country. Ah, here is Jason. We'll talk later, Katherine. I want you to know how pleased I am, for both of you, that Derek had the inestimable good sense to step in where he perceived a vacuum. Jason, a merry Christmas to you.'

Shocked, Katherine raised a hand to call him back, but Ann was hugging her, telling her how glad she was to see her. Katherine barely heard her. *He thinks Derek and I are sleeping together. Do they all think that?*

Jason and Curt shook hands; brothers who barely resembled each other. In a whisper, Ann confided, 'They've seen each other only three times in fifteen years. They never were close, you know. Brothers, of course, but not friends. That was their father's fault: Hugh always preferred Curt. Jason never forgave him for that. Fathers shouldn't favour older sons, don't you agree? It leaves scars that never heal.'

Involuntarily, Katherine looked from Ross to Derek just as Victoria, standing beside the tree, clapped her hands. 'We shall distribute the gifts. Polk, please bring in the children.' She looked doubtfully at the vast array of packages. 'Derek, will you organise them? Tobias and Ross will help. I shall watch.'

The next hour was a flurry of wrapping paper, ribbons and shouts of glee. The gifts for the children ranged from books and clothing to Erector sets and skis and, for Jennifer and Todd, a present that struck them momentarily dumb: a complete home computer with a video screen, disk drives for recording, games and school programmes, and its own printer. Jennifer read the card aloud. 'From Derek.'

'It's too much,' Katherine said to him. 'We can't accept . . .' Her voice trailed away. If he had told her in advance, she would have refused it, but now, as Todd and Jennifer looked at her with faces like two bright suns, she could not take it away.

'Mom!' They scrambled to their feet and rushed to her. 'Come look at it! We can play games and do maths and write papers for school and do puzzles –'

'How about a thank you?' Katherine said.

'Yeh, but who to? The card says Derek. Who's Derek?'

'Why, sweetheart,' Melanie said in tender amazement. 'You mean you haven't met your mother's very good friend Derek? He's standing right next to you.'

Katherine's face was hot. 'You met last June. When we were here the first time.'

Todd looked up at Derek. 'You're who Mom goes out with at night? And you bought us the computer?'

Derek held out his hand. 'How do you do? Yes, I bought it.'

'Maybe we shouldn't take it,' said Jennifer reluctantly. 'It's an awful big present from somebody who doesn't even come in the house when he takes Mother out.'

'Jennifer!' Katherine exclaimed.

'Well said.' Derek smiled faintly. 'I shall come inside, most properly, from now on. With your permission.'

'Don't ask me!' Jennifer protested. 'I don't have anything to do with it!'

'Maybe you could help us with the computer,' Todd said. 'Learn how to program it and stuff.'

'No.' Derek's face was expressionless and for the first time it occurred to Katherine that she had never heard him laugh. 'But if you have trouble with the instruction book, I'll give you the name of someone in my company who can help.'

Rebuffed, Todd stepped back. Then his face lit up. 'Bruce! He runs the whole computer at Heath's! I'll ask him!'

'Todd,' Katherine said.

'Oh. Yeh. Thanks a lot. We really – thanks a lot.'

'Thank you,' Jennifer said politely. 'If you'd like to use it sometime, please do.'

'Now,' Victoria said. 'The children have had their turn and I am anxious to see what Katherine has brought me.' She unwrapped the small round package and held up a jar, tied with a red bow, labelled 'Preserved Ginger'. 'My dear,' she said after a moment. 'Did you make this?'

Katherine nodded, unable to speak. She had known her preserves and jams and jellies would be outshone, but there was nothing else she could afford for the whole family. She had thought of making jewellery, but rejected it. Not until she was established with Mettler's, or somewhere else. And when she had arrayed the colourful jars on her coffee table at home and tied them with gaily coloured ribbons, they looked so bright and festive she thought they would be all right.

But when Victoria held one in her hand and Katherine saw how tiny and plain it looked, she knew with a sinking heart that this family would find her gifts stingily small. She'd been dreaming when she thought she might fit in with people who had enough money to buy anything they wanted.

But Victoria came to Katherine, laid a gentle hand along her cheek, and kissed her. 'How did you know preserved ginger is my favourite?' She spoke loudly enough for all of them to hear. 'Others have bought it for me but no one ever took the trouble to make it. And Tobias recently found a superb recipe for chicken with preserved ginger. You will come to dinner and the three of us will be quite gluttonous and share it with no one. Thank you so much, my dear. Now please open your gift.'

Katherine would rather have waited, but Tobias took her

234

hand and led her to a stack of boxes. 'But which one?' she asked.

'All!' he announced, his face bright with anticipation. 'From all of us – Victoria, Ross, Ann, Jason, and me. Open, open, open!'

Not Derek, Katherine thought. Not Melanie. Self-consciously, she knelt and opened the first box. Lying before her, in symmetrical order, was a complete set of American and Swedish files for use on metals – oval, square taper, knife edge, lozenge, cant, pippin, barette and crochet – in different lengths and seven degrees of fineness. Beside them lay a set of handles. Almost fearfully, Katherine touched the gleaming rows.

'They won't break, you know!' said Tobias, almost dancing in delight. 'And now the other boxes!'

She could guess what they contained. Quickly she pulled off all the wrappings until she was surrounded by open boxes of pliers, dapping die blocks, chasing tools, sanding materials, a saw and set of blades, and two small motorised wheels for buffing and polishing. She stood up, then, in the midst of a collection of jeweller's tools she had not been able to buy for herself, and looked at the family – *my family* – with a face so radiant that Derek drew in his breath and Victoria and Tobias came to put their arms round her.

'You haven't opened my gift,' said Derek, handing her a narrow box. Katherine unwrapped it and took out a strip of gold, one inch wide by ten inches long. Wonderingly, she met his watchful eyes. 'Mettler likes gold,' he said casually.

'Gold –!' Melanie exclaimed. 'Why, that must have cost –'

'I'd guess about a thousand,' said Curt approvingly.

'Vulgar commentaries have no place at Christmas,' Victoria declared. 'Or any time. Derek? Will you move the gift-giving along?'

'But I haven't thanked you,' Katherine said. She held the cool strip of gold, and stood beside the shining tools on the

235

carpet. 'You've given me the freedom to work. I don't have to borrow; I can work in my own home, in the daytime or at night; I can try different techniques and styles because I have the tools for them. Do you know what this means to me?' Tears filled her eyes. 'It's as if you've given me a life. The tools to shape a life. I can't really say it –'

'You've said it quite well,' Melanie commented sweetly. She was standing beside Derek. 'You like your freedom. I wonder if we ever heard the real story of why Craig disappeared.'

In the shocked silence, Tobias was the first to recover. Drawing himself up, he roared, " 'Farewell, farewell, you old rhinoceros! I'll stare at something less prepocerous!" '

The four children, huddled around the computer, burst into laughter. Jason, Ann and Curt laughed with them. Victoria's lips twitched, Ross chuckled, then grew quiet, and Derek smiled, watching Katherine. But she had turned away, embarrassed, because she had laughed and then seen the helpless fury in Melanie's eyes. The children rocked back and forth, repeating 'prepocerous rhinoceros!' until Victoria, holding her lips tight, signalled the butler to help them carry their gifts to the library.

'We owe Katherine an apology,' she said, but Katherine vigorously shook her head. 'Then we shall finish with the gifts and go in to dinner. Ross, I thought you and Derek were managing this. Where have you been while Tobias clowned?'

'Applauding him,' said Ross quietly, and knelt to distribute the remaining gifts.

Christmas was the one time Victoria allowed the children to eat with the adults. Everyone sat at the long table decorated with berries and chrysanthemums twined among white candles in crystal holders, and ate goose and duck, fresh cranberries with orange rind, and the largest *Bûche de Noël* Katherine had ever seen. When coffee was served, the children and Tobias

236

slipped out, to the library. Soon after Victoria and Katherine followed. By the light of a dancing fire, Tobias was reading *A Christmas Carol*, abridging it since they had begun so late. Standing, squatting, hopping and prancing about the room, he acted all the parts in a dozen different voices. Glancing at her children Katherine saw tears streaming down their rapt faces, and her own tears welled up as memories of Craig's voice mingled with Tobias's, reading those same words at their small family celebrations in Vancouver. *You had no right to leave*, she told him fiercely. She moved back into the shadows to let her tears come, and saw Ross sitting quietly near the door. An hour later when Tobias ended with Tiny Tim's 'God bless us, everyone!' she looked again, but he was gone.

'Melanie has many virtues,' Derek said on the telephone. 'But common sense, perception and discretion are not among them. Craig has nothing to do with my wanting to be with you.'

'Nothing?'

'Even if it were true, what difference would it make? When we met, you were intriguing; now I find you irresistible. And you are too intelligent to take Melanie seriously. We have plans to see the New Year in together. Nine o'clock?'

'Yes.'

A month before, in his apartment, she had known she wanted him, and she knew it when he walked through her door on New Year's Eve, reminding Jennifer that he was coming for her mother in a proper manner, nodding when Todd told him something about the computer, but never taking his eyes off Katherine. She watched him watching her, as if they were playing a game: Katherine telling him with her eyes that she wanted him, and Derek's eyes appraising and caressing the exquisite vision in black and white, lace and taffeta, and the strong yet delicate lines of her face that at last, freed of despair and a sense of inferiority, glowed with an arresting beauty. He took a long breath. 'I think I will not make love to you in front of your children,' he murmured, and swept her out the door.

They kissed in his car. Katherine felt the rush of her body's demands before they pulled apart and Derek started the car. She rested her head against the back of the seat as they sped up steep Christmas-wrapped streets to a white mansion ablaze with candles and technicolour lights.

The three floors had been transformed into a carnival. Crowds of guests tried their skill at sharpshooting and base-ball-pitching booths, darts, bowling, and fishing in a tub for sterling silver dolphins; others watched a striptease show in a tent on the third floor, acrobats in another tent, and, in a third, trained dogs doing mathematical calculations and barking rhythmically to Christmas carols played on a trumpet by a foot-tapping clown.

'Slightly overdone,' Derek commented dryly. 'But they were afraid of being anonymous among the rich.'

'They've made everyone else anonymous,' Katherine said, as they made their way through the rooms.

'Good God, Derek!' exclaimed a thin, moustached young man. 'How have you discovered this beauty before me? I thought I was always a step ahead of you.'

'No one is ever ahead of Derek,' said a dark, burly man. He bent over Katherine's hand. 'Brock Galvez. A pleasure. Derek –' They shook hands. 'Have you been upstairs? Some madman has taught dogs to bark "The First Noël" '.

Derek looked at Katherine. 'Shall we avoid them? Or would you like to go up there and work our way down?'

'After the dogs.' Katherine said, 'perhaps one can only go up.'

As Galvez laughed, they smiled at each other. 'What would you prefer?' Derek asked.

'Whatever you like.' Swaying towards him, her eyes meeting his, Katherine was strung as tight as a fine wire. The sensuous play of taffeta and lace against her skin, the open admiration on all sides. the deafening chatter and music, left her open to the wild fantasies of the carnival and the dreamlike evening. There were no responsibilities, no restrictions – and no Craig. She was alone with Derek.

At midnight they toasted the New Year, kissing lightly, and ate dinner with some of Derek's friends who were in the state legislature. At one-thirty, when they left, Katherine discovered that a crowd was coming with them to Derek's apartment. 'Tired of the dogs,' said a redhead. 'You can't have a romantic New Year's Eve with a bunch of dogs barking Christmas carols. Pretty fucking unromantic, in fact.'

They all settled themselves in the leather and chrome and glass of Derek's living-room. The doors to the Victorian room were closed. 'Katherine,' said a woman whose long black braids were wrapped about her throat like a scarf. 'Could I have a gin and tonic?'

Katherine looked for Derek but he was in the den, putting on a tape of music. So she became his hostess, moving through the rooms, showing guests to the bathrooms, and helping them fix their drinks. When the telephone rang she started to answer it, but stopped. After all, it wasn't her house. But by three-thirty, when Derek had smoothly urged the last guest out, she felt almost as if she did live there.

'Well done,' he said. 'You were magnificent.'

She raised her head higher. 'Was that a test?'

'Not after the first five minutes. Come with me.'

He opened the doors to the Victorian room and she followed him to the red velvet couch. 'Derek,' she said. 'Do you turn everything into a drama?'

'Only for those who can play it out. Do you want a drink?'

'No.'

She leaned towards him, then paused, fearful of the surge of her passion, but Derek held her, his mouth on hers, forcing her back against the arm of the couch. Katherine opened her mouth and kissed him, her arms tightening around his shoulders as his hand covered her breast.

But she felt suddenly that she could not breathe, and pulled her mouth free. 'Wait,' she whispered. 'I don't –'

'Oh yes you do. You want this, you've missed it, and you've known all evening you would lie under me tonight. My God you were superb – it's not often I'm taken by surprise but you –' He kissed her again, his tongue possessing her mouth. 'My exquisite creature,' he murmured.

Like a pause in a storm, Katherine's passion was arrested in its flight. Derek's words echoed starkly. My creature. My possession. No, she thought. But the fantastic carnival still throbbed within her, and when Derek slid down the zipper on her blouse and it lay like a black lace cloud about her waist, her thoughts fled; she knew only that for six months she had been starving, and now held in her arms . . . a feast.

Slipping off her camisole, Derek held her breasts in his hands and bent over them, his tongue playing slowly on one nipple and then the other. Katherine gave a low sigh as the long surf that was like his voice swept through her.

'My God,' he said, and something in his voice told her he did not usually wait so long for a woman.

'Why –?' she murmured but he was leading her to the bedroom, and the question drifted. He laid her on the bed and bent over her, his mouth opening hers, his tongue deep against hers, as he pulled off her skirt. The sounds from outside grew faint, carried away like pebbles in the windstorm that roared in Katherine's ears.

And then, cutting through it, the telephone rang. Derek did not move. 'Derek,' she said against his mouth.

'Ignore it.'

'No, wait.' She struggled to sit up. She had heard the telephone earlier and ignored it. Now it shattered the last spell of the carnival and stilled the roaring in her ears. 'Please answer it.'

'I will not answer it; are you mad?'

'Then I will.'

Expressionless, he contemplated her.

'I should have answered it earlier. I left this number with Annie. Something may be wrong at home.'

Without a word, he reached down to the lower shelf of the nightstand and handed her the telephone. She picked it up at the start of another ring. 'Yes?' The word was a whisper. She cleared her throat. 'Yes?'

'Mommy!' Jennifer cried. The words reverberated through Katherine's head. 'Come home in a hurry! Daddy's here!'

Chapter 10

Past all the revellers weaving homeward, Derek drove in
silence, his face a mask. Occasionally, disconcertingly, he
chuckled.

He had begun in his bedroom, when Jennifer's piercing
voice reached him. In one swift motion he was off the bed and
across the room, chuckling, then laughing aloud. 'Did it again,
by God! Fifteen years and he's still cutting me off, that son of
a bitch. Still doing it, as if he never left. It's almost comforting,
knowing how little the world changes. Come on; I'm sure
you're in a hurry to get back to hearth and home.'

She was pulling on her skirt. 'You don't have to take me.'
His laughter and his words clanged against the guilt swelling
inside her, making her feel sick. She wanted to be alone. 'I'll
get a cab.'

'You'll go in my car.'

They drove in silence, his low car flying along the

Embarcardero to Market Street and then across town, cutting off other drivers, barely slowing at red lights, until they reached the Sunset, where Katherine's neighbours had long since gone to sleep and the only light that burned was hers. Braking sharply at her building, he smiled thinly. 'Give him my regards.'

Katherine opened the car door, but a sudden reluctance held her back. 'Thank you for –' It was lame and feeble; there was nothing she could say. 'The party,' she finished, and began to step out.

He stopped her by lifting her hand to his lips. 'Katherine, you were magnificent. At the party, at my home, with me.' She shuddered. 'And I wish you joy with your husband.'

'I don't know . . .' she said, and stepped onto the sidewalk. As soon as she closed the door, Derek slammed the car into gear and tore away, leaving her to meet Craig.

But when she walked in, she was met with silence. No one saw her come in; no one greeted her. The room was empty. No, not empty; Jennifer and Todd were curled up on the couch, asleep. As if a vice had been released, Katherine's thoughts flew in all directions. *Where is he*? She crossed the room to look into the kitchen. Empty. She felt a premonitory chill. The bedroom. A husband would wait for his wife in bed. Her skirt rustled in the silence as she took three long steps and jerked open the door. But the two beds, neatly made, were empty.

'Jennifer,' Katherine whispered, kneeling beside the couch. 'Jennifer.'

'Mommy!' Jennifer sat bolt upright and looked about the room, squinting in the light. 'Where's Daddy?'

'He's not here. Jennifer, are you sure he was? You didn't have a dream that seemed so real –?'

'He *is* here! He is! He's been here since midnight! Todd and I were waiting for the New Year and Daddy came and we called you. We called and *called* but nobody answered, and

Daddy said he had to leave but finally you answered and he said we should go to sleep 'cause it was so late and he'd sit with us and wait for you. He can't be gone! He said he'd wait! *Why did it take you so long to get here?*'

'I was on the other side of town.'

Todd woke, rubbing his eyes. 'Dad?'

'He left!' Jennifer cried. 'Without even telling us!' She clenched her fist and looked narrowly at Katherine. 'Daddy doesn't like Derek, does he?'

They're going to blame it on me. 'Did he say that?' Katherine asked.

'No – but he said he was lonely – he called us in Vancouver in *October* and the phone was disconnected and he asked somebody to get our address from the post office and that's how he knew where to send the money. But then he asked where you were and we said a New Year's party with Derek, and Todd said you went out with Derek all the time, and when you answered the phone at Derek's house that was when Daddy said we should go to sleep.' Her eyes met her mother's with a woman's knowing look. 'So he could leave. Just like he did before.'

'Don't imagine things,' Katherine said sharply. 'Just tell me what happened. He came here at midnight?'

'He knocked on the door,' Todd answered. 'So I looked through the window like you said to when we're alone, after Annie goes across the hall. And there he was! Just the same as ever!'

'Thinner,' Jennifer said. She screwed up her face. 'He promised he'd wait for you!'

'He hugged us and hugged us,' said Todd. 'And he looked in the kitchen and the bedroom and everywhere. He opened all the closets and drawers and he asked where his big desk was –'

'He asked if we sold it!' Jennifer said loudly. 'What does he

244

think we are, anyway? We told him it was waiting for him in Vancouver, in storage, 'cause there's no room for it here.'

'And then?' Katherine asked. She was sitting on the hassock, head bowed, arms around her knees. Her children's voices drifted to her as if from far away; she tried to picture them with their father, but instead she saw a stranger poking through her house.

'He looked all over your worktable,' Todd went on. 'And picked up his picture and looked at it and then, real careful, put it back and said he knew you wouldn't forget. And then we all sat on the couch and he gave us our Christmas presents. Only –'

'Only what?' Katherine asked.

Todd opened a box and took out an Icelandic sweater. He held it against his shoulders. 'It doesn't fit.'

'It's too small,' said Jennifer scornfully. 'So's mine.' She dangled another sweater by a sleeve, trying to turn disappointment into anger. 'Doesn't he know we've grown up? He didn't think about that! He just pretended everything was exactly the same as when he left!'

'He didn't know,' Katherine said. Clasping the soft wool sweaters between her hands, she buried her face in them, tears burning her eyes. 'But he tried.'

'He said Christmas was awful.' Todd's voice was sombre. 'Awful lonesome, and he missed our house and he missed us . . .'

'What else did he say?'

'He told us about Alaska – he's working there – he didn't say doing what. Maybe the pipeline. Or something else. He wasn't real definite.'

'Not about anything.' Jennifer looked at her mother again with the same woman's look: a child growing up too quickly. 'He was hard to talk to. It was like he had all these secrets and the more we asked, the more he closed up. He kept changing

245

the subject the way you do when you don't want to talk about something. He'd ask about school and stuff. Or you. Mainly you.'

'What about me?'

'Everything –'

'Boy, was he surprised!' Todd broke in. 'We were talking about Christmas and we showed him the computer and your jewellery tools and we told him about Carrie and Jon's train and the Atari games in the library and he kept saying, but who? Who? Like an owl.' He laughed, then hiccupped, and his eyes filled with tears. 'Mom, he looked so sad.'

He crawled into Katherine's lap, crushing the two sweaters and she held him tightly in her arms. 'Jennifer,' she said. 'What did you tell him?'

'He didn't know we knew the Haywards. He didn't even know we knew about them being his family. You know that story about the man who slept for twenty years – Rip Van Winkle – and then woke up and didn't understand why everything was different? Daddy didn't understand either. He looked all confused and he kept shaking his head. We told him how we sold the house and moved here, and Leslie helped you get this job at Heath's and about your jewellery order that's going to make you famous and Todd said you looked all different, like a princess, and started talking about dinner at Great Grandmother's –'

'And Daddy said, in this loud voice, "Who?"' interrupted Todd. 'And I said Great Grandmother Victoria, of course –'

'And Daddy shook his head real hard and we said that was what she told us to call her, and she is our great grandmother, isn't she? And Todd told about Tobias and the prepocerous rhinoceros and –'

'And Derek.'

'Sure. Everybody. Then when you answered the phone at Derek's house, Daddy said something real quiet, we couldn't hear it, and he said we should go to sleep while he waited for you. I didn't want to go to sleep, Mommy, but I was awful tired. And it took you so long to get here.'

'He brought you a present, too,' said Todd, picking up a small box from the floor. 'Oh, here's a letter. I didn't see it before.'

Slowly, Katherine opened the box. Wrapped in cotton lay an ivory bracelet, delicately carved with flocks of birds. Inscribed on the inside were the words 'I love you'.

'Oh, beautiful,' Jennifer breathed.

'Well, you shall wear it,' said Katherine. 'Since your sweater didn't fit. Here. Try it on.'

'Too big.' Jennifer turned it on her narrow wrist.

'No, it's perfect; it's not supposed to be tight. You keep it, for special occasions.'

Jennifer looked at her shrewdly. 'When will you wear it?'

'Someday. I'm busy making my own jewellery right now, remember?'

Todd had opened the envelope. 'It says "Dearest Todd and Jennifer," but I can't read it.' He handed it to Jennifer.

' "I'm sorry",' Jennifer read. ' "I can't – can't wait for –" ' She shook her head. 'It's hard to read.' She gave it to Katherine. 'You can read it. It's probably really for you, anyway.'

' "Dearest Todd and Jennifer",' Katherine read aloud, making out Craig's hurried scrawl.

' "I'm sorry I can't wait for your mother after all; it's late and I have to leave. But I promise someday we'll all be together again, for good, the way we used to be. Remember what I told you: sometimes things happen to us that we can't help, and then we have to go away. I love you and I love your mother and I didn't want to go away but I had to. Please believe me. Maybe I can make you understand when I come back – as soon as I get everything straightened out. That's what I'm trying to do now. Tell your mother that, she'll believe it because she believes in me and she loves me and as long as I know she's waiting for me, I know I can work everything out and we'll be happy again. I'll see you as soon as I can get back. Take care of your mother, tell her XXXXXXXXXXXXXXXXXXXXXXX I love her. And I love you, and miss you all. Dad".'

Craig's letter lay on the worktable for a week, while Katherine tried to make out the words he had crossed out. The first was 'Derek'. The others had been marked out so heavily the paper was torn. *Take care of your mother; tell her Derek* – what? Tell her Derek does not like her husband? Derek already told her. Tell her Derek will want to take her to bed? She knows that – and she wanted it, too. Tell her Derek holds the power in the family? She knows it. Tell her Derek has a streak of cruelty? She knows it. Tell her Derek quarrelled with Craig on a sailboat fifteen years ago? She knows it; she knows it; she knows it. *Tell your mother* – what?

Each night, after Jennifer and Todd were in bed, she stared at the letter until she could no longer sit still, then, asking Annie to keep her door open for a while, she walked the short distance to the ocean. Beneath the steady beat and whoosh of breaking and receding waves, her fury grew. *He was still keeping secrets from her.* The blackened space in his letter was just like the spaces in their marriage.

But he did say he'd be back, she told herself, and help us understand what happened. He'll tell us what he's been through, what he's been thinking –

How can he, if he couldn't even face me, or write down what was in his mind?

He might have been able to, a small voice responded cuttingly; if you hadn't been with Derek.

I don't know that for sure, she thought angrily. I don't know why he left. I don't know why he crossed out what he started to write.

Her tears mingled with the salty mist from the ocean. How could she ever know what he was thinking if he kept shutting her out? I'll never know who he is, she thought despairingly, if he keeps running away. *Tell your mother –*

Damn it, tell me yourself!

There was no one she could talk to. Victoria and Tobias were in Italy for a month; Leslie knew the family only through Katherine's eyes; Ross didn't seem to have time to talk to her; and Derek – how could she ask Derek what he thought Craig might have written? Besides, Derek had not called.

'So call him,' Leslie said a week after New Year's Eve. 'Times have changed, you know; we no longer languish beside the telephone, faint and frail, waiting for our master's voice.'

Katherine shook her head. She was twisting a soft piece of wire around her wrist, imagining it in gold. 'I don't want to call him. I'm not proud of myself. I don't think I like either of us very much right now.'

Leslie sat back on the couch. 'Don't you think you're making too much of it? You only wanted a simple screw, not something that – OK, I'm sorry, don't look at me as if I'd suggested roast thumbs for dinner. You don't mind not seeing him? Or having him around?'

'No.'

'My, my,' Leslie drawled with a grin. 'What a change from the early days.'

Katherine took off the wire bracelet, and laid it gently beside a sketch of a matching ring. 'Sometimes I think so . . . and sometimes I don't. Last summer I was terrified at having to make my way without Craig. In some ways I still am, because

I don't understand myself. What kind of woman lives with a man for ten years and doesn't see through him? I feel like a blank slate, starting from scratch. Not even a name. Fraser isn't Craig's name, so it isn't mine either.'

'You've used it for ten years; it's yours. And about seeing through a man – I don't know. We see what we want to see. You knew he had secrets, but you liked what you had with him, so you didn't push. I don't think you'd be that way if you met him now. You're more demanding. Not so anxious to be protected. If you hadn't changed, you'd be calling Derek.'

Katherine laughed slightly and picked up the gold. 'Do you think his gold would make a good substitute?'

'You could try. I know a lot of men who love it more than sex.'

They laughed, but in fact it was Derek's gold that Katherine thought most about in the next two weeks. She had been afraid that Jennifer and Todd would slip back to their early sullenness after Craig left a second time, but instead they were strangely cheerful and, after the Christmas vacation, very busy at school. When Katherine talked to them about Craig, they answered politely, but she saw they were uncomfortable with what they had discovered: their father was alive and had come to see them; he said he loved them and loved their mother; he sent them money. But he would not stay with them.

Awed by the immensity of those facts which they could not understand, they pushed them out of sight. 'Vancouver is gone,' said Todd one day. 'A fleet of a hundred dolphins came along and swallowed it up. Once in a while, when they burp, a piece of our old house might come up, but Vancouver is *gone*.'

'You know it's still there, Todd,' Katherine said gently.

'Not for us,' he insisted, and she let it go. In a way he was right; Vancouver didn't exist for them. There would be time enough to resuscitate it if they were ever to go back. Right now, it was more important to Katherine that the three of them were busy and looking ahead, instead of back.

Every day she carried books to read on the bus and on her lunch hour: art books and books on design, architecture, folk art and archaeology. At night and at the weekends, she was at her worktable until twelve or one o'clock, and by the third week of January, she had finished her sketches and models. The day she made her first cut in the gold strip Derek had given her, Leslie came to watch.

'An important moment; I didn't want to miss it. If you don't mind an audience.' Bent over her work, Katherine shook her head. Leslie looked about, a puzzled expression on her face. 'Something's changed.'

'I did some rearranging,' Katherine said, concentrating on the lines she was scoring in the gold. 'I needed more room.'

'I should say,' murmured Leslie. Shelves now filled the wall above the worktable, stacked with boxes holding Katherine's new tools. Other tools hung from hooks or were spread on her worktable and a new folding card table nearby. Empty Heath's shoe boxes on the floor beneath the worktable held wires, string, solder and other supplies. Craig's picture was gone.

'It's in the children's room,' Katherine said as Leslie eyed the spot on the worktable where it had stood since August. She bent to her work again, scoring lines in the soft gold where she would make cuts.

Leslie watched in silence. When Katherine picked up one of her new saws and fastened a blade in it, she said, 'It is a substitute for Derek, isn't it? And maybe for Craig? The way you handle that gold.'

Katherine laughed. 'No, it's not a substitute. But if you don't have love, you ought to have work you love to do.'

'I read that somewhere,' said Leslie. 'That the two things we

251

can't do without are love and work. I wish to hell I wasn't battling all the time at Heath's. Since love does not cast a rosy glow over me and Marc, or me and anybody, I could use a fun job. That's all I ask.'

'I wish you had one,' Katherine said, and then concentrated on making the cuts in her piece of gold. But later, after Leslie was gone, the words still echoed in the room. Love and work. She gazed at her collection of shining tools, her sketch pads and the materials she had gathered, waiting to take shape under her fingers. Craig was in the background; Derek was gone. I have my work, she thought. And at least for a while – she smiled to herself – it's plenty.

Heath's profits were down for the six months ending in mid-January. Even the post-Christmas shopping spurt had not changed the percentages; profits were below what they should be. Someone had to be at fault, and at the Tuesday morning executive meeting, fingers were pointed at Leslie McAlister, vice president for Personnel and Payroll.

'The computer and I have become one,' she said wearily to Marc on Friday night, collapsing beside him in a booth in a lounge high above Union Square. 'I pushed that crew to buy it; now I do nothing but defend it.'

'Why bother?' he asked.

Looking through the window, she said wryly, 'You could have chosen a place where the view wouldn't have included Heath's.'

'Look beyond it.'

'You mean literally.'

He shrugged. 'You could get a job anywhere. If they attack you for your pet project, why waste your time on them?'

'Because we took inventory yesterday and got some crazy numbers, and one explanation might be that my pet project fouled up.'

He looked at her with the shrewdness that sat so strangely on his plump face. 'Pet project or pet programmer?'

'Both.' She sighed. 'Bruce scares me sometimes; he's so damned laid back I'm not sure what he'd think is a joke. Like feeding false information into the computer.'

'What false information?'

'That theft is only one and a half percent –' She stopped abruptly. 'I don't see a drink before me. Has everyone gone on strike?'

'I'm sorry. Your usual?' She nodded and he ordered for both of them. 'My dear Leslie, you can talk to me.'

'It's confidential. You know that.'

'Then let me guess. The computer says theft is one and a half percent. Considerably below industry average. Most stores would cheer at such news. Why, then, is Leslie McAlister worried? Because she thinks someone is giving the computer false information so that it pumps out a false figure. And if someone is going to all that trouble, the correct figure must be higher.' Taking out a pencil, he began figuring on his paper napkin. 'Retail stores . . .' he murmured. 'Average theft . . . Heath's annual volume approximately one hundred million dollars . . . an additional loss of . . .' He eyed Leslie. 'I'd guess that what worries Leslie McAlister is that someone is robbing Heath's of approximately a million dollars in merchandise and fixing her pet project so the numbers balance and it doesn't show up. How close am I?'

She put out her hands and let them fall. 'On the button.'

He nodded with satisfaction. 'And you propose to investigate a million dollar loss and keep it confidential?'

'I don't propose; I hope, and I try. Marc, it's my job; anything that happens from now on is going to be dumped on my doorstep. One of my fellow executives even reminded me today that I got my brother a job as a programmer. Any way you look at it, or any way *they* look at it, I'm responsible.'

'Not for computers, for God's sake. No one even understands them, much less willingly takes responsibility for them. Blame the devil. The tides. Sun spots. The Lord. Who probably doesn't understand them either, but at least is big enough to shoulder the blame for them.'

She laughed. 'Thank you, Marc. You do put things in perspective. And yes, though you haven't asked, I would like another vodka martini. Well!'

'Well?' He gave the order to the waiter as Leslie bent to look more closely through the window. 'What attracts your attention so far below?'

'A sports car that looks familiar. And a woman getting into it. I think I know that coat.'

'What woman?'

'It's not important.' She turned back to him and thoughtfully ran her finger around the edge of the glass the waiter put before her. 'Just that I didn't know they were seeing each other again. They had a – misunderstanding on New Year's Eve and I thought she'd have told me if they'd cleared it up. Maybe I'm just feeling left out; things happening without my knowing it.' As she took a drink, she saw his quick frown. 'I gather I'm talking about myself too much. Sorry. Your turn.'

'No. I have no intention of spending the evening with a nervous woman. I want you at your best or not at all. So tell me – you aren't really frightened of those idiots at Heath's.'

'You're damn right I am; I'm scared stiff. Marc, can't you understand that those idiots, as you call them, control my future?'

'You should never allow anyone to control your future. Go elsewhere.'

'I don't want to go elsewhere. I want to stay at Heath's. It's been my whole life for ten years; I've built a small power base there and I won't throw it away or let anyone take it from me.'

She looked at her hands. 'As for allowing others to control my future – you're right: I don't like it. But it goes with the way I make my living and I can deal with it. It might be different if we were talking about my private life.'

'My dear Leslie, are you asking me to marry you?'

'God forbid.' She laughed. 'I don't want to marry you, Marc, any more than you want to marry me. But I've been thinking –' She sipped her drink and said carefully, 'My life doesn't seem to have much . . . shape. Or meaning. Other than making Heath's bigger and better, of course. I need something more.'

'A hobby? Leslie, if you're thinking of making jewellery –'

'No; good Lord, no. I'm thinking of making a baby.'

'I beg your pardon?'

'Don't look so shocked. Women often think about having babies. It's easy when they're married; harder when they're not. I've been thinking about this a long time, trying to figure out what I need, and I've decided what I need is to be responsible for someone else. The way I live – most of the time I'm thinking about me. It's a little . . . narrow. Maybe it's being with Katherine and her kids; whatever it is, I want more than what I have now.'

He nodded. 'I see that. And why are you telling me?'

'Because I'm not so young. I have to decide pretty soon and there aren't many men I like well enough to ask. Marc, if I decide to have a child, would you be the father?'

He looked at her, momentarily paralysed. 'I thought I was beyond surprises.' She waited. 'With what strings attached?' he asked.

'Not one. My child, my little family, my income, my cherishing. I'm talking about a seed, not a contract.'

'You understand, it would change everything. I would not adjust my schedule to fit an infant's. It would be impossible to continue what we have now.'

'Of course.'

'Well, then,' he said amiably. 'If you're serious about attaching no strings, and if you put that in writing, I would consider it.'

'Fair enough.' She put her hand on his. 'Let's talk about something else. Make me laugh and forget profits and computers and my advanced age. Tell me about the jewellery business.'

'It prospers. No matter how bad the economy, there are always people who make money, and spend it, especially on jewellery. Mettler tells me he can't keep enough twenty thousand dollar watches in stock. He sold two necklaces at a quarter million each within a week of showing them. There are those who worry about groceries and those who worry about satisfying the greed of wives, mistresses and lovers. Fortunately, I deal with the second group.'

'The rich are always with us.'

'Thank God. You need them as much as I. How else would Heath's survive?'

'It wouldn't. Marc, what is the matter with the waiters tonight?'

'The waiters are the same as ever, but you are impatient. And since when do you have more than two drinks before dinner?'

'Only when I need them. I've worked every night this week and after the inventory yesterday I stayed until three in the morning, getting preliminary reports –'

'My God, why didn't you tell me? You shouldn't be in a restaurant at all. Come. We're going home.'

'Whose home?'

'Mine. I will provide a massage and a sauna, champagne to clear the head, and then dinner. And bed. If you feel like it.'

She looked at him curiously. 'You know, Marc, for a selfish bastard, you can be exceedingly thoughtful.'

'My foolish, beautiful Leslie,' he said, standing up. 'Why else are you here? How many men understand that even bright, aggressive women are worth a little thoughtfulness? You yourself said there aren't many like me. I agree.' And he held her coat so they could leave.

Derek drove with his customary speed, slowing only when he turned into a short curved street. As he stopped the car before a stucco house in a manicured yard, Katherine heard the pounding of ocean surf. 'Sea Cliff,' he said, opening her door. 'The four of us grew up a block from here.'

Inside the house, enormous rooms looked out on a steel-grey ocean below a fading sunset. Among the guests Katherine recognised familiar faces, but as soon as they greeted their hostess, Derek steered her through the house to a table in a deep bay window. 'We need some privacy. I have to show myself at one of these Mardi Gras dinners every year, but that doesn't mean we can't find some quiet. And it won't be easy to talk later, at the race track.'

'Talk about what?'

'Why you're here with me,' he said. 'After deciding not to see me again.' A waitress brought an open bottle of Fumé Blanc and two glasses. Derek poured, and sat back, watching Katherine smooth the surprise from her face. Learning fast, he thought. Another few months and she could hold her own with any of them: as beautiful and carefully-dressed, her emotions as controlled, her wit as sharp. And something even more interesting: a seeming vulnerability that made others want to help her. Clever woman. Assuming she planned to give that impression.

'And why *am* I here, ' Katherine asked. 'If I'd decided not to see you again?'

'Because you're infatuated; because you've been starved for a long time and you know I can satisfy you; because I

257

bring you excitement and introductions to people who are important to your profession.'

She contemplated him over her wine glass: a different man from the one she had hungered for on New Year's Eve – harder, the flashes of cruelty closer to the surface, but his charm undiminished, his magnetism so powerful that she realised with dismay she was still attracted to him. 'Is that all?' she asked.

He smiled. 'As for why I am here, though you have not asked, it comes from wanting you. And because I expected you to call after our New Year celebration and it interested me that you did not.'

'You left out something,' Katherine said. 'You want to hurt Craig by sleeping with his wife.'

'Well I'll be damned.' The waitress paused in passing their table, hoping to hear more. But Derek waited, patient and amused, until reluctantly she moved on. 'A curious idea,' he said. 'I wouldn't have expected it from you. Did you get it from someone else?'

Katherine's voice became as cool as Victoria's. 'I'm learning not to depend on others. It was something you said, when Jennifer called.'

'That Craig had come between us? I thought it an accurate description. Craig often did that when we were children: he would smile slyly – others said sweetly – and say, to Victoria or Ann or anyone in authority, how wonderful it would be if he had – whatever it was. He never whined or complained, he almost never asked outright. He just let it be known that shy, innocent Craig would be so happy *if* . . . When it didn't work, he simply walked away. Or ran. That's his style: to run from confrontation or crisis. By now you ought to recognise it a mile away. Yes,' he said, seamlessly changing his tone of voice as a waiter approached.

'The buffet is in the dining room, but if you prefer, I can prepare some plates for you.'

'Katherine?'

'Whatever you like.' She looked at the ocean. She was ashamed, as if Derek's scorn had been for her as much as for Craig, and it made her feel stifled, closed in, wanting to run away. And she knew, as if Craig were telling her, that this was how he felt when he couldn't face whatever was happening. Craig hated it when people analysed him. He held his thoughts close and despised people who told him they could have guessed what he'd do because they knew his style. Craig, she thought, would despise Derek.

Evidently he did. And evidently it was mutual.

'Now listen to me,' Derek said when the waiter had left. 'I don't lie to women. I want you. Not because you're Craig's wife or because Ross was the one who brought you here –'

'*Ross*?'

His eyes became hooded. 'It has nothing to do with Ross. Or anyone else. I find you enchanting and elusive; if you knew me better, you would know that those are the qualities I cannot resist in a woman. It's as simple as that. I told you: I do not lie to women.'

You're lying to me, Katherine thought. But at the same moment she knew that it didn't matter. She lied, too, every time she pretended she was free. She wasn't free; she was tied to Craig, dogged by his presence and the loose ends dangling from their marriage. Earlier, when Derek called to ask her to the Mardi Gras celebrations, all she could think of was that it had been three weeks and she wanted to see him. Now, looking at his lean face and dark blond hair and unrevealing eyes, she remembered the precision of his hands holding her breasts and knew her body hungered for him, even though she did not like him as much as before. But none of it mattered. She was not free to sleep with him. 'I think we should be friends,' she said evenly.

His eyes flickered. 'Friends,' he repeated.

She nodded. 'Not lovers.' And as soon as she said the words, in spite of her hunger she felt a burden lift from her.

Derek raised his wine glass. 'In that case,' he said with a remote smile that meant he was already moving to other thoughts, 'To friendship.' And he touched her glass lightly with his.

The jewellery gleamed in the lamplight – necklaces, lapel pins, a linked bracelet. Nine pieces, ready to be delivered. In the quiet room, where the only sounds were the rain against the window and the muffled tapping of her hammer, Katherine sat in a circle of contentment, making a tenth piece. Beneath her fingers, the pliable gold seemed alive, shaping itself through her thoughts, as if it were part of her.

She had never worked with gold and as she curved its sensual gleam into a bracelet she felt the exhilaration of working with what jewellers called the king of metals. For centuries it had beckoned toward exploration and conquest; in Katherine's living-room, it meant something else. Professionals used gold.

She had dipped into her savings to buy silver, so the gold would last longer. but not even worries about money could invade her contentment. She was shaping beautiful things to be sold in one of the finest shops in the city; in the other room her children slept after the three of them had spent the evening reading and laughing together; she saw Leslie frequently, and once or twice a week Derek took her to dinner or a party. That, she acknowledged, was not always easy. He was charming and cool and made no demands, but, though her mind knew what it wanted, her body still wanted Derek and sometimes she thought it would be easier simply to stop seeing him. But that would mean giving up the gilded evenings he offered. She wondered whether Derek and his evenings were inseparable. Probably. When she got over one, she would no longer need the other.

The golden bracelet lay with its matching necklace of thin gold textured discs in a cotton-lined box. Eight other pieces lay in separate boxes. Katherine stood beside her worktable, studying them, listening to the rain. She knew they were good; tomorrow Mettler would tell her what he thought. Tomorrow, she repeated; tomorrow.

The rain was still falling the next morning, blowing in long sheets across the pavement. Katherine heard it behind her as she entered the store, and then it was gone. In Herman Mettler's office, the only storms were those he made himself.

'They're very good,' Mettler said, turning Katherine's jewellery in his splayed fingers as if he were inspecting fruit for rotten spots. 'Very good technique. Excellent technique. More than Tony has taught you – individual touches here and there – very good – very good technique.'

'Thank you.' Katherine shifted in her chair.

'I place great emphasis on technique,' Mettler said, putting his palms together beneath his chin as if he were praying. 'The best design in the world can be ruined by poor technique.'

She nodded, twisted inside so tightly she thought she would snap, waiting for him to talk about design.

'However, the reverse is also true. The best technique in the world cannot disguise weak design.'

Katherine sat on the edge of her chair, her back straight.

His hands still praying, Mettler looked down at the boxes of jewellery, jumbled from his handling. 'These pieces, now. Excellent technique. Very impressive. But the design, I fear, leaves something to be desired.' He paused and gave her the same cool inspection he had given her jewellery. 'Frankly, I'm surprised that a woman as attractive as you would be so cautious. Beautiful women can afford to take chances other women cannot. So why do you bring me safe designs similar to those I see in other fine stores?' He leaned back in his chair. 'Customers only buy technique when they pay a high price for design. Am I making myself clear? These are nice pieces, pleasant pieces, superbly made. I have no doubt that I can sell them, and I intend to, but in the cases in the rear, not those up front. Our customers expect uniqueness at Mettler's. They are willing to pay for it. I see nothing here that is remotely unique.'

Furious, Katherine bit her lip to keep quiet. He could have softened his criticism. But suddenly Victoria's voice came to her. *You need a little eccentricity. To be so proper . . . at your age . . .*

Mettler was waiting. Hastily, she said, 'I was worried that you might not buy anything too different, from someone new . . .'

'No, no, no: what nonsense. You've studied our display cases? Then you know how much we value the avant-garde. The excellent avant-garde, of course; we are not interested in the merely sensational. Your designs are neither. They are simply – rather ordinary. In any case –' Shooting his cuff to look at his watch, he became brisk. 'As I said, I intend to sell these. And you brought prices. Good.' Reading from her list, he jotted figures on his notepad. 'One hundred for the bracelet . . . not much for your labour there. I'll have to charge five hundred; my competitors would run me out of town if I charged less. And you want fifty for the . . .' He talked to himself for a while. 'All right. Your total is fine; twelve hundred for the ten pieces. And I can take another dozen, even if they're like these. There is always a market for the tried and true. I need them by June, for our fall collection. Thank you, Mrs Fraser. I'm sure we'll work well together.'

'But –'

Mettler's secretary appeared in the doorway, invisibly sent for. Katherine stood up. Twelve more, four months from now. Not enough to quit her job; not enough to make a name for herself. All her dreams were sliding away. But Mettler, looking again at his watch, would not know that. She held out her hand, surprising him into shaking it. 'Thank you,' she said, her voice strong. 'I'll get them to you as early as possible.'

And downstairs, lingering beside the glass cases at the front of the store, she vowed to herself that that was where her next twelve pieces would be displayed. Somehow, she thought as she left to face Lister's sarcastic wrath for being late – next time, I'll find a way to make Herman Mettler sit up and take notice.

Victoria and Tobias had been back from Italy only a few days when they called, separately, to invite Katherine to dinner the following week. It was a blustery night, the beginning of March, and when she arrived the butler led her to the library, where she found them in front of the fire, with Ross.

'My dear!' Victoria exclaimed. rising to kiss her, and Ross turned, as startled as Katherine. In the flickering light, she had thought at first it was Derek; then, in a swift comparison she was barely aware of, she saw that the cheekbones were not as sharp, the shadowed hollows not as deep, the mouth, even unsmiling, wider and a little fuller. His face was gentler than Derek's but not soft; in fact, as Katherine sat between Victoria and Tobias, she thought he looked as severe as he had in Vancouver, when he was forcing her to accept the truth about Craig.

He stood and greeted her formally and brought up Craig's New Year visit. 'Victoria and Tobias told me about it. He still won't give you a chance.'

Tears sprang to Katherine's eyes. He was the only one who saw exactly why she had been so hurt and angry.

He asked about her children. 'Jon and Carrie enjoyed seeing them at Christmas.'

'We might get them together some time,' Katherine said.

'We might.' They were silent. Victoria and Tobias watched with interest. Ross asked about Katherine's jeweller's tools and she asked about BayBridge and then silence fell once more. 'I was just leaving,' Ross said at last. 'I'm expected at home. I only stopped by to greet the returning travellers. I'm sorry –' He paused. 'I'm sorry we've seen so little of each other.'

'So am I,' Katherine responded, puzzled by the strain in his voice. 'But I know how busy you are. And I've been busy, too . . .'

He nodded. 'So I've heard.' Their eyes met and still he lingered. Then, turning abruptly, he bent over Victoria and kissed her. 'Lunch on Friday. Don't forget. Katherine . . . it was good to see you. Tobias, I'd like to ask you about some books I'm thinking of buying.' Tobias shrugged in silent apology to Katherine and left the room with Ross.

Victoria raised her eyebrows. 'Ross isn't usually so abrupt. But he's concerned about you, you know.'

'I doubt it,' said Katherine.

'Oh yes.' Victoria handed her a glass of sherry. 'We all are.'

Katherine was puzzled. 'Why? You can't know anything about Mettler yet.'

'Mettler? What about him? No, wait; Tobias will want to hear it, too. What we are worried about is you and Derek.'

'*Derek*?'

'Well, my dear, it's been four months. People talk when a beautiful woman is seen about town with Derek for one month, much less four. They talk to me, anyway, and to Tobias, and we were discussing that when Ross came in.'

'But what difference does it make if I go out with Derek?'

'None, as long as you don't fall in love with him.' Katherine was silent. 'Are you in love with him?'

'No. And I don't expect to be. I have a husband, you know.'

'When was that ever a guarantee –? In any event, you haven't seen your husband for almost nine months. It's natural that you would be attracted to other men. But it should not be Derek.'

Katherine drank her sherry and looked at the flames in the fireplace. 'A strange way to talk about your grandson.'

'I am saying he's not good for you. Is it strange for me to tell my granddaughter that?'

A rush of love swept over Katherine. *My granddaughter*. 'Thank you,' she said. 'You make me feel as if I belong.'

'But of course you belong,' said Tobias cheerfully, taking his seat and pouring more sherry into their glasses. 'Though we were slow to see it at first. How have you been while we romped through Italy?'

'Something is wrong about Mettler,' Victoria said, and while the butler set the table beside them Katherine described what had happened the week before.

'A pox upon him!' Tobias thundered.

'What you must do, Katherine,' Victoria pronounced as they sat at the table, 'is choose one style and one material – gold would be excellent – which will give you an identity with customers. I've been thinking about your career, my dear, and I've decided you should take advantage of your charmingly old-fashioned quality which I find so endearing.'

'Old-fashioned?' Katherine asked.

'My dear, I may be as old as the century but I am aware that, today, when a woman says she will not fall in love with someone because she has a husband, that may safely be called old-fashioned. I find it charming. Most people would, at least privately, because they long for what seems to have been a simpler past. If you pattern your designs, for example, on my antique jewellery, women will buy them.'

'No men?' asked Tobias mildly.

'Some; but women wear most of the jewellery, Tobias, you know that. You yourself wear none.'

'Who buys most of it?'

'Ah.' Victoria sat back to allow the butler to remove her soup plate. 'So you think jewellery is aimed at males. That might be. Male fantasies?'

' "Hopes and fears and twilight fantasies –" ' Tobias quoted.

Katherine was struck by the words. 'Who wrote that?' she asked.

'Shelley.' Tobias smiled, grateful for an audience. 'From *Adonais*. Would you like to hear more of it?' Without waiting, he quoted, ' "Desires and adorations . . . Splendours and Glooms, and glimmering Incarnations of hopes and fears, and twilight Fantasies; And Sorrow, with her family of Sighs –" '

'Yes,' said Victoria abruptly, her keen eyes on Katherine's sombre ones. 'But I thought we were talking about Katherine's career. Katherine, before you do anything else, you must speak to the other important jewellers in town. Herman Mettler may think he's the only one, but I myself often shop at Xavier's and Laykin Et Cie. I'll call first and tell them you're coming. Take your sketches. A pity you have no more finished pieces; it's possible no one would agree with Mettler. Especially if he made such a point of your technique.' Without warning, she struck the table. 'Bastard! To praise your technique and then call you ordinary! I remember when he was peddling fake pearls during the Depression. I shall buy nothing more from him. In fact, I shall write him a letter. If he thinks he can speak that way to my granddaughter –'

'No, please. Don't do that.' Katherine looked troubled. 'I have to make my own way. Craig forced me to do it, but now I really want to.' She smiled. 'You did say I needed to be eccentric. And my pieces really weren't unusual. I mean, I thought they were beautiful, but I wasn't trying to be different –'

'You don't need to be different,' Victoria declared. 'You must only be yourself, no one else.'

'How about a younger, successful Victoria?' asked Tobias, and the room was silent except for the whisper of the fire.

'I am not trying to force Katherine into anything,' Victoria said at last. 'She does not have to be successful for my sake. But' – she looked at Katherine through half-closed eyes – 'you want a place to belong, yet you insist on going your own way.'

'Finding my own way,' Katherine corrected quietly. 'I need a place to belong, I need your help, or, at least, your concern and interest and –'

'Love?' suggested Tobias helpfully.

'Love,' Katherine echoed. 'It makes me feel wonderful when you swear at Mettler, but I don't want you to swear at him in person. I need to win him over myself, with my work. Otherwise, I'll never know whether I'm any good or not.'

'Even if you fail?' Tobias prompted.

'Of course. I'm sorry,' she said to Victoria. 'I know you want me to succeed. But I have to know.'

After a moment, Victoria took her hand. 'Be sure to tell me when Mettler puts your pieces on display. I shall be the first to buy one.'

For a month, rumours had drifted through Heath's. Business was bad or the chain was about to be sold or somebody on the fifth floor was playing a hell of an April Fool's joke. Whatever it was, an outside accounting firm had been hired to examine the sales records of all departments, and inventories were being ordered in different departments without warning.

When an inventory of the design department was called, Gil Lister went into a frenzy. 'Do the windows!' he ordered Katherine the minute the store closed. 'Everything! Merchandise, props, every fucking champagne bottle in the wedding scene! By God, they want an inventory, I'll give them one they'll never forget!'

In the strange, cave-like windows, screened from the street, Katherine stood in the centre of a gala wedding reception, with memories of her own wedding flooding over her. She could feel Craig's arm around her waist as they stood in the judge's living-room; she could see Leslie and the judge's wife: their witnesses. In the corner a Raggedy Ann doll stared at the ceiling. Craig had said there was no one he wanted, and so they had begun their new family in a strange living-room with only Leslie as Katherine's link with her past.

In the curtained window, Katherine walked around the vacantly smiling mannequins, jotting down department and style numbers of dresses, men's cutaways, shoes, purses and gloves, glasses and bottles of champagne, trays of Polyethylene hors-d'oeuvres, silk and paper flowers. Long ago she and Craig had given parties, though never very many, and after a while they had stopped altogether. Katherine had loved every part of them, planning, cooking and cleaning for days in advance, grateful to Craig for letting her do it even though he was uncomfortable with groups of people and always breathed a sigh of relief when the last guest was ushered out.

She'd always been grateful to Craig, Katherine realised, standing in the window beside the bride and groom. First because he loved her and married her, and then, over the years, for giving her a home, for taking care of her, for being a loving father to Jennifer and Todd, for building a beautiful house and encouraging her to buy whatever she wanted to make it perfect. She gazed at the mindlessly grinning groom. She had even been grateful for her orgasms. When I had them, she thought; usually I didn't. In the last two years, when Craig had been so rushed and preoccupied, there had been almost none.

But he hadn't known that. He would have been hurt if she'd told him she wasn't satisfied. The groom leered at her, and suddenly the thought came to Katherine – no, he wouldn't. He wouldn't have been hurt at all. He'd have found some way to make it seem my fault. *He would have run from it.*

It was as if she'd turned a corner and come upon a familiar view from a different angle. 'I have to stop this,' she said aloud. 'I'm beginning to sound like Derek.' She hurried through the other window displays, scribbling numbers on her lined paper. With a final look around, she went back into the store and walked through the aisles, so eerily empty, her footsteps echoing as she went down the stairs to the basement.

The display storeroom was empty. 'Gil?' Katherine called. When there was no answer she put her clipboard on his desk and stood uncertainly, wanting to go home but afraid to leave anything undone. There was no new paperwork on her desk, but along one wall was a row of merchandise cartons packed with materials they'd removed from the windows the day before, when they created the wedding scenes. Perhaps he expected her to check them. They should have been sent back to the warehouse that morning, but the driver had been sick and though Lister had been offered a replacement, he had refused, saying he'd wait for the regular man.

I'd better do them, Katherine thought, or he'll sneer at me for being in a hurry to leave.

The dresses and shorts were neatly folded, layered with tennis rackets and hiking gear, and Katherine went through them rapidly, marking them on her master list. But halfway into the second box, she came upon a plastic bag with six Perry Ellis cardigans that had not been used in the window displays. Damn, she thought. If somebody's got new things from the receiving room mixed up with ours, it could take hours to straighten out.

Methodically, she began emptying all the cartons. In the next four, she found merchandise that had not come from window displays or the display storeroom: Francesca of Damon dresses, Anne Klein blouses, ten boxes of Hermes silk scarves. She was about to begin the fifth carton when Lister walked in. He stopped short, a doughnut halfway to his mouth. 'What the fuck are you doing?' he screamed. 'Who told you to do that? Get away from there!'

Katherine sprang to her feet. 'I'm sorry, Gil; I didn't know if they'd been done and I thought –'

'You thought! You thought! You're not supposed to think! You're supposed to do what I tell you and I told you to do the windows!'

'I did the windows! I didn't have anything else to do and –'

'And you didn't wait for my orders! How many times have I told you never to do anything unless I order it? Well? A hundred? A thousand? Ten thousand? But you've never liked that, have you, all ga-ga'd up with your new haircut, and looking down your nose like the Queen of Sheba – you and your high and mighty ideas about art and design and window decorating – but I'm the one in charge here, whatever you may think, and your sucking around a certain person on the fifth floor won't help you –'

'That – is – enough!' Shedding all her caution, Katherine strode across the room. Lister, a gleam of alarm in his eyes, scuttled backwards until he was against his desk. 'Leslie is my friend,' Katherine said deliberately. 'But I've never used that in my work here and you know it. I've taken your insults and rudeness and offensive jokes and I've never told anyone about them. I've never told anyone how many window ideas you steal from other stores. I've never told anyone how many of *my* ideas you've used and claimed credit for. Because I needed this job –' My God, she thought; I still need this job. But it was too late; the resentments of the past months were a torrent that drowned out everything else.

'You are a mean, vulgar little man, always trying to prove how important you are by crushing someone. It's usually me, because I'm the closest, but you've made life miserable for everyone who's ever worked with you. You have no artistic sense; you don't even have the tiny bit of talent that nasty people need to make others tolerate them. You have a minuscule imagination and an inflated ability to copy from others and nothing else –'

'That's enough, that's enough, that's enough!' Lister pushed himself off the desk as if it were a diving board and scampered to the other side where he sat in his high-backed leather chair, glaring at Katherine. 'Not another word! I knew you would go too far! And now you've done it; you've done it; you've gone too far! You were foisted on me and you've spent half your time on personal telephone calls and lunches –'

'That is a lie.'

'Don't call me a liar! I knew from the first day you were a social climber and a trouble-maker and a fraud and now you have the gall to criticise my artistic ability, which has *won prizes* –'

'The last one was for a window I designed.'

He began to sputter. 'You think you can hide behind McAlister – you think you know so much – you're an unreliable, stubborn, insubordinate bitch, and I want you out of here! This minute! I want you gone!'

Katherine opened her mouth but no words came. Frantically she tried to think of something to say, but all she could think of was pleading, and she could not bring herself to do it.

'Did you hear me? I want you gone!' he screeched as Katherine looked at him numbly. 'Are you deaf?'

'You're firing me.'

'Dear God, I have finally gotten through to her. Yes, yes, and yes. You are fired. Dismissed. Terminated. I have wasted enough energy on you; you are untrainable. Get out! Did you hear me? Out! Out! Out!'

The last thing Katherine heard as she walked blindly down the corridor, was Gil's high voice, following her with furious syllables. '*I want you gone!*'

271

Chapter 11

By seven o'clock in the morning, the line stretched from the front door of the building down Mission Street and around the corner. The people in front of Katherine and behind her knew each other and as the line inched forward she listened as they compared experiences with the state unemployment system. It's only a bad dream, she tried to tell herself; but the hours passed, the morning fog gave way to sunlight and a mocking blue sky, her feet hurt, and by noon, when she had learned the names of all the people around her, she admitted it was real. She was out of work and almost out of money and she was standing in line to ask the state of California for help.

It had taken her a week to decide. The first thing she had done, the day after Lister's screech followed her out of Heath's, was call Leslie and tell her she had been fired. And Leslie had been furious. But also, distracted.

272

'Shit, that little fart . . . But, Katherine, you've got along with him up to now. Why all of a sudden —?'

'I don't know; I can't even remember how it started. He was screaming at me for something — worse than his usual, I guess — and I blew up and told him off. And he fired me. I suppose he's just been waiting for me to give him a chance to do it. He said he knew one day I'd go too far; he even accused me of trying to use my friendship with you.'

'Did he?'

'Leslie? What's wrong?'

'My job and my evasive brother. But let's talk about your —'

'No, wait.' Katherine heard the note of alarm in Leslie's voice. 'Why is he evasive?'

'How do I know? He's always trying to be cute, but this is something else. Everytime I try to talk to him about his work, he scampers away. Literally.'

'As if he's up to something.'

'That's it. Katherine, I'm sorry about Gil; what do you want me to do? I'll give you a reference — and call some people in other stores —'

'What about Heath's? Aren't there any other jobs open? I'd do anything, Leslie.'

'There isn't a thing. Damn, we just filled a job in accounting.'

'Well, I don't know bookkeeping anyway.'

'Listen, can I call you back? I'm up to my eyebrows in problems over here; if you can give me a day or two —'

'Leslie,' Katherine said. 'You don't think Bruce is a criminal.'

'I'd rather not. But when I look at the evidence —'

'Real evidence? Solid? He can't be a criminal, Leslie; Jennifer and Todd are crazy about him.'

Leslie laughed. 'We'll put them on the witness stand. No, it's not solid. But it's pretty damning.'

273

'But if you believe in him . . . You did believe in him, didn't you? When you hired him?'

'And even after. Until this business started.'

'But why should that change your mind? You must have had good reasons for trusting him; were you wrong or did he change?'

There was a pause. 'Neither. He just got evasive.'

'But Bruce is like that a lot of the time, isn't he?'

After another pause, Leslie said, 'He is indeed.'

'Well, if you know that, and if you don't think you were wrong when you hired him, I think you shouldn't worry about him.'

'Be the loyal and trusting big sister?'

'What's wrong with loyalty and trust?'

Again they were silent, both of them thinking about what Katherine had said. 'Nothing's wrong,' Leslie said at last. 'Except my head. You're wonderful and I should have talked to you weeks ago. Now listen, lady, we have to find you a job.'

'Let me try on my own; you've got enough on your mind. I'll take you up on the reference, though. I won't get anything from Gil.'

'Nothing you'd want to use. I'll make some phone calls, Katherine, and get back to you in a few days. Let me know if you find something.'

And so, feeling as if she were back in Vancouver, Katherine began reading want-ads.

'Inventory clerk,' she told Tobias on the telephone a few nights later. 'The only office skill I've learned. I applied to a company in Oakland; they'll let me know tomorrow.'

'Long hours and low pay,' he said. 'When will you work on your jewellery?'

'At night. I did it before.'

'Yes indeed. And if you fail again that would be your excuse.'

'Tobias!'

' "God loves to help him who strives to help himself." '

'Oh, Tobias, don't quote things at me. If that's why you called –'

'No, no, my dear. I merely point out that as early as 500 B.C. Aeschylus was saying that we have a duty to help ourselves. Now tell me: when have you ever put a total effort into your work?'

'You might remember that I have to earn a living.'

'I haven't forgotten it. Victoria and I have been discussing a fund for you and the children while you complete the order for Mettler; it would pay your bills and buy whatever materials you need. We would deposit it directly in –'

'Tobias.'

'My dear?'

'I wish I could –' The temptation was so strong Katherine could almost taste the freedom he offered. But how much freedom did she have if she was always dependent on others, always being grateful? Leslie had found her a job, the Haywards had given her tools, Derek had given her gold. When was she going to stop taking handouts? '– but I can't. I appreciate it, I love you for offering, but I can't do it.'

But Tobias' challenge to put all her efforts into her work stayed with her. He was right, of course; she never had. Other things had always come first. But how else did anyone succeed, except by working full-time, overtime, whatever was necessary?

I could give it a few months, she thought. And that was how she found herself in the unemployment line.

It still stretched behind her as she reached the building after waiting six hours. And then she discovered it was only the beginning.

'Fill out the form on top,' a harried young woman recited, handing Katherine a packet. 'Turn it in to any one of us for orientation. Next?'

275

When Katherine returned the filled-out form, another harried young woman skimmed it. 'Looks OK,' she said. 'Earned more than $900 in the last fifty-two weeks . . . name and address of last employer . . . you didn't quit; you were fired . . . well, here's what you should know.' She rattled off four regulations requiring Katherine to look for work and to report any income during the time she was receiving unemployment. 'Any questions, read the booklet in that packet you got. It's all there. Now you'll need an appointment in two weeks . . .' She turned the pages of a calendar.

'*Two weeks?*' Katherine repeated.

'This goes to Sacramento,' the young woman said, writing Katherine's name on the folder. 'Computer there checks your salary information and to see if you were fired because of misconduct. Takes a couple of weeks, so we'll give you an appointment –'

'Misconduct.' *Unreliable*, Lister had said. *Insubordinate*. 'What kind of misconduct?'

'I don't know; they have a list.'

'If that was the reason . . . if someone is fired for misconduct –'

'Not eligible,' said the young woman. 'Usually. Might depend on the circumstances. Let's give you an appointment. April 27th. Two weeks from today. They'll figure your eligibility then and how much you get. You ought to start getting cheques a couple of weeks after that.'

A month from now, Katherine thought, writing down the date. If someone doesn't decide I've been guilty of misconduct.

And that was when the lure of Craig's money – all of it – became too strong to ignore.

'Well, why not?' agreed Tobias, cutting another piece of chocolate cake and lifting it precariously to his plate. 'If he didn't want you to use it, he wouldn't be sending it.'

'But I didn't want to use it for myself, until we were together. It isn't *money* I want to share with him.'

'Yes. Perfectly sensible. But now?'

'Now I'll use it until I know I can earn my living in jewellery . . . or get another job.'

He tilted his head quizzically. He had invited himself to Sunday dinner, bringing steaks and artichokes, and Katherine had made dessert. It was raining and the two of them sat at the kitchen table while Jennifer and Todd watched a television programme in the living-room. A regular family, Katherine thought. And in a way it was, because she could not think of any other man she would rather be with at that moment than Tobias smiling at her, his white beard wagging. 'And why will you use it now?' he asked.

'Because I owe it to Jennifer and Todd. They were terrified when I told them I'd lost my job; I could just see them thinking: first Dad, then Mom; who's left to take care of us? I had no right to talk to Gil that way as long as I'm responsible for them. Do you know, I don't even have medical insurance now? It went with my job. I have to buy some tomorrow morning and I can't afford it without Craig's money. Don't you see? I had no right to put us in this position.' She shifted uncomfortably in her chair. 'I think about Craig all the time. He must have felt this way when he began taking money from his company. There we were, the three of us, depending on him to bring home a big cheque every couple of weeks – so somehow he had to bring it home. I never realised how vulnerable people are when others are dependent on them.' She gave a small laugh and got up to refill their coffee cups. 'I don't much like it.'

'Being responsible for Jennifer and Todd?'

'Being vulnerable.'

'The same thing. Wonderful cake; should I have a third piece? No.' Sadly he pushed away his plate. 'I can still hear –

after seventy years – my first grade classmates laughing at my waddle in the gymnasium. Even after I thinned out, their laughter stayed with me and all my life it has forced me to refuse third helpings of chocolate cake. How the past does haunt us! Yes, of course Craig hated vulnerability. He hated being responsible for making Victoria and his parents happy by living up to their expectations: triumphant long-distance runner, all-A student, dutiful son and grandson . . . Well! Who wouldn't hate it? The only one he seemed happy to be responsible for was Jennifer, because she wanted only affection and companionship and gave as much as she got. Except for Ross, I think she was Craig's only friend. You should have seen those two race a sailboat! Ross sometimes went along, watching and taking lessons, and he said they were the greatest team on the water. But all of that was certainly a mixed blessing.'

Katherine watched Tobias' face change as he thought back. His beard had stopped fluttering and the lines around his mouth had deepened. 'Why?' she asked.

'Because when Jennifer took up with Derek it wasn't only Ann and Jason who were upset; Craig was nearly out of his mind. What a stew they all made!'

'*Jennifer and Derek?*'

Tobias gave her a quick look. 'That's right, you didn't know. But you should; it's part of our history. The one you were going to help me research, remember?'

'What does that mean – Jennifer took up with Derek?'

'Do you know, I'm really not sure. I was living in Boston and everything came to me secondhand. Victoria said that Ann felt a seventeen-year-old girl should go out with boys her own age, but Derek was only twenty-one, so it was probably Derek, not his age, she was unhappy about. Even then, you see, Derek was a . . . forceful person. He certainly could terrify me when he fixed me with one of those looks I could feel in my toes. But then I grew my beard, and it seemed to give me a magic

278

power to resist both his scorn and his charm. Or perhaps it was staying away for four years. The next time I came back was for Jennifer's funeral. She, poor child, had no magic powers. Victoria says she adored Derek. Actually, I think I'll have one more small piece of cake . . . Will you join me?'

'What? Oh. No thank you. Did Derek adore her?'

'I doubt it, but I wasn't privy to his thoughts or emotions, nor was anyone else. And if Jennifer was, she told no one. But, according to Victoria, her schoolwork had slipped badly and two or three months before graduation Jason and Ann forbade her to see Derek again. Always a mistake, I think. In years of teaching, I've learned that direct orders often cause mysterious chemical changes in youngsters that make them totally deaf in the presence of adults. Which is exactly what happened to Jennifer. She went right on seeing Derek, pretending to be with her girl friends at night and at weekends. Of course Jason and Ann found out and went to Curt, who told Derek he thought they should break it off. So Derek became deaf. It never fails.'

'Derek refused –'

'Ignored them all. Girls right and left calling him up – hand-some fellow, whatever you think of him – but he wanted Jennifer. And she was a lovely little thing, so alive and laughing. I've often wondered whether that quarrel on the boat between Derek and Craig was about Jennifer. Ross says he didn't hear it and Derek becomes deaf when I ask him.'

'It was about a building they were working on.'

'Is that so? Did Derek tell you that?' She nodded. 'Well, I shall ask you to tell me all about it. Still, a researcher looks for the story beneath the story. I think there was more to it. Don't you?'

'I don't know. The more I hear about your family, the less I know.'

'Or like?'

279

Her chin in her hand, she studied his face. A small chocolate crumb was caught in his white beard. She reached over to remove it. 'I like you,' she said.

'Close the door,' Leslie told Bruce as he came in. She pushed a button on her intercom. 'No calls, please.' Taking a file folder from her desk drawer, she held it out to him. 'Can you explain this?'

'Golly gosh gee sis,' he said, taking it from her. 'What's so serious you can't even give your loving bro a kiss?' But, flipping through the papers in the folder, he scowled. 'How the hell did you get this?'

'Is it yours?'

'Sure but it was in my desk – how the hell –?'

'What's inside it?'

'Is this an inquisition, sis – do I get a lawyer or what?'

'Don't be funny, Bruce. What are those papers?'

'Notes I made, I told you I had an idea – remember? – about how somebody could use the computer to rip off the store and I was going to write a program to see how it might be done, and these are my notes for it, to see if maybe for instance you could steal hot-selling stuff and change figures in the computer on just that stuff without leaving a record – are you following me? – I am of course a genius for thinking of it –'

'You are a goddamn fool. Are you saying you don't know we've suspected that something like that has been going on for months?'

Stunned into rare silence, Bruce stared at his sister. 'Those spot inventories!' he cried at last. 'Somebody is doing it? Ripping off the store?'

'Keep your voice down, damn it. Don't you understand what it means that a blueprint for stealing was found in your desk?'

'Now wait – sis, I swear in thirty extinct languages I did not know about any stealing going on and I didn't write a program to do it; I only made notes for a program – and I told you I was going to do it – *last summer!*'

She looked at him steadily. 'I don't believe you.'

'For Christ's sake my own sis –!'

'Look: you asked me to get you a job in Data Processing and then you told me you were investigating the new system – and God help me, I encouraged you – to see if it could be used to rip off the store; to close any loopholes, *you said*. In less than a year, profits are down; an audit of sales records gives figures that don't match the computer sales figures; you just said you had the idea of changing figures without leaving a record; and handwritten notes for doing it are found in your desk. Why should I believe you?'

'Search me, it sounds pretty devilish – how about the fact that your brother tells you on his honour it ain't so? Damn it sis, listen, I have to my great shock discovered that after my wild youth I really like working – *I like working here*, I wouldn't steal a fucking pair of socks because I don't want to get fired, and even if I did why why *why* would I leave the damn notes in my desk for someone to find?'

'I don't know.' Leslie sighed, watching his agitated pacing. 'Why were you trying to write your own program?'

'Sis, what is the matter with you, *I wanted to see if it could be done*, then I could write a program to *prevent* it!'

'You didn't write one that could be used?'

'Sis! I swear on the great goddess Mary Jane I didn't –'

'Well, who else could do it?'

'Only a few people in Data –' He cocked his head, thinking, then hitched up his pants. 'Time for a little detective work.'

'No. Bruce, I'm sorry, but I'm going to put you on temporary leave of absence. And it has to be without pay.'

'What the hell –!'

'Listen to me. You are in trouble around here. Your boss

281

took these notes to my boss and by now everyone thinks you're part of some theft ring. So for a while you're out.'

'Hey, now –'

'*No arguments!* I'm doing the best I can, but I've got my own problems and I can't take much more from you. You disguise your fantastic brain under a lot of bullshit, you drive me crazy, and I want you out of here while I do what I can to protect both of us. Why don't you go to San Francisco State, take some computer courses, maybe get a degree?'

'I know more than they do.'

'Probably true. Then take other courses. Or find another job. Just keep out of trouble.'

'If I'm in so much trouble, how come the police aren't hauling me off in handcuffs?'

'Because we're keeping it quiet while we try to solve it. And I'm counting on you not to talk. That's part of the deal. You don't come back if I find out you've been talking.'

'Why would I talk, I'd be arrested. Christ, my first decent job and this has to happen, shows what you get for being a good boy.'

'What you get for being a good boy is a sister who will help you and keep your job waiting for you. Go on now, I have work to do. Take care of yourself. Come to dinner on Sunday.'

He pushed out his lower lip and squinted at her. His shoulders drooped. 'You're the boss, sis, see you Sunday.'

Leslie watched him drag himself through the door. The first time, she thought, that I've violated a direct order from the President of the store. And an executive committee already trying to break my contract and kick me out. I think I need a lawyer. I think Bruce and I both need a lawyer. She debated. Katherine, she thought. Katherine knows one of the top lawyers in the city. He's practically a member of the Hayward family. She turned and picked up the telephone.

*

Crumpled papers filled the wastebasket; the worktable was piled with notes, crossed out drawings, string, and bent and broken wire. Nothing was finished. Nothing, Katherine thought in frustration, was ever begun. In the three weeks since Tobias challenged her to work full-time, she had not created one design good enough to turn into a piece of jewellery. She was blocked. Trying to think of curves and whorls and angles, of gold and silver and precious stones, she relived instead the cumulative shocks of Mettler's cool response, Lister's fury and the sense of defeat that descended on her the first time she used Craig's money and knew she hadn't come so far after all: she still wasn't making it on her own.

When Derek called, she was grateful for a reason to get up from her worktable. 'Friday night,' he said. 'I have to make an appearance at a benefit at Ghirardelli Square. We don't have to stay long; there's a new jazz trio at –'

'Derek, I'm sorry, but I'm busy Friday night.'

'*Busy?*'

Annoyed, she said, 'I do have a life when I'm not with you.'

'I apologise,' he said smoothly. 'But there are times when I expect you to be available. Friday night is one of them.'

'I'm sorry; I can't change my plans.'

I expect you to be available. Meaning, she owed him something in return for his tolerating her abstinence. But abstinence was a problem for both of them; he wasn't the only one who wanted to go to bed. Katherine had thought it would get easier once she made up her mind, but it didn't; the more courteous and distant he was, the more her hungers gnawed her.

But whenever she wavered, something would happen to remind her of the other side of Derek: his cutting comments and contempt for others; his cold assumption that in some way she was his possession and owed him her availability in exchange for his tolerance and letting her into his glamorous life where she could meet the women who might someday buy her jewellery. And there was Tobias's story about Jennifer. Katherine had been trying to bring it up since she heard it, but lately Derek had refused to talk about the accident at all, abruptly changing the subject whenever she mentioned it.

She was pulled too many ways by Derek, and it was a relief to refuse him for Friday night, even if it meant missing a benefit where she probably would see many of the women she was beginning to know by name. But, as it happened, she spent that evening at Ghirardelli Square, after all. 'I didn't plan this,' Leslie said as they arrived and saw the mass of people in front of them. 'But with things as they are, when my President tells me to represent the store, I can't refuse.'

As they struggled through the crowd to an elevator and then to the doorway of The Mandarin, Katherine thought she had never seen the place so crowded. Once a chocolate and spice factory and a woollen mill, the red brick building had been renovated years before to a delightfully quirky ten-storey maze of boutiques, theatres and restaurants built around open squares, with small stairways and sudden corridors that made it seem endless and endlessly inventive. Always a tourist attraction, when it became the site of the May benefit for the Family Welfare League, its normal population was instantly quadrupled.

But the crowds and the noise receded as Katherine and Leslie were led through The Mandarin, past softly lit rose brick walls and silk tapestries to a table overlooking the bay. 'Almost as private as a Chinese tomb,' Leslie said with satisfaction.

Katherine, happy to be with Leslie, was happy even with the crowd; its electric vitality helped her forget that she had been feeling sorry for herself for much of the past month. 'It's wonderful to be here. In fact, it's funny, but I would have been here anyway; Derek asked me to come with him. I don't suppose I'll see him in this crowd.'

A waiter poured their wine and in the lull Leslie asked, a little too casually, 'Did you talk to your friend?'

'He said he'd meet us here. I didn't tell him very much.'

'Thank you. Isn't it odd: Heath's has a dozen lawyers, but when I need one for myself I come to you for help.'

'I think Claude is supposed to be very good.'

'Good? He's one of the best. Very posh firm, very solid.'

'But if you knew that, why didn't you call him?'

'I'm small potatoes compared to his other clients.'

Katherine shook her head, watching the waiter arrange skewers of marinated meat on a small tabletop stove. 'If you're fighting Heath's executive board to keep your job, that's not small potatoes.'

'The point is, he'd rather have Heath's as his client than Leslie McAlister.'

'He didn't refuse when I asked him to meet you.'

Leslie lifted her glass. 'To better times. I've seen him at parties, you know. Tall, handsome, silver hair, blue eyes. He collects nubile maidens.'

'He what?'

'He's one of those fifty-ish bachelors who won't look at anyone but young lovelies in their twenties. To the collective despair of those of us who are single and approaching forty.'

'I didn't know that about him.'

'Not important. It's my neck I care about, not his sex life.'

There was a quaver in her voice that Katherine had never heard before. Ever since she drove to San Francisco in her rented truck, Leslie's positive, forceful presence had encouraged and cheered her; she had been the friend Katherine could cling to and the successful woman she could look up to because she had everything Katherine did not have: beauty, confidence, independence, a future she was sure of. But now a tremor ran through Leslie's voice and Katherine recognised the same uncertainty that had trailed through her own voice for months. 'Tell me about it,' she urged, and realised they had traded places: she was the one offering support.

'The pack is closing in,' Leslie said, trying to keep her voice light. 'And I've probably given them the last excuse they need to kick me out – though they haven't discovered it yet.'

'What did you do?'

'It's what I didn't do. In the last few days so many arrows started pointing at Bruce for manipulating our inventory programs that his big sister was ordered to fire him on the spot. Hello.'

She was looking at Claude, who had materialised in the dim light beside their table.

Katherine stood and kissed his cheek, feeling like a magician who conjures people from thin air. She barely knew Claude; she had not seen him in months; but because Leslie asked, it had been easy to make a telephone call. For the first time since Craig disappeared, Katherine was helping someone else instead of worrying about herself. She smiled quietly. She hadn't realised what a burden she'd been to herself until she forgot herself for a few minutes.

Claude was looking from her to Leslie and she saw the two of them through his eyes: red-haired Leslie, green-eyed, sophisticated, her beauty as polished as a fine gem despite faint curved lines, like parentheses, on either side of her mouth and a jaw that jutted slightly, especially when she talked about Heath's; and Katherine, dark-haired, hazel-eyed, her head high, wearing a soft wine-coloured dress from a designer resale shop – in almost no way resembling the woman Claude had seen in June at Victoria's and in October when he bought her a drink and tried to find out what she was up to. She smiled again and said, 'I'm so glad you're here. This is Leslie McAlister. Claude Fleming. Have you eaten? We haven't ordered yet.'

'I haven't eaten.' Claude shook hands with Leslie as he sat

down. 'I heard the last few words. You were ordered to fire your brother from his job. I gather you didn't.'

Leslie's eyebrows shot up – exactly like Bruce's, Katherine thought. 'Why do you gather that?'

'Katherine told me you need a lawyer because you think an effort is being made to oust you from a job for which you have a three-year contract. Those trying to oust you must think you've given them a reason. Such as disobeying an order. Did you fire your brother?'

'No. I couldn't do it. He's never had such a good job and he was doing so well – I've never seen him so happy with himself. He'd tried everything else – drugs and as much booze as he could drown himself in and bumming around Europe and Asia, but nothing made him content with himself. Until he discovered computers.'

'Predictability,' said Claude. 'Logical, reliable, programable. Correctible. Much better than drugs and booze.'

Leslie looked at him with interest. 'That's impressive, to understand that about a kid in his twenties.'

He chuckled. 'I know something about people in their twenties.'

'Oh yes,' Leslie said coldly. She tilted the wine bottle. 'We need another. Or would you rather we just talked about my problem so you can leave? I'm sure you have other plans for the evening.'

'I have no other plans.' He stopped a passing waiter and ordered another bottle. 'You care for your brother very much.'

'True. He's related to me.'

'Simple family obligation? It sounded to me like love.'

She turned the stem of her wine glass in her fingers. 'Well it is. Bruce is very special to me. We had a family once, but as soon as we got to voting age our parents and cousins and uncles scattered around the planet, doing this and that. Bruce, like a fool, went looking for them. The ones he found were

287

very busy, so finally he came back, looking like he'd met up with a gang and lost. Not that our busy family beat him up; they just ignored him to a pulp. So he came to me and it happened to be a . . . difficult time in my personal life and I wasn't at all busy. I gave him a bed to sleep in and an ear to listen to him and a kiss when he started crying. We took to each other.'

'You're older than he.'

'Oh yes.' Leslie gave a short laugh. 'Ten years older than his twenty-six.'

Claude nodded. 'And you gave him a home.'

'No. He had his place; I have mine. What I give him is a door that's always open, and someone to hang onto when he needs it. We give those to each other.'

Quietly, Claude repeated, 'A door that's always open. Not easy to find. What did you do,' he asked, 'if you didn't fire him?'

'Put him on temporary leave of absence without pay. I didn't tell him I was supposed to fire him; I just told him to get out until he heard from me again.'

'That's all you told him?'

'I told him to come to dinner on Sunday.'

They laughed together. Katherine wondered if she had become invisible. 'I'm very hungry,' she said mildly. Without hesitation, Claude centred himself between the two women and made himself their host, conferring with them on the menu, beckoning a waiter, and, all through the meal, punctiliously including both Katherine and Leslie in his conversation. It was so pleasant that Katherine was sorry when they were finished and Leslie said she had to leave. 'I've been assigned to accept an award for Heath's, for being the top donor of the past year. I think a most boring ceremony awaits me. If you two would like to wait here . . .'

'No,' Katherine said.

Claude pushed back his chair. 'We haven't finished the

business part of the evening. Unless you've changed your mind about retaining me as your attorney.'

'I would be delighted to retain you as my attorney.'

'Then we still have a great deal to discuss. Perhaps after your ceremony? There's a club not far from here . . .'

Walking from the restaurant and down the stairway, Katherine decided not to go with them. She shouldn't, anyway; she wasn't involved in their discussion. Suddenly she felt depressed, and it deepened as they merged with the crowd. Everyone was part of a couple. The whole world was a huge Noah's ark. She'd been part of a couple, too, but the other half had run off – evidently because she wasn't good enough for him to ask her help in solving his problems and keeping their marriage together. Keeping their family together.

I'll go home and cry, she thought. I haven't done that for a long time.

'My, my,' Leslie said as they reached the ground floor. 'That's a flashy lady Derek found to take your place tonight.'

Katherine followed her look in time to see Melanie put her arm through Derek's and whisper in his ear.

Claude made a sound between a cough and a snort. But his voice was level. 'I suppose Ross was too busy with his new Plaza. Good of Derek to accompany his sister-in-law.'

'The protective family lawyer,' said Katherine, as much to her own surprise as to Claude's. 'Leslie, we should get to your ceremony.'

But Derek had seen her and with a quick word to Melanie, who turned a frozen face to Katherine, he made his way towards them through the crowd. 'Claude,' he said as they shook hands. Leslie forced him to shake hers by holding it out and waiting. 'Leslie . . . Katherine . . .' He glanced from one to the other as if trying to decide which one was Claude's companion. 'A pleasant surprise.'

289

'An understatement,' Leslie murmured, the words almost lost in the noise of the crowd.

Claude heard. He smiled and took her arm. 'The sooner you get that award, the sooner we can escape these crowds. Katherine?' He offered her his other arm.

Katherine was looking at Derek, her thoughts racing.

Derek and Melanie.

Derek and Katherine.

Derek and Jennifer.

'Katherine?' Claude repeated.

'If you could wait,' Derek said to her.

She nodded. 'Do you mind, Leslie? I'll catch up.'

'Lovely dinner,' Leslie said, kissing her cheek. 'Thank you.'

'It was your dinner. I should be thanking you.'

'You know what I mean. See you soon.'

Katherine watched them disappear in the throng, then turned back to Derek. 'Was there something special you wanted?'

'Don't talk to me that way.' He put his arm around her waist and began to lead her towards a nearby coffee house.

'Derek, you can't – Melanie is –' She looked, but Melanie was gone. 'Where is she?'

'I assume she's gone home or found other friends. I told her I wanted to talk to you. She's very understanding.'

That is a joke, Katherine thought as Derek moved ahead to talk to the hostess. Somehow, in the crowded room, an empty table appeared. He held her chair. 'Was there something special *you* wanted?'

'Yes. I want to ask you –'

'Wait.' He ordered cappuccino for both of them and sat back. 'You look very lovely. How curious, that we are together here after all. As soon as we drink our coffee, which will give us time to adjust to our sudden good fortune, I shall introduce you to some friends upstairs who can be very useful to you.' He contemplated her. 'What *is* the matter?'

'I was wondering . . . about Melanie –'

'Here you are now,' the waitress said gaily. She set mugs of the foaming coffee before them, with spoons and paper napkins.

'Melanie,' Derek said flatly. 'What would you want to know about Melanie?'

'Not only Melanie. Jennifer, too. Jennifer and Melanie – and me. I wondered why – when there are so many women in the world – you've gotten involved with the three who are closest to your brother and your cousin.'

Not a muscle moved in his face or his body as he looked at Katherine through the steam curling up from their coffees. Then she saw the taut vein in his neck. 'You've gone somewhat beyond your territory, my dear,' he said at last. His voice was light, almost pleasant. 'You know very little about us, or, indeed, about anything, you've been Craig's sheltered little weed for so long. You seem to think that because you've learned to look like a flower you understand the garden. You have neither the knowledge nor the authority to speak about the things of the world. They are far beyond your comprehension.' He drank from his mug. 'I've been patient with you; the smallest reward you could give me would be to understand that it is better to remain silent than to demonstrate that you are a fool.'

His light voice, almost a monotone, was a thin blade, cutting through the noise and laughter at the crowded tables, sliding coldly into Katherine. Her breath came faster. She remembered the desire that had eaten at her for so long and wondered at it. Surely it had been for someone else. 'It doesn't help to call me a fool. That won't change the fact that you've been using me. You have been, haven't you, Derek? Because I'm married to Craig and fifteen years hasn't been long enough for you to stop hating him. And you don't like Ross either. I don't know why, but it doesn't matter. And Melanie is married to Ross. And Jennifer was Craig's favourite.'

291

'Katherine.' His face and voice had not changed, but the muscles in his neck were quivering ropes. 'You are in a singularly poor position to talk about being used. For months you have used me as your guide into a world that otherwise would have been completely closed to you. You have used me for lessons in behaviour and for satisfying your insatiable need for praise; as an escort to replace the husband who discarded you, and for sexual titillation without a sexual liaison. You're a good match for your husband; both of you run from responsibility.'

Katherine's face burned. 'You mean my responsibility was to pay for your services with sex.'

He let out a long breath, relaxing the explosive pressure behind his rigid muscles. 'This will stop. Now. I am not ready to end our curious affair –'

'But I am.' Breathing rapidly, Katherine leaned forward. 'I couldn't go on now. Because even though I did use you – you're right, of course; you've given me a great deal – but did I really take anything from you that you didn't want to give? You never said a specific coin was necessary to pay for what you did for me.' Feeling ashamed, she held her head high. 'How could I go on after this?'

'Are you asking for advice? Listen to me. You have grandiose ideas about making something of yourself, but you are no one in this city; you have nothing. The best thing for you is to go back to Vancouver, get some simple job that you can keep for more than a few months, and wait for your pathetic husband to crawl back into your lap, where he belongs and where you probably like him best.'

Katherine looked at him in disbelief. 'Is that a threat?'

'I never threaten.' He picked up his mug and showed a flicker of surprise as he found it empty. 'But if you were not a fool you would have learned something about power by now – in our family and in this city. That, too, was offered for your use; you had a choice between your husband's cowardice and the terms I might have offered if you'd been willing to be what I wanted. But you were afraid of that and threw it away.'

'I didn't –' A wave of revulsion made her choke. She fumbled blindly in her purse to take out a five dollar bill and put it on the table. 'This is for my coffee.' She stood, looking at him as if he were a small figure in a painting. 'I won't try to pay for the food and drinks you've bought me since October; I paid for them in the last few minutes by listening to you insult me. I don't know anything about your kind of power because I don't care about it. I want a family, not a battlefield, and I wanted companionship from you, not a contest. If you do have power, that only proves to me that a man can be handsome and charming and powerful, and still, underneath, crude and vulgar. And that kind of man I don't want to see again.'

She took a step back as his face darkened with fury, then turned, forcing her way through the crowd. Unexpectedly, violently, she began to tremble, and she let herself be carried along with the brightly-coloured mass of people to an arch across the square, and through it, to the street. It was quieter there, almost peaceful. It's all right, she said to herself. It's all right. Everything is all right.

And as a cab came to a stop in response to her raised arm, she knew that, in fact, everything *was* all right. Once before, after she decided she would not sleep with Derek, she'd felt as if a burden had been lifted from her. Now another was gone. She did not want him; she did not need him. She was free.

PART III

Chapter 12

Ross swivelled his chair to look through the window behind him. His gaze took in the steady stream of traffic on the Embarcardero, and beyond it the city's bustling piers, stretching like thin fingers into the choppy, deep blue bay. Two years earlier, when he was expanding his company to work on BayBridge Plaza, he had moved into this building, a former icehouse converted to bright office suites with interior brick walls and tall windows reaching exposed-beam ceilings. He had furnished his own office in rosewood and leather, with patterned American Indian rugs on the floor. No outside sounds breached the thick walls, and in the silence Ross let himself daydream about Paris.

'Work with me,' Jacques had urged earlier, on the telephone. In college he and Ross had shared an apartment; since then, across the thousands of miles between them, they had shared ideas about work, wives, their countries, and those thoughts often expressed more easily with someone far away. Now Jacques Duvain, believer in the new and modern, was in the midst of renovating a forty-room Parisian townhouse built in 1605, converting it to four apartments of ten rooms each. 'You always preach to me – "Keep the past; as much as possible, keep the past". Here is the past and I am being paid to keep it. Work with me on the Place des Vosges; be my consultant.'

'I know nothing about renovating seventeenth century French townhouses,' Ross had said.

'And I,' Jacques promptly replied, 'know little of new American renovation techniques. We will learn from each other. Besides, is this not a perfect way to prise my friend from his American draughting table to visit with me?'

Place des Vosges. Ross pictured in his mind the magnificent square of brick and plaster townhouses surrounding a park, once the Paris residences of the royal court, lately – having survived almost four hundred years of use and misuse – being bought by investors for renovation as condominiums, shops and restaurants. On his last trip to Paris, two years earlier, Ross had been given a tour of the square by Jacques, and he remembered still the elegant dimensions of the rooms, the grandeur of curving stairways, carved mouldings and ceilings, and the intimacy of private courtyards hidden in the centre of each of the houses.

He had wanted to go back, but work on BayBridge intervened. Over the two years, Jacques had sent him progress reports that in many ways matched the progress of BayBridge; now he was ready to make his detailed plans, and he wanted Ross to join him.

But I have two major projects already, Ross thought, brooding at the view from his window. BayBridge, which is just taking shape, and my marriage, which is losing whatever shape it had.

'Mrs Hayward is here,' his secretary said over the intercom. 'Should I call the others to tell them the meeting will be
late?'

Her words were carefully chosen. Ross knew, from past
experience, they meant there was a storm on Melanie's face
that probably could not be dealt with in five minutes before his
scheduled meeting. 'Yes, do that,' he said. 'I'll let you know
when we can get started. And tell Mrs Hayward –'

But Melanie was already there, closing his office door as
she walked in. With her ebony hair and tanned skin, wearing a
white silk blouse and red suit cut geometrically to make her
shoulders broader and her hips narrower, she looked like a
drawing in a fashion magazine – even, Ross thought, to the
cold, faintly defiant look with which she swept his office just
as models sweep the audience as they glide down the runway.

Melanie glided across the office to drop her purse and
gloves on his desk. 'I was shopping and had some extra time,
so I decided to stop by and talk.'

Flattering, he thought. But probably not true; she came
expressly to talk, since we don't talk at home. Which means
there's a crisis. He went to a credenza near a leather couch and
chairs grouped besides the high windows. 'Coffee?'

'You could offer me a martini.'

'If I had it. The best I can do is coffee.'

She shrugged and sat on the edge of the couch, drumming
her fingernails on the glass coffee table. 'Wilma tells me your
Mr Macklin is getting a divorce.'

'He's not mine. I don't even know him well enough to be
interested in his affairs.' Ross handed her a cup and carried his
own around the table to sit beside her. 'Do you?'

'I'm interested in divorce.'

'So you've told me. Wilma's stock in trade.' He was playing for time; he knew she had not meant Wilma's gossip. 'Was
there something special you stopped by to talk about?'

299

With an exasperated clatter Melanie set her cup on the glass table. 'Do you have to be difficult? Couldn't you once, just one goddam time, be understanding? I'm not talking about Wilma; I'm talking about me. *I* am interested in divorce because *I* want a divorce. I've –'

'Just a minute. Wait.' They had always stopped short of this point. 'We've never talked about this; we never even talked about finding a way to –'

'What difference does it make? I've found somebody who's better for me than you, somebody who really cares about *me*, about what *I* want and how *I* feel and what's good for *me*. So I want a divorce. Right away.'

'Someone else?' He hadn't heard any gossip; he'd never thought of that. 'Who is it?'

'It doesn't matter. All that matters is that I've found someone who really cares about *me*, who pays attention to me and satisfies me –'

'Can you control your teenage tantrum?' Ross asked bitingly. 'And use a few words besides *I* and *me*?'

'Damn you,' she spat. 'That's what you do every time. You *treat* me like a teenager – a baby – you make me feel *little*.'

Instinctively Ross put out a hand. 'I know. Melanie, I'm sorry; I know I –'

'I don't want your fucking apologies; it's too late for that! Don't you understand? I'm sick and tired of feeling like I'm not smart enough or grown up enough for you. I'm as grown up as you are, and I want somebody who'll treat me like that, somebody who knows how grown up I am –'

'Who is he?'

'Somebody special.'

'*Goddam it*, who the hell is he?'

'You can swear at me all you want; I'm not afraid of you. It's somebody wonderful who's going to take care of me and buy me presents and bring me breakfast in bed –'

'Melanie. I asked you who he is.'

At the low steel of his voice, she took a quick look at his face. 'Guy Walker.'

'Guy Walker?'

'He's a very famous champion tennis player. He gives lessons at the club, but when he's on tour he wins trophies. He's going to marry me.'

The words struck an odd chord. 'What about you?' he asked. 'Are you going to marry him?'

'Don't try to make me look silly. Of course I'm going to marry him.'

It registered then. Ross sucked in his breath, feeling as if he had been punched in the stomach. He'd known how far apart they had moved; even Carrie and Jon knew it, watching, listening, moving through the house with delicate footsteps, as if afraid of making a noise that would bring the whole structure tumbling down. Already tumbled, Ross thought; the evidence had been there for a long time – the spaces, the quarrels that came up like thunderstorms and were as quickly spent, their silences, the way their eyes never quite met.

But he'd wilfully ignored the signs, assuming that however bad it was, they would work it out; assuming that because it was familiar and predictable, it would be easier to repair than to destroy.

Wrong. All the assumptions: wrong. Panic welled up, and he turned from Melanie, staring out the window. He remembered the day he'd moved here and first looked at this view. He was beginning BayBridge and was boundlessly confident: sure of his wife, his home, his profession. Idiot, he thought. Secure, satisfied – blind.

I miss knowing the boundaries of my days. Where had he heard that? In a moment it came to him: Katherine, at The Compass Rose. *I miss being sure of what will happen tomorrow and the day after. I miss knowing the boundaries of my days. None of it was true, nothing was certain, but it was so comforting to think it was . . .*

I knew as little as she did, Ross thought.

'*Are* you listening?' Melanie demanded.

Frowning, he turned back to her. 'I was thinking of something else.'

'Something else! Something more important than your children?'

'What about the children?'

'I'm keeping them. How many times do I have to repeat it? They'll stay with me and you'll move out. I'm keeping the house. I don't want Carrie and Jon changing schools and doing all those upsetting things that make children hate divorce. We'll stay in our own house and everything will be the same for them.'

'Except that their father will be gone.'

'Well, yes. But the really important things won't change – their house and school and friends. And me of course. And they'll have Guy. Don't worry about them, Ross; they'll be fine.'

She said it with such earnestness, mixed with defiance, that Ross felt a flash of pity. But then he thought: what if she's right? What if they would be fine without him? His panic grew; spreading through him, cold and heavy.

Melanie was still talking. '– And visitation rights, because I suppose they'll want to see you, once in a while. Our lawyers can settle that –'

Visitation rights? A schedule for telling your kids you love them? How do lawyers work that out? He felt sick – and then the coldness inside him froze all feeling. Facing Melanie, he felt nothing. 'We'll settle it now, between us. I'll want them every weekend, one night a week for dinner, and at school holidays. Thanksgiving, Christmas, spring vacation, long weekends, and of course all summer –'

'Are you crazy? They can't always be running off to stay with you! How can we make a new family if we're not together at Thanksgiving and Christmas? You can have them – my lawyer said if you made a fuss you could have them every other weekend – if you really want them that often – and a week in the summer . . . well, maybe two weeks, but no more because of camp. And you'll pay for camp; that's on a list – my lawyer has it – things you'll take care of, alimony and child support and the dentist and all those things. Ask my lawyer; he'll show it to you; here's his card. See him tomorrow Ross, or get your own lawyer to call him; don't wait because Guy's impatient –'

'To get his little family started.'

She shot him a look. 'Don't use that tone of voice with me.'

'You've forfeited the right to tell me what tone to use.' What emotions had broken through that cold barrier to make his hands tremble? Anger? Pain? He stood and walked to his desk, his back to Melanie. 'You'd better leave.'

'Well, I guess I've said what I had to say.' There was a pause. 'Did you think you'd come home tonight?'

'I hadn't thought about it.'

'Well, you'd better not try. I've had the locks changed.'

He whipped around. 'Change them back. Or give me a new key. That is my house and I haven't moved out.'

'I'll do what I want! It's in both our names!'

'Until I move out, I have the right to enter that house and use it and I advise you not to try to stop me. Give me the key.' She wavered. 'I won't rape you,' he said, his voice grating.

She flushed. 'I didn't think you would. I just don't want you around! But if you'll call first –'

'I'll be damned if I will; *that is my house*. Give me the key!' When she still hesitated, he said evenly, 'I don't think you'd want your friends to hear that your husband called the Tiburon police to witness him breaking into his own house.'

'God damn you to hell,' she said, and held out a key.

He crossed the room to take it, clenching it to hide the trembling of his hands. 'I'll pack when Carrie and Jon aren't home. Probably tomorrow while they're at school.'*To go where*? He held open the door. 'One more thing. I'm not leaving them. I intend to be with them far more often than you and your lawyer think.' *Where? Doing what?* 'You'll have to organise your new family around my schedule. Remember that. I'll make you spend the next five years in court if you try to keep those children from me.'

'You bastard. You must want to ruin my marriage to Guy the way you ruined ours.' She ducked, as if expecting a blow, and scurried out.

Ross watched her stumble and catch herself. Tripped, he thought, by the wreck of our marriage. He wondered if she was right: that he could have prevented the destruction if he'd been different – better, kinder, more patient . . .

'– The meeting?' his secretary was asking.

He rubbed the back of his neck. 'I had a reason for scheduling it today. Do you remember what it was?'

'We couldn't get everyone together for at least another two weeks.'

He nodded, prodding his thoughts like a shepherd herding reluctant sheep. 'We'd better have it then. But give me half an hour. I have to pick up some pieces, and put myself together.'

Across the bay from San Francisco, the houses in the Berkeley Hills climb so steeply they look over the roofs of those below offering a vista stretching as far south as San Jose. The house Ross rented stepped down from the front entrance hall, past two airy bedrooms to a long living-dining room and a square cedar deck screened by trees and bushes but still giving a clear view of the Golden Gate and Oakland-Bay bridges, the San Francisco skyline, and the softly-rounded hills of Tiburon where, only five miles away, his wife entertained her tennis-playing lover.

Carrie and Jon sniffed suspiciously the first time they explored his new home. 'It doesn't look *anything* like our house,' Carrie declared. 'Was this the best you could find?'

'What's wrong with it?' Ross asked mildly, hiding the panic that still gripped him when he let down his guard – *What if they refuse to come here? Lawyers can forge agreements but who can make my children want to be with me?* 'I thought it felt like a home.'

Slowly, Carrie turned in place, her head tilted, considering the heavy, worn furniture in half a dozen different fabrics and colours, with soft cushions that retained the shape of the last person to sit in them. No interior decorator had ever set foot in those rooms; the professor's family had simply collected furniture over the years, never throwing anything out, and Ross knew, seeing it through Carrie's critical gaze – exactly like Melanie's – that no place was more unlike the perfectly modulated velvet and silk rooms of his Tiburon home.

But, unlike Melanie, who would have scornfully dismissed it, Carrie began to smile. 'It's not bad,' she conceded. 'It's kind of friendly. Of course,' she added hastily, not wanting to betray her mother. 'It's not as beautiful as home. But it's . . . *comfortable*. Like you could jump on the furniture.'

'Dad!' shouted Jon from the deck. 'They've got a jacuzzi!'

'*We've* got a jacuzzi,' Ross said as he and Carrie joined him. 'Thanks to the professor.'

'But it's his, isn't it? You didn't buy it.'

'Until he gets back, a year from now, it's ours.'

'Yours,' muttered Jon, becoming very busy with the controls. 'We're only visitors.'

'Jon.' Ross sat on the edge of the round tub and turned his son to face him. 'This is your house as much as mine. You'll be spending a lot of time here; we'll all be here, together.'

305

'But we don't *live* here.' Jon turned red, then blurted, 'Dad, we were wondering if maybe you'd come back.'

A deep ache filled Ross's lungs. 'I can't do that, Jon. When a marriage dies, there's no way to bring it back to life.'

'Why did it have to die?' Carrie demanded. 'It used to be fine. Didn't it?'

'We thought so. But then something made us go in different directions. We started having separate ideas and thoughts, even separate feelings and dreams about the future. As if –' He paused. 'If each of you tied the end of a cord around your waist and began to walk away from each other, the cord would stretch tighter and tighter, and if you kept on walking it couldn't take the stress. It would fray and then snap. That's what happened to our marriage.'

Carrie chewed the end of a blonde curl. 'You could tie a knot in the cord.'

'Some people try.' Ross put an arm around her shoulders. 'And sometimes it works. But you have to move closer together to do it. And if you've been too far apart, with too many different thoughts, the chances are you'd start straining against the cord again and the knot wouldn't hold.'

'You shouldn't pull apart in the first place,' Jon muttered.

'You're right.' Ross drew his son to him and he and his children leaned against each other. 'I don't know why we did. When we were married, and the two of you were born, I thought my life had a shape, like a house I'd designed, with rooms for the people I loved and the work I loved, and places for friends and holidays and sailing . . . I was so excited with my imaginary house, because everyone and everything that was dear to me was in it. And I think your mother felt the same way.'

'You're not sure?' Carrie asked.

'I'm pretty sure she was at first. Later – I don't know exactly when – she began worrying about all the things she might be missing. But I think for the first few years she was happy. I know I was.' The three of them were silent, holding each other. 'But then we went in different directions and the cord between us snapped. And we've gone too far to mend it; you mustn't wait for that to happen. The only good thing left from our marriage is you, and how much we love you.'

'Love,' snorted Jon.

Ross tightened his arms around them. 'That's what we've got. We're held together by cords, too, the strongest I've ever seen. And if we spend lots of time together, they'll never get frayed; they'll never come close to snapping. I promise that.'

Carrie turned and flung both arms around his neck. Ross tried to keep his voice firm. 'That's why this is your home, too,' he said. 'You'll have a key for when you're staying here, and you can be here whenever you want.'

Jon shook his head. 'Mother said –' he stopped.

'What did she say?'

'Never mind.'

'You started to tell me.'

'Never mind.'

'I'd like to know, Jon.'

'It's not important.'

'It might be.'

Stubbornly, Jon shook his head and Ross sighed, seeing his son begin to build a wall between two houses, two families, two loyalties. 'Maybe someday you'll tell me. In the meantime, *I'm* going to call this our home, and I hope one of these days you will, too.' He looked over Jon's head, past the pines in his yard, at the distant silhouette of Mount Tamalpais rising above the misty Tiburon hills. The air was fragrant with roses and narcissi; the flamboyant beauty of cymbidiums and flowering plum covered the bushes beside the deck. A stairway led to a lower garden where a neglected hedge of thorny raspberry bushes grew. Deep foghorns blasted through the

Saturday morning quiet; a dog barked; someone was practising piano scales. Our home, Ross thought. And tears filled his eyes.

His days became fragmented, like shards of a broken bowl. In his office he worked with the BayBridge contractor, going over the final plans, and with his staff on proposals for new projects. In his lawyer's office, meeting with Melanie's lawyer, he laboriously negotiated downward her demand for ten thousand dollars a month alimony and child support, worked out a schedule for visiting his children, and arranged to have his huge collection of books and recordings packed and shipped from Tiburon to Berkeley, leaving Melanie the house and everything else in it.

At night he sat in his new living-room, with piles of work he had brought home and lists of people and companies to whom his secretary would send change-of-address cards. But he spent most of the time trying to think logically.

What the hell was wrong with him? He hadn't had a real marriage in years; he didn't miss the glossy magazine atmosphere of the home Melanie had made – in fact, he'd never liked it – and he didn't miss Melanie. So what was he mourning?

Twelve years ago, he'd married a beautiful, ebony-haired debutante who had enthralled him with her carefree gaiety in the dark days after Jennifer and Craig had died. By the time Carrie and Todd were born, the carefree debutante had become a restless wife; and after they moved to San Francisco it seemed the only way a Tiburon housewife, as she called herself, could allay her fears of missing out on life was by spending large sums of money, even though the things she bought always seemed to lose their desirability once they were hers. Soon Melanie's beautiful lips had tightened at the corners into perpetual disappointment and dissatisfaction, at least when she was with her husband.

All this Ross had known and lived with, finding more satis-faction in his work as he got less from his marriage. Melanie would not listen when he tried to talk about the gulf between them, and after a while he let it go; it was easier not to try. They'd do it later.

It had not occurred to him to leave her. Why not? he won-dered now, gazing absently around his new living-room.

Because they were married. Because they had two children. Because his life was devoted to restoring, not destroying. Because he'd thought if they could work out the biggest prob-lems, an imperfect marriage was probably better than none.

'But it's over,' he said aloud. 'And it should have been, long ago.' He listened to himself and understood why he had spoken out loud: to force himself to face the truth about the woman his wife had become and his own failure to do any-thing but drift through the years, preferring that to change.

More and more often he thought of Katherine. She must have the same kind of mourning for a marriage, and even something like the shame Ross felt at his ignorance about Melanie; she had had to face her own, about Craig. He won-dered if she carried on silent dialogues, as he did, trying to understand, and to calm the turmoil within.

I could call her, he thought, and find out. But he did not. She had Derek – that was lasting a long time. He didn't understand how a woman as bright and proud as she was hadn't yet seen through his brother, but he wouldn't seek her out to find the answer – at least not now. It was the wrong time: there was too much he was wrestling with already. He knew he wanted to see her, but until he understood what had happened to him, and why, and where he was going, he'd stay away.

The more he thought about it, the blacker his mood became. He took to sailing at night, having to drive to Tiburon Harbour for his boat because he hadn't yet found a slip close to Berkeley. The drive made his mood even worse and once on the water he brooded at the dark waves lapping his boat, the brilliant white stars above, and the gold lights below, embracing the bay.

He was a superb sailor. Tobias had called it his obsession when, after Jennifer was killed, he grimly took lessons and crewed for others in races or on long trips. For a year, there had been no pleasure in it; he fought the boats as if they were enemies. But as he became technically skilled he discovered that each boat had its own characteristics – almost its own personality – and if he worked with it he could use the wind and the currents instead of being their victim. Then sailing lost its horrors and he understood Craig's passion for its freedom and power: the joy of skimming silently between sky and water, part of the earth, yet flying, controlling, yet bending to the wind.

But after the separation from Melanie, Ross sailed simply to be alone and to wear himself out. One night he sailed for the practical purpose of moving his boat, at last, to a slip in the Emeryville Marina, down the road from Berkeley. But mostly he sailed to get away from everything on land.

Still, it wasn't enough; he needed something else. He was too wound up with doubts about himself, too angry without a specific target, too lonely, with a feeling of isolation that neither his friends nor Victoria nor Tobias could ease. He thought he would explode from the energy trapped inside him if he could not find a way to work it off. And that was when he discovered gardening.

In Sea Cliff, when he was growing up, there had always been gardeners, almost invisible except when Ross and Craig and Derek needed gardenias or camelias for the girls they took to dances. Now, trying it whimsically, then more seriously, he was amazed at how satisfying it was. It gave him a sense of accomplishment and wore him out even more than the easy sailing the bay had offered in the two weeks since he moved from Tiburon. With the vigour of a convert, he dug and hoed and chopped. At first he killed as many flowers as weeds, but soon, after a week of studying a garden encyclopaedia propped at the breakfast table, he began to tell them apart and even felt confident enough to plant two rows of radishes and red peppers. Leaning on his hoe one morning before leaving for the office, he surveyed his territory and gave a short, satisfied nod. He might have made a mess of his marriage, but he sure as hell could keep a garden in order.

On June 16th it was one year since Craig had kissed Katherine goodbye and driven off in a taxicab, waving to her through the rear window. Todd had drawn a fierce X with a red Magic Marker beneath the date on the kitchen calendar and he and Jennifer shot nervous glances at it whenever they walked past. By the time the day arrived, they had worked themselves to a pitch of anticipation, anxious and quick-tempered from the minute they leaped out of bed, spilling their cereal at breakfast and snapping at Katherine when she suggested they try not to walk through it.

'Now hold on a minute,' she said calmly, though their anxiety had proved contagious and she was as jumpy as them. Already keyed up about delivering her new jewellery to Herman Mettler on Friday, she also had begun to wonder, like Jennifer and Todd, if Craig would choose June 16th to return. One year, she thought, remembering back to Vancouver and the long nights when the porch light had blazed while she waited, curled up on the couch. Her memory sped forward – dinner at the Haywards, the trip to San Francisco in a rented truck, their first dismayed look at this apartment, the strength of her friendship with Leslie, Gil Lister's daily insults, lunch with Ross, Derek's fantastic box lunch, the Exploratorium with Jennifer and Todd, her first sale to Mettler, her love for Victoria . . . A long, crowded year. A long way, Katherine knew, from the fears of those first dark nights. And as she thought that, a new idea came to her: if June 16th was the anniversary of Craig's disappearing, it was also the anniversary of her beginning to find herself.

He left and I came out, she thought whimsically, then pushed the thought away. 'Maybe it would be better,' she suggested to Jennifer and Todd, 'if we didn't think about today being different from any other day.'

'It's an anniversary!' Todd protested. 'People celebrate anniversaries – everybody knows that!'

'It seems different to us,' said Jennifer reprovingly. 'It's like a birthday. You're the same age all year, but your birthday is still different from other days. *Daddy* would understand that.'

Katherine felt a flash of impatience. 'I understand that, too. But I don't think a birthday is very much like the anniversary of a man deserting his family.'

'*Mother!*'

Todd jumped up and stomped in a circle on the spilled Rice Krispies. 'You *said* we didn't know why he went away and we had to wait till we heard his story.'

'That's still true.' Her chin in her hands, Katherine gazed at the pulverised cereal. 'I shouldn't have said what I did, at least not quite that way. But it doesn't help to lie about what happened. Your father did leave us a year ago, without a word – we even thought he might be dead, remember? – and it took us a long time to get ourselves put together. I think we should take credit for what we did and not forget how hard it was, how unhappy we were, the trouble you had in school, the problems I had with my job . . . Even if we don't know why he disappeared, I think we ought to remember that he did just . . . leave us.'

'So you can stay mad at him?' Jennifer asked shrewdly.

'So someday we can find out the truth,' Katherine said steadily. 'Whether he really had to leave or not.'

It was the first time she had said it aloud. Jennifer's eyes narrowed. 'You shouldn't talk that way about Daddy. He tried to come back on New Year's Eve but you were too busy with Derek to get here in time, so he left. He thought you didn't want him. It was your fault he went away; he probably knew you were going to bed with Derek –'

'Jennifer!'

'Well, everybody does, don't they? When they're out late and go to somebody's apartment? I used to wake up when you came home and look at my clock and see how late it was and the kids at school always talk about it so what else were you doing? Daddy knew. That's why he left; he felt awful and he went away again.' Stonily she looked at Katherine. '*What did you do to make him go away the first time?*'

Stunned, Katherine stared at her. Once, they had asked what they had done to make their father leave. 'What did *I* do?'

'Well, you and Mr Doerner lied that Daddy stole money, so we figured you made that up so you could pretend it wasn't your fault he left – you did something that got him mad – because why else would he go away from us unless you made him –?'

'Stop it, Jennifer! This instant! You don't know what you're talking about!'

Jennifer burst into tears. 'I know I don't! But you never tell us anything!'

'Mom,' Todd blurted, looking from Jennifer to Katherine. 'Should I sweep up the cereal?'

Katherine's eyes met Jennifer's and unexpectedly a small laugh escaped them both. 'In a minute,' Katherine said. 'First, we'd better talk.'

She contemplated them across the breakfast table, her bright beautiful children who had to pick their way through the mine-fields of adult behaviour. Children ought to be happy and

313

carefree, Katherine thought, but how can they be, if they're caught in our complicated lives?

'I didn't lie. It does seem that Daddy took money from the company; I told you, I'm waiting to hear what he says about it. But that's separate from everything else. I didn't want him to leave; we didn't fight; he wasn't angry at me. We loved each other, and we were happy. All of us.' As vividly as if she were in Vancouver, Katherine saw the slanting afternoon sunlight bringing her living-room to life – the flowered furniture, the patina of Craig's oak desk, the gleam of black Eskimo sculptures – and Craig's smile when he held her close, telling her he loved her. 'We were happy,' she repeated and her voice broke on the words. It hadn't seemed so real for months.

'What about Derek?' Jennifer asked, her voice subdued.

'Derek was exciting,' Katherine answered truthfully. 'I told you about those enormous houses we went to, with fancy food and bright lights and people wearing beautiful clothes. All those parties, where no one was poor and no one ever seemed worried about anything . . . Going out with Derek was like being in a fairy tale.'

'I guess that was wonderful,' Jennifer said.

'A lot of the time it was. But Derek turned out to be not so wonderful, and after a while I didn't want to be with him any more. You know that, because I told you when I stopped seeing him, almost two months ago.'

Wordlessly, Jennifer scrutinised her. 'No,' Katherine said. 'I didn't go to bed with him. I thought about it, but I didn't.'

'You thought about it?'

'Everybody does,' Katherine replied, using Jennifer's words. 'It's one of the important things men and women do together. But every woman doesn't do it with every man and I didn't do it with Derek.'

Jennifer's eyes were bright with relief and gratitude. 'Now,' Katherine said, looking for a change of subject. 'Could you

314

give me some help this morning? I'm trying something new for my last piece for Mr Mettler and I'd like your opinion, and some help in polishing. And I thought tonight we'd have dinner at the Hippo; I could use a good hamburger. How about you?'

'Me too!' Todd grinned.

'Jennifer?'

Shamefaced, Jennifer looked at her lap. 'You're so nice. But I wasn't nice to you.'

'Not very,' Katherine agreed. 'But you were unhappy, and you tried to spread it around. Remember what we decided at the Exploratorium? Don't keep things bottled up; let's talk about them.'

'Dad kept things bottled up, didn't he?' said Todd, making a discovery. 'Maybe if you'd asked him to talk about them –'

'I did,' Katherine replied shortly. 'Now I'm going to work. After you sweep the floor, come on in.'

Filled with sudden resentment, she sat on the stool at her worktable. Please go away, she begged Craig silently. Stop creeping into all our conversations; let us get on with the things we have to do. But then she added quickly, I'm sorry; I didn't mean it. Of course we should talk about you. Jennifer and Todd need you and I know you're still part of our lives. But you make it very hard for us.

She picked up a piece of polished Lucite and closed her hand around its cool surface. The tightness inside her began to ease. This was where she was happiest. The frustrating weeks of April, when she could not draw a sketch or begin a piece of jewellery, had ended, astonishingly, almost as soon as she walked away from Derek in Ghirardelli Square, seven weeks ago. It was as if in escaping from the web of his charm and cruelty, the dominance of his power and sexual magnetism, she suddenly discovered herself. By freeing herself of needing Derek, she had freed her own energy and inventiveness, and since that night, her imagination had soared. Images came to her: bold shapes and vivid colours, exotic combinations and fantastic designs too complicated for jewellery, but containing some single idea that she could use – and those were the ones she put on paper. Sketches flowed from her pencil as fast as her hand could move, followed by watercolour paintings of the best of them and, finally, models of the twelve she chose for the collection she would take to Mettler.

The hours and days had passed in silent absorption, in the same circle of contentment Katherine had felt when she made her first gold bracelet. She was satisfied to be alone. Now and then she thought of Derek, but only fleetingly and always with relief that it was over. Leslie stopped by occasionally, to share a quick supper or cup of coffee, but she always left, with an indulgent laugh and a kiss, when Katherine's attention wandered to her worktable. At dinner one night Victoria and Tobias told Katherine that Ross and Melanie had separated, but she felt only casual interest and a flicker of regret that she and Ross had never become friends. She was caught up in the excitement of her work; it tugged at her demandingly, making everything else seem distant and faint. And so she spent most of her time alone or with Jennifer and Todd in their small apartment until eleven pieces of jewellery lay nestled in individual boxes and the twelfth, almost finished, was in her hand: a necklace of clear Lucite ovals alternating with small, irregularly shaped chunks of Lucite in deep shades of burnt orange, like small pieces of the setting sun.

'Sensuous and aloof,' Mettler said admiringly soon after Katherine arrived on Friday morning. Leaning far back in his chair, he let the necklace slip slowly through his fingers and glanced across his desk at the boxes lined up in front of Katherine.

He had reached for them when she first came in, but after shaking hands, she had moved away and sat down even before he invited her to. Gone were the days when Katherine would

316

give over her jewellery or sketches to be viewed at the whim of someone else while she clenched her hands and waited for criticism. She had learned from watching Derek manage encounters so that they included only the subjects he wanted, and lasted only as long as he wanted. She had learned from Derek how to withhold something – a comment, a smile, a handshake, a piece of information – until the time when it could be used to control.

She had never put his tricks into practice until Herman Mettler reached for her jewellery boxes. Smiling, she shook her head. 'I'd rather show them to you,' she said softly and casually rested her arm along the gleaming surface of his desk, the sleeve of her suit jacket pulled back just enough to reveal two bracelets on her wrist.

Mettler frowned with sudden concentration. 'I'd like to see those.'

'Of course.' Removing them slowly, making him wait, she laid the two bracelets in the palm of his hand. He picked up one of them – strands of ivory beads twisted with strands of red and dove-grey stones in different sizes and shapes, fastened with a silver clasp like a small palette embedded with three red stones. 'Bone, cornelian and grey agate,' Katherine said as Mettler examined the strands. 'The clasp is silver, set with cornelian. It could be gold, if a customer wished, though in that case I would replace the grey agate with black onyx.' He gave her a piercing look and she returned it calmly, one hand clenched so tightly in her lap it was numb. He turned back and picked up the other bracelet, a smoothly curved band. 'Gold,' Katherine said, though of course he knew it. 'Bisected by a strip of onyx marble.'

Mettler slipped the bracelets over the upraised fingers of his hands, and examined them. 'Why did you wear them together?'

'To get your attention.'

He began to smile. They both knew the bracelets – one flamboyant, the other exquisitely restrained – should not be worn together. 'You succeeded. What else did you bring me?'

'Do you have any other questions about these?'

He sighed – amused, annoyed, curious – and let her run the interview. 'Not at the moment.'

'You'll want the price list.' Katherine slid a blue folder across the desk. 'You'll find photographs and descriptions of each piece. Now, for the necklaces . . .' Opening one of the boxes, she took out the strand of clear Lucite alternating with burnt orange, slipped it over her head so he could see it against her black turtleneck sweater, then removed it and handed it to him.

He slipped it through his fingers. 'Brilliantly simple. And a different medium from the others. Have you mastered them all?'

'Not precious stones; I won't be working with them. I like semiprecious stones, glass, gold and silver. And Lucite now and then, for relaxation.'

'Indeed. Relaxation.'

Katherine had stopped trembling. Bringing out her other pieces one at a time, she described them in a voice that grew increasingly confident as she saw Mettler lower his eyes like a poker player to hide their gleam of excitement. But he gave in to emotion when Katherine held up her last piece: a necklace of gold segments, roughly shaped, hammered to an antique finish and fastened together with short double strands of tiny, geometric, bezel-set stones in amber, blue and deep green.

'Magnificent!' he burst out, almost snatching the necklace from her. He turned it in his hands, murmuring to himself. 'Totally new, yet almost ancient. Modern, but echoing of the past. Katherine.' He looked up and for the first time his voice was without pomposity. 'I salute you. An extraordinary collection free of the commonplace, free of other influences. Excellent throughout.'

Katherine flushed, her heart pounding. She had sometimes

been alarmed by the flights of her imagination, but she had trusted them, and, combining them with the techniques she had mastered in Tony's studio, had done what she dreamed of: created pieces that were completely new and beautiful.

'We'll feature you, of course,' Mettler was saying. 'In the showcases at the front of the store. A full frontal attack,' he added, chuckling with satisfaction. 'We can't market you to a specific clientele, since you fit in no narrow category, but we'll make that a virtue and introduce you as a designer for all our customers – the same way we handle Marc Landau and Angela Cummings and Paloma Picasso. And the publicity! My God, I can get stories on these designs wherever I want. Spectacular photos, and your own story, of course: human interest. Divorced, are you? Beautiful woman, children – you do have children? – they help. Struggling night and day to support your young children with the work of your hands – and such work! Such talent! We'll get you in *Vogue*, *Cosmo*, *Savvy* – different markets – and I'll take full page ads . . . "Jewellery by Katherine Fraser – exclusive at Mettler's".'

'But if my designs are exclusive at Mettler's, I won't be able to sell my work anywhere else.'

'True. But obviously you understand it is to your benefit to be connected with one store where you are well-treated, where customers know they will always find your work, where your newest pieces will get immediate exposure. I'll have a contract drawn up and of course you'll want to read it; if you want a lawyer to look it over, let me recommend –'

'Just a minute, please.' Katherine tried to imagine how Derek would regain control of a conversation after he had lost it. 'I'm afraid this is a little too fast for me. We haven't discussed the price list I gave you.'

'Katherine. I am offering you a showplace. I won't quibble over prices and you won't try to rob me. After all, I know what the market will bear. We'll get along, never fear. But I

319

want you exclusively. The same thing you want: security.'

'I just don't know.' It might be all right, but it bothered her. It's like a marriage, she thought wryly; locked into one person, whatever happens . . . And Mettler was pressing her – all business, no jokes – which probably meant he knew others would want her, too. Would it increase her value, or decrease it, to sell only through one store? I've never had to cope with success, she thought, and said, 'I can't decide this minute. I never even thought of an exclusive contract, I wasn't that far along. If you won't wait for me to get some advice, perhaps I should go somewhere else.'

'My dear Katherine,' said Mettler hastily. 'You shock me. I never give ultimatums. But if you reflect a bit, you'll see that it is to your advantage. In fact, I can't imagine why you would refuse. Unless' – he frowned at a sudden thought – 'is it possible these are not actually your own designs? I would have to be privy to that information. Tell me, Katherine, is all this truly yours? It is quite amazing, you know, for someone to create highly original designs only a few months after making a collection that was quite ordinary. A transformation, you might say. I could not, of course, advertise the line as Katherine Fraser's if you used other – Katherine!'

Shaking with shock and outrage, Katherine was sweeping the jewellery across his desk, letting it fall over the edge into her purse. 'I cannot believe,' she said icily, 'you would jeopardise a business relationship you were so anxious to make exclusive. It's a strange way to do business and I don't want to have anything to do with it. I'll find someone else to carry my jewellery. My . . . grandmother, whom I think you know, Victoria Hayward, says she frequently shops at Laykin Et Cie and Xavier's; it will be interesting to see what they think of my designs. *My* designs, Herman; Katherine Fraser originals. I'm sorry we wasted so much time this morning; it won't happen again.'

'Now Katherine, just a minute. Just a minute.' Mettler

walked around the desk, holding his splayed fingers in a small gesture of apology. 'I regret seeming to impugn your integrity. But *my* integrity is on the line in every display case in my store and I must guard it religiously. If I say an item is an original, my customers believe me. Marc Landau is an original; unscrupulous manufacturers copy him – he expects it, in spite of the fact that jewellery designs are copyrighted – but Marc Landau copies no one; that is why his pieces command exorbitant prices. I am not interested in jewellery copied with minor variations from Marc Landau or Elsa Peretti or – as inevitably will happen – Katherine Fraser; I am interested only in originals. My customers trust me; I must be able to trust my designers. But come now; we mustn't get too excited.'

Pulling up an armchair, he sat close to Katherine. 'Your work is superb. If you say it is yours, I accept that. I will not press you for an exclusive contract, but in the long run, you will do better with me if you have one. I'm making myself clear?'

'Yes.'

'Good. Now, I am buying these pieces, but I want at least a dozen more before I introduce you to the world. I'll wait until fall and feature you then. Is that acceptable?'

'Yes.'

'Then we will shake hands. We have just begun the career of Katherine Fraser, jewellery designer *extraordinaire*.'

Holding back the excitement rushing through her, Katherine shook his hand. She would have to sort everything out, ask Claude what he thought about exclusive contracts, and Victoria and Tobias, too. But there was time for that. For the moment, even as she and Mettler talked about the pieces she would make for September, she savoured his words. Katherine Fraser. Jewellery designer. *Extraordinaire*.

*

'Katherine and I are celebrating at dinner,' Leslie said, pouring coffee for Claude and herself. 'Which gives us all day, but not the evening.'

'We'll be done by evening,' he responded, settling back on the blue suede of Leslie's couch. 'I'd invite myself, but I gather it will be just the two of you.'

'Just the two of us.' She sat beside him. 'We miss each other when we don't get together often.'

'I like that,' he said. He was admiring her, thinking she was like a summer flower: white jeans, yellow shirt, bright red hair against the blue couch. 'And I envy it. How many men can say, without embarrassment, that they miss each other when they're not together often enough?'

'Maybe they don't miss each other.'

'I think they do. But it doesn't sound manly. Whatever that means.'

Leslie sliced coffee cake. 'I made this. First time in years. Oddest thing.' But what was truly odd, she knew, was that after six weeks of dinners with Claude, drives in the country and weekends at Tahoe, she was feeling domestic urges she hadn't felt since she was a romantic twenty, wondering which of a dozen handsome up and coming professionals she would marry. 'Bruce!' she exclaimed as the front door opened, and she leaped up to hug her brother.

Claude looked at the two flaming, curly heads close together, and at the slice of spiralled coffee cake on his plate, and had in his mind Leslie's warm voice, talking about her friendship with Katherine. My God, he thought, I'm in love with her. Tough, aggressive, beautiful, but with a sharp jaw, and an unladylike vocabulary – and thirty-seven this fall. A long way from fantasy. He laughed silently as he became aware of the relief surging through him: never again to have to keep up with a twenty-year-old.

'Welcome home,' Leslie said, her cheek against Bruce's. 'I

missed you. This is Claude Fleming – my brother Bruce McAlister. Have some cake and coffee. How was the vacation?'

'Not vacation, sis, a sincere attempt to be a wild youth again with my cohorts in Los Angeles – only it failed. I kept thinking about Heath's and the bastard who stole my notes and ripped off the store – so here I am, ready to solve your whodunit, clear my name, and go back to work and by the way, when it's all finished, I want to be the new head of Data Processing.'

Hiding a smile, Claude said, 'It sounds like you think someone framed you.'

'Bright fellow, got it in one.' Bruce took a piece of cake. 'Sis warned me not to talk; sounds like she talked to you.'

'Claude is my lawyer,' Leslie said coolly. 'Yours, too, if things get rough, so be polite.'

'I'm a gentleman, sis, you know that. Why a lawyer?'

'Because everything pointed to Data Processing or store security – or both – and either one meant me. Rumours were flying and I was on the verge of being forced out – until Claude threatened to sue everyone including the mannequins if they broke my contract. Then my president piped up that he really believes in me, and nothing would be done until we have a store-wide inventory after the June sale. So I'm being left alone. At least until July.'

'Most important,' Claude put in. 'The thefts have stopped.'

'Since when?' Bruce demanded.

'Since the day someone brought your notes to Leslie.'

'Ah ha! You see, when they aimed the finger at me they had to stop their evil doings . . . what's wrong, sis?'

'You don't seem to understand. The thefts stopped at the same time you stopped working there.'

Bruce gaped at her, his eyebrows moving as if on a spring. He looked from Claude to Leslie. 'What half-assed son of a bitch would believe that?'

'My fellow vice presidents,' Leslie said, thinking: And I nearly did, until Katherine talked to me about things like loyalty and trust.

'Christ, sis,' Bruce sputtered. 'I did good work there, doesn't my record count, how can they look at everything I've done for them and think –'

'Cut it out,' Claude snapped. 'Everything points to you, and running off to Los Angeles didn't help. What are you going to do about it?'

'Tough lawyer, sis.' Bruce sighed deeply. 'Well, I see it's up to me. I have figured out that the villain is Dick Volpe, my boss, head of the department, and I'm the only one who can check it by going through his programs because I cracked his password one day when I was bored –'

'Password?' Claude asked.

'We each have our own, like a code, that lets us work on our own programs; you can type all day and get nothing on the screen if you don't know the password – supposed to keep out spies and such –'

'But you figured out Volpe's.'

'I'm smarter than your average spy; so sis how's about you give me your master key and I'll take a look around my old office.' He held out his hand.

'Bruce, you're out of your mind. I can't give keys to non-employees. I can't even *take* you into Data Processing.'

Claude coughed. 'If you'll excuse me . . . back in a minute.'

After a bewildered pause, Leslie burst out laughing. 'You know where it is.' As he went upstairs, she stood. 'OK, let's go. Seems Claude trusts you and thinks you ought to take a look around but he doesn't want to know we're violating company policy. He'll wait for us here. Come on, damn it! How long do you think he can stay in the bathroom?'

'Forty seconds, if he pees normally. How come he knew where it was?'

'He's been there before.'

'How often?'

'Often enough to keep a spare shaver in the cabinet. Are you being protective, Bruce?'

'Hell no, I'm being approving – best choice in a long time – tough and cool and think of all that free legal advice.' He kissed her loudly. 'Good for you, sis.'

'Hey,' she protested. 'Nothing's settled.'

'Good vibes, though. OK, all is well; let's go solve this thing.'

With no children to keep him company in the morning, Ross began arriving at the office earlier each day. He liked the cool morning quiet of the streets as he drove down the hill from his house, everything hushed and still, like a painting about to burst into life. Only the joggers were out, their shoes slapping the pavement. As they passed, Ross returned their exuberant greetings with a wave of his hand, sharing with them that private moment suspended in sunlight above the fog that obliterated the Golden Gate Bridge and the skyline of San Francisco. Others slept, but they savoured the morning.

Driving down the hill, Ross followed the boundary of the University campus with its smooth, sloping lawns and earth-tone buildings. Above it all, rose the slender Campanile Tower, a white beacon visible for miles. In the afternoons, when Ross reversed the trip and the tower came into view, it beckoned telling him he was almost home.

Amazing how we adjust, he thought, parking his car and taking the stairs to his office. A year ago I wouldn't have believed I could do it. A year ago, he realised, he had been in Vancouver, meeting Katherine Fraser. Her life had been crumbling; his had been under control. He wondered if she'd commemorated the year: not an anniversary, but a milestone of sorts. She might even have heard from Craig. Maybe he should call her, to find out. No; what difference would it make? If Craig showed up, they'd all hear about it. From Derek.

Sitting at his desk, he looked out the window at the Embarcardero. Few cars; empty sidewalks. Down the street, the red brick buildings of Levi Plaza still slept; behind them, in his apartment on Lombard Street, Derek presumably slept. In Tiburon, Carrie and Jon were probably awake, perhaps making breakfast, since the cook didn't arrive until seven-thirty. Across town, Katherine might be awake by now, especially if Jennifer and Todd –

Damn it, why did he keep thinking of Katherine? Turning from the window he pulled out his Monday morning agenda. He probably wanted sympathy and thought she would understand him well enough to provide it. But he'd find sympathy elsewhere: on Sunday he and Tobias would be cooking a sumptuous farewell dinner for Victoria before she left for France. Considering how those two felt about Melanie, he'd find sympathy to spare.

He concentrated on his work until the members of his staff arrived and he gathered up his papers and strode down the hall to the conference room. It looked as if a tornado had blown through. Papers, charts, computer printouts, blueprints, sketches, pencils and notepads covered the oval table and draped to the floor; a few lay on the rolling table in the corner where an automatic coffee maker sputtered and gurgled as its carafe filled to the top. Twenty men and women stood about chatting, holding styrofoam cups as they waited for the coffee. 'Breakfast,' one of them announced, handing a box of Danish pastries to Ross. 'I figured you'd be hungry since you get here at the crack of dawn.'

'I am,' Ross said. 'Thanks, Will.' He sat in the centre of one side of the table and waited until the others were seated. 'Let's start with the latest crises on BayBridge. Who goes first?'

'I'd better,' said one of them. 'You won't believe this, but when the crews began gutting the Number Three warehouse yesterday they found a structural column fifteen feet from the southwest corner – a goddamn column through all ten floors, in the goddamn middle of what's going to be a goddamn living-room!'

'*Christ*,' someone whispered. 'How the hell –?' someone else began. The rest sat in stunned silence.

Feeling his anger build, Ross got up to refill his cup, moving slowly and deliberately, keeping his face calm. He was supposed to be the steadying influence around there. But it wasn't always easy. You design a massive project, he thought; you put your best people on it; you get the approval of half a hundred committees, agencies, and everyone else who's interested; you get written up in the newspaper as innovative, bold, brilliant – and then you spend the next year or two putting out fires that no one could have foreseen.

He returned to his chair. 'If it's a structural column,' he said quietly, 'I'd guess it was added during construction, fifty years ago. Probably the warehouse began settling while they were working on it and they stuck in a support column and then forgot it. No one bothered to re-draw the plans to show what they'd done. Any ideas on how to get around a concrete column in the middle of a living-room?'

They began to bounce suggestions around the table as Ross listened.

'Make the living-room smaller and hide it in the wall.'

'A twelve-foot room on that corner, with that view? You want your biggest room there!'

'So make it longer. What's wrong with a twelve by twenty foot living-room? If you take five feet from the east bedroom –'

'You just eliminated the east bedroom's closet.'

'Shit.'

After a while, Ross said, 'How about going up?' They

looked at him. 'Multi-storey apartments. If you can't have a modern loft, build a Victorian house. Two rooms wide, two or three storeys high. Spiral staircases if we don't have room for conventional ones . . .'

They caught the idea, liked it, enthusiastically began embellishing it. Ross scheduled a meeting for later that week to work on final drawings. 'Any more crises?'

No one spoke. No more fires, he thought. Until tomorrow. 'I have one item before we go to other projects. Donna, I just got a copy of the engineering report on the Macklin Building. You've seen it?'

'Of course, Ross. I ordered it.'

'You ordered it. And it says the northeast corner has settled two inches.' She nodded again. 'Damn it, I knew that already. You would have, too, if you'd gone to look at it. I don't need a consultant to tell me what I can see from the cracking pattern on the walls.' He was aware of the surprise on the faces around the table; he wasn't being the steadying influence they expected. But he was worried and didn't hide it. 'The question isn't *if* it's settling; it's *why*; and if there's something wrong with the foundation, what should we do about it? Is that building in danger of collapse? Should we halt the renovation work until it's fixed? That's what I asked you to find out last December, what the hell are you waiting for? Where's the foundation engineer's report?'

'It hasn't been done,' Donna said defensively. 'You said there was only one company you wanted to use, in Los Angeles, and they have more work than they know what to do with. I gave you a memo on this, Ross; it looks like they won't get to us until July. I did look at the building, and I tried to get the engineers here earlier, but they can't do it. If you want, I'll call someone else.'

'No, I remember now. I know you don't let things slide, Donna and I know you wouldn't work on a building without

328

inspecting it. I apologise.' He looked around the table, at faces that were sympathetic, even solicitous, and he knew they were telling themselves he was tense because he and his wife had split and he was living alone, spending weekends with his kids . . . he needed understanding in this difficult time.

And probably they were right, he thought later, as he went back to his office; there was a lot going on at once. 'Derek Hayward called,' his secretary said. 'He'll be a few minutes late.' Ross nodded. Something else going on: why had his brother, who had never set foot in his office, made an appointment for this morning?

'Good job,' Derek said, looking around the renovated office as they shook hands. 'How are you? Melanie is telling her friends you are devastated, callous and obstreperous.'

Ross chuckled. 'What does that mean?'

'No one knows. Probably not even Melanie. It may, however, have something to do with money.'

'It may indeed.' They smiled together and Ross felt a moment's regret that they were not close. They looked close, he knew; a stranger would have noted the physical likeness, the easy way they sat in their chairs, the smile they exchanged, the quick, almost intuitive way they sometimes communicated. Like good friends, Ross thought. But we aren't. We're only brothers. And there is nothing either of us likes about the other.

He made a fresh pot of coffee and they sat on the leather couch. Derek deliberated a moment, then asked amiably, 'Who's controlling the BayBridge contracts?'

'A number of people.'

'But you're pulling the strings.'

'I'm not even trying to pull the strings. Your spy is giving you false information, Derek.'

'I don't need spies; I know everybody in this business.' The brief amiability was gone; his voice was metallic. 'And from what I hear, the Hayward Corporation is getting the contract for a four million dollar parking lot and deck. Four million out of a three hundred million dollar project.'

'That's not public knowledge.'

'I heard it.'

Ross was silent, wondering who was feeding Derek information. Someone in the contractor's office, or one of the developers.

Derek sat back. 'It's true, then.'

'As far as I know.'

'You son of a bitch. Where did you learn to play like the big boys? You made yourself a nice little reputation since you moved here – you can't imagine how many people think they'll please me by praising my little brother to the skies – but you never played for stakes like these. And it went to your head. One of the biggest projects this city ever had, and you couldn't risk competition. *I should have been the contractor on that project.* But you kept me out of it.'

'You're wrong. I wanted you in.'

'Bullshit. You had the developers eating out of your hand; all you had to do was point in my direction.'

The first time in our lives, Ross thought, that I had any influence over something Derek wanted. 'They chose the contractor on their own. I wanted you in as a subcontractor, to build the shopping mall. But I only made suggestions, none of the final decisions. You know everything else, you know that, too.'

'You're lying.'

'Goddamn it –!' Ross took a breath. 'Use your common sense. Most of them never backed a project like this before. They didn't know how long it would take, or how much they'd have to spend, before we could begin. The day we got commitments for federal money they bought champagne; five years later, when we were still waiting for final approvals from federal and city agencies and community groups, and they'd spent twenty million dollars on land, feasibility studies, schematics, all the rest, *and we still hadn't dug the first hole*, they were too cautious even to buy beer. All of them were on edge, swearing this was going to be the cleanest project since cave dwellings; they didn't want any hitches. So how do you think they felt about giving a seventy million dollar contract for the mall to a corporation owned by the architect's family, with the architect on its board of directors?'

Derek's mouth was a thin line. 'Who the hell do you think you're talking to? I know developers; I was handling them while you were still kissing professor's asses in college. Nobody's clean, little brother. And all this fucking piety about the family corporation . . . you might show some piety about getting your family a chunk of your three hundred million dollar baby. Why didn't you call me at the beginning? We could have set up a front company to funnel contracts through, and a fund to pay off the bush league politicians in Sacramento –'

'Why didn't you call me and suggest it?'

'Call you? Ask favours from you?'

'What are you here for now?' Ross asked evenly. There was a pause. 'It doesn't matter. I wouldn't have done it; I don't work that way. But it wasn't –'

'Don't give me that choir-boy bullshit –!'

'Derek.' Ross's voice was low but it cut through the room. 'We're in my territory, not yours.'

There was another silence, long enough for Ross to reflect that it had been more years than he could remember since he and his brother had argued. In the past, when Derek charged like a bull, accusing or attacking, Ross had retreated – once as far as New York – reluctant to confront him, revolted by his tactics. But something had changed. BayBridge, he thought; giving me a sense of what I can achieve. And Melanie; forcing me to be alone, and find out who I really am. He leaned against the wall, contemplating his brother's rigid face. 'The decisions on contractors for BayBridge were never up to me. The developers made it their game, their baby – not yours, not mine. And they decided to award the Hayward Corporation the contract for the parking lot and deck; nothing else. They didn't ask me; they told me. Whatever you heard, that's the way it was.'

Derek was silent, the muscle beside his eye pulsing in the smooth mask of his face. 'What about Brock Galvez? Didn't he have anything to say to your brave band of developers?'

'A lot. He even suggested setting up a front company to funnel contracts through. He did his best. How much did you pay him? No, never mind; it doesn't matter.' A wave of revulsion swept through Ross and he turned to the windows, his back to his brother, watching the noon crowds gather with their lunches on the grassy knolls and benches of Levi Plaza. Galvez could buy and sell the Haywards; if Derek had bought him, it wouldn't have been with money, but services – drugs, sex, insider information – and Ross didn't want to know about them.

'If we're going to talk about payment,' said Derek softly. 'How much did you pay for advance information on BayBridge before you bought the Macklin Building?'

Ross turned. 'I didn't know about BayBridge when I bought it.'

'Didn't know,' Derek mocked. 'The way I heard it, you bought it in 1976 and didn't do a damn thing with it; even let Macklin keep his office space. And one year later developers begin buying land just behind it for a three hundred million dollar development. Amazing coincidence – or someone selling information.' He waited, but Ross made no answer. 'Why else would you buy it?' he demanded.

His brother was worried, Ross thought, about the Macklin Building. But he wasn't ready to talk to him about it. 'I'll tell you someday. As for Galvez, he did his best for you; I suppose he'll go on trying. But he's not a fool; when he's outvoted he backs off and goes with the majority. And they're not about to bend.'

Derek nodded thoughtfully and turned to leave. Cutting his losses, Ross thought. He seldom made mistakes as serious as this – counting on one developer without gathering information on the others – but when he did, he didn't waste energy; like Galvez, he knew when to back off. Besides, after swallowing the bitter pill of coming to his brother to ask for help, he wouldn't stay a minute past the time he knew he had failed.

But at the door, Ross held him back, asking, before he could hold back the words, 'How is Katherine?'

Imperceptibly, Derek's face changed, as if a thin cloud had passed over the sun. 'Quite well.'

Ross waited. 'And her jewellery? Is she selling through Mettler?'

'Yes.'

'Enough to make a living?'

There was a brief pause. 'With an allowance.'

Their eyes met. It had not occurred to Ross that she was taking money from Derek.

'You should call her,' Derek said pleasantly. 'Now that you live alone. She's extraordinarily accommodating.'

Ross drew in a sharp breath. 'You crude bastard.'

'My, my, such sensitivity.' Derek smiled in cold amusement. 'It must come from being cuckolded by a younger man. Don't bother to see me out; I can find my way.' He strode through the reception room, and then was gone, his diminishing footsteps echoing on the wood floor of the corridor.

Ross was gripping the edge of his office door so tightly it left a ridge on his palm when he went back to his desk. Because no matter how much he thought he had changed, his brother still had the power to infuriate and frustrate him. Derek might have lost the round on BayBridge, but it was Ross who felt battered, even sullied, by the encounter.

Sitting at his desk, contemplating the paperwork demanding his attention, it was a long time before his muscles loosened and he could begin to relax. Because he knew it wasn't only Derek who was the source of his frustration. It was also Katherine, and as Ross turned to the piles of paper on his desk, he wished to hell he could forget her and concentrate on more important things.

When Katherine arrived, Victoria was supervising the packing of a dozen suitcases and garment bags. Dresses, skirts and blouses lay everywhere in the white and gold bedroom like exhausted figures that had flung themselves on the wide bed and the silk loveseat and chaise to catch their breath. 'Just look at it,' said Tobias, quoting wickedly,

> ' "Dresses to sit in, and stand in and walk in;
> Dresses to dance in and flirt in and talk in –
> Dresses in which to do nothing at all."

Dear Victoria, do you or do you not have full closets awaiting you in France?'

'Most likely,' she said. 'Though when one has not been there for a year, one cannot be sure of anything. Lily, may I have those?' The maid handed her two knitted suits. 'St John and Castleberry,' she mused. 'So very much alike. Why did I buy them both?'

'To support the knitting industry,' Tobias hazarded.

'I know nothing about the knitting industry, Tobias; as you are well aware, I must have had a reason, though I cannot imagine what it was. This is quite wasteful; Katherine, they're your size: please take one.'

'I'd love to,' Katherine said easily. 'Thank you.' Once, she would have refused, instinctively, even rudely, thinking every offer of help was a criticism of Craig or of her own

334

helplessness. But now, more confident of herself, she admired the superb cut of the two pale blue skirts and cardigan jackets, and the silk blouse hanging beneath each one, and kissed Victoria's cheek. 'I shall look quite elegant, thanks to you.'

'You always look quite elegant. But of course clothes do help. I have several other –'

'Victoria,' Tobias warned.

She gazed at him. 'I do not flirt,' she said. 'Where did you find that ridiculous poem?'

'In a book of forgotten poets. It amused Katherine; I saw her smile. We haven't seen you for a while, my dear. What have you been doing?'

'Working, and borrowing money,' Katherine said ruefully. 'I didn't want to, but I was afraid of using the household money for buying gold and silver.'

'Well done,' Tobias declared. 'Much better to borrow than use your own. Which bank?'

'The Bank of America.'

'Very solid.'

'But I used Mettler's order as collateral. If he doesn't buy the whole collection –'

'Katherine, you are better than you think you are. Always. If you remember that, you will age less rapidly.'

'Never worry about a loan, Katherine,' Victoria said peremptorily. 'Until it's time to pay it back. What is this?' She took a long dress from a pile on the bed. 'Satin. Why is it here? I would never wear a satin dress in Menton. The rest of the Riviera perhaps, but I keep the villa in Menton precisely because it is unpretentious. And where is my black sweater with the pockets? Lily, this is not well organised. Come with me.'

As they disappeared into the dressing room, Tobias said cheerfully, 'She has twenty sweaters in the bureau to the left of her bedroom door in Menton. After this summer, she will no doubt have thirty. Are you feeling melancholy, my dear?'

'About the loan? No –'

'I was not thinking of the loan.'

Katherine gave a little laugh. 'It's not fair that you can read my mind, Tobias; I can't read yours.'

'Of course you can. Why do I think you might be melancholy?'

'You think I'd like to go to the unpretentious south of France and stay in my own villa and take side trips to Paris and the wine country and the Alps.'

'And wouldn't you?'

'Yes.'

'Quite right. I would be profoundly worried about you if you didn't. What are you going to do about it?'

'Nothing, Tobias; what can I do? I'll feel better when Victoria has left for her villa. I have plenty of work to keep me busy, and you'll be here to cheer me up; I won't brood all summer, if that's what you mean.'

'Of course you won't brood; you're not the type. I was simply wondering why you don't go to the south of France.'

'I cannot afford to go to the south of France.'

'True. But Victoria does not demand rent from her guests, and three airline tickets could be called an advance birthday present – your birthday is in August, is it not?'

'Three airline – ? To France? To stay with Victoria? But she's never said a word about it.'

'Ah, but she has. To me. Since Christmas, she has fretted over how to ask you to join her in Menton. Why do you think she is going in July when her usual time is April and May? She waited until Todd and Jennifer were out of school. But still we kept debating how to ask you. Victoria is not timid, as you no doubt have noticed, but after your severe refusal last March of her offer to help your jewellery career, she tiptoes around you, wanting to give, but afraid to try. You are so fierce in your rejections, my dear. But just now you graciously accepted a

336

knit suit and it occurred to me that you might accept a trip to France if I explained it carefully, which I have just done. Now, my dear, quickly, before you have time to think of obstacles: would you like to go to France with Victoria?'

'Of course I'd like it – I'd love it. I've never been there, I've never been anywhere in Europe. But how can we? I haven't made arrangements –'

'No obstacles allowed! Of course we should have asked you earlier, but each time we talked about it, we put it off. Two old people afraid of being turned down. But it's not complicated; you don't need much time. Let me think. Passports. Are they current?'

Katherine shook her head. 'We never travelled. And we didn't need them to move here . . .'

'Oh dear, oh dear. Well, we have friends in the government offices; we'll manage. What else? Your jewellery. You can work on designs in France and make the pieces when you return. You could stay quite a while and still accomplish that. Three weeks? Four? The children, of course, are out of school, and you said you would not be sending them to camp.'

She nodded.

'Yes?' Tobias asked.

'Yes, I'm not sending them to camp.' They laughed.

'And you told us some time ago you are no longer seeing Derek, so unless you have returned to him or found someone else –'

'No.'

'Then there is not even a romance to keep you in the city.'

'Not even that,' Katherine said. 'There's really nothing to keep me in the city.' *Except Craig.* The words were dark against Tobias's bright confidence. *If he comes looking for us, he'll find another empty house.* But excitement was running through her like quicksilver, and thinking of Craig only reminded her of the times, long ago, when she wanted to plan

337

trips to Europe and Craig refused. He preferred trips in Canada, he said, though when she asked why, he gave no specific reasons. Now, suddenly she understood why. He didn't have a passport. He couldn't get one without a birth certificate . . . and there was no birth certificate for Craig Fraser. I suppose he could have had one forged, Katherine thought. But perhaps he thought enough of his life was forged already. She felt a rush of pity for him. He wasn't free to travel about the world, and he couldn't explain that to me without telling the truth about himself. So there was one more secret, one more space between us . . .

'Nothing to keep you here,' Tobias was echoing with a gleeful smile and Katherine felt her excitement return as Victoria, who had been listening, came out of the dressing room, her arms filled with clothes, saying, 'Of course, Katherine, you will want your blue jeans and your own casual things, but I have far too many sweaters and shirts and all of them are perfect for you –' She stopped as Katherine and Tobias burst into renewed laughter. 'As part of your birthday present,' she went on calmly. 'I cannot imagine why you two should find that hilarious. Katherine, it will take a day or two for you to get passports, but after that, how soon can you come? You will fly to Nice, the limousine will meet you, and you and I will take a separate shopping trip to Paris. Did Tobias say four weeks?'

'Yes,' Katherine breathed. 'But I'm not sure –'

'Four weeks sounds quite satisfactory. Can you be ready to leave in a week? July fifth. My dear' – Victoria laid her hand on Katherine's cheek – 'forgive me if I seem a trifle autocratic, I am so very happy that you will let me give you this. It has been so long since there were young voices at the villa . . . We think we become self-sufficient and tough, but we never stop longing to share the things we love. Without it, we're only half-alive. How wonderful that you are coming!' She coughed and impatiently wiped her eyes. 'Well, then' – briskly she turned back to the piles of clothes on the bed – 'it's settled. Tobias will arrange for passports and three tickets for July fifth. Unless, of course, you have a serious objection –?'

' "Take the good the gods provide thee",' murmured Tobias urgently. 'Dryden. Wise man. Valuable advice.'

'Of course,' said Katherine softly. 'After all, she only seemed to be a trifle autocratic.' Their eyes met in a smile. Then her excitement was too much to contain and jumping up, she put her arms around Victoria. 'Thank you. Thank you. Oh, it sounds so *pale* – how can I tell you –?'

'Quite sufficient, dear Katherine. As long as you are pleased.'

'I love you,' Katherine said. 'And now I'm going home because I can't wait to tell Jennifer and Todd. Or may I help you pack?'

'Lily is here. And Tobias helps by telling me I need nothing, which reduces the amount I pack. I'll call you tomorrow morning before I leave.' Victoria kissed her on both cheeks. 'Tell your children to practise their French. Oh, my dear, what fun we are going to have!'

Katherine was smiling as she left the building, her voice dancing with such delight when she said goodbye to the doorman that his face creased in an answering grin. It was still there a few minutes later when he opened the door to let Ross in. 'Happiest young lady I ever saw, just left Mrs Hayward,' he said, shutting the grille on the elevator and starting the stately ride to Victoria's floor.

Ross had seen her, walking down the steep pitch of Washington Street. Her distinctive beauty drew glances from passersby, but it was the brightness of her face that had struck him, and the eagerness of her step. At a stoplight, she had crossed in front of him, her eyes looking to the distance. A happy woman, he thought: joyously anticipating, hurrying – probably because someone is waiting.

'You just missed Katherine,' Victoria said, kissing him. 'You'll have sherry with us, won't you? Tobias thinks it is sustenance for packing.'

'Otherwise I grow faint from your exertions,' said Tobias. He handed Ross a glass. 'Derek was here earlier, to wish Victoria a good trip, and Ann and Jason called, from Maine. It is astonishing how the solicitude over Victoria's well-being has increased in the past year.'

'Has it?' Ross asked. 'I didn't know.'

'Do you know why?'

He reflected. 'Craig, of course. The chance that he might come back. Odd, how he hovers over the family.'

'Disruptive,' said Tobias sagely. 'Thoughts of him bring thoughts of emotional and financial disruptions.'

Ross pictured the Craig of his youth; brown eyes watching for approval as he busied himself with model aeroplanes, wood carvings and intricate matchstick houses, or sailed his boat on the bay, dreaming of the skyscrapers he would build, and the trips he would someday take to Europe and Asia, as far as he could go. Disruptive? Only Derek had found him disruptive in those days.

'Derek mentioned BayBridge Plaza,' said Tobias very casually. 'He seems to think we're being frozen out. Where would he get that idea?'

'He got it from me. Don't be cagey, Tobias. Derek told you he came to see me.'

'So he did. I thought I should hear your side of the story before forming an opinion.'

'The Hayward Corporation will have a small part of BayBridge. The rest will be built by other subcontractors. The developers are afraid of the appearance of a conflict of interest. That's all there is to it.' Ross began to pace from one end of the bedroom to the other. 'I didn't think, Tobias, I'd have to make excuses to you. There's never been any reason for you to doubt my honesty. Or my family loyalty.' His strides grew longer. 'Of all the places where I hope to find acceptance this is the one I count on most; I don't expect to walk in at the end of a hellish week and be grilled about my relationship with my brother.'

'Whoa, whoa, now, dear friend. ' Tobias looked keenly at Ross. 'I was speaking of the corporation, not you and Derek. However, this is not the time. You seem tired –'

'– Seem!'

'And fuming. Would you care to dump your problems – as the young people say?'

Ross gave an apologetic laugh. 'I'm sorry, Tobias. You didn't deserve that. Do you really want to hear about my week?'

'Does it have more plot than Victoria's discussion of what she will pack – which I have listened to all day?'

They laughed. 'Well, then.' Sitting on a hassock, his elbows on his knees, Ross described his staff meetings on crises at BayBridge, and his session with Derek. 'And at least a dozen times this week I started a letter to Jacques Duvain, telling him I can't be his consultant in Paris.'

'Started?' Tobias asked. 'Not finished?'

'Not yet. For some reason I keep putting it off. I'll do it tomorrow. But I haven't finished with my week. Friday evening I picked up Carrie and Todd. Do you know what it feels like, Tobias, to knock at a front door that was mine for years?'

'You said Melanie gave you the new key.'

'I won't use it unless I have to. I don't live there anymore, so I knock.'

'Correct but depressing.' Tobias poured more sherry. 'And how did the three of you get on?'

'Acrimoniously. We squabble over little things – trying to get used to everything, I suppose. This afternoon, when I was

341

driving them home, Carrie said, "Mother goes around singing about Guy what's-his-name, and you have a house with a jacuzzi: we're the only ones who are unhappy, and what's fair about that?" '

'What indeed?' asked Tobias. 'How did you answer?'

'I told them life wasn't fair.' Ross began to pace again. 'On my way over here, I bought a stack of books on divorced fathers. Do you think they'll help?'

'They'll show you you're not alone. That should help.'

Quietly, Victoria had come up behind them. She put a hand on Ross's hair. 'Poor boy. So many pressures on you.'

Tobias glanced up sharply at the note in her voice. No one knew Victoria as well as he; no one else, hearing her sympathise with her grandson, would have been aware that her thoughts were racing ahead with plans. 'Yes,' he agreed. 'A difficult time for Ross.'

Victoria smiled at him with a glint of conspiracy, then as if suddenly inspired, exclaimed, 'Ross! I have a grand idea!'

Ross looked up. 'You mustn't worry about me; I'll be all right. You're supposed to be thinking about France, and taking a rest from all your Boards of Directors.'

'I am thinking about France! How clever of you to understand. You shall come to France! You have work to do in Paris –'

'I'm turning that down.'

'Please do not interrupt. You just told Tobias you put off writing your letter. Why? Because you want to go. *Voilà*! You shall go. Do your consulting in Paris and when you are finished come to Menton. You haven't been there in far too many years. We will have a visit. Are you listening?'

'I am listening. Carrie and Todd are spending July with me.'

There was barely a pause. 'Bring them. The Riviera is very healthy for children. And their fathers. Your staff can handle

342

your new Plaza for a while. You haven't had a vacation since Melanie began refusing to go away with you; I am offering you one, with a chance to do the work you wish to do. There are other reasons –'

'Stop,' Ross laughed. His head was up, his body felt lighter and more buoyant than it had in weeks. 'You don't need any more reasons. You've convinced me. I don't know why I never thought of going; it's exactly what I need.' He stood and hugged Victoria, kissing her boisterously. As he turned, he saw the glance she and Tobias exchanged. 'What is it? What don't I know?'

'How happy you've made me,' Victoria said smoothly. 'How much I look forward to seeing you in Menton. How sorry Tobias is that he is not going. Oh, my,' she added with a tremulous sigh. 'What fun we are going to have!'

Chapter 13

Hugh Hayward had dreamed of a villa near Nice since spending several months there during the first world war. Not yet mobbed by tourists, it had a leisurely pace, vivid beauty and year-round golden warmth that he remembered for the next thirty years. The Depression and another war intervened before he could return, this time with Victoria, to explore the region of Provence from Marseille to Nice until they found the Villa Serein. At the time, in the spring of 1948, it hardly matched its name, being far from serene as it huddled, empty and desolate, behind tangled weeds. Its stucco walls were flaked, its windows broken, the roof pocked with holes, and all its doors had been used during the war for firewood.

But the villa stood near the top of a hill overlooking Menton and its harbour, long a favourite of European royalty, and its rooms were large and solid. Besides, so soon after the second world war, properties on the Côte d'Azur were bargains, especially those in disrepair. Before returning to America, Hugh bought six, and some years later sold five of them at a handsome profit.

There never was any question of selling Villa Serein. Once the weeds were gone, the trees tamed, and the rooms newly whitewashed, Victoria had fallen in love with it and undertook its renovation with the experience and enthusiasm that had been pent-up since she had run the Hayward Corporation.

After Derek and Ross were born, the villa was enlarged to fourteen rooms with a terrace in front and a garden with a small pond at the rear. Over the years it was refurbished many times, and when Katherine and the children arrived, they found square, low-ceilinged rooms, bright and inviting, filled with plump furniture in the sun-filled colours of Pissarro and Matisse, painters who had lived in Provence and whose paintings, bought by Hugh when he was a soldier, hung on the walls of the villa as well as in Victoria's apartment in San Francisco.

'*Magnifique*,' pronounced Todd. '*Merveilleux. Beau.*' Having nearly exhausted his French vocabulary, he added a final, '*Merci.*'

Victoria laughed. 'Well done.'

Jennifer, remembering instructions from Katherine, said, 'It's very good of you to have us here.'

'It is a pleasure,' Victoria responded. 'I want you to have a wonderful time, so we shall begin by going over your choices . . .'

There was swimming in the olympic-size pool in Menton, tennis lessons in town and sailing lessons at the harbour, badminton and croquet which Victoria had imported from England, the villa's own library, with French and English books, down the hall from their bedrooms ('Our own rooms,' Todd said, jabbing Jennifer with his elbow), and a garden filled with vegetables to pick for lunch and dinner.

To help them choose, the next morning Victoria gave them a supply of francs to pay for lessons or to go shopping in town. And finally she introduced them to the gardener, and Sylvie and Charles, the couple who cooked and managed the villa, and who would watch over them for the next few days. 'Because your mother and I are going shopping in Paris,' she announced.

'We just got here,' objected Todd. 'And you're already leaving.'

'We will be away for three days,' said Victoria calmly. 'I am confident you will cope quite well.'

Katherine let her thoughts drift while Victoria took charge. How pleasant, she thought, to let someone else take over for a while.

It was a little space of time in a fantastic place like none she had ever known. Tropical palm trees along the harbour; cypresses and ancient, gnarled olive trees on the steep hills, shading flat-roofed villas covered with climbing roses; the narrow dusty-pink houses of Menton stopping just short of the harbour's edge, beyond which huge, gleaming yachts and sixty-foot sailboats rocked gently in the soft breeze. A little bit of time in a place so beautiful and warm, the sun heavy and golden, the air spicy and sensuous, it was impossible to believe anyone could frown or worry or weep. Far from familiar routines and problems; far from everyday thoughts; far from memories.

Far from Craig.

He wasn't there, Katherine realised. And the next morning, when she and Victoria flew to Paris, it was still true. His shadow had not followed her. Crossing an ocean to a different world, she had broken away from him. For a while.

The next morning, as the plane climbed rapidly above the white crescent of Nice, Victoria said, 'I waited for you, so we could go shopping together. One of the few joys of being old is introducing the young to new pleasures. It would take you months of wandering to discover the best places by yourself, while I can show them to you in three days. So unfortunate, the tourists who have no one to direct them.'

'Perhaps they enjoy wandering,' Katherine suggested.

'Nonsense. Without a plan? I cannot imagine it.'

Katherine smiled. 'You always have reasons for what you do. What is your reason for bringing me to Paris?'

'I told you,' Victoria said coolly. 'A shopping expedition.'

Katherine felt a clang of warning – *she's hiding something* – but it faded as she watched the mountain ranges of central France give way to dairy farms and wheat fields and then, suddenly, Paris: the soaring, echoing concrete of the Charles de Gaulle airport, and then the crowds and noise of the city – the sidewalks jammed, traffic nearly immobilised, and outdoor cafes crammed with small tables, each a centre of vigorous discussion. Even the noble lobby of the Hotel Meurice was a shifting mass of people carrying on rapid, high-pitched conversations.

'Now,' said Victoria with a sigh in the silence of their suite as the maid hung their clothes in the wardrobe and Katherine, striving not to gape, took stock of the lavish adjoining rooms. 'We shall go shopping. We lunch at two at Maxim's with Henri Flambeau. An old friend,' she said at Katherine's questioning look. 'Who, it so happens, owns a number of fine jewellery shops. You must always expand your circle of acquaintances, my dear. Especially in France. Nothing makes an American designer more desirable than being desired by the French.'

Katherine laughed. 'Thank you; I'd like very much to meet him.' That was Victoria's surprise, she thought; her reason for the trip to Paris. A rush of gratitude and love swept through her, mingling with the excitement of being in Paris, and when they left the hotel and walked in the sunlight past the great

347

gardens of the Tuileries, it was as if every fairy tale she knew had come to life, and she was the heroine of all of them. Her feet began skipping into little dance steps and she had trouble matching her pace to Victoria's dignified stroll.

On the Rue Cambon, Victoria stopped at the House of Chanel. 'Why don't you go ahead?' she suggested a little too brightly. 'You shouldn't be burdened with my dawdling. I'll tell you how to get to Maxim's, to meet for lunch.'

'No,' Katherine said swiftly. 'I'd rather you showed me your favourite places.'

'Well.' Victoria put her hand on Katherine's arm. 'Of course, you must not say that just to please me.'

'I want to be with you.'

'Well,' she said again, and beamed. 'What a lovely day. So often it is too hot in Paris in July. We'll browse for a moment in Chanel and then go on.'

Victoria's Paris was almost entirely contained within a triangle with Napoleon's column in the Place Vendôme in the centre. Here were the narrow streets and wide boulevards dedicated to culture and consumption: the world's most elegant stores, with discreet entrances and displays, alongside the national library and the Opera, with its domes, columns, and extravagant stonework. 'The Opera is open to the public now,' Victoria said in passing. 'Most impressive. We shall visit it if we have time.' And when they passed the *Bibliothèque Nationale*, 'The dome of the Library reading room is quite astonishing. We shall visit it if we have time.' And, 'Madeleine: one of my favourite theatres; we shall visit it if we have time. But the plan for today is to visit shops.'

Katherine wanted to linger everywhere, in buildings and at intersections where carefully-planned vistas stretched down long streets, but she stayed with Victoria and got a succinct lesson in European designers, and the best places to shop. She wished Leslie were there – with her flair and income she could have used Victoria's guidance far better than Katherine, and taken back to America enough clothes for a decade. Or Katherine amended, remembering Leslie's closet, at least a year.

At Maxim's, Henri Flambeau was waiting. He watched the two women walk towards him in the sunlight – of equal height and slenderness and a certain way of holding their heads that made passersby look twice – one old, with sharp bones, her skin finely scored, her beauty fragile, fading, like a painting seen in the failing light of dusk; the other young, her loveliness arresting in its opposites: a face delicately-shaped yet strong, a complexion pale but flushed, magnificent eyes, knowledgeable but as wide and eager as a young girl's. Such different kinds of beauty, Henri mused and – as he saw them exchange a smile – how they love each other.

'Tell Henri about your jewellery,' Victoria commanded as soon as they were seated.

Self-conscious, Katherine was brief, but he was attentive, at first to her beauty, then to the designs he asked her to sketch as she talked. 'Ah,' he said, studying them and nodding non-committally, until Victoria demanded, 'Are you interested or not? This is not a game, Henri.'

He spread his hands. 'Of course not; Madame Fraser is most serious in her profession. But she understands that I do not commit myself until I see her work. The designs are interesting.'

'Interesting!' Victoria raised her eyebrows. 'So cautious – and you a Frenchman.'

'The French are the most cautious of all people,' he replied. 'It is the Americans who like to think we are reckless. Madame Fraser, when you wish to sell in Paris, please let me see before anyone else what you are making.'

Smoothly, then, he changed the subject, asking them if they had seen the Beaubourg, a modern museum of outrageous architecture built inside out with exposed pipes, structural beams, and escalators running up the outside of the building. 'The entire Marais has been rediscovered,' he said. 'All those grand mansions that had been used as factories are being restored as homes and apartments. Imagine: after two centuries of neglect, it is once again acceptable – indeed, chic – to live on the Right Bank.'

'Someone told me,' said Victoria thoughtfully, 'of a royal square in the Marais being completely redone. The oldest in Paris . . . what *is* its name . . .'

'Place des Vosges,' said Henri. 'You have not seen it? But it is quite extraordinary; in all the tourist books, in fact. If you have time for a visit –'

'We'll make time,' Victoria declared. 'Perhaps this afternoon. Katherine? Would you have any objection?'

A little bewildered by how suddenly they had time, Katherine shook her head. 'Whatever you would like.'

And that was how it happened that Katherine and Victoria were standing before Number 21 Place des Vosges at four-thirty in the afternoon, just as Ross Hayward emerged from a nearby archway and looked up from the photographs he was studying into Katherine's wide, uncomprehending eyes.

They stared in silence. 'Well, Ross,' Victoria said with mild surprise. 'I thought the name of this place sounded familiar when Henri mentioned it. Is it the project your friend Jacques asked you to work on?'

Awareness grew in Ross's eyes as he looked from her to Katherine. 'You know perfectly well it is,' he said, kissing Victoria on one cheek and then the other. Slowly he shook his head. 'Couldn't you have told me the truth, instead of going through that play-acting?'

'One should never take chances,' she said calmly.

What truth? Katherine asked herself. Ross was watching her and she met his gaze, waiting for him to explain. She had not seen him since those few minutes in March, when she had arrived at Victoria's and he had left almost immediately. Now she was struck by his looks. Carrying a suit jacket, his shirt open at the neck, his skin bronzed and his light hair lightened by the sun, he was more relaxed than she remembered: tall, with an athletic stride, his face strong and expressive, his deepset eyes studying her with curiosity and a promise of warmth. 'You didn't know I'd be here – and was invited to Menton?'

'No.' Katherine understood then. Turning to Victoria, she said, 'You should have told me.'

'*Should*? Indeed not.' Victoria tilted her chin. 'Since when must I report to my grandchildren? Tobias told you I've wanted to bring you to France for months – I thought it would help you break your relationship with Derek, though you did manage to do that on your own' – Ross's head snapped towards Katherine, brows drawn together, and she realised he had not known about it – 'and I wanted to share with you a place I love. But I had to wait until your children were out of school. I asked *you*,' she told Ross, 'because you were in despair over your children and pressures at work and Lord knows what else; you desperately needed to get away and any-one who cared a fig for you would have helped you; it would have been peculiar if I had not.'

Imperiously, she eyed the two of them, daring them to respond, but, wisely, they were silent. 'In addition,' she said tartly, 'I expect harmony in my family and I've waited quite long enough for the two of you to become friends on your own. If you cannot do that – for whatever unseemly and unac-ceptable reason – you certainly can tolerate each other during the few days you will be together at the villa. Now.' She took a breath. 'I am finding it quite tiresome to stand here. Is no one going to take a frail old woman in off the street and buy her a glass of wine?'

Katherine and Ross glanced at each other, exchanging a smile. Sighing, Ross took his grandmother's arm. 'The privileges of age are often abused. Come this way; it's just a few steps.'

Katherine lagged behind. She was uncomfortable; her dancing delight at being in Paris had faded. Henri wasn't the reason for their visit; she'd been brought here so she and Ross could 'run into' each other. It didn't help that Ross had known no more than she; Katherine felt used, not trusted to share in a decision.

I've been treated that way before. By my husband.

Silently she joined Ross and Victoria at Ma Bourgogne, a small café under an arcade in one of the buildings of Place des Vosges. They sat in rattan chairs at a round table and, as Katherine watched Victoria and Ross chat about Paris, she felt like an outsider. Ross kept glancing at her but she could not participate in their gossip and talk about a city they both knew well and she knew nothing about. She wished she were alone.

The waiter brought a bottle of Bordeaux and filled their glasses. Ross and Victoria talked on. Katherine sat back in her chair, sipping the mellow wine, contemplating the aloof elegance of the mansions on all sides of the grassy square, speculating about the people who lived behind their tall, many-paned windows, dreaming about living in such a place herself someday.

'Katherine?' Victoria said.

She started. 'I'm sorry. I didn't hear you.'

'Dinner, my dear. We decided on Tour d'Argent. Too many tourists, but I want to watch your face when you see it for the first time. And it will be my dinner: I shall treat you both, to compensate for not confiding in you.'

She began to tell Ross about their lunch with Henri. Half-listening, Katherine wondered what Victoria expected to happen. Were they supposed to fall in love – or just become instant friends? Her carefree sense of adventure had disappeared; she didn't know how she was expected to behave. 'Nine o'clock, then,' Victoria said at last, gathering her purse and gloves and rising as the waiter held her chair.

Swiftly, Ross came to hold Katherine's chair. He had sensed her discomfort, and knew she'd rather he weren't there. 'Only dinner,' he said, his voice low. 'Then I won't interfere with any more of your trip.'

She looked at him, silenced by surprise and embarrassment.

'It's important to Victoria,' he added, leaving out the fact that he was looking forward to the evening. He had thought about Katherine so long, and stayed away from her for so long, that discovering her in Paris seemed almost magical – even if it were no wizard but his grandmother who had brought her there. But he would not tell her that; she was uncomfortable, whether from Victoria's secrecy or because she didn't want Ross intruding on her holiday, and he had no wish to add to her discomfort. 'The Tour d'Argent is spectacular,' he said. 'Enough to make up for even unwelcome dinner companions.'

Victoria took Katherine off so quickly she had no chance to respond and there was no chance that evening, either. First Victoria insisted on absolute silence as they were led to their table so she could watch Katherine's delight in the view. For a few moments the three of them gazed without speaking at the barely rippling water of the Seine, reflecting the darkening sky, and the brightly-lit Notre Dame cathedral looming from its thickly wooded island, so close it seemed they could touch its square towers and needle-like spire.

'Lovely,' Victoria sighed. 'I never saw it with Hugh. I wish I had.' She turned to Katherine. 'There is a famous story about this restaurant –'

The story was lengthy, about a visiting chef and a foreign dignitary, and Katherine tried to follow it while studying the shapes and shadows of Notre Dame and the other ancient buildings on the two islands in the Seine that had been the original city of Paris. She felt Ross watching her, and wondered what he was thinking, and wished she were having the uncomplicated holiday she'd expected.

But suddenly Ross and Victoria became charming companions, as if apologising for leaving her out that afternoon, entertaining her all through dinner with a colourful history of the kings and queens of France and the duelling, lusting, sniping, gossiping courts that revolved around them in the palaces of Paris. They took turns telling stories, from books they had read, from theatre-going in Paris, and evenings with Parisian friends, all for Katherine, who was content to listen and laugh with them. By midnight, when the waiter presented Victoria with a bill that made even her worldly eyebrows rise, the evening seemed as friendly and uncomplicated as Katherine could wish.

'Thank you,' said Ross, kissing Victoria as they waited for a taxi. 'For a most pleasant evening. I haven't told so many stories since I was in college.'

'And these were probably far less bawdy,' Victoria smiled. 'It was a pleasure, dear Ross. I had a delightful time.'

At the Meurice, Ross walked with them into the lobby and took Katherine's hand. 'I hope your trip is everything you want it to be. You have the best companion in the world. And the villa is a perfect retreat.'

'Such formality,' said Victoria with a trace of anxiety. 'You'll see us in Menton in less than a week.'

'I'm not sure.' He looked at Katherine's slender hand, still enclosed in his. Nothing she had said all evening indicated she wanted to see him again. 'There's more to do here than I'd expected. And my children will be here soon and I thought I might introduce them to Paris. We'll come if we can,' he said quickly, as Victoria opened her mouth to reproach him. 'I'll let you know, one way or another.' Briefly, he tightened his hand

354

on Katherine's. 'Have a wonderful time. If there's anything I can do for you before you leave Paris, please let me know.'

'In my day,' Victoria snorted as she and Katherine walked into the elevator, 'a gentleman would have offered to buy us a lavish breakfast in the morning.' She lapsed into silence. 'It would have been pleasant if Ross had done that.'

Yes, Katherine thought, surprising herself, as they reached their floor. It would have been very pleasant.

Place des Vosges is a green park surrounded by thirty-six tall brick and plaster townhouses, or *hôtels*, of dusty pink to deep red, with wrought-iron balconies and round windows in steeply pitched slate roofs. White stone arches lead through each *hôtel* to a private courtyard. Four hundred years ago the park was the scene of royal tournaments and festivals; two hundred years ago the mansions were abandoned for new residences across the Seine, on the left bank; in the 1960s they were rediscovered and slowly reclaimed from the factory owners who had boarded up windows, bolted heavy machinery to the rich parquet floors, torn out ornately-carved doors, and dumped trash in the inner courtyards.

When Ross first saw it, a few *hôtels* had been bought and were beginning to be restored. When he returned fifteen years later as Jacques Duvain's consultant in restoring one of the *hôtels*, the Place had become a lively blend of new and old. Some of the buildings were still in disrepair, but many had been renovated, hiding, behind identical exteriors, private homes, apartments, schools, restaurants, a synagogue, and a number of fine, small shops.

The second floor of Number 9 Place des Vosges was owned by the Architecture Society, and through Jacques, who was a member, Ross had been given his own quiet corner with a desk, drawing table and two armchairs for as long as he was in Paris. On the day after his dinner with Victoria and Katherine, he sat at the desk, trying to work. *In my day*, he had heard Victoria scoff as he left them, a *gentleman would have invited us to breakfast*. He had considered it, then decided against it, but still, throughout the day, he thought about Katherine, heard Victoria casually say she had broken with Derek, pictured her as she had looked at the Tour d'Argent – poised, yet eager and curious, making no attempt to seem worldly. She was without pretence, willing to admit there was so much she did not know, yet firmly determined to be independent. And in that contradiction, she was both strong and vulnerable. In the past year, Ross thought she had been different each time he saw her, changing from Craig's protected wife to the elusive woman he had dined with last night. And he realised he knew nothing about her.

But competing with those thoughts was a busy day. He and Jacques worked on various plans for putting an elevator in the four-storey *hôtel*, they spent an hour with specialists in matching segments of broken mouldings on the fifteen-foot-high ceilings and restoring the parquet floors to their original lustre; they met for another hour with the contractor, discussing ways to install modern plumbing and wiring in plaster walls that had withstood wars and revolutions but often crumbled at the bite of an electric drill. Since he had arrived, Ross had studied, read, learned, from early morning until late each night; he had inspected other buildings marked for restoration; he had given advice. He was having a wonderful time. And even when distracted by Katherine's sudden appearance, he was absorbed by the special fascination of bringing into the twentieth century a building constructed in 1605.

'Yes, yes,' Jacques admitted when they met for Lunch at La Chope des Vosges, at one corner of the Place. 'Certainly it is fascinating. And yet – ' He paused as they heaped their plates from the hors-d'oeuvres buffet near the entrance and found a table. 'This elevator – weeks I have spent on this elevator! And now I am trying your idea of hiding it behind the staircase, but of course we must not disturb the sweep of its curve – impossible!'

'I'm working on that.'

'I delight to hear it. I also am working on your other suggestion – that we put it at the front of the entrance hall. But you say I may not use the cloakroom. A perfect space! A perfect size!'

'Well, we may have to use it. But it means moving a wall on the third floor.'

'Precisely the problem! Why all this effort and cost? It is cheaper to tear down and begin afresh!'

'Not always.'

'I concede that. But consider: buildings are made for specific times and people, with specific customs and idiosyncrasies. No one builds for people who will not be born for four hundred years.'

'Jacques, working on this *hôtel*, you'd still erase it if you could?'

'Whoosh it out. Begin fresh. An odd debate, is it not? The Americans are the best at tearing down, even buildings only thirty or forty years old. Occasionally they are wrong, but most often I agree. Begin afresh. No clutter of old ideas, no rubble from other generations, no messy traditions, no –'

'Variety,' Ross finished helpfully. 'Or contrast or history or excitement.'

'Well –' Jacques shrugged. 'So you say. But what we lose we replace with what is truly ours. Look at us, you and me. Did we not start all afresh? Of course people are not the same as buildings, but what do you think ? Was it not better that you and I left wives who were not congenial so we could begin again and improve our situations? Should we not seek perfection? We change; we require new marriages and new buildings. The old no longer satisfies. Who would pay ten

357

million francs for a *hôtel* of four floors with no elevator? Who will tolerate a marriage that is all uphill?' He grinned. 'That is not bad.'

'Not bad,' Ross agreed, then said, 'I have two children who are part of my old marriage. Would you have me throw them out . . . give them up?'

'No, no; that is different. You would regret it; so would they. Allow me to speak from experience. My wife and I own an art gallery together. We are good partners, yes – but ferociously bad at living together. So we kept what was good: we are together often, we dine, we laugh, we shake hands and go to someone else for love. One must leap to new adventures; one does not look back, even if occasionally one regrets losing something along the way. You comprehend? Here is the bill; is it my turn to pay?'

'No, mine.' Ross pulled out his wallet and smiled. 'You're the real consultant, Jacques. We disagree, but without you I'd have no ancient building to study; and you also offer me the bonus of your curious philosophy. I don't give you half as much.'

'Not so. You bring me friendship and American technology. As for ancient buildings, it is not your fault America has nothing from the sixteenth century on which you can practise.'

'Only wigwams,' Ross said and they were chuckling as they walked through the shadowed arcade into the sunlight. Shading his eyes. Ross turned toward the *hôtel* and for the second time in two days found himself face to face with Katherine.

He stopped short. His grandmother's idea – or hers? But why would she let Victoria manoeuvre her a second time? Then he saw her eyes, self-conscious, determined, a little wary, as if she had steeled herself to be here and feared he might turn his back on her. Ross took her hand. 'Welcome back.' He looked around. 'Are you alone?'

'Yes.' She glanced inquiringly at Jacques, who hovered at Ross's shoulder.

'Jacques Duvain,' said Ross, piqued by the intense admiration that lit Jacques' face. 'Katherine Fraser.'

Jacques lifted Katherine's hand and brushed it with his lips. 'How pleased I am to greet you.' He smiled broadly and, through him, Ross saw Katherine as if for the first time, separated from the familiar background of San Francisco, with no husband shadowing her, no grandmother as chaperone, no Derek. In a low-necked sleeveless blue dress with a white jacket over her shoulders, she stood alone, tentatively, as if on a threshold: a young woman of unusual beauty, hesitating before opening a door onto the unknown. Ross understood why Jacques was intrigued. 'I have heard you are visiting,' Jacques went on innocently, with barely a sidelong glance at Ross. 'I do not wish to intrude, but if at some time you desire a guide who has lived here always . . .' A movement from Ross caught his eye. 'Of course, my friend Ross knows Paris almost as well as I. So I leave you' – again, he touched Katherine's hand with his lips – 'but I hope to see you again . . .' He looked at Ross and grinned. 'I spoke of starting afresh. I did not realise my admirable friend was far ahead of me. Perhaps dinner one night, the three of us, if it becomes possible –?'

He drifted off. Silence filled the space left by his chatter. 'Why don't we walk?' Ross suggested. 'You didn't get to see the whole square yesterday.' Katherine nodded. She was nervous and he wondered again about his grandmother as they strolled through sunlight and shadow. On one side was the green park with its fountains and benches, on the other the stately old *hôtels*. They paused to look through a shop window at a craftsman restoring a clavichord. 'What time are you meeting Victoria?' Ross asked.

'I'm not.' Katherine watched the man's quick fingers. 'She went back to Menton this morning.'

He turned sharply. 'Was she ill?'

'No.' Katherine met his eyes and smiled. 'She thought she was being cool and crafty.'

Ross chuckled and then Katherine laughed with him. 'Well,' he said as they walked on. 'Maybe she was. Here you are.'

Katherine stopped, her face deeply flushed. 'I act on my own,' she said. Her nervousness gave way to anger; her large eyes were clear and unwavering. 'I'm not a puppet to be manipulated; I make my own decisions.'

Ross cursed himself. 'I'm sorry; I didn't mean that. I thought you didn't want me to share your time in Paris, and it was so clear that Victoria wanted –'

'Of course it was; she even admitted it. But she left without making any suggestions, without even a hint. She knows I wouldn't have come to you because it was something she would have liked, especially after yesterday.'

Ross looked at her averted eyes. 'Why did you come?' he asked quietly.

'Because I wanted to.' For the first time, her voice wavered. 'Because I wanted to see you.'

The words struck him with their simplicity. Just as simply, he responded, 'I'm glad to see you.' In a moment they walked on. 'How did Victoria explain her sudden departure?' he asked.

They were passing a sculpture gallery and Katherine paused to look through the window. 'She said she'd give me a chance to explore on my own.' She smiled, almost to herself. 'In a way, she was telling the truth, because yesterday she knew she was holding me back. But whatever her reasons, she gave me our hotel suite and two days in Paris, and that was wonderful. *She's* wonderful, and I'm grateful, and I love her.'

'Yes,' Ross said. 'That's something we share.' His eyes had the same tenderness Katherine had seen in Vancouver, the first time she heard him speak of Victoria. 'When did she leave?' he asked.

'After breakfast.'

'And left you *no* instructions for touring Paris? That doesn't sound like my grandmother.'

Katherine laughed. 'She left me names of her favourite restaurants and the finest buildings, the places to go for the finest views, small boutiques for the finest of –'

'Everything,' he finished and they laughed together. Ross put his hand on Katherine's arm and led her into a restaurant filled with flowers. 'Have you followed all her instructions?'

'I'm afraid I forgot most of them. I bought a map; I walked; I took the Métro . . .' She hesitated. 'And I took a bus tour.'

'A bus –!' He caught himself. 'And what did you see?'

'A great many buildings and statues that all looked alike after ten minutes.'

He smiled. 'That happens on most bus tours. And then?'

'I came to find you.'

How natural she made it sound. 'Why?' he asked.

'I was thinking about you. I never really knew whether you liked me or not, and it bothered me, and this seemed a good place to find out, but I knew you'd never call me; I knew I had to come to you.'

A strange lightness was spreading through Ross. 'Why is this a good place?'

'Because it isn't San Francisco. I couldn't have done it there.' The waiter brought a carafe of wine and filled their glasses and Katherine raised hers, looking through it at the colourful flowers surrounding them. Seen through the pale gold wine, the petals were elongated and curved, oddly changed. 'I feel as if I've broken away from everything I knew, everything I've done. Whatever I look at is new. Even ordinary things like groceries and street signs and price tags are exotic and mysterious. So it seems all right to behave differently. In fact, I feel that I ought to, since everything around me is different.' She gave a small laugh. 'It sounds so foolish.'

'No.' Ross sat back, stretching his long legs. 'When I work with Jacques on the building he's renovating – it's around the corner; I'll show it to you later – we stand in front of fireplaces more than three and a half centuries old, large enough for three men to stand comfortably, and we walk on parquet floors that were laid long before the Pilgrims came to America. It's not easy for me to hold on to twentieth century thoughts when I stand there; nothing seems quite real.'

Katherine's eyes were bright. 'Yes. That's exactly it.'

'But you didn't think I'd understand. Since I might not like you.'

She flushed, then challenged him. 'Do you?'

'Yes,' he said easily. The waiter reappeared, dividing the remaining wine evenly between their glasses. 'We can talk about it, if you'd like. At dinner. Will you have dinner with me? And tomorrow, if you'll let me, I'd like to show you my Paris. It's quite different from Victoria's, but I think you'll enjoy it. If you have no other plans, of course. And if it would please you . . .'

For the first time, Katherine's smile was relaxed. 'It would please me very much,' she said.

Dinner was at Chez Philippe, small, casual, crowded, with vociferous conversations bouncing off the stone walls, beamed ceiling and red tile floor. Ross had reserved a table in a quiet corner. 'It's not always so noisy,' he said as they were brought a bottle of country wine. 'But it's a neighbourhood place and when it's crowded it's like one big family gathering. Are you disappointed?'

'No,' Katherine said, surprised. 'Why would I be?'

'It's a long way from Tour d'Argent or Taillevent or

L'Archestrate. I should have told you I'm not fond of spectacular restaurants. It doesn't matter how special the food, I can't enjoy it when it takes second place to mirrors and silks and black-tie waiters who whip silver covers off the plates like penguin magicians.'

Katherine was smiling, but uncomfortably, she remembered how impressed she had been when Derek took her to San Francisco's most glittering restaurants. And it was true that she had expected one of the places Victoria or Derek would have chosen, and had dressed for it. And pale yellow silk seemed excessive in the simple room.

'You look wonderful,' Ross said, watching her look at the other women. 'And not out of place. Chez Philippe prides itself on individualism. Is that a Parisian dress?'

'Yes; is it really all right? I found a wonderful shop yesterday; one of the designers Victoria introduced me to told me about it, a place called Miss Griffes – ' Ross nodded, and she said, 'You've heard of it?'

'Melanie heard of it. Designer clothes that had been used on mannequins in store displays – isn't that it?- sold for next to nothing. Melanie never went there; she said she didn't like used clothes.'

'Victoria told me you'd separated.'

'Yes,' he said shortly. 'So you liked Miss Griffes?'

'Liked it? I went into a trance. I didn't even count dollars – I just spent francs. I haven't spent so much on myself since – for more than a year.'

'It's about time you did. You're very lovely, Katherine.' Her colour rose and she looked again around the room as Ross contemplated her. Her beauty was softer and less vivid than Melanie's, her gestures less sharp, her dress, though exquisitely cut, simpler than one Melanie would have chosen. But perhaps because of that she seemed steadier than Melanie, more steadfast, more –

Damn it, he cursed silently. Why the hell am I comparing her to Melanie? They have nothing to do with each other.

'I'll order, shall l?' he asked as the waiter approached. 'The food is Basque and you might find it unfamiliar.'

'I might,' she agreed. 'Since I don't even know what it is.'

He laughed. 'It's from the Pyrenees, a cross between Gascony France and northern Spain. Do you like roast quail?'

'I have no idea.'

'We'll share, then.' He ordered it, then added, 'And *cassoulet*. With a Pomerol or a Saint-Emilion. I leave the choice to you; the best year of the two.' He sat back. 'If you dislike any of it, we'll order something else. But I think you'll find it worth giving up the showplaces.'

'I wish you'd stop expecting me to be disappointed,' Katherine said mildly. 'I like it here. I don't need showplaces; that was exactly what I didn't like about the bus tour. Everything I saw was magnificent, but it was the public face of the city. I kept wanting to see the hidden part, to make discoveries –'

'– To turn a corner and find real people –'

'– Doing the laundry or making dinner –'

'– Or eating together in a neighbourhood restaurant.'

They were laughing. As the waiter brought glasses and the Pomerol, Ross put his hand on Katherine's. 'You have my promise,' he said, 'that for the next two days, you will see only the hidden side of Paris.'

He kept his word, beginning at seven-thirty the next morning. 'Victoria would be appalled at the hour,' he grinned when he met Katherine in the Meurice lobby. 'But she would approve of my buying you breakfast.'

'I don't think this is quite what she had in mind,' Katherine commented as they stood at the bar of a small café while having their croissants and coffee. But she laughed as she said it, because the morning was sunlit and cool, the croissants hot and buttery, and she was as eager as Ross to begin – not to sit in a restaurant at the mercy of a waiter's deliberate pace, but to hurry into the city that awaited them.

There are so many cities called Paris that no one can count them, for no two people view it the same way and no one views it with indifference. Brilliantly beautiful, deafeningly noisy, jammed with people and traffic, stunning in its vistas, grubby in its corners, infinitely varied and experimental in food, couture, culture, churches and erotica, it is a city that prides itself on being at once a vast museum and a vibrant, living part of the modern world.

Ross's Paris embraced it all, but especially the hidden *arrondissements* behind the city's grandeur: narrow, twisting streets where generations of families have lived and loved, worshipped, worked, died and been buried. Over the years, in trips with his parents and then alone or with Melanie, he had explored those labyrinthine neighbourhoods, each centred on a church and a small square or park, listening to conversations in the bistros, making friends, reading French history and literature, and studying the architecture that religion and everyday life had inspired.

These were the streets he and Katherine walked, while he told her their legends and histories. It was as if he were peeling off layers of the past, revealing the quirks and dreams of centuries. 'The owners found eighteenth century torture instruments in the lower cellar,' he said as they stopped before the massive double doors of a renovated building. 'If you can picture it – revolutionaries suspended over vats of boiling oil, while, three floors up, in the kitchen, the cook measures olive oil for the salad dressing. An eerie symmetry; death and life, killing and creating . . .'

Katherine gazed at the carving of the Greek goddess of

365

justice above the door. 'I wonder if every family has a cellar it would like to forget.'

A smile lit Ross's eyes. It was a thought he'd had often when restoring old buildings, but he had never talked about it with anyone. 'People, too,' he said. 'We have our cellars inside us – things in our past we try to bury and ignore.'

The words hung in the air. Repeating them silently, Ross thought of the one person they best described. He scrutinised Katherine, trying to think of her as Craig's wife. But Craig was remote; absent. Nothing seemed real but Paris.

Katherine looked past him. His words had tugged at her, but the pull of the present was stronger. Just as she had at Victoria's villa, she felt cut off from everything that had happened before. At least for a while, it had been left far behind. She met Ross's eyes. 'I'm sure we all do,' she said easily.

Slowly, he let out his breath and together they turned and walked on. In the Rue de la Bucherie they came to a wall that Ross said had been part of the Faculty of Medicine five hundred years earlier. 'Only monks practised medicine then,' he mused. 'They prescribed eating earthworms in white wine to cure jaundice, droppings of mice for bladder stones and the blood of a hare for gallstones.' He glanced at Katherine. 'In a classic case of discrimination, women weren't permitted medical care.'

'Fortunate women,' she murmured, and they laughed as they moved on. A few blocks farther, Ross touched Katherine's arm.

'Here's the other side of the story of torture in the cellar.' He ran his hand over a dark stone embedded in the corner of a new building. 'Buried treasure. When the old building was condemned, and wreckers ripped open the wall, a torrent of *louis-d'or* gold pieces poured out – over three thousand twenty-two-carat gold coins – and the will of a man who'd disappeared in 1757, bequeathing it all to his daughter. Eventually eighty or so descendants of the daughter were found, and they divided up the fortune.'

'The other side of the story,' Katherine repeated slowly. 'Torture and treasure, balancing each other. Symmetry. Is that what you look for in your work?'

Ross felt the rush of joy that came with having someone to share his thoughts. 'In my work and for myself. To be able to juggle things so that, even if I go off half-cocked over something, eventually I can come back to a balanced centre. That's probably why I love Paris, because it exists by its own balancing act: some of the bloodiest history of all time alongside a reverence for life; memorials to hermits next to monuments to the family; the wildest post-modernism a few feet from the most lovingly preserved works of ancient times. All those wonderful contradictions that add up to symmetry.'

The idea intrigued Katherine. He had described not only architecture, but jewellery design as well. They strolled on and she thought about it, exhilarated by having a new way of thinking about familiar things. 'Ross,' she said impulsively. 'I'm having a wonderful time.'

His eyes swung to her, almost stunned with surprise. 'I'm glad,' he said. 'There's so much more I want you to see . . .' And as they walked Katherine wondered what had surprised him: that she was having a good time, or that she had told him she was.

They walked all that day, the hours passing for Katherine in a reverie of the past intertwined with the bustle of a modern city. She and Ross persuaded sextons to show them through ancient churches, and concierges to let them look into renovated apartment buildings with their inner courtyards and formal gardens; they stopped at kiosks where Ross translated the colourful posters plastered on all sides, announcing everything from operas to protest marches; they dawdled at open bookstalls on the Left Bank of the Seine where neither could resist buying. ('Just a few,' Katherine kept vowing. 'I'm getting heavier by the minute.') They paused beside sidewalk artists and musicians; after lunch in the small bistro they climbed steep steps to the plateau at the top of Montmartre where Paris disappeared in the crooked streets of a small village of dilapidated studios of earnest young painters and sculptors. And they walked along the quays beside the Seine in the soft, silver light of early evening that lay like a delicate veil over the river and its arched stone bridges, and the people, lingering before going home.

For two days they traversed the city, on foot by bus or on the Metro, with its wide, brightly-lit corridors lined with huge paintings and enlivened by young musicians sitting cross-legged, playing guitars or saxophones or flutes. But most of the time they walked and Ross talked, and as he did, Katherine's eyes kept returning to his face. The harshness she had often seen there was gone. Except at their first lunch, when he had told her about BayBridge, she had never seen him look so relaxed, his deep voice warm and animated, with a boyish delight in sharing what he knew. But what struck her most were his hands when he ran them over ancient stones and grillework: warm and sensual as if the material were alive. Mine must look like that, she thought, remembering the feel of warm gold as she shaped and worked it, and she knew they both felt they could touch the hidden life of stone and metal through their fingertips. But Ross had something more, she thought enviously; he also touched the work of others, as if he clasped hands, over the ages, with builders long dead but living still in the structures they left behind.

'It's a way of staying close to my grandfather,' Ross said, startling Katherine by seeming to respond to her thoughts. They were standing in a small courtyard tucked away on the Rue Jacob, facing two houses, one restored and inhabited, the other empty and crumbling with the ravages of three hundred years. Ross ran his hand over one of the two stone lions guarding the restored house. 'Every time I bring a building to life, I'm keeping him alive. In fact,' he added half-humorously, 'I can hear him criticising me or approving the kind of restoration I'm doing, as if we're still having the long conversations we had when he was alive. It's almost as if we're working together.'

'I wish I'd known him,' Katherine said.

'He would have loved you.' Ross opened the gate and they left the courtyard. 'You would have reminded him of Victoria.'

Katherine flushed with pleasure, and was silent, treasuring his words as they walked together toward Rue Bonaparte and Ross pointed out details on houses and shops that he admired. Watching his long fingers trace fanciful wrought iron gates and stone figures from mythology or the Bible, Katherine wanted to put her hand on his, to share his sensual touch on the material and his connection with the past. Instead, she shared them by talking with him and watching the movements of his hands, his mobile face, and the sights he pointed out, liking him more and more for his concentration and depth of feeling. We share that, too, she thought, remembering her own absorption in her work, until she realised that in Ross's concentration there were times when he seemed to forget she was there. Which is more important to him, she wondered – the past or the present?

Which is more important to me? The thought sprang out, but no sooner was it there than she pushed it back. She was thinking about Ross; later, she'd think about herself.

When they went to their separate hotels to change for dinner, Katherine lay in her marble tub, soaking muscles that had carried her through countless Parisian miles. The next morning, she would fly back to Menton. She thought about the past three days, and about Ross Hayward – who avoided fancy restaurants but was expert in fine cuisine and wines; who moved easily in international social and professional circles but sought out the hidden streets of Paris; who built the most modern urban developments while preserving buildings from the past; who had a family but avoided talking about it; who was handsome and successful but who almost never spoke about himself, who had given her two of the most companionable days she had ever known after months of being cool and distant in San Francisco. And she knew she did not understand him at all.

'One last hidden part of Paris,' he said that evening as they walked through the kitchen at Allard and were shown a table. 'One of my favourites.'

The waiter knew Ross, jovially calling him *Monsieur le President* as he did all his favourite customers, and conducting a vigorous debate with him over their after-dinner drink. 'Of course it doesn't matter,' Ross confided to Katherine. 'They bring Calvados whatever one orders, because that's what they consider proper. But debate comes first; one must honour tradition.'

The past and the present, Katherine thought. 'Is that most important to you?' she asked. 'Tradition? The things of the past?'

'They endure,' he said.

'But they don't. They crumble.'

'You were in St Julien le Pauvre today. Built in 587.'

'But – what does that mean? That you trust stone because sometimes it endures?'

'It's a better bet than paper. Better than metal, clay, wood . . . Or love,' he added lightly. 'Or marriage.' The waiter brought their Calvados and garrulously poured from the bottle into two snifters, addressing Katherine as *Madame la President* and complimenting them on what a *harmonieux* couple they made.

Swirling the brandy in his glass, Ross said, 'You deserve an

370

answer. The things of the past are important to me for the same reason I became an architect; because I need to feel there's a continuous line holding us together, all the generations and ages. We aren't in a void, spinning out our lives and then disappearing; we're part of something that stretches behind us and ahead of us, that gives meaning to our lives and everything we create. We all want to leave something behind – that means we need to believe others will see what we've made touch it, bring it to life. In a way, that's what keeps us alive.'

He smiled and took Katherine's hand. 'I didn't mean to lecture. At the moment I'm very much enjoying the present. Which reminds me. I'm meeting Carrie and Jon at the airport tomorrow. It's occurred to me' – his voice grew casual – 'that they'd probably enjoy the country more than the city. And Todd and Jennifer's companionship. Would you mind if we join you tomorrow – when you fly to Menton?'

Chapter 14

Ross had telephoned ahead, so Victoria was prepared for the invasion when the limousine arrived from the airport in Nice, and few would have guessed, from her unruffled smile and calm kisses, that she had not planned from the beginning to spend the month of July with four children under the age of twelve. But Ross, feeling responsible, whispered as he greeted her, 'They won't bother you; I'll keep them on a leash, never out of my sight.'

'Oh, but you mustn't,' she said in alarm. 'You'd have no time for yourself.'

Or to be with Katherine, he thought, which was what she really meant. Amused, he watched her welcome the children. Stubborn, tenacious, trying to manage her family's lives, so she could live through them. And clever, he reflected; she knew Katherine and I would get along. 'We'll make time for everything,' he promised, bringing a smile to Victoria's face as she watched them go to their rooms to unpack.

The children were in a wing of four rooms and a playroom with its own courtyard, that Hugh and Victoria had added to the villa, anticipating noisy visits from grandchildren. Craig, Jennifer, Derek and Ross had stayed there every summer, and as they grew older the playroom grew with them: rocking horses and Tinker Toys replaced by motorised Erector sets, model aeroplanes and, finally, draughting tables, a television set and stereo, and a cabinet filled with chess, backgammon, Scrabble, Chinese Checkers and Monopoly.

From the doorway. Ross shook his head wonderingly. 'She hasn't changed a thing,' he told Katherine as they walked into the room. 'The last time I was here was 1966; the four of us came for a couple of weeks when school ended. The next month Jennifer was killed and Victoria closed the whole wing. But' – gently he touched a chessman and a model of the Wright Brothers' first plane – 'she didn't change anything.'

Katherine picked up a small open box with a strand of black pearls coiled inside. 'Jennifer's,' Ross said. 'She left it behind when we went home.'

'She forgot it?' Katherine asked.

'She didn't want it. Which rooms are yours? Did Victoria ever tell you she has a scheme for assigning suites to visitors?'

'No.' He had cut her off. Too personal, Katherine thought. They walked out of the playroom and turned a corner into a wide corridor. One side was entirely of glass, looking through horizontal wooden slats into the villa's flower gardens and, beyond, the badminton court, croquet lawn, and vegetable gardens. In the mornings, the slats were closed to keep out the sun. On the other side of the corridor, doorways led to three suites, each with sliding glass doors opening on to the terrace that overlooked the pink-beige roofs of Menton, the crowded harbour and the azure Mediterranean. Wooden slats formed a canopy over the terrace, and were tilted after lunch to shade the house from the blazing afternoon sun. 'Here's mine,' said Katherine, turning into a bedroom and a sitting-room in sage green and ivory: a cool oasis amid the blinding colours of the Riviera. 'And what was Victoria's scheme in choosing it for me?'

Ross sat on the arm of a chair and looked about the two spacious rooms. 'When we were growing up, the villa was always full of guests – writers, painters, diplomats, businessmen – coming and going, all summer long. Mostly we didn't pay much attention, but those who were given this suite we watched, because Victoria made it clear they were her favourites. What we didn't know was whether she put them here because they were special, or whether they became special by staying here. Finally we decided the rooms were magic and each of us, I guess, dreamed of the day Victoria would ask us to stay in them.' He smiled. 'Of course it never occurred to her; why should it? We had a whole wing to ourselves. And she had her special people. Not many – Victoria doesn't love easily or casually – but a few every summer, enough to make me remember these rooms. Do you know what her plans are for dinner tonight?'

'No.' He'd done it again, she thought; offered a glimpse of himself, then skidded away to something else.

'Because, I thought we might take a drive after dinner,' he went on. 'Monte Carlo is a few miles down the road; worth seeing once and then avoided. Unless you had enough sightseeing in –?'

'Dad,' said Jon, charging in. 'Carrie says I have to unpack. We're gonna be here all month: why do I have to unpack this minute? Why do I have to unpack anyway? I can find everything in my suitcase. Carrie's only dumping on me because she's mad at Jennifer.'

'Why is she mad at Jennifer?' Katherine asked.

Jon looked up dubiously, not sure how to behave with

374

Katherine. She was butting in on their vacation, but his Dad seemed to like her, so he and Carrie had talked it over and decided it would be smart to be careful. 'Just 'cause she and Todd were here all week,' he said, 'they act like they live here and we don't belong.'

Seeing Katherine's dismay, Ross said quickly, 'I think this requires some diplomacy. Do you mind if I handle it?'

She shook her head and watched the two of them leave the room. *Did she mind!* For a year she'd been forced to settle every squabble and soothe every anxiety by herself. Now she stood in the perfect silence of her room, content to let Ross deal with her children. And that, she thought, makes this a real vacation.

Sheltered from the gusting north winds, in an almost tropical climate, lush palm trees grow in Menton; citrus orchards yield oranges, tangerines, grapefruit, kumquats and lemons the year round, and pines, olive and cypress trees grow thickly on the hills beyond the town, hiding the villas tucked among them. A short drive away, the world's wealthy gamble all night, and tan by day; a two-hour drive away, skiers find snow all year long in the Alps. Aloof from them all, the villas of Menton, reached by paths and steep staircases, guard their privacy and ignore the tourists below.

At Villa Serein, Victoria attempted to impose her benevolent rule. 'I have a complete list,' she told Ross and Katherine, 'of the music and art festivals between Menton and Aix-en-Provence – a fine day's trip – plus the museums and churches and Roman ruins you will want to see. Hugh and I loved poking through them; Katherine, you must take your sketch pad; you'll find extraordinary formations. As for the children –' She spread a sheaf of papers on the table. 'I've arranged private sailing and rock-climbing excursions, and swimming and diving lessons in Menton's pool. In addition, I've spoken to a friend in Monaco who has tennis courts and his own coach; the children are welcome there any time. And of course, there are movie theatres, the library in the villa, and the games in the playroom. I presume they are appropriate.' She looked up. 'If not, I will buy whatever . . .' Her voice faltered as she saw Ross shaking his head. 'What is it?'

'You know what it is; we've been through this before. You cannot organise every hour of everyone's day. I need time with Carrie and Jon; I have to return to Paris for a few days; I want some time with you and with Katherine; I'd like some time alone. I think it would be best if we work out our own schedules and then try to put them together.'

'It would not be best,' Victoria said tartly. 'I become exceedingly nervous when I don't know what is happening under my own roof. But I understand about the children; I should have realised. You and Katherine could take them sailing, in place of some of their sailing lessons; I'll arrange that –'

'I don't want you to arrange it,' he said. 'You've been arranging since you took Katherine to Paris.'

'And what was wrong with that?' she demanded. 'You had a fine time –!'

'Couldn't we decide this together?' Katherine asked. 'Everything you've thought of is wonderful, but it doesn't leave me any time either; I have to design at least a dozen new pieces of jewellery. And you didn't say what you're going to do. Couldn't we discuss it? Ross?'

'A good idea. We'll have a conference.'

'Would that make you less nervous?' Katherine asked Victoria .

'Most likely,' she said. 'Often I think I'm most nervous when I don't get my way.'

Ross laughed. 'Often I think so, too. Well, let's see what we can organise.'

Uphill of the villa, with a view of the terrace where the adults were talking, Jennifer, Todd, Carrie and Jon sat cross-legged in the shade of a cypress tree, eating oranges and playing Scrabble. It was a morose game. Jennifer and Todd thought Carrie and Jon had been foisted on them, cutting into the exclusive attention they got from their great-grandmother while their mother was in Paris; and Carrie and Jon, remembering their mother's biting comments, thought Katherine and her children were intruders and troublemakers. But Ross had practically ordered them all to get along, saying he expected a peaceful vacation and they could be peaceful separately or together, but they had to understand that sailing and rock-climbing and tennis weren't for one person at a time. Either they did them as a group, or not at all. It was up to them.

So they were a group, playing a glum but determined game of Scrabble. They watched Todd ponder his letters, then place three tiles on the board. 'B-U-X,' he spelled aloud, adding in a rush, 'That's fourteen points and it's doubled so I get –'

'There's no such word,' Jennifer said indignantly.

'There is too.' He looked sideways at the others and began to giggle. 'It means lots of money.'

A smothered laugh burst from Jon, and in spite of themselves Carrie and Jennifer laughed, too. 'Not bad,' Carrie conceded.

'Then I can have it?' Todd asked. 'Twenty-eight points?'

'No,' they all said in unison.

'Nuts.' He pondered, found another place to make 'bull', then watched sternly as Jennifer took her turn and made 'fil-ial'. '*That's* not a word, either!'

'It is too. Just because you never heard of it –'

'It is a word,' said Carrie.

'Meaning what?' Todd demanded.

'Being a son or daughter.'

'Oh. Well, it isn't a word for everybody.'

'It *is* for everybody!' Jennifer said impatiently. 'When you have a mother and father you're a –'

'I don't have a father. Neither do you.'

'That is the stupidest thing I ever heard!' Furious, Jennifer shoved aside her letters. 'We do have a father. He just isn't here right now.'

'If he isn't here we don't have him.'

'Hey,' scowled Jon. 'My dad doesn't live with us but we still have him.'

'That's not the same,' Todd retorted. 'You know where your dad is, even when you're not with him. That's a lot better than with my dad –'

'It isn't better, it's worse, 'cause I know he's there and it's crazy that he's not living with us – I mean, you know he's just across the bay, you can sort of see where he lives – but he's not with you when you want him and that's *crazy* . . .'

'It's better than not even knowing if your dad is alive or not!'

'How do you know!'

'Oh, stop it!' Jennifer cried. 'The worst thing of all is never seeing your father and we haven't seen ours in months and months –'

'Yes, but then you get used to it,' said Carrie. 'I mean, with our dad we're always saying goodbye. We spend a weekend with him or have dinner or something and then he takes us home and he never comes in, he stays outside and we say goodbye. Everytime I turn around I have to say goodbye!'

'You say hello, too,' Todd countered.

'Yes, but I'm always thinking about later, how I'm going to have to say goodbye all over again. It's awful and I start to cry because I never get used to it.'

'Well I'd rather cry,' said Jennifer flatly, 'than not have a father at all.'

'You said we did have a father!' Todd yelled.

'Not close by, like Carrie and Jon. We have a father some-where, and he sends us money, but we never talk to him or go places with him like they do . . . they see their dad every day!'

'Only here,' said Carrie. 'Not at home.' Her eyes filled with tears. 'And if you want to know what's really the worst of all, it's looking out your window and watching your father drive away. Seeing the *back* of his *car*.'

'You think *that's* bad,' Todd declared. 'Try thinking you'll never see your father again.'

Silence fell. Orange peels lay on the wild grass; a bee circled over them, buzzing loudly before disappearing into the bushes nearby. 'This is silly,' Jennifer said in a small voice. 'We all have things that are bad. I don't want to have a contest about them.'

'I don't either,' said Carrie. 'Nobody would win.'

Todd was staring glumly at the Scrabble board. Suddenly he raised both hands and furiously rubbed his head, making his hair stand on end, as if he were vehemently washing it clean. He looked at them challengingly. 'I'd win,' he said. 'If any-body would let me use "bux".'

There was a startled pause, then a shaky laugh from Jennifer and then they all were laughing, louder and louder, unable to stop, their screeches echoing off the cliffs and reaching the adults below, who smiled at the sound. Gradually, the laughter slowed and faded away. They wiped their eyes and smiled at each other – and were friends.

The days fell into a rhythm that turned out, not surprisingly, to be similar to Victoria's plans. Most mornings, Katherine worked on her jewellery designs; Ross was with his children; Jennifer and Todd entertained themselves, or were with Katherine when she wasn't working, or were invited to join Victoria in the garden, where the three of them had a glorious time picking their way through vegetables and flowers and pulling a weed here and there while the gardener stood by in silent agony, waiting for the moment when he could reclaim his private kingdom.

In the afternoons, everyone went in different directions. Victoria read in her sitting-room; the children went off on whichever excursion or lesson she had scheduled for that day; and Ross and Katherine explored the countryside.

They had begun the first night, after dinner. Ross had rented a car and they drove along the coast to Monte Carlo. 'Not impressed?' he inquired when Katherine stood silently before the marble and bronze, gilt and crystal of the palace-like Casino and Hôtel de Paris, glaringly lit against the black Mediterranean night.

'Very impressed,' she answered. All around them, between the Casino and the hotel, a constantly shifting stream of people paraded in glittering evening dress, tuxedos, capes, and feathered hairpieces that nodded like the palm trees above. 'It's a little like a bakery,' she added thoughtfully.

It pulled him up short. Once more he surveyed the chandeliers, curlicued balconies and decorations of plaster caryatids and exaggerated flowers. 'A bakery?'

'At Christmas. Puff pastry, meringues and layer cakes. Iced, sprinkled, tinted, decorated, absolutely gorgeous, and festive, because they're overdone and unreal. And they look so expensive.'

'And they are.' Amused, Ross surveyed the crowd as he and Katherine walked through the rooms of the Casino where bored gamblers sat at the tables or wandered in the smoky air, peering over shoulders or stopping to exchange a tidbit of gossip. Ross pointed to a croupier spinning the roulette wheel. 'The chef?'

'Or a spun sugar Santa Claus,' Katherine responded and they were laughing as they walked back to the car.

The next day at breakfast, Ross casually mentioned the hill

town of Saint Paul, an easy drive from Menton, a pleasant way to spend an afternoon. His afternoon was free, was Katherine's?

Katherine looked inquiringly at Victoria. 'Certainly you should go,' Victoria said promptly. 'Nothing else is scheduled. Stay for dinner, if you wish.'

'I'd like to be back for dinner,' Katherine said.

They left after lunch and spent the afternoon in the old village that clung to the top of a craggy peak, surrounded by the stone wall built a thousand years earlier to protect it from invading armies. 'I used to come here when I was in high school,' Ross recalled. 'Usually alone. My grandfather was the only one who found it as fascinating as I did, but even he had had enough after a while. I never tired of it.' His voice echoed off the stone arches above the narrow, climbing streets. 'I made up stories about the people who lived here, the battles they fought, the games they played . . .'

'And you were the hero,' Katherine said.

His eyebrows rose. 'How would you know that?'

'I made up my own stories. I didn't have a wonderful stone village on the top of a hill – I only had Golden Gate park – but I had battles and games and imaginary friends, and a family . . . I can't picture you being alone, with your family around you.'

'I was alone when I wanted to be; I escaped from them and came up here. I had a place like it in San Francisco, not as remote, but private enough to suit me. Special places,' Ross added thoughtfully. 'I loved being alone.' He laughed shortly. 'I seem to have lost that, as an adult. I've had to learn it all over again.'

'Did you?' Katherine looked at him curiously. It was the first time he had volunteered something about himself. 'You've always seemed to me so self-sufficient and sure of yourself; I thought there was something wrong with me

381

because I had such a terrible time getting used to being alone.'

'Probably something wrong with you if it came naturally.' Ross told her about the first time Carrie and Jon had come to his house in Berkeley. 'Jon still refuses to call it ours. And that reminds me that they'll leave and I'll be alone and I'm still not used to it.'

'I know,' Katherine said in a low voice. 'I used to talk to myself –'

'Did you? I wondered about that. Especially when I found myself doing it.'

'– And then I'd be embarrassed and turn on the radio.'

'I didn't think of the radio. I ordered myself to get used to the silence.'

'And did you?'

'No.'

They had walked beyond the town, and in a few minutes reached the Maeght Fondation, where they strolled through the art museum and its sun-washed sculpture gardens, comparing notes on the pieces they liked best, agreeing, they discovered, far more often than not. Later, they returned to Saint Paul, for wine and cheese at La Colombe d'Or. 'Also a museum,' Ross said, as Katherine admired the colourful Leger mural in the courtyard where they sat. 'Wait until you see the paintings inside. It all began when the owner, Monsieur Roux, allowed his poorest customers, who were also his friends, to pay for dinner with their paintings when they had no money. The customers were named Picasso, Braque, Miro, Matisse, Dufy – among others.'

'A wise man,' Katherine said. Mischievously, she asked, 'Which would he have said endures best? Friendship or stone?'

'Appetite,' Ross replied ins antly. 'It's his livelihood.' They shared a smile in the shadows lengthening across flower-filled stone urns and glossy dark ivy cascading over the walls behind them. 'I thought we might drive to San Remo tomorrow,' he

382

said. 'Just over the Italian border. The drive along the corniche is supposed to be worth seeing.'

Victoria confirmed it at dinner. 'Magnificent. The most
wonderful palms at Bordighera, and flower gardens covering
the slopes beside the road . . .' Her voice became soft. 'Hugh
always bought me flowers. He couldn't stop, he admitted it
was like a disease – but a most benign one. Every time he saw
a flower vendor he'd stop the car and buy a bunch of everything. By the end of the day people would see our car heaped
with flowers and stop us to buy. When I'd tell them my husband had bought them for me, the tourists would say, "Where
will you put them all?" but the French would nod wisely and
say, "*Folie ou amour*". Madness or love.' She laughed softly.
'*Folie ou amour*. But they knew it was *amour*. Well, then.' She
looked contentedly at Ross and Katherine. 'San Remo. I most
certainly recommend it.'

After San Remo, each morning at breakfast Ross would
casually mention another town, or one of the modern art museums strung along the Riviera, or a drive through the Alps.
Occasionally, gingerly, Victoria would make a suggestion
from the store of her memories, but usually she smiled quietly
as Katherine and Ross pored over maps, making plans. On
weekends, when the children had no activities, they took the
four of them along, but the rest of the time they went alone,
each day roaming a little farther, taking different turns in the
roads that twisted through the hills to explore a château or a
garden with a thousand tropical plants growing on cliffs and in
underground caves, or a ruined olive mill with ancient wooden
sprocketed wheels and grinding stones in stone troughs. The
scents of Provence were everywhere: herbs, olive oil, tomatoes
and garlic, orange and rosemary, fruit trees and lavender,
baguettes fresh from the oven. One morning, Ross brought a
round-handled basket to the breakfast table and that day they
left the villa before lunch, carrying the basket that Victoria's

cook had filled with a Niçoise onion tart, cheeses and fruit, and a bottle of Provence rosé wine.

Two hours later they opened it beside a stream in an Alpine meadow, sitting beneath a tall pine on a carpet of silken wild grass. The stream was bright with hundreds of tiny waterfalls spilling over rocks and boulders in its rush down the mountain; the air was clear and warm. 'I feel so lazy,' Katherine said, lying on the grass. Above her, the rough branches and dark needles of the tree were silhouetted against a deep blue sky. 'And not at all ashamed.'

Ross handed her a cluster of grapes. 'Why should you be ashamed?'

'Because I'm not doing anything.'

He settled his back against the tree and looked down at her. 'You're relaxing. Contemplating nature. Enjoying sun and shade. Giving great pleasure to your companion. Busy enough for a summer day. You can't mean you've never taken a holiday before.'

'No, of course I have. But I don't think I ever let myself feel really lazy. Part of me was always thinking ahead, making lists of all the things I should be doing, planning schedules . . . there were so many *shoulds* in my life . . .'

'And now?'

'Mostly questions.' Katherine sat up, crosslegged. 'They all begin, "Can I –?" ' She looked at Ross. 'Isn't that odd? I thought I had more restrictions now, because I'm responsible for the three of us. But somehow I don't. I have fewer.'

'Because you've proved what you can do.'

Katherine shook her head. 'I haven't proved anything yet. But I'm finding out.'

Still not sure of herself, Ross thought. But, after all, how could she be? She'd only had a year. And a good part of that must have been spent just getting used to being alone. He watched her gather pine needles into a fragrant bundle in her

384

palm, and wondered when she would begin to take her accomplishments for granted, as well as her beauty and all the other changes of the past year. *When she's convinced her life is settled,* he thought. *Until then, who can blame her for being uncertain and a little tentative?*

Without warning, Ross thought of Derek. How uncertain had she been with him? Contemplating Katherine's pensive face, asking himself the question, Ross couldn't make sense of it: the more he learned about her, the more impossible it seemed that she had been one of Derek's conquests. He started to ask her about it, then stopped himself. What would he say? *Who are you, really, that you could embrace my brother?* If I want to understand her, he thought, I'll do it by understanding who she is with me, not who she might have been with Derek. I owe her that much.

But still, he could not prevent the thought from slipping through: *Someday I may have to ask her.*

'Tell me about your life in New York,' Katherine said, when she looked up and found Ross watching her.

She was, as he had discovered, a good listener. Ross told her about his apartment on the West Side with its glimpse of the Hudson River between two other buildings; his friendship with Jacques Duvain; his work on urban redevelopment projects in Boston and Philadelphia that had gained national attention. 'By then Victoria was calling once or twice a week, asking me to come back, not to the company – she knew I didn't want that – but to start my own firm. She said she needed me, for friendship, companionship, the family; and I knew I needed her for the same things. Besides, I was confident enough to think I was ready for my own firm. She clinched it by offering to recommend me to her friends and fellow board members –'

Katherine laughed. 'She did the same for me, with jewellery store owners.'

385

'One of her most lovable qualities is her consistency. You turned her down?'

'It was important to me that I do it on my own.'

'Because you were just beginning. But I'd had those years in New York, and enough success behind me, to take her up on it. Some of my best commissions came through her contacts, and most of them came back for second homes or office buildings. My favourite is a real estate tycoon whose house I designed in Mill Valley. The second job I did for him was a shopping centre he named after himself. He was so proud, he said he never wanted to leave it, so he had a mausoleum built for him and his family beneath the main store.'

'Cash registers instead of gravestones,' said Katherine wryly.

Ross laughed. 'We never put it that way, but that's perfect.' He laid the empty wine bottle in the basket. 'We'd better get started if we want to be back for dinner. Although we don't really have to, you know . . .'

'I want to.' Katherine stood up, brushing off her jeans. 'It's a good time to be with the children, and I think it's important to Victoria.'

Ross picked a fragment of pine cone from her hair. 'It's also important to Victoria that we have time together.' She looked quickly at him and he smiled into her clear eyes. 'She's a very wise lady.'

Katherine returned his smile but did not answer. He had talked about everything, she thought, except his wife, whom he had met and married in New York. She wondered about it through dinner, and afterwards, on the terrace, while she and Ross played Chinese Checkers with the children under Victoria's critical eye, but she thought mostly about Ross and his grandparents. He had moved back to San Francisco because Victoria needed him, and because he missed her. The year before, in Vancouver, almost his first words had been that he was there because his grandmother had sent him. And, he felt he was still connected to his grandfather. *A continuous line – holding us all together, all the generations and age.* Katherine had never known anyone who moved comfortably across the generations, who knew where he fitted within them, and it seemed to her that Ross's world was infinitely larger than hers, with more places to belong.

But her world was growing, she thought; it was expanding, stretching ahead with more possibilities, more people to consider, so much more to think about . . .

'Ha!' cried Jon, using his marble to leap over four others to reach the coloured triangle that was his goal. 'First one in.'

'Not for long,' Ross responded with a wicked gleam and jumped over six marbles to his own goal. 'Katherine? Are you with us?'

'Oh. Yes. Let me see . . .'

'Dad,' said Jon as Katherine surveyed the board. 'There's a party this weekend at the Casino in Monte Carlo. We've been invited.'

Ross raised his eyebrows. 'They don't allow youngsters in the Casino.'

'One of the kids' fathers rented a private room and they're putting in roulette and blackjack and everything. Really neat. It starts at eight o' –'

'Hold on,' Ross said. Jennifer, Todd and Carrie watched him, almost holding their breath. 'This party is for nine and ten year olds?'

'Well . . . most of the kids are like sixteen and seventeen but they asked us 'cause we're good on the diving team. So can you drive us?'

'No. I don't want you at the Casino, even in a private room, especially with an older crowd.'

'Dad –!'

'I doubt that you'd even be allowed in, but we're not going

387

to find out. You have plenty of things to keep you busy; gambling isn't one of them.'

'But, Dad –!'

'No, Jon. That's final. It's no place for any of you. You're not going.'

'Jee-sus,' muttered Jon.

'I told you,' Carrie said. 'I knew he'd say no.'

At the obvious relief in her voice, Ross and Katherine exchanged an amused glance. 'About the diving –' Ross began.

'Maybe I'll just go home,' Jon muttered. 'If you won't let me do what I want, maybe I won't stay. Or visit you anymore on weekends, either.'

'Jon!' said Katherine sharply. Ross was frowning, his mouth tight, and for the first time she saw in practice the power of his children.

'Jon,' she said again. Jennifer, recognising the tone in her mother's voice, became so nervous she dropped one of her glass marbles and as it rang on the flagstone terrace, she and Todd scrambled down to look for it. Katherine waited until Jon looked at her. 'Blackmail,' she said softly, 'is a nasty means of persuasion. And when it uses love as a weapon it is disgusting. Do you understand that?'

Ross had turned, his eyes fastened on Katherine. Victoria, too, was watching her, uncharacteristically silent.

'Do you?' Katherine repeated.

'No,' Jon muttered.

'It means it is disgusting when you threaten to withhold love from people who love you and need your love.'

'I didn't –!'

'Yes, you did. You said if you didn't get your way you'd walk out. And your family would be left behind, missing you. Don't play hard-to-get, Jon; it hurts the rest of us, and it hurts you. Is any party worth all that?'

After a moment, Jon mumbled, 'I don't want to go home anyway.'

'That's not the point,' Katherine said gently.

'She means apologise,' Carrie whispered loudly.

Ross put his arm around Jon's shoulders. 'Why don't we talk about this later? Katherine's right, you know: if you threaten to go home every time I say something you don't like, we'll have a hard time getting along. You'll end up like a yo-yo, back and forth so fast we can't keep track of you . . .'

Below the table, Jennifer and Todd began to giggle, mostly in relief at the easing of tension. 'Can we get some cake from the kitchen?' Jennifer asked, standing up now that the air was clearing.

'A fine idea,' Victoria said crisply. 'And Sylvie made more lemonade; help yourself.'

'Come on,' urged Todd when Jon still sat in his chair.

'I'm sorry, Dad,' Jon said. 'I didn't mean it.'

Ross tightened his arm around his son's shoulders. 'Good thing,' he said casually. 'This place wouldn't be the same without you. Go on, now; get yourself some cake.'

As the four of them walked into the living-room, Carrie's piercing whisper could be heard on the terrace. 'Wow, did Katherine ever tell you off?'

'She's gotten real tough since Dad left,' said Todd. 'She used to be careful, but now sometimes she just lays it on us. I don't know . . .' His voice diminished as they went through the swinging doors into the kitchen. 'Mostly she's great, but she sure is different.'

Ross took Katherine's hand. 'Thank you. For caring, and for giving me a chance to catch my breath. I live with that damned fear every day, wondering when they'll decide they have better things to do than stay with me . . .'

'I don't think they will,' Katherine said. She wanted to lift her hand and smooth the lines between his eyebrows; instead, she said quietly, 'I've watched them follow you around – they're crazy about you and they need you. I think they're testing their weapons. Jennifer and Todd do it, too, only with different ones. I just hope Jon doesn't pull that one too often.'

He chuckled. 'Now that he knows he has Jennifer and Todd's tough mother to contend with, I doubt he'll ever do it again. Thank you,' he repeated, his voice low, and later, when he went to talk with Jon, his step was light.

The children's diving team was scheduled to practise the next day from morning until late afternoon, and Ross and Katherine took advantage of the day, leaving before breakfast for Aix-en-Provence and its international music festival. Ross took an inland road that was, at that hour, almost empty, and they drove in silence amid the green and gold splendour of the countryside. The air was soft and caressing; the sun spilled like honey over orange and olive groves that parted suddenly to reveal small stone villages with steep rust-coloured roofs and flocks of pale brown sheep watched over by a single shepherd, hands clasped behind his back, his staff sticking out as if he, too, had a tail.

Aix was filled with the music of the festival, and it was market day, with stands crowded together in the Place de Verdun beneath a rainbow of parasols. Ross bought a bouquet of carnations and pinned one to the collar of Katherine's cotton shirt and when they turned to walk on, their hands touched and their fingers twined together. They strolled through the market and the quiet side streets, along worn stone walks shaded by enormous plane trees, and then to a concert in the courtyard of the Archbishop's palace, and when they sat down Katherine took another carnation from the bouquet and pinned it to the lapel of Ross's sports jacket. In the afternoon, blue shadows lay across the town, and fountains in the courtyards reflected the sunset. And much later, on the drive back along the Mediterranean, the brilliant lights of the Riviera blocked out all signs of the small towns, the orange and olive groves, and the single shepherd with his flock.

Everyone was asleep when they reached the villa. At the door to her rooms, Katherine sighed, resting her head against the wall. The spicy scent of carnations was all about them, and the pungency of the almond paste *calissons* they had brought back for Victoria and the children. 'We brought the day home with us,' she said, and laughed softly. 'Such a perfect day.'

His face was shadowed in the dim corridor. 'More than any I've ever known.' He held her face between his hands. 'Thank you.'

Katherine shook her head. 'I'm the one who should thank you. For all the perfect days.' She stepped back, into the doorway, wanting more than his hands; refusing to admit it. 'Goodnight, Ross.'

'Goodnight, Katherine.' He lingered a moment, wanting her, knowing she wanted him. Not yet, he thought. We have time; there's so much we still want to know about each other. 'Is tomorrow the diving competition?'

'Tomorrow morning.'

'I'll pick you up at the breakfast table.'

She laughed and watched him walk down the corridor and turn into his own rooms.

They had avoided the populous vacation areas and the next morning for the first time they encountered the impenetrable crowds of the Riviera's high summer season. 'July,' Ross murmured as they descended the steep stairway from Victoria's villa and found themselves surrounded. 'Don't fight it; don't even try to walk; they'll carry you.'

The crowd was cheerful and noisy, exchanging shouted itineraries and names of restaurants. Everywhere, strangers held out their cameras to other strangers, asking them please to take their pictures. A large round man with a Polaroid snapped a picture of Katherine and kept pace with Ross as the image

391

developed. '*Bella, bella,*' he said. '*Uomo fortunato.*' Amid a torrent of Italian he handed Ross the photograph, nodded amiably and turned to walk on.

'*Grazie,*' said Ross, and he and Katherine looked at it together. Katherine's eyes widened. *Is that really me – that woman laughing in the sunlight? She looks so happy. I didn't know she was so happy.* She felt vaguely uneasy – as if everything was speeding up and she was not sure she was in control.

But then they reached the pool, and she saw Jennifer and Todd standing near the diving board, lean and tanned, chattering excitedly with a swim-suited group that included Carrie and Jon. We're all happy, she thought, and nothing is out of control. With another glance at the picture, she asked Ross, 'Did you understand what he was saying when he took it?'

'Most of it.' Ross pulled two chairs together near the edge of the pool. 'He looked at you and said you were beautiful. And then he told me I was a fortunate man.' The crowd milled about them but there was a small space of silence around their chairs. He tucked the photograph in his pocket and took Katherine's hand in his as they turned to watch their children's diving skills. 'And, of course, he was absolutely right.'

The shapes and colours of the Riviera glowed in the sketches spread on the drawing table Victoria had bought for Katherine's sitting-room. There were fishes and birds, exotic cactus flowers, the scalloped edges of the orange overlapping roof tiles of Provence, the symmetrical arches of Roman bridges, the swirl of water rushing over stones in a mountain stream.

Katherine had redrawn the sketches she liked best, then, tried different variations of the basic shape until she had one that was bold, simple, striking: uniquely hers. When she was satisfied, she coloured it with oil pastels – a cross between coloured chalk and crayons, with subtler shades and a permanent finish.

She had been holding a blue-black oil pastel in her fingers for half an hour, wondering if the soaring bird she had drawn, with wings outspread, should be a perched bird with wings folded back. A simple problem, but she could not resolve it because her thoughts kept returning to Ross. Finally, she threw down the coloured stick and raised her head to gaze through the glass doors at the sailboats swaying in the harbour. 'Ridiculous,' she said aloud. 'I'll finish it tomorrow.'

She walked down the corridor to Victoria's room and knocked on the closed door.

'Yes,' said Victoria. 'Ah, Katherine, how lovely; come in. I thought you would have left by now.'

'We put it off for half an hour. Ross had some telephone calls to make before he goes to Paris tomorrow.'

'How nice. For us, I mean. A quiet time together.' Lying on a silk chaise beside the open doors to her terrace, she tilted her head, inspecting Katherine's madras shirt and khaki jeans, her dark hair held by a gold band, her hazel eyes flecked with blue in the Mediterranean light. 'You look delightful: a week in the sun has put colour in your face. Where do you go today?'

'Ross said the Turini Forest and Vesubie Valley. Does that sound right? My pronunciation . . .'

'Is improving. Ross is invariably sensible. You will have a memorable afternoon.'

'And it's been two weeks in the sun.'

'I beg your pardon?'

'We've been here almost two weeks for the sun to put colour in my face.'

'When time goes too quickly, Katherine, I make a practice of ignoring it. What else has Ross planned? Has he mentioned the folk festival at Nice?'

'We're taking the children when he gets back from Paris. And we want you to come along.'

'No, my dear, how pleasant that you thought of it, but no; I shall stay here and wait for you to tell me about it.'

Katherine sat on the edge of the chaise. 'You haven't gone anywhere with us, except to dinner, twice. After Paris, I don't want to accuse you of being obvious, but –'

'Katherine. I am never obvious. I may occasionally become careless and tip my hand, but I am not obvious. My dear, I do not go with you because I no longer enjoy all-day excursions, or even half-day ones. I'm too tired.'

Worried, Katherine asked, 'Is something wrong? You always seem to have so much energy.'

'The only thing wrong is my age. As for my energy, I have plenty, so long as I know when to rest and preserve it.' She grimaced. 'It's dreadfully tiresome; I get so annoyed at my body. Until recently, I could force it along and think I'd fooled it into renewing itself. But it was going its own way, wearing out, and then one day I could no longer ignore it. I'm eighty-two, my dear, and I can no longer romp through the Vesubie Valley. And if I cannot romp, I refuse to go at all.'

'Are you sure you're all right?' Katherine pressed. 'You haven't even gone out with your own friends since we arrived.'

'Oh, that has nothing to do with me; they're not here. Most of them scatter to their other homes in July and August.'

Katherine remembered something Tobias had said. 'You came in July because of us. So you missed all your friends.'

'I have you; I have Ross. Who is more important to me? And if I know where you are *and what you are doing*, I may be lying here like a piece of crumpled tissue paper, but I can imagine myself with you. I remember all the places, you know, so clearly. And it gets easier to pretend, the older I am.'

'I'm sorry,' Katherine said. 'I didn't realise ... So much has been happening and I've been selfish, only thinking of myself instead of spending time with you.'

'But you must be selfish! Don't you understand, the more

you do, the more pleasure you have, the more successful you are, the more of everything *I* have. I did think *that* was obvious! Now, my dear' – she patted Katherine's hand – 'be off and have a wonderful day. If you're too late for dinner, I will entertain the various offspring; but I'll expect a full report tomorrow. Every detail.'

Katherine bent to kiss her forehead. 'Every one.'

'I hope not,' Ross laughed when Katherine repeated the conversation as they drove through a mountain valley. 'It's a bad precedent.'

'Why? If it's all she has –'

'Did she say that?'

'Not exactly, but –'

'All she said was she wants to be part of our lives because it makes her feel less old and limited. Katherine, Victoria is the majority stockholder in the Hayward Corporation and she sits on four other Boards of Directors, helping manage and raise funds for some of the most powerful institutions in San Francisco. That's hardly a picture of a helpless little old lady lying like a crumpled piece of tissue paper while the busy world passes her by.'

Involuntarily, Katherine smiled. 'Hardly.' Her face grew thoughtful. 'But she wasn't really lying.'

He shook his head. 'Bending the truth. She's intelligent and wily enough to know that the one thing her wealth can't do is slow down the years, so she uses whatever means she has to hold onto parts of the world she can no longer experience directly. Like the Vesubie. It's all right, you know; it's a benign form of tyranny.'

Katherine looked at him. 'That's not kind.'

'It's accurate,' he said simply. 'She's using our love for her to make us feel responsible, to keep her at the centre of our lives, even though she knows that's impossible – ultimately we'll have to pass her by. But she tries. And I admire her persistence, and love her deeply, but I have no intention of telling her everything that fills my time. And if you do, and I see you whip out a pencil to take notes to report to her' – Katherine began to laugh – 'I'll probably become silent and quite possibly immobile. Whereas, if you agree with me, I will take your hand, so, and hold it while I get us through the Brevera Valley.'

He took his eyes from the road for a split second, to share her smile, then, holding her hand firmly in his, he drove slowly along the narrow road that looped back and forth as it climbed through the mountains. The scenery grew wilder and they were silent, awed by the maze of deep, shadowed gorges separated by sunlit meadows. Twisted trees clung to the rocky slopes, while in the meadows pines grew amid boulders that crashed from above each spring when melting snows set off avalanches. The air turned cool and Katherine pulled on her sweater. As the atmosphere thinned, the farthest craggy mountains came into sharp relief. And then they drove into the Turini Forest – dim, cool, dense with huge trees and twisted undergrowth.

Ross kept going on the zigzagging road until they rounded a curve and came upon the tiny village of La Bollene-Vesubie, where he pulled the car to a stop. 'The backpacks are in the trunk. From here on, we hike.'

From the village, the trail climbed rapidly through forests and meadows, leaving the last vestiges of civilisation behind. The air was chilly but as they climbed, they were almost too warm in their sweaters. Once Katherine leaped from one boulder to another, weightless; when she landed lightly, bending her knees to cushion her fall, Ross held out his hand and she took it, sharing with a smile the joy of their isolation. They hiked for an hour, pushing through bushes, jumping across streams, following a trail that sometimes disappeared among rock outcroppings or underbrush, and reappeared farther on.

They barely spoke, except to point out, now and then, a soaring bird haloed in gold against the blue sky, tangled skeins of brilliant wildflowers weaving about grey boulders with orange, grey and black lichen covering their north sides, wide pastures smooth as velvet, the flick of an animal on the trail, and over everything the crystalline air and vast silence, broken only by the piercing songs of birds.

The sun moved higher, warming the sheltered valley. They stuffed their sweaters in their backpacks, moving on into a landscape less rugged, trees and bushes shimmering in the dazzling sun, until at last Ross said, 'I don't know about you, but I'm famished. If you see a good spot –'

'There!' Katherine exclaimed, pointing as they came to the crest of a small ridge. 'Just waiting for us.'

They clambered down the slope to a grassy nook protected on three sides by high rock formations. Nearby, a stream widened into a clear blue-green pool before narrowing again and disappearing among the trees. 'The old swimming hole,' Ross murmured. He looked at Katherine, eyebrows raised. 'What do you think?'

'I think it will be freezing and we ought to try it.'

He laughed. 'You're wonderful.' Dropping his backpack on the soft grass, he seemed not to notice the flush on her face and the brightness of her eyes. 'Right away, don't you think? Better to do it before we eat.'

Katherine set her backpack next to his. 'I'll beat you in. Unless you feel it's a man's job to test the waters.'

'It's a man's job to know when to let the woman go first.'

Laughing, she disappeared behind a cluster of pine and chestnut trees. But as soon as she pulled off her shirt and khaki pants and felt the sun burning on her bare skin, she was swept with a dizzying surge of desire and anticipation, and reached out to steady herself against a tree. The rough bark was solid, deeply textured, and she clung to it, aware of Ross, close by, as

397

if she could feel him as sharply as she felt the bark of the tree. I didn't know, she thought. I didn't know how much I wanted him. But deep in this valley, cut off from distractions and carefully constructed reasons, protected in the sunlit niche from the cool air beyond the rock walls, she knew that all their days together had led to this one, and that Ross knew it too.

The dizziness was gone. Katherine left her clothes on a rock and, in silk underpants and brassiere, she slipped from the cluster of trees to the wild grass bordering the pool. She did not see Ross, but rather than give herself a chance to think twice, she took a breath and made a shallow dive into the clear water.

She gasped in the shock of the icy cold. Every cringing muscle seemed to curl into a tight defensive knot. 'Once,' she gasped aloud. 'Once across, then out.' In a strong crawl, kicking hard, she cut through the mirror images of trees that seemed to grow down from the surface, and reached the other side, where she grasped a low-hanging branch, pulled herself out of the water and, shivering in the shade, turned to look for Ross.

Across the pool, the water broke into a long wake. Katherine heard his shout as the cold struck him, and she watched him swim towards her with powerful strokes, bursting through the water to grab the same branch she had used. 'I'll race you back,' he panted.

'I thought I'd walk around,' she said through chattering teeth.

'Sensible. No risk of losing.'

'Oh!' Without warning, she dove back in and kicked away from the shore, leaving Ross in a fury of droplets.

'Unfair!' he yelled, and followed, within a moment pulling even with her. Her lips were blue, he saw, but her body was strong and sinuous in the freezing water. They swam together until he gave a final spurt and finished half a length ahead of her.

'You're wonderful,' he said again as they staggered from the water. Exulting, they laughed through numb lips. 'Do we have any towels?' She shook her head. 'Damn. Poor planning. Sit here; I'll see what I can find.'

She leaned against a warm rock. The molten sun dried her almost instantly, but her skin was still covered with small bumps from the cold that seemed to have soaked into her bones. Staring vacantly at the deceptive, sun-sparkled pool, she thought of nothing at all, but there was an image in her mind, like a photograph, of the two of them, swimming side by side with matched strokes.

'One towel,' Ross said, returning. 'Wrapped around the wine. Not very big, but enough to share.' He looked down at her. His muscles quivered from the cold that pervaded him, but he stood still, gazing at her. 'My God,' he breathed. 'You are so lovely.'

Katherine's thoughts stirred and she saw herself as he did: half-lying on the grass in transparent wet underclothes. Brushing her dripping hair from her eyes, she made a move to stand up. 'No,' Ross said and, kneeling, he began to dry her hair with the towel.

'The sun . . .' Katherine murmured. 'It will dry –'

'I know.' Holding the towel, his hand moved rhythmically, caressing her hair in long strokes and then her neck and shoulders. She was beginning to feel warm again. From Ross's own drenched hair, a drop of water fell like an icicle on her breast and she flinched. He laughed shakily. 'Dangerous . . .' With a swift motion he ran the towel over his hair, then, bending, put his lips to the spot on her breast. For a long moment they stayed that way, barely breathing, engulfed in sunlight, their flesh beginning to glow, as if, at last, the sun ran through their veins.

'Katherine,' Ross murmured. 'My God, how many times I've said your name to myself . . . dearest, lovely Katherine.'

He pulled off her wet brassiere and pants and Katherine put her hands on his soaked cotton underpants and pushed them off. They lay on the fragrant grass, bodies burning hot, cool where their wet clothes had been, and Ross slid his arm beneath Katherine's shoulders and brought his open mouth down to hers.

They held the kiss, prolonging it, letting their desire grow, letting it flow through them, like the sun. Katherine's arms kept Ross close. 'I thought of this,' she said, her lips against his, 'before I went in the water. I wanted you –'

'I thought of this in Paris,' he said. And then, lying on her softness and delicate strength, he felt her legs part for him and he thrust into her, into the darkness of her body while sunlight spun in brilliant wheels behind his closed eyes and Katherine whispered his name in the clear mountain air.

There was so much to say they chose silence, lips meeting in small kisses as they lay quietly, Katherine's head on his shoulder, one of Ross's legs lying across hers, its heaviness as pleasurable as their caresses. Ross moved his palm slowly up the curve of her hip to her breasts, brushing the nipples, and then to her throat and face, as if sketching the lines and textures of her body; and Katherine lightly slid her hand along his back to his shoulders and muscled arms, and stopped with her fingertips in the blond hair of his chest. She raised herself on one elbow, looking down into his dark eyes. 'I feel so greedy,' she said, embarrassed.

'Not greedy,' he said, and smiled at her, the sun running through his veins. 'Alive, marvellous, part of me . . .' He kissed the fullness of her breasts, taking her taut nipples, rose and pink in the sunlight, into the warmth of his mouth.

A long sigh came from deep within Katherine, freeing the last of the hungers and fears she had restrained for so long. Everything was all right; everything was wonderfully right between them. She was filled with a joy that was like the sun warming her after she had been so cold, and the joy sang within her as Ross's mouth moved from her breasts to her stomach. 'You taste like pine trees,' he murmured, his mouth on her soft skin. 'And wild clover and mountain streams.' A heavy languor held her still, while his touch swept through her in widening ripples; he was everywhere a part of her, surrounding her, and she felt herself press against the earth, melting, open, waiting, as his hands parted her thighs and his tongue whispered against her.

The touch, sharp and soft, leaped through Katherine's body; a low moan escaped her and she dissolved into feeling as his tongue moved lightly, exploring, pushing inside her – *alive, marvellous, part of me* – until she felt herself draw together, like a flower curling to hold within its petals the golden liquid of the sun. She drew together to one blazing point until it was too great to be contained and with a cry, her body arching, Katherine felt it burst, spinning through her veins, then slowly fading away.

They lay together, and kissed. For a moment Katherine drowsed in the sun, and then they murmured together about dressing, eating, hiking back – but instead they looked at each other through half-closed eyes in the brightness and let their bodies waken in a long embrace. 'If I could take you onto me,' Ross said. 'And hold you there . . .'

'Yes,' Katherine said. 'Yes.' And when his hands went to her hips, she moved on top of him.

His arms enfolded her so tightly her breasts were crushed against his chest, her face buried in the curve of his neck and shoulder. Stirring, she raised her head so her lips could make tiny kisses along his neck. 'Your skin is so warm,' she murmured. 'Hard and smooth and warm – and I can kiss your heartbeat here –' She kissed the hollow of his throat and then his mouth, open and as demanding as hers.

He lifted her and Katherine sat astride him, lowering herself upon him, feeling him slide upward filling her. She smiled down on him, his dark blond hair still damp, his deepset, dark eyes as warm as the sun, his lips curving on her name.

'. . . Lovely, magnificent woman,' he murmured. His hands held her breasts, his palms against her erect nipples as their bodies found a rhythm as perfect as the one they had found in the water. Katherine bent over Ross again, her dark hair falling in a curtain about their faces as their mouths met and clung and they moved together, faster, merged in a haze of sunlight and pure feeling, faster still, climbing, to the narrow peak of a mountain against a clear sky, until, together, they leaped free and trembling, came gradually to earth.

Night falls quickly in the mountains, the sky flaming to crimson, orange and amber, fading to violet, smokey-grey, and then black, blotting out everything but the ghostly outlines of snow-covered peaks. Driving through the valley, Ross and Katherine watched the sunset fling its brilliance across the sky and then retreat leaving them in a darkness broken only by the brightness of their headlights.

At the small crossroads town of Sospel, they stopped for a late dinner and lingered over coffee on the terrace of a hotel overlooking a cobblestone square. Hands clasped, chairs touching, they watched the play of light and water from a fountain covered in a mosaic of brightly-coloured pebbles. Relaxed, sated, filled with a soft, glowing happiness, Katherine rested her head against the back of her chair and gazed at the black sky, so close above them, crowded with brilliant clusters of stars, and the pale frozen lace of the Milky Way. We're always outdoors, she thought idly, remembering how everything with Derek had been inside: restaurants, hotel ballrooms, night clubs, private homes. But she and Ross were almost always outside – everything open, fresh, limitless. She started to tell him, but stopped. They'd never talked about Derek. Long ago, Victoria had said Ross was concerned about her, because of Derek. We'll have to talk about him, she thought. And they'd never talked about the reasons she'd been unsure whether Ross liked her or not. And they'd never talked about –

'We have to talk,' Ross said when they were in the car again, descending on the corniche to Menton. 'So many things we've been avoiding. At least, I have.'

Katherine laughed softly. 'I was just thinking of all the things I want to talk to you about. But not tonight. Tomorrow.'

'Tomorrow I'll be in Paris.'

'Oh.' She had forgotten. 'But you'll be back.'

'In three or four days.' The road made a few final twists, then straightened, the car raced forward. 'I'd rather not go at all,' he said, his hands relaxed on the wheel as they sped faster, passing other cars. 'It's the wrong time. If I'd known, when Jacques and I made our plans –' He paused. 'Why don't you come with me? You'd have the days to yourself and I'll cancel my dinner meetings – why not?' he asked as she shook her head.

'Because we have things to think about. And it might be a good idea for us to be apart for a little while.'

'Before we talk?'

'I don't know. Yes. Before we talk.'

They fell silent, preoccupied with their own thoughts Suddenly Katherine began to laugh. 'What?' Ross asked.

'Victoria. Remember? She gave me strict instructions to tell her every detail of our day.' Simultaneously they pictured their bodies twined together on the grass. 'And you said it would be a bad precedent –'

'And I didn't want you taking notes,' he finished, his laughter joining hers.

At the villa, they parted at her door. 'I'll be gone before

you're up,' he said, and the next morning, when she woke, she found a spray of carnations and roses on her draughting table, with a note written across her sketch pad.

'Thank you for the most wonderful of days. I'm taking you with me, because from now on you'll always be inside me. One more thing for us to talk about when I get back. Soon.
Ross.'

'Well,' said Victoria, searching her face when she came in to breakfast. 'You found the scenery satisfactory?'

'Magnificent.' *I'm taking you with me.* But he was still here – as if he had become part of her – and Katherine was uncomfortable. Too much, too fast, she thought, and remembered feeling, just a few days earlier, that events might be out of control. She wondered what Victoria had seen in her face, and knew she was not ready to talk about Ross. Pouring juice and coffee at the sideboard she asked, 'Where are the children?'

'I believe in the playroom. Two of them grumbling, two being sympathetic.' Katherine looked puzzled. 'When Ross said goodbye early this morning, he told Carrie and Jon to call their mother. They were supposed to do it once a week and they missed last week. They say they have nothing to tell her – though they're busy every minute of the day – and for some reason Jennifer and Todd understand this perfectly. So they sympathise while the other two grumble. Does this make sense to you? When my children were young they would have had no difficulty calling me; they told me everything.'

Katherine smiled. 'Did they really?'

'Well, probably not. Probably I was better off that they didn't. And I suppose children would never become independent if they didn't have secrets. But from you, my dear, I want to hear about everything that gave you that radiant look. Come,

404

sit down, sit down, I want to hear it all, from the beginning. Where did you leave the car – La Bollene or St Martin? And where did you hike? Sit down, my dear, drink your coffee, eat something, and tell me all about it.'

'I will. But if you don't mind, I'd like to check on the grumbling, first. I'll be right back.'

Walking down the wide corridor to the children's wing, she shivered, as if a chill breeze had found its way through a crack in the wall. Melanie, San Francisco, the outside world. Craig. For three weeks they had barely existed, invisible in the glare of the Mediterranean sun, the unfamiliar landscape, the force of Ross's presence.

Now the chill breeze brushed her and she almost turned back. But then she heard Carrie's voice and caught a quick glimpse, in the playroom, of Jennifer and Todd on the couch, watching gravely as Carrie spoke on the telephone with Jon beside her. Katherine stepped back, not wanting to make them self-conscious. She wavered between going and staying, then stayed. She would just listen for a minute; just to make sure everything was all right.

'Nothing much,' Carrie was saying. 'We go swimming and there's Scrabble and stuff in the playroom and that's all.' She listened, tapping her foot. 'Well I suppose we're bored. I don't know.' She listened again. 'No, she's nice. She lets us do lots of things and she jokes with us and she's funny . . . she drives the gardener crazy by picking vegetables he thinks aren't ripe, or flowers that aren't – what? Oh. Well, I can't help it if you don't care about the gardener. Here. Jon wants to say hello.'

Scowling, she thrust the phone at Jon. 'Hi, Mom, we're fine. What? I don't. I don't think I'm bored. We do things all the time with Jennifer and Todd and – Carrie, cut it out! What are you doing?'

'Hitting your head, stupid! Oh, never mind.'

'Wasn't I supposed to tell Mom they're here?'

'I don't know. I just thought maybe we wouldn't.'

Jon frowned at the telephone, then said into it, 'Sorry, Mom, Carrie was beating on me. What? Jennifer and Todd Fraser, you know them.' He looked at Carrie and rolled his eyes. 'We didn't *know* they'd be here, so how could we tell you? Sure she's here; they all came together. We don't see her a lot though 'cause she works every morning and then in the afternoon she and Dad go places. How do *I* know where? They don't tell us. I guess everyday; we do our own stuff; we don't watch them. I don't know what time they get back. Usually for dinner. Mom, I gotta go. There's another diving contest and we have to practise. No, I can't get Dad to the phone; he's in Paris. He left this morning. I don't know. Carrie, when will Dad be back?'

'Three or four days.'

'Three or four days. I don't know; Carrie, what's Dad's hotel?'

'L'Hôtel on the Rue des Beaux Arts. The same one he was in before. You know all that.'

'Yeh, but – Mom? L'Hôtel. The same one he was in before. OK? Gotta go; talk to you soon. 'Bye.'

Melanie hung up the telephone and stared, unseeing, at the lights of San Francisco.

Across the room, Derek took ice cubes from the refrigerator behind the bar. 'I didn't get all of that, but I gather Victoria has imported someone to entertain Ross.'

'Katherine Fraser,' she said, still looking out the window.

He stood still. 'Ross and Katherine? How clever of Victoria.'

Melanie turned. His face was smooth, but his eyes were dark with fury, and she felt a stab of jealousy. 'Does that bother you? Katherine and your brother? I must say, it didn't

406

take long; we only split in May.' She watched his expression-less face. 'Jon says they're having quite a time, every afternoon and night . . . sending the kids off to play tennis or whatever so they can be alone. He leaves me stuck with this house while he plays on the Riviera . . . and he certainly isn't spending time with his children, which was the reason, *he said,* he wanted them in France for the month. I should demand them back; they both say they're bored; they don't have a mother or a father.'

Derek was looking off in the distance, the muscle beside his eye jumping erratically. He put back the ice cube tray. 'It's after eleven. If you want to get to this party we'd better go. When is your tennis champion due back?'

'Tomorrow.'

'And what are you going to do with him?'

'Marry him, I suppose.'

'Why?'

'Because I love him.'

'Bullshit.'

Standing at the vestibule mirror, Melanie smoothed her hair with nervous fingers. 'Because he's young and makes me feel young.'

'That's not all. What else?'

'Damn you, Derek.' She took a silk shawl from the closet. 'I'm afraid of being alone.'

He nodded. 'I wish you well.'

'No you don't. You don't really care anything about me. You used to make love to me – you *pursued* me – and lately you won't. Even though I ask you. I *never* ask! *Anybody!* But I ask you, and you turn me down!'

'Katherine said I wanted you because you were Ross's wife.'

'*Katherine* said! What does that bitch know about any of us?'

'Considerably more than you do.' He opened the door, his thoughts cold and bitter. Derek understood himself well enough to know when someone saw through him. Ordinarily he was indifferent to what others said, but on the rare occasions when someone got past his barriers and reached the Derek Hayward he took care to hide from the world, he reacted with fury. It had been bad enough when Katherine did it in April; now, knowing she was with Ross, imagining them talking about him, he felt his insides twist with rage and knew he had to be careful until he calmed down. Abruptly, he said, 'Are you ready?'

Melanie swung upon him. 'Are you in love with her?'

'No.'

She persisted. 'Were you, when you were going out with her?'

'No. And what difference does it make?'

'I don't know,' she said. They walked to his car. 'I'd just feel better if you weren't.'

He made no answer and after a moment, unable to endure silence, Melanie began to talk of something else. She talked all the way across the Golden Gate Bridge into San Francisco and to the top of Nob Hill where Derek parked on the steep street in front of Herman Mettler's town house.

It was a very large party, the kind Mettler gave every summer when business was slow. Assuming everyone else was bored, too, he provided various entertainments: a choice selection of pornographic films in the basement projection room; an orchestra playing dance tunes in the living-room that took up most of the first floor; and Polynesian hors-d'oeuvres served by circulating waitresses in grass skirts. Upstairs, a glass case held a sampling from Mettler's fall line of jewellery.

'Of course, she doesn't do your kind of thing,' Mettler said to Marc Landau as their gaze fastened on a gold necklace labelled 'Katherine Fraser'. 'But she's got quite a talent, no doubt about it. Might even rival you someday, Marc. Make her own mark.' He chuckled. 'Especially if her work keeps changing as incredibly as it has so far.'

'No one rivals Marc Landau,' Leslie said slyly. 'He's told me so himself. But that necklace is spectacular, isn't it?' She turned as someone called her name. 'Excuse me; I'm going to mingle.'

Landau studied the necklace. 'Her work changed?'

'Like night and day. Her first batch was nice, well-made, the kind you see at Williams and Baylor, or Corfert's. The second . . . well, you see it. Inventive, bold, unique . . . fascinating use of materials. The first time she kept to safe channels; the next she broke free. Astonishing. And you know, I nearly ruined it. I was so surprised I made the almost fatal mistake of asking her whether they were really hers. Ah, Derek.' He interrupted himself. 'Good to see you.'

They shook hands. 'Have you been accusing someone of stealing designs?' Derek asked.

'God forbid! I only asked. Your friend Katherine Fraser; she didn't tell you? She seemed angry enough to tell the world, just because I made an innocent comment when she brought in *totally* different work and refused to consider an exclusive contract. What a high horse she got on! It made *me* hoarse apologising. I'd let on how impressed I was, so she knew she could go elsewhere, and she almost walked out on me. Hard to believe she didn't regale you with the whole story, Derek.'

'She didn't because she didn't see me,' Derek said, thoughtfully contemplating Katherine's necklace. 'The last time we saw each other was sometime in April.'

'Lover's quarrels,' said Mettler whimsically. But his curiosity was like a persistent itch. 'I'm sure you'll patch it up . . . or has it gone too far?'

Seemingly absorbed in the necklace, Derek said softly,

'Herman, I never talk about young women's problems.'

After a pause, Mettler asked, 'Problems?'

Landau frowned. 'Leslie said she was settled and doing well.'

'Problems about her work?' Mettler asked Derek.

'No. Personal. I wouldn't worry. Herman; chances are they won't affect you at all.'

In the midst of the party's gaiety, a small, dark silence fell among the three men.

'*Chances are*,' Mettler repeated. 'Shouldn't I be the judge of that?'

Derek shrugged.

'Goddamn it, Derek, I asked a civil question. I'm investing in this woman and if she has problems that might affect her work, *I want to know about it!*'

'There's no cause for hysteria, Herman; I only know some isolated facts. Nothing more.'

'Facts! Facts! What the fuck are you talking about? Marc, if you don't mind . . . Derek, in private –' Taking Derek's arm he led him to a corner away from the crowd. 'Now, what the hell is going on?'

Derek drank half his Scotch. 'I haven't the faintest idea whether something is "going on", as you put it. Katherine is a troubled young woman, with more than her share of problems. Her husband is an embezzler who disappeared over a year ago after admitting to his partner that he'd stolen from the company for years. Less than two months after he disappeared, Katherine sold their house at a loss and fled Canada; soon after she arrived here she started receiving money every month from her husband. And last New Year's Eve he came to see her. We've asked her to tell us where he is, so we could help him, but she insists she doesn't know. More likely she's afraid to trust anyone.'

Mettler passed his hand over his face. He had heard parts of

410

that story – though nothing of embezzling – but coming from Derek it sounded far different. 'Are you saying . . .' He cleared his throat. 'She might be involved in her husband's embezzling? She might be a thief?'

Derek shook his head. 'Doubtful.'

'You're not sure?'

'One has only her word. She seems honest.'

'But you're not sure. And if she's a thief, she could be stealing other things. Like jewellery designs.'

Derek smiled thinly. 'That's quite a leap, Herman. I wouldn't accuse her of any such thing.'

After a moment, Mettler blurted, 'She married into your family!' Derek was silent. 'That's why you're so cautious! Protecting your family!'

'Pull yourself together,' Derek said coldly. 'You're going off the deep end. I don't know how this came up; you have nothing to worry about.'

'I have plenty to worry about! You know how much my customers pay for the assurance that they're buying originals! Jewellery designs are copyrighted, damn it; my customers know that; they didn't get rich by being naive! Do you know what they'd do to me if they thought they were investing in copies or – my God – stolen designs? They'd find someone else to trust! Then where would I be? Goddamn it, if I'd known –!'

'Has Marc wandered off?' Leslie asked, pushing through the guests to reach them. 'I thought he was with you. Good heavens, Herman, has someone died?'

Mettler looked at her blankly. 'Marc went off. I don't know where he is.'

'Thanks,' she said dryly. 'I'll find him. And do let me know if it was someone important who died.'

She found Landau fending off a short man with heavy jowls who wanted him to design a necklace for his wife. 'Must go,'

411

Landau said in relief as Leslie came up. 'Drop me a note with a sketch; never do business at parties. He won't write,' he muttered to Leslie as they made their way across the room. 'Because he can't. Inherited all his money, plays a pathetic game of golf and never learned to write. That's all I know about him. Except that his wife likes emeralds. Are we eating dinner here or will you come home with me?'

'Here, if you don't mind.'

'Leslie.'

'Yes?'

'When were you last in my home?'

'April twenty-ninth.'

An eyebrow went up. 'Extraordinary memory. Or something happened to fix the date in your mind. And to keep you from my bed for nearly three months. Who is he?'

'You don't know him.'

'Even so, I assume he has a name.'

'Claude Fleming.'

Landau studied a manicured fingernail. 'You're right; I don't know him. But I know his firm. Shall we eat?' In a walled garden a buffet held ice sculptures of birds, weeping as they melted above hot and cold kebabs and hollowed pineapples heaped with fruit. 'You're moving up,' Landau said as they filled their plates. 'From a humble jeweller to a partner in one of the stuffiest law firms in the country. Isn't that a rather old-fashioned way for a woman to get ahead these days?'

'Don't overdo it, Marc,' Leslie said, walking ahead of him to a table. 'If you're nasty, I might think you really care what I do.'

'Or is it that he is willing to father this mythical child you once prattled about? That sentimental tale of longing for single motherhood. Have you been looking all this time, while I continued to escort you, for someone who longs for fatherhood?'

'I'll be damned,' she said. 'You do care. Marc, you're as jealous as a teenager.'

'Don't talk nonsense. I'm saying I don't allow anyone to take advantage of me.'

'That's what you were saying? You could have fooled me.' She pushed her plate away and stood up. 'I'm sorry, Marc; I wanted to stay friends. You're the only son of a bitch I know who sometimes has a heart of gold. But I wouldn't want you to feel taken advantage of, and whatever you may think I don't want you to be unhappy. If I'd known you cared a hoot in hell about me – well, I don't know; Claude might not have made such an instant impression. We'll never know, will we? But damn you anyway, Marc, for sleeping with me for years and keeping all your feelings to yourself. God, I'm so tired of cool, clever people. No, don't get up; I can find my way out; you stay and enjoy the party. Cheer up our host; he looked like Derek gave him a dose of poison. Goodbye, Marc; thank you for a pleasant few years.'

She strode through the living-room to the foyer. Shouldn't have gotten upset, she thought. But she felt light with relief. For three months she'd been unable to break it off – still unsure enough of Claude, and her own feelings for him, to cut loose entirely from someone as reliable as Marc. But now it had happened almost by itself and she gave a small skip as she went outside, stood for a minute, debating, then walked briskly two blocks to the Mark Hopkins to catch a cab.

She got home early, spent an hour on paperwork, and had it organised when she arrived at Claude's office the next morning. 'Here it is,' she said, handing him her typed notes. 'All but the last chapter. I don't suppose Bruce is here yet?'

'Bruce is here. Crisis inspires him to rise early. Can I get you coffee?'

'Yes.' She sighed with pleasure. Everything was coming together; everything would be all right. She hadn't felt so well protected in years.

413

'Morning, sis,' said Bruce from the floor where he sat yoga-style. 'I'm meditating if you want to try –'

'Bruce, could we go over this once more?'

'You're nervous,' he said accusingly.

'There's a lot at stake. I don't want to be wrong.'

'We're not wrong! I know everything – well, almost everything –'

'Bruce.' Claude sat on the arm of Leslie's chair. 'Go through it again.'

With a glance at the two of them, Bruce sighed. 'Right. Here goes. You want to steal merchandise from a store – not just a sweater or a purse, but maybe a million bucks' worth a year – what do you do? First you write a special computer program that lists each week's high-priced stuff that's selling fast – it's on sale or specially advertised or whatever. Then you give the list to somebody who goes through the store lifting the stuff, a dozen sweaters, maybe, or two dozen scarves or a couple of five-hundred-dollar jackets . . . not enough to be noticed when things are selling fast. He'd have to do it after store hours –'

'Night watchman,' Leslie interrupted.

'Or security guard, whatever. At the same time another part of this special computer program changes the inventory record for the store – *showing the stuff as sold!* Got that? If you used the regular program to do this you'd leave a record, but this special program bypasses all the controls we put in and doesn't leave a trace of tampering! Clever bastard, but I was almost on to him, when he found my notes and stole them –'

'That's what the special program does?' Claude asked. 'The one you found, but won't tell me how?'

'Damn it, you know where I – oh. Right, all the king's horses couldn't drag out of me how I got into the office to find it, right that's what it does, without leaving a clue. But I confess I'm stumped on how they got it past the sensors and

414

television cameras and out of the store. Janitors, using trash cans? Carpenters? Painters, with paint cans?'

'Leslie and I have an idea,' said Claude. 'We have to call Katherine to check it.'

'Katherine in France?'

'Yes. But first I have some questions. This special program took an expert, is that right?' Vigorously, Bruce nodded. 'How do we know it wasn't you?'

Bruce sprang from his meditative position. 'By telling them who really did it! My boss, Dick Volpe – the one who framed me by stealing my notes – I told you all this!'

'Grow up, Bruce,' Claude snorted. 'Who'll believe you?'

'Fuck you, Fleming! I thought *you* believed me! If you think I'll let you marry my sister if you call me a –'

'Bruce!' Leslie cried. 'No one's said anything about marriage!'

'Stick to the subject,' Claude ordered, but the corners of his mouth twitched as he tried not to smile. 'What's your defence when someone accuses you of lying about your former boss?'

'Oh – that's what you're doing? – working on my defence? A lousy defence lawyer, scaring the shit out of me . . . I told you, Volpe and I are the only ones who know enough to get past the controls on these programs, and Volpe has his own way of writing arrays – you don't know what that means, but never mind – we always knew which programs he wrote because of his style – wait, I'll show you –'

'Just explain it,' said Claude. 'Is it like different styles of painting or writing books?'

Bruce nodded.

'Different handwriting?'

'Not quite, but close.'

'Could computer experts identify one person's style?'

'Yes, damn it! That's what I'm saying!'

415

'And yours is different from Volpe's?'

'Every which way.'

'We can go with that,' said Claude. 'I'm satisfied. Leslie, are you?'

She nodded. 'I apologise for my brother's wild fancies.'

He met her eyes. 'I didn't hear any wild fancies.'

In the silence, Bruce cried, 'Well? Are we calling Mademoiselle Katherine in her French hideaway?'

'Leslie is,' said Claude. 'But only a question, Leslie. Not a word about Bruce's theory.'

'Why not? Claude, she's my friend and she knows what I've gone through –'

'I want to finish it first. Make sure we have the whole scenario, and that we're right. Leslie, I'm thinking of what is best for you. And Bruce.'

'You're thinking of getting a conviction,' she said.

'Which will keep your job and perhaps make Bruce head of Data Processing if that's what he wants. Damn it, Leslie, Heath's hasn't hired me; I don't care if they're robbed to their foundation. All I care about is you.'

Leslie remembered coming home one night and curling up in her window seat, thinking how lovely it would be to have someone who gave a damn. 'A convincing argument,' she said with a small laugh, and picked up the telephone. Claude lifted the receiver on the extension at the other end of his office as she dialled the number Katherine had left her for Victoria's villa in Menton.

'Hi,' she said casually, when Katherine came to the telephone. 'I called to say hello and –'

'Leslie! Good heavens . . . a voice from the outside world! How are you? Have you gotten my letters?'

'All of them, and they're wonderful. But, Katherine this is really a business call. The social one comes later. I'm in a meeting and I need to know why Gil fired you.'

'Gil? Of all the people I never think about –'

'I know, but it's important or I wouldn't ask. Could you tell me what happened? It was the night you took inventory, wasn't it?'

'I did a wedding scene in the window,' Katherine said thinking back. 'When I finished I went back downstairs . . . Gil wasn't there but he'd been in such a terrible mood I was afraid to leave if there was still counting to do. There were some cartons on the floor – display materials from the windows we'd taken down that week. They hadn't gone back to the warehouse because the regular driver was sick and Gil refused a substitute, so I thought I'd better count them. About then he came back and started screaming at me.'

'While you were going through the carton?'

'I'd gone through two or three: it was taking longer because there was new merchandise mixed in with the display materials . . .' Leslie and Claude exchanged a triumphant glance, as Katherine's voice faded. 'Leslie?' she said. 'I thought at the time the receiving room had made a mistake, and then later I was so shaken up by Gil that I forgot about it, but . . .'

'Katherine, I'm sorry,' Leslie said hastily. 'I know what you're thinking but I can't talk about it now. Not yet – pretty soon. I'll call you as soon as I can; is that all right?'

'Of course, but –'

'I'm sorry – so much is happening – goodbye, Katherine, I promise I'll call you back.'

She and Claude hung up simultaneously. 'Well?' Bruce cried, squirming in frustration. 'Well, damn it?'

'Very well,' said Claude with a smile seen in courtrooms when he was closing in on a trail of evidence.

'Window display cartons,' Leslie told Bruce. 'The stuff was packed in them just before they were sent back to the warehouse – past the sensors, past the guards and television cameras – and nobody asking any questions because those

417

boxes were *supposed* to go out of the store. Katherine found them because they were there longer than usual; the regular driver was sick and Gil refused –' She looked at Claude. 'Gil refused a substitute. And fired Katherine when he saw her going through them.'

Claude nodded. 'I would imagine either he or Volpe was the leader. They needed two others: someone to take the merchandise from the departments to the basement storeroom, and the driver. A wonderfully simple scheme.'

'So that's all?' Bruce demanded. 'You don't need anything else?'

'We need to have a chat with Gil Lister. And then, if all goes well, Heath's president. And then, Leslie, you can call Katherine back, and tell her your news.'

Katherine and Victoria were on the terrace when Leslie's second call came. 'Be prepared for a spectacular story,' she said abruptly as soon as she heard Katherine's voice. Rapidly, she outlined what they had found. 'And then we went to the little man himself, sitting in his high-backed leather throne in his little kingdom, and he collapsed like a punctured soufflé. My only regret was that you weren't there to savour it.'

'And then?' Katherine asked.

'We told the story to the executive committee, and Bruce explained the computer program – without a single vulgarity, by the way, which proves he can do it, and I got a huzzah from my president and grudging grunts from the others. The whole thing went beautifully. Bruce behaved, and Claude was perfect – cool and smooth and devastating. Very impressive.'

'Only professionally impressive?'

'Oh, hell. You mean you can hear it in my voice?'

'What I hear is that a lot seems to have happened while I've been away. I'd like to hear more.'

'I'll tell you all about it when you get back. Mainly I wanted you to know that I'm in the clear and so is Bruce. They did a nifty job of framing him – Lister let slip that they thought he was the type who'd run from problems, which would incriminate him even more – and it almost worked: it almost convinced his own sister. But in the end Bruce was the one who did them in. What do you think of that?'

'I think you're right: it's spectacular. Now tell me more about you and Claude.'

'When you get back. It's only a few more days, isn't it?'

'Five.' The word jolted Katherine. Five days. Ross would be back from Paris in two days, and three days after that she and Jennifer and Todd would leave. Even while she said goodbye to Leslie, those words repeated themselves. *Five days. And then we'll be part of the world again.*

'Sad news?' Victoria asked when Katherine rejoined her on the terrace. The dinner plates had been removed and crystal bowls of strawberries with orange zest and curaçao were at their places. Below, the tall masts in the harbour swayed against a russet sunset, and through an open window the two women could hear the children giggling as they invented dire predicaments for their characters in Dungeons and Dragons.

'No,' said Katherine. 'Good news.' She told Victoria the story, from the time Gil Lister fired her to Leslie's description of the executive board meeting that morning. 'And there's more. She and Claude seem to have become very close.'

'But isn't she your age? Claude likes young, wide-eyed maidens.'

'That's what we thought. But perhaps he's changed?'

'If so, she must be a remarkable young woman.'

'She is. I hope Claude knows it. I want her to be happy and she's been wishing for a family a long time.'

'Ah.' From a fluted silver dish, Victoria spooned a small mound of whipped cream and set it floating on her coffee. 'I noticed a postcard for you in today's mail.'

Katherine burst out laughing. 'Yes. From Ross. Now what could have made you think of that?'

'I can't imagine,' said Victoria calmly. 'You know how an old woman's thoughts skip about. Is he busy?'

'Busy and happily watching walls being torn out. And collecting postcards for all the children. The one he sent was a picture of a place we had dinner the night before we came here.'

'Postcards for the children,' Victoria said ruminatively. 'When Craig was a boy, he collected postcards. I remember the first time we took him to Tahoe, he insisted someone had drained the lake because it looked so much smaller than its picture on postcards we'd sent. Hugh roared about the difference between reality and pictures but that only terrified the poor child, so finally they went out in the boat and spent the day motoring around the circumference of the lake. Hugh never sent any postcards after that. I'm not sure what Craig learned from it all.'

Craig. Katherine looked at the harbour, lit now by floodlights: a tangle of masts and ropes, and sails wrapped in bright canvas shrouds. All that month she'd barely thought of him; no one had spoken his name; his shadow had not followed her. But now it was here. What was he doing now? she wondered. What was he afraid of now?

'If Ross buys postcards for the children,' Victoria was saying, 'He should tell them they're not the real thing. Do you miss him?'

'Yes,' said Katherine quietly. She had been avoiding Victoria's questions, but now, in the chill of Craig's shadow, she wanted to talk.

'And you think about him?'

'Yes.' She smiled. 'Enough to interfere with my work.'

'And what is it you think about?'

'Nothing specific. Just – about him.'

'What you do with him, or what you would like to do with him?'

'Are you asking me if we're sleeping together?'

'No, no, no, I would not ask that! It may be modern to discuss such matters, but in that respect I am most emphatically not modern. That is no one's business but your own, and his. I meant, do you think of him as a husband?'

'No.' Agitated, Katherine stood, and went to the low stone wall bordering the terrace, holding her face up to the faint breeze. 'I don't think of him as a husband because I already have a husband –'

'Whom you should divorce.'

'– Who is also my children's father . . . What? What did you say?'

'I said you should divorce Craig. Why should that surprise you? He deserted you thirteen months ago and except for some money and one visit, from which he ran away again, you haven't heard a word from him. Do you really call yourself married?'

'I don't understand. In the past, you've always defended him.'

'So I have. In some circumstances I still might. But I also have you to think of now. And it has become obvious to me that you cannot think clearly about Ross, or indeed any man, or make an unobstructed future for yourself, until you are free of this shadow that follows you about, clouding your view.'

'I can't do that.'

'Of course you can: it is not at all difficult; Derek has done it three times. I've asked Claude about it – of course he is the perfect person to help you: discreet, almost a member of the family – and he explained it to me. In the first place, it is not "divorce" any longer, but "dissolution", and all you need do, since you cannot find Craig to serve him the papers in person, is place a legal notice in the Vancouver newspapers, for one month, that you are petitioning for dissolution. If he does not respond in that time, you will go to court. accompanied by Claude, declare that your differences with your husband are irreconcilable, and the judge then issues the order. Claude says it takes about three minutes. And in six months it becomes final.'

'Very simple,' Katherine said. 'But that isn't what I meant. I can't divorce Craig because he isn't here.'

'I have explained that he doesn't have to be here –'

'Victoria, you know what I mean.'

'Yes. Of course.' Victoria laced her fingers together. 'I suppose I was trying to prevent you from talking to me about fidelity. It does not seem applicable.'

Something was nagging at the back of Katherine's mind. Something Leslie had said. She sat on the stone wall, staring through the swaying masts at a boat coming towards the harbour, running with the wind. Running. Bruce. Someone thought Bruce would run. *They thought he was the type who'd run from problems, which would incriminate him even more.* Someone framed Bruce for a crime because he seemed like the type who would run away.

They did a nifty job of framing him . . . it almost worked . . . it almost convinced his own sister.

The boat had come into the harbour; Katherine could see the small figures of the crew pulling down the main sail and furling the jib. Dizzily she gripped the rough stone. 'Katherine,' Victoria said sharply. 'What is it? Come here, before you fall.'

But Katherine was thinking back, a long way back, remembering someone shouting at Carl Doerner. It was at her party for Leslie, that Friday night when Craig didn't come home. Someone had shouted . . .

Pretty free with your accusations, Doerner! You're known for that, aren't you? Especially when they're false –

Listen you bastard, that was two years ago. And I thought I

422

was right. When I found out I wasn't I paid the costs and it was over.

'Katherine!' Victoria commanded.

Obediently, Katherine returned to the table, but she did not sit down. 'Would you mind if I go out for a while?' she asked. Her voice was very soft, as if she were afraid of breaking something. 'I'd like to take a walk. There are some things I have to think about.'

'Of course, my dear, if you're all right. If I said too much, I apologise –'

'No. It was nothing you said.' Bending down, she kissed Victoria's soft cheek. 'I love you. I won t go far.'

But she had already gone a long way, all the way back to Vancouver, to the day Craig left. The day he ran away. Not necessarily because he'd committed a crime but – perhaps – because he'd been framed for one.

But Carl said Craig had confessed. Katherine remembered his shaggy presence in her living-room as he held out an envelope with what he said was proof. And then later she'd found all those bills, past-due notices, sheets of scribbled numbers . . .

But still . . . Why hadn't it occurred to her that he might have been framed? For ten years she had known him as a good man; he'd been good to them and she loved him. *Why was I so ready to believe my husband was guilty?*

Because he wasn't there. Because he ran.

Why would he run, if he was innocent?

Maybe because he didn't know what to do, and had no one to talk to about it.

I was there, she reflected angrily; he could have talked to me. Whose fault was it that he was better at keeping secrets than sharing?

His. But maybe I didn't make him feel I really wanted to know them. What was it Leslie had once said? *You liked the life you had with him, so you didn't push*. I tried to get him to talk, but after a while I stopped, and let him have his secrets. If I'd asked more questions, maybe he would have told me about the Haywards, and about our overspending – and maybe other secrets that I haven't even thought of.

Walking along the harbour, a silent figure among crowds of vacationers, Katherine knew it was not an excuse for running. There was no excuse for Craig's deserting them. But if he thought he couldn't talk to her about what happened – whether he was framed or really did steal – didn't she have something to do with that?

Can you be married for ten years without sharing some responsibility for what happens?

If I'd been different – would Craig have run?

Chapter 15

Somehow Victoria saw to it that everyone was occupied and out of Katherine's way from early the next morning until well after dinner. 'I don't know what is bothering your mother,' Katherine heard her answer Jennifer's question, 'but if she needs a quiet time to think, we can help by leaving her alone.'

They all left her alone. She took the car that Ross had left for her to use and drove into the hills behind Menton, where ancient 'eagles' nest' villages clung to the rocky peaks. In Eze, she stopped and sat for hours beside an old stone house hundreds of feet above the sea. Below, on the Corniche, cars rolled like tiny marbles on a narrow strip between the beach and wooded hills. Behind the houses of Eze, the cactus gardens were in full bloom. But for Katherine, the magic and dreamlike isolation were gone. All the questions that had haunted her before, had found her here; she hadn't escaped them after all – she'd only pushed them aside for a brief time.

She remembered thinking, in Sospel, that she and Ross ought to talk about Derek – but it was Craig they really had to talk about. And when she'd been uncomfortable, at breakfast with Victoria, thinking Ross was becoming a part of her – it was Craig she was uncomfortable about, still with her, shadowing her, part of her life. And it was Craig she had to deal with, no matter how important Ross had become.

'What time do you expect Ross tomorrow?' Victoria asked after dinner.

'He said sometime in the morning.'

Victoria nodded and returned to her book and in a moment Katherine returned to hers. They were sitting opposite each other in deep, soft armchairs, and now and then they glanced up and smiled, happy with each other. But Katherine was restless and just before midnight, when Victoria kissed her goodnight and went to bed, she went to her own rooms. The housekeeper had turned down the bed and left small lamps on, casting a soft glow over the sage green and ivory furnishings. Unbuttoning her shirt, Katherine walked from the sitting-room to the bedroom and back, thinking of Jennifer and Todd asleep in their own rooms just off the playroom. She pictured the three-room apartment awaiting them in San Francisco and thought ruefully that they'd have to get used to it all over again, as they had the year before.

She paced restlessly, then, pulling on a robe, went back along the corridor to the darkened living-room where she had left her book. As she reached for it, a key turned in the front door and Ross walked in, a suitcase in one hand, a bunch of packages in the other, dangling like balloons from a loop of string.

'Hitched a ride,' he said, as casually as if he had not been gone at all. He dropped the suitcase and packages and strode across the room to take Katherine in his arms. 'I missed you. I woke up missing you and went to sleep missing you. Did you get my postcard?'

'Yes –'

'I wrote twenty. The other nineteen are in my suitcase. I didn't want you to think I was overdoing it.' And as she laughed, he kissed her.

Enfolded in his arms, Katherine held him in her own, her lips opening with his in a long breathless kiss and then small, murmuring ones. Their arms seemed like a charmed circle, she thought, with no secrets or doubts. Ross untied her robe and pushed it open. The buttons of his sports jacket had left faint impressions on the smooth skin of her breast and stomach and he kissed each one, lingeringly, before Katherine took his hand – not thinking, not planning, dizzily wanting him – and they walked down the corridor to her rooms.

But once inside, when he had shut the door, they moved apart. Katherine saw the sombreness of his dark eyes, intent on her face. 'All the way back from Paris,' he said, 'I wanted you. And I knew we'd have to wait. We have too much to talk about.'

No charmed circle after all, Katherine thought. She nodded. 'I spent hours yesterday at Eze, wondering where we'd begin.'

'Could we begin with some food? I flew down with a friend who was in a hurry to leave, so we didn't take time for dinner.'

'Of course,' Katherine said. And added softly, 'Thank you,' knowing he would understand that she was grateful to him for giving her something to do, giving them both something to do, until their bodies cooled and they could talk. And then she thought how rare it was to find someone she could trust to understand her. We can tell each other the truth, she reflected. Remembering Craig, nothing seemed more important.

In the lower half of an olive-wood cabinet in her sitting-room was a small refrigerator. Katherine knelt in front of it. 'I'm not sure what's here. We may have to go to the kitchen.'

'My wants are simple,' said Ross beside her, then laughed

'and what could be simpler than this?' – as he pulled out three kinds of cheese, sliced Westphalian ham, locally-grown clementines and dates, and a crusty loaf of French bread. He piled everything on a platter and from the upper shelves of the cabinet chose a bottle of Côtes du Rhone, and they carried it all to the terrace, returning to the cabinet for plates and wine glasses, cheese knives and napkins. 'Who could resist a woman who provides such a midnight snack?' he murmured.

'Her name is Sylvie,' said Katherine. 'She's run the villa for Victoria for fifteen years, and seems content, but she might consider an offer if you wanted to make one.'

He chuckled and kissed the top of her head, then sat beside her at the round cypress table. 'I don't think I'll steal Sylvie from my grandmother. Though if she has a sister, I could use her in Berkeley; I'm ashamed of how little I know about keeping house. How do women know these things? Their mothers can't possibly prepare them for every crisis that crops up.'

'I think they got the message a few thousand years ago,' Katherine said dryly, 'that if they didn't pay close attention and learn on the job, they'd be *out* of a job.'

'You mean out of a marriage.'

'Probably. But it's mainly attention and practice. You'll learn very quickly.'

'Of course. I've already begun.'

'And how are you getting along?'

'Carrie gives me advice.' They laughed, and then were silent.

The soft air was fragrant with roses and pine, and an elusive breeze brought whispers of the sea. The terrace was deeply shadowed, lit only by the glow from the sitting-room and bedroom, and when Ross leaned forward to fill Katherine's glass, her face filled his vision – pale, faintly flushed, with dark hollows: as fine as a delicate etching. 'You are so lovely,' he murmured, then let out his breath in a long sigh. 'Do you know, the whole time we've been together, with everything we've talked about, we've managed to avoid talking about Craig – and Derek.'

'We talked about us,' Katherine replied. 'About our feelings. As if no one else were real.' She looked at him gravely. 'What do you want to know?'

'I want to know you. What you were before I met you, what you were with Craig, what you were with Derek.' He paused. When he spoke again it was as if the words were wrenched from him. 'I have no right to ask about Derek. But from what I do know about you, it makes no sense . . . that you stayed with him as long as you did.' He waited, but Katherine said nothing. 'I know what he offered you, and I know how much you needed it. But I don't understand how it lasted, why the glamour didn't fade when you got to know him, how he uses people –'

'He didn't use me.'

'Derek uses everyone; he sets up power plays and manoeuvres people through them. He always has, even in our family.'

'Jennifer,' Katherine murmured. 'Melanie. Myself.'

'What? What does that mean?'

'Once I asked Derek why he pursued women who were close to you and Craig.'

'How did you know about Jennifer? What made you think he was ever involved with Melanie?'

'Tobias told me about Jennifer. I saw him with Melanie one night, and guessed.'

As if struck, Ross sat back in his chair. Phrases, looks, small details from his marriage ran through his mind and he knew it could be true. He'd never suspected, because Melanie talked about Derek so much – too much, one would have thought, for a woman burdened with the guilt of an affair. But why should he assume that Melanie had any guilt?

A flash of rage tore through him, then, surprisingly, faded, and he realised how little importance Melanie had for him now – even when his brother was involved. Once, that might have crushed him; now, sitting beside Katherine, he found his thoughts moving beyond Melanie and Derek to something even more surprising. 'You said that to Derek and he took it? I've seen him destroy reputations for less.'

'I didn't stay to give him a chance.'

'But you'd stayed a long time.'

'Ross, you said you understood what he offered me: glamour, excitement, a chance to be with people who controlled events instead of being jostled by them . . . And you must know how charming he can be, and how clever. I needed all of that; I enjoyed myself with him.' Seeing his dark frown, she sighed. 'You want to know if I slept with him.' When he was silent, she said slowly, 'You think I did.'

Ross refilled their glasses. 'I told you I have no right to ask. But I spent a lot of time in Paris thinking about you, about being in love with you and wanting more than picnics and swimming holes. So I had two choices. I could say the past is unimportant, that you and I begin from our time in Paris; or I could say it's more important than ever that I understand the past, because it means understanding you. I decided I had to understand. That was why I came back early. I couldn't wait.'

His words were like heartbeats beneath Katherine's thoughts. *In love with you.* 'I didn't sleep with Derek.' But then she knew that wasn't enough. If we don't have the truth, she thought, we don't have anything. Taking a deep breath, she said, 'But I wanted to.'

Quickly, looking beyond him, at the harbour, she said, 'Craig had been gone for almost seven months, Derek was the only man I was seeing, and he hadn't pressured me. I suppose he thought he wouldn't have to. Instead he took me into his world and made me feel beautiful and desirable, instead of like a housewife who'd been deserted. And there was something

430

else.' She gave a small, embarrassed laugh. 'He had none of Craig's virtues. He wasn't gentle or kind or loving or anxious to please . . . I never knew exactly what he expected of me. He was like the dark side of my husband and somehow that was so exciting – I felt like a child, sneaking cookies from the cupboard. And I think Derek knew that; he encouraged that feeling of something forbidden . . .' Again she paused. 'I didn't love him, but he was hard to resist. Then, last New Year's Eve, he invited a crowd back to his place after a party and I became his hostess. It was as if all my fantasies had become real. By the time everyone left, there was only one thing I didn't have, and hadn't had for months. But then . . . Jennifer called. Telling me to come home. Craig was there.'

She turned. Ross's eyes were shadowed. He sat still, saying nothing, his face hard and unyielding.

'Why can't you understand?' she burst out. Springing from her chair she walked the length of the terrace. 'What is it about Derek that makes you pull away? Both of you – he's just the same – you can't talk about each other . . . you become cold and distant . . .'

Ross stared fixedly at the distant lights of Menton. It was so quiet they heard the scurrying of a small animal through the wild grass below the terrace wall. 'I do understand.' He spoke without turning. 'I'm sorry I didn't make that clear. I'm sorry I seemed cold.' His voice was gentle, with a thread of sadness. 'I've never talked to you about Derek; I've never told you how he dominated us, all the years we were growing up . . . Katherine, please sit with me.'

Slowly, Katherine came back to her chair, and Ross went on. 'Derek always seemed so sure of himself, like a pile driver. even when he was wrong. He had a way of taunting us that made us feel we'd bungled something . . . and the damnable thing about his power was that we'd feel that way even when we knew we'd done it well. He can still do that to me – at least

431

momentarily, until I catch myself. The only ones he didn't do it to were my grandparents, but when Hugh died and Derek and Curt took over the company, there was no stopping him.' He brooded at the dark shapes of olive trees, barely visible against the starlit sky. 'Melanie always held Derek up to me as the kind of man I should be, who'd protect her, coddle her, give her what she wanted.' He laughed shortly. 'I didn't take that well. I knew she was wrong – Derek wouldn't protect or coddle anyone unless it served his own purposes – but I didn't try to tell her that; instead I found a way to punish her for idolising him. When she'd come running to me, bubbling with excitement over a party she'd dreamed up, or taking a trip to the Caymans – something she'd spent days or weeks thinking about – I'd cut her off with a few words. Her excitement would disappear and the life would fade from her face, and I'd hate what I'd done. But with you' – he turned to Katherine – 'I didn't mean to pull away. I never want to pull away from you. I don't know what the hell got into me.'

'You didn't want to know that I'd had any pleasure with Derek.' Katherine's voice was muffled and she cleared her throat. 'I didn't finish. After New Year's Eve, the spell – I suppose it was a spell – was broken. I still went out with him once or twice a week, but finally I broke it off. In April.'

'April? I saw him in June. He said he was giving you money.'

'He never gave me money! Once he told me to buy clothes and charge them to him and I refused. I never took a penny from him! Why would he tell you I did?'

'To wound, I suppose; to cause pain; he'd failed to get something he wanted and he was lashing out –'

'He thought he'd hurt you by lying about me?'

'He was right.'

'Even last June you cared what he said about me?'

'Even then.'

'But how did he know?'

Ross shrugged slightly. 'He knew I'd cared about you since I met you in Vancouver. And Derek always has been able to identify the vulnerable spot in people.'

'But you didn't ask me about what he said.'

'I should have. I was swamped with my own affairs. That's probably why Victoria didn't tell me you'd broken off with him. She was waiting for a time when I was less preoccupied, more receptive.' He thought a moment. 'New Year's Eve . . . Victoria told me you didn't see Craig.'

'He was gone. Jennifer told him I was with Derek, and he left before I got there.'

'Oh, Christ! Poor Craig. Whatever he'd done, whatever he came back for, to find his wife was with the person he hates most in the world . . .' Katherine winced. Startled, Ross realised that, for the first time, he was thinking about Craig as if he were alive, and part of their lives. He glanced at Katherine and saw her watching him. 'I told you I didn't call you because I was swamped. But there was another reason. I wasn't sure how to think about you – my cousin's wife – how much I could risk getting close to you. But it wasn't a real issue. I haven't had a cousin in sixteen years. It's strange,' he mused. 'I was in your house in Vancouver; I saw those photographs you brought the first night you came to Victoria's; and you and Jennifer and Todd are part of us now . . . but Craig had no reality for me. I mourned him too long, accepted him as dead for too long, to feel that he was alive. There were only memories that had no connection with me or anything I did or thought.'

'He's alive for me,' Katherine said. Restlessly, she walked to the stone wall, then back to the table, repeating Ross's words to herself. *No connection with me* . . . She'd felt that, too, the past few weeks. But not any longer. 'He's alive and . . . everywhere. No matter what I do, he follows me. The same as before. Everything is the same. I still don't know what he was really like; sometimes I think the more I hear, the less I know. Because I don't know what to believe. Ross,' she said abruptly. 'Tell me about the sailing accident. I've heard Claude's version, and then Derek told me his, but I never knew whether to believe it or not. I've wanted to ask you, but in the past few weeks . . .'

'You didn't think about Craig. Neither did I. Katherine, do you know, I'm still hungry?'

'You've been talking instead of eating.'

'Then I'll make up for lost time.' He heaped his plate with cheese and dates and bread. 'Is there anything left in that bottle?'

She filled their glasses and nibbled on dates while he ate. 'Is all this to avoid answering my question?'

'All this is to provide the narrator with sustenance. It's not an easy story. Do you want to tell me how Derek told it?'

'No. I just want you to tell me.'

'Well, then.' Hitching his chair closer to the table, he took a few more bites, then once again forgot the food. 'The four of us were sailing home from Sausalito, across the bay. It was July – my God, sixteen years ago this month – a cool, clear evening and Craig decided to take a longer way back, making a loop through the Golden Gate. He was in charge; he always was, on the water – the best sailor I've ever seen. I think it was the only time he was really happy, absolutely confident, cut loose from people making demands on him. In those days I was more interested in swimming and tennis, and Derek had just bought his own speedboat, so Craig was in charge when he took us sailing. That day, when Derek wanted more speed, he said we could put up the spinnaker. Have you ever sailed under a spinnaker?'

'I've never sailed.'

'You've –' Stunned, he said, 'That never occurred to me. We'll correct that when we get back.'

'Ross, please tell me what happened.'

'Well, with a spinnaker and a good wind, you skim the water weightless, flying, but with the waves at eye level. The most fantastic feeling . . . Jennifer was ecstatic; she threw her head back, laughing into the wind. That's the picture I carry in my mind: her hair blowing, her face bright and laughing, her arms wide when she burst out "I love all of you so much." We . . . loved her, too. So much.'

After a moment, he went on quietly. 'When we were more than halfway home, Craig asked me to go below for a winch handle and Derek called down to bring him a bottle of Scotch from his pack. Then Jennifer came down, saying Craig had ordered lifejackets for everyone; the currents are tricky near the Golden Gate and the wind was coming up. "Derek is so unpleasant when he drinks too much," she said. "Could you . . . forget to bring up the bottle?" She was trying to be cool and sophisticated, but she couldn't quite make it; she was young and impressionable, full of life and love, one of the dearest people I've ever known.' He drew in his breath. 'Incredible, how grief stays fresh. I said I'd forget to bring the bottle and she kissed me. It was the last time Jennifer ever kissed me.

'When we came up from the cabin, Craig and Derek were arguing about the spinnaker; Craig said it should come down; it could get ripped apart in a strong wind. And by then the wind was very high: wild and sometimes gusting, with a kind of whistle – sometimes we had to shout to be heard – and the boat was heeling, with spray coming in the cockpit. Derek put his arms around Jennifer and told Craig – his voice cut through the wind – they liked living dangerously; the only one who was afraid was the captain.

'Craig's face, when he saw Derek holding Jennifer . . . I'd never seen him look like that: enraged but terrified, his mouth working as if all the words were trying to rush out at once. He

435

screamed at Derek – "Get your goddam hands off –!" and started towards them but he couldn't let go of the wheel. He had to stay there, shouting to Jennifer to move away, and to Derek to take his hands off her. Neither of them moved; they stood still, staring at him. Everything had changed, in just a few minutes, from laughter and exhilaration to something terrifying. I was scared to death, because *Craig* was scared – I didn't know of what, which was even more frightening – and he didn't look as if he could control himself or the boat. I had to do something, so I yanked Jennifer away and asked Craig if I should take down the spinnaker.

'The sound, roaring in our ears – you have no idea what it was like: wind and spray breaking over us, Derek and Craig yelling at each other – it all mixed together into a nightmare. Craig couldn't stop: he shouted at Derek that he was the captain and if Derek didn't like it he could swim to shore, if he had the guts to try it – he found a dozen ways to doubt Derek's courage and skill – and then he told me to go forward and take down the spinnaker. But Jennifer grabbed my arm, begging me to stay and stop Derek, because he'd begun taunting Craig in that way of his that always drove us mad. I didn't know what to do first – comfort Jennifer, who was starting to cry, or slug Derek, or tell Craig to ignore him, or go forward and take down the spinnaker – and then I remember thinking that it didn't matter what I did; something was going to happen and *there was no escape*.

'We were crammed in that sailboat, flying over the water in a roaring wind, heeling at a crazy angle, soaking wet from waves washing over the cockpit, and Derek stood there, absolutely still, his voice like a knife, calling Craig the little golden puppet, his grandmother's toy . . . well, a string of brutal insults. Jennifer was crying and when Craig saw that he got so livid I thought he'd burst. He roared out – making sure Jennifer heard – that Derek was a liar and a crook – he'd cut corners to save money on a building we were putting up, and bribed an inspector to OK the job. I hadn't worked on that building and I asked what the hell he was talking about and Derek, like ice, said "Golden boy changed the specs on the Macklin Building to be grandma's hero – even bribed the inspector – but now he's scared and shifting the blame. Running away," he said. "As usual." And then, out of the blue – the damnedest thing – Craig laughed. I've never known why. He said he cared about the Hayward reputation more than Derek, and he was going to tell the family and the city officials what Derek had done. He was still laughing when he told me again to take down the spinnaker.

'I got about halfway forward when I felt the boat change course. I turned around to see what the hell Craig had done and saw him with his hands on Derek's throat. Jennifer was pulling at his arm. And then everything happened at once. The boat had changed course because no one was at the wheel, and the wind pushed the mainsail to the other side. The boom swung across and slammed against Jennifer's head. There was blood – like a rose, bursting into bloom just beside her eye – and then she stumbled and fell overboard. She never made a sound. She just fell. But Craig and I screamed – my God, I still dream about this – the blood and the two of us screaming – "JENNIFER!" and Craig lunging at the life preserver and marker pole to throw them over the side. Jennifer was floating face down; the water was choppy all around her. It looked so cold – it hadn't looked that cold all day – and we were moving away from her. With that wind and all the sail we had, we were going so damned fast . . . I raced to the spinnaker and hauled it down. Slashed my hands on the ropes and never knew it until I saw the blood when I ran along the deck back to the cockpit.

'Derek was at the wheel, cursing because he couldn't get the boat to respond; it wasn't like his speedboat. He told me Craig had jumped in after Jennifer. I grabbed the wheel from him; I didn't know much more than he did, but with the spinnaker down we slowed, and I managed to turn us around. Then I told him to take the wheel again and I took down the mainsail and started the motor.'

'But Derek said –'

Ross turned, suddenly aware of her. 'Derek stood by the cabin, looking at the water, and never moved a muscle or said a word while I turned the boat. I remember thinking he was figuring out how all this would affect him, because that's how Derek looked at everything, but I didn't have enough energy even to be angry: I was dizzy and sick and trying to get back to Jennifer and Craig. It took me ten minutes – ten minutes, when today I can do it in three! – and that was too long. It was too late. We got back to the marker pole and Jennifer . . .

'She was . . . tucked into the opening of the life preserver . . . like a doll . . . her eyes were staring . . . The wind was a steady screech, and Jennifer was staring at us, not seeing us . . . And I was crying. I couldn't stop. I stood at the wheel, crying.'

Katherine felt her own tears well up, and she closed her eyes.

'I shouted to Craig, but there was no answer. I thought he'd be close by, waiting for us after he put Jennifer in the life preserver, but I couldn't see him or hear him. It was almost dark and I was still crying. I told Derek we had to get Jennifer. It was the only time in our lives I gave orders and Derek followed them. He went in the water and tied a rope around her; and we got her into the boat and put a blanket over her. Derek tried to find a pulse but he couldn't. That was all, really. We shouted for Craig and Derek called the Coast Guard on the radio and I kept the boat close to the marker pole while we waited for them, shouting for Craig. Our voices seemed so small in the darkness, with just the circle of our spotlight moving over the black water, and in the distance the lights of San Francisco and the lighted bridges strung across the bay – so damned beautiful, but I kept thinking, "Jennifer can't see it" –

438

and we kept shouting Craig's name into the wind . . . But, my God, we sounded so infinitely small. The night swallowed our voices. I don't know if Craig heard us. He never answered.'

Katherine was crying, her muscles tensed, as if she stood beside Ross on the boat, calling to Craig. Ross put his arm around her. 'That night we were all at Victoria's. I suppose we talked about what happened, but I kept hearing Craig's voice. In a room full of people, all I heard was Craig shouting Jennifer's name, and I kept seeing Jennifer's eyes.'

His voice became dry. 'The next morning, I went to see my father in his office. I hadn't slept, but at least I was thinking again, and I had to know what Derek and Craig had been talking about. My father had been with me all night, of course, but I hadn't said anything about a fight on the boat and it took him by surprise. Not for long; he never takes more than a few seconds to recover from surprise. Derek is like that, too. I asked him to have the Macklin Building checked, and just then, Derek came in and heard me, took a quick look at our father, sitting behind his desk like a judge, and said to him, "Craig changed the specs: I didn't tell you at the time because it wasn't serious, and I took care of it." I asked him what he did, and he said he'd strengthened the footings and there wasn't anything to worry about.

'My father asked him if he was sure he'd corrected the problem. Those were his words. And Derek said it was all taken care of. They were very smooth, except that the nerve next to Derek's eye was jumping. I thought they were lying, but I didn't have any evidence to back me up. My father gave me hell for doubting my brother, suggested I was distraught over the accident, and offered me a trip to Europe, after the funeral. I took it.

'Probably I shouldn't have. But I was exhausted and sick of all of them; I just wanted to get the hell out of there. When you're twenty years old, it's hard to accept the fact that your father might be a liar or dishonest; especially if you're already having trouble coping with nightmares about seeing your two cousins die in the same afternoon. So I went to Paris.

'In the fall I went back to school and when I graduated my father asked a friend in New York to hire me as a junior architect. It occurred to me today, for the first time, that he wanted to keep me away from the Hayward Corporation.'

'So you wouldn't ask questions?'

'So I wouldn't snoop around and discover that Derek hadn't repaired anything, and my father knew it. And there was another reason, I suppose, why they wanted me out of the way: to make sure that Derek would take over the company.' He reached for the wine and poured what was left into their glasses. 'If they'd asked, I would have told them I never wanted to take over the company. But I did worry about that building, and finally managed to buy it and get it vacated. It was inspected this week, I got the report yesterday in Paris.'

After a moment, Katherine asked, 'What didn't Derek repair?'

'The footings that supported the building. We hired a foundations engineer to check them and the first thing he found was a column . . . damn, I'm sorry, I didn't mean to get into this.'

'Tell me,' she said. 'I want to hear it.'

Ross smiled at her. Nice words, he thought. 'He found a column that hadn't been sunk deep enough and then, under it, a footing that was cracked because it hadn't been reinforced with enough steel. We assume that if it's true of one, it's true of all of them, which means the building is in danger. Do you remember the accident at a Hyatt Hotel in Kansas City, when people were dancing on a skyway and it collapsed? The reports say it was the same problem: shortcuts in construction that made it unsafe. In other words, someone deviated from the original specifications to save time and money.'

'And that's what happened in the Macklin Building?'

'We think . . . What the hell, that's what it had to be. The footings are substandard, which means the specs were changed, which means, I suppose, an inspector had to be bribed to approve them.'

'Was it Craig?'

The name echoed on the terrace. 'I don't think so,' Ross said slowly. 'I always had trouble believing Craig would knowingly do anything to jeopardise a building's integrity; he was absolutely straight in construction. He thought of money last. I always felt I could trust Craig with any building I designed.'

Trust Craig. Katherine rested her head against Ross's arm feeling drained. A faint glow made her look to their left. 'Sunrise,' she said wonderingly. The sky brightened: a wash of pale pink and apricot spread above them, and then the sun burned through, turning the cypress and olive trees to burnished red-gold. 'So beautiful,' Katherine murmured. 'But everything followed us here, after all.'

She left the circle of Ross's arm and perched on the stone wall, gazing down the hill at the sand-coloured buildings of Menton, growing brighter as the sun rose. Ross watched her, the downcast curve of her neck, the tremble of her lips. 'Divorce him,' he said bluntly. She swung around. 'Katherine, somewhere in all the talk tonight, I told you I love you. Did you hear it, or did it get lost in the conversation?'

'I heard it,' she answered. 'And . . . I'm grateful –'

'Grateful!'

'I mean . . . oh, damn, how can I say this? Ross, it doesn't change anything. I can't say, "Ross loves me, so I'll divorce Craig . . ." I can't just walk away from him.'

'He walked away from you.'

'Is that why I should do it? Whatever he does, I do in return?'

'It's hardly the same. You have a reason; he had none. And you've given him more than a year to come back.'

'But there's so much I don't know. He's in trouble but I don't even know what kind, or how it happened.' She told Ross about Leslie's call, and Carl Doerner's quarrel at her party in Vancouver.

He looked at her in disbelief. 'You can't be serious. Because a kid at Heath's was framed and a year ago some people quarrelled . . . Katherine, they have nothing to do with Craig!'

'How do you know? Isn't it a possibility? You just said you don't believe he altered those specifications – he was absolutely straight, you said; you trusted him. Why would he have been any different in his company? If he was framed, and he ran because he thought no one would believe him, he was right, wasn't he? Everyone, including his wife, believed he was guilty. And now you say I should divorce him.'

'You don't want to divorce him?'

Katherine slumped, her energy deflated. 'Sometimes I've wished I could. No, that's not right. Sometimes I've wished he would just be gone. Really gone. Not –'

'Clinging.'

'Yes, that's how it feels. But I've never thought about divorcing him. How could I? What would I tell Jennifer and Todd? I got tired of waiting for Daddy? I'm cutting him from us, even though he's sending us money and probably trying to find his way back to us? Is that what I should say?'

He did not answer. 'Ross, I can't leave Craig because I owe him something after he loved me and took care of me for ten years. I don't see how I can erase that because he did something I don't understand.'

Steadfast, Ross thought, remembering their dinner in Paris, when he had found himself comparing Katherine to Melanie. Steadier; more steadfast.

'And something else,' Katherine said. She came back to him, putting out a hand to smooth his hair. She hardly knew what she was doing, but she felt she had to touch him to make

442

him understand, and then he had pulled her to him and she was on his lap, her arms around his neck, her face against his, crying quietly. 'Don't you see – I can't make a future with you, I can't even think of one, until I finish with the past. Everything is dangling. I don't have any answers, I don't know how much I'm responsible for, *I don't understand what happened and who I am now*. Ross, don't you see? When you said you loved me, you said your choices were to wipe out the past or to understand it. You decided you had to understand it. So do I. I can't make a future until I understand the past, and finish it.'

Ross pushed back her hair and kissed her closed eyes, her cheek, her lips, tasting her tears. He tried to think what it would be like if he and Melanie had not gone through a final confrontation, wound things up through their lawyers, signed documents – finished their marriage. 'Yes,' he said. 'Of course I understand. But I don't know how you're going to do it.'

'Craig and I will do it. Together. When he comes back.'

'And how long will you wait for that?'

'I don't know.'

The piercing trill of a bird broke the silence. Within the house, a door opened; water ran in the kitchen; the fresh smell of coffee reached them. The day had begun.

Chapter 16

San Francisco was cool and airy after the Riviera's molten heat and, his first evening back, Ross walked from his office to the top of Telegraph Hill to reacquaint himself with his city. It spread below in soft pastels and the fresh green of eucalyptus trees, tinged with pale gold from the slanting rays of the setting sun. Sighting down the hill, past the roof gardens and sun decks of the houses covering its slope, Ross saw the city as a canvas, always changing, always waiting to be changed. He picked out the site of BayBridge Plaza, where he had spent the morning inspecting work begun while he was in France, and other neighbourhoods around the city he and his staff planned to work on in the future.

Restore and renovate, he reflected. Our days are spent remaking and rebuilding. And when necessary, destroying. When nothing can be saved, we tear down.

He wondered which one Katherine would decide to do.

His memory held the image of her beauty in the coral glow of the sunrise over Menton, and the troubled look in her eyes. She had to finish her marriage, she said, and understand it. But what if understanding gave her a reason to try to rebuild it? Steadfast, he reminded himself. And loyal.

Walking back down the hill, Ross thought about Craig. Why the hell hadn't someone found him? The money came every month, and even though it was always mailed in a different town, some enterprising investigator should have figured out a way to trace it. Claude had hired one, long ago, but after four months he'd had nothing to report. No one had anything to report. But Craig had a profession; he had habits, and contacts —why the hell hadn't someone put all those together and found him?

Maybe because no one cared enough anymore. Doerner's loss must have been covered by insurance, and not enough money was involved to keep police on it full time for fourteen months.

But I care, he thought. More than the police, more than Doerner, even more than the tax people. Because I want Katherine to be free.

I can't make a future with you until I understand the past.

Find him, then. Help Katherine put an end to her past, or rebuild it. Either way, it's better for both of us than not knowing.

I could call Carl Doerner; get the names of people Craig worked with. Maybe someone knew something, but didn't want to help the police find him. Maybe that someone would help Craig's cousin.

Ross considered it. He had three meetings tomorrow; he could be in Vancouver the next day. But that was when Katherine and Victoria would be home from France. But he'd only be gone a day or two. And impatience was pounding inside him. He had to do something; Katherine would understand that.

He thought of her, in the Vesubie Valley, leaning over him, his hands holding her breasts, the sun beating down –

He went back to his office to call Carl Doerner.

He found him at home. 'My name is Ross Hayward,' he began. 'I'm trying to locate my cousin, Craig Fraser –'

'Aren't we all?' Doerner said flatly.

'– And I'd appreciate it if you'd give me some information.'

'After fourteen months? There isn't anything I can tell you that I haven't told every policeman in Canada and the States. I'd love to find the son of a bitch – you know how I trusted him and he let me down? – if you want to try, lots of luck. You'll need it.'

'I grew up with him,' Ross said. 'I knew him pretty well at one time. I might be able to figure out his thinking if I knew what he was working on when he disappeared.'

'Skipped.'

Ross was beginning to dislike him. 'What was he working on?'

'The police have that information. Look, I'm about to eat my dinner –'

'I'd like the names of contractors he worked with in other cities.'

'The police have that, too. I gave them a list a year ago.'

Evasive and unhelpful, Ross noted, and wondered why. 'I thought you might have remembered some other information,' he said. 'If we find my cousin, or even hear word of him, my family is thinking of repaying the money he took.'

There was a pause. 'What does finding him have to do with repaying it?'

'We'd want him to share in the repayment.'

After another moment, Doerner said, 'There was one thing. Nothing definite, just peculiar. I told the police about it – they checked it out and said it wasn't anything – but I still wonder.'

Ross waited.

446

'I think something was going on in Calgary. Craig was there an awful lot the last two years – the whole time he was stealing from me. He said he was making contacts, getting new clients – but he did it in his own time. I called around after he skipped, to see if he was working for a competitor.'

'And?'

'Couldn't find one. But there's no doubt in my mind he was. Obviously he needed a lot of money, and untrustworthy once, untrustworthy twice, I always say.'

'Profound,' Ross murmured. Aloud, he said, 'Do you know of a contractor he might have gone to?'

Carefully, Doerner replied, 'There was a Len Oxton we worked with once or twice. But I told you, the police have a list.'

'I remember,' Ross said. 'Thanks.'

He was about to hang up when Doerner's voice, a little anxious, burst from the receiver. 'What are you going to do next?'

Gently, Ross touched a picture of Katherine he had taken in Saint Paul, smiling in a field of flowers. 'I'm going to Calgary,' he said.

Two days later, catching his first glimpse of Calgary from his plane, he thought it looked like a steel island floating on the wheat fields of Alberta, where the Bow and Elbow Rivers met. It was bigger than he had expected, even though he knew that oil and gas had made it the fastest-growing town in Canada for years. 'About six hundred thousand,' said the man beside him when he asked its population. 'And growing, eh?'

A habit of Canadians: to end their sentences with a little explosion of air. Ross wondered if Craig had picked it up. He wondered what he would do if he found him.

Bring him back to Katherine and hope she doesn't decide to rebuild.

Last month, he recalled, I was arguing with Jacques, saying it was better to restore than to destroy.

When possible, he amended. There are times when it's not. It depends on where you're standing.

From a telephone in the airport, he called Len Oxton. 'Police talked to me, eh?' said Oxton. 'Couldn't tell them much; I liked Fraser but I never worked with him and wouldn't have the faintest where he might be. Noah Johnson, now, he might; I think he and Fraser worked on a bank building a few years back.'

Noah Johnson was a man of few words. 'Fraser, eh? Knew his stuff, easy to work with, kept to himself. Never got friendly. Bob Vessen knew him better.'

Bob Vessen liked to talk. 'Fine fellow, Craig; low-key, good ideas, loved to use glass. We put up an office building with a combined greenhouse and cafeteria; sensational in the winters. Craig carved me a little horse once – now there was something else he really knew: sculpture, especially Eskimo. But if you're asking me where he might have gotten to, that I couldn't say. He wasn't much for giving away feelings or private thoughts. Hold on, though; he did seem friendly with Danny Nielsen . . . Nielsen Builders, you know. Danny might have an idea.'

And so, late that afternoon, Ross found Danny Nielsen. And Danny took him to Elissa.

Elissa Nielsen, Craig's mistress for almost two years, before he disappeared.

'Of course I never told the police anything,' Danny said as they drove from his office to the outskirts of the city. 'Crocodiles couldn't have dragged it out of me. All they wanted was to make Craig look bad, like a real bona fide criminal, you know; they didn't want to clutter their minds with the possibility that he wasn't guilty or maybe had serious reasons for doing what he did. It was easier to think he was just an ordinary crook.'

Hardly ordinary, Ross thought in disbelief as Danny drove

on towards yet another of Craig's lives. San Francisco, Vancouver, and now Calgary. Had Katherine suspected? Of course not; she would have told him.

'You think he wasn't guilty?' he asked as he watched the city speed by. New construction was everywhere, cross-hatched girders reaching to the blue-white prairie sky. Enough to keep Craig busy for years. But of course that wasn't why he came here.

'No,' said Danny. 'I don't think Craig was guilty. But I don't like to think about it. We cost him plenty, you know. Here we are.'

The house was a small cottage with four rooms and a screened porch. A tricycle lay on its side in the front yard; on the coffee table in the living-room was a wooden carving of a large sleepy-eyed turtle with a gleeful little boy astride it. 'My sister,' said Danny. 'Elissa Nielsen; Ross Hayward.'

'Well,' she said and put out her hand. 'I've heard so much about you I'm glad to see you're real.'

She was as tall as Ross, large-boned, with long, light brown hair and wide-spaced blue eyes – clear, honest, appraising. Not quite pretty, she had such an open look, ready to be friends, that Ross, holding her hand, found himself liking her, wanting her to like him, even though, driving there, he had been blaming her for all of Katherine's problems. 'Heard about me?' he asked.

'Craig told me all about you,' she answered. 'How about a drink? We're having chicken for dinner; did Danny tell you?'

'I didn't,' said Danny. 'And I'm not staying. You two have plenty to talk about. Ross, call me later and I'll drive you back to your hotel. I'm glad you found us; I always thought Craig was the best guy in the world. See you later.'

When he was gone, Ross said, 'I'll take you out to dinner.'

'No,' said Elissa. 'Thanks, but no. It's quiet here and anyway I've already cooked the chicken. What will you drink? I have

449

Scotch, left from Craig's last visit – but it's better when it ages, isn't it? – and sherry.'

'Sherry, thanks.'

'Keeping a clear head, I see. Danny said you're looking for Craig.'

'He thinks you know where he is.'

'He's wrong. I don't know where Craig is; I haven't seen him or heard from him since a year ago June. He called to tell me he was going to Toronto and he'd try to fit in a couple of days with me on the way back. I haven't heard from him since. All I've heard is about him. The police talked to Danny in July; they said he was an embezzler. I never believed that.' She handed him a glass. 'To your good health. And welcome to Calgary.'

'But he disappeared,' Ross said. 'You didn't see him again. If he hadn't committed a crime, why has he gone?'

'Well. You wouldn't understand, but if you're a woman and your guy is married and has a family and all, you expect it. I mean, you know that one day he's going to choose his family over you. His wife will get suspicious or he'll run out of excuses or he'll just get tired of running back and forth – and he'll stop coming around. So you prepare yourself. It doesn't really work; it still breaks your heart when it happens; but at least you think you know what's going on.'

'Did it break your heart?'

'Of course it did. I love him.'

She said it so naturally that Ross felt a stab of pity. 'Why didn't the police find you?'

'Because Craig always registered at a motel in town before he came here. In case he got telephone calls, you know. I mean, his kids could have been sick . . . some emergency . . . When the police checked, they found the registrations. And my neighbours, and people in the shops around here, knew him under another name.' At Ross's exasperated sigh, she became

450

defensive. 'He had to; he was protecting his family. Anyway, he thought he had to, and I understood, and that's how everyone knew him. And when he stopped coming around, well, they just thought we broke up. It happens, you know.'

Ross walked about the small living-room, crowded with memorabilia; dolls and stuffed animals from amusement parks, glass paperweights embedded with the names of Canadian cities, a bowl filled with restaurant matchbooks, pictures of Elissa and Craig, some with a young boy grinning happily between them. Ross looked at her.

'He's not Craig's.'

I hope not, he thought, and moved on, stopping in front of a calendar from Vancouver Construction. 'Last year's,' he murmured.

Elissa gave an embarrassed laugh. 'I should take it down. But if I throw that out, what about all the other things Craig brought me? I mean, where do you stop, if you're trying to forget someone? Everytime he came here he brought a paperweight or a carving or . . . Well, anyway. Did Katherine throw out the things he brought her and the kids?'

Startled, Ross said, 'Do you know her?'

'Katherine? Good lord, no. Craig would have died if I'd even come near Vancouver. But I heard so much about her I might as well know her. I mean, she's sort of like a relative you hear about but never meet. So I talk about her like that. More sherry?'

'Thank you.' Ross saw her hand shake as she poured. 'What did Craig tell you about Katherine?'

'What didn't he, would be more like it. He didn't tell me he'd leave her, if that's what you're asking. That was the last thing on his mind. He was crazy about her.' She saw Ross look again at the photographs around the room. 'You don't understand.'

'No,' Ross replied. 'I don't.'

She sat on the couch and motioned to the space beside her. 'Don't you want to sit down?'

Sitting with her, Ross felt her warmth, the comfort of her strong body and calm gaze. Remembering Craig, he began to understand what had drawn him here.

'You knew Craig,' Elissa said. 'So you know he wasn't really happy unless somebody needed him. Not demanding things of him – he hated it when people told him what he ought to do or how he ought to behave – but just needing to be taken care of. It made him feel good to take care of people who were in trouble. That was me when he met me: I was in trouble and I sure needed to be taken care of.'

She took a sip of sherry. 'Do you want some crackers or pretzels or something?'

'No, thank you.'

'Well, when we met, I was three months pregnant and no one was around to be the father. Isn't that the damnedest luck? First my little boy's father and now Craig. Good thing I'm not superstitious. This guy, the father, was working on an oil rig and he got transferred and said he'd send for me when he got settled, but he never did. I have a feeling he was a little scared by the idea of fatherhood. I tend to take up with men who scare easily; I wonder why that is. Excuse me.'

She left the room and was back in a minute. 'Turned on the oven. Whenever you start getting hungry, let me know. I met Craig when Danny took me drinking with them one night. I was pretty down and Craig tried to make me feel better and I ended up telling him all my problems. I'd been sick with some kind of anaemia – pernicious anaemia, does that sound right? – and I'd lost my job and there I was pregnant with no man around. Little did I know I was practically seducing Craig; he couldn't resist a sob story like that. The next night he showed up on my doorstep with a couple of steaks and two pints of cherry vanilla ice cream and some bottles of Scotch and wine.

452

He said in my condition I needed protein and good cheer and he was providing them. He provided them for almost two years.'

In the silence, Ross asked, 'How old are you?'

'Twenty-nine.'

'And where is your little boy?'

'I sent him to a friend's house for the night. He's just about gotten over missing Craig; he didn't need to hear any of this.' She looked sombrely at Ross. 'What you have to understand is that Craig didn't come here because he liked a roll in the hay with someone who wasn't his wife. He came here because he needed me as much as I needed him. I'm not criticising Katherine; she sounds like somebody I could be friends with. But Craig said she thought he was perfect and if he told her the truth about himself – *any* of the truth, way back to the sailing accident . . . oh, sure,' she said as Ross's eyebrows shot up. 'He told me about that. He couldn't tell Katherine because he was sure she'd stop believing in him, stop loving him, if she knew that he caused his sister's death and ran away and let his whole family think he was drowned. And he said he was going to be blamed for some building that wasn't built right – I never understood all of that, but he said he couldn't fight his son of a bitch cousin Derek, and Derek's father, to prove he wasn't the one who did whatever Derek did. He was so full of hate for Derek you wouldn't believe it. There was something else – something he couldn't even tell me, it hurt so much – but most of it he talked about over and over. He had to; he said he'd never told anyone and he could hardly stand it.'

'He had a wife who loved him,' Ross said. 'He could have told her.'

'Didn't you hear what I said? He couldn't tell her because he loved her.'

'So he shut her out.'

'Is that how she felt? Well, I can see how she might. But

Craig didn't think of that. He was just scared of telling her.'

'Why wasn't he scared of telling you?'

'Because he didn't love me,' Elissa said simply. 'He needed me to talk to; he was comfortable with me; he was *happy*. But he didn't love me. He loved Katherine and he couldn't risk disappointing her.' In a moment she stood and said briskly, 'I think I should put the chicken in the oven. About fifteen minutes until dinner. Is that all right?'

'Yes.' Preoccupied with his thoughts, Ross absently followed her into the kitchen, perching on one of the stools at the linoleum-covered breakfast counter.

'Craig used to do that,' said Elissa, putting a covered dish in the oven. 'He sat there drinking Scotch and talking away while I cooked the food he brought. He always brought food; he always acted like he had plenty of money. Do you know, I can tell you what every room in his house in West Vancouver looks like? I used to dream about how it would be to live there.'

'Did you ever tell Craig that?'

'Of course not. It would have made him feel bad and then he couldn't talk about it anymore. What I was best at with Craig was listening. He never thought of me envying his house because . . .'

'Because he never thought of you.'

'That's not true! He thought of us all the time! When my boy was born and this anaemia thing of mine came back, he took care of us. He bought us things – he paid the mortgage on this house! – And never refused me anything. And it seemed we were always needing something. He didn't steal because of us, did he? Do you think it was my fault? I've thought and thought about it and I don't believe he stole at all. He wasn't the kind. He was so good to us . . .

'Danny, too,' she said, putting pickles and olives on a plate. 'He and a friend had saved some money to start their own

454

business and Craig loaned them the rest, without even being asked. He heard them talking about borrowing money and said he'd take care of it. He liked doing things for people.'

'He liked showing people how much he could do for them.'

'It's the same thing, isn't it? He didn't even tell Danny when to repay the money, but Danny started anyway; he'd made two or three payments when Craig disappeared. It's too bad he always ran when things got difficult – and I know it wasn't right that he spent money on us instead of his family – but he acted like he had plenty, and when he'd say he couldn't tell Katherine things, and smile that sad little smile of his . . . Well, I loved him, and wanted to make him feel good about himself. Oh, damn, damn, damn – Ross, I keep wondering where he is, and if he's all right, and what I did wrong to make him disappear. Everywhere I go, he's sort of there . . . but not really . . . and I *miss him*.'

Standing beside Elissa in her kitchen, with his arms around her, Ross silently cursed his cousin, who twice had found wonderful women, and had hurt them both.

And I'm at a dead end, he thought. Which Craig would I look for from here – Craig Fraser or the one Elissa's neighbours knew?

All I've found is another shadow.

Their three rooms looked even smaller than Katherine had anticipated, and Jennifer and Todd wandered through them reminding her how great it had been to have separate rooms. 'We're getting too old to be in the same room,' Todd declared after dinner. 'Especially Jennifer. Girls need privacy for intimate matters.'

Katherine laughed. 'Who told you that?'

'Carrie. And Jon told me I need my own space, too.'

'They're right; we all need privacy. I sleep in the living-room, remember? But we can't afford a bigger apartment yet.'

'When can we?'

'Pretty soon, maybe. If I get my jewellery made this month, and Mettler's customers buy it . . . I guess then we could look for a place with lots of room.'

'And rooms,' Todd grinned.

'That too. ' Katherine began to sort the mail they had picked up from the post office that afternoon. 'Here's something from school for you and Jennifer.'

'Is that all? No letters?'

'You have to write letters to get letters.'

'I would, if I knew where to write.'

'Oh.' Katherine put her arm around Todd and held him close. 'I'm sorry, sweetheart. I guess I gave up expecting a letter from Daddy a long time ago.'

'So did I, I guess,' said Todd. 'I was just asking. I'll be out in front with Jennifer, OK? Mom? Is that OK?'

'What? Oh, yes, fine. Just don't wander off; it's getting close to your bedtime.' Katherine looked back at the letter she had just opened with *Mettler's* embossed at the top. 'Dear Mrs Fraser,' she read.

'When we discussed your jewellery, I hoped we were beginning a profitable relationship. However, the recession has forced me to change my plans; like all prudent retailers, I must reduce my inventory; and since I cannot alter my relationship with trusted, long-standing suppliers, I must reluctantly withdraw my verbal offer to you of last June. I am returning your jewellery by special messenger. Please do not think unkindly of me; someday we may yet work together. With all best wishes for a successful career, I am –'

He can't do this. Katherine crumpled the letter in her hand. *I was so sure I'd made a start . . . He can't . . . Of course he can;*

456

it's his store. She hurled the letter across the room. *Bastard.* He was lying; the economy hadn't changed in two months. Anyway, Leslie had told her that Marc said people like Mettler held their customers even in bad times.

Her thoughts racing, she held her head in her hands. He decided he didn't like my work after all. It wasn't what he wanted . . . it wasn't as unusual or as good as he thought at first . . .

That's not true!

She jumped up and went to the kitchen and with furious energy began washing the dinner dishes. 'It's not true,' she repeated aloud. She remembered Mettler's face when he saw her pieces; they *are* good, she thought fiercely. I know they're good.

But he knows more about jewellery than you do, a small voice said. Maybe he had reasons . . . She shook her head. I know how much I've changed; I know what I can do. Whatever happened while I was in France, I know my work is good.

Then she thought: I shouldn't have gone to France. Maybe, if I'd been here, I could have found out why he did this, and turned it around.

But then, I wouldn't have had a month with Ross.

The telephone rang and, answering it, she heard his voice, distant, with static on the line. 'I tried to call you this afternoon,' he said.

'We went grocery shopping and to the post office. Are you out of town? You sound so far away.'

'I am. I have a lot to tell you. I just got back from dinner with –'

'Ross, will you be away long?'

'I'll be back tomorrow. What's wrong, Katherine?'

'Nothing –'

'Something is; I can hear it in your voice.'

457

'Nothing that can't wait until tomorrow. Where did you say you are?'

'I want to know what's bothering you.'

She gazed at her soapy hand on the telephone receiver. 'Herman Mettler cancelled my order.'

'Cancelled —! Why?'

'The recession, he says. I think it must be something else, but I can't imagine . . .' Her voice broke.

'Katherine, he can't arbitrarily cancel it. You have a contract.'

'Only verbal, as he carefully said in his letter. I never insisted on a written contract.'

'And you didn't ask Claude about it? Or any lawyer?'

'I was going to; I just didn't think it was urgent. He was so excited, talking about where he'd advertise my work, and display it, it never occurred to me there was anything to worry about. And then Victoria invited us to France and I just forgot about it. But I wouldn't have worked all month on new designs if I didn't think we had an agreement.'

'That son of bitch — what the hell got into him? My God, for you to come back to that . . . Katherine, dearest Katherine . . . damn it, I should be there, to help you.'

Dearest Katherine. 'I'd rather just have your arms around me.'

His warm laughter seemed to fill the room. 'Tomorrow. As soon as I can get a flight.'

'Ross, I haven't let you talk at all. You had something to tell me. Dinner with someone. Did you tell me where you are?'

He laughed again. 'No. I'll tell you about it when I get back. You have enough to think about right now. Katherine, could you have Jennifer and Todd looked after this weekend? I want to be with you. We'll have lots of family weekends; this time I want you to myself.'

'Yes,' she said. 'I'd love it. I'll see what I can do.'

'Try Victoria,' he suggested. 'They all had a good time together in France; she and Tobias can't spoil them too badly in one weekend.'

Her despair began to lift, and the next morning she went to Victoria and Tobias. She found them at breakfast in the sunroom. 'Ah, Katherine,' said Tobias, kissing her on both cheeks. ' "Journeys end in lovers' meeting." I understand yours did. Sit down, have coffee with us, and tell me everything.'

Katherine flushed and glanced at Victoria. 'It seems there's nothing left for me to tell.'

Victoria was unruffled. 'I gave Tobias no details, since you gave me none. I did mention your wonderfully expressive face, which was radiant most of our time in France.' She looked closely at Katherine. 'And now it is not. What is it, my dear?'

Briefly, Katherine told them about Mettler's letter. Tobias began to sputter. 'But – but – but –'

'Wretch!' Victoria exclaimed. 'Viper!' She cast about. 'Reptile!'

A laugh broke from Katherine. 'Much more creative than I.' She leaned over to kiss Victoria. 'All I thought of was bastard.'

'Of course,' Victoria replied. 'But it is not sufficient.'

' "When angry count four",' Tobias quoted through clenched teeth. ' "When very angry, swear." Mark Twain.' He sighed. 'I cannot swear in the presence of women. My mother would be proud, having drilled that into me, but it is terribly frustrating. Why did he do this? We don't really think it is the economy, do we?'

'No,' said Katherine. 'Something made him change his mind about my jewellery. Maybe he decided it wasn't good enough for him after all –'

'Poppycock!' snapped Victoria. 'I shall call him this instant! He has lost my business forever . . . and my friends' –!'

'My dear –' cautioned Tobias, his eyes on Katherine's face.

459

'By all means stop buying from him, but beyond that . . . perhaps we should ask Katherine what she would like.'

'Katherine!' Victoria glared at him. 'Katherine would not stop me!'

'I think I would,' Katherine said hesitantly. 'At least for a while. I think I should talk to him, and then – keep going. I believe in my work more than I did before – I want to believe in it – I want to believe in myself. But I'm still finding out what I can do on my own. If I give in to a setback –'

'Setback!' Victoria exclaimed. 'Treachery! I shall speak to him – I shall not allow that scoundrel a moment's peace of mind.'

Tobias sighed deeply and loudly. Victoria frowned. 'Well,' she said. 'You think it should be Katherine's decision.' He nodded solemnly. 'Katherine?' Victoria asked. 'You are sure of yourself?'

'Mostly,' Katherine said. 'You see . . . even if he gave in, to keep you as a customer, he wouldn't be very happy with me. He might put my pieces in a display case at the back of the shop, and forget them, and I wouldn't be much better off. You can't force him to be enthusiastic, however angry you are.'

'Wise Katherine,' said Tobias softly.

His praise was as warm to Katherine as Victoria's indignation. 'I'll see if I can find out the truth,' she said. 'And then I'll go to some smaller shops. Maybe I shouldn't have tried to start at the top.'

'No, no, no!' Victoria punctuated each word with her fist on the table. 'Always the top, never anything but the top! I will remain silent, since you and Tobias are so sure that is best for you, but you must not temper your ambitions; you must not let that donkey defeat you! Where is Ross?' she added abruptly. 'I called and his secretary said he was out of town.'

'He'll be back some time today,' Katherine said.

'Where did he go?'

'I don't know; he said he'd tell me when he got back.' Katherine hesitated, then asked them about the weekend. 'I can't leave Jennifer and Todd alone, even with Annie across the hall.'

'Alone!' Tobias exclaimed. 'Of course they must come here; we'll have a delightful time . . . they can alphabetise my file cards on the Hayward family tree.'

'No,' said Victoria firmly. 'They might never come again. But of course we'll take them, Katherine; they'll brighten our weekend. And a pleasant diversion is just what you need.' She put her hand on Katherine's cheek. 'I wish I could go with you to Mettler.' She grinned like a small girl. 'Give him hell, my dear.'

Walking down the steep hill, past lush purple and pink gardens cooled by silver-blue ice plants, Katherine repeated it to herself – *Give him hell, my dear* – smiling, to keep from knotting up inside. And so she was smiling as she walked into Mettler's and climbed the spiral staircase to the balcony.

It seemed the secretary did not know what had happened. 'How nice to see you, Mrs Fraser,' she said. 'He's not busy; I'll let him know you're here.'

'Don't bother,' Katherine said, and swiftly reached the closed door, swung it open and walked into Herman Mettler's office.

He was reading a brochure on the French Riviera and looked up, frowning. 'Mrs Fraser!' His face went through a series of rapid transformations. 'An unexpected pleasure! What can I do for you? I am at your service, though only briefly; some customers are due to arrive at any moment . . . and due customers are better than don't, are they not?' A brief chuckle came and went. 'So.'

Katherine stood near his desk. 'I found your letter yesterday, when I returned from France.'

'France!' He waved the brochure. 'I leave this weekend for

Monte Carlo; I cannot resist the gambling. As a recent traveller, you must tell me what else I can do there.'

I'd love to, Katherine thought with grim humour, but aloud she said, 'I'd rather you tell me what your letter means.'

'It means what it says! Dear lady, times are bad! Unemployment is up, interest rates are up, bankruptcies are up. Sales are down. The future is uncertain. What more can I say?'

'Monte Carlo is very expensive.'

'Well, but one must get away for one's health!' He coughed. 'Mrs Fraser, I thought my letter was clear. If you have nothing else to ask me –'

'Of course I have; I'm asking for the truth.' Katherine moved closer to his desk. In a slim blue linen dress belted in white that she had found at the discount designer shop in Paris, and wearing a broad-brimmed white straw hat, she stood over him. 'The last time I was here, you called me Katherine and talked about advertising my work in *Vogue*. Two months later you cancel my order and call me Mrs Fraser. Something happened in between and it wasn't the economy. I want to know what it was.'

'Mrs Fraser, I am a busy man,' he said, and pushed back his chair. 'I can't waste my time –'

'You've wasted my time,' Katherine retorted, gazing coldly at him from beneath the brim of her hat. 'I spent the month of July working on designs you'd contracted for – '

'We never had a contract!'

'We had a verbal agreement between two professionals, but you behaved badly, without good faith –'

'I always act in good faith! And if you knew what was good for you, you would not insult Herman Mettler!'

'What is good for me is selling my jewellery. I spent valuable time working on designs you requested and now I'm forced to spend more time visiting your competitors –'

'You won't get far! They know about you, too!'

462

Bewildered, Katherine stared at him. His gaze dropped. 'What do they know?' she asked.

After a moment, he shrugged. 'What the hell. Mrs Fraser, there's a cloud over you.'

Katherine's chest tightened. 'A cloud,' she repeated.

'You don't have to pretend with me. I know about your husband; I know he's on the run; I know you ran away, too – sold your house at a loss and got out of Canada.' He sighed. 'It's just too much, Mrs Fraser. You know how demanding our customers are – how jealous of the uniqueness of their possessions. I can't take a chance on designers with questionable backgrounds; I can't risk buying jewellery that might be . . . copied.'

'You mean stolen,' Katherine said, keeping her voice steady. 'But you have no reason to think that of me. If you're worried because someone told you these stories, why didn't you ask me –?'

'I did! I asked you about the authenticity of your designs!'

'And I answered you.'

'Not to my satisfaction.'

'You were satisfied at the time.'

'Mrs Fraser, listen to me. The truly wealthy live in a very small world. They meet at the same parties, dinners, weddings – no matter what country they're in. And their memories! My God, they remember the dress each woman wore at a dinner party nine years earlier . . . they even remember who her husband was then. So, of course they remember jewellery. And would they come back to Mettler's if they paid three thousand or three hundred thousand for a necklace and then saw it on someone else?' He sighed again. 'There is no malice in my heart; you are an attractive young woman, but I must protect my business and myself. I will not take a chance when the shadow over you is so dark. And now, Mrs Fraser, I have customers due . . .' He held open the door. 'Good of you

463

to come in; I do wish you well. I hope you and your husband work out your problems so you can go back to Canada.'

Katherine gazed at him. 'You're a coward, Herman.'

'True,' he agreed. 'But even if I took risks, Mrs Fraser, it would be for someone more important than you. Now will you please go?'

Numbly, Katherine walked through the outer office and down the stairs to the main floor. The store sparkled with gems and gold and silver, but she saw it dimly, as if a shadow obscured her view.

There is no escape from Craig.

The boat gleamed a pale white in the dense fog, the roar of its engine bouncing back at them as Ross steered through the harbour. Seven o'clock in the morning and they were the only ones out, avoiding the traffic jam of weekend sailors. They moved past the ghostly shapes of other boats, out of the harbour, and then there was only fog and a small clear space around them. Ross slowed the engine. 'It's all yours,' he said to Katherine. 'Keep a straight course while I get the sails up.'

'I can't see a straight course,' she said, trying to sound casual. 'I can barely see the land behind us.'

He put his arm around her. 'You have the compass. But the fog isn't so bad. Look.' He pointed and, straining her eyes, she saw a faint shape in the distance. 'Treasure Island,' he said. 'I've been out on days when you couldn't see it until you were practically part of it. Watch the compass and keep us west north west, heading for the island. It's a big target. Hard to miss.'

'I'd rather miss it,' Katherine said.

He chuckled. 'I think we will; I'll take over before we're even close. You'll do fine; I trust you.' He kissed her lightly and moved away from the wheel. Katherine took his place, watching him jump easily from the cockpit to the deck before she turned to check the compass heading and the faint shape of the island. Relax, she told herself. Everything will be fine. She shivered and zipped up her jacket against the damp fog. But it wasn't only the fog. She was nervous – about sailing, about telling Ross what Mettler had said, and about Ross's odd reluctance to talk about his trip.

'You have enough on your mind,' he'd said when he called the night before, soon after he got home. Then he suggested ways to spend the weekend: driving to Big Sur, staying at his house, or on his boat. 'We can sail up the coast on Saturday, and come back on Sunday. The weather's fine and even though you might think living on a boat is a bit primitive, I think you'll enjoy it.'

As nervous as she was, Katherine knew what sailing meant to him. 'I think I'll enjoy it, too,' she replied.

And as she steered the boat, looking alternately at the misty outline of Treasure Island and then at Ross, bracing his feet to pull on the mainsail halyard and then turning the winch to raise the huge sail to its full height, she found her nervousness fading. The wheel was solid beneath her hands; the compass told her she was on course. She surveyed the gangway leading down to the cabin, the benches with blue cushions on three sides of the cockpit, the side decks with thin steel railings shining dully in the fog, the bright aluminium mast where Ross stood, tying the halyard – and began to relax. Ross had shown it all to her before they cast off, naming and explaining everything, moving lithely and confidently around ropes and railings and jutting obstacles that seemed to leap out just in time to trip Katherine. She had been tense and anxious, and he had said gently, 'We sold Craig's boat after the accident. This one is quite different.'

'If you've never sailed –' Katherine began.

'– All sailboats seem alike,' he finished. 'But try to remember that this is mine. It was new when I bought it and its only

465

history is the one I make for it. The one you and I make,' he amended.

You and I. As Ross stood at the mast, looking up at the tall sail that had billowed into a white curve, Katherine watched his face – absorbed, serene, content. The wind blew his dark blond hair, his lean body was as taut and graceful as the sail. It was as if he had become a part of his boat, and she wished she could share that with him.

'– The motor!' he shouted.

'What?'

'Turn off the motor!' He pointed to the key and she reached down and turned it. Instantly, the engine stopped, and silence, like a clear glass bell, enclosed them. Ross grinned. 'I always wait for this,' he said in a conversational voice. 'So quiet you can feel it.'

Katherine felt it. The only sounds were the whisper of wind in the mainsail and the soft slapping of waves. 'I'm going to put up the jib,' Ross said. 'I could use some help. Lock the wheel when I tell you; then come up here and pull on this rope.'

He went forward and fastened the jib to the slanting cable at the bow. 'Ready,' he said. Katherine locked the wheel, climbed to the deck and pulled hand over hand on the rope. When she realised she was pulling the jib up the cable, where it caught the wind and snapped into its own curve, she felt a surge of exultation. The rope scraped against her palms, she pulled harder against the force of the wind in the sail, and then Ross took over, winching the sail tighter and fastening down the rope. With both sails in place the boat was picking up speed. 'Four knots,' Ross said. 'Do you want to keep the wheel?'

'Yes.'

He put his arm around her and they smiled at each other. 'Head northwest until we're past Treasure Island, then we'll go

466

around Alcatraz, straight to the Golden Gate Bridge.' He sat on the bench behind her. 'I'll watch your technique.'

Katherine laughed. They floated in the fog, completely alone. Nothing on land seemed real . . . Herman Mettler receded to a character in a play; Craig to a figure in a painting. Even Ross's evasiveness about his trip seemed unimportant in the vast silence of that shrouded world. All that mattered was her happiness at being with him, cut off from land.

Ross took the wheel when they were beneath the bridge, keeping to the centre of the channel until they had passed the headlands. And then they were in the ocean, turning to follow the coast. Within minutes the fog began to come apart, as if torn into large pieces. They sailed through the ragged openings, long tendrils of mist swirling about the boat, and then, suddenly, the sun burst through, flooding them with gold. Katherine gasped with the beauty of it and Ross reached out to her. She stood within his arms, facing forward as he held the wheel, his lips in her hair. 'Thank you,' he said. 'For sharing this with me.'

The waves were tipped with gold beneath a cloudless sky; the boat skimmed through the water, alone in the sun-filled, sea-scented air. Katherine turned within the circle of his arms and kissed him. 'Thank you for letting me be a part of it.'

His lips smiled beneath hers. 'You're a part of everything I do. Haven't I told you that? But there is a problem, at the moment, of seeing where I'm going . . .'

'Oh, that.' Laughing softly, she ducked under his arms. 'What can I do? Tie a rope or untie one or hook something . . .? How can I learn if you don't give me assignments?'

He took her hand. 'There is a moment of perfection in sailing, when the wind and water are in harmony with the boat. A wise sailor never interferes with that. We'll have a lesson some other time. When you're ready for lunch, you'll find sandwiches and beer in the refrigerator; until then, there's nothing

467

to do but relax. And talk. Do you want to tell me what happened with Mettler?'

'Later. Do you mind?'

'Of course not.' He pulled off his jacket. 'Would you toss this in the cabin?' He watched her take off her own and lean into the gangway to drop them on one of the bunks. 'Katherine.' She turned to him. 'Do you see a time when everything is in harmony for us?'

'Now,' she said swiftly. 'If we can just be together, one day at a time . . .' She searched for other words, but at last said only, 'It's perfect. Now.' And that was the closest they came that weekend to talking about the forces that drove their lives on land. Katherine refused to let Mettler interfere with their serenity, and whenever Ross thought of Elissa he put her aside. She'd been there for the two years Craig knew her and the year since he had disappeared; there was plenty of time for Katherine to hear about her.

They ate lunch in the cockpit, their voices mingling with the wind and waves and the calls of curious, swooping gulls. All afternoon they followed the cliffs that came to the water's edge, taking turns at the wheel. Occasionally they passed a small beach, or rocks with sea lions sunning themselves. As the sun dropped lower, a fiery streak of orange blazed across the water and the breeze quickened. Katherine threw back her head, her skin red-gold in the brightness, the cool air caressing her throat She heard Ross pull in his breath and at the same moment she felt unsteady with the heavy pull of wanting him. She put out a hand to support herself. 'Are you all right?' he asked.

'I'm fine.' She smiled at him. 'I was just thinking how much I'd like to make love to you.'

A slow smile lit his face. He held out his arm and Katherine moved inside it. 'We'll dock at Drake's Bay,' he murmured holding her against him. 'There's a cove I remember from years ago . . .'

It was dusk by the time they dropped anchor and stowed the sails. They worked together, Ross giving instructions, Katherine memorising each step, and as they moved about the boat the shared tasks were another kind of love-making.

In the cabin, Katherine lit kerosene lamps and pulled shut the blue and red curtains on the small windows above the bunks, while Ross prepared dinner by transferring food from the refrigerator to the oven. Together they set the table between the bunks with a checked cloth and pottery dishes, and Ross poured wine and served a platter of tiny crabmeat cakes and stuffed mushrooms. He touched Katherine's glass with his. 'To primitive living.'

She laughed. 'If the Pilgrims had lived this primitively, you couldn't have dragged them off the Mayflower.'

'And none of us would be here,' Ross said, taking their dinner from the oven. He handed her a plate. 'Chicken breast with Dijon sauce, wild rice and glazed baby carrots. I warn you; I did it all myself, without Carrie's help or advice. If it's inedible, we go over the side and catch whatever we can find.'

Katherine shook her head. 'It's wonderful. You'll spoil me.'

'I hope so.'

The small cabin was snugly enclosed within its curtained windows, softly lit by flickering lamps reflected on mahogany panelling. As they finished their coffee, Ross said, 'Do you want music? Our primitive home has a radio . . .'

'No,' Katherine said. 'I want the silence.'

He held her face between his hands and kissed her eyes, the tip of her nose, the corners of her mouth, the small hollow of her throat, holding his lips against the pulse that beat there. Katherine's arms tightened around him, then she pulled away, laughing into his eyes. 'Close quarters. There's the table, but . . .'

'You've discovered the primitive part,' he said. 'You have to get rid of the dinner dishes before you can make love.'

They piled the dishes in the sink, lowered the table and extended the double bunk over it. 'Better,' Katherine said and they undressed each other and lay on the bed, their mouths meeting, tongues exploring as their hands explored their bodies, sliding slowly along warm hollows, the hardness of muscle, the softness of hair.

'Dearest Katherine, I love you,' Ross said, his mouth on her breast. He murmured 'I love you' on each nipple, taking them lightly into his mouth. His hands slid beneath her hips and Katherine turned so that he barely had to move to lie on her and enter her; effortlessly, they flowed together and the sharing of the day became the sharing of their bodies, until Ross heard Katherine cry out beneath his mouth and in another moment, clasped in her smooth, throbbing warmth, he let himself go, his cry meeting hers.

They lay still, their lips touching, until Katherine said lazily, 'Is the boat moving?'

'Rocking.'

'Not floating away?'

'No. Don't worry; we won't go anywhere.'

'I wish we would. So far nothing could follow us.'

'Someday.'

His voice was so low Katherine was not sure she heard it. 'What?'

He raised himself on one elbow and looked at her in the soft light. 'You're going to make a wonderful sailor.'

After a moment, she said, 'And then?'

'Then, with a good set of sails, there won't be any place we can't go.'

She smiled faintly. 'A lovely dream.'

'Katherine. Tell me you love me.'

She touched his lips with her finger. 'I'm afraid to. I'm almost afraid to think it. I was so settled; I never thought of myself as falling in love again. It's as if, when I think about you, I become someone else – I move farther away from the person I was. And I get frightened: who am I now, and what do I want and how can I dream of you and long for you and still feel bound somehow to Craig . . .? And,' she added, trying to speak lightly, 'I haven't loved – I mean, fallen in love – for ten years. I've forgotten what it's like to be pulled out of myself, towards another person. I like it – I think – but it's confusing. It's all so new – and so *enormous* –'

Ross leaned over her. 'Thank you.' He kissed her slowly, lingeringly. 'As long as that's true, the words can wait.'

Katherine ran her finger down his throat, to his chest. 'I love the way you feel.' Her fingertips brushed the skin of his hard, flat stomach and the softness of his groin. 'Your body is so wonderful – you move on the boat like a lion, smooth and graceful, never looking at your feet . . .'

'That's to show off. Sometimes I take a flying leap that way. And if we're going to talk about wonderful bodies –'

'We're not going to talk,' Katherine said. Sliding out from under him, she kissed his lips, then followed with her mouth the path her fingers had taken, down his throat to the blond curls of his chest, his narrow waist, the smooth skin of his stomach and groin. She held her lips to that soft hollow – her hands slid up his thighs, and she felt his fingers encircle her breasts as she ran the tip of her tongue along warm flesh and clustered hairs and then took him into her, deep into her throat, so that he filled her once again. A low moan broke from him and she exulted in arousing him, giving him pleasure, even as she lost herself in the sensuality of enclosing him in her mouth, feeling with her tongue the solid smoothness and ridges, the hot, throbbing life of his penis. Her hands held his buttocks, pulling him against her, pulling him to the back of her throat where small murmuring sounds rippled, like the pleasure spreading through her. Then, abruptly, Ross pulled away. Sliding down on the bed, he entered her, fiercely, insistently –

one body, not two, with blinding streaks of passion joining them like jagged lightning, raising them higher and higher until they stopped, balanced on the thin edge of pure feeling, and then fell, through a dark echoing tunnel, to lie motionless, gazing at each other with small, wondering smiles.

'I never realised how long I've gone without love,' Ross said at last. 'More than a year . . . Married, but alone.'

'Both of us,' Katherine said. 'In different ways . . . Ross,' she said drowsily. She touched her lips to his. 'I love you.'

He cradled her in his arm, their faces together, and they slept.

They woke twined about each other in a tangle of sheets. 'Playing hard to get,' grumbled Ross. 'One minute you say you love me; the next you set up an obstacle course.'

'Love conquers obstacles,' Katherine said, her eyes bright, and together they pushed the sheets off the bed. She lay back, her slender body open and waiting for him to lie on her and begin the day with love. 'But is there an obstacle to breakfast?' she asked a little later. 'And sailing again?'

'I knew you'd make a good sailor,' Ross said resignedly. 'All they're interested in is sailing and food.'

'When tempted,' Katherine pointed out. 'I make time for other things.'

But they waited for breakfast until they had motored away from the fog that was a regular feature of Drake's Bay and had put up the sails. Then, heading south, at ease in the sunny cockpit, they divided oranges and rolls and coffee, and watched shifting shadows on the cliffs along the coast and wheeling sea gulls grey and white against the deepening blue sky. All day they sailed in a haze of lazy talk and timeless, contented silence.

It shattered when they were in the channel that led to the Golden Gate Bridge. Leaving the emptiness of the ocean, they were suddenly surrounded by boats: dozens of white sails bobbing and circling about them. Taking the clearest path, Ross steered under the northern end of the bridge. Katherine idly watched them draw near a group of rocks thrusting like spires near a spit of land with a lighthouse, and a tiny beach beyond. Unaccountably, she began to feel anxious. A memory tugged; she turned questioningly to Ross and found him watching her. 'Lime Point,' he said quietly.

The weekend was over; they were home.

Carrie found Melanie on the deck, her eyes protected from the sun by a mask. 'Mommy,' she said.

'Yes, sweetie.'

'I need two more cards for the country club.'

Melanie raised the mask an inch and squinted at her daughter. 'Have you and Jon lost yours?'

'No –'

'Well, then?'

'I need them for Jennifer and Todd.'

Melanie sat up and replaced the mask with dark sunglasses. 'Who?'

'You know who I mean! Jennifer and Todd Fraser!'

'Why should you get cards for Jennifer and Todd Fraser?'

'Because they don't belong to a club and there's all of August before school starts and we want to be with them. We're friends.'

Melanie contemplated her daughter. 'They're not our kind, Carrie. They'd be uncomfortable at the club.'

'Oh, mother!'

'Don't "Oh, mother" me. These things are complicated and children don't understand them. Someday you will.'

'I don't see why,' said Carrie.

'That's what I mean. You're not ready to understand.'

'So can I have two more cards?'

'Carrie, what did I just say?'

473

'I don't know, because I didn't understand it.'

'Oh, my God.' Melanie walked to a table where tall glasses and a pitcher stood on a tray.

'Can I have some, too?' Carrie asked.

'It's gin and tonic; you aren't ready for that, either. Carrie, the club doesn't like strangers coming in.'

'Lots of people brings friends from out of town.'

'Your friends aren't from out of town.'

'They live in San Francisco; the club is in Mill Valley.'

Melanie drained half a glass and refilled it. 'Why are you asking me? Let your father get them in on his membership.'

'He resigned from the club when you made him resign from our house.'

'That's not funny,' Melanie snapped. 'I suppose this was his idea for you to bring those children.'

'It's my idea! Mine and Jon's! We can't help it if you don't like Katherine –'

'*Katherine?*'

Carrie stamped her foot, 'She said to call her that. We're friends! And I don't see why you care if Daddy likes her; you like Guy, don't you? He's always in your bed so you must like him –'

'Carrie!'

'Well, isn't he? When your door is closed? But it's OK; everybody's parents do it; we don't care except why get mad at us just because you're mad at Daddy or whoever? Can't you just leave us alone? You like us to leave you alone and we don't get in your way; I mean, we mostly do what you tell us and we don't bug you when you've got problems – all kids have mixed-up parents – so you could let us do what we want with our friends – it doesn't have anything to do with you anyway – and *I want two more cards for the club!*'

Her drink halfway to her mouth, Melanie stared at her daughter. When did she get so fiery? she wondered. And how

474

does she know so much? She used to be soft and cuddly, telling me I was her pretty mommy, with her little arms around my neck. What happened to her?

'*Well?*' Carrie demanded.

'Does their mother know how long a drive it is?'

'They don't have a car. The club has a van that picks people up at Union Square. You know that. Mother, *please.*'

'Well, that's the first time I've heard that word today.' Melanie shrugged. 'I'll call the manager; I don't suppose they'll mind two more kids. Just make sure your friends behave themselves. They probably aren't used to private country clubs.'

Carrie bit back a reply. 'Thank you,' she said. 'It's very nice of you. I'll bring you the phone.'

'How come you aren't with your father this weekend?' Melanie asked when she returned.

'He went sailing with Katherine. We're going to his house next weekend. Here; do it now. I want to call Jennifer and tell her we can go swimming tomorrow.'

'All *right*,' Melanie said. But when she lay back on the chaise, she wondered, as she did so often these days, why everything seemed so difficult when she'd been sure that from now on she would live happily ever after.

The sketchbook was crammed with drawings from the Riviera; the portfolio contained a dozen designs ready to be worked in gold and silver; a felt-lined box held the twelve pieces of jewellery Mettler had returned. Beside them was a pad of paper with a list of jewellery store owners.

Katherine had called two of them. Both said they had heard of her interesting work; both said they were not taking on any new people just then. 'The economy,' they said. 'You understand how it is . . .'

Katherine understood. She sat on the stool at her worktable, chin in hand, absently rearranging the jewellery she had made for Mettler. It gleamed dully in the grey light filtering through morning fog: very expensive, highly original, vibrant in its perfect balance of shape, texture and colour. But she couldn't sell it.

So, in spite of Victoria's declaration that only the top would do, she had to move down from the top, and go to smaller, less prestigious shops. But not with these pieces. She needed what Mettler would call nice, ordinary ones.

For two weeks she worked from breakfast to midnight. She saw Ross for a few late dinners, Tobias and Victoria only once. Leslie was out of town for the opening of a new branch of Heath's, and, miraculously, Jennifer and Todd were occupied. The friendship with Ross's children had endured past the trip to France and somehow Carrie and Jon had got country club privileges for them. Each morning at eight o'clock, a club van picked them up in Union Square; each afternoon it returned them there. They took a bus home, arriving happily worn out and bubbling with their adventures. That left Katherine free, and, using sketches from the Riviera, she spent two weeks in concentrated energy, making up another collection. At the end of that time she had ten pieces, ready to be sold.

Travelling from one of San Francisco's shops to another, her samples tucked in a slim shoulder bag, Katherine avoided the glittering displays at Mettler's and Laykin Et Cie, Saks Fifth Avenue and Xavier's, and the half-dozen other exclusive shops she had once dreamed of. She kept her eyes firmly on small stores that specialised in mass-produced jewellery but also offered their customers a small selection of original pieces. By the time another week was up, she had visited nine of them. Three had bought her pieces, and ordered more.

Not quite a triumph, she thought, getting off the bus at her corner at the end of the week. In a way, she'd gone backward:

she was no farther than she'd been eight months earlier, when Mettler first bought from her. And this time she'd sold to stores less prestigious than his.

But a little over a year ago, in Vancouver, she had given up. Katherine remembered the feeling of defeat that had swept over her when the last envelope came in the mail, containing her sketches and a letter of rejection. She'd been convinced she was no good; she'd had fun with a hobby but hadn't been a professional.

All that was behind her. Now she had a profession, and she'd begun to earn her living at it. Not at the top, but still – three good stores; three written contracts. She might not have escaped Craig, but she'd gone around him. I can make my way, she told herself, walking home with a light step. Three jewellers believe in me; and Ross, and Tobias, and Victoria. And so do I.

Chapter 17

Ross called while they were at breakfast. 'Happy birthday,' he said. 'I'm making sure we still have a dinner date for tonight.'

'Of course,' she said. 'How could I forget?'

'I can't imagine, but the way you've been working I thought it possible. I planned, if this meets with your approval, to include Jennifer and Todd, so they can share their mother's birthday dinner. Then we'll drop them off at home and go to my house for dessert.'

'Dessert,' Katherine said and began to laugh.

'Often the best part of the meal, but it must be savoured very slowly. You sound happy. Did you sell to another store yesterday? I'm sorry I didn't call; my meeting went on until all hours.'

'It was a good day. I'll tell you about it tonight.'

'Six-thirty?'

'We'll be ready.'

'We?' said Jennifer, and Katherine told them about dinner.

'But what about today?' Todd asked. 'Aren't just the three of us going to celebrate?'

'Of course we are,' Katherine said, dropping her plans to work. 'What would you like to do?'

They spent the day riding rented bicycles through Golden Gate Park and picnicking on the island in Stow Lake. 'It's nice when it's the three of us,' Jennifer said as they walked home. 'Most of the time you're working or out with Ross, and we're with Carrie and Jon – it hasn't been just our family for a long time.'

Our family, Katherine thought. Just the three of us. How naturally Jennifer had said it. 'You're right,' she replied quietly. 'It's very nice; it's been a lovely birthday.'

Her thoughts were moving ahead to the rest of her birthday – dinner with Ross, an evening with Ross – as she unlocked the door. 'What's that smell?' Jennifer asked, sniffing.

'Perfume?' Katherine guessed. 'No, flowers.' The scent pervaded the apartment.

Annie opened her door across the hall. 'They came while you were gone. I put them in the –'

'Hey!' Todd shouted and staggered in from the kitchen, almost hidden behind a vase of white roses. A small envelope stuck out from between his fingers.

'Golly,' Jennifer breathed. She began counting. 'Thirty-six. That's how old you are. Are they from Ross? Or . . .' She saw Katherine's face. '*Oh.*'

Katherine was reading the familiar handwriting. "Happy birthday, sweetheart, with love." And he had signed it as he always did, with his initial.

'It's Daddy, isn't it?' Jennifer asked in a small voice.

Katherine nodded.

'What does he say?' Todd asked. 'Like – to us?'

'Nothing, silly,' Jennifer said when Katherine was silent. 'It's not our birthday, after all.'

'Well, but still –'

The doorbell rang and Todd ran to peer through the window. 'It's Ross,' he said, and opened the door.

Ross looked from Katherine's stunned face to the mass of white roses and the card in her hand. Anger welled up in him as he understood what had happened, but he kept his voice calm as he said to Jennifer and Todd, 'There's a surprise for you in my car. Do you want to get it now?'

'Sure,' Jennifer said. 'And you want us to stay there.'

'I'd appreciate it. While your mother and I talk. Then we'll go to dinner. Is that all right?'

'Sure,' Jennifer said again. 'I just wish I understood all this.'

'So do I,' said Ross. 'Off you go now.'

Todd, strangely quiet, followed Jennifer. Ross took the roses into the kitchen, out of sight; then he came back and sat beside Katherine and took her in his arms. She buried her face against his shoulder and burst into tears. 'Damn him,' she sobbed, her voice muffled. 'Damn him for his hide-and-seek games and . . . *hanging on*. Damn him for not being honest with me. Damn him for *being*.'

Ross held her until her sobs quieted. At least she's angry, he thought. It's about time. He considered telling her about Elissa, as he did every time they were together. But again it seemed the wrong time to force her to face another shock about her husband.

'Katherine,' he said firmly. 'I have brought you a birthday present; I have made arrangements for dinner. If you're too distracted, we can skip dessert at my house, but you should be able to handle the rest of the evening. And I want to hear about your triumphs with jewellers this week.'

Katherine raised her face to his. 'How did you know I had triumphs?'

480

'Because you deserve them. Are you going to change for dinner? I'd like to be festive.'

'Yes . . . I'm sorry; we just got home before you –'

'I was early. Go ahead and change; I'll wait.' He picked up a book. 'Are you reading this? I've been meaning to buy it. I'll read; you take your time. We have a seven-thirty reservation at Fisherman's Wharf.'

'Oh, Jennifer and Todd will be thrilled.' At the door to the bathroom, she turned back. 'What did you get me for my birthday?'

He laughed. Recovering fast, he thought. 'Do you want it now or later?'

'Now, please.'

He handed her a paper bag he had left inside the front door. Katherine pulled out a silver-wrapped box: a shoe box, she saw, when the elegant paper was removed. Giving him a puzzled glance, she lifted the lid and took out one shoe, then its mate: handsewn leather with white rubber soles, and leather thongs laced through brass eyelets all around and tied in a bow at the instep. A card was propped in one of them: 'Steady feet and a steadfast heart – I love you.' 'Deck shoes!' Katherine cried and burst into delighted laughter. 'For the boat!'

'Safer than those tennis shoes you wore,' he said. 'You aren't disappointed? I thought of perfume and silk and other luxuries, but you'll be spending so much time with me on the boat and if you want to move around without worrying about slipping –'

'Oh, Ross, I love you,' Katherine said and, holding a shoe in each hand, put her arms around him. 'No one has ever given me deck shoes for my birthday; no one has ever given me shoes. Thank you, thank you –' She kissed him and he thought how natural those words sounded in this small apartment that she had made for herself and her children. She tilted her head.

481

'I'll wear them to dinner with my yellow silk from Paris, shall I? And set a new style?'

'Why not? It might be just the thing for Fisherman's Wharf.'

'Don't tempt me,' she said, laughing again as she disappeared into the bathroom. And by the time she was towelling dry after a quick shower, thinking back over the past week, it seemed to Katherine that she had everything: work, Ross, her children, the love of Tobias and Victoria, the friendship of Leslie. She opened the door a crack to let out the steam and was struck with the pervasive scent of white roses.

No, she thought. Not everything. I have it all – except my freedom.

'He's out on bail,' said Leslie, helping herself to more pasta as she answered Katherine's question about Gil Lister. 'Working in a warehouse in Oakland.'

'A warehouse?' Katherine asked.

'I think he tells the robots which merchandise to pull down from which shelves. Or maybe the robots tell him. One of these days he'll go on trial and we'll all be called as witnesses, but until then I don't pay much attention to him.'

'Will he go to jail?' Todd asked.

'I hope so,' Leslie said cheerfully. 'He's the one who fired your mother, you know. We wish only discomfort for him.'

Katherine handed the platter to Bruce. 'And what about you?'

'Head of Data Processing,' he said promptly. 'As of today September first, a memorable date. My sis has more clout than ever, so my well-deserved promotion came through – of course, as l predicted, I am doing an admirable job, in fact, offers are pouring in for my unique services from far and wide.'

'You're not going away, are you?' asked Todd.

'Ah, afraid of losing your private instructor.'

'No,' Todd said. 'Well, partly. But mostly, I'd miss you.'

Bruce's eyebrows danced up and down. 'Well, now, that's mutual. No, I'm not going, at least not yet – my sis needs my protection until she makes up her mind to get married.'

'Bruce,' Leslie sighed.

'And anyway the truth is I don't want to go anywhere – I don't want to leave my family.'

'Your family?' asked Jennifer. 'Who do you have besides Leslie?'

'No one. Leslie is all I need. A family is one person who loves you and cares who you are and makes your private world a rich and boundless garden. Of course the more the merrier, but if you've only got one, be thankful. Does anyone mind if I finish the spaghetti?'

'I do,' said Todd, and they divided it. 'Our family's weirder than yours,' he said, slurping in dangling strands. 'There's Mom and Jennifer and me, and there's Dad, who's gone, unless you count last New Year's Eve and last week when he sent about a hundred roses for Mom's birthday that smelled up the whole house, and then there's Victoria and Tobias who are kind of funny, but fun, and Carrie and Jon who are great, and Derek who nobody likes, and then there's Ross who Mom is in love with and is probably going to divorce Dad and marry.'

Seeing that Katherine was speechless, Leslie said casually, 'When?'

'What?' asked Todd.

'When is your mother going to divorce your father and marry Ross?'

'How do we know?' he said indignantly. 'Nobody tells us these things!'

'Then how do you know she's going to do it at all?'

There was a pause. 'Carrie and Jon say that's what all the parents in their school do.'

'Most of them,' Jennifer put in.

'Well, most of them. But anyway.'

'What I think,' Leslie said thoughtfully, 'is that your mother isn't about to do that.'

'Why?' asked Jennifer.

All of them, even Katherine, looked at Leslie, waiting for her answer. Hell, she thought. Look who's a guru; I can't even answer my own questions about me. 'Because,' she said wisely, 'when you're in the middle of a tornado, you sit quietly and wait for things to settle down so you don't get clobbered.'

'Tornado,' mused Bruce. 'Tornado, tornado – why, sis, what a clever thing to say.'

'There isn't a tornado,' Todd declared, but doubtfully, since Bruce had approved it.

'A tornado,' Leslie stated, 'is turbulence sending things flying in all directions. Your Dad is in Canada or Alaska or somewhere; you're in San Francisco, in the Sunset; your great-grandmother and Tobias live on Pacific Heights and you never even knew you *had* a great-grandmother until a year ago –'

'But –' Todd began.

'Don't interrupt; I'm just getting started. You go to a country club in Mill Valley, across the bay; you've just come back from France, across the ocean; your mother worked at Heath's and then had a contract with a scoundrel named Mettler and now has contracts with three other stores; Carrie and Jon live with their mother in Tiburon and spend most weekends with their father in the Berkeley hills; Ross and your mother seem to have become very good friends while they were in France – maybe they even fell in love – but she's still married to your Dad . . . good Lord, are things going in all directions or aren't they? A wise person makes no predictions. Everything could change tomorrow or next week or not until next year. The best

484

thing to do is sit tight, don't worry, and remember to duck when unidentified flying objects come your way.'

Katherine had been smiling, then, as Leslie went on, she grew thoughtful. Everything could change, she repeated silently. Remember to duck. *Someone is going to get hurt, no matter what happens.*

Jennifer and Todd were giggling. 'Sis,' said Bruce. 'You are a genius. I am proud to be your family.'

'I'm proud to have you.' She gave him a long, prodding look.

'Oh, right,' he said, remembering. He turned to Jennifer and Todd. 'You want to talk about mothers and fathers and turbulence? I can tell you a thing or three about all that – and I can do it while beating you at underhand-overhand frisbee.'

'You can not,' said Todd.

'I can indeed and I say it so confidently that I declare the loser will buy ice cream cones – do we go to the park or don't we?'

In a minute they were gone. 'Planned in advance?' Katherine asked Leslie.

'Of course. Isn't he impressive? I told him I wanted a private talk with you and he managed it like a pro. He is a pro. The best thing that ever happened to Heath's Data Processing department.'

'You're the best thing around here, today. Thank you, Leslie. Every time I think I'm getting better at handling whatever comes up, something new comes up.'

'It certainly does. Are you going to tell me about it?'

'I wrote to you and last week I told you on the telephone –'

'Yes, but not how you felt. Not the inside Katherine. If I hadn't been out of town I'd know everything by now. Are you in love with him? Well, I see you are. Was Todd right about divorce and so forth?'

'No.'

485

'You're not going to divorce Craig?'

'No. And you haven't told me anything about you and Claude.'

'My loose-lipped brother did it for me.'

'It's true then? You are going to marry him?'

'It sounds like college, doesn't it? Comparing our love lives. All we need is a dormitory and a box of candy. Am I going to marry Claude? Sometimes. My mind changes itself, depending on the day of the week. I assume Todd exaggerated the number of birthday roses that arrived from Canada.'

'You're changing the subject.'

'Not anymore than you did. Anyway, we're both talking about husbands, aren't we? One potential; one absential.'

Katherine laughed. 'You sound like Tobias.'

'I couldn't; I don't read poetry. Katherine, are you in love with Craig?'

'With Craig?'

'Your husband. Remember?'

'I don't think so. I mean, of course I remember, but I don't think I'm in love with him anymore. I'm not the same person I was; I don't suppose he is, either. Whoever he is. Craig Fraser. Craig Hayward. I've learned more about him in the past year than in all the years we were married.'

'*Were* married?'

'Living together; we're still married.'

'And he's been gone almost fifteen months. Katherine, what the hell are you waiting for? You just celebrated – or deplored – your thirty-sixth birthday. When you get to those numbers you stop dallying and make quick decisions. Haven't you noticed how the years slip through your fingers? You barely grab one and it's gone.'

'What about you? When are you getting married?'

'I told you, my mind changes each –'

'And what about a baby? You were thinking of having one.'

'I haven't decided yet.'

They broke into laughter. 'OK,' Leslie conceded. 'I may not be the one to give advice on quick decisions. But what are you waiting for?'

Katherine's laughter dropped away. 'Less turbulence,' she said.

'Less? Oh. My tale of a tornado. That was only to divert your kids; it wasn't serious.'

'It was to me; I do feel as if we've been tossed around by a storm. We're still being tossed – when those roses came, that's how I felt. And if you recall, you said we should sit tight and remember to duck. It was good advice. A tornado is no place to make a decision.'

'So you're not going to do anything.'

'I'm going to work, spend time with Jennifer and Todd, wait for Craig . . .'

'Without Ross?'

Katherine shook her head. 'I can't stop seeing him. I love him . . . and I haven't felt this way in so long – as if I have the most wonderful secret that's always there, with me, whatever I'm doing . . . It makes everything more complicated, to love him, but it makes everything so wonderful . . . I can't push him away.'

'That sounds like a decision, lady.'

'Half of one. He thinks I should divorce Craig.'

'Sensible man. Katherine, what are you worried about? Someone getting hurt? Someone always gets hurt. Even when you least expect it. Let me tell you about Marc when he wormed Claude's name out of me . . .'

Curled up in a corner of the couch, Leslie told Katherine the story. 'Now you tell me,' she said at the end of it. 'Did I owe Marc anything after all those years when he spent money on me, squired me all over town and a good part of Europe, and was a most pleasant companion in bed?'

'Hardly a marriage,' Katherine said dryly. 'He didn't support you; you didn't have two children and a home you'd made, you never made a commitment to spend the rest of your life together.'

'True. So you owe Craig undying loyalty and I owe Marc nothing?'

'I don't know what anyone "owes" anyone,' Katherine said feeling frustrated. 'It's what we *feel* that's important.'

'And you don't feel that you want to be free?'

Katherine looked at her in silence. Finally, she asked. 'Why can't you make up your mind about Claude?'

'Because I'm not sure I trust my feelings, and that means I'm not sure what's best for both of – oh, well.' She grinned at Katherine. 'I see what you mean. All right, I shouldn't push you. But, Katherine –'

'Yes?'

'Think of yourself first. I know you have to pay attention to your kids and all those other people around you, but you owe it to yourself to take care of yourself. You're the only one you can really trust to do that.'

After a moment, Katherine said, 'In a good marriage, or a good friendship, people take care of each other.'

'There aren't many good marriages or friendships. When women think of themselves last, which they usually do, men and kids think of them last, too.'

With a glint in her eyes, Katherine said, 'Were you thinking of yourself first when you didn't fire Bruce?'

'Well, but sometimes . . . Oh, hell,' Leslie admitted ruefully. 'Love messes it up. You start wanting to protect someone, or help, or just *do for* . . .'

'And doesn't Claude want to help you, and do things for you?'

'He does. I'm not used to it yet. Maybe! I don't trust it. After all you thought Craig wanted to protect and do for you . . . damn I'm sorry, Katherine.'

488

'It's all right. It's true. But he did take care of me for a long time, and I still don't know what forced him to stop doing it. And even if I was wrong about him, does that mean I shouldn't trust anyone else?'

'No, of course not.'

'Then why not try trusting Claude?'

'When you put it like that – damned if I know. But that's enough of Claude; I want to talk about you.'

'No, it's enough about me, too. Tell me about Heath's.'

'All right; if you tell me about France. Your letters were wonderful, but I want more. All the details. What is it?' she asked when Katherine began to laugh.

'You sound like Victoria.'

'Well, whatever that means, tell me what you think I should hear. Bruce promised to make the game and the ice cream last at least a couple of hours. God, lady, I missed you – I haven't had a good talk since you went away.'

Ross had talked about BayBridge so often that Katherine thought she had a clear picture of it in her mind. But, on Saturday morning, when she stood with him and saw its length and breadth, with twenty-five buildings gutted but still standing, and construction equipment scattered about like huge yellow insects beside excavations and newly-poured foundations, she was stunned. 'I had no idea. I remember saying it sounded as if you wanted to build small towns . . . but I never thought I'd see one coming to life, all at once.'

'It's not ideal,' Ross said. 'I wanted a larger park, and wider walkways between the townhouses, but that would have meant fewer units to sell, and the developers balked. Next time if I can get more control, we'll have more air and light, lower buildings, more parks and fountains –' He caught himself. 'Why don't you gag me, or better still, kiss me, when I start lecturing?'

489

'Because I like listening.'

'Dad!' Jon shouted. 'What's this?'

Ross looked and saw nothing. 'Where are you?'

'Here!' Four grinning faces peered from behind what looked like a miniature oil rig on a yellow flatbed truck. Drills like huge corkscrews, and long flexible pipes, were strapped to its sides.

'Come down from there,' Ross ordered. 'That's not a play-ground.'

They clambered down. 'But what is it?'

'A drilling rig. The foundation engineers use it to drill holes for pumping concrete around building supports.'

'This building?' Todd asked. Contemplating the Macklin Building, Ross nodded. 'What for? Doesn't it have concrete under it already?'

'I think it needs more,' Ross said. 'I can't vouch for its safety in case of a tremor.'

'Tremor,' Carrie said. 'Earthquake?'

'When it's big enough it's called an earthquake.'

Todd ran his hand over one of the drills. 'It digs down like a corkscrew?'

'Exactly. Then one of these pipes is fed through the hole –'

'Like a snake,' said Jon.

'Right. And the concrete is pumped through the pipe, under tremendous pressure. It's like an injection, forcing concrete around the footings under the columns that hold up the build-ing, making them bigger and stronger.'

Jennifer and Carrie stood nearby. 'Even in an earthquake?' Carrie asked.

'In most earthquakes.'

'Then why wasn't it done that way the first time?'

Ross paused. 'We don't know. But it has to be done now before it's an office building again, or we'll always have it hanging over our heads, like a sword about to fall.'

490

In a dramatic voice, Todd intoned, 'The surgeons are ready to vaccinate the Macklin Building. Will it work? Or will it still come tumbling down, cutting off our heads like a sword?'

'Does it cost a lot to do?' Carrie asked.

'Yes,' Ross replied.

'How much?'

'About a quarter of a million dollars.'

Todd whistled.

Katherine was watching Ross. 'Who pays for it?' she asked.

'I do,' he answered. 'It's my building.'

'But you weren't the one –' She stopped as he shook his head in warning. 'Wouldn't it cost less to tear it down?' she asked instead.

'No. It's almost always cheaper to repair a building. Let me show you what we're doing.'

He led them through a rough opening in the building. 'New front door,' he said, then described the arcade that would cut through the building from Mission Street to the shopping mall on the other side: 'An atrium going through all ten floors to the roof, with a glass dome on top. The workmen had opened it up through the second floor when we stopped the work. We'll start again after the concrete is pumped in.'

Todd and Jon walked over to a forest of beams shoring up the ceiling and, tilting back their heads, looked through the jagged hole above them. 'If you cut out the middle of the floor, what keeps the rest of it from collapsing?'

'These.' Ross pointed to the temporary beams.

'On every floor?'

He nodded.

'Forever?'

Smiling, he said, 'Only until the atrium is built. Look, here's how it works.' He squatted down and in loose sand on the floor drew a quick sketch of the building. The four children squatted beside him as he described the problems he and his

491

staff faced, making them sound like puzzles and challenging the children to find solutions. He was enjoying his audience, Katherine saw, and his seriousness as he considered their guesses, and offered his own ideas, held them like a magnet. She looked from one rapt face to another. *I wish Jennifer and Todd had a father.*

'So the atrium frame helps support all ten floors,' Ross finished. 'And then we take away the temporary beams.' He stood, stretching the kinks from his muscles. Leaning casually towards Katherine, he whispered, 'I love you.' Then he said aloud, 'I'm cooking dinner tonight. And I have a couple of scale models of this building at home, if you want to take them apart and put them together your own way.'

They walked outside and as the children ran ahead to the car Katherine asked hesitantly, 'Ross, shouldn't Derek pay for the work? At least part of it?'

'None of it. I haven't even told him I'm having it done.'

'But – why not? If you think he was the one who didn't build it properly – '

Their steps slowed as they approached the car, and they lowered their voices. At the same moment, their eyes met and Ross felt a rush of love and gratitude. 'I'm glad you're here,' he said. Automatically, their hands met, their fingers interlocked and then they saw the children look their way and quickly pulled apart.

'I'll tell you why I haven't told Derek,' Ross went on. 'If I asked him to share the cost, he'd smile and say he didn't know what I was talking about. I can't prove anything and he'd figure out in a few seconds that I've kept quiet because I don't want it to become public knowledge that the Hayward Corporation was involved in bribing an inspector and putting up a substandard building.' He laughed shortly. 'Derek's legacy. It's going to be all I can do to handle the cost, but I don't see that I have a choice. Victoria is eighty-two years old; I'd do a lot more than spend some money to keep a scandal from ruining however many years she has left.'

Katherine was silent.

They reached the car and Ross opened the door for her. 'Does that sound irrational?' he asked.

'No,' she said. 'It sounds loving.'

By the middle of September, they had settled into a pattern, spending three or four evenings a week together, alone or with the children. One night, after dinner at Ross's house, the four children were leafing through Katherine's sketchbook, reliving the month in France through her drawings. 'Could I have this one?' Carrie asked, lingering over a vivid watercolour of the cactus gardens at Eze.

'Of course,' Katherine said.

'Me too?' asked Jon, holding up a charcoal sketch of a Roman olive mill.

Katherine's face was bright with pleasure as she took both pictures and wrote on them, "With my love, Katherine."

'I'll hang it up,' Carrie said, holding it at arm's length, admiring it. 'Of course not at home,' she added with a shrug. 'You know. But –'

'Here,' said Jon. 'At Dad's house.'

'Whose house?' Katherine asked.

'Our house,' Jon grinned. 'I meant our house.'

Ross met Katherine's eyes with such love she caught her breath in wonder. 'Thank you,' he said quietly. 'For making us a family.' And looking at the six of them at the table, Katherine thought she had never been so happy.

Some nights they took the children to outdoor concerts in Stern Grove, or for an evening sail, but mostly the two of them were alone, on the boat, going to the theatre, driving to the wine country, making love. Katherine remembered when Derek's whirlwind had seemed magical, but she knew now that this was the real magic: the love that grew slowly, steadily, beating within her, inseparable from the beating of her heart. And Ross found it impossible to get through a day without talking to her on the telephone or sending her a flower, a note, a newspaper clipping that had amused him, a magazine article he wanted to share.

Occasionally he called to ask her to lunch, but Katherine was reluctant to take time off during the day. With Jennifer and Todd back in school, she was concentrating on making and selling as many pieces of jewellery as she could, because she was afraid Mettler's story would reach other shops, and no one would do business with her.

'It won't happen,' Leslie assured her. 'Only a few shops specialise in copyrighted originals. You don't have to worry.'

Still, each morning, as soon as Katherine sat down and began to sketch and shape bracelets and bar pins, pendants and earrings, Mettler's voice would echo in her mind, reciting the evidence that inescapably linked her to Craig.

'Divorce him,' Victoria said at dinner. 'Then you can sell through the top stores. How else will you make a reputation? You must divorce him. Cake, my dear?'

'Yes, thank you. Divorcing him wouldn't help. I'd still be known as the woman who was his wife when he was charged with embezzling; who fled Canada, according to Mettler; who gets money from him every month –'

'But it might help you to be yourself,' said Tobias, cutting an oversize piece of cake and transferring it to his plate. 'Help you get away from the past and look ahead. "In the deserts of the heart, let the healing fountain start." '

The words struck Katherine and she was silent, repeating them to herself. 'I don't know,' she said finally. 'It seems that the happier I am, the harder it is to . . . drop him. Because I don't believe he's happy; and if he had to run away because he was framed –'

494

'He could have stayed,' Tobias said. 'He could have fought.'

Victoria shook her head. 'We never forced him to learn that.'

'Then I don't think,' Katherine said gently, 'that you're the ones to tell me to divorce him.'

But the urgings from everyone stayed with her. And so did her memories, appearing unexpectedly, bringing back the best parts of Craig and their marriage as well as his brooding silences, the spaces that kept them apart. Derek's exasperated voice stayed with her, too: *Must you always feel guilty?* And Mettler's accusing voice, tying her to Craig. And Ross's, deep and warm: *Dearest Katherine, I love you.*

'I can't make the decision for you,' he said as they lay in bed the night after her dinner with Victoria and Tobias. They had eaten on the deck of his house, and made love on the wide chaise beneath the stars, and then, in the white light of a full moon slipped naked into the jacuzzi, letting the jets of hot water massage their muscles into almost total collapse before they climbed out and ran through the chill air into the warmth of Ross's bed.

'How can anyone make a decision after that?' Katherine asked languidly, her head on his shoulder. She didn't want to move. 'I have no energy for decisions.'

'Did you know,' Ross murmured, 'that Todd asked me today if I'm trying to make him and Jennifer forget Craig?'

Her lethargy vanished. 'What did you say?'

'That I wanted them to remember their father, and their love for him, but that was separate from the fact that he isn't here and we have no expectation that he will be here again; that I love him and Jennifer and would like to take care of them; and that I am deeply in love with you and would very much like to marry you.'

Katherine lay still. 'Todd didn't tell me any of that.'

495

'I asked him not to. A man ought to do his own proposing.'

She laughed slightly. 'Was that a proposal?'

'No.' He pulled away to look at her. 'You'll recognise it when it comes. I'm waiting for you to make up your mind about Craig. With him or without him.'

'With him,' Katherine said. 'I can't do it without him. Not yet, anyway. Can't I make you see that I want to do this decently, that I want to end our marriage as equals? We began that way; I want to end that way.'

Ross thought of Elissa, and Katherine's loyalty, and his own responsibility. I should tell her, he reflected; she should know all of it. But she'd been hurt enough by Craig's lies and pretences. Knowing about Elissa would change nothing; she already had plenty of reasons to divorce him. 'Treating him as an equal is more than he's done for you,' he said at last.

'Maybe that's why I want to do it.' Turning up her face, Katherine kissed Ross with small, leisurely kisses. 'I love you. I might even propose to you someday. But not now. Not yet.' After a moment, she sighed. 'What I have to do now is go home.'

'It's early.'

'What time is it?'

'A little after midnight.'

'How much after?'

He laughed reluctantly. 'About an hour and a half after. All right. Get dressed, my lovely one; I'll drive you back.'

Later, in the car, he said, 'I hope you noticed that I didn't say I would drive you home. Home is wherever the two of us are together. Do you believe that?'

'Yes,' she said simply. And they drove across the bridge and into the city in silence, content with each other, and in silence kissed goodnight in front of her door.

But it's not enough, Ross thought, making the return trip. Contentment isn't enough. Even love isn't enough. We have to build something together and we can't do that when we date like teenagers, jumping apart when our children find us close together, making love almost furtively, driving home at one-thirty in the morning so the children won't know we've been in bed.

At home, pulling off his clothes for the second time that night, looking at the empty bed, wanting Katherine there, her eyes dark with passion, her body opening to his, he thought how ridiculous they were. The children knew exactly what they were doing. One of these days, the sooner the better, they'd all sit down together and have an honest – The telephone rang and he lunged for it. Katherine had found something wrong at home –

'Yes,' he said loudly. 'What's happened?'

'Ross?' said a familiar voice. 'Can I talk to you? It's Craig.'

PART IV

Chapter 18

The years fell away. Craig's voice had not changed and for a moment Ross felt as if they were boys again and he had called to make plans for the day, saying, 'Ross? Can I talk to you?'

'Sure,' he said casually, as if they truly were in that long-ago time, but his body was as tight as a clenched fist as he struggled to think clearly through the numbing shock of hearing a voice, when for so long there had been only a shadow. 'Of course we can talk. Do you want to come here or meet somewhere?'

'No, I meant now. On the phone.'

'Craig, after sixteen years we ought to be able to talk face to face.'

'I'm not in San Francisco.'

'Where are you?'

'It doesn't matter. Ross, I need help and there isn't anyone

501

else I can call. If you won't talk to me on the phone –'

'Of course I will; whatever you want. Are you all right?'

'Fine.' Craig laughed. 'How does that sound? I'm fine. I've lost everything, but I'm fine.'

Ran away from everything, Ross corrected him silently. But he was aware of changes in Craig's voice that he had not heard at first: it was deeper and stronger than he remembered. 'What kind of help do you want?'

'I need advice. And money. I wouldn't ask – I never thought I'd be able to come to you again, after leaving you . . . with Jenny . . .' He stopped. 'I can't talk about it. I've tried to write to you, or call, so goddamn many times, but I couldn't – and I still can't. Someday I will; I swear it; but this is more important . . . Ross, I've got to have my wife and kids back. I want to start over again. The mess with Carl got out of hand; I could have straightened it out – we'd had misunderstandings before – but I panicked. And then there's –'

'You mean you didn't –?'

'Katherine.' Craig went on without pausing. 'I need to explain to her – make up for . . .' His voice faded.

'Craig?' Ross said loudly.

'Sorry. I get stuck on telling Katherine. I don't know how the hell I can explain . . . It was bad enough last year, when I left, but now . . .'

Stiffly, Ross said, 'She's your wife.'

'That doesn't guarantee anything; that was part of the problem. I have to think of the right way to tell her, otherwise she won't . . . Ross, can you loan me some money? There's a high-powered lawyer in Vancouver, but he wants a retainer. Can you do it?'

'Of course. How much do you need?'

'I don't know. Probably five thousand to start. But I may need a lot more.'

'I'll try to get you whatever you need. Craig –'

'I was crazy to run; I know that. I could have worked everything out, found a way to keep the whole mess from Katherine –'

'Keep it from her? You should have told her!'

'You wouldn't say that if you knew her. But you see her now and then, don't you? Do you know if she got the roses I sent on her birthday?'

'She got them . . .'

'The kids told me she works at Heath's but she can't be earning much – my God, have you seen that apartment? She ought to be able to do better, with the money I send. That's one thing: as hard as it's going to be to work everything out, at least she knows I helped support her all this time.'

Ross paced as far as the telephone cord would stretch, then back the other way. *Call her; come back; she wants to talk to you.*

No, stay away.

Steadfast Katherine. What would happen when she heard the plea in Craig's voice and took pity on his aloneness, and saw her children greet him and call him Dad?

'Ross, are you listening? I've got to know how things are before I call her. Is she still seeing that bastard? When I came last December, to take her back to Canada, the kids told me she was with him, *at his place* . . . they said she saw a lot of him. Christ, I thought I'd gotten away from the son of a bitch – that he'd never get his knife into me again – and then almost the first thing I hear is my kids talking about him . . . I won't go through that again; I don't want to come back and find out she's with him. Or someone else.'

Ross was silent.

'Well? *Is she still seeing him?* Damn it, he'll chew her up, destroy her; she's so naive . . . she doesn't understand . . .'

'She broke off with him,' Ross said.

Craig sighed. 'I thought she would. Katherine's too smart

not to see through him. She probably didn't spend much time with him anyway. After all, she's not a young girl who could be taken in, hypnotised . . . So is that it? She hasn't got anyone? Or is there someone else?' He paused. 'I'm asking you, Ross. Is my wife waiting for me or has she found someone else?'

Poor Craig, Ross thought involuntarily. He hasn't changed. He can't take the risk of calling his wife without making sure of what he'll find.

'Ross, did you hear me? It's a simple question. Or is it? Are you trying to protect someone?'

'No –'

'Then what the hell is going on?' He waited. 'Damn it, Ross, *I'm asking for help! I* counted on you; we were friends once. At least I thought we were . . . What's going on with Katherine? Who are you covering for?'

'Craig, she's been waiting for you –'

'Who is it? You're a lousy liar, Ross; something's going on and you're lying about it. *This is my wife we're talking about* . . . and you and I used to be honest with each other. I wouldn't be so surprised if it was that bastard – I'd expect him to lie to me, make me squirm, keep me in the dark . . . but you! For Christ's sake, you're no better than he is. When did you start acting like your brother?'

'You damn fool,' Ross exploded. 'Katherine and I are in love with each other. I want to marry her, but she won't divorce you. She has a kind of loyalty you couldn't begin to comprehend, and she won't marry me or even live with me until she understands why you left her, until she finishes with the past, finishes her marriage –'

'She said that?'

'Damn it, do you think I'm making this up? She wants to finish her marriage with you, but only face to face, as equals – that was how she put it – which is a hell of a lot more than she ever got from you –' A small click broke through his torrent of

504

words. 'Craig? CRAIG!' he shouted, but there was no answer, only dead silence from the telephone in his hand.

Ross flung himself from the house and strode through the darkened hills, going over the conversation in his mind, cursing his clumsiness. He'd bungled it. With Craig in his grasp, he had let him go.

Towards dawn he was home again, thinking of Katherine, repeating the conversation over and over in a bitter rehearsal for when she would arrive. She'd be there in a few hours to spend the afternoon with him; a time they had planned lightheartedly in bed the night before: Friday, the end of the week, a chance to spend a few daylight hours without the children. 'And this time,' Katherine had said, 'I'll pick you up; Leslie loaned me her car while she and Claude are in New York. I'll be there about noon.'

Waiting for her, Ross prowled from room to room and was outside, on the deck, his back to the house, when he heard her footsteps. 'Hi,' she said softly, coming up behind him. 'What requires such deep thought you can't –' He turned and she saw his eyes. 'Ross, what is it? What's happened?'

He put out his hands and took hers. 'Craig called me last night.'

The sunlight lurched. Everything around them, from their clasped hands to the great bridge below, snapped out of place, then slowly settled back. The world grew still. A solitary bee dived into the silence, its buzz a deafening roar. Gently, Katherine pulled her hands away and walked across the deck. 'When is he coming back?'

'I don't know. Perhaps not at all.'

'Not at all!' She swung around. 'He must be! Why else did he call? Why *did* he call? Why didn't he call me?'

'He wanted to know if you were still seeing Derek.'

'He could have asked me . . . Oh. He couldn't take the chance . . .?'

'He wanted my help. And I made a mess of it.'

'But you told him to come back.'

There was a pause. 'No,' Ross said.

'You didn't – Ross, you know I must see him!'

'*I was afraid!* Can you understand that? Of course I know you have to see him, but when I heard his voice, I thought of what might happen when you were all together again, the Fraser family –'

'But . . . what about embezzling? Being framed? What did he say?'

'We didn't get to that.'

'Ross!'

'Damn it, I tried to ask him but he kept changing the subject –'

'You didn't ask him about embezzling and you decided not to tell him to come back.'

'I didn't decide anything. That was the problem. Katherine. I've gone over it so many times I can repeat the whole thing. If you'll just sit down . . .'

Slowly, she came back to him. In the fragrant sunlight, they sat apart from each other and Ross repeated the conversation.

When he finished, Katherine was looking past him, shaking her head, her hands gripped together. 'How could you tell him about us? That was for me to do!'

'I know; I hadn't intended –'

'You had no right to tell him! I was going to –'

'I know that! I hadn't intended to tell him anything!'

'Then why did you? Oh, Ross – to have him so close and then to make him run away –!'

'Katherine, no one makes Craig run away; he does it by himself.'

'But you knew that; you've always known that. Of all people, you should have known how to talk to him.'

'Right. I should have known.' Slowly, he said, 'He goaded

me. But I might have told him anyway. I remember thinking, at one point, that you might not do it yourself.'

'You knew I was just waiting until he got here –'

'That's what you said. Maybe I didn't believe it.'

'Didn't –!'

'Katherine. Look at yourself. Your husband deserted you more than a year ago; you love and you're loved by me. But you still cling to someone who's betrayed you –'

'You think I should pay him back. Has it occurred to you that the only thing left of my marriage is knowing that *I* haven't destroyed anything, that I haven't been the one to cut him off from his wife and children?'

'He doesn't deserve them!'

'That's not the point! I'm not thinking of Craig; I'm thinking of myself – what kind of person I am. Do I run away as he did? Or do I wait for him –'

'So you can be better than he is.'

'Well, why not? What's wrong with trying to be better than someone who's hurt you? Are we only supposed to be loyal when it's reciprocated?'

'It's not a bad idea.' Ross studied his hands. 'I started to ask you – when I said you should look at yourself – what if it's not loyalty at all?'

'What are you talking about?'

'I'm talking about a woman who's so afraid of marriage she hides behind an absent husband rather than risk another failure.'

'That is ridiculous!'

'Just think about it for a minute. I'm going to get us something to drink.' He disappeared into the house and returned with a pitcher and two glasses. 'Iced tea. With home-grown mint.' He filled the glasses. 'What do you think?'

'About the tea?'

'Katherine.'

'I'm not hiding behind Craig. Maybe I am afraid – a little. Everything's happened so fast, I'm not sure where I am – how far I've come. I still don't know how well I can do on my own, I don't know if I can support the three of us by myself; I don't know how strong I am without a man. Maybe that's why I'm not sure I want to trust love yet. But I'm not hiding behind Craig; you're wrong about that. I *owe* him something.'

'Whatever it is, you've paid it.'

'It's not that simple. I have to think of Jennifer and Todd; of what's best for them.'

'A stable family is best for them.' He stopped abruptly. 'Are you saying you *might* go back to him? To have a stable family? God damn it, he deserted you!'

'*I know that!* And I haven't thought, for a long time, that I'd go back to him. I told you I was just waiting . . . I told you I still don't understand what happened to us. We loved each other and had a life together and were happy – I think we were happy – and then everything collapsed . . . *and I don't know why!* And until I do, I'm not going to start another marriage.'

Katherine's eyes were hurt and angry. 'I told you all that – I thought you understood – but then, when he finally called, you drove him away! Ross, do you know what you've done? I had a chance to talk to him, to ask him so many questions . . . but now I'm still where I was before – wondering, imagining, waiting, *not knowing*. And I don't know how long it will take for him to try again, to get up his courage, the way he did after Jennifer and Todd told him about Derek.' She began to tremble. 'I don't know what he's thinking; I can't even imagine what it will be like to see him again if – when – he does call again; I don't know what we'll say to each other or how I'll feel or how I'll tell him . . .' The glass of tea, wet with condensed moisture, slipped from her shaking hand and shattered on the deck. Katherine burst into tears. 'I'm sorry, I'm sorry, I just don't know how everything is going to end . . . I don't know what's really best for the children . . . and I worry about Craig . . . he's all alone and I have you, and Jennifer and Todd, and Victoria and Tobias . . . I have a family and he has no one and he knows it now, because you told him about us . . . Ross, you think all you have to do is remind me that he deserted us, but it isn't that simple . . .' After a moment she wiped her cheeks with the back of her hand and sat up straight. 'I'd better get a rag and clean up this mess.'

'Sit still. I'll take care of it later.' Ross had not moved, though his arms ached to hold her; he sat apart from her, his anger growing as she wept. 'He isn't worth your tears. He doesn't know the meaning of love or loyalty or steadfastness –'

'Don't, Ross. You hardly know him anymore, or anything about him. I don't find it admirable when you attack him –'

'Admirable –! Good God, he kept another woman for two years while you were married! Was that admirable? That was why he needed so much money he had to steal it!'

'That's not true! I don't know where you heard it, but it isn't true! Craig would never. . . he told me he never wanted . . . *I would have known!*'

Ross looked at her in silence.

'All right, I didn't know everything about him, but I would have known that! Two years?' she cried wildly. 'You expect me to believe . . . *two years?* He couldn't have; he was always home.' She fell silent, then looking at her hands, asked, 'Where did he – where was he supposed to have someone else?'

'In Calgary.'

'He spent a lot of time there, on business. And he always left me the number of his motel.' A thought struck her. 'Did he tell you . . . he didn't *tell* you this!'

'Of course not. Craig never admits anything unless he's forced to. I discovered it by accident.'

509

'Well, whoever told you was lying.'

'Katherine, listen to me. I went looking for him; I wanted to find him so you and I could be alone, without his damned shadow following us all the time. What I found –'

And so, starkly, he told her about Elissa, leaving nothing out.

At first Katherine kept shaking her head, murmuring, 'No, no no,' beneath his words. Then she was silent, her eyes closed. Another Craig. Even another name. Another space separating them. But something else was bothering her . . . something Ross had said . . . And then she had it. 'August. That trip you took – you called me from there, the day I got back from France.'

'And I didn't tell you about it,' Ross said, before she could. 'I meant to, but you'd just found Mettler's letter cancelling your order, and you had enough to worry about –'

'But that was August; this is the middle of September. When were you going to tell me?'

'Look, you've had a lot on your mind –'

'Ross, Craig had secrets, we don't! I want to know the truth about the world I live in!'

'All at once? I was waiting until things calmed down; I thought it would be best if you didn't have to tackle everything at the same time.'

Katherine shook her head. 'You decided to look for Craig without telling me, and then you decided not to tell me about Elissa – you even decided to tell Craig about us – all on your own. Don't I have anything to say about decisions that involve me?'

He gestured helplessly. 'Of course you do. You're wrong about my deciding to tell Craig about us – that was an accident. But the rest, and looking for him, and finding Elissa – you're right; I did those on my own and I suppose I should have told you. But it was done from love –'

510

'Ross, I've spent all these months trying to find out who I am, what kind of a woman I can be on my own, without being shielded, as if I were in some kind of cocoon . . . I've been through that with Craig!'

'So you never want protection again, is that it? You think it's some kind of a weakness. If you weren't still tied in knots over Craig and his secrets, you'd know better. It isn't all or nothing –'

'All right; maybe that's true. Maybe I am exaggerating because I'm afraid of going backwards, but –'

'And you're lucky,' he went on, 'when you find someone who cares enough about you to try to shield you. How many people spend their lives looking for that? How many people – men or women – find someone to protect them from pain?'

'I don't know what that means anymore.' Katherine twisted her hands together.

'It means – at least this time – that I kept putting off telling you what I'd done because I didn't think it would change the way you feel about Craig; it would just make you more unhappy to discover another hidden piece of his life, another lie –'

'But I have to know all the pieces! All the lies! And you know that!' Katherine looked beyond him, at the skyline of the city across the bay, and the towns extending down the peninsula, fading into mist. 'How do I know how many other lies there are? *Can't you see – I lived with him for ten years and I was blind to all those lies! How can I understand myself until I understand him?* And you let him go! I'm sorry, I keep coming back to that, but that was the worst of all . . . he was so close! And I don't know when he'll be that close again . . . when I can break free and move ahead . . .'

Tears streamed down her face. She made no attempt to wipe them away, but sat still, looking past Ross and past the city, as if she could not bear to look at anything nearby. Watching her, Ross hurt inside with love, and anger at Craig, and frustration. 'You understand more about him now than you ever did. Katherine, you've changed so much – what difference does it make what you were with him, now that you've found out what you can be without him?'

'I'm still finding out,' she said doggedly. 'You always make things sound so simple, when they aren't.'

'I know they're not simple. But one of these days you may have to decide it's enough anyway.'

Katherine turned to him. 'You mean if he doesn't come back. But he's tried twice; I can't believe he won't try again.'

'And in the meantime he's always with us.' Ross gave a short, bitter laugh. 'I had the wrong sword over our heads: it's not the Macklin Building; it's your husband. We can't make any plans; we can't think about the future. We argue when we should be enjoying each other, sharing the kind of love we've never had before . . .' He stood and paced the length of the deck, furiously kicking aside some small stones near the edge. 'We can't even go back, can we? It used to be that he was in the background; now he's between us.'

'Yes.' Katherine's voice was almost inaudible. 'He's so far away, but he's . . . here. And then I look at you and I can't even think straight anymore . . . Oh, if I could find a way out –!'

From the opposite end of the deck, Ross said flatly, 'I make it harder, don't I? I can't help you; I can't tell you what to do; I can't even try to protect you from pain because we don't agree on what that means. I only confuse the issue.' When she was silent, he said slowly, 'It might be better if I got out of your way. You'd be able to concentrate on thinking about your husband and your marriage. Maybe you'd even decide you do know all you need to know – about him, and yourself, and us.'

Katherine gazed at him, her heart pounding.

'And maybe I could use some time, too,' he went on carefully. 'To think about how I feel about sharing with you. If I'm making too many decisions on my own, I ought to know it and do something about it.'

Katherine breathed deeply to slow the pounding of her heart. *Not to see Ross. To wake up in the morning and not be able to think, 'Today I'll see him; today we'll talk; tonight we'll make love . . .' Not to see Ross.* She swallowed hard, feeling her heart beat in her throat. *But – to be alone for a while, with no wild swings of emotion, with no pressure to decide, to act, to choose, to do . . .* 'Yes,' she said, forcing it out. 'I think it would be a good idea.'

His breath escaped in a small burst; he had been holding it. 'Whatever you think is best.' Swiftly, he went to her and took her hands between his. 'I love you. I'll do whatever you want –' He turned her hands and kissed one palm, and then the other, her skin cool and soft beneath his lips, rippling with the tremor that ran through her.

I don't want to leave you; I want to be close to you . . . 'No,' she murmured.

He stood, bringing her with him, enfolding her in his arms. But she remained motionless, her arms at her sides instead of embracing him, as if already she had begun to withdraw. In a moment of panic Ross wondered what the hell he'd done. To be without Katherine; to go through the days without her smile, without seeing her eyes light up in response to something he said, without feeling her beneath him . . . What the hell had he done? And what would he do if she did find Craig and began to rediscover, with the children, the bonds that had held them for ten years?

It won't happen. They've gone too far. We've gone too far.

Katherine moved within the circle of his arms and immediately he dropped them. He would not force her to stay. 'Whatever I can do to help you –' he said.

Tremulously, she smiled. Teardrops glistened in her dark

eyelashes. 'I think I'll just be alone for a while . . . and think about the three of us . . . and everything that's happened . . .' She reached out, touching his face with her fingertips. 'I love you, Ross.' Then she turned and walked quickly across the deck and through the glass doors into the living-room. In another moment Ross heard her open the front door, and close it firmly behind her.

He stood where he was. Be well, my dearest Katherine, he told her silently. I'll be waiting.

Elissa saw the taxi driver peer at the address, then stop at her front gate. Not Craig, she thought; he'd tell the driver which house. She saw a woman step out and pay the driver and she knew, even before she saw her face, that it was Katherine.

Hell, she thought, feeling her stomach grab, there's nothing to be scared of. She held the door open, watching the prairie wind lift eddies of dust and carry them along the street like tops. She saw Katherine turn and give an appraising glance at the house – I know it's not his type, Elissa told her silently; and he didn't want me to paint the door red, but I did it anyway, when I decided he was gone for good – then Katherine was walking towards her. She was more beautiful than Elissa had thought; her pictures didn't do her justice. 'I'm Katherine Fraser,' she said, holding out her hand.

'I know,' said Elissa. 'I've seen your picture. I'm Elissa Nielsen.' Gravely, they shook hands. 'Please come in.' She led the way. 'I wondered if Ross would tell you about me.'

'He only told me yesterday.' Katherine gave a swift glance at the living-room.

'Why don't you take a good look around?' Elissa asked. 'I won't be insulted. You want to know where Craig lived part-time; I would, if I was you. Ross only told you yesterday? He took his time.'

'He didn't want me to be hurt,' said Katherine. Turning, she met Elissa's eyes. They looked away at the same time and then fell silent.

Elissa fidgeted with a candy dish as Katherine picked up the carved wooden turtle and ran her finger over the small boy on its back. 'He's not Craig's,' Elissa said. 'I guess Ross must have told you. And that Craig helped me when I was pregnant? Without Craig . . . well, without Craig, I just don't know.'

Katherine walked about the crowded room, seeing small touches identical to those she remembered in their Vancouver house. She felt disoriented, as if the two houses had merged and she'd got lost among objects that were strange but somehow hers. 'Would you like something? ' Elissa asked. 'Tea or coffee? There's sherry and Scotch, but I thought, before lunch, you know.'

'Coffee would be fine.' She followed Elissa into the kitchen. 'Is it true that you haven't seen Craig since June – a year ago June?'

'True. Haven't seen him or heard from him.' She ran water into the percolator, gazing out the window until it ran over, splashing her dress. 'Damn, damn, damn. I guess I'm a bit nervous.' Carefully, she plugged in the pot. 'Ross is in love with you.'

'Did he tell you that?'

'No, but it's all over him, like measles. Well, prettier than measles.' Involuntarily, they smiled at each other. 'It's nice, to see a man in love. I just wondered if you're in love with him.'

'Why?' Katherine asked.

Elissa hesitated, then shrugged. 'No special reason. Do you take cream? Or sugar?'

'Just black, thank you.' She watched as Elissa put mugs on a tray, arranged doughnuts on a plate, dropped one, made an exasperated sound and threw it away. 'Let me help,' Katherine said. Gently she took the package from Elissa's hand and put out the rest of doughnuts. 'Where shall we sit?'

515

'In the living-room; there isn't anywhere else. Craig wanted to build a nook off the kitchen – a breakfast room, you know – he'd drawn the plans for it, but then . . . he didn't come back.'

Katherine heard the tears behind the simple words, and she knew that Elissa still missed Craig, still longed for him and waited for him. And that was why she had asked if Katherine was in love with Ross; she wanted to know if Craig would be free when he came back. 'I'll carry the tray,' Katherine said, and this time she led the way to the living-room. There were things she wanted to know, too.

'Did Craig really steal from his company?' she asked bluntly as they sat down.

Surprised, Elissa said, 'You don't know?'

'Only what his partner told me.'

Elissa considered it. 'I don't think he did.'

'But you don't know.'

'He didn't tell me. He told me most everything else. But I don't believe he's a thief. I don't think he took a damn thing.'

You don't want to feel responsible for his needing money, Katherine thought, remembering what Ross had said. 'Then why did he disappear?' she asked.

Elissa looked at her directly. 'I guess you ought to be able to answer that better than me.'

'I didn't know who he really was. I didn't know about you. How could I know why he left?'

'You must have known something. If I lived with a man for ten years I'd sure know a hell of a lot about him.'

Yes, you would. And I didn't.

The questions that had haunted Katherine before, rushed back with Elissa's words. Why hadn't she known more? Why hadn't she asked questions about Craig's past, and their house, their bills, their finances? Why hadn't she forced herself into his silences?

Maybe because I didn't really want to. Or didn't want to

enough. Maybe it was more pleasant not knowing. Not worrying. Like a little girl.

The silence was stretching out. 'Tell me about Craig,' Katherine said. 'You know him better than I do.'

'That's true,' Elissa responded frankly. 'He was pretty relaxed and easy around here. Like somebody who's been locked into a suit and a tie all day, very proper, and then he comes home and puts on an old T-shirt and jeans – and kind of slurps his soup?'

'Locked in,' Katherine echoed.

'Well, it was more like he felt *burdened*. He said you needed somebody to look up to, who'd protect you from things that were ugly or scary, and he couldn't always do that. Though I must say you look a lot more able to take care of yourself than he made you out. I might have guessed he was exaggerating. Anyway, he said when you two met, you were so innocent all you wanted was love. You didn't ask how much money he made or anything about his future – or the past either, for that matter; you didn't ask a lot of questions about his so-called orphan childhood; you were just happy to love him and have him love you. He was pretty impressed with that except he thought it made you awfully vulnerable. But it was a powerful force on him; it was why you were the only woman he was in love with.'

She was so matter-of-fact that Katherine was embarrassed. 'He didn't love me enough to be honest with me.'

'He loved you too much to be honest with you. Can I ask you something?'

'Of course.'

'Were you a virgin when you met him?'

'Yes.'

'Well that explains part of it. He always talked about you as if you were a virgin in everything – not just sex, but getting along in the world.'

517

'But that's nonsense,' Katherine said. 'I'd been to college – I had a job; I had friends . . .'

'Not to hear him tell it. He kept saying all the things he'd taught you, the kind of life he gave you. I had this crazy idea that he sort of thought of you like his sister – you know, kind of frozen at her age? So, he had to believe he was first in everything, I guess: not just your bed. But then he was always afraid he'd make a mistake and you'd be disappointed in him and stop loving him.'

'A mistake in what?'

'How he behaved. Acting like his family, showing his anger.'

'But he wasn't an angry person. The times he did get angry, he usually controlled it and it passed.'

'It didn't pass. It dug in deeper. He said all the men in his family were like that. He remembered his grandfather, Hugh, roaring at him about something real silly, like picture post-cards, I think, and then there was Derek – the all-time champion of anger. And Craig was like them but at the same time he was afraid of angry people. Scared to death of Hugh and Derek, and Derek's father – Curt – and even himself. He was scared of being angry.'

Restlessly, Elissa stood and moved about the room. 'Do you know, I could tell you the story of every Hayward all the way back to Hugh's grandfather? I know every piece of jewellery Hugh bought Victoria; I know the colour of the dress Jennifer wore when she graduated high school; I know . . . oh, damn, I'm sorry . . . I didn't mean to hurt you.'

'It's all right. I was just thinking – he told you the things he missed, the people he loved and couldn't forget. After fifteen years.'

'He didn't love all of them, you know, and they didn't all love each other. He told me about Derek's girls and how Jennifer cried –'

518

'Derek's girls? Jennifer?'

'That was the last time they were in Menton. They had their own apartment, sort of, with bedrooms around a kind of play-room, and there was a garden with a wall, and a door in the wall, and Derek would sneak girls into his bedroom. Didn't Ross tell you? He knew about it. Jennifer didn't, until one night she found out and ran into the garden, sobbing, and no one could get her to stop, not even Craig. And the next day, when they went home, she left behind a necklace Derek had bought her in Monte Carlo. She didn't like it anyway, Craig said; it was black. Death around her neck, Jennifer called it. So she left it there. Derek was furious – he'd paid a lot for it – but *he* wouldn't take it home, so it stayed there. That was only about a week before she died. Scary, isn't it?'

Katherine recalled a black necklace, coiled in a jewellery box in the playroom of the villa. Everything is a circle, she thought, coming around to its beginning. And when Craig comes back, the circle will be complete.

Elissa talked on, quoting Craig, showing Katherine a shelf of his wood carvings in her bedroom, and his plans for the breakfast room. She made lunch, still talking about Craig; they ate in the living-room, talking about Craig, and after lunch Elissa brought out a photo album of the two of them. They had made a marriage, Katherine realised, and in the small, cluttered room, listening to the love in Elissa's voice, she understood why Craig had not been able to give it up.

Finally, she said, 'I have to leave soon; my plane is at five. But I want to ask you something.' She paused. 'I'm grateful for everything you've told me, and I believe you when you say you haven't seen Craig, but I think you must have heard from him. I think he needed you too much to cut himself off – the way he did me.'

Elissa's eyes filled with tears. 'Thank you for saying that. I thought you'd hate me and think I was trying to ruin your marriage; I didn't think you'd understand. But I needed him, too, you know. I still need him – he was my friend and my son and my brother and my lover and my husband – I'm sorry, but he was – all the same time and I miss him . . . oh, hell and damnation.' She wiped her eyes. 'Anyway, I swear I haven't heard from him. I kept thinking I would; there'd been times before when a few weeks would go by and he couldn't get here, so I kept thinking he'd show up and everything would be back to where it was – but it never happened. I'm still waiting. Silly, maybe, but that's how I am. Are you?'

'Am I what?'

'Still waiting.'

'Of course.'

'To live with him?'

'I don't know. I don't think we can live together again.'

'But you're still waiting. Even though you haven't heard anything, either.'

'Well, yes we did –' Katherine stopped at the look on Elissa's face. She was terrified. She had talked on and on, filling the hours, giving Katherine no chance to say she had heard from Craig. And now, seeing that terrified look, Katherine couldn't bring herself to tell Elissa that Craig had called Ross, wanting his wife back. 'He sent me roses,' she said. 'On my birthday.'

Elissa's face cleared. 'White ones, I'll bet. Craig told me you liked white roses.'

'Did he?' Katherine said dryly. 'Didn't he ever talk about anything but his family – his two families?'

'He talked a lot about Eskimos. Didn't he talk to you about them? He loved the kind of life they led: harsh, uncomplicated, close-knit. That was how he saw it. He and Hank used to talk about Eskimos all the time.'

'Hank?'

'Hank Aylmer. He travels to Eskimo villages in Alaska and

Canada and buys soapstone sculptures to sell in the States. You met him; Craig told me you did.'

Katherine stared at her. 'I'd forgotten,' she said slowly. Hank Aylmer. A long time ago, Craig had said Hank Aylmer had invited them to go with him on a buying trip to Eskimo villages. Scattered all over, he'd said; a real sightseeing vacation. Scattered all over. Hank Aylmer travelling from village to village, from one province to another – *mailing money to Craig's family from a different post office every month*. 'Where is he?' she asked. 'Hank. Where is he?'

'Home, last I heard,' Elissa replied. 'But he doesn't know anything about Craig; I've asked him.'

'Home? Where?'

'Calgary,' said Elissa. 'The other side of town. Do you want to call him?'

'Yes!' Excitement was stirring in Katherine. Of course Hank knew where Craig was. If he hadn't told Elissa, it was because Craig had asked him not to. But he would tell Katherine; he would tell Craig's wife. 'If I can use your phone . . .'

'Here's his number. I'll be in the kitchen if you need me.'

'Thank you,' Katherine said, and dialled, tightening her grip on the receiver when he answered.

'Hank Aylmer here.'

'This is Katherine Fraser, Hank. We met a few years ago, if you remember. My husband introduced us. Craig Fraser.'

There was no response.

'Hank?'

'Right here. Katherine Fraser, did you say?'

'Hank, don't pretend with me. You remember the name and tribe of every Eskimo from Alaska to Hudson Bay; you remember me, too.'

A rumbling laugh came over the wires. 'Right, then, I do. And your two little ones – Jennifer and Todd, right? – how are they?'

'Fine. They'd like to see their father.'

'Well, now. Well, now. Sometimes we lose track of friends, Katherine. I haven't seen Craig for an age.'

'Where is he, Hank?'

'Can't say. I know he left Vancouver some time back –'

'Fifteen months ago.'

'Right, then, it was that long ago. But I can't say where he is now, you know. I don't keep track of him.'

'You see him every month. He gives you money and you mail it to me, always from a different town.'

'Well, now, that's . . . very imaginative. I wish I could help you, Katherine, but I can't.'

'Hank, I want to see him. I want to talk to him. Would you tell him that?'

'Katherine, you're jumping to all sorts of conclusions.'

'All right, don't answer. Just listen. Tell him I got the roses he sent for my birthday; thank him for me. Tell him I want him to come to San Francisco. He knows where I live; tell him I'm waiting for him. Are you listening?'

'Right, but you mustn't get your hopes up, Katherine.'

'Just listen. Tell him the three of us are waiting. Just the three of us. Remember that, Hank; it's very important. Tell him it's just me and the children. No one else.'

'You mean you're not bedded down with anybody, is that it?'

She sighed. 'That's it. You'll tell him?'

'I didn't say that. I was just clarifying what you said.'

'And I want him to come to San Francisco! Will you tell him that? Please, Hank; if he won't tell me how to come to him, he'll have to come to me.'

'Right.'

'You'll tell him that?'

'If I see him, I'll tell him.'

'When?'

'Katherine, if I see him, I'll give him all your messages. That I promise. More than that I cannot do. Right?'

'Right,' Katherine said.

'Goodbye, then, and give my regards to those fine children.'

'I will.' She hung up the telephone, staring into space.

Elissa came to the doorway. 'He didn't know anything?'

'He wouldn't say. I left a message with him.'

'For Craig to call you?'

'For him to come to San Francisco. I have to see him.'

Elissa reached out her hand. 'If he shows up . . . and you decide not to get together again . . .'

'I'll tell him you're waiting.' They looked at each other for a long moment.

'I wish we could be friends,' Elissa said.

Katherine gave a small smile. 'I think we are, don't you?' Moving swiftly across the room, she laid her cheek briefly against Elissa's, then turned and went to the front door. 'Thank you,' she said, and later, flying home, she silently thanked Elissa again – for making her acquainted, after ten years of marriage, with her own husband.

Once again the days and evenings were spent at her worktable. More confident with each piece, Katherine worked more quickly than ever before, and when an idea came to her and she began to sketch it, she knew immediately whether it belonged with the jewellery she was selling now, or whether it was so striking and distinctive that it had to be put aside in a separate folder, kept on a shelf above her table, marked 'Henri Flambeau.'

'I'll never sell to the top people here,' she told Victoria at dinner a week after she had seen Elissa. 'They won't take a chance on me. And the small stores I'm selling to now won't buy my so-called "far-out" designs. So when I have enough of them, I'll see what I can do in Paris.'

'You don't need Paris,' Victoria said tartly. 'I intended Henri to offer you a second country; your first reputation should be made here.'

'Not with Herman Mettler talking about me.'

'He won't do it forever; he's too indolent and self-centred to pay attention to anyone else for very long.'

'But I haven't got forever; I'm barely making enough money now, and I promised Jennifer and Todd we'd look for a larger apartment. And I'd like to take a trip, just the three of us, over Thanksgiving.'

'To avoid a family dinner,' Victoria declared. 'Why are you so foolish? Why can't you and Ross be together while you resolve your dilemma?'

'We're not ready,' Katherine said.

'Nonsense! Love isn't like a roast turkey that is or is not ready. It simply *is*, and you must let it guide you. Why don't I call Ross now? He can join us for dessert.'

'No,' Katherine said. But she was smiling, thinking someday she'd tell Ross that Victoria had compared them to roast turkey.

There was no word from Craig, nor from Hank Aylmer. Ross did not call and she did not call him. Reluctantly, Victoria honoured her request and did not invite them to dinner on the same nights, so there was no place they might run into each other. Without him, Katherine's days seemed choppy: everything that happened was cut short because it could not be shared with him – a newspaper item, one of Todd's wild fantasies, a special piece of jewellery. She would feel a surge of longing, and then frustration over his allowing Craig to slip away, and then impatience because Craig had not called – until the space around her worktable was crowded with feelings and images and voices, clamouring to be heard.

But all the time, her hands were steady, adding to her collection of jewellery, boxed, priced, and lined up on a shelf. As an experiment, she had made two belt buckles of randomly shaped silver cut out in delicate patterns like lace and scattered petals. To display them, she bought a strip of dark blue velvet and another of wine-coloured silk and made two wide belts by gathering the ends into the two halves of her buckles. She wore one of them – for good luck, she told herself – the day she went to the bank, to talk about her loan.

She had pushed it out of her mind, but when September was almost gone and she added up her bills, and what she thought she could get for her new jewellery, the numbers did not balance. They hardly ever do, she reflected wryly. But if I extend my loan for twelve months, the payments will be smaller. Then we can go somewhere at Thanksgiving.

At the bank, she filled out the application and gave it to a loan officer, waiting for more of the probing personal questions she had answered when she first applied for the loan. But this time it was different. The officer scanned the application, typed rapidly on his computer keyboard and in a few seconds read aloud her name and address from the screen. 'Loan made in June,' he went on. 'Payments made on time in July, August and September. And the loan recently guaranteed . . .' He read silently. 'Well, Mrs Fraser, I see no problem: we'll begin with October fourth, next Monday, for twelve months. We'll have a new agreement for you to sign in a few minutes; the computer does it, you know; wonders of technology, aren't they?' He turned back to the terminal and began typing.

'Just a minute,' Katherine said. 'I think there's a mistake. No one guaranteed this loan; that's why I brought the contracts I have with three jewellery stores –'

'Guaranteed by Ross Hayward, according to our records, Mrs Fraser; on September 25th. Just three days ago, in fact. So of course, there is no impediment to the extension.' He returned to his typing.

Katherine opened her mouth, then closed it. Ross knew she

would refuse money, so he found another way to help her. Clever, she thought; no one with any sense would reject a guarantee on a loan.

As soon as she was home, she called him at his office. 'I was just at the bank,' she said, rushing through her words to get past the jolt of longing she felt at the sound of his voice, and his surprise and delight when he heard hers. 'I found out you'd guaranteed my loan. It was wonderful of you. Thank you.'

'You're welcome,' he replied. 'How are you? Victoria says you're working very hard.'

'I am. That's what she tells me about you.'

'Then she's right both times. Have you sold to any new stores?'

'No; I'm still working on the collection for Henri. Are the engineers working on the Macklin Building?'

'They had to put it off for two or three weeks.'

'Oh. That's too bad.' There was a silence. 'I went to Calgary,' Katherine said abruptly. 'I spent the day with Elissa.'

'Did you! That must have been difficult.'

'It was easier than I expected. She's a very easy person to be with. And she told me so many things I never knew . . .'

'You liked her?'

'Yes. And I understood why Craig went to her. She loves him so, and she's still waiting –'

'Even after you told her about Craig's call?'

'I didn't tell her,' Katherine said ruefully. 'I couldn't; it would have made her so unhappy, and it wouldn't change anything for her, at least not now, before Craig and I . . . have had a chance . . .' Her voice faltered. 'To talk.'

There was a long silence as they both recalled her anger at Ross for not telling her about Elissa. 'Well,' Ross mused aloud. 'That sounds like something I once said.'

'I should have told her,' Katherine said faintly.

'Probably. But you cared about her feelings. She's lucky to have such a friend.'

Don't rub it in, Katherine told him silently. After a moment she said, 'I guess I'd like to think about that.'

'Good.' His voice was warm.

'I wanted to tell you something else. I talked to a friend of Craig's, the man who's been mailing the money each month –'

'He said he had?'

'No. But he didn't deny it, either. I'm sure he's in touch with Craig and I left a message, asking Craig to come here.'

'To come back to you?'

'I said I had to talk to him. I'd hoped to hear from him by now but it may take Hank a while to reach him. If he does. But I think he'll be here soon.'

'Do you know what you'll say to him?'

'I'm thinking about it.'

'Good,' he said once more.

'Ross, I haven't told Victoria and Tobias about Elissa.'

'Of course not.'

Katherine heard the door open; Jennifer and Todd, home from school. 'I'd better go,' she said. 'Thank you again. I'm grateful for your help.'

'I was glad to do it. Take care of yourself, Katherine.'

Hanging up, she turned to see two grouchy faces. 'What's wrong with you?' she asked.

'Nothing,' said Todd, and went to the refrigerator.

'Jennifer?' Katherine asked.

'They announced the Father's Dinner today; it's in two weeks.'

'Father's Dinner?'

Todd slammed the refrigerator door. 'Some dumb teacher thought it up; they didn't have it last year. You're supposed to bring your father and there's this big dinner in the gym and then some of the fathers and their kids put on a show.'

'It's to honour fathers,' Jennifer added. 'Whatever that means.'

'We thought we'd borrow Ross,' said Todd off-handedly as he cut a chunk of cheese. 'But he hasn't been around lately, has he?'

'No,' answered Katherine. 'Do you want crackers with that?'

'Sure. Where is he?'

'Where he always is. He's pretty busy . . .'

'Yeh.'

Katherine took down a new box of crackers and handed it to Todd. 'Sometimes people stop seeing each other for a while. They're still friends; it's just that they aren't together all the time.'

'Or ever,' Jennifer said. 'Did you have a fight?'

'We had a disagreement. And then we decided we were . . . getting in each other's way when we needed to think about some important things.'

'Like what?' Todd asked.

'Like whether we should be together so much when I'm waiting for your Dad to come back.'

Todd screwed up his eyes, then blurted, 'Do you love Ross more than Dad?'

Katherine's throat tightened. I should have expected that, she thought. 'I love them in different ways,' she said at last. 'And I love you in another way. And Victoria and Tobias in another –'

'Then why can't you be with Ross while you're thinking about waiting for Dad?'

'Because I get distracted,' Katherine said a little frantically. 'It's hard to explain . . .'

Todd shook his head glumly. 'It's a crock.' He tilted his head at Katherine. 'How come you can't find a man who'll stay with you?'

'Todd!' cried Jennifer. 'That's mean!'

'It sure is,' Katherine said, feeling bruised. How much do you excuse, she wondered, because they're young and bewildered and don't have much control over their lives? Not much. I get bewildered, too, and I didn't have much control when Craig decided to leave. 'It was a low blow and I think I deserve an apology.'

Todd scowled. 'Well, I'm sorry. It was just that I was wishing we had a father.'

'You're not the only one,' said Katherine.

'How about Uncle Tobias?' Jennifer giggled. 'We could borrow him.'

'I think you'd have a wonderful time,' Katherine replied.

'Seriously?'

'Seriously. He's never been a father; it would be a new experience for him.'

'I want him!' Todd shouted. 'He's better than Ross!' He glanced at Katherine's expressionless face. 'I mean, nobody else will have a father *anything* like him.'

'Can I call him?' Jennifer asked.

'Why not?' said Katherine. 'And then I'd like some help in the kitchen. We're having guests for dinner.'

'How will they taste?' Todd asked, trying to make Katherine smile.

She did, and gave him a hug. 'Tough but sweet. It's Leslie and Claude.'

They laughed. And as Jennifer went to the telephone, and Todd finished the cheese and crackers, Katherine gave a small, private sigh. Another crisis bypassed – at least for a time.

Jennifer stood beside Claude, waiting, while he opened the bottle of Spanish sherry he had brought and filled three glasses. He looked at her grave face. 'Would you and Todd like some?'

'No thank you. I hope it doesn't hurt your feelings, but we think it tastes awful.'

He smiled. 'No hurt feelings. Did you want to ask me something?'

'Todd and I would like to borrow you to be our father, just for one night.'

A stunned look settled on Claude's face. Across the room, Katherine looked puzzled; Leslie alert and curious. 'Was this planned with someone?' Claude asked.

'Just us,' Jennifer said. 'We need a father for the Father's Dinner at school, and our own father is gone, and we can't ask Ross because he and Mother get in each other's way when they think about important things so he doesn't come around anymore, and I did ask Uncle Tobias but he has to be at an Alumni dinner that night. And you're here.'

'So I am,' Claude agreed. Jennifer and Todd stood side by side watching him. 'I'd be honoured to be your father. But I've never been one and I'm not sure I can do it in a way that will please you.'

'Just stay around for a while,' muttered Todd.

'Longer than one evening?' Claude asked.

'No,' said Jennifer. 'That will do. Two weeks from tomorrow – that's a Wednesday night, is that all right?' He nodded. 'Could you be here at five-thirty? Then we could walk to school together. We should be finished by eight o'clock, so if you have more important things to do that night you can still do them.'

'That will be the most important thing I have to do that night,' said Claude. 'Am I supposed to perform? Sing or dance?'

'Do you sing or dance ordinarily?' asked Jennifer.

'No. Definitely no.'

'Then you don't have to. Just be with us.'

'It will be a pleasure. Now, if you'll excuse me—' He

carried the tray of sherry glasses to Katherine and Leslie, who had been whispering and now watched him with small soft smiles.

'You're amazing,' Leslie murmured as he sat beside her on the couch. 'Where did you learn to talk to children?'

'I don't talk to children. I talk to people. Leslie, did you and Katherine plan that?'

'Damn it, of course not. You know I'm not that devious.'

'What does that mean?' Katherine asked.

Leslie held her glass by its stem. 'Katherine, will you drink to our momentous decision to marry?'

A smile lit Katherine's face. 'How wonderful! Of course I will. To all the joys you'll have together.' After they drank, she said, 'But I still don't understand –'

'You see, we've been having a dialogue. I want a child. Claude, being fifty, doesn't think –'

'Fifty-one.'

'Almost fifty-one, doesn't think he is at an optimum age to become a father. So when we walk in your front door and almost immediately he is asked to be a father, even for one night, he is naturally, or unnaturally, suspicious. I, on the other hand, think it's wonderful. Dress rehearsal.'

'What's wrong with fifty-one?' Katherine asked Claude.

'I'm set in my ways, I've never had to take infants into consideration when I schedule my days and nights, I've long since forgotten what the anxieties of childhood are like, and I'll be sixty-one when this child wants to play baseball. What kind of a father is that?'

'A little slow at running bases,' Katherine said. 'But if you learn how to throw a fast one – and lawyers often do, don't they? – the rest won't matter.' Claude chuckled. 'What's more,' she went on, 'you just said you don't talk to children; you talk to people. If you want to know about children's anxieties just think about people's anxieties; they aren't much different.'

'Faultless reasoning,' he said admiringly. 'Do you think Leslie will be happy as a homebody?'

Katherine looked at her. 'You'd give up your job?'

'How do I know?' Leslie asked crossly. 'Claude thinks I can be president of Heath's if I fight for it. Maybe I don't want to fight. Or maybe I do, but not right now. Maybe I want to be domestic for a while. Maybe I'll decide to do both, like a four-armed mythological wizard. Do I have to decide this very minute?'

'No,' Claude said. 'And I'm sorry if I was pushing.' He put his hand on the back of Leslie's head, caressing her red curls and the nape of her neck. 'I adore this woman,' he told Katherine. 'I want to give her vacations in Italy and moonlight cruises in Scandinavia and balloon flights over the Himalayas, but all she wants, at least right now, is a child. I have a suspicion she really wants two, but so far I've managed to refrain from asking. Well dear Leslie, I think we should have a child and see how we like it. If things don't work out, we'll give him or her to Jennifer and Todd.'

'You'll what?' cried Jennifer from across the room.

Leslie kissed him. 'I'm marrying a clown. Things will work out. We can always come to Katherine for words of wisdom.'

Katherine jumped up. 'I forgot about the wild rice,' she said and went to the kitchen.

Leslie followed. 'What's wrong?'

'Nothing.' She turned down the flame a fraction. 'You two looked so happy. And settled.'

'And you're not. What happened with Ross? Can't I go to New York for a few days without you getting into trouble?'

Katherine laughed slightly. 'We decided to stay away from each other for now. Jennifer and Todd act like it was a divorce.'

'They're fond of Ross.'

'I know. He's very good with them.'

'So what are you going to do about him?'

'Nothing. Until I do something about Craig.'

'Like divorce him?'

'Maybe.'

'The alternative is to go back to him.'

'I know.'

'Listen, lady, you wouldn't do that.'

'I don't think so.'

'What do you *want*, Katherine?'

'I think I want Ross. I'm still trying to work it out; I don't understand it all, yet. I can't even talk about it, Leslie. Let's talk about something else.'

Leslie paused. 'OK.' Something cheerful, she thought. 'I was going to ask you anyway. Where did you get that belt? Did you make it?'

Katherine looked at her waist. 'Yes. I'd forgotten I had it on. I wore it for good luck.'

'Did it work?'

'Yes.'

'Can you make me one?'

'You mean for good luck?'

'I mean because it's sensational and I want one.'

'I'll give you one now. Burgundy silk or blue velvet, whichever you want; you can put in any fabric, to change the look.'

'How many do you have?'

'Two.'

'How fast can you make them?'

'I don't know. I didn't keep track. Why?'

'Because I want to sell them at Heath's. Can you make me a dozen?'

'I can make as many as you want. You really think you can sell them?'

'Damn right; in fine jewellery or the Empire Room. I might even design my wedding dress around one.'

533

'When?' Katherine asked. 'Leslie, I'm sorry; I got side-tracked and never asked when it would be.'

'You would have been told; you're part of it. Christmas, we think. By then, you'll have your problems solved and you and Ross can be best man and best lady. Will you?'

Katherine lit the candles on the table and turned down the lights. 'I'd love to be part of your wedding. I can't speak for Ross. Can I ask a favour?'

'Name it.'

'I'd like to make your wedding rings.'

'That's a favour? I was going to beg you on bended knee to fit us into your schedule! Why is it a favour?'

'Because I can pretend,' Katherine said. 'I always do, when I make my best pieces; I pretend I'll be the one who wears them, for some special event.'

'Then I have a suggestion.' Leslie put her arm around Katherine. 'Make two sets. You can pretend twice as hard, and you'll have an extra pair – in case a special event should come along.'

Katherine laughed. 'I just might. Why not? Now let's get the children and their borrowed father to the table. We'll have a family dinner.'

Chapter 19

On Friday, the first of October, at 9:34 in the morning, an earthquake sent shock waves rumbling across San Francisco and the surrounding area. Centred beneath the bay and registering 4.7 on the Richter scale, it was not considered severe, especially by those who remembered a more damaging one fifteen years earlier, but it was strong enough to shift furniture, knock groceries off shelves, cause doors to open and shut, and slosh coffee out of thousands of cups. In a warehouse at BayBridge Plaza, Ross was perched on a sawhorse, going over blueprints with the construction manager, when he felt the shock. The sawhorse jolted beneath him and he fell. 'Ross!' someone yelled. 'Look out!' Instinctively he rolled to the side as a stack of lumber toppled and crashed, grazing his arm, covering him with a cloud of dust.

For ten seconds the ground shook. Buildings creaked and a brown haze of plaster dust and wood shavings filled the air.

Then walkie-talkies began to chatter as workers reported to each other from one end of the construction site to the other. 'OK in Number One . . .' 'Pile of bricks down in Number Two –' 'Bag of Oreo cookies crushed in Number Ten –' Ross chuckled as he stood and brushed himself off; then he froze. 'Couple of guys hurt in the Macklin Building! Get some help over here!'

He dashed through the building, jumping over piles of lumber, bypassing the construction elevator to take the stairs. Outside, the dusty haze blurred buildings and equipment and workers hunting for tools that had fallen and bounced away amid scattered lumber and bricks. Ross ran past them to the Macklin Building, where a cluster of workmen stood just inside the door, arguing loudly among themselves. The floor was littered with debris below a gaping hole in a corner of the ceiling. 'Let me through,' Ross ordered, shoving the men aside.

'Who the hell do you think you are?' one of them demanded.

'I own the building; now stop that damned shouting and somebody tell me what happened.'

'Ceiling fell,' a voice said caustically. 'Couple of guys underneath got hit.'

A man was lying on the floor. Ross knelt beside him. His eyes were open; so was his mouth. 'Shit,' he muttered. 'The fucking ceiling . . . '

'He ain't the worst,' someone said. 'It's Bud –'

Ross followed his pointing finger and saw a pile of shattered concrete, with a man's leg jutting from it. Christ, he thought. Not dead; please God, not dead. 'Has he moved?'

The men nodded. 'We pulled some of the shit off, but we can't get at him. But he moved and he said something . . .'

'He did not!' a voice yelled. 'He ain't said a –'

'Has somebody called the fire department?' Ross demanded.

'Yeh, sure,' a heavy-set man said. They heard the wail of a siren. 'Fast work,' he joked nervously. He pulled a flask from his back pocket and knelt beside Ross. 'Medicine for my friend,' he said.

The man had pulled himself partway up and sat slumped against the wall. He saw the flask and reached for it. He was all right, Ross thought. But the other man's leg had not moved.

Another, closer siren was heard; the undulating sound pierced through the building, then stopped as if cut with a knife. Two firetrucks pulled up, then an ambulance. In a few minutes the space was crowded with firemen and paramedics. 'Cutters!' one called and they began cutting through the twisted steel bars that had reinforced the concrete ceiling.

'A hoist, damn it, you can't lift that concrete!'

'You want a rope?'

'Damn right I want a rope! Over that beam –'

'Have to get something under the concrete to lift it –'

'A sling.'

'Right; and the hooks in the truck . . .'

'Tie the fucking rope to the hooks! You think we got all day?'

Ross and the workmen slid the makeshift sling beneath the largest slab of concrete as the firemen made a hoist with a block and tackle attached to an overhead beam. 'Everybody keep that slab from swinging sideways when we pull the rope,' the fire chief ordered. 'Got that?'

'Do it,' Ross said, gritting his teeth, and with the workmen he strained to steady the slab as it stirred and began to move.

'Little more! Little more!' grunted the fire chief. He and his men pulled on the hoist. 'More! Keep it up –!' And slowly the slab rose a few inches above the still form lying beneath. 'Grab him!' yelled the chief, as Ross and one of the workers already were shoving aside small pieces of concrete and then easing the man from beneath the hanging slab.

'OK,' Ross gasped and the slab crashed back into place as the hoist was released. Two paramedics laid the limp figure on a stretcher and as they inserted an intravenous tube into the vein on one of his hands Ross grabbed the other to find a pulse. He found it, strong and steady, and closed his eyes in relief counting for a full minute. 'OK,' he said again, and stood up. 'No, wait a minute.' He turned to the workman with the flask. 'How come you were in here? All the work in this building had been stopped.'

'Came to get some wire we'd left.' The man rubbed his head. 'Just for a minute. That's when it hit.'

Just for a minute, Ross thought. So much for precautions. He took a note pad from the inside pocket of his jacket. 'Can you give me that man's name and address? And phone number; his family has to be notified.'

'Sure. He all right?'

'Looks like,' said one of the paramedics. He held the intravenous flask while the other strapped the man to the stretcher. 'Small pieces kept the big one from crushing him. Lucky guy,' he added as they lifted the stretcher and carried it to the fire department ambulance.

Ross squatted beside the other workman. 'Names and addresses,' he said. 'For both of you.'

'My cousin's a lawyer,' the workman said. 'I gotta call him.'

'Names,' Ross said again, and he was writing them as the construction manager came. Ross gave him the paper. 'Greg, would you make this call?'

'Right.' He stood there, looking with Ross at the gaping hole in the ceiling. 'If somebody fucked up –' he muttered.

'Is that what you think?'

'Tell you the truth: I don't know. I thought your engineer did an OK design for the temporary support beams – he said a herd of elephants could do a polka on it and tell you the truth:

I thought so, too. Course we weren't figuring on a quake, but still and all, I wouldn't of thought that little bit of shaking would make this much mess. Shit, now we'll have lawyers all over the place.'

'Probably,' Ross said. 'How about making that call?'

'Sure. Be right back.'

Ross stood amid the debris. His throat was dry. He'd thought he could repair the building and keep its history a secret, but now it would all come out. Because he knew there was too much damage for a minor earthquake: it had to be more. It had to be what he had worried about from the moment he read the engineer's report: some of the support columns had settled just enough to cause the ceiling to break apart. And because the temporary supports weren't designed to hold the entire weight of the ceiling, when it pulled away from the columns, they collapsed and a chunk of the ceiling came crashing down.

And two workmen were in the way.

If they sued BayBridge, there would be an investigation. One earthquake, one investigation, and out into the open would come a sixteen-year cover-up by his father and brother of illegally changing specifications and bribing an inspector – and a two-month cover-up by Ross Hayward after he had the building inspected in July and could no longer say he only suspected problems.

The Hayward Corporation could survive it; Ross Hayward Associates might not. If he had to pay damages to those two workmen he could be wiped out. And Victoria would be forced to watch a dream splinter in scandal.

Unless they could settle out of court.

With the force of a physical pain, Ross wanted Katherine beside him. I wouldn't keep it from her, he thought; I'd share it; I'd ask for her help. I'll have to tell her that.

Except that he wasn't telling her anything these days. He

was waiting for her to make up her mind about her husband.

So this one he'd have to handle by himself And in fact, the solution was really very simple. All it took was money.

Katherine had asked if Derek was going to help pay for the repair of the footings. Ross had said no. But now everything had changed. Now, after sixteen years, Derek and their father were going to share the responsibility for the Macklin Building.

He went outside, to see if any other buildings had been damaged. And it was then that television came to BayBridge.

All that hectic Friday reporters raced about the bay area, gathering earthquake stories for the evening news and a later special report. 'Thank God it was in the morning,' they told each other. 'Nothing worse than late-afternoon disasters; no time to get them on the air.'

By the time Ross got back to the Macklin Building, Greg Thorpe, the construction manager, was looking with loathing at two cameras and the microphones thrust in his face. He waved in relief. 'Ross Hayward,' he told the reporters. 'Architect for BayBridge, and he owns the Macklin Building.'

They switched to Ross: reporters from two different television stations, flanked by bored men in shirtsleeves holding mini-cameras on their shoulders. Shooting questions, the reporters kept an eye on their watches; they had a quota of earthquake stories and the Macklin Building wasn't really news: no one had died. They wouldn't even have come if BayBridge weren't so important.

'The beams,' one of them began. 'They were temporary?'

'While we cut the atrium,' Ross said. 'We had to –'

'Yes, sir, what I meant was, were they safe?'

'Of course.' Quickly, without letting them interrupt, he described the shoring up of the ceiling. 'I wouldn't have allowed work to start in there if I didn't think it was safe. No one should allow workmen in a building that isn't secure.'

'You're defending your engineer, then, and saying it was only the earthquake, is that right?'

'We'll be reviewing the plans, but I have no doubt the earthquake caused the damage.'

'Thank you, sir. You don't mind if we do a few interior shots –?'

Ross saw the televised story, cut to thirty seconds, while sitting in Victoria's library. 'Today's earthquake also caused injuries to two workmen in the Macklin Building,' the reporter said. 'Part of the BayBridge Plaza development south of Market.'

The camera panned across the BayBridge site to the Macklin Building, then moved inside, pausing at the hole in the ceiling and the debris on the floor. Greg Thorpe appeared glumly on the screen. 'We followed the plans on the temporary beams,' he said. 'Though I think at the time I would have made them stronger.'

Ross shot up in his chair. 'Liar,' he said.

'But that wasn't up to me,' Thorpe added. 'It was the engineer on Mr Hayward's staff.'

'Ross Hayward Associates,' the reporter's voice said as Ross appeared on the screen, 'are architects for BayBridge Plaza and the renovation of the Macklin Building.'

Watching himself, Ross thought he looked dishevelled and faintly guilty. 'No one should allow workmen in a building that isn't secure,' he said. 'We'll be reviewing the plans –'

The reporter replaced him on the screen. 'The Department of Inspectional Services had no immediate comment. In other earthquake news –'

'Son of a bitch!' Ross exploded as Tobias snapped off the set. 'That wasn't what I meant and he knew it.'

'Have some more Scotch,' said Tobias. 'You could use it.'

'I could use a new construction manager. If I carry any

541

weight around there, the contractor's going to fire Greg tomorrow morning. But Scotch will do for now. Thanks.'

'Ross,' Victoria said anxiously. 'You're not really worried about this, are you? It will be forgotten in all the other earthquake news. There were far worse incidents than yours.'

Ross kissed Victoria's cheek. 'I'm concerned about it, but you shouldn't be. I'll take care of it. I won't stay for dinner, though; I'm going back to the office for a while.'

'Mr Hayward,' the butler said from the doorway. 'There's a telephone call for you.'

Ross thought of reporters. 'I'm not here.'

'It's Mrs Fraser,' said the butler.

'Take it in here,' Victoria said quickly. 'We'll be in the dining room.'

Ross grabbed the telephone. 'I saw the television report,' Katherine said. 'I was worried about you. I called your house, and your office . . . Why didn't anyone mention the work on the footings?'

'It hasn't started.' Listening to her low voice, he wanted her so desperately his words seemed to stumble. 'They'd rescheduled it for next week.'

'Then it might not come up at all. But – if people are looking for reasons, do you have to say your engineer was at fault so no one looks any further and maybe gets to the footings?'

She'd seen it all, Ross thought; the whole of his dilemma. Protect Victoria and the company by keeping the footings out of the story; or point to them to get his own company off the hook for the design of the temporary beams. 'We may be able to blame the earthquake by itself. Especially since there was damage in the whole area.'

'The reporter made you seem responsible.'

'He was looking for a good story and he distorted what I said. Victoria thinks it's too small a disaster to be remembered. She may be right.'

542

'But she doesn't know about the footings. Ross, is there any way I can help you?'

'You can come to me. Help me get through this mess and whatever it leads to. No one else knows enough about me to understand everything instantly, the way you just did. I need that. I need you. I love you, I want you with me, I want you part of me.'

He heard her long sigh. 'I'd come now. But it would be the way we were before.'

'That's not good enough. I said *part of me*.'

'I haven't heard from Craig or Hank. I'm still waiting.'

'And calling me up.'

'I was worried about you. I can't just turn off my feelings –'

'Katherine, there has to be a time when you make up your mind, in spite of Craig. You can't wait indefinitely.'

'No . . .'

'Well, when is it? When will you say it's been long enough?'

'I don't know. That's one of the things I'm thinking about. Ross, please trust me. I have to do this. If you don't want me to call you anymore, I won't.'

'Of course I want you to call me. I reach for the phone a dozen times a day to call you. Whenever something happens, good or bad, I turn around to tell you – and you're not there.'

'But you don't call.'

'No. Because I'd begin pushing you about timetables and decisions, the way I just did. And then you'd tell me this is something you have to do, the way you just did. And I understand that. Katherine, you're a remarkable woman, you've made a new life with pride and dignity from the rubble your husband left behind; you hold up your head and face whatever comes instead of hiding or running away; you're honest with yourself. I don't want to try to force you to see things as I'd like you to see them. I don't want to stand in your way and prevent you from finishing what you've begun. Does that make sense to you?'

'Yes,' Katherine said softly. 'Do you know, the more you tell me what you want for me, the more I miss you?'

'I hope so,' he said, and she heard the smile in his voice.

When they said goodbye, nothing had changed, Katherine was no closer to coming to him than she had been before, but Ross was still smiling when he stopped in the dining-room to say goodnight to Victoria and Tobias, and her words – *I miss you* – stayed with him as he went back to the office to organise his strategy on the Macklin Building.

'Sit down,' said Derek, gesturing towards a chair while continuing to talk on the telephone. Ross chose one of the couches at the other end of the office, leafing through a copy of *International Architect* while waiting for his brother's conversation to wind to its leisurely end. The office was in glass and chrome and burgundy leather: desk, chairs and conference table at one end, a simulated living-room at the other. Track lighting illuminated blown-up photographs of bridges, shopping malls aqueducts, office buildings and expressways built by the Hayward Corporation since its founding in 1918. In a corner, almost hidden by a massive ficus tree, was a photograph of the Macklin Building.

'Well, what a pleasure,' Derek said, swivelling his chair to face Ross. 'You don't often pay us a visit. Haven't seen you since you went to Paris, in fact. Place des Vosges, wasn't it?'

Ross closed the magazine. 'And Menton.'

'So I heard. Melanie said the youngsters had a fine time.'

'We all had a fine time.'

'And did Katherine finally learn to order from French menus? They always used to intimidate her.'

'Katherine learns whatever she puts her mind to,' Ross said

544

evenly. 'She's not easily intimidated. I came to talk about the earthquake damage in the Macklin Building.'

Derek's faint smile did not change. 'I heard about it. We had some damage, too: displacement of a roadbed in Daly City; nothing serious. Well? What is it you want to talk about?'

'Two workmen were injured by falling concrete. I had a letter this morning from their lawyer; they're going to sue my firm, and me, for negligence. Five million dollars.'

'Insane. Are they permanently disabled?'

'I haven't talked to their doctors. I doubt it and their lawyer isn't claiming it – yet. He mentioned time lost from work, medical bills, rehabilitation therapy, psychological trauma, pain and suffering to the family, and one or two others. It's all in the letter; I brought you a copy, since you're an interested party.'

Derek shook his head. 'Nothing to do with it.' He was no longer smiling. 'I haven't much time; is there anything else you wanted to tell me?'

'You know there is.' From his briefcase, Ross brought out photographs he had taken on Friday and printed in the office darkroom Saturday morning. He laid them on the coffee table one at a time. 'The south side of the Macklin Building, showing settling cracks in the wall . . . the first floor interior where the wall and ceiling separated; also the collapsed ceiling... basement floor showing the amount of column settling. And this is the report of the foundation engineers who tested the soil and inspected the footings in July. You can keep it. But don't take the time to read it now; you already know what it says.'

Expressionless, Derek gazed at him. He had not glanced at the photographs. 'I have no idea what it says. Nor any interest in it.'

Ross closed his briefcase. 'I've contracted to stabilise the foundation by pumping concrete under and around the column footings; it should be done by mid-October. I'm paying for it.

And I'll pay for repair of the earthquake damage. But I'm going to try to settle the suit out of court, and whatever that costs, you're going to pay half. Or you and Dad, if you can get it from him.'

'What the hell are you babbling about?' Derek's voice was contemptuous but Ross noted he was not demanding that he leave. 'I'm going to pay? Like hell I am. You can clean up your own shit.'

'It's yours, too, and you'll help clean it up. These columns wouldn't have settled if you'd built them the way they were originally designed.'

Derek shoved back his chair and strode the length of the office to pick up the photographs. He leafed through them. A corner of his mouth twitched, then he forced it still. 'Would you care to explain what these have to do with me? You're demanding that I hand over a couple of million – for what? To help you pay off a pair of cretins who see dollar signs because their fucking lawyer says they can hold you hostage? Why in hell would I touch that with a ten foot pole? Brotherly love?'

Ross stood, and their eyes were level. 'To keep it out of court.'

'What the hell do I care whether it goes to court? What do you care? Let it go; you'll win. There was an earthquake, dozens of buildings were damaged, a few people were killed, a few more were hurt. So what? That's what people expect. There's a mob of lawyers out there giving dumb workmen visions of sugarplums, and engineers and architects are going to go down like tenpins, unless they're smart. So get yourself a sharp lawyer – not Claude; he's too straight – and if you're still worried, find an inspector whose wife wants a vacation in St Croix and buy them one. He'll swear to the design of your temporary support beams and he won't look any further; he'll say it was the earthquake. Christ, why do I have to explain all this? It's mother's milk in this business.'

546

'That's not the way I work. Who got the vacation when you changed the specs on the Macklin Building?'

Derek flung the photographs on the table. 'Listen, you sanctimonious ass, the Hayward Corporation wasn't built by prayer; I doubt your little firm was, either. But I don't ask where you put your dollars; and it's none of your business where I put mine. You look after yourself, little brother, and don't worry about the family corporation. The value of your stock is just fine.'

'Until city inspectors start looking at damaged buildings where there are lawsuits. What's mother's milk for city officials for God's sake? They're primed to look for fraud, and sixteen years doesn't mean a thing if they find it; there's no way the Hayward Corporation could come out of that clean. That means you and Dad. Hugh had died two years earlier; the two of you were in charge. And it won't be as easy to brush off the city as it was to get rid of me when I asked you about it.'

'We told you there was nothing to worry about. We believed that.'

'You lied. Both of you.'

'Don't call me a liar!' Derek lashed out, but his eyes were focussed inward; he was weighing his options. Of course they had to keep it out of court; no one had more to lose than Derek Hayward, who was liable because he'd built the damn building, and also could be cut out of his grandmother's will, if she found out. But Derek knew Ross was worried about Victoria for a different reason; like a fucking white knight he wanted to shield her from the whole mess. Which was why he wanted to keep it out of court as much as Derek did, perhaps even more. Good enough, Derek concluded, and almost casually called Ross's bluff. 'It was Craig's little game; we had nothing to do with it. If you want to pay off those workmen, go ahead. But you're on your own. I'd let it go to court.'

'Craig had nothing to do with changing those specs.'

547

'Is that a revelation from on high? Craig floating down on a sunbeam to whisper sweetly in your ear?'

'No, damn it, it came from you: that pack of lies you told Katherine about the sailing accident. The sanitised version of your fight with Craig – that he didn't like the way you managed the Macklin Building. Why didn't you tell her you accused Craig of being a crook? Why didn't you tell her the story you and Dad made up the next day for my benefit? For months you'd been trying to make her see Craig through your eyes and hate him the way you do. There was your big chance to completely blacken him, and you passed it up. You never pass up a chance like that; why did you do it then? Because you couldn't take the chance she'd tell Victoria. Or me.'

'Horse shit. That's one of Katherine's fairy tales. I told her Craig lost his temper when I showed him up in front of Jennifer.'

'That's a lie.'

'I told you – don't call me a liar! Are you so besotted you don't know she makes up stories as she goes along? She lies when it suits her, to get what she wants, and now she wants to get back at me by twisting what I told her about her spineless husband. She must regret her passion more than I realised – those worshipful eyes, her extraordinary body, offering itself –'

Rage exploded in Ross; the room spun in red streaks. 'You son of a bitch!' He grabbed Derek's jacket, jerking him towards him but Derek wrenched free and backed away, his face taut, his breath coming in hoarse gasps.

'Don't touch me – God damn you – if you come near me –!'

Ross caught himself. Breathing hard, he flexed his fingers. *Don't hit him; don't let him make you react.*

His voice still hoarse, Derek said, 'Everyone lies. Craig made up a whole new life, all lies. And even before that, the two of you all those years we were growing up, turning

Victoria against me with lies . . . so you never had to fight for anything . . .' His eyes darkened as he stopped himself. 'Fairy tales,' he said, his voice rasping. 'Like the one you brought me today. I don't believe in fairy tales.'

Deliberately he turned his back and walked to his desk. Ross stood where he was, his thoughts racing. *Turning Victoria against me . . . you never had to fight for anything.* The room had stopped spinning; the red streaks of his rage were gone. His muscles loosened and he felt the lightness that came when he cut the motor on his boat and silence descended. He looked at Derek's rigid figure: the tight, narrow face and contemptuous smile that hid a maelstrom of anger, competitiveness, and fear.

Fairy tales, he thought, hearing again the fury in his brother's voice as he had said it. But it was Derek's life, he realised, that was the fairy tale: an intricate web of wishes and fabrications to get attention, love, admiration, deference from his father and grandparents, clients, business associates, women, even – though Ross had never suspected it – his cousin and his brother.

Ross looked back through the years, as far back as he could remember. Derek had perfected his skill at manipulating people by practising on his family, forcing Ross and Craig to feel they were competing with him – and losing. And so from the time he was a boy, Ross had feared and envied his brother, longing to have his compelling power and magnetism, even, sometimes, his single-minded ruthlessness that seemed to sweep all obstacles aside. But at the same time his fierce dislike of Derek had grown and he had tried to keep a distance between them – even refusing to consider working in the family company because that would have meant working with Derek. But there could never be enough distance, even when he moved to New York. All his life, Ross had been tied to his brother by the strongest bonds of envy and hatred.

549

Now, for the first time, he saw that Derek's magnetism was desperation, that the brother he had feared and envied was a chameleon furiously plotting, lying, changing colours to snare and impress others. With a shock he realised how much Derek was like Craig. No wonder they hated each other; they understood each other too well.

'Well?' Derek demanded. Usually he used silence as a weapon, making others so nervous they would say anything to break it. But Ross had outwaited him. 'Well?' he repeated.

Ross picked up his briefcase. 'I think we've finished for today. I have work to do.' He saw uncertainty flicker in his brother's eyes. He had never seen that before, and he knew that Derek was fighting to regain his balance: to recover from that brief moment of letting down his guard, and to recapture control of their conversation. But Ross would not let him. For once he had called Derek's bluff, and he was the one who was leaving.

Derek watched him cross the room to open the office door. 'What the hell are you going to do?' he burst out.

From the doorway, Ross looked at him thoughtfully, without answering.

'You're not going to let it go to court!'

'I'm not sure. I have to make some plans. You'll hear from me.' He opened the door. 'Good luck with repairing your displaced roadway. It's always best to have a straight path, isn't it?'

He strode down the corridor. As he reached the elevator, the image of his boat returned: pushing away from the dock with no constraints or ties. Whatever he needed to do, however he had to do it, he had left the bonds of competitiveness and envy behind. Derek could no longer touch him; he was free.

Victoria handed the portfolio of Picasso lithographs to Katherine. They sat together on the silk couch in the library; a low fire burned in the fireplace though the evening was mild.

550

'A wonderful collection,' she said. 'Hugh and I bought them in Paris so long ago I can't remember. I'll miss looking at them each day.'

'So why donate them now?' Tobias asked as he poked a log and laid a new one upon it. 'Put them in your will. The museum can wait.'

'Board members are expected to make donations to set an example. Besides, I want to be able to see people enjoying them.'

Katherine looked up from a picture of a bull and a young woman that would have been called obscene if anyone but Picasso had drawn it. 'Why are you doing this now?' she asked.

'Because I'm getting old and the years vanish and there's so much I still want to do. I've promised our nineteenth century collection to the Palace of the Legion of Honour and the rest to the Museum of Modern Art and I want to space it out so I can see them all mounted, and hear experts pontificate about the Hayward collection and my generosity.'

'I mean, why do you talk about dying? It makes me think I'm about to lose you.'

'Dear Katherine, I'm shockingly healthy; I don't intend to die for years. Although worrying about you and Ross makes me feel very old.'

'That's blackmail,' Katherine said.

'The older you get, my dear, the more weapons you are willing to use to get what you want.'

'Actually,' Tobias put in. 'We are most worried right now about Ross.' Mournfully, he quoted, ' ". . . the shrivelled hopping, loud and troublesome insects of the hour." Certain injured workmen, that is, and their lawyers.'

'The ones in the Macklin Building?' Katherine asked. 'What about them?'

'They are suing Ross,' said Victoria bitterly. 'For five million dollars.'

Katherine drew a sharp breath. 'Has he said how he'll fight it?'

Tobias gave Katherine a keen look. 'If it goes to court, which it may not, he'll say the support beams were strong enough and anchored properly, and the damage was caused by the earthquake. Is there any other explanation?'

Five million dollars, Katherine thought. And no one to help him. She put the portfolio of lithographs on the table and stared into the fire. *What do I do now? Ross wants to protect Victoria . . . but I want to protect Ross. Or at least do whatever I can to help him.*

Which means telling Victoria and Tobias, because they're the ones who can do something for him.

And, after all, why shouldn't they know? Victoria is a pretty tough lady. Ross told me that himself, in France. *It's not accurate to think of her as a helpless little old lady who lies like a crumpled piece of tissue paper while the busy world passes her by.* But still he thinks she needs to be shielded.

He thought I did, too, when he found Elissa.

But he underestimated us. We're stronger than he thinks. And families should be told, when one of them is threatened; they shouldn't be prevented from helping each other.

But who am I, to make that decision? Maybe Ross had other reasons for keeping quiet; how do I know what I might be starting? For the first time in months Katherine felt uncomfortable, almost like an outsider again, involved in events she shouldn't know about, telling a story she had no right to tell, violating a confidence without any idea what train of events she might be setting in motion.

I don't know what to do!

'Well, my dear,' said Tobias mildly. 'Is there a way we can help you solve whatever dilemma keeps you in silent dialogue with yourself?'

Katherine started. 'I'm sorry. I was being rude.'

'No, no. Something is troubling you and you are not sure whether you should tell us. Of course we think you should, because we love you. But you must do whatever you think best for all of us. Your whole family.'

The weight of the dilemma slipped from Katherine; she began to smile. *Your whole family.* She wasn't an outsider; she hadn't been for a long time. *I'm sorry, Ross. I hope you'll understand. I love you; I want to help you; and I want Victoria and Tobias to be able to help you, too.*

'There is another defence,' she said at last. 'But Ross won't use it.'

'Yes?' Tobias was alert.

'And that is –?' Victoria demanded.

'The building was weak,' Katherine said, choosing her words carefully. 'The support columns, or the footings under them weren't as strong or as deep as they should have been. Ross suspected it and when he had the building checked in July he found he was right. But the repair work kept being delayed, and then the earthquake came. The problem wasn't the design of the temporary beams; it was in the building itself.'

'*That's* why he bought it!' exclaimed Tobias. 'He suspected – '

'Just one moment!' Victoria raised a peremptory hand. 'Katherine, are you suggesting the Macklin Building is substandard? It was built by the Hayward Corporation!'

'I know. The specifications were altered to cut costs.'

'But the building inspectors . . .?' Tobias asked.

'Ross thinks they must have been bribed.'

'Rubbish,' declared Victoria. 'Curt or Jason would have known about it.'

Katherine nodded.

'Curt,' Victoria said, her voice blank.

Katherine nodded again.

They were silent, locked in their own thoughts. The butler

appeared in the doorway and announced dinner. Victoria roused herself and as they moved into the dining-room, she put her hand on Katherine's arm. 'This has been difficult for you. Ross told you he thought he could keep it a secret?'

'He was going to have the building repaired as part of the renovation. He didn't want you to face a scandal –'

'– In my declining years,' Victoria finished, scoffing. 'Of course I am not nearly as delicate as my grandson thinks; how fortunate that you knew that. But my dear Katherine, what a dilemma – keeping Ross's secret or telling me! Thank you, my dear, for choosing me. I promise you will not be sorry. But, of course, now that you know I will not faint upon the spot, you must tell us everything, wherever it leads. We want to know it all.'

As Katherine smiled gratefully, Tobias asked, 'How long has he known, or suspected?'

There was a pause before Katherine replied, 'He's suspected, for sixteen years.'

'Sixteen –!' Victoria exclaimed. 'And told none of us! He should be ashamed of himself!'

'No, that's not fair. He couldn't tell you then, because –'

'The sailing accident,' Tobias broke in. 'That's when he began to suspect? You told me Craig and Derek quarrelled about the Macklin Building.'

'Good God in Heaven!' Victoria burst out. She whipped open her napkin and laid it across her lap. 'Was I the only one who knew nothing?'

'I know no more than that,' soothed Tobias. 'Katherine. Please.'

'Craig accused Derek of altering the specifications on the footings in the Macklin Building; Derek came back and said *Craig* had done it, and bribed an inspector to approve the work.'

'But more likely it was Derek.' Spearing a wedge of mango,

Tobias had a gleam of discovery in his eye. 'Always was impatient – and thinks he's above the law.'

Victoria toyed with her food. 'And of course Curt knew about it. He and Derek always worked closely in those days; I remember how confident I felt: Hugh was dead but my son and my grandson were there . . . My son and my grandson!' she repeated contemptuously.

Her face was drawn, her eyes looking to the distance.

'Hugh always insisted on safety. Our reputation, he said; the lives of the people who trusted our buildings . . . He never violated that trust. He was scrupulous in following city regulations, earthquake safety codes – he even helped write some of them! And now . . . my son and my grandson . . . cutting corners . . . bribery . . . Dishonourable! Despicable! Playing on the desperation or greed of others . . . Damnation!' she burst out. 'An old woman should be able to relax; she should be able to trust her heirs to protect her name and the company she and her husband built from nothing and made famous and respected . . .!'

'This old woman,' Tobias said pointedly, 'insists on being chairman of the board of the Hayward Corporation.'

She looked at him imperiously. 'I am the majority stockholder in the corporation.'

'Then perhaps you are not ready to relax.'

'Ah.' She gave a small laugh. 'You have a point.' The butler offered a silver platter of veal and tiny potato puffs to each of them. Serving herself, Victoria frowned thoughtfully, then said, 'Of course that suit against Ross cannot go to trial. It is intolerable to contemplate others poking through our affairs. So we must settle it out of court, which will require . . . Tobias, Ross said the workmen were injured but not crippled. What is a realistic sum their lawyer would be likely to accept?'

'Perhaps a quarter of a million.'

'And it is Derek's responsibility. Do we agree on that?

Katherine? Didn't you bring us this information so we could bring pressure to bear on Derek?'

'Not only to settle the suit,' said Tobias quickly. 'But to pay for the repair of the building.'

Uncomfortably, Katherine said, 'I'm not sure what I expected. I just thought you should know, so Ross wouldn't be alone.'

'Ah.' Victoria sighed with satisfaction. 'Then we must decide what to do. Obviously Derek must assume the responsibility for various expenditures. Can he be blackmailed?'

'Good heavens!' Tobias exclaimed. 'After seventy-five years, to find I still do not know my own sister . . .'

'Surprise keeps us young,' Victoria said. 'It's the glue that holds people together.' She smiled at him with such tenderness that Katherine felt a spurt of envy. After years of separate lives, how lucky they were, she thought, to find companionship and love.

' "He is as deaf to angels as an oak",' Tobias quoted. 'How do you reach a man who loves no one, who has more money than anyone needs, and who finds morality boring? His only enduring passion is power. Might we threaten that?'

'Derek runs the Hayward Corporation admirably,' Victoria said. 'He makes a great deal of money for all of us.'

'Yes, yes, very practical. But –'

'In fact,' she declared suddenly, 'if I'd paid more attention to what he and Curt were doing, all along, none of this might have happened. I've been complacent; quite satisfied to let them run the company –'

'Come, come!' Tobias exclaimed. 'You cannot blame yourself. We all are responsible; none of the board members, myself included, asked enough questions. Now we will. Derek's leadership has threatened us with a scandal, possibly a large cash outlay, serious damage to our name; perhaps the ruin of Ross's reputation. I must say, when Derek does something, the repercussions are not small. And I have another thought. How do we know where else Derek has taken it upon himself to cut costs? What other surprises might be in store for us? Perhaps our Derek needs his wings clipped.'

'Perhaps he needs an overseer,' suggested Victoria.

'Ah.' Tobias cogitated. 'It would be better if we had proof. Katherine says he accused Craig, and Craig is not here to refute that.'

Katherine had been watching the two of them. Now, hesitantly, she said, 'Wouldn't building inspectors have forms to sign, approving the jobs they inspect?'

'Indeed!' Tobias tipped back his chair, his beard wagging vigorously. 'On file at City Hall. Indeed.' Then he frowned. 'Why wouldn't Ross have dug them up to persuade Derek to pay?'

'He wasn't going to ask him,' Katherine said. 'He didn't want to stir anything up since he thought the repair would be part of the renovation.'

Tobias shook his head. 'Stubborn.'

'We shall deal with that,' Victoria said calmly. 'Tobias, dear, would you call Claude and Ross and arrange a conference? The time has come for the chairman of the board to make some decisions.'

Leslie called at the weekend. 'I have no problems left. Tell me yours. Unless you've solved each and every one –?'

'Hardly,' laughed Katherine. 'But I have no new ones to offer.'

'Then we'll share glad tidings instead. I got your grandma's Hallowe'en invite today; it sounds like one of those parties people will talk about for years. What are you wearing?'

'I don't know. I don't much like costume parties.'

'It's not costume and you'll like it. Claude says she and Hugh used to give one every year and those who weren't invited committed suicide, went into mourning or slunk away in humiliation. Since we are among the favoured throng, all we have to do is look magnificent.'

'Leslie, where can I get a magnificent dress at a less than magnificent price?'

'Have you tried Val's?'

'Not lately. Their prices have tripled.'

'Well, I have some hot information. The prices were tripled by a new manager who took one look at those designer seconds and went gung ho for profits. He has been booted. His replacement is at this very moment marking everything down. Get there early Monday, before the mob scene. I'm off; dinner with Claude. Oh. No word from Craig, I take it?'

'No. You'd be one of the first to know.'

'I hope so. See you soon.'

No word from Craig. Katherine had been so sure he would call within a few days of her trip to Calgary that she had sat by the telephone, jumping every time it rang, just as she had a year and a half earlier, in Vancouver. But the silence was unbroken. *Back where we started*, she thought.

No, not the start, she corrected herself. Because she knew, from Ross, that Craig wanted to come back. Whether he stole the money or was framed, he wanted to come back and make amends for leaving her.

Well, jibed an inner voice; isn't that nice of him?

Her thoughts argued with each other: all the voices of those who had urged her to make up her mind, to do something, to divorce Craig, to cut herself off from the past. So what if parts of it were still dangling; so what if her marriage was unfinished; so what if –?

What's the hurry?

Why were they all rushing her? Craig had been gone a little over a year. She and Ross had been together less than four months – and for the last three weeks they'd been apart.

If I want to take some time to think about all this – sort out who I am and where I'm going – what's wrong with that? Why is everyone rushing me?

'Mom?' said Todd. 'Could we get started? You said you'd help us, and all this stuff is due on Monday.'

'Right away,' Katherine said. 'Give me a minute to clean up.'

She found the two of them waiting for her at the kitchen table, surrounded by bits and pieces of clay models they had volunteered to make for a school diorama on space exploration.

'Actually, we volunteered because we knew you'd help us,' Jennifer confessed as they watched their mother's skilful fingers fashion a clay model of Voyager II. 'We didn't think you'd mind too much.'

'I don't mind at all,' Katherine said. 'I'm having a wonderful time.'

'Really?' Jennifer asked. 'How come I don't think it's so much fun?'

'Because for you it's a school assignment. For me it's like going back to mud pies and childhood.'

'Oh.' Jennifer thought about it. 'I don't want to be a child again. Why do you?'

Katherine kept herself from smiling. 'I had less to worry about in those days.'

'We have a *lot* to worry about,' said Todd. Looking intently at his slightly deformed model of the Columbia space shuttle, he added, 'Carrie and Jon brought Ross to the club yesterday; he went swimming with us and bought us lemonade.'

Katherine's heart skipped. 'I hope you thanked him.'

'He asked how you are.'

'And what did you say?'

'That you miss him.'

'Todd!'

'He said he missed you, too,' said Jennifer.

'So do Carrie and Jon,' added Todd. 'They wanted to know where you were. They like you.'

'They got used to all of us being together,' Jennifer explained.

'The same way we did,' said Todd.

'I like Ross,' Jennifer commented.

'Me, too,' Todd chimed in. 'He's nice to be with.'

They were tossing the conversation back and forth like a beach ball. 'Have you two rehearsed this?' Katherine asked.

'We talked about it,' Jennifer admitted. 'We told Ross about the computer program we're writing.'

Katherine pictured the three of them talking together and felt jealous of her children. 'The one for maths?' she asked.

'No.' Todd looked at Jennifer. 'The one to see if you'd marry Ross or get together with Dad again.'

The clay model slipped and she grabbed it. 'What are you talking about?'

'We made a formula. Dad equals X, and Ross equals Y, and the number of months Dad is away equals N, and the times you ask us about Carrie and Jon when you really want to hear about Ross, equals R, but we haven't got an answer yet –'

'I'm not surprised.' Katherine went to the sink and rinsed off her hands. 'Why don't you finish up? I guess I'm getting a little old for a whole afternoon of clay modelling.'

'You said you were having a wonderful time,' Jennifer reminded her. 'Mud pies and all that.'

'I was just reminded that I'm a long way from mud pies and all that.' Standing at the sink Katherine studied them. 'What do you think I should do?' she asked abruptly.

Taken aback, they stared at her. 'I'd like Dad home again,' Todd said finally. 'The way everything was.'

'I guess I would, too,' said Jennifer slowly. 'Except I don't think things would be the same. Ever again.'

'Sure they would,' Todd said. 'Oh, you mean our house? We'd build another one. That's easy.'

'No.' Jennifer met her mother's eyes. 'I don't think Mother and Daddy feel the same way about things anymore. Neither do we.'

'So?' Todd demanded. 'We're older.'

Furiously, Jennifer dashed a piece of clay against the wall. 'I don't trust him anymore!' she cried and burst into tears.

Katherine swept her into her arms and held her tight. 'Jennifer,' she whispered. 'Dear Jennifer –'

'I'm sorry!' Jennifer sobbed. 'I'm an awful person to say that! I shouldn't even think it –!'

'You're not awful. If someone makes you unhappy, it's natural to worry that he might do it again. It doesn't mean you're awful. It just means you're worried about what's going to happen; you're not sure of the future. And once upon a time you thought you were sure.' Katherine pulled back from Jennifer and said seriously, 'That's what childhood really is: a time when you think you're sure of tomorrow. And I guess, in that way, you aren't a child any more.'

None of us is, Katherine thought later, sitting at her worktable. We all grew up when Craig left us. And Jennifer is right: nothing can ever be the same again.

She bent to her work, concentrating on linking together the segments of an amethyst bracelet. By now she was making jewellery for four small stores, and belts for Heath's. She was earning almost enough to rent a larger apartment, though not yet enough to take time each day to make enough jewellery to send Henri – and also other designs that crowded her imagination: wrist watches, pen and pencil sets, desk sets, even candlesticks and napkin rings. Her fingers itched to make them all. She might still feel trapped by Craig, but in the evenings,

561

after her other work was done, when her pencil flew across empty expanses of paper, she was free of everything, soaring in a world of her own making, without limits or bounds. Someday she would make them all. Now she could not afford the time, or the materials.

But – Victoria was giving a party. She ran her fingers over the square white parchment envelope addressed in gothic lettering, and re-read the invitation inside.

' "So hallow'd and gracious is the time",' it quoted from Shakespeare, and Katherine smiled at the evidence of Tobias's hand. 'All Hallows Eve . . . a time for celebrating dreams . . . for dining and dancing in the Fairmont Ballroom and Garden, Saturday, October 30, at 9:30 p.m.'

For Victoria's party, she thought, she might make some jewellery for herself. Eventually she could sell it, perhaps in Paris. She'd never made herself a special piece. And if she found a magnificent dress . . . why not?

The telephone rang and, thinking of jewellery, she answered it. 'My dear,' Victoria said. 'I'm calling to invite you –'

'The invitation came in the mail,' Katherine said. 'And of course I'll come; how could I stay away from your party?'

'Party? Oh, yes: All Hallows. Tobias's secretary sent those out; we have been occupied with other matters. Katherine, there is a time for parties and there is a time for business. I am calling about business. There will be a special meeting of the board of directors of the Hayward Corporation, next Thursday. I would like you to be there.'

'But . . . I'm not a member. I know nothing about it. Why would I . . . why would you want me there?'

'Because you are part of us. Because if it were not for you, and the information you brought us the other day, there would be no meeting. Because I want you beside me. I have not forgotten the frivolity of the All Hallows ball. We will have that, too. But this is more important. And it could be extremely important to you. Please, Katherine. Ten-thirty, Thursday morning, the twenty-eighth. And please don't be late.'

Hanging up, Katherine stared into space. Ross would be there. And Derek. And the shadow of Craig. And Katherine Fraser – still finding out exactly where she fitted in with all of them, for now and the future.

Chapter 20

It was the first time since Christmas that they were all together. Jason and Ann flew in from Maine, and Curt from Palm Springs; Ross walked the mile from his office near Telegraph Hill to the Hayward Corporation's offices in Embarcadero Centre where, on the thirtieth floor, Derek strolled the hundred paces from his office to the conference room; Tobias and Victoria were driven in a limousine from Pacific Heights, stopping in the financial district to pick up Claude; Katherine took a bus from her house.

They were there because Victoria had summoned them as directors and shareholders of the Hayward Corporation. Refusing to give a reason, or an advance agenda, she had simply demanded their presence. And so they came, greeting each other with questions as they poured coffee from the large pot on the slate-covered sideboard ('Enough for all day,' Derek muttered to his father) and took their seats at the long rosewood conference table where each place was furnished with a pad of paper, newly-sharpened pencils and a water glass.

Ross poured a cup of coffee and took it to Katherine, who was sitting in a corner of the room. When she thanked him, he shook his head. 'I'm the one to thank you. I wanted to call you, but it seemed better to wait until today. I was wrong about Victoria and you knew it; you did what I should have done long ago.'

'I'm glad it's all right,' she replied. The coffee cup trembled in her hand as she fought back the longing for him that pulsed through her. 'I thought you might be angry. And I didn't know what I might be starting – with the family.'

'You started quite a bit. But I wasn't angry; how could I be angry with you? You took the burden from me. What I really feel is a strong desire to hold you in my arms.' He saw the startled look in her eyes, and smiled. 'I see I'm not the only one.'

Tobias came up and almost apologetically suggested Ross sit down. 'Claude and Victoria will be here any minute,' he said. Ross touched Katherine's hand briefly, then took his place at the table, where the others were all talking at once.

'. . . . heard from Craig,' Ann suggested tentatively. 'Why else would she call us?'

Brusquely, Jason growled, 'Probably called his grandmother so she'd smooth his way back to the company. But he's wrong if he thinks I can just forget, as if he'd never run away . . .'

'I doubt he'll want to come back,' said Curt. 'Derek runs the company and Craig would know there's no place for him. Though Victoria may try to force us to take him . . . Or she's simply rewriting her will.'

Simply! thought Derek.

Ann twisted her hands. 'I don't like the way any of you are talking. We have to welcome him back –'

'Welcome,' Curt snorted. 'What has he done to deserve a welcome from any of us?'

'He doesn't have to do anything,' Ann replied with spirit. 'You don't have to earn your way into your own family.'

'You have to earn your way everywhere,' said Derek contemptuously. He was tense, every nerve taut and ready – to react, retreat, attack, plan. He didn't know what was happening – a rare and infuriating situation – and so he had to be prepared to respond to whatever was proposed: to buy Craig off before he had a chance to dilute Derek's power in the company; to handle the Macklin problem if Ross had gone running to Victoria with the story; to counter any rearrangement of Victoria's will that could inhibit his total control of the company once she was dead.

His eyes met Tobias's. 'If only I were a playwright,' said Tobias with relish. 'What I could do with all of you!'

'But you're not,' Derek said.

'True,' said Tobias penitently, and fell silent, but the atmosphere was no calmer. Katherine felt it, sharp with speculation and apprehension, as if hundreds of tiny knives were flashing beneath the fluorescent lights that reflected on panelled walls and the rich rosewood table. It touched her, too, in her chair in a corner, away from the table, as everyone shot covert glances at her while hazarding suppositions about Craig. Across the table, Ross watched her and when their eyes met she stirred restlessly with vivid memories of their times together. Derek sat a few feet away, and she was aware of his glances, not only because Ross was there, but because his wariness was unnerving. She had not seen him in months and he reminded her of a tightrope walker – thinner than she remembered, withdrawn into himself, rigidly controlled as he scribbled on his pad of paper.

Victoria walked in, followed by Claude, and stood at the head of the table. Wearing a black silk suit with an ivory blouse, and a bar pin of silver filigree with coral that Katherine had made her, she stood regally erect, her eyes piercing and unsmiling, resting briefly on each of them.

Stiffly formal, as if giving advance warning of the bombshell she was about to throw, she said, 'The special meeting of the Board of Directors of the Hayward Corporation is called to order. Tobias will take the minutes. I have called this meeting because I have recently gained information which is dangerous, disgraceful and repugnant. It demands immediate action. Our agenda is to deal with this information, which affects the reputation of the corporation, its liability for past misdeeds' – Derek's mouth tightened – 'and its future shape and direction.'

'Future shape and direction?' Curt queried. 'Not in one meeting, without advance notice so we can prepare suggestions.'

'Perhaps,' said Victoria distinctly. 'I was not understood. I gained this information only recently. It is intolerable. And as long as I am alive and own fifty percent of this corporation, when I find something intolerable, it will be changed. Immediately.'

No one spoke. Standing perfectly straight, hands clasped loosely before her, she was imperious and formidable. Katherine loved her and was in awe of her. She looked at the others: Ann and Jason puzzled, Curt suspicious, Derek withdrawn, Ross, Tobias and Claude watchful – they know, Katherine thought; they know what this is about.

'Claude?' Victoria said. 'If you please.' She sat in the leather wing chair at the head of the table, her head high, observing all of them.

Claude was seated at the other end of the table. 'Sixteen years ago,' he began in his resonant courtroom voice that reminded Katherine of the first time she had heard him, at dinner in Victoria's apartment, 'the Hayward Corporation built the Macklin Building on Mission Street. There were delays due to a strike, and to make up for lost time and money, the specifications were altered in such a way that the building was constructed in violation of city codes.'

'What's that?' Jason said. 'Nothing like that ever –'

'Highly unlikely,' Curt rumbled. 'Claude, I'd like to know to whom you've been talking –'

'Over the years,' Claude continued, 'the building settled, causing cracks but no immediate danger, until the earthquake of October first, when part of the second floor collapsed, injuring two workmen. Together, they are suing for five million dollars.' He raised his voice as Curt and Jason exploded with questions. 'They are suing Ross, who bought the building some years ago, and his company, which designed its renovation. However, an investigation – and there will be one if this goes to trial – will reveal that the floor collapsed because of excessive settling of the foundation, which occurred because the Hayward Corporation, under Curt's presidency, with Derek as construction manager, knowingly and illegally put up a substandard building.'

'You lying bastard,' said Curt tightly.

Jason pounded the table. 'Why the hell wasn't I told this?'

'Jason,' said Ann. 'It was 1966.'

'God damn it, I know what year it was. But when did this happen? Before or after the sailing accident? Before or after we left for Maine?'

Derek seemed to pay no attention. He jotted an occasional note on his pad, but otherwise sat absolutely still.

Curt shoved back his chair and hunched his shoulders, facing Claude. 'You won't be able to practise law in a stable of shit when I get through with you. I know a conspiracy when I see one; Derek warned me something was going on –'

'Curt!' Victoria flared. 'How dare you speak like that in front of me? Sit still and behave yourself! I will accept an apology.'

After the briefest of pauses, Curt said suavely, 'I apologise. I forgot myself.' He pulled his chair to the table, cursing whatever weakness in him made him feel, at sixty-four, like a schoolboy when his mother scolded him.

'It is curious, however,' said Derek lightly, turning to a fresh sheet of paper, 'that someone has fabricated this story at this time.' He glanced up. 'When Ross is being sued. Could that someone be his little friend and companion – trying to make sure we all contribute when the hat is passed – so she spreads a pack of lies that would virtually force us to pay and be silent?'

'You rotten son of a bitch!' Claude roared – calm, careful unemotional Claude – violently shoving back his chair, beating Ross to it by a fraction of a second, shocking everyone into momentary paralysis.

In that small pause, Tobias sent his voice like a trumpet down the table. ' *"Envy's a coal come hissing hot from hell!"* '

Nervous laughter erupted around the table. Victoria, who had briefly closed her eyes, fastened her gaze on Derek as she said, 'Thank you, dear Tobias. And my dear attorney. Now may we continue?'

A mistake, Derek acknowledged. Unsure where Claude was heading, he'd thought he could force him to admit the danger to the corporation if they publicised the Macklin Building. He hadn't known that Claude, like Victoria, had been mesmerised by that woman. Fuck her. Every time he thought he knew what she could do, he discovered he'd underestimated her again.

Claude had sat down, reluctantly passing up his first and probably only chance to feel his fist ram Derek's mouth. 'I don't waste my time on a pack of lies,' he said shortly. 'The history of that building is no longer a secret.'

Derek's pencil tapped his pad of paper, making small specks, like a storm of insects. His head had begun to pound from the frustration of not knowing what was happening, and he went on the attack, to retrieve what he could. 'This has nothing to do with personalities,' he told Victoria, as if they were alone in the room. 'My first concern is the corporation. From what I've heard, Ross's engineer was incompetent in his

569

renovation design and then had the misfortune to have it tested by an earthquake. Bad luck, but not ours: it wasn't our project or our engineer. We can't risk the corporation's reputation by accepting responsibility for the incompetence of others.'

Jason glared at him. '*Whose* incompetence? What about yours and' – he shot a glance at Curt – 'my brother's, sixteen years ago, that nobody bothered to tell me about?'

Derek's pencil skidded across the sheet of paper. 'God damn it, you were Vice-President; you hadn't run away yet to the backwoods of Maine. Weren't you paying attention to business? Were you blind? *Or are they lying?*'

'You and Curt,' Jason muttered, his face dark with embarrassment and anger. 'You worked together; shut me out.'

'We filled a vacuum, uncle,' said Derek smoothly, feeling his power return as Jason's slipped. 'You weren't paying attention.'

'I was working on other projects! And I was worried about my daughter, sneaking out at night, after her mother and I ordered her to stay away from you!'

Derek gazed at him, his mouth twisted in a tight smile.

Claude's courtroom voice sliced between them. 'I have a statement to read that will clarify matters and speed our proceedings.' He picked up a sheet of paper. 'This past week I located and interviewed a former city inspector. This is his statement, dated October eleventh, and signed Frank Beecher.'

Derek's head jerked up, the tiny nerve beside his eye beginning to flicker.

' "On July 11th and 12th, 1966",' Claude read,

' "Working for the city of San Francisco, I inspected the foundation columns and footings of the Macklin Building being constructed by the Hayward Corporation on Mission Street in San Francisco. I signed four reports saying they met the engineering specifications and plans already approved by the city and the state Seismic Commission. But the fact is, based on my experience, I thought the columns weren't sunk deep enough in that particular soil, and the amount of steel reinforcing in the footings didn't seem adequate. I checked the specs, and the columns and footings met them, so I thought the specs might have been changed after the city approved them. I talked this over with the construction manager, Derek Hayward. He suggested I approve the work in exchange for ten thousand dollars cash, and I did. That was my only contact with the Macklin Building." '

No one moved. Jason's face was dark with fury. 'Is that public knowledge – what he wrote?'

'Not yet,' Claude replied.

'Then how did you know enough to look for this guy?'

'Katherine gave us the background –'

'*Katherine?*' said Derek. 'So I had the right woman but the wrong man.' His twisted smile flickered again, but Katherine heard a change in his voice; he was losing control. 'It was her husband she was protecting, not Ross. How disappointing for Ross to discover she's still turning loyal somersaults for the runaway.'

'Derek –!' Victoria began icily.

But Derek could not stop. '*None of you can believe that tripe!* Christ, only a lawyer could read it with a straight face. A child could see through it. Who the hell is Frank Beecher? A piece of fiction dreamed up by Craig and his faithful little woman, with Claude's help, to ruin me and bring their golden boy back in a blaze of glory. *Craig* was the one who altered the specs on the Macklin Building and paid off that beer-bellied liar to approve the whole thing; *that's* what we've known for sixteen years!'

571

A stunned silence settled on the room. No one moved. But in that moment, as in an earthquake, the power and alignments of the Hayward family shifted, and everyone felt it.

Victoria sighed. 'Katherine,' she said, without turning. 'Please sit beside me.'

Katherine brought her chair to the table. Victoria's regal posture had not wavered, but her eyes had filled with tears, and her hand shook as she sipped from her glass of water. She reached for Katherine's hand and held it tightly. 'Now,' she announced, keeping her voice cool and steady, 'I shall talk about the future structure of the Hayward Corporation.'

The stillness in the room was as heavy as the morning fog. Katherine saw Derek and Curt exchange a glance, then look away, staring into space, waiting. 'Hugh and his father built it,' Victoria said. 'Hugh made its reputation for excellence. And Derek, for the most part, has managed it brilliantly, built it to its present size, and increased the wealth of all of us.'

She drank again from her glass. 'Once, for a few years, I ran the Hayward Corporation. Ever since then, I have felt quite proprietary about it. And when Hugh died and left half his stock to me, it was his way of telling me that *the company and the family were mine to care for*.'

She contemplated them. 'I waited almost fifty years to put my mark on this company. Even after Hugh died, I waited. Curt took over; when Jennifer died I lost interest . . . then Curt retired and Derek took his place... and things were going well . . .' Her voice had wandered into the past and she caught herself. 'But now I'm getting old. I cannot leave to chance, or even to tomorrow, the affairs of a company and a family I love.'

She put down her glass, her hand steady. 'Everyone has always assumed Derek would have full control after I die, that I would divide my shares between him and Ross, and, since Curt gave Derek some of his shares when he retired, and also votes with him on all issues, Derek would have a clear majority. However, nothing is obvious any longer.' She paused. Prolonging the drama, Katherine thought; just like Tobias. 'Because of what we have discovered, I have decided on a complete reorganisation of the company.'

Curt grunted, as if he had been hit in the stomach. 'Talked into it,' he muttered.

'*I* decided!' Victoria blazed. 'Is that clear? This is *my* decision, which I have worked out with our corporate attorney over the past two weeks. He will describe it to you. I want no questions or comments until he is finished. Is *that* clear?' Her breathing was rapid and she clung to Katherine's hand, but still she sat erect. 'I expect silence and attention; I am tired of hearing you wrangle like children and I am disgusted by obscenities which demonstrate nothing more than infantilism and limited vocabularies.' She paused. 'Claude? If you please.'

Claude unfolded a chart and pinned it to an easel beside him. 'The Hayward Corporation will be reorganised as the parent company of three subsidiaries: Hayward Construction, Hayward Development, and Hayward Associates. Victoria is transferring eighty-two percent of her stock in the Hayward Corporation to Ross, and eighteen percent to Derek. Added to the stock they already have, Ross will own fifty-one percent of the Hayward Corporation, and Derek twenty-nine percent. Curt will still have ten percent, and Jason and Ann, five percent each.'

A rustle, like an autumn wind, moved through the room, but no one spoke.

'The Hayward Corporation will own fifty-one percent of each of the three subsidiaries. The remaining stock will be divided as follows:

'Derek will own forty-nine percent of Hayward Construction. He remains president and will continue to lead the company in large-scale construction, as in the past.

'Ross and Derek will divide equally forty-nine percent of the stock in Hayward Development, an entirely new company which will concentrate on major urban redevelopment projects.

'Ross will bring in his architectural firm, Ross Hayward Associates, as one of the subsidiaries, and will own forty-nine percent of it.

'I have corporate and tax details worked out in these booklets, which I'll give all of you later.'

'He got everything,' Curt seethed.

'Not at all,' Derek said tightly, understanding more quickly than his father how masterfully it had been done. *Damn them. God damn their clever hides.* His thoughts twisted and turned, looking for a way out through the pounding in his head. The walls were closing in. He flung himself from his chair and left the room.

Claude barely paused. 'Put simply, Ross has majority ownership and control of the parent company, the Hayward Corporation, which, in turn, controls three subsidiaries. I might add that all the shareholders in the Hayward Corporation will realise substantial financial gains by this reorganisation.'

But Ross has control, Katherine thought, understanding the rage in Derek's face. They took away the only thing that really means anything to him: his power. He'll make more money than before; he can build his bridges and highways and aqueducts; he'll still be pursued as a wealthy, charming bachelor. Outwardly his life won't change. Except that his brother is now at the centre of power.

But – Ross hadn't wanted this. He hadn't wanted to be a part of the Hayward Corporation.

Katherine remembered the look between Victoria and Tobias. *Perhaps Derek needs his wings clipped.* They had talked Ross into it. Because there was no one else. And in fact, wasn't it what Ross had always wanted? A wealthy corporation, with the resources to build as he dreamed, to remake large landscapes, changing the look of cities . . .

'It won't work,' said Curt, clipping his words. 'I won't let you remake this company overnight, and I won't let you give it to Ross. He doesn't have the experience to run the whole show. The idea of a development subsidiary isn't bad, and if you want to merge Ross's firm with ours, I'd go along with that. But not with the rest of this scheme the three of you have cooked up.' Coolly he pushed back his chair. 'That so-called statement of Beecher's doesn't mean a damn thing. You wouldn't let this go to trial; too much damage to the corporation. If I know Claude, he's already working on an out-of-court settlement, and of course, we'll contribute to that if Ross needs help in paying it. As for the rest, you've gone too far. I'm voting against it. And you need a unanimous vote of the shareholders for this kind of reorganisation. Claude will remind you of that, in case you've forgotten the bylaws.'

Victoria gazed down the table. 'You were such a pleasant child, Curt. Hugh and I had twelve years of enjoyment from you before you grew hard and quite unlovable. Now I have discovered that you lied to Ross after the sailing accident, telling him there were no problems with the Macklin Building; you kept it from all of us, all these years; and you and Derek tried to shift the blame to Craig. You have been irresponsible and corrupt and I am ashamed of you, as my son and an officer of this corporation. Look at me when I speak to you! And listen carefully because what I am about to tell you is in your interest.' She looked at Derek's empty chair. 'Will someone find Derek and bring him back?'

Tobias slipped out and a moment later returned. 'He'll be –'

Derek came in, his face remote, his eyes shadowed, and took his seat.

'First,' Victoria said. 'Derek and Curt will pay the cost of

575

settling the suit against Ross. You were quite right, Curt; we intend to keep it out of court. You will pay whatever is required to do that. In addition,' she said calmly, 'You will vote for the reorganisation of the corporation. The vote will be unanimous. If it is not, I will strip Derek of the presidency of the Hayward Corporation and appoint Ross in his place, and I will sign over to Ross my fifty percent ownership in the corporation. Derek will then have no place in the company at all. Do you wish to have me clarify any of that or do you understand it?'

Derek sat without moving. His mind raced one last time around the walls that had closed in, then came to a stop. There was no way out. At least, not that he could see. Next year perhaps, or the year after. Or in five years. But not yet.

Curt gave Victoria a long look. 'Do you know,' he observed. 'You are a formidable woman. I always wondered why my father stayed with you. Now I understand.'

'I am not flattered,' she said, and turned away from him.

'Is it going to be unanimous?' asked Ann.

'Of course,' Jason said, 'And not a bad idea, either.'

'Is that so?' she retorted. 'Tell me this. Where in this plan is a place for Craig?'

Softly, Tobias quoted, ' "Your shadow at evening rising to meet you".'

'I'm so weary of all this,' murmured Victoria.

Katherine felt the coldness of her hand. 'You should lie down.'

'I will, as soon as we vote. Too much emotion; quite exhausting. Ann,' she said, raising her voice. 'The Board of Directors will discuss Craig's place in the Hayward Corporation. I will no longer be a member, and I will not try to influence anyone on it. However, there is also my personal estate. That has troubled me deeply. My love for Craig was intact for many years, but I have learned too much about him, and too much time has passed. He has forfeited it all.'

'No –!' Ann began, but Victoria stopped her with an upraised hand. How strange, Katherine thought, that these two women, who had done the most to burden Craig with demands that he perform, excel, live up to the image of their golden boy, had grown so far apart in their thoughts of him. 'He has forfeited it all,' Victoria repeated. 'His wife and children – oh, how absurd to call her "his wife"! Katherine has made her own place in this family, and a larger one in my heart, and she and Jennifer and Todd have a major place in my will. What you and Jason decide to do with your stock is your affair, but of course you have too little to make any difference in the structure of the new company.'

'You're shutting him out!' Ann cried. 'Katherine, you could convince –'

'She cannot,' Victoria said impatiently. 'Why must I keep repeating myself? I make my own decisions. I want this company to be exactly as Claude described it. And I want it voted on. Must I make the motion myself?'

'I move,' said Derek flatly – for the second time that day causing a stunned silence at the table – 'that the reorganisation of the Hayward Corporation as described be accepted unanimously.'

'Second,' said Claude quickly.

Victoria stood. 'All those in favour, please raise your hand.'

The hands went up: Victoria, Ross, Claude, Tobias, Jason, Ann, Derek. Victoria raised her own. She looked at Curt. Slowly, his hand went up.

Victoria sighed. 'The motion is carried.' Turning, she said, 'Ann, if I could speak to you a moment?'

Derek pushed his chair away from the table. The walls hadn't closed in completely after all; the possibilities were enormous. Managed properly, the corporation could be transformed: rich, versatile, powerful, international. When they combined the base he'd established in construction with what he had to admit was Ross's architectural genius, plus the vast market for urban development . . . *that* would be a company to fight for. I'll work my ass off to help him build it up, and then I'll find a way to take it over. He looked up, and met Ross's eyes.

Gathering his papers together Ross stood and tilted his head towards the corner of the room, telling Derek to join him there. The son of a bitch, he thought. Cutting his losses, probably planning already how to take the company from me. We'll fight every step of the way. Briefly, he recalled their last meeting, when Derek's fear had cracked his composure. If it hadn't been for that, Ross reflected, I wouldn't have accepted Victoria's offer. But now that the company was his, and he had the chance to do what he'd always wanted, the way he'd always wanted, he knew it would be worth even the battles with Derek that loomed ahead. And he could use Derek; he was damned good; he just had to be controlled.

In the corner of the room where two armchairs stood beside the coffee maker on the sideboard, Ross poured a cup of coffee, and waited. There wasn't anything he would worry about in the months ahead, not even the battles with his brother, if Katherine were with him. He'd enjoy winning them all the more if she could share the victories.

He glanced at her, but she was listening to Victoria and Ann. I'll see her at the ball, he remembered. By then I'll be able to tell her about the first session between the president of the Hayward Corporation and the president of Hayward Construction. The first time in our lives I'm controlling our direction. We have a lot of adjustments to make.

At that moment, Derek rose and walked slowly over to join him. 'You wanted to see me,' he said smoothly, and, pulling out the armchairs, they sat down and began to talk: two businessmen in a neutral corner, discussing the future.

'– want you to understand,' Victoria was saying to Ann. 'We've needed something new for a long time. A company. A family.' Her glance lingered on her grandsons. 'Maybe they'll learn to get along with each other. Or at least fight constructively. And now it's done. I won't have anything more to do with the company; I'd only be in the way.' She stepped back. 'Ross will sit at Hugh's desk and make his dreams and mine come true. And now, Katherine, you too must be part of it –'

Katherine smiled and shook her head. 'You've just organised a new company. Isn't that enough for one day?'

'Well, we can talk about it tomorrow. Oh, I forgot to mention . . . Ross! If you and Derek are defining the activities of the subsidiaries, you should include Claude for tax purposes –'

'That had occurred to us,' Ross said gently. 'Do you want to join us?'

'No.' She laughed ruefully. 'An old woman has trouble letting go. The finality of it . . . like giving away the art collections of a lifetime. Relinquishing one thing after another; dying one step at a time. Oh, if I could be seventy again! Go on, go on with your talk. Katherine will help me to the car. After all, you're in charge now: why aren't you presiding over the meeting?'

She went to the two of them. 'Derek, I'm pleased that you stayed. I was afraid you would resign in a pique and that would have been unfortunate.'

Expressionless, he bowed his head slightly. Victoria put her hand on Ross's shoulder and he stood and walked with her to the door. 'Dear Ross,' she said. 'You are like Hugh in so many ways. Take care of what he built. Take care of what we made together.' He held her close and kissed her. 'Bless you,' she whispered, and, on Katherine's arm, nodding to the rest of her family, Victoria left the board room of the Hayward Corporation for the last time.

Chapter 21

On Saturday afternoon, Victoria called to ask Katherine to be the hostess for her All Hallows party that night. 'I've organised it all; it only needs someone to make sure everything is running smoothly. Tobias will be there, of course, but he does get lost in his quotations.'

'But you'll be there,' Katherine had protested. 'It's your party!'

'Naturally I'll be there; I wouldn't miss it. I intend to sit on a gilded throne, graciously accepting greetings, allowing my guests to touch my hem, and sending you forth as my other self. Can you be there early, to check on the table settings?'

'Yes, but –'

'Don't be alarmed, Katherine; there won't be much to do. And if you need help, Tobias and I will be there. And Ross.'

When they had said goodbye, Katherine shook her head at Victoria's stratagems to team Ross and Katherine as replacements for Hugh and Victoria. The two of us, she thought, and our four children, starting a new Hayward dynasty. She's forgotten Craig.

Or she hadn't forgotten; she was simply ignoring obstacles, trying by sheer force of will to make events go the way she wanted. Katherine was never sure, with Victoria, how much was pretence and how much was real. Maybe it didn't matter, if in the end she got her way, as she had at the board meeting.

'Mom, we're going,' Todd said. 'We're helping Annie make hamburgers for dinner.'

She hugged them. 'Have a good time.'

'You have a good time,' Jennifer said. 'Will Ross be there?'

'Of course. His mother is giving the party.'

'Tell him hello for us.'

'All right.'

Todd said brightly, 'You can even kiss him hello for us.'

'All right.'

'You can even invite him to dinner,' Jennifer said. 'We'll make hamburgers.'

'We'll see. You could make hamburgers for Leslie and Claude some time.'

'Sure.' Jennifer and Todd looked at each other. 'But we promised him dinner that day he went swimming with us.'

'You didn't tell me that.'

'We like him.' Todd said. 'That's all. And it's fun going places together. We just like him, and we thought – after what we said before – about Dad – you might not understand. That's all.'

'Understand what?' Katherine asked.

'That you need sex and companionship,' Todd blurted. 'Carrie told us. They really hate the guy their mother has – his name's Guy, which is weird – and we really like Ross, so we figure if you have to have somebody . . . Well, anyway, that's what we meant.'

'Thank you,' Katherine said.

'And have a wonderful time tonight,' Jennifer said. 'And don't rush home. Be as late as you want.'

'Thank you,' Katherine said again.

Now I have permission from everyone, she thought, taking her new dress from the closet. At least for sex and companionship.

'You're not dressed!' Leslie said, swooping in half an hour later. 'I came to help; Claude's picking us up in a few minutes. He told me about the board meeting; I'd like to bow down before Victoria and kiss her feet. My God, is this your new dress? You'll be the star of the party. Turn around; let me zip you up.'

They stood in front of Katherine's mirror. 'Look at you,' Leslie said quietly.

Katherine was all in gold: the dress a strapless silk sheath in antique gold, with a lace overblouse, pale gold and longsleeved. Her dark hair, tumbling to her shoulders, was a deep burnished brown against the fragile gold lace and her pale skin glowed softly, barely touched with colour.

She had removed the button that fastened the blouse at her waist and replaced it with a miniature gold seahorse with an opaline eye and a slender coiled tail nestling a fleck of abalone shell. But it was the necklace and matching bracelet that Leslie reached for with shining eyes.

'Incredible. They're art, not just jewellery. Why the hell you're wasting your time at those little shops . . .'

'You know why.'

'Your belts are selling at Heath's. I'll have to talk to our jewellery manager again.' They heard the doorbell. 'Claude come to take his ladies to the ball. Can I try on the necklace first?'

'Go ahead.' Katherine went to the door and when she and Claude came in they found Leslie sighing at her reflection. Her dress was wine taffeta leaving one shoulder bare; around her throat flowed the slender, curved gold segments of Katherine's necklace, held together with small clusters of tiny bezel-set gems – tear drops, triangles and circles – in amber, pale blue, deep green and black. Leslie sighed again. 'It belongs in a palace – seventeenth century Italy or France – on a woman wearing a crown or at least a tiara.'

In a low voice, Claude asked Katherine, 'Is it for sale?'

'No.' She smiled. 'This was my present to myself. But I could make a similar one.'

'I'll buy it.'

'Sight unseen?'

'Of course; I trust you.'

'It's very expensive.'

'I don't doubt it. I want it, whatever it costs. My wedding gift to my bride. I congratulate you, Katherine; it's brilliant.' He stood beside Leslie. 'You belong in a palace. But not tonight. Victoria asked Katherine to be early; we should leave.'

'I'm ready. Katherine, Tobias would say "A thing of beauty is a joy forever," and he'd be right. My God, your jewellery has me quoting poetry. Here; take it back before I break into song.'

By the time they reached the Fairmont, Katherine was thinking only of the party. It would be her first social event since the whirling months with Derek, and she wasn't even sure what Victoria expected her to do as a hostess. Check the tables, she thought, and whatever else it takes to make four hundred guests happy. A cinch, as Leslie would say. Just a little gathering, like the one I gave for her in Vancouver.

She stopped short in the middle of the ornate lobby marble-pillared, floral-carpeted, velvet-upholstered, remembering the softness of the summer night as she stood on the terrace of her home in Vancouver, telling Leslie it was too bad she couldn't stay over, to see Craig. I was waiting for him then, she thought.

I'm waiting for him now. Two different parties. She glanced in a mirror. Two different women.

'Katherine,' Leslie called. 'Didn't you want to be early?'

'Yes,' she said. She might still be waiting for him, but nothing else was left from that other party. Go away, she told his shadow. I have so many other things to think about right now.

She walked with Leslie and Claude along what seemed to be endless corridors to the glass doors that led to the ballroom. Only the bartenders were there, but in the adjacent dining-room waiters and waitresses were setting wine glasses on forty round tables set with ivory damask cloths, white and gold china, floating candlewicks, and centrepieces of russet and white chrysanthemums in woven baskets. Clusters of Norfolk pines stood like miniature forests along the walls, in the corners, and below the stand where an orchestra was tuning up. Chandeliers glowed with amber lights. The Fairmont dining-room had been transformed to a New England autumn forest.

'Tobias,' Claude said, surveying the scene. 'He misses Boston in the fall so he's re-created it in San Francisco.'

A large man in a tuxedo approached, looking inquiringly from Katherine to Leslie. 'Mrs Fraser? I'm Arvin Wallace, assistant caterer. Mrs Hayward said I was to discuss any problems with you.'

'We'll be in the garden,' Leslie said.

Traitor, Katherine thought. 'Is there a problem?' she asked Wallace.

'The caviar mousse, madame. The chef used Beluga instead of the American Golden that Mrs Hayward ordered.'

Katherine looked at him blankly. Beluga instead of American Golden. When a woman puts on a new gown and the most elegant of jewellery, she does not anticipate a lesson in sub-species of caviar. 'Have you tasted it?' she asked.

He looked offended. 'But of course, madame. How else would I know which caviar had been used?'

584

'You could have asked,' Katherine said mildly. 'How did it taste?'

'Excellent, of course,' he said. 'It is, of course, the finest caviar one can buy.'

'Then what is the problem?' Katherine asked.

'But, madame, surely it is clear . . . Mrs Hayward originally asked for Beluga, but we thought it was unavailable and therefore the price we quoted for the dinner did not include it. I thought of course madame would see that immediately.'

Snob, Katherine thought. He's worried because he's going to be stuck with the extra cost. Well, he's not going to make himself feel better by making me feel inexperienced, even if I am inexperienced. She raised her chin and calmly scrutinised him until his eyes flickered. 'Mr Wallace, at this moment, is the most important consideration cost or excellence?'

'Madame, there is no question –'

'Good. It seems inappropriate, then, to raise the issue of cost two hours before dinner. I am confident the mousse will be as excellent as you claim, and tomorrow we will study the matter. I will, of course, discuss this with Mrs Hayward.'

He lowered his eyes. 'Of course, madame.' He turned to go.

'Mr Wallace, about the centrepieces –'

He looked up and Katherine saw the flash in his eyes. 'The centrepieces, madame? Did Mrs Hayward –?'

'Mrs Hayward didn't mention them. But they're skimpy. And the two colours aren't bright enough against the ivory cloths. I would guess that flowers are missing.'

He looked at her with grudging respect. 'Yes, madame. By mistake the florist sent red dahlias instead of yellow asters. Quite gauche; I left them out.'

'Let me see them.'

He sighed, left her, and was back in a moment with a handful of ruby-red dahlias with yellow centres like tiny suns.

Katherine arranged four of them among the chrysanthemums

in one of the woven baskets. The centrepiece sprang to life, brightening the entire table. Silently she looked at Wallace.

'It does seem pleasant,' he said.

'Please take care of the other tables. Four to a basket; five if you have enough. Is there anything else?'

'No, madame.' He hesitated. 'Thank you.'

Flushed with success, Katherine wandered about the dining-room, admiring the tables. She pointed out to a waitress a place setting that lacked a wine glass; she straightened a centrepiece that was perfectly straight; she spoke to the orchestra leader about his selections and asked him to include the Autumn section of Vivaldi's *Four Seasons*. By then the beautiful room seemed hers and she walked toward the ballroom feeling sure of herself, in charge, a hostess – until she saw the first guests arriving, and quailed. I can't do this alone, she thought, and went to find Leslie and Claude. 'You have to stand there with me,' she pleaded. 'I can't possibly greet four hundred strangers without support. Why isn't Victoria here?'

'She makes a grand entrance at ten,' said Claude. 'Come along; I'll fill you in on personalities.'

He stood at her shoulder, with Leslie beside him, and whispered capsule descriptions of approaching guests. 'Just came back from Majorca . . .' 'And how was Majorca?' Katherine asked, smiling, as she shook hands. 'Owns a pool with flamingoes . . .' 'Are the flamingoes flourishing?' Katherine asked, smiling. She was beginning to have a good time. 'Mounts stuffed elks in his hunting lodge,' Claude whispered. '*Whole* elks?' Katherine asked in astonishment. The guests looked bewildered as she and Claude and Leslie burst out laughing. 'I'm sorry,' Katherine said to the dignified man standing in front of her. 'How nice to see you; I've heard so much about your elks.'

When Ross came, Claude whispered, 'In love with a brilliant

jéwellery designer,' and so she was smiling when she put out her hand to him. He held it tightly. 'Is Victoria ill?' Katherine shook her head. 'Claude says she'll make a grand entrance at ten.'

'And she asked you to do her chores?'

'Yes.'

'But we'll have time –' He hesitated, then, as others came in behind him, said, 'Later', spoke briefly to Claude and Leslie, and went on.

Finally, Claude said, 'That's most of them. Come; I'm parched. The three of us have earned champagne.'

By ten o'clock, four hundred guests in tuxedos and lustrous gowns strolled in the ballroom and garden. Waiters and waitresses circulated with mirrored trays of champagne and hors-d'oeuvres; the orchestra played show tunes; and in a pause between numbers, Victoria appeared in the doorway, in ivory velvet edged in silk. On Tobias's arm, she walked to a high-backed chair on a small platform between the garden and the ballroom, where she could observe everyone.

A few feet from her, on the other side of the glass, was the garden, a luxuriant oasis of towering palms like thickly-feathered umbrellas, raised circular beds of flowers separated by grass and walkways, an illuminated fountain, lamp posts topped with softly-lit spheres, and six-foot Bird-of-Paradise bushes covered with brilliant blue and orange flowers like birds in flight. As guests came to greet her, Victoria saw Katherine at the far end of the garden, standing with Leslie and Claude, Marc Landau and his newest companion, and a group of board members of the San Francisco Symphony. They stood beside one of the Bird of Paradise bushes, but, in Victoria's eyes, Katherine outshone the flowers and more than held her own with the women around her.

It was a different crowd from the ones Katherine had met with Derek. This was Victoria's élite: the wealthy benefactors

587

of the city's museums, concerts, ballet, theatre, colleges and universities. Many of them had several homes in or near the world's great cities; most of them represented wealth that had been transmitted through generations; all of them gave away more than most people earn in a lifetime. Katherine stood among them, smiling, chatting, listening, learning.

'Look at her,' Victoria said to Tobias. 'Would you guess she grew up over a grocery store?'

'I would guess,' he mused, 'that she is terrified and exhilarated in equal measure.'

'Nonsense. Well, perhaps so. But how well she carries it off!' She saw Katherine break into laughter, her face glowing. 'How full of life she is! Tobias, I do love her so.'

'Yes, quite right,' he agreed, thinking how extraordinary was the train of events that began with the cowardice of Craig and led to the love between two women who needed each other.

'Where is Ross?' Victoria demanded. 'I don't see him anywhere.'

Tobias chuckled. 'Whatever made you think of him?'

'Katherine made me think of him, as you well know. Well, would you bring her to me, Tobias? I haven't greeted her and I want a look at her jewellery; several people have mentioned it. Please, my dear.'

Tobias wended his way through the crowd, nodding and smiling at the sleek, successful guests who treated him with respect because he was Victoria's brother and had written a number of scholarly books, but who also thought him amusingly eccentric because he had been content as a professor, unconcerned with what they called serious money.

I am serious about books, Tobias mused, and as greedy about acquiring them as others are about acquiring money. He chuckled. Perhaps they would admire me more if they knew I was as covetous in my way as they are in theirs.

At that moment he found Ross beside him. 'Can you share your joke?' Ross asked.

'No, dear boy; it was on me, so I keep it to myself. Have you seen Katherine?'

Ross looked at the group beside the Bird-of-Paradise bush. 'Yes. Would you introduce me to her? If we pretend we're just beginning, with no past to deal with, I could ask her to dance.'

'Ask her anyway. Tell her you're doing it not for yourself, but to please Victoria.' Ross laughed. 'It *would* please Victoria,' Tobias said. Almost to himself, he quoted, ' "However long we were loved, it was not long enough." '

Ross came to a full stop. 'Say that again.'

Tobias repeated it. 'You should always listen to the wisdom of poets, Ross. And of old men. There is never enough time. Damn it, boy, ask her to dance!'

'Have you a poem that explains loyalty and betrayal?' Ross asked quietly. 'And a fear of repeating the past? And a shadow that darkens everything it touches? Of course I'll ask her to dance. But after that . . .' He shrugged slightly. For the past hour, as he moved among the guests, finding old friends, making new acquaintances, fending off commiserations and probing enquiries on his separation from Melanie, he had continually found himself near Katherine. How it happened he was not sure, but wherever he turned, her vivid loveliness was not far away, surrounded by broad-shouldered tuxedos and glittering gowns and jewels. She was a slender, golden flame, swaying slightly in the currents of the crowd, drawing others to her, as he was drawn, to stand close to her glow and the lilt of her voice and laughter.

As he and Tobias walked towards her, the thought suddenly came to him: She doesn't need any of us. She's come this far without Craig, without me, without Victoria. She's done it all herself. She can go as far as she wants, by herself. He felt the emptiness of loss. He'd thought he was protecting her when he kept Elissa a secret, but that had only shown her one more step she could take on her own; she could do without him.

But then Katherine looked his way and he saw the swift succession of joy, love and caution in her clear hazel eyes, and he thought it might be all right after all. She didn't depend on him to survive and make her way in the world, any more than he depended on her, but if she needed his love to be a whole person, as much as he needed hers, that would be more than enough on which to build a life.

'May I introduce Ross Hayward?' Tobias was saying. 'Ross, this is Katherine Fraser; I think you two should get acquainted. But first' – he tugged lightly on Katherine's arm – 'Victoria demands your presence. If I can spirit you away, just for a moment . . . '

'Tobias,' Katherine said as they walked into the ballroom. 'Was that a private joke?'

'Ross wants to start from the beginning,' he explained cheerfully. 'A good idea. When he asks you to dance, tell him you'll accept not for yourself but because it will please Victoria.'

Katherine looked at him closely. 'That sounds like something you'd tell Ross to say to me.'

'Great heavens!' Tobias expostulated. 'Am I condemned to live my entire life with intelligent women who see through me? Victoria, here is your granddaughter. I leave her to you. I go in search of gullible guests.'

The pitch of conversation had reached a level that almost drowned out the orchestra, and Katherine had to lean close to Victoria to hear her. 'The dahlias are perfect,' she said, kissing her cheek. 'Wally tried to tell me they were his idea, but I know better. You seem to have put him properly in his place. He is the worst kind of snob: a small-minded and very dull man who looks down on others because he moves among people who happen to have money. Salespeople at certain exclusive shops are the same; I avoid them.'

'I should tell you,' Katherine said. 'The caviar –' Quickly she explained it. 'I don't know how much more it costs –'

Victoria waved it away. 'They'll make it up; it's their mistake. They knew they'd have to; Wally tried to intimidate you because you weren't arrogant enough to impress him. You handled it perfectly, my dear; I'm sorry I missed seeing you do it. Have you seen Ross?'

Katherine nodded.

'Will you dance with him?'

'Of course.'

'Excellent. Let me look at your jewellery. My friends are asking me where you bought it.' Katherine took off her bracelet, a small version of the necklace. 'Ah, my dear, the feel of it, almost as if it breathes. Have you ever done anything like it? No, of course you haven't. Neither has anyone else. Do you know, Katherine, I almost *covet* it.'

Katherine laughed and kissed her again. 'It's yours.'

'No, no. But if you would make me something like it . . .'

'You know I will.'

A trumpet call from the orchestra announced dinner and the crowd surged towards the dining-room. From Victoria's platform, Katherine had a full view of the mosaic of richly-coloured gowns interspersed with black and white tuxedos – patterns forming and dissolving, shifting, flowing, thinning out until the last of the guests had gone through the doors and she and Victoria were alone. 'I should have brought my sketch pad,' she murmured.

'You'll remember,' Victoria said serenely. 'You have an artist's eye.' As they walked to the dining-room, she said, 'Katherine, dear, when you make my necklace and bracelet, will you also make the seahorse? Such simplicity; almost Florentine. How did you learn that?'

591

'I don't know.'

'It just comes to you? How exciting that must be. And satisfying.'

'And demanding,' Katherine said. 'I can forget whatever else is happening – at least while I'm concentrating on it.'

Victoria nodded. 'I think of you working at your table, the way I once worked at Hugh's desk. It gives me such enormous pleasure to think of you at work.'

In the centre of the dining-room, Ross sat at a table with seven people Katherine did not know. Two chairs were empty. 'For us,' Victoria said, and as Ross held the one beside him, she took it.

A burly man with masses of waving hair and a moustache to match held the other chair for Katherine. Ross introduced him. 'Brock Galvez – Victoria Hayward – Katherine Fraser. Brock is one of the developers of BayBridge Plaza, Katherine; he talks about it almost as much as I do.'

'More,' Galvez declared. 'My wife Brenda here, she gets upset; says a mistress she could handle; BayBridge has her stumped.'

In the general laughter, as waiters served the caviar mousse, he said to Katherine, 'We've met. New Year's Eve, wasn't it? Some crazy shindig with dogs barking Christmas carols. You were with Derek. Haven't seen him tonight. He out of town?'

'I don't know,' Katherine replied. 'He's been very busy lately.'

'Good man, Derek, knows how to run a construction team. He built us a helluva – excuse the expression – office building down Cupertino way. Doesn't have the – how would you say it – vision of Ross, but I had a drink last night with Curt – known him for years – and he says they're all getting together a new company. Quite a team, that'll be. Where'd you find that necklace?'

'I made it.'

'*Made it?*'

'I design and make jewellery.'

'I'll be damned. Can you make me one? And' – he peered at her waist – 'don't mean to be impertinent but could I see that thingamajig?'

Katherine unpinned the seahorse and handed it to him. Brenda Galvez asked to see it, and it was passed from hand to hand. Ross watched, a thoughtful expression on his face, and when a woman across the table said, 'I'd love to buy one for my daughter,' he held a quick whispered conversation with Victoria. 'Who carries them?' the woman asked.

'It's one of a kind,' Katherine answered. 'And I don't sell these to –' Ross raised his hand slightly, and, puzzled, she broke off.

'Well, one of a kind is what I prefer,' the woman across the table was saying. 'It's unbearable to see just everyone wearing something I've spent a fortune on to be different. Do I order from you?'

As a slow, wicked smile spread across Victoria's face, Ross said casually, 'You'll find the Fraser collection at Xavier's in about a month.'

Speechless, Katherine stared at him. Victoria looked at her with dancing eyes. 'Try the caviar mousse,' she urged. 'It is quite the best I've had in a long time.'

But as superb as the mousse was, and the watercress soup and fillet of duck in calvados that followed, and the dessert of *Crème Brûlée* and lacy almond tuiles, Katherine barely tasted any of it. Xavier's? What was Ross talking about?

Cognac and port were offered as the orchestra in the ballroom struck up a waltz. Gradually, the dining-room emptied. Brock Galvez asked Katherine to dance. Marc Landau followed; then a string of men she did not know, all animated, flattering, light on their feet, successful in business – and none of them Ross. An hour passed, then two. Katherine went to sit with Victoria. A few minutes later Ross joined them. 'Will you dance with me? For no one's pleasure but my own. And, I hope, yours.'

She gave a low laugh, so intimate his hands felt the curve of her body even before he held her on the dance floor. 'I want to carry you off,' he said. 'And hold you and tell you I love you and let no one come near to distract us, until you say we're so much a part of each other you can't imagine a life without me.'

'Ross, please don't –'

'Katherine, your jewellery,' interrupted a tall woman Katherine did not know. 'Xavier's? In November?'

'I don't think –'

'Well, even December . . . as long as it's in time for Christmas.' The woman and her partner spun away.

'– Handsome necklace,' said the president of the Bank of California, pausing in the dance with his wife.

An electronic flash went off as a photographer captured Katherine in Ross's arms, chatting with the president of the Bank of California. Within the next half hour, photographers from *Chronicle* and the *Examiner* circled the room to give their readers a pictorial report of Victoria Hayward's All Hallows Eve celebration, while society reporters eavesdropped and scribbled notes.

Victoria watched with a wide smile, and Katherine said, 'Ross, what is that all about? It's not true . . .'

'Not yet. But what do you think will happen when these people call Xavier's next week asking about the Fraser jewellery collection?'

'They'll be told there is no such thing.'

'My dear love,' he smiled. 'More likely, the astute people at Xavier's will be delighted to take the names of the callers, to notify them when the collection is available and when they have a list of potential customers, they will call you.'

Katherine shook her head. 'Only in fairy tales.'

'Business isn't so different from fairy tales; they both have obstacles, rewards, coincidences, fairy godmothers and godfathers, winners and losers . . .'

'But fairy tales have happy endings.'

'I'm working on that.'

They danced in silence. 'You had your own happy ending,' Katherine said. 'I meant to congratulate you after the board meeting.'

'Not an ending,' he said. 'A beginning. With a long and very bumpy road ahead. If I were smarter, I'd be scared.'

She tilted her head and studied him. 'But you're not. You're excited; you can't wait to get started.'

He kissed the top of her head. 'Do you know what it means to me when you understand me, without explanations?'

Tobias materialised beside them. 'Katherine, my dear, I have again been commanded to deliver you to Victoria. She wants to say goodnight.'

'Goodnight?' Katherine asked. 'But it's only –' She looked at her watch in disbelief. 'Three o'clock?'

'So it seems. And the two of us are ready for bed.'

Victoria was fastening a cape at her throat when they found her at the cloakroom. 'A highly satisfactory evening,' she said. 'You did very well, Katherine. Now kiss me goodnight and go back to your dancing.'

'I think I should go home, too. There's no such thing as sleeping late on a sofa bed in our living-room.'

'Stay a while,' Ross said. 'I'll take you home whenever you're ready.'

'Very sensible,' Victoria commented. 'My dear,' she added to Katherine. 'Promise me something. Don't make any sudden decisions about your jewellery. Take your time.'

'All right,' Katherine said.

'Promise me.'

'I promise.'

'And you'll tell me what happens.'

'I promise that, too.'

'Excellent. Goodnight, my dears. I'll talk to you tomorrow.'

The music was soft and slow and they glided in a gentle, swaying rhythm. Katherine touched the smooth cloth of Ross's sleeve. 'Do you know, I've never seen you in a tuxedo? You look exceedingly handsome.'

'And you are wonderfully beautiful,' he said quietly. 'You haven't responded to what I said earlier.'

'You mean about becoming a part of you. Ross, I already am – as much as I can be. I miss you and I want you, and I find myself reaching out to share with you –'

'Katherine –!'

'– But you said you wanted to let me finish what I began. That was why you weren't calling me, you said. And then tonight – to tell me you want me to be part of you . . .'

'It's not consistent.'

'Or fair.'

'It would be easier to be consistent and fair if I could stop worrying about what you might do when Craig comes back.'

'Has it occurred to you that you worry about that more than I do?'

He thought about it. 'No. I don't think you know how you'll react to him any more than I do when he starts playing on your memories and sympathies, and his needs and your kids . . . Katherine, we don't have to be so far apart; if we love each other we can find a way –'

'Ross, please, I'm trying to do what's right.'

It struck him like a blow. *Trying to do what's right.* If she thought she knew what that was, how could he tell her she was wrong?

He repeated it as he drove her home. *Trying to do what's right.* In fairy tales, Ross thought, that was always rewarded; happy endings, Katherine had said. They walked to her front

596

door and he held her for a moment, as he had when they were dancing. 'I hope, whatever happens, it is what you want,' he told her, and waited until she had closed the door behind her before he went back to his car, and drove home.

Monday morning's newspapers were strewn about Victoria's chaise as she sat on her sunporch, clipping the society pages. 'Most satisfactory,' she said, almost purring, as Katherine came in. 'Especially the photograph of you and Ross talking to that bank president . . .' She kissed Katherine soundly, then looked closely at her. 'Something has happened. Come, come, what is it?'

Katherine's eyes sparkled. 'I had a telephone call this morning. From Herman Mettler.'

'Ah.' Victoria grinned. 'He's read the papers. I'll bet it spoiled his breakfast, to read about Katherine Fraser and see her picture as she moves in the highest society among people who will buy her jewellery. But he gets no sympathy from me; he does not deserve it. What did he say?'

'He called me Katherine –'

'Cosy,' Victoria observed scornfully.

'And wanted to buy back the jewellery he'd returned, and any more I had. He also said my husband had nothing to do with our business dealings.'

Victoria laughed delightedly. 'And what did you tell him?'

'That I couldn't decide right away.'

'Quite right.' Victoria nodded vigorously. 'How pleasant it is when people get what they deserve! You did well.'

'I followed your advice.'

'It was good advice; therefore, you did well.'

Katherine smiled. Restlessly, she walked to the windows looking down at Lafayette Park, the sun glistening off its dark green leaves and the white uniforms of nurses pushing buggies and strollers. She considered telling Victoria about the rest of

597

the conversation with Mettler; that he had let slip that it was Derek who had given him the idea Katherine Fraser might be a thief But what good would it do? Victoria knew what Derek was like, and she had already punished him, in the board meeting, by stripping him of most of his power and putting him beneath Ross's authority. There was nothing more anyone could do to Derek. It doesn't matter anymore, Katherine thought. It's over. I can't even be angry. I've got past him.

Turning from the window, she asked Victoria, 'Why did you tell me not to make any quick decisions about my jewellery?'

'Ross told you why. To give Xavier's a chance to get requests from customers.'

'Victoria, do you and Ross tell each other everything?'

'Certainly not. There are many things a grandmother and a grandson do not share. But others we do. He would make you very happy, Katherine. I am not trying to force you; I am simply saying he would make you happy. And he needs you; the next years are not going to be easy for him, putting together that company I forced him into. You could help him; you would be good for each other.'

'And Craig?' Katherine asked.

'Craig is a fool!' Victoria exploded. 'And Ross is a romantic. How can you even hesitate in choosing between them?'

Katherine laughed ruefully. 'It's so easy for you to forget I'm married to one of them.'

'Not any more, you foolish girl. Craig ended it, long ago. You are the only one who clings to it.'

Katherine had not told her about Craig's telephone call; neither, she realised, had Ross. I don't want to repeat it now, she thought, and said only, 'Then it's my foolishness. May I ask you about something else?'

Victoria looked up, her eyebrows raised.

'Why did you give that party last night?'

'Hugh and I gave one every year. It was our tradition. Besides, I wanted to watch you take my place.'

'That was my initiation?'

'An odd way of putting it, my dear.'

'And if I had failed?'

'If I thought you would fail, there would have been no party. I knew you would not.'

'But you don't know what will happen with Craig.'

'For sixteen years I thought Craig was dead; for the past year and a half I haven't had any idea what would happen with him. But I trust you. Whatever you decide – whether you are with Ross or Craig or someone else – or alone – I trust you. When I die, Katherine, I am leaving you this apartment, complete with Tobias, if he outlives me; he must be able to live upstairs as long as he wishes. But the rest will be yours, and more than enough money to end your worries. No don't say anything now; I won't change my mind. Just listen.'

She held out her hand and Katherine took it. 'Sometime in the future, when I am no longer here – will you keep all of them together? Even when they wrangle and compete and run off to Maine or God knows where . . . keep them in touch, keep them feeling like a family. For the children, you know, to give them a haven. The world spins so wildly, we're thrown apart, we lose each other – unless we have a solid core to hold on to. No one knows that better than you, my tenacious Katherine; you don't let go easily or lightly.'

She touched Katherine's cheek. 'When Craig and Jennifer died – were gone – I thought I'd stopped caring. But you've made me believe we can be a family again. It is maddening!' she burst out, 'that I won't live another fifty years and see the four children marry and have children of their own . . . see what becomes of the Haywards. It's like being forced to leave a movie in the middle. I can't even convince myself I'll be sitting somewhere watching all of you after I die –'

'You couldn't bear that,' Katherine said. 'Watching us without being able to comment or organise our affairs . . .'

'Good Lord, you're right; I would go mad. So I must arrange as much as possible while I'm here. Promise me you'll do this, Katherine. There is no one else I can ask. Keep a family for the children, and their children. Don't let everyone get trampled by private needs, and then scattered like dust.'

Katherine put her arms around her, aware of her own youth, the firmness of her skin, the vigorous pulsing of her blood, demanding to run and dance, to accomplish, to love. She kissed the cool parchment of Victoria's cheek. 'I'll do my best,' she said then gave a small laugh. 'And even if you aren't sitting somewhere, watching us, you'll always be inside me, telling me what I should do.'

'Of course,' Victoria said serenely. 'I'm counting on that.'

It was nearly five o'clock when Ross's prediction came true and the manager of Xavier's telephoned Katherine. 'I have been inundated with requests for jewellery by Katherine Fraser,' he said. 'I do have the right Katherine Fraser? Victoria Hayward gave me this number.'

'You called her?' Katherine asked.

'Just a few minutes ago. She wondered why it had taken me so long.'

'She couldn't have said that.'

'We've known each other many years and she said exactly that. Mrs Fraser, my customers have excellent taste, and all the cities of the world in which to shop. If they are impressed with your jewellery, I want to see it, everything you have, including designs or sketches. Unfortunately, I'm busy tomorrow, but can you come in on Wednesday? Christmas isn't far off, and we should begin as soon as possible.'

Excitement was rushing through Katherine, warm and

heady like red wine; she could barely sit still. 'Wednesday is fine. In the morning?'

'Ten o'clock, if that's convenient.'

'That's fine.' Any time was fine, Katherine thought, hanging up; whatever time he wanted. She phoned Victoria and told her; Victoria called Tobias to the telephone and Katherine repeated her news; at dinner she told Jennifer and Todd and because she was so excited she did not try to dampen their fantastic plans for castles in the sky.

All evening her excitement raced at its high pitch. She tried to calm down by sorting her jewellery and sketches, but when the thought came to her that she was finally escaping Craig's shadow, she became so restless she could not sit still. She called Leslie, but even talking to her was not enough, and at last Katherine admitted to herself that it was Ross she most wanted to share her excitement. Without thinking further about it, she dialled his number, and then listened to the empty ringing of his telephone. She called again and again, and at midnight was trying once more when the doorbell rang. It can't be Ross, she thought; he said he wouldn't even call. But still, her heart was pounding as she ran to open it – and saw Craig, standing on the doorstep.

Chapter 22

T hey did not touch. Craig's hand made a small movement towards her, then dropped back, and he stayed in the doorway, waiting, until Katherine stepped aside and he walked in.

'You're so beautiful,' he said wonderingly. 'And the way you stand . . . I remember, Jennifer and Todd told me you were different, that night I was here.'

His eyes were hungry and restless, fastening on Katherine's face, darting about the small room, then back to her face and slender figure in the white velvet robe Ross had brought her when he came back to Menton from Paris, then down, down, lingering on her bare feet. Katherine watched him, her mind in a turmoil. *I waited so long, and now I don't feel ready* . . . 'But I didn't think you'd be this different,' Craig said, and smiled – the gentle smile that brought everything back to Katherine, almost as if he had never been gone.

'Would it be too much trouble to make some coffee?' he asked. 'I feel like I've been travelling for weeks.'

'Of course,' Katherine said. Her voice seemed to come from a stranger. 'I mean, of course it's not too much trouble. We can sit in the kitchen.'

The oak table was the one they had used for ten years. Craig sat down and pulled his chair forward exactly as he always had and watched Katherine make coffee as he always had. And when she brought the mugs and a plate of coffee cake to the table, and sat with him, he looked just the same, his beard full and brown, his eyes eager, his smile tentative, waiting for approval and love.

'Thank you,' he said and sipped the hot coffee as he always had.

Dizzily, Katherine looked away. *This is my husband.* She was sitting in the kitchen, drinking coffee with her husband, and nothing had changed.

Everything has changed. Remember that.

'Katherine,' Craig said. 'I love you. You've got to believe me: I love you.' He leaned forward. 'I've never stopped thinking of you, needing you . . . Even when I couldn't find a way to come back, you were always the centre of my life; I never stopped loving you and wanting you.'

Katherine looked at him across the table. *This is my husband.* All the feelings of being married were rushing back – love, companionship, the comfort of familiarity – but tangled with them was the feeling that this was a stranger. Which is he? Katherine thought with a surge of panic. I don't know who he is, or how to talk to him.

'I've said that to you every night for the last sixteen months,' Craig was saying. 'Told you I love you, talked to you, told you what I was thinking . . . Katherine, I'm sorry for what I did to you; I'm sorry for the mess I made of things, for letting you down . . . Christ, all I ever wanted was to take care of you. But I'll make it up to you, I promise. Just give me a chance. I know how much I destroyed, but I want to –'

'Why did you leave?' Katherine asked.

'Why did I –? *You don't know?*'

She shook her head.

'But you must. Hank sent me the newspaper stories; he told me reporters were badgering you and the police were in and out of our house . . . and I can't believe Carl didn't come looking for me, that hypocritical bastard, full of thunder and lightning and sanctimonious talk of trusting me . . . Didn't he? Didn't he tell you what happened?'

'He told me you'd embezzled seventy-five thousand dollars from the company over two years, and admitted it when he confronted you, and you told him you were going to Toronto to borrow money to pay him back.'

He was watching her steadily. 'Clear and concise. And you still don't know why I left?'

Puzzled, Katherine realised she had been wrong about him: he *had* changed. Tanned and lean, his hands calloused, wearing slacks, a white shirt open at the neck, and a corduroy sports jacket, he was handsomer than she remembered, and more assured. When had Craig ever talked so directly, especially when it was about something unpleasant? 'Craig,' she burst out. 'Did you really steal it?'

'My God,' he said staring at her. 'You didn't believe him?' *'Did you steal it?'*

'Yes. And Carl had proof.' Almost sadly, he said, 'I didn't think you'd have so much faith . . .'

'I know,' Katherine said shortly. 'And I did believe it at first, when you didn't come back. But then something happened this summer . . . it's a long story. But it made me think you might have been framed.'

He looked stunned. 'Framed. I never thought of that. Did you ask Carl?'

'I didn't want to ask Carl. I wanted to ask you. I wanted to believe in you.'

'Why?' he asked bluntly. 'I'd left you.'

Katherine looked at him in astonishment. She had never heard Craig talk like that. 'I loved you,' she said.

'*Loved.*'

'And you still haven't told me why you left us.'

'I thought it was obvious.' He drained his mug. 'Is there more coffee?' Katherine refilled it and, without being asked, made another pot. He watched her as she stood at the counter. 'It all came crashing down. Carl screamed at me that I'd betrayed him and he'd see me in jail and make sure everyone knew what an ungrateful bastard I was. I thought a trial would mean an investigation and they'd dig up my past, and you'd hate me, if you didn't already, for stealing . . . There was no good ending to it! Do you know how many hundreds of letters I've written to you, trying to explain all this?'

'I didn't get any letters,' said Katherine.

'I never mailed them. Hell, I never finished them. How do you tell someone you love that you deserted her because everything was crushing you and you felt trapped and helpless? That morning I left I didn't even realise what I was doing until I told the cab driver to stop at the bank on the way to the airport. That was when I knew. I told him to go on, I deposited the money for you, and then I walked – two or three hours, I think – until I hitched a ride with a truck driver.'

'*Two or three hours . . .!*'

He shrugged. 'You're right; I had time to change my mind. But how could I? The more I walked, the more I thought about it, the more everything closed in, crushing me. I couldn't tell you I'd stolen; I couldn't tell you about my past; I couldn't ask anyone for help. I couldn't do anything but run. And once I'd started I had to keep on, keep moving, because when I stopped, I couldn't stand the loneliness and I'd turn around to come back to you and it would all come back – all the things I couldn't tell you crushing me, so I couldn't breathe . . .

Katherine, if I could make you understand . . . whenever I tried to come back *I couldn't breathe.* I had to keep running . . .'

His voice stopped. Katherine was silent, feeling his panic.

'But I got past that,' he said. 'Because I had to see you. Katherine, I want you to come back to Canada with me. I'll get the money to settle with Carl and we'll start again, make a home . . . I know you sold the house; we'll build a new one, a better one, and start all –'

'Craig, wait . . .'

'You can't be surprised. Why do you think I came back? Why do you think I called Ross? Ross did tell you I called, didn't he?'

'Yes.'

'I told him I love you. And want you back. Did he tell you that?'

'Yes.'

'Well.' His voice became flat. 'He told me he's in love with you. I'm not surprised; you're so lovely, and proud, the way you hold your head . . . and it's natural that you'd look for help and affection. I know it's been a rough time for you; you have nothing to be ashamed of. And Ross is as decent as they come and trustworthy . . . at least, I always thought so.' He paused. 'What are you thinking?'

'What about your family?' Katherine asked. 'If you go back to Canada.'

'You're my family! You and Jennifer and Todd!'

'And Victoria and Tobias, Ann and Jason, Derek and –'

'Not Derek, God damn it; he's no part of me and never will be!'

Katherine shrank from the fury in his voice and instinctively put her finger to her lips. 'Todd and Jennifer –'

'Sorry.' He stood up. 'I'd like to take a look at them. You don't mind –?'

'Of course not.'

Katherine watched him cross the living-room and inch open the bedroom door. She felt a stab of pity at the stiffness of his back as he stood in the doorway; then, very gently, he closed the door and came back to her. 'They look wonderful.'

'They are wonderful. They felt betrayed when you disappeared on New Year's Eve.'

Embarrassment and anger swept over his face. 'You were with Derek. I couldn't handle that. All I could think of was that if I'd told you about him you would have been warned.'

Katherine frowned. 'What are you talking about? You never told me about any of them. You lied about being an orphan; you kept yourself locked inside your secrets. For ten years . . . *What was so terrible that you couldn't tell me about them?*'

'Something . . . a long time ago. I thought about telling you but after a while it wasn't important. I didn't have to talk about them, Katherine – I didn't even think about them – as long as I had you. It never occurred to me you'd meet them. You can't imagine how strange it is to hear you talk about Victoria, Tobias, my parents – it's all wrong; you never were supposed to know about them.' Slowly, he shook his head. 'I put so many years and miles between us. How did you find them?'

'Ross found me.' Katherine brought the fresh pot of coffee to the table. 'It was Jennifer, wasn't it? The terrible thing, a long time ago. On the sailboat. When she died.'

He jerked back, as if stung. 'Who told you about that?'

'Derek. And Ross. But I want to hear it from you.'

He cupped the mug in his hands, looking at the trembling surface of the coffee. 'I didn't know they'd talk about it.' The room was silent. The building slept; the street slept. There were only the two of them, facing each other across the oak table – until Craig began to talk, slowly at first, then faster as the story poured out.

'We were sailing home, across the bay. We'd been invited

607

to some damn party in Sausalito and Jenny asked Ross and Derek to sail across with us. It was a dull party with nothing to do but drink, and by the time we left I felt rotten. We all needed to clear our heads and it was so peaceful on the water I wanted to stay out as long as possible, so I decided to sail past the Golden Gate Bridge and then in again, to the harbour. But Derek decided he was in a hurry, and he harped on it, so I put up the spinnaker. Derek usually got what he wanted, one way or another. Jenny loved it. She put her head back and laughed into the wind; she opened her arms and said "I love all of you so much." She was so lovely and happy. Oh, God . . .'

He was looking past Katherine, at the dark window. 'Near the Gate the currents were strong and the wind started to pick up, so I told Jenny and Derek to put on lifejackets, and sent Jenny down to the cabin to tell Ross. I shouldn't have; it left us alone. Usually I made sure Derek and I were never alone. We fought all the time – mostly over power, I suppose, but there were other things, too. Love, attention, money . . . I was a year older but we were both first sons and Derek made it a war: enemies and rivals from the start. And he could always get to me – make me lose control – so I tried to keep others between us. But that day, for some reason, Jenny stayed below with Ross for a few minutes, and I said something about the wind, and taking down the spinnaker, and Derek called me a coward, said I was afraid to sail at anything more than a crawl . . . said if I didn't have my mama and grandma around I couldn't even shit by myself. Crude bastard, when he wanted to be . . . smooth when he wanted . . .'

He contemplated the coffee pot. 'Do you have any Scotch?'

Katherine shook her head. 'Only wine.'

'Well, then, if I could –?' She brought a bottle to the table and a corkscrew, and pulled out the cork. 'That always used to be my job, remember? Thanks.' He filled the glass she gave him. 'I told Derek to shut up – the spinnaker had to come down. It was too much sail for that wind; a bad gust could rip it apart, might even overturn us. That was when Ross and Jenny came up from the cabin. Derek reached out and pulled Jenny to him . . . put his arms around her . . . standing sideways so I could see . . . Ross couldn't . . . his hand on her breast . . . Christ, I can't make that go away! – I still see it, at night, when I'm trying to sleep . . . his thin fingers curled over Jenny's breast, his cold eyes, daring me . . . "Jennifer and I like living dangerously," he said. "The only one who's afraid is the captain."

'It made me sick – it was the first time I knew for sure there was something between them. I yelled at Derek – because I couldn't let go of the wheel – to get his Goddamn hands off Jenny and I yelled at Jenny to get the hell away from him. It looked like she was trying, but he held her – she looked like a scared little bird caught in a trap –

'God knows what my face looked like; it scared the hell out of Ross. He yanked Jenny away and asked me if he should go forward and take down the spinnaker and I think I said yes, but I was yelling at Derek – I couldn't stop – telling him to get below or get off the boat; he could swim to shore for all I cared, if he had the guts to try it in that water . . .

'Derek came back at me in that voice he used on all of us, high and light, like fingernails on a blackboard, calling me a puppet, a doll, grandma's toy . . . who could only get it up when grandma stroked it . . . The wind was roaring, we were all drenched from the waves and spray breaking over the cockpit, and that bastard stood there like a Goddamn soldier, absolutely straight, his voice like a knife, talking, talking, and I was shouting back and Jenny started to cry. "Don't," she said. "I love you both; don't fight."

'I went crazy, I guess. First seeing Derek hold her, and his voice, cutting into me, and then hearing Jenny say she *loved us both* – I had to stop her, make her despise him, see what he

609

really was under that fake charm . . . so I screamed at him – so Jenny would be sure to hear – that he was a crook; he'd changed the specs on a building we were putting up after the city had approved them; he'd violated a pack of laws and was a rotten crook who didn't give a shit if he built a dangerous building. His face was like stone. I'd seen the changed specs that week and couldn't figure out how they'd gotten past an inspector, so I made a wild guess and accused him of bribing the inspector on the job.

'When Ross asked what the hell I was talking about, Derek turned it around – he could recover and attack faster than anyone I ever knew – and in that damned scraping voice he said: "Golden boy changed the specs on the Macklin Building to be grandma's hero – even bribed the inspector – but now he's scared and shifting the blame. Running away, as usual." That was when I knew I was right, and I laughed. I remember how good that felt, to laugh in Derek's face because he'd given himself away. I told him I cared more about our reputation than he did and I was going to my father and his and would get him kicked out of the company before he got us into real trouble.

'That was when I told Ross to go forward and take down the spinnaker – while I was laughing at Derek. And while Ross did that . . . while Jenny huddled in a corner, and spray and waves washed over us and the wind roared . . . Derek came up to me, close to me, and told me . . . so Goddamned soft and friendly – that Jenny was in love with him and . . . pregnant . . . by him . . . *pregnant by Derek* . . .'

Katherine drew in her breath sharply, but Craig did not hear. '. . . and they hadn't decided what they were going to do, but if I got in his way, he'd tell the family . . . and anybody else who might be interested . . .

'I broke apart inside. The pain was so terrible I couldn't stand it. I saw Derek's eyes watching me and I had to close

610

them – crush him – so I went for his throat and got my hands around his neck. I could feel Jenny pulling on my arm, and I was sick, thinking, *Derek's child, Derek inside you, Derek's child*, and I exploded – "You whore, Jenny! You damned whore; damn you, damn you –!" and then suddenly she was gone. Everything was gone . . .

'I didn't see it, but I felt it: when I left the wheel, the boat changed course and jibed, and the boom swung across and slammed into Jenny. I heard it, a terrible thud, and saw her stumble – blood, a starburst of blood, next to her eye – and then she went over. She didn't make a sound. She just . . . fell. I dropped Derek and got to the life preserver and the marker pole and threw them to Jenny – she was face down and I screamed at her to grab the preserver – JENNY! JENNY! JENNY! –I still hear that scream inside me. I screamed it when I dove and swam to her– and when I held her head out of the water and saw her eyes, staring at me, not seeing me, not seeing the sky . . . not seeing ever again . . . Because she was dead.'

He was crying. 'The boat was gone. There was no one but Jenny and me and the water – choppy and dark, so cold – and an awful silence.

'I got Jenny to the life preserver and tucked her into it so her face was out of the water and I stayed with her. It was so cold, but I had to talk to her . . . I was crying and treading water and telling her I was sorry. I had to make her understand that I didn't mean what I said, I'd been crazy because I hated Derek and he'd used her the way he used everyone . . . I kept saying, "Please, Jenny, forgive me – please, *please* –" '

Tears ran down his face and caught like raindrops in his beard. 'I saw the boat, coming back, and I heard Ross calling me, and I thought how it would be getting into the boat with him and Derek, taking Jenny home, her eyes staring through everyone . . . and I couldn't do it. I'd destroyed everything and

I couldn't go back to them. If I hadn't jumped Derek, Jenny wouldn't have been killed. My parents and my grandmother had asked me to watch over her when she started going out with Derek. They said, "Craig, stop her; she listens to you." And I failed. I didn't try hard enough to stop her because I couldn't let myself believe it was serious. I let everyone down, and then I killed Jenny. I hated Derek so much I let him become more important to me than Jenny. And Jenny died.

'And even when I was asking her to forgive me, I was still sick and furious because Derek had been inside her. And once – only once – I thought, "It's good that Derek's baby is dead." I couldn't face myself after that – or anyone else – so when Ross called, I swam away. I didn't know which direction I was going; I didn't care. I thought eventually I'd just go under. But instead, after a while, I don't know how long, I came to a spit of land with a flashing light . . .'

'Lime Point,' Katherine murmured, and Craig's head shot up. He had forgotten her, forgotten where he was, and he squinted through his tears as he looked closely at her.

'You're crying,' he said. 'For Jenny?'

'And for you,' Katherine said. She had cried for Jennifer before, but now she was crying for all of them – for Jenny and Craig, for Ross, calling into the darkness, even for Derek, gnawed inside, all his life, by jealousy. Bit by bit, she recalled the pieces of all the stories she had heard, and as she put them together, she felt another rush of pity, stronger than before, for Craig.

'I'm sorry for breaking down,' he said. 'I've never told the whole thing.' He wiped his face with his handkerchief. 'How did you know about Lime Point?'

'Ross and Derek told me. When they learned you were alive –'

'When was that?'

'Not until last year, when I came here the first time. Then

they thought you must have made it to Lime Point. Everyone told me how strong you were. Ann said she had your trophies from college. For running.'

He nodded. 'She was always so proud of those.'

'And you left them behind. With everything else. You made yourself into another person . . .?'

He shrugged. 'It's not hard, you know. A social security card, a driver's licence, a job . . . anyone can get them. And Vancouver was big enough; I could be anonymous.'

'I didn't mean that,' Katherine said. 'I was thinking of inside . . .'

'It takes longer.' He shrugged again. 'You shed bits of yourself, and it hurts, but you do it. You begin to live a different kind of life and after a while you think of yourself as a different person. If you do it long enough, you wake up one day and you know you can't go back to your other life. It's too late.'

Katherine stared at him. *Which one of us is he talking about?*

The bottle was empty. Katherine had made another pot of coffee and absently Craig filled both mugs, glancing at the clock as if they were a normal couple wondering if there was time for one more cup before leaving for work. 'My God, it's two-thirty. I'm keeping you up.'

It was so absurd that they looked at each other and laughed, a soft laugh: the first they had shared. Memories rushed in on Katherine, overwhelming her with images, words, laughter, hope . . . the brilliant light of nostalgic love that burned away the bad times, leaving only the good ones.

She forced herself to stand up and walk away from the table, away from that warm spell. 'If you'd told me all this . . . years ago . . .'

'Why? For a while I wanted to, but then I realised that I wanted even more to get away from it, not to be forced to think about Craig Hayward ever again. Why should I tell you

613

about him when I was happy as Craig Fraser? We were both happy; we had a full life together; how would a long confession have helped us?'

'It would have let me share part of your life.'

'A part I hated and wanted to forget.'

'But you never forgot it! You just kept it from me. And then you kept our finances, and other things –'

'You hardly made a point of asking,' he said coldly. 'You enjoyed the way we lived without asking if we really had the money to pay for it, or where it came from –'

'I know.' Katherine's face was burning. 'I've thought about that. You're right; I should have asked; I should have known what was happening. But that was what you wanted, Craig; someone who wouldn't question your decisions; someone who wouldn't ask questions at all.'

He shook his head. 'You wanted someone who wouldn't burden you with answers.'

They were silent. 'Well,' he said with a short laugh. 'An impasse.'

'It always was,' Katherine responded. 'But I should have insisted. I've learned that. Then we would have been two grown-up people instead of a husband shielding a little-girl wife.'

Craig leaned back in his chair and gazed at her. Then he smiled, almost wistfully. 'Do you know, Katherine, I'm not sure it would have made a damn bit of difference what you did or how you behaved. I don't think I could have told you. I never was able to show my weaknesses to people I love.'

Slowly, Katherine walked back to the table and stood beside him. Almost fearfully, she put out her hand and touched his. 'That's the first time you ever told me a simple truth about yourself,' she said.

'But it's not true anymore.' He grasped her hand. 'I've had sixteen months to think about it; I know what I did to you, to both of us, and I won't let it happen again. I've changed, Katherine; everything will be different now.' He stood and faced her, still holding her hand. 'We have a lot invested in each other: ten years, ten wonderful years, and the children – we can't just throw it all away.'

'But that's what you did when you left.' Confused by the tenderness she felt, Katherine eased her hand away and stepped back until she was standing against the counter. 'You turned your back on all of us.'

He shook his head. 'I did the best I could. It was a lousy solution, but I never really turned my back. I sent you money; I tried to come to you in December. And I thought about us – how we could both change, and start again . . . Katherine, listen to me. I love you. There was a time when we had so much together, we did so much for each other – you haven't forgotten that.'

'No,' she replied. Studying his face, she thought he *had* changed. He was stronger, more open and direct, without having lost the gentleness she had loved. And he looked so much like Todd she found herself wanting to comfort him.

'I'm asking for another chance,' he said. 'For the children, for the years and energy we've invested in each other, for the good things we did for each other. We can build something together that we could have had from the beginning, if I hadn't been such a fool, and if you'd been more involved . . .'

Katherine was dizzy under the hammer blows of his reasons. And the question came to her – why not? He'd learned, he'd changed, he was her husband, he was Jennifer's and Todd's father – and surely this tenderness she felt was more than pity . . . wasn't it just as likely a revival of memories, and a renewal of the love she once had felt, or the first step back to it?

Watching her intently, Craig said again, 'Another chance. To make up to you and the children for what I did –'

'Craig,' Katherine said faintly. 'Give me a minute to catch my breath. You're piling everything on –'

'I'm fighting for my life!' he said. 'Can't you see that?'

'No,' she answered as another memory returned. 'I thought I did. I believed you. But – all this talk about change – even now you aren't being honest with me.'

'What does that mean? After I went through that whole story tore myself apart over it – told you about everything –'

'Except Elissa.'

He stiffened. His shoulders drew together; his face became smooth and blank as if he were a deaf person pushing through a crowded street. Finally he said, 'What are you talking about? If someone's been telling lies about me –'

'Stop it!' Katherine cried. 'Craig, *don't run away*!'

Another minute went by. Stiffly, he shook his head, looking past her. 'I don't know what you're talking about.'

'Oh, Craig.' She moved in front of him to force him to look at her, but he turned his head. They stood that way as the silent moments passed, Craig's features rigid and stubbornly defensive. Poor, frightened Craig, Katherine thought. And with that, the same feeling swept through her that had lifted and carried her along when she left Derek in Ghirardelli Square. She was free.

She knew all the stories, now; all the evasions. She knew she had played a part in them, but she also knew that she had learned enough, grown up enough, to leave that passive child-wife behind forever. But Craig still created his evasions, weaving them into a screen of lies and silences that shut out reality whenever he could not face it. And he would never change.

'I spent a day with Elissa, in Calgary,' she told him. Drooping with fatigue, she did not even try to soften it. 'I liked her – we liked each other. She's still in love with you. Your carving of the turtle with the little boy is still on the

616

table in front of the couch. All the mementoes of your times together are still there. Her little boy had a hard time when you left. He missed you. Probably as much as Todd and Jennifer did.'

Craig's shoulders slumped. He sat down again, turning his coffee mug around in his hands. 'She promised me she'd never call you.'

'She kept her promise. She never called any of us. Ross found her.'

Dully, Craig echoed her words. ' "Ross found her. She never called any of us. *Any of us*".' His head came up; he looked at her accusingly. 'You've lined up with them.'

'This isn't a war,' Katherine shot back. 'They're my family. And yours, if you'd let them be.'

He shook his head. 'I can't be part of them.'

'But you don't know what's happened; there have been so many changes –'

'I don't want to know! Can't you understand? I've cut them out of my life; I don't want to know anything about them! I got over them! It took years, but I got over feeling sick from missing them mostly because I had you to love me and help me make a new family. Katherine, you're all I want – you and the children –'

'And Elissa.'

'My God, can't you let go? You *have* changed. Not just your hair and the way you walk and hold yourself – you've gotten hard. You used to be soft and loving and grateful, but that's all gone.'

'Is it?'

'You act like you don't want anyone to care for you; you don't need anyone . . .'

I need Ross.

'Hank gave me your message; he told me you were waiting for me. What did that mean?'

617

'I had to talk to you.'

'To finish our marriage. Right? That was how Ross put it.'

'To finish with the past. I wasn't really sure about our marriage.' Katherine hesitated. 'Craig,' she said softly. 'When you left us, why didn't you go to Elissa?'

He shook his head.

'Because you love her. That's right, isn't it? You couldn't go to her because you couldn't tell her what you'd done.' He sat still, and Katherine sighed. 'Earlier tonight you said you didn't have to talk about your family, you didn't even think about them as long as you had me. That wasn't true. You never stopped thinking about them, you had to talk about them, and so you went to Elissa. And after a while, you fell in love with her. Why can't you face that?'

'I love you,' he said. 'I came back because you told Hank you were waiting for me. *I'm asking for help.* I keep ruining things – I just did it again, didn't I, trying to deny Elissa? You were leaning towards me – I saw it in your face – until I . . . ran away again. Katherine, I want to repair some of the damage I've done, but I can't do it alone. Don't make me do it alone. Stay with me; help me.'

'I can't. I'm sorry, Craig.' Katherine felt her tears again. He wasn't evil or cruel or even bad; he was a good man too easily overwhelmed by events. He was a man she no longer loved. 'We'll do everything we can to help you. Whatever you need, we'll give you –'

'You're speaking for the family?'

'Yes.'

'You mean you're choosing Ross.'

'I mean I can't go with you; I can't live with you.'

Craig pushed back his chair and stood up. 'Just a minute.' Katherine watched him close the door of the bathroom behind him. Her muscles ached, her head ached, and she walked through the living-room to the front door, opening it to feel the cool, damp air on her face. The sky had grown light; she looked at her watch. Six o'clock. *We talked more in the last six hours, she thought, than in all the years of our marriage.*

Craig came out of the bathroom and stood beside her. 'And the children?' he asked.

'They love you. Wherever you are, they'll come to you, as often as possible, and spend time with you –'

'Visits.'

After a moment, she said, 'A lot of children do that, these days.'

'But they'd be visiting. I wanted to live with them again.'

She felt a tug of impatience. 'You'll see a lot more of them than you have in the past year and a half.'

'Right,' he said. 'You're right. I deserved that.' He went to the door of the bedroom. 'I'll just take a quick look goodbye. I won't wake them – I'm not ready to talk to them – I have to figure out what to say. But when I've decided where I'll be, and when I'm settled, you'll let them come?'

'As often as possible.'

He nodded. 'Yes, you said that.' He stood in the doorway, as he had hours before. 'They curl up in their sleep. I remember that. But they're growing so fast. Jenny is going to be as beautiful as her mother. And Todd . . . Todd looks like me, doesn't he?'

Distantly, a foghorn sounded. 'Dad!' Todd shouted. 'Dad!' Katherine saw Craig bend down and take in his arms the pyjama'd form that flung itself at him.

'*Daddy*?' Jennifer asked. Her voice was clouded with sleep and doubt. Instead of dashing to him as Todd had done, she appeared in the doorway, frowning, reaching out to touch Craig's arm, testing its solidity.

'Hello, dear Jenny,' Craig said softly.

Wordlessly, she put up both arms. Craig knelt and held his

children, his eyes meeting Katherine's over their tousled heads, accusing her. They love me, his eyes said. And you want to keep us apart.

'Where's your suitcase?' asked Todd as they sat on the couch. 'Where are you going to put everything? We'll have to move, now, won't we, Mom? Are we going back to Canada?'

Jennifer looked at her mother and then at her father. 'You're not staying,' she said flatly.

'He is too!' Todd cried. 'You are, aren't you. Dad?'

'No,' Craig said. 'I'd like to but I can't. Your mother –'

Katherine caught her breath. Don't run away from it, she begged silently. Don't blame it all on me. Face it, Craig. *Please.*

'Why aren't you?' Todd demanded.

'Are you going to get a divorce?' Jennifer asked.

'We haven't talked about it.' Craig's skin was tight over his face, like a mask; his mouth worked. And then a long sigh broke from him. 'But, you see, I left all of you – which was a terrible thing to do – and then I stayed away too long. And your mother and I changed. People do change, you know,' he said, looking directly at Katherine. 'We really aren't the same people we were. It's nobody's fault, but it happened. So that's what we're going to do. Get a divorce.'

'Shit,' muttered Todd, and no one scolded him.

After a moment, Jennifer asked, 'Why did you go away?'

'Because I got myself into a mess and didn't know how to get out. I was scared. Too scared even to ask your mother to help me. It wasn't very smart. In fact, it was stupid. If you're lucky enough to have people love you, you ought to be smart enough to let them help you when you need it.'

Katherine sat on the arm of the couch and touched Craig's cheek. 'Thank you,' she said softly. 'I wish –'

He looked up quickly, but she stopped. It was too late for them. She clasped her hands in her lap.

Todd scowled, furiously blinking back his tears. 'What's going to happen to all of us?'

'I'm going back to Canada,' Craig answered. 'And as soon as I find a place to live, with an extra bedroom, you'll come for a visit. Lots of visits. All you have to do is tell me when you want to come, and I'll be ready.'

'Like Carrie and Jon,' said Jennifer. 'They see Ross a lot.'

'Ross has children,' Craig murmured. 'Funny; in my mind he's still twenty years old, a college kid. Do you see them often?' he asked Jennifer.

'Sort of.'

He gave a small smile. 'It's all right if you like Ross, Jenny. He and I grew up together, you know. I always thought he was . . . I loved Ross and my sister better than any other people in the world. That was a long time ago.'

Abruptly, Katherine turned away. Nothing is simple, she thought.

'We love him, too,' Jennifer said. 'Not the same as you. Different.'

Craig nodded. 'I'll bet he loves you, too. Hold on.' He took his arms from their shoulders and stood up, wiping his eyes with his handkerchief. No one moved. Then he turned briskly. 'If I'm going to find a place to live, I'd better start. I have a lot to do. I'll call you very soon –'

'When?' Todd demanded.

'In a day or two, as soon as I've decided what I'm going to do.'

'Tonight,' Todd insisted.

Smiling, Craig leaned over to kiss them both. 'I won't disappear again. But I'll call you tonight, if you want. And tomorrow. And as often as you like. I'll even write to you if you promise to write back.'

Jennifer and Todd looked at each other. 'We're not much good at writing letters,' said Todd.

621

'Then you need practice,' Craig declared. 'Now, would you do something for me?' They nodded watchfully. 'Go on into your bedroom. I want to say goodbye to your mother.'

Todd sprang up and threw his arms around him. 'You'll call *tonight?*'

'I promise,' Craig replied, holding him tight. 'I love you, Todd.' He let him go and held Jennifer. 'Goodbye my lovely Jenny. I'll see you soon.'

When they were gone, he said, 'They're so wonderful. Like their mother.' He cleared his throat and tried to smile as he and Katherine walked to the door. 'A man couldn't ask for a better family. And I threw it away. Dear God, Katherine' – he put his arms around her – 'isn't there any way –?'

'No.' She raised her hand to brush the hair back from his forehead, as she had done countless times in their years together. 'You were wonderful, with them. Thank you.'

He grimaced. 'What difference does it make? It's too late.'

'Not for the life you make from now on. And I'll help you, any way I can.' She smiled. 'You can tell me anything now. I'll be here, if you need to talk –'

'But that's all,' he said.

'That's all. But I care about you. You'll always have that.'

He tightened his hold, pulling her close again, and Katherine put her arms around him, her cheek against his. They stood that way, without speaking, as the air grew lighter and the fog pushed in from the ocean, and then they moved apart, and in another moment he was gone.

Chapter 23

The night was so quiet Ross heard his footsteps echo through the house and out to the hushed coolness of the deck. He had tried to sleep and given up; some nights were worse than others, and this night, for some reason, seemed the worst of all: filled with longings and memories.

In the living-room he poured himself a drink, then wandered through the rooms, turning lights on and off, seeing Katherine wherever he looked.

In his bedroom, an enlarged, framed photograph stood on the dresser: Katherine, on the boat, her hair lifted by the wind, her eyes laughing into his. Beside it was another, snapped surreptitiously by Carrie on the terrace in Menton: Ross and Katherine in conversation, absorbed in each other, smiling, in love. He ran his finger along the glass over their two faces. *Katherine*.

On the living-room desk was a Lucite paperweight

Katherine had made in the shape of a curved sail; engraved on it was a sketch of Ross's boat, with a seagull wheeling above. Holding the polished curve on his hand, Ross sat on the couch, staring at the wall. *To take up such a large space in my life, in so short a time . . .*

The telephone was beside him. His hand touched it, then drew back. Ridiculous; it was two-thirty in the morning – she'd be sound asleep. Besides, he had promised he would not call. He'd gone too far as it was, at the Hallowe'en Ball, because he was so damned impatient.

On the table was a book he had bought the day before; he lay back on the couch and opened it. And then suddenly a misty early morning light was coming through the glass doors and Ross awoke, the book still in his hand, and thought, as if he had not slept at all, *Katherine*.

It was six o'clock. The bridges were shrouded in fog, their towers jutting above it like miniature steeples floating above the clouds. Ross went through his morning routine, listening to a newscast as he dressed, reading the newspaper while drinking his coffee. And then he left the house.

He was backing his car out of the driveway, when a taxi approached. He stopped to let it go by, drumming his fingers on the steering wheel as it slowed to a crawl, but in the next moment he knew. *Katherine*. And then she was there, opening the door and jumping out before the taxi came to a full stop.

After all the hours of imagining her before him, he could not move. Then he saw her smile. Through the pounding of his heart he took a deep breath and threw open his car door to take long strides across the grass, his eyes on her.

'Lady?' the taxi driver's voice was rising. 'Lady, did you hear me? You owe me –'

'I heard you,' said Ross, and pulled out his wallet.

'No,' Katherine said. 'Wait. I have it, I just – for a minute, I didn't hear him.'

Ross held out some bills. 'Keep it.'

The driver's eyes brightened. 'No kidding. You want a receipt?'

'No. This is a special occasion.'

'No kidding. That's what the lady said.'

'Did she?' Ross murmured. He put his arm around Katherine to lead her to the house. 'You look like you didn't get enough sleep.'

'I didn't get any.'

He stopped, his hands on her shoulders, searching her face. 'He called? Or came to you?'

'He came about midnight. We talked all night.'

'And he left?'

'Yes.'

Ross felt his pounding heart slow: he took a long breath, almost weightless with relief and love. With their arms around each other, they walked through the house to the deck. Looking at her pallor, he asked. 'Have you had breakfast?'

She shook her head. 'Jennifer and Todd had an early rehearsal at school, and I fixed them something, but I wasn't hungry. And I was in a hurry to get here, before you left.'

'I would have waited if you'd let me know you were coming.'

'I didn't want to let you know. I wanted to surprise you.'

He laughed softly. 'And so you did. Wait here; I'll get you some food.'

'Just coffee would be fine.' When he was gone, Katherine lay back on the chaise. 'Don't do that,' she said aloud. 'You'll fall asleep.' She forced herself upright, half-closing her eyes against the glare of the sun, floating on the golden light and the early-morning fragrance of roses and carnations. She took off her jacket, the heat flowing through her, making her bones feel liquid. Her head began to droop and then she heard footsteps and opened her eyes to see Ross putting a tray on the table in front of her.

625

'Orange juice and coffee. I didn't want to take the time for something dramatic, like waffles. Are you all right?'

'I came to propose to you,' she said.

'Yes.'

'You knew that?'

'I mean, my answer is yes.'

She laughed and rested her cheek against his tweed jacket. 'I was hoping it would be.'

Ross kissed the top of her head. 'Can you tell me what happened?'

'So much happened. It seemed like a lifetime, in one night.' Waves of sleepiness lapped at Katherine and she swayed against Ross. 'I didn't really understand how much I'd changed until I talked to Craig – heard him talk – about himself, and us.'

'We've all changed,' said Ross. 'But you more than anyone. I tried to tell you that.'

'I know. But I couldn't put it all together – what I had been and what I'd become and why I hadn't been able to do it before. Then Craig came and every time I looked at him it was as if I were looking at what I used to be. Remember,' she went on sleepily, 'once I told you I missed being able to predict tomorrow? That was only because I was afraid.'

'And you're not afraid now?'

'No. Not since some time last night, when I saw how far I'd come by myself. That was when I knew I wanted you.' Over the edge of her coffee cup, she smiled at Ross. 'I knew I could be a whole person by myself, but I knew my life would be richer with you in it. I want you to let me face things on my own, the way you did when you said we should stay away from each other, but I want you to care about me, too, and protect me – and I want to help you when you need it . . . the two of us, sharing the good times and helping each other through the bad ones . . . Ross, I'm so sleepy . . . am I making sense?'

'You're promising,' he said gravely, 'to be less fierce about your independence as long as I help you without diminishing it – and let you do the same for me. As long as we keep a balance between us.'

'Not easy,' she murmured.

'We'll probably manage it about half the time, and work on the rest. Is that good enough?'

'It's wonderful,' Katherine laughed, her love for him welling up through her sleepiness, making everything seem possible. She looked at the fog, burning away in the hot sun, and the skyscrapers across the bay, shimmering like an enchanted city filled with happy endings. 'If you're lucky enough to have people love you,' she said softly, 'you ought to be smart enough to let them help you when you need it. Craig said that, when he was explaining to Jennifer and Todd why he'd been wrong.'

'Then he's learned more than I thought he could. Will he go to Elissa?'

'I don't know. I hope so.'

'And Jennifer and Todd?'

'They told him they love you. Not the way they love him, but . . . Oh, *damn*, I wish there was a way to build happiness without sadness somewhere underneath.'

Ross took her in his arms and they held each other. 'Katherine, I love you,' he said, moving his lips slowly against hers. He kissed her eyes as she fought to keep them open. 'My sleepy darling, I promise to share with you everything I am and everything I dream of, if you'll do the same for me.'

Katherine's eyelids flew open. 'I forgot to tell you. Xavier's called. I have an appointment tomorrow.'

'Another beginning.' He smiled. 'We'll have a celebration. Trumpets and fireworks and champagne. And eventually, when the laws of California are satisfied, a wedding. With four offspring in the cheering section.'

627

Katherine put her arms around him and opened her mouth beneath his. Their bodies met, remembering, and they stood together and walked with their arms around each other into the house, to the shadowed coolness of Ross's bedroom. But the instant the mattress yielded beneath their weight, Katherine drooped.

'Ross, do you mind –?' she asked. 'I'm so sorry, but would you mind very much if I just went to sleep?'

Holding her, he laughed with pure joy. 'Dear one,' he said, 'we have a lifetime ahead of us.' He took off her shoes and laid her on the bed, her head on his pillow.

'But wake me up,' she said drowsily. 'I promised Jennifer and Todd I'd be there at three . . .'

'I'll go. I want to stop at the office; I'll pick them up and bring them here.'

'And we have to call Victoria and Tobias.' Her voice was barely a murmur. 'They'll be hurt if we don't tell them right away . . .'

'I'll invite us there for dinner tonight. Would you like that? The four of us, and Carrie and Jon, and Victoria and Tobias. A family dinner.'

Katherine's lips curved in a smile. 'A family dinner. I love you, Ross.'

He put a light blanket over her and drew the drapes, then stood for a moment beside the bed. Katherine held up her arms. Bending down, Ross kissed her closed eyes. 'Sleep well, my love. You've come home.'

PRIVATE AFFAIRS

Judith Michael

EVERY WOMAN WANTS HER FANTASY TO
COME TRUE – UNTIL SHE LEARNS THE
COST...

The Lovells had everything: demanding and absorbing
careers, two teenage children, a lifestyle of enviable
affluence. And they still had their youth. But for sixteen
years they knew their most treasured dreams had been
put aside in deference to others' needs. Now, before it was
too late, they knew they had to act.

And so Elizabeth and Matt risk everything to buy the
newspaper they'd always longed to own, rekindling both
their youthful ambitions and the passions of their
marriage. Yet in their new-found paradise of power,
glamour and wealth they meet temptations that never
before existed in their small, private world. And the one
thing they both desperately need is fast slipping out of
reach – each other ...

<u>INHERITANCE</u>

Judith Michael

IT WAS LIKE A DREAM COME TRUE. SHE HAD
DISCOVERED LAUGHTER, LUXURY, AND THE
LOVE CF HER LIFE. AND THEN THE
NIGHTMARE STARTED . . .

When the fabulously wealthy Owen Salinger died, he left
an inheritance to Laura Fairchild. But Laura already had
a legacy – a hidden secret from her past. And the
Salingers used that legacy to destroy her life – and claim
her inheritance.

Laura didn't want revenge, she wanted the fruits of
power, passion, worldly success – and her lost love
regained. And so she built an empire – an empire that
stretched from fashionable Boston to the fabulous haunts
of the European jet-set. But the past is forever present –
and the stakes are perilously high . . .

SLEEPING BEAUTY

Judith Michael

Anne Garnett is no longer the weak, frightened teenager
she was when she last faced Vince Chatham. Now she is
proud, beautiful, and a high-powered divorce lawyer.
And Vince is the new US senator from Colorado, exuding
vitality, vigour and charm – and ambitions for the White
House. Both of them have carefully constructed public
faces that conceal a bitter, tormented past – and a
nightmare that has haunted Anne for years.

Now, as they face each other over the grave of Ethan
Chatham, old wounds are savagely reopened, and a
conflict that began twenty-four years ago enters its final
stages. A conflict that sweeps away their professional
media images and reveals the raw, savage enmity between
them. A conflict for control over the family empire and
name, and for the leadership and love of the family.

Tamarack, Colorado, the beautiful mountain playground
of the rich and famous, the jewel in the family's empire, is
the paradise that turns into a battleground. From there to
the treacherous political enclaves of Washington and to
the remote reaches of Egypt, Anne must struggle to
awaken from her past; to fight, to win – and to love
again . . .

Other bestselling Warner titles available by mail: